THE YEAR'S BEST SCIENCE FICTION & FANTASY

2016 EDITION

OTHER BOOKS BY

RICH HORTON

—◆—

Fantasy: The Best of the Year, 2006 Edition

Fantasy: The Best of the Year, 2007 Edition

Fantasy: The Best of the Year, 2008 Edition

Robots: The Recent A.I. (with Sean Wallace)

Science Fiction: The Best of the Year, 2006 Edition

Science Fiction: The Best of the Year, 2007 Edition

Science Fiction: The Best of the Year, 2008 Edition

Space Opera

Unplugged: The Web's Best Sci-Fi & Fantasy: 2008 Download

The Year's Best Science Fiction & Fantasy, 2009 Edition

The Year's Best Science Fiction & Fantasy, 2010 Edition

The Year's Best Science Fiction & Fantasy, 2011 Edition

The Year's Best Science Fiction & Fantasy, 2012 Edition

The Year's Best Science Fiction & Fantasy, 2013 Edition

The Year's Best Science Fiction & Fantasy, 2014 Edition

The Year's Best Science Fiction & Fantasy, 2015 Edition

War & Space: Recent Combat (with Sean Wallace)

THE YEAR'S BEST SCIENCE FICTION & FANTASY

2016 EDITION

EDITED BY
RICH HORTON

PRIME BOOKS

THE YEAR'S BEST SCIENCE FICTION & FANTASY, 2016 EDITION

Prime Books
www.prime-books.com

ISBN: 978-1-60701-470-6

In memory of my father, John Richard Horton (1931-2015).

CONTENTS

CONTENTS

THE YEAR IN FANTASY AND SCIENCE FICTION, 2015

RICH HORTON

Let's Not Let Custom Stale Our Infinite Variety

We've seen a lot of talk about "slates" in the field the past couple of years, much of it disparaging a couple of prominent nomination slates for the Hugo Awards. I was disturbed by the "Sad Puppy" effort last year, and much more so by the "Rabid Puppy" slate (which went so far as to direct a strategic nomination ballot). But all along I've been keenly aware that I have engaged in recommending stories for the Hugo for years. Of course for the past decade that has primarily been merely by publishing this series of books—you can certainly assume that any story I reprint is a story I'd be thrilled to see win an award. And in the past I have also, on occasion, posted my own nomination ballot. So what is wrong with slates?

Well, really, nothing, as long as they are presented as a set of recommendations, and as long as one presumes that people will use the recommendations as a spur to further reading, and not as a voting guide similar to those political parties publish. All my lists, for one thing (and certainly the tables of contents for these books), include more stories than anyone can nominate for a Hugo. The point is to promote reading great stories! That's all my anthologies are about—a way to put great stories in front of more readers. And in the end, that should be the main point of awards of all sorts: a way to bring great work to wider attention, to wider readership. That's worth much more than a shiny rocketship!

I will confess that I have always enjoyed nominating and voting for the Hugos. The process is, for me, fun. But I remain at some level uneasy about a strict ranking of works of art. How can I say that, to take examples from this book, "Mutability" is *better* than "Little Sisters"? Or "The Karen Joy Fowler Book Club" *better* than "Consolation"? I can't! And not because "it's all a matter of taste." Individual taste is a factor, to be sure, but I still believe that some stories are better than others, and not just because I like one kind of thing more than something else. But, also, each story is trying to do something different, and there's no reason the lush, linguistic larks of "The Long Goodnight of Violet Wild" are intrinsically better than the tense and twisty hard science fiction of "Twelve and Tag." There's no reason a dark and emotionally fraught piece like "Please Undo This Hurt" is to be necessarily preferred to a romp like "Cat Pictures Please." (There is, however, reason to prefer a well-written story to an ungrammatical mess, or an original work to a pile of clichés, or a tightly executed plot to one with holes you could parade ogres through.)

All this is partly why I publish both fantasy and science fiction in these books and a reason my definitions of the genres are pretty broad and why I like to make sure there's a range of tones to the stories I reprint and a range of sources and a range of writers. Variety is a pleasure in itself. This field is very rich, and we should celebrate its riches at every chance. This book has exotic fantasy. It has steampunk (and dieselpunk!). It has near-future speculation. A Lovecraftian story! Something as indescribable as Nike Sulway's "The Karen Joy Fowler Book Club," which is about intelligent hippopotami of all things! Interplanetary science fiction. Several stories about art. (Lots of stories about art or writing . . . that may be a matter of my own personal inclinations, I admit!) A nonstop action-adventure piece. Strange but plausible biology. Far future science fiction, a time travel story, a story about a TV show. Military science fiction.

The variety of the field is confirmed by the variety of sources for new short fiction. Starting with the traditional print "Big Three" magazines in the US: *Analog*, *Asimov's*, and *The Magazine of Fantasy & Science Fiction*. *Analog* publishes, by preference, "hard science fiction" with a fair amount of adventure-oriented stories and military science fiction. It also, these days, seems to me to prefer near-future sociological speculation that reminds me of the early years of *Galaxy*: speculation often based on quirky exaggerations of current trends or the possibilities of new technology. The content has been increasingly interesting under new editor Trevor Quachri. *Asimov's* also publishes mostly science fiction (with an occasional fantasy mixed in), but a generally broader mix. For my taste, under long-tenured editor Sheila Williams, *Asimov's* remains consistently the best print magazine in the field. *F&SF* also has a new editor, C.C. Finlay. As the title suggests, it publishes a fairly even mix of fantasy and science fiction.

The leading UK magazine for quite some time has been *Interzone*, edited by Andy Cox. *Interzone* publishes both science fiction and fantasy, and under Cox it seems to have a tropism for more highly colored science fiction, stranger stuff. Cox also edits *Black Static*, a horror magazine, with what seems a perhaps cliched British quietude and generally excellent writing. The newest notable magazine is *Galaxy's Edge*, which publishes mostly science fiction, a lot of new writers, and some outstanding reprints.

From Australia comes *Andromeda Spaceways Inflight Magazine*, which— among a wide variety of styles—shows a certain predilection for comic stories.

And from Canada comes *On Spec*, perhaps a bit on the staid (or, dare I say, polite) side, but worthwhile and generally quite well-written.

It's no secret nowadays that much of the action in short fiction is online. I have a personal stake here, as I'm the reprint editor at *Lightspeed*, so I won't try to rank the sites. *Lightspeed* itself publishes a purposely even mix of science fiction and fantasy, and an even mix of reprints and new fiction; a fairly broad approach to the field. We also reprint a longer story each month in the ebook edition. *Clarkesworld* is another highly esteemed ezine, publishing more science fiction than fantasy as a rule. It also publishes some reprints, and it tends to publish longer stories than many ezines. In the past year, it has been publishing a lot of translated science fiction, mostly from China—much of this very good indeed. The oldest surviving prominent ezine is *Strange Horizons*, which has a reputation of hospitality to slipstream and more overtly literary stories. That said, in reality it features plenty of science fiction as well as fantasy and slipstream. Another important ezine is *Apex*, which began as a print magazine with a focus on horror (particularly science fiction horror), but migrated online and turned to a broader mix, perhaps not dissimilar to that of *Strange Horizons*. *Uncanny* is a new online magazine with an express intent to publish truly weird stories—an intent it has achieved so far. For fantasy, particularly adventure fantasy, the top online magazine is probably *Beneath Ceaseless Skies*, though we shouldn't neglect a couple that are more purely focused on adventure fantasy: *Swords and Sorcery Magazine* and *Heroic Fantasy Quarterly*. For horror, look to *Lightspeed's* companion, *Nightmare*, and also to *The Dark*, not officially a companion of *Clarkesworld*, but co-edited by one of *Clarkesworld's* editors (and the publisher of this book), Sean Wallace. *Daily Science Fiction* publishes a lot of new stuff (as the name suggests) and quite a wide variety. *Abyss and Apex* is another long-running online 'zine with a broad remit. And for longer fiction, *Giganotosaurus* is a great place to go: long novelettes and novellas, both fantasy and science fiction, much of it very fine.

I haven't mentioned one of the most important sources of new short fiction: *Tor.com*. They publish stories of all sorts, including occasional reprints, some longer stories as well, and also some graphic stories. Their quality has been consistently high. Last year Tor began a series of novellas as well: a great way to get more fiction of that tricky length to us.

Of course beyond the magazine field there are still plenty of anthologies. This year saw excellent outings from Ellen Datlow (particularly **The Doll Collection**), Jonathan Strahan (particularly **Meeting Infinity**), Sean Wallace (**The Mammoth Book of Dieselpunk**), the very busy John Joseph Adams (**Operation Arcana, Press Start to Play, The End Has Come,** etc.), and the team of Gardner Dozois and George R.R. Martin, who gave us **Old Venus**. That just scratches the surface. I ought also to mention a few very near-future oriented hard science fiction anthologies: the continuing series from the *MIT Technology Review,* **Twelve Tomorrows**; and a fine book from Microsoft, **Future Visions**. Finally, a number of stories were published in standalone ebook format, many of these novellas: "The Two Paupers" and "Little Sisters" (both included here) and also a new long story by Lois McMaster Bujold, "Penric's Demon."

This variety of sources, styles, and forms of new short science fiction and fantasy can be imposing. It certainly contributes to the fractioning of the field, so much so that few, if any, can really say they've read anything significant. (Which contributes to the controversy over awards: much of it consists of partisans for one story or another arguing with other partisans, neither side having read the other side's favorites.) But in the end, that's a feature, not a bug—better to have great stories you can't get around to reading than to run out of great stories! At any rate, here's hoping that this book will introduce you to a new set of great science fiction and fantasy!

MUTABILITY

RAY NAYLER

We are as clouds that veil the midnight moon;
How restlessly they speed, and gleam, and quiver,
Streaking the darkness radiantly!—yet soon
Night closes round, and they are lost forever:
                                    —*Percy Bysshe Shelley*

It was an almost perfect café. It was in a red brick building built sometime in the early twentieth century: a mass of art deco, faux-Moorish and Russian influences, punctuated with stained glass and onion domes. You entered through an Arabian Nights archway into an anteroom of cracked hexagonal tiles and robin's-egg plaster. Here, you could take off your coat and hang it on one of the brass hooks along the right-hand wall. Turn left through another arch—this one crawling with chipped plaster grapevines—you were in the main room. This room had a domed ceiling like a mosque or a Turkish bath house, blue Byzantine tiles on the floor, and layers of crumbling posters on the walls interspersed with framed pictures and notes signed by customers. The age-spotted mirrors and dusty bottles of an ancient, hand-carved bar dominated one side of the room.

The bar was where the owner was always to be found, rubbing his shaved head, staring at a game of chess. He always played against one of three different opponents. Opponent One was a gaunt man in a dirty collared shirt who chewed, repulsively, on a piece of string hanging from the corner of his mouth. Opponent Two was a heavy, slope-shouldered man. He kept his coat on and played quickly and impatiently. Opponent Three was a girl, thirteen or so, with a nose she was trying to grow into and blonde hair that looked like it had been rubbed in ashes. One so rarely saw children these days. Very serious, she always came in with a book—a real book. Where was she getting them?

It was unclear who won any of the long, silent games. Once they were over, Opponent One or Opponent Two would get up and leave, with no hint of triumph or desolation. Opponent Three would stay and read her book for hours, accepting the occasional cocoa on the counter nearby while the owner busied himself with other things. His child? Who knew? The owner never spoke to the café's customers, with the exception of these three.

The rest of the room was filled with tables, chairs, and light. The tables were an assortment of round café tables, square or rectangular tables from restaurants or offices long since gone, high tile-topped wrought-iron tables of the kind you might find in a garden or on a balcony somewhere, big scarred oaken slabs that might have come from a warehouse or factory. The chairs were also a mix: some straight-backed, some cane, some wicker, some just plain stools. All were defective in their unique way, and all demanded different techniques for getting comfortable. The chairs and tables were never to be found in quite the same configuration when Sebastian came in in the mornings. The light was never in the same configuration either: it fell piebald through the stained glass panels at the top of the windows in a moody shift along the tiles and tables and chairs, dependent on cloud and season.

And so the café had the feeling, at once, of agelessness—its ancient building, its collection of rescued furniture like a museum of other places, its continual game of chess in the corner—and of change: the patterns of color-stained light and the restless puzzle of tables and chairs. All this, and the coffee, sandwiches, and macaroons were excellent. All this, and the service was good.

But what made it nearly perfect was Sebastian's place in the corner, against the wall furthest from the entrance, by the windows. Here there was an enormous, worn, purple-velvet armchair and a massive oak table. There was enough room on that ancient table to spread his work out; the terminal and the notebooks he liked to use when he wanted the mechanical action of writing by hand, the cup of coffee brought steaming to the table by one of the students from the nearby universities who worked here (they were like the light and the chairs and tables, moving always elsewhere). The waiters never came around to ask if he wanted anything else, but they were always near the bar, scanning the customers for a motion that meant something was needed, that meant it was time for the check.

He had found the café at a terrible time in his life. He felt, in a way, as though the café had saved him. The long days of work, or of just watching the light slide across the floor, or just watching other customers—in hushed conversation, or bent over their terminals, or just staring off at nothing—made him feel a quiet part of something. He was welcome here. He was known, but left alone. He could work here in a way he could never work at home. At home, when he tried to attack a particularly difficult problem in the work, something would distract him. Hours later he would find himself staring blankly into his terminal, reading about god knows what insignificant detail of research on something completely unrelated to what he had been looking for. Here, surrounded by pleasant, human-scale distractions, he found his focus.

Sebastian had noticed her long before she approached him. More exactly, he had noticed her notice him. He'd looked up and caught her staring at him. Later he would examine the moment: rain outside that the wind occasionally drove against the windows, streaking through the dust in alluvial fans toward the bottom of the glass. A special feeling of refuge in the café that day. The smell that the rain brought in along with new customers seeking shelter—one of whom was this tall, dark-haired woman in a gray dress and moss-green scarf. It was a hard, autumn rain that said winter was coming, a rain that drove the loosening gold leaves from their branches to the ground. He had not seen her before, and he caught her looking at him—really looking at him, in a way at once rude and mystifying. She looked away when he looked up, but he was aware of her glancing at him while he worked. The rain hammered the streets and the buildings outside and the place filled up with more dripping refugees. When he came home that evening, the maple in the courtyard, which that morning had been wrapped in red and yellow, was a winter skeleton.

The next day she was there early. She stayed most of the day, with a terminal for company. Also the day after. On the fourth day she stopped him in the anteroom. Outside, the evening street was shadow-colored. Above the buildings, the flushed undersides of clouds were dark blue and salmon. He was lifting his ancient shooting jacket from a hook. She came in, reached for a threadbare peacoat. Then she stopped, resting her hand on the collar of her coat, and turned to him.

"I have a strange request."

He had the jacket on and was shifting it to fall correctly over his shoulders. There was a little whirring blade of cold air in the anteroom, and it nipped at his wrists and climbed up his pant leg. The world, hesitating between fall and winter, all brown, dry leaves and flights of migrating birds headed south. "How strange is it?"

She had small crows' feet around her eyes, a vertical worry-line between her high, dark eyebrows. Longish hands, unpainted fingernails cut short. She could have been a musician, or many other things.

"I live near here. I wonder if you would come to my apartment so I can show you something."

What did he read in her face? Impossible to say. There should be a class offered in reading the expressions of others. Perhaps there already was: he would ask his terminal. "All right. Now, you mean?"

"If it's not too much trouble." She began, quite clumsily, to put on her coat, dropping the mossy scarf and grey gloves on the floor in the process. He picked them up for her, handed them back. She carefully avoided touching him when he did so. The impossibilities of reading other people. Were some people able to do so? He thought yes, certainly better than he. They went out into the cold street.

Her apartment was on the next block—but because the apartment buildings (most of them in this section of town very ancient) were enormously long, it was a ten-minute walk. The days were shortening, and the chill filled him with positive melancholy: winter was hot drinks and flushed cheeks and good books. Leaves scuttled across the pavement. Overhead, the dark spiderweb of the Nanocarbon Elevated Metro (NEM) striped black through the indigo air, a train dopplering past. For some reason, they did not speak much. She was tense. She seemed to be working herself up to something. She did tell him her name: Sophia.

Her apartment was on the third floor of an unobtrusively upgraded old building. The lack of draftiness inside was probably due to insulating nanofiber injections into the walls. The modern voice/ret scanner near the entrance to her stairwell posed as an antiquated *domofon*. The dismal authenticity of the concrete stairwell had been maintained. The apartment was high-ceilinged but small, just one rectangular room furnished with a *matroshka* furniture cluster, which she converted with a touch to its table and chairs format. A kitchenette near the windows overlooked the street. Refrigerator unit, old-fashioned teakettle, instantheat, a cabinet from which she drew two mugs and a teapot. While she was making the tea he politely scanned the room. Besides the *matroshka* unit, a bookshelf along one wall held a selection of music theory books, two terminals not of the latest make, a violin, and a shelf of carefully collected, vintage psychoanalytical works—not first editions, but well-known translations. On the opposite wall, a painting hung in which several female forms dissolved in a grey-and-red-streaked fog. Difficult to place its period: eccentric and not of any particular school, artist likely an unknown, but fantastically talented: the piece moved him. He looked away from it.

Sophia set the two mugs and the teapot on the table. The apartment was full, now, of the scent of the steeping tea, black with some sort of berry in it. The window near the electric kettle was obscured by steam: the other windows mirrored the room and Sebastian and Sophia standing in the room. He sat down on the backless cube of a chair. She poured him tea. He looked up to find her deep in thought, staring hard into his face. She caught herself and looked away.

"You must think I'm very strange," she said.

Sebastian stared into his tea. Miniature leaves floated, unfolding in the heat of the water. "Who isn't, these days?"

She was holding an envelope in her left hand. She placed the envelope on the table.

"First of all," she said, "please take a look at this."

Sebastian opened the unsealed envelope and drew out a photograph. It was a color photograph, very old. Its tones were shifting toward orange and red as it aged. The edges were yellowed, although it had been printed on supposedly archival paper. It had been badly bent a number of times, and creased once diagonally, then re-straightened. The two people in the photograph were wearing laughably out-of-fashion winter coats: coats that would have been normal now only in some sort of historical drama. They were grinning into the camera. The man was wearing a wool watch cap, the woman a beret. Behind them there were some very neat, tiny houses almost entirely obscured by snow. Judging by the architecture of the houses, the picture was taken somewhere in northern Europe. A very pale light. Very far north. The couple looked truly happy: their arms around one another, their heads leaned in to one another, the crown of the woman's head against the man's jaw.

It was a photograph of Sebastian and Sophia. Their hair was significantly different (his was just terrible, unflattering. What could he have been thinking? Hers looked nice). Their clothes of course were different, but there was no doubt at all that it was the two of them. He looked for a long time at the photo, turned it over and looked at its back. Nothing there but the digital printing from the machine—a series of numbers, some kind of internal code from wherever it had been printed, barely legible now. No date, but he could guess by the clothes that it was . . .

"The first thing you think. The first thing that comes to mind."

He looked up. She was leaning in a bit toward him, both of her hands wrapped around her mug of tea.

"Well . . . it's us. I mean . . . it appears to be a picture of you and me. But I don't . . . "

"No, you wouldn't remember it, Sebastian." She said his name strangely, like a person afraid to pronounce a word incorrectly that they had only read in books. "I don't remember it. I don't remember anything of it. It's . . . " She stood up suddenly and went to the window. "It's well beyond my memory horizon. I've researched the picture. Looked up the fashion of the clothes. Not . . . obsessively. Just—because I've always had it with me. I found it in my things, I think . . . I can't remember exactly. But this picture . . . which I've carried with me as long as I can remember . . . I think it's about four hundred or so years old. That's just a guess. It could be three hundred ninety and their—our—clothes are out of style, but it's probably closer to four hundred. I need to walk. Do you want to go for a walk? I can't be in here with you."

• • •

They walked along the river embankment. There was no ice yet on the river, but a serpent of freezing air coiled down its length, winding winter into the city. They crossed the river via an escalator and an enclosed pedestrian footbridge. Below, the black mirror of river reflected the city up at them. There were, of course, no stars.

"I don't know how long ago I found it. I have a vague recollection of pulling it out from the pages of a book. The book is battered"—she was walking with her eyes shut—"and it has a white cover. With only text on it. Like handwritten text. And green stripes? I remember green stripes. The book is gone now—I can't recall what I did with it, but it's been gone a long time. I've tried as hard as I could to remember the title of the book, and I can't."

She stopped walking and turned to him suddenly. "Tell me your oldest memory."

"Clear or muddled?"

"The oldest one you are sure is not a dream, but an actual memory."

"Okay . . . " In the distance, down a turn of the river, the sections of a residential skyscraper slowly rotated, changing which of its balconies had a view of the river below. "I'm standing on the deck of a ship. It's massive—almost the size of a city, and its deck is covered with stacked containers. You know the ones. Apartment containers, with catwalks and gantries between them. I've examined the feelings around this memory: I'm at the end, maybe, of a long period of being sad. I look at my hands. I'm holding pieces of something in them. But I can't see what it is, closely. Whatever it is, it's mostly white and orange. I can't identify it for the life of me—I've spent hours trying. I open my hands, and the stuff drifts out of them, is caught by the wind, and then falls down along the huge side of the ship and out of sight. And I remember feeling disappointed: I had wanted the drama of seeing it hit the water, but I could not see it. It just—went away under this enormous bulk. Gone.

"The next clear memory is months afterward, and after that they get clearer and clearer, of course. That one must have been very strong to have lasted for so long. I sort of keep retelling it to myself. To see if I can remember it. Forever . . . "

"It must have been one of those round-the-world container-home trips," she said. "I remember the ads: 'Travel around the world for five years, all in the comfort of your own home.' The whole idea was a bit unwieldy, a lot of diesel fumes and seedy ports, but people signed up who had the time and the money. They were popular for a long time. Until one of those liners went down in the Atlantic, remember?"

"Fifty years ago."

"Sixty, I think."

"It could easily be. I keep so little track, these days." They were on the down escalator, across the river now. Outside, cobblestones and cold. The entire center of the city had been restored to the way it was hundreds and hundreds of years before anyone could possibly remember—even the professional mnemosynes. He liked that about it: it was why he lived here: and also why, he imagined, Sophia lived here. Their gloved hands bumped against one another as Sophia changed direction, leading them up a narrow side street. There were bicycle stations everywhere, of course: no cars allowed within two hundred fifty blocks of here. His own bicycle was at a station not so far away. They were within walking distance of his place. He blew through the fabric of his gloves. Time to switch from the fall to the winter pair. He felt a sense of dread opening in him, and he wanted to be away from Sophia and home among his SAE texts, pushing himself through another hour of studying, closed off in that little, specific world. She put a hand on his shoulder as she turned, stopping him, blocking the sidewalk in front of him.

"I'm not a superstitious person, you know." A gust came off the river and hissed evilly through the dry-leafed trees. They both laughed. "No matter how hard the world tries to make me one. I don't think I believe in fate or anything else. But I want to say a few things. Can I?"

He blinked. "Why wouldn't you be able to?"

"Right. What I want to say is: my oldest memory is of finding that picture. And they say—all the books say—that the memories that survive for the longest are the ones that are somehow important. Some even say, the ones that carry some sort of a key inside them to something else. I don't know if it's true—but it makes sense that you remember the more important things for longer. That's one." She counted it on her glove.

"Two is—we look really happy in that picture, in a way that I know I haven't felt for as long as I can remember. Which is a long time. And I'm not saying that I haven't been happy . . . but not like that picture. Nothing like that. Those people . . . we . . . were happy.

"Three is—I've kept the picture, but I haven't been looking for you. Maybe keeping an eye out, half-consciously, but how would I ever find this person in a photo I couldn't remember taking? Hire a detective? So I just kept it. I was maybe hoping. But not . . . looking. And the picture was taken a long way from here and a long time ago. And the fact that I went into that café—because it was raining, only because it was raining—and saw you there—not looking for you—makes me feel—although I'm pretty terrified of you—that this seems right."

Standing still was pushing the cold all the way up his thighs. It would be time to switch to long underwear again, as well. "It does. It seems right."

She started backing up the street. "Okay. Go home, it's cold. I'll see you tomorrow."

He just stood there for a while, after the shadows under the furthest trees had drowned her shape. She was not walking toward her apartment, but farther away from it—he wondered how much farther. He turned left and went down the embankment, turning details over in his mind and trying to remember things. Did he remember her? Now that he had seen the picture, it seemed as if he did, but he knew the way these false memories could be constructed by the mind: you would remember a moment, but in the memory, you would be looking into your own face, or looking down at yourself from above—which meant it couldn't possibly be real. And they said that every time you remembered something, you subtly changed the memory to suit the present moment. He had no independent recollection of her. A hoax? There were memory con artists, some of them incredibly skilled; whole volumes had been written on them.

But he felt sure that Sophia was exactly who she seemed to be. It was a stubborn, ignorant sureness, but it was all he had. He walked a long way down the cold, concrete embankment, very much aware of his fragile, warm form along the riverbank.

At five in the morning he clambered clumsily out of bed in the dark. He was sweating. He must have been dreaming, but the dream was gone, only the impulse remained. He searched desperately in the dark, not even thinking to turn on the light. It was here, somewhere. . . .

Today it was Opponent Three, the little girl. Sebastian was earlier than usual: after waking up at five, he had not been able to sleep. Finally, at seven or so— much earlier than he usually got up, these days—he forced himself into the shower tube, then flung on the old shooting jacket, took his bag, and went out for breakfast to a little Greek place on the corner. For some reason he did not want to go to the café yet. The book on SAE theory was a blur; he kept reading broken bits of sentences, backtracking over whole pages, closing the book and staring out into the quiet, early street. Finally he just got up, leaving the breakfast half finished, and went to the café to wait. It was not a morning café; not the kind of place that people came to for a quick cup of coffee before work, but more the kind of place people just—came to. There was just a smattering of customers reading their terminals, and the owner at the far corner of the bar, playing chess with the serious little girl. At first, Sebastian would be quiet. He would let Sophia talk first—get whatever it was out of her system. Then he would show her. And then what? He couldn't know. For the first time in a very long time, he was frightened of making a mistake, and he realized that there was something in him, some capacity, like a forgotten function, like an unused piece of programming.

Outside, it started to rain. Not a normal autumn rain, or an early winter rain—but a rain of surprising force. Wind came hammering down the street and awnings flapped, then hail rattled and smacked against the windows. The little girl looked up from the chess game with a look on her face of joy and wonder at the horrible weather—Sebastian's reaction too, normally. But now the storm threw him into a panic as the rain mixed with sleet, then snow, then freezing rain, and shellacked the windows with distorting ice. Everyone looked around. Customers ordered second cups of coffee. Nobody was worried yet, but nobody was going anywhere. In books in the old days he knew that this was about the time that the power would go out, candles would be brought around, and they would begin to tell stories to one another, or some such thing. The beginning of a one-act play. Of course, the last time there had been a power outage in the city was well beyond anyone's memory horizon. Still, a few people did look up at one another, acknowledging for the first time that other humans were also in this room. A banner across his terminal announced a temporary reduction of NEM service. The city was in the midst of a major ice storm.

Within two hours, much of the storm had passed, without real damage done to anything. The streets were mechanically cleared thirty minutes after that, and the city returned to its normal, subdued level of activity—but Sophia did not come. Sebastian went home in the dark, up streets forested with icicles. It occurred to him that poems, like eucalyptus trees, poisoned the ground beneath them. Eventually, there would be no soil left where anything new could grow. Eventually, there would be no writing about human feeling left to be done at all—only reading.

There was an Opponent Four. This was something new. Sebastian had come in very early. He dropped into his usual place and ordered a macaroon and a Japanese coffee. How long had the place been a café? Longer, possibly, than he had been alive, which was a very long time. He had moved so long from one obsession to another. Now he thought that, underneath all that concentration—all the papers for peer-reviewed journals, all the attention to syntax and SAE peculiarities and dialectical variations—all the careful research, decades of it—was something else. Some sort of breadcrumb trail he hadn't even been aware of following, leading off into the darkness. In the meantime he had been analyzing, in excruciating detail, the symbolism in the presentation of the contents of a medicine cabinet, the details of a young man shaving in the mid-twentieth century, the typology of Manhattan apartments, haiku in SAE translation, Western appropriations and reinterpretations of Buddhist thought, twentieth century traditions of suicide . . . Simply to justify his existence, he had thought, when he no longer had to work for money because some version of himself that he could not remember had done all the work for him. Only now did he realize what it was he had really been doing.

A bicycle went past, a manual type, as mandated by city ordinance, making a pleasant, nostalgic clatter over the cobbled street. Opponent Four was a woman in a nurse's uniform, but without her hat on, and in regular walking shoes. Just off a night shift? She was standing, bent over the board. A sky-blue wool coat was thrown over a barstool next to her, as if she had just swept in off the street and didn't intend to stay long. " . . . and . . . *mate*," she said, clapping her hands together.

"You're good," said the owner.

"Well," said Opponent Four, "I've been playing for as long as I can remember."

The owner rubbed his shaved head. "So have I. A lot of good it's done me."

The nurse put her jacket on and turned. Seeing Sebastian in his usual place in the corner, she walked over.

"You're Sebastian."

"Yes," he said, swallowing macaroon. "Yes. Do I know you?"

"Sophia asked me to stop in here and tell you she's in the hospital. Central District Hospital #2, just up the street. She slipped on the ice yesterday, broke her elbow very badly. Surgery's tomorrow. Glad I caught you in time." She turned and walked out.

Sophia looked like she was being eaten, right arm first, by a white, ovoid machine. The machine was suspended over the bed at the end of a multi-jointed armature. A slight green glow spilled from it and across the side of Sophia's face.

"Latest of the latest," Sophia said. "Same technology they use in limb regrowth—it's supposed to shorten healing time by about ninety-five percent—I should have full mobility in four days. You brought flowers, which is incredibly antique of you. This thing feels weird."

He sat on the chair next to the bed. "You have surgery tomorrow?"

She frowned. "No, just more of this. Is that what they told you?"

"The nurse told me."

"That woman has a very strange sense of humor."

"What does it feel like?"

"It feels like . . . ants crawling up and down the bones of my arm and massing at my elbow. Crawling through the marrow of my bones. But it doesn't hurt—it tickles. Very strange. Very unpleasant, without being painful. I'd rather not experience it again. This is all very dramatic—ice storms and broken limbs and messengers."

"And strange requests in anterooms, and photographs."

She smiled. "My hair is greasy, and I've done nothing with my life for about the last hundred years except diddle around on the violin and pretend to write a book on Freud. I can't even be bothered to learn German. So . . . embarrassing."

"Possibly of more use than what I have been up to."

"Which is?"

"An obsession. I've built a minor career around it. In fact, I might be, because of it, the world's foremost expert on Specific American Englishes of the Period 1950–1964, especially those related to the works of one author."

"Okay, that rivals my idiotic Freud project. Why?"

"I came across a translation of a book. Maybe it was sixty years ago now. I wasn't living here at the time, but out East at a cataloguing dig. One of the abandoned cities. Another archaeologist loaned me this old book he had—this was just at the time when the fad for paper books was coming back around. I read it, and read it again, and again. I felt drawn to it. And I couldn't really understand it: the sentences seemed tangled. The book seemed to be about nothing at all, or about something that I couldn't possibly grasp. But these little glowing pieces that I did understand—fascinated me. I was sure that it was the translation getting in the way. So I decided I would learn to read it in the original."

"Why?"

"I wouldn't have been able to tell you. I thought at the time that it was because I desperately needed something to do. This thing was as good as any other thing. But it's what I've done now for decades. I've studied this very particular, dead version of English. It isn't really that different from the kind they speak nowadays—maybe half the words are the same, maybe more. The grammar has changed, of course. Mostly, the challenge lies in understanding the world they lived in, which is so different from ours. Their world is so shadowed by inevitabilities, especially the inevitability of death, which covers everything. And of course everything moves so urgently. Everything is so compressed. Yet they waste time with a terrible determination, as well. I knew at least a little modern English, so that was a start. After a few years, I began to forget exactly why I had started the project. I'd become fascinated with all of the little details along the way. Complex, endless little problems. And I started to publish in the field, after a while. Then it became about that—about the academic side of it. The very fine distinctions.

"Several years ago, I was digging around in one of the little antique shops here in the city center, and I came across a paperback copy of the book. The same one that had gotten me started. In decent condition—and you know how rare they are these days, though they were very common at the time. It wasn't a first edition or anything, but it was of the period, in the original language, and it was in decent shape. I honestly thought I would never find one. Before that, I had always worked from my terminal on electronic texts.

"I was so happy—I remember being happier than I had been about anything in—well, in a very long time. I walked down to the park and I read it—in the original—cover to cover. It was dark when I finished. I remember that I sat there, for it seemed like hours afterwards, trying to hold on to this—mode— that I had slipped into. A particular shape of the world, a tone to things. Like when someone says 'it struck a chord' in me. That must be the rough, dead metaphor for this feeling—but it's nothing like the thing itself."

He looked at Sophia. She was staring back at him. The machine on her arm bleeped. She turned her head and scowled at it. "Oh, shut up, machine. What do you know?" She turned back to Sebastian. "Keep talking, you."

"It had taken me fifty-three years to get to that point, where I could read it like that—understand every word, know their world almost as if I had lived in it. I felt like it had all been worth it. And I felt as if I had been following some kind of trail into the dark. I had been following that trail for so long that I had forgotten what I was doing. I had begun to think that I was just walking aimlessly. And then I had come across something that I was looking for. It didn't feel like the end, the final thing. But it was like . . . a waypoint.

"Then that night, after we talked . . . I didn't realize it right away . . . "

He reached into his bag and withdrew a paperback book. It was crumpled, curved of spine, and fragile-looking, packaged carefully in a sleeve of clear plastic. There was, unusually, no illustration on the white paper of the cover— only the book's title and the author's name, printed to look as if they had been hand-written with a fountain pen, and a pair of green stripes bisecting the cover, about three-quarters of the way down its white surface.

He put it in her good hand. "This," he said. "I didn't realize this. It's the thing that I've been studying for all these years. You see? The trail that led off into the dark. The SAE English, the haiku, the contents of a medicine cabinet . . . they all lead here, to a silly little book that shouldn't have had any meaning for me at all."

She held the little book in her hand, moving her hand slightly up and down, as if testing the weight of the thing. She turned it over. The back cover was the same as the front cover, except for a bar code near the bottom—the sort of thing not seen on a book for three hundred years, at least. The lower corner of the back cover was torn.

"I feel like I've seen it before."

"You have," he said. "It's the book you took our picture from. You described it to me. In your apartment. A white cover. Only text on it. Handwritten text. And green stripes. It's the book you put on a shelf once in a little bookstore, meaning to forget it."

She set the book down on the bed sheet. Then picked it up again. Then put it down, adjusted it a bit. "Yes. This is it." She shook her head, closed her eyes for a second. Opened them again. "This is it."

It was an almost perfect café. It was in a red brick building that turned burgundy in the rain, when the rain streamed down its onion domes and its stained glass. Through the archway of chipped grapevines, under the dome of the main room, stood the old, mirrored bar with its bottles gathering dust and the silvered mirrors growing darker every year.

The bar was where the owner was always to be found, rubbing his shaved head, staring at a game of chess. He always played against one of three different opponents. Opponent One was a nurse who stopped by in her uniform around lunchtime. She played quickly, and when she won—as she nearly always did—she clapped her hands together, said "Ha!" and walked out. Opponent Two was a woman with a nose she had never quite grown into and blonde hair like ashes. She would finish the game and, win or lose, sink her pointed face into a book, sipping her coffee in silence. Opponent Three was Sebastian. He played slowly and carefully, with a sort of desperate concentration. After three decades he still had not won a game.

The rest of the room was a shifting dance of tables, chairs, and light. The chairs and tables were never in quite the same configuration when Sebastian came in. He suspected that, after the café closed, the owner moved them around, just for the sake of moving them. The light was never the same either: it fell through the stained glass in a moody shift, dependent on cloud and season.

But what made it nearly perfect was the place in the corner, against the wall furthest from the entrance, by the windows. Here there was an enormous, purple-velvet armchair, a battered wicker high-backed chair, and a massive oak table. When he lost, as he always did, Sebastian would cross the room, shaking his head, and settle into the armchair. Sophia would look up at him from her terminal and sigh.

"One day, you'll give up."

"One day, I'll win."

And so the café had the feeling, at once, of agelessness—its ancient building, its collection of rescued furniture, its continual game of chess in the corner— and of change: the patterns of color-stained light and the dance of tables and chairs. All this, and the macaroons were excellent. All this, and the service was good.

AND YOU SHALL KNOW HER BY THE TRAIL OF DEAD

BROOKE BOLANDER

The mobster has a gun pressed to Rack's forehead. The mobster has a god-shitting *gun* pressed to her partner's fucking forehead, and the only thing Rhye can do is watch and scream as the man smiles at her and pulls the trigger and blows Rack's perfect brains out from between his ears.

Rhye has her guns drawn before the other Ganymede fuckers can twitch, but it's way too late—the damage is done and smeared across the walls and floor and ceiling. Synthetic blood and bone look exactly the same as the real deal. She puts three shots into the flesh slab that did it *(he's dead he's dead gods fuck it no nononono)* and then the rest of his pals are on her like the three-times-fucked human jackals they are, pulling her down. The room stinks of blood and gunsmoke and fear-sweat. For the first time in her life, those smells make Rhye want to gag. Her ears are ringing—whether from the gunshots or god knows what else—and it feels like the floor is falling away beneath her motorcycle boots.

She's still struggling against their meaty fingers to reach Rack when the head goon breaks her nose with a squared-off fist the size of the moon he's from. She barely feels the bone snap. He's dead. He's dead and the world is grayscale, all the color leaching from it to pool around her feet in a red puddle.

"He was trying to crack it, you *fucks*. The fuck is wrong with you? He was coming out, he was going to try again, it was just a fucking hiccup! Jesus *fuck*, do you think you're going to get your cunting kid back now?" Her throat hurts from screaming. Blood from her nose is backing up into her sinuses, half-choking her. She doesn't care. "I'll kill you, I'll fucking kill all of you. You're fucking *dead*, do you hear me? Let me go, let me fucking *go*—"

"We hired you and your partner to finish job. Nothing was ever said about quitting," the man says. His voice is heavily accented, breath reeking of onions and vodka. "If pretty boy couldn't bring what we need out, pretty boy is useless, like tits on bull or useless cyborg bitch. His consciousness can stay inside box and rot for all I care. But!—" he pokes Rhye in the forehead with one of his blunt fingers—"I think *you* care. I think you care very much, yes? Yesyes?"

"I'm going to kill you, you fuck." She says it slowly, pronouncing every word with deathly clarity. "I'm going to shove my gun up your ass and blow a hole so fucking wide a whale's *prick* wouldn't fill the gap."

"Not if you want partner back," he says, throwing an uplink cable at her. "Plug in, get data out. Get pretty boy, too, if you like. Fail, and you die together. Is very simple."

And because she *does* care, cares too fucking much, cares, and the sight of Rack slumped over in the chair with a neat round hole scorched into his forehead is squeezing at the heart she's always claimed not to have, Rhye spits blood and hate in their employer's face and jams the jack into the port at the base of her skull.

The first time she meets Rack, Rhye's fresh out of the army and fresh back from one of the meat-grinders the humans pay her kind to fight in. The children of wires and circuits aren't worth a tinker's fuck compared to the children of real flesh and bone, so far as the world's concerned. The recruitment agents pluck her off the streets when she's twelve and send her to a training camp and she's good with linguistics and better at killing, so they keep her hands busy until she's twenty-five and then they spit her back out again like a mouthful of cum. She has gray curly hair cropped short and gray dead eyes and calluses on the inside of her palms worn hard and horny from years of holding pistol grips. She's small and lean, which makes people underestimate her, but she's cool enough and don't-fuck-with-me enough that most know to jump the fuck out of the way when they see her coming. The ones that don't get flashed a warning glimpse of her teeth and holsters.

There's nothing funnier than watching some drunken fleshsack piss his drawers when that happens. One minute he's trying to grab a skin-job whore's ass, the next he's looking his own death in the face and wetting himself like a goddamned baby. It never fails to tickle the shit out of Rhye.

She bums around the city looking for something to do, gets in a moderate amount of trouble in every district she lands (her and the cops are on a first-name basis; it's touching), and finally ends up at the deathmatches, fighting her own kind for a quick buck in front of a bunch of screaming yahoos. Rhye doesn't really do it for the cash, although money for smokes is always nice. She does it because killing is the only thing she's good at, and quite frankly, she enjoys it. If the poor fucks she gunned down didn't want to be there, they wouldn't be. They're all fucked, everything is fucked, and the pain at least makes her feel something.

Then one night in the arena her foot slips and the hulking musclebound mountain of nano-technology she's peppering with shots catches up and busts three of her ribs and one of her wrists. Rhye still manages to take him down one-handed, but even with the purse prize she doesn't have enough money for a fixer. They toss her out into the alleyway behind the joint like a kid's broken toy and there she lies, soaked to the skin from the oily rain that never seems to stop falling in this fucking gray ashtray of a city.

And that's where Rack finds her, that clean-fingered, mild-mannered motherfucker. Why he's even there in the first place is beyond her. All she knows is that one minute she's huddling in a puddle, exhausted and hurting, and the next there's a hand extended her way and a pair of sad brown eyes looking down at her (*fucking puppy-dog expression, clean-shaven and thoughtful and for fuck's sake he was wearing a tie and carrying a briefcase, can you believe that shit*) and no matter how hard she glares at him, he won't fucking go. Rhye shows him the grips of her pistols and he just looks at her, just fucking *looks*. That surprises her; she's not expecting young Mr. Salaryman to be stubborn.

"Fuck off, White Collar," she says. "Do I fucking know you?"

"No," he replies, exasperatingly patient, "but I know what it looks like when somebody needs a hand. C'mon. Let's get you out of the rain."

She's hurting too bad to put up much of a fuss. He loops an arm beneath her own and together the two of them limp back to his flat, her getting oily water and blood all over his nice white shirt the entire way.

If he had been smart, he would have left her where she lay. Fucking dumbass. Stupid fucking noble idealistic kind-hearted dumbass.

Outgoing Connection detected!

Initializing Connection Handoff to Interpretive Interface . . . Handoff Completed!

(Hey, Rhye, c'mere. I made you something.)

It's like floating in black static, and all the pressure is sitting on top of Rhye's head sumo-style, pushing her further down. Lines of code play across the insides of her eyes. Floaters are annoying; this is fucking maddening. And it *hurts*. She can't keep a straight thought, scalpels of pain are slicing through her brain over and over and she fucking hates this cyberspace bullshit. It's Rack's thing, not hers. Rhye likes her shit concrete. Rhye likes having a *body*. North, South, East, West. You use your feet to walk in a direction and then you shoot some motherfucker at the end of it. Finding Rack in here is gonna be like finding a seed in an elephant's ass, especially if he's tangled up with the security system. He had sounded scared shitless over the comm-link before that waste of jizz up top had done what he did. Thinking about it makes Rhye's currently non-existent asshole clench.

So. Find Rack, get him out of whatever pile he's stepped into, and also somehow free up the data their employers want. Piece of cake. No problem. As soon as Rhye figures out what form any of that is gonna take, how to move forward, and which fucking way forward *is,* she'll go ahead and do that. Should've paid more attention in school. Should've actually gone to school.

(It looks like a chip, a tiny little chunk of plastic and wire no bigger than a .22 shell. He drops it into her palm, looking like a cat that's just robbed a canary store at gunpoint. She glances down at the thing, then back at him, the smile tugging at the corners of his mouth and the pride in his eyes.)

(The hell is it?)

Establishing parietal operculum loopback . . . SUCCESS

Establishing posterior parietal cortex loopback . . . SUCCESS

Something about the script is nagging at Rhye. A memory half-clouded by booze, disinterest, and the obscuring fog of being so embarrassed by something she had willed her brain to forget all about it. Good god, had she actually *blushed?* Like a fucking schoolgirl with a Valentine?

Rhye never has been good at accepting kindness. Being loved doesn't suit her.

(It's art. It's art and it's one-of-a-kind and it's all yours. It's an interface, like mine, but I cut out all the rendering hardware and installed a direct path to the somasensory cortices of your brain. You interpret the stimulus naturally, like poetry, or music, and—Rhye, there are no words for this. Here, hook yourself up to the test deck. Log in with me. You need to see for yourself.)

(Just say what it does in fuckin' English, Rack, baby.)

(It develops metaphors for abstract environments. I put it together just f—)

(Oh. Huh. Well, that's somethin'. You're a sharp motherfucker, Rack. You want a drink?)

And she had slotted the thing away in one of the ports beneath her hair so his feelings wouldn't be too hurt (not that she cared, of course) and turned away so he wouldn't see her blush (fuck) and promptly gotten herself so completely fucked up on the cheap whiskey they kept in the fridge that the rest of that night was an indistinct blur. That he had wanted her to plug in with him was not something she dwelled on, not something she had let herself dwell on. Fucking sentimentality. It was that sort of shit that got you killed.

But it sure as fuck seems to be coming in handy now, this little gift of Rack's. The static shudders and flashes and things begin taking shape. She has a body again, and guns, and she thanks her brain for that because she'd rather hop around in here on fucking stumps and hooks than be without some representation of her weapons. Another twist of the big empty and there's dirt beneath her boots, a gray sky above and a river ahead, and—

Enhanced local motor/sensory homunculi detected, offloading rendering tasks . . . complete!

Filling input buffer . . . 60% . . . 85% . . . 100%!

Rendering buffer contents . . .

Dead trees, dead grass, and a skeletal ferryman in a boat, cowled and waiting.

Joining up with Rack hadn't stopped her from doing much of anything, at first. She played the part of the hired gun on whatever jobs he asked her to—beneath that quiet boy scout front was a mercenary mind the criminal underworld would spread their cheeks and wallets for, if and when they needed his skills—but Rhye's time was her fucking time, and if she wanted to spend it getting blackout drunk or fighting in deathmatches until the street sweepers came out to mop up the hobo piss, that was none of his fucking concern. And, to Rack's credit, he never gave her any shit about it. He just bundled her into her bed when she came staggering home stinking of bourbon and sweat, sewed up her cuts and swabbed out her wounds, and watched. Always with the fucking watching.

Maybe she got a little reckless (more so than usual). Reckless or sloppy. The outcome was the same: She went into the ring with two good eyes to fight some knife-throwing motherfucker and came out a cyclops, blood and goo leaking from the sliced-up socket like candle wax. She's never been able to remember how the fuck she made it back to the apartment that night on her own. There's a big "scene missing" card and then she's perched on the bathroom counter while Rack dabs gently at the hole in her head, tight-lipped and trying so fucking hard not to let his concern show.

Neither of them says anything for a while. But a question is gnawing at Rhye, and she's drunk enough and light-headed enough from losing all that blood to finally just ask.

"Hey. Rack."

He wrings the washcloth out and a slaughterhouse swirls down the plughole. "Yeah?"

"Why the fuck do you care? About anything, I mean." She shakes her head. Bloody water and antiseptic splatter the walls. "You know what humans say about us? We're just fucking garbage to them. God created their ancestors, but ours were made by Tom, Dick, and motherfuckin' Turing. We don't have souls and they can just use us and throw us out"—she snaps her fingers, bang—"like that. Better than ruining a real person's hands in the factories, right? That kid on the assembly line, she's just a goddamned piece of synthetic trash, she doesn't dream about getting the hell out of the slums to somewhere better. So why give a fuck if that's all the world expects out of you?"

A beat. "Do you believe them?"

"Fuck no. For one thing, there's no such thing as their fucking God. Load of horseshit. The only things you can rely on are these babies." She pats her guns, solid and safe in their holsters. "But they got one thing right. Our lives ain't worth shit in a sewer, and mine least of all. So I'll ask again: What's with the caring act? What's in it for you? You think you're gonna fix me or something?"

"No, Rhye. I don't think that."

"Then why? Why give a fuck?"

He shrugs, shooting her that wry little smile that never reaches his eyes.

"Hey," he says, finally. "Everybody needs a hobby, right?"

That was the last deathmatch Rhye ever fought in. She kept the empty socket, got an eyepatch, and aimed just as well with one eyeball as she ever had with two.

She pays him in spent brass, the kind that gathers in your pockets and shirt cuffs after a day at the range or a night spent turning people into raw red meat. No reaper in Rhye's head would ever bother asking for fuckin' pennies. He stretches out a bony hand and the empty shells clatter into it like beer cans bouncing off a fence post, *ting ting ting*. Lead on, motherfucker, lead on. Down the river and through the woods and if the Big Bad Wolf jumps out, you give him a lead tampon in his pisshole before he can say *hey baby, what's shakin'*.

It looks like all the rivers and canals she's ever known, choked with old shopping trolleys and used condoms and rafts of yellow-brown foam. Styx by way of The City, stinking, oily-slow, full of shit and bodies and about as good a metaphor for life as you could find. The only difference here is that all of the faces beneath the water belong to people Rhye put there. She's not guilty— most of them deserved it—but it's still a little fucked up. They stare at her with accusing, fish-nibbled eyes. Some claw at the bottom of the boat. She doubts shooting them again would help anything, so she saves her bullets, lighting a cigarette instead. The smoke is warm and fuzzy inside her chest, comfortingly familiar, like sucking down a carcinogenic teddy bear.

"Do many of those fuckers get out?" she asks Reaper Man. She can be fuckin' polite, no problem. But Mr. Skullhead doesn't give her a second look, not even when she offers him a smoke (less out of kindness and more because she's curious to see how the hell something without lungs would manage the trick), so she scowls and stares across the water with the coffin nail dangling moodily from her lips, chin in hand. To entertain herself she starts trying to identify every dead person she sees.

There are foot soldiers and foreign agents, low-level punks and pirates and even a police officer or two. Other bounty hunters. Cartel bosses. The kid that couldn't have been older than fifteen that tried to stick her up that one time, not recognizing Rhye for what she was. And yeah, even her first kill, the kiddy-diddling adoption agent with the wormy smile and the good-looking face. Nobody had suspected a goddamned thing. As long as they're good-looking, they never do. Who the fuck were they supposed to believe, the street rat skin-job with a rap sheet at age nine? It had been his blonde-haired, blue-eyed word against hers.

He wasn't fucking pretty with all that blood spurting out of his mouth, though, and he sure as fuck ain't looking too good now with half his chin rotted off. Real or not, it gives Rhye some satisfaction to see him stranded like a rat in the aftermath of a wrecked ship. She reaches down, avoiding the grasping hands. Her cigarette hisses and sizzles as it grinds into his bloated forehead. He sinks back into the water like one of those poor amusement park androids, stuck on a rail with a beam up their ass.

"Waste of a fucking cigarette," she says, and lights another. She actually feels kind of good after that, at least until she sees Rack's face down there too. The drag curdles behind her ribs and sticks like grime clotting a gun barrel.

He's not real. She knows that for a goddamned fact. But Rhye can't tear herself away from those sad eyes, the round hole dribbling black blood and river water down his nose. She watches him as they pull away, until the distance between them stretches and he's just another face in the crowd her hands have made.

The river goes along, as rivers do, and then, out of fucking nowhere, like cockroaches circling the last can of cat food before a paycheck, suburban neighborhoods begin popping up along the banks. They stare down the bluffs with broken window eyes, yards gone to weeds and dog shit and strips of old paint. Who would have thought Hell had pink flamingos?

The ferryman lets Rhye out on a shore made of splintered bone and more spent brass. Why the fuck he needed that shit for a toll when there are dunes of it lying within easy reach, Rhye doesn't know. She sets out for the houses without looking back. They'll meet up again soon enough for real, she figures. No need for handshakes when she'll be probably be back in the boat before her shelf life hits forty.

Keep moving. Keep searching. Wading through drifts of dead leaves and candy wrappers, glancing into doorways, further up and further in, uneasiness growing with each SLOW CHILDREN AT PLAY sign passed and bombed-out, rotten-tired station wagon peered under. Rust, dust, plaster, Styrofoam. Two-story brick hulks sagging at crazy angles, their multi-car garages gaping like slack-jawed drunks at a nudie bar. Shadows everywhere:

beneath grimy windshields, in the alleyways, stacked thick behind brokeback venetian blinds. Rhye's been in friendlier combat zones; at least there you'll spot the occasional buzzard or scuttling cat.

She's being followed by *something,* but that's not surprising. A good sign: If she's suddenly interesting enough to be getting the hairy eyeball, maybe it's the security system crawling out from under its rock to do some territorial pissing. She puts up with the peeping for another couple of blocks, then stops in her tracks.

"Look. You wanna ask me to the fuckin' dance already instead of trying to peek up my skirts?"

Nothing. Not a big talker, her stalker.

" 'Cause, y'know, if you're too chickenshit to give me an invitation, I'm just gonna go with the football captain, that motherfucker is *dreamy* and I hear he's got a dick like a goddamned science experiment."

Nada but tree shadows, all the way down the block. Nothing—and then, three or four houses down, a shape stepping out into the street. It stands there on the curb, watching quietly, silhouetted against the ashtray sky. The sharp, familiar scent of a lit cigarette punches through the stale air.

"Rhye? Is that you?"

But it's not the figure speaking to her. This voice comes from behind, one she's been wanting to hear ever since she plugged in. Her breath snags barbed wire. She half-turns to look back over her shoulder, against her better judgment.

"Holy shit, Rack! Where the fuck are you, man? I've been looking all over the place for you! Are y—"

"No, look, *look,* Rhye, you need to get out of here. You need to get out of here right now. I made a huge mistake, I underestimated the security protocol, and she's going to come after you, too, if you don't go. Don't worry about me. Rhye?"

The shadowy shape is walking towards her. Rhye's pretty sure it's not out selling cookies or spreading the word of the Lord. "That's assuming I know how to fucking get out of here without you, man," she says. Her hands are already on her guns. "And what the fuck do you mean by *she?*"

The purposeful walk has turned into a wolf-trot. The light still isn't great, but she can see now that it's a girl. About her height, about her build, same hair color, same way of moving—

Wait. Wait just one fucking minute.

"Rack? This security program. I'm just, like, seeing my subconscious or some bullshit again, right? Right?" The other woman is running now. "Because if you've done what I think you did—"

"I, uh . . . "

Mother*fucker*.

". . . I may have cribbed heavily from existing source material, yes."

The woman grins as she sprints. Still has both of her eyes. Four years ago, maybe? A copy of her at her most bitter and burned out, thirsty for blood and not caring whose.

"Let's do this, then," she says, sighing, and then there's no time for talk anymore.

So there's this skin-job kid that gets adopted by one of those high muckity-muck Ganymede mobsters. He isn't exceptionally bright and he sure as hell ain't a looker, but Don Whoeverthefuck has a bug up his ass 'cause his biological clock is tick-tick-ticking away like a block of C4 is tenderly bearhugging his testicles. Old fart needs an heir. All those years of pushing baby carriages into traffic ain't gonna count for shit if he doesn't have an heir to pick up the slack when his heart valves do their last dance with the extra-lard pork belly. He throws some money around, which is how he's solved every other problem in his bloated life, and hey voila, instant son. The boy is dumber than a sack of skullfucked squirrels, but that just makes him fit in with all the real Mafioso squirts that came from ballsacks and bad decisions.

Things go on swingin' as they usually do. Little Johnny Electronuts gets in his share of trouble, but Daddy is always there to yank his ass out of the fire with greased palms or greased dicks or a carefully administered dose of goon muscle to somebody's knees and groin. Then, one day, kiddo gets the idea that he's some kind of fucking hacker. He's nineteen and he's better protected than the Virgin Mary's holy of holies and he's got a chip on his shoulder and a hard-on in his lucky rocketship underoos just crying to fuck something up. He tries to bust his way into a rival family's black box so he can crow about it to all his knuckle-dragging script kid buddies. This is what is known in the business as a Giant Fucking Mistake, 'cause the security system in this motherfucker was set up by another motherfucker by the name of Rack, and Rack is a goddamned super genius when it comes to that sort of thing. It grabs the kid by the short hairs almost as soon as he plugs in and slams the door behind him, and when the Don's cavalry comes busting in to save his ass, their nuts land squarely in a bear trap. His consciousness is all locked up like a gold bar inside a treasure chest. They've got the box, but nobody seems to be able to get through to the toy inside.

Nobody but the motherfucker who designed the system in the first place, that is. They offer him money. They offer him a lot of money. And less because of the money and more because he likes a challenge, Rack bites.

And that's where things get fucked up.

• • •

Dodge for dodge and feint for feint and bullet for bullet they come together, the woman that was and the woman that is. The Not-Rhye is laughing like a kid at the circus as she spins her hand-cannons, laughing and twisting and breathing in that gunsmoke that turns your snot black like she's a barracuda and it's seawater. She doesn't give a shit whether she lives or dies and Rhye knows this because it used to be *her,* and she suddenly realizes, with something like shock and something like mild disgust, that this is no longer a truth that applies. Something inside Rhye wants to make it out alive, wants to go home to the shitty-ass flat with the bullet holes in the air conditioner, wants to taste bourbon and cigarettes and go right on living alongside that dumbfuck brainiac like she has every day for the past five years. Dangerous. Very dangerous. The moment you start wanting is the moment you slow down. And the moment you slow down—

Not-Rhye lands close enough that Rhye can smell the burning wire and ozone stink of her over the reek of cordite and hot metal. She flicks one of the pistols like a gecko lapping up a mosquito and it coughs emphysema and tuberculosis and Rhye's cheek is laid open to the bone even as she rolls behind a row of trash cans, ears ringing like pulled fire alarms. She's a fucking idiot. She should've been scrapped at construction. She's going to die here, soft and stupid as a human cop, and Rack is going to be trapped inside this box forever. The mobsters are going to be fucking pissed when nobody comes back. Good. Fuck 'em, and fuck their wives and moms and childhood pets for good measure.

"Were you trying to hit me, or did one of those pink flamingos do something to piss you off?" she says. If she can irritate Not-Rhye into making a mistake she might have a chance. Anything is worth a shot. "The neighbors are gonna talk, y'know."

No response. Too smart for her own good. God *damn* she wishes Rack had held a less flattering view of her when he programmed this fucker. "Oh well. We'd have made shitty Home Owners Association members anyway. Rack! You alright?"

"I think so. I wasn't exactly expecting this to happen when I went in. I thought—"

"That was your first fuckin' mistake, Rack baby. You do too much of that anyway." She rubs her blistered, lead-stained fingers clean on her cargo pants and digs for a fresh magazine. "Is there any way for me to disable her easier than giving her brain airholes?"

You could hear a gnat fart in the pause that follows.

"Rack, say something before I come over there and do some kinky shit to your ass with this gun barrel, please."

". . . I don't know," he says. "I think I can do it, but you'll have to free me up first."

"Fuck a row of baby ducks, is that all? Lemme send Little Miss Red Rover a fuckin' engraved invitation to move her psycho ass to a new neighborhood and I'll be right over with a bundt cake and a goddamned meat loaf."

But she's already tensing to spring back into the line of fire, because of course she is.

Up and at 'em, knocking the bins over clitter-clatter like a fuckball of feral cats, and sure enough there's her shadow racing to greet her, four years younger, one eye richer, and meaner than a limp-dicked drill sergeant. No time to fire off a good shot; she says *fuck it* and goes ahead and launches herself straight into the other woman's knees and down the two of them tumble in a muddy heap of fists and flailing motorcycle boots like a pair of overturned shot glasses, the world reduced to rubber soles squeegeeing shins and knuckles glancing off grittywet concrete. Rack's yelling something. Little-known fact, though: It's pretty fucking hard to focus on anything but the task at hand when the task is trying to club your teeth out with the handshake-end of a pistol. She dodges the blow and it glances off her temple instead with a hollow *thwonk*. Gasoline stars and flat-tire sparks shimmy-shake across her vision.

No fucking way I'm blacking out. Her bone-sickle grin hangs overhead, the last thing so many other unlucky motherfuckers have seen at the end of a fight. Rhye focuses on that sliver, wills the darkness back with clenched fists and a gas leak hiss. The thing with her smile is still laughing, but it's not some kind of mad villain cackle. She sounds like she's having the time of her life.

"What the fuck are you laughin' at, dumbshit? See something funny?" Not the wittiest thing to ever rasp its way out of her nicotine box, but whatever. Wit's the first thing to go when you've just gotten pistolwhipped in the side of the head so hard your brain thinks it's being skullfucked to death by a rhinoceros. The grip comes down again, misses her by an asshair, and judo-chops the pavement so that little bits of gravel spray up like buckshot.

If the girl-slash-security-system-that-was-her is sharp and not a dumbfuck, she'll use these precious seconds to turn her guns around and shoot Rhye in the face, like she's wishing she had just done herself. But oh, glory of glories, blessed be the almighty fuckin' cockiness of youth. This little asshole right here—with her two dead eyes and her don't-need-nobody jock walk—curls her lip back in an *are you fuckin' serious* sneer and swallows the bait deep.

"Aw, come the fuck *on,* man!" she crows. "You can't fuckin' tell me the thought of actually going up against somebody who can give you a fair fight isn't gettin' you all tingly in your grandma-bloomers! Why the hell else would you come here? For *him?*Fuck's sake, I'm you, aren't I? You live for sweat running under your tits and blood splattering your face, not some soft-hearted fuckhead can't tell which way a magazine loads."

Is that what he thinks I thought? Shit. *There's* a nasty little spoonful of glass to chew on. No time for guilt, though.

"You got one part of that right, sister," she says, and jams her thumb into the girl's left eyeball. It's all executed in one smooth motion: jabtwistpull. And then she's rolling across the wet ribbon of tarmac while her not-self flails and shrieks gurgling stray cat curses, rolling and back on her feet and bringing up her guns to make an end of this, but even in a considerable amount of pain the other her is fast in an unnatural, make-the-flesh-of-your-ears-crinkle sort of way, slither-snarling back beneath the rainy evening's skirts before Rhye can give the triggers a good hard prom-night fingering. She starts to go after her, blood boiling.

Y'know what? A little voice in her head, the one that sometimes says things like *are you sure getting into that gimp's windowless white van is a good idea?* or *maybe we should go get that festering bullet hole checked out,* or, of late, *don't punch Rack in the face, the poor bastard hasn't done anything to deserve it this time.* In other words, her inner killjoy.

What?

Fuck pride, man.

And just what is that supposed to mean, exactly?

Pride is for jackoffs who aren't being hunted from the fucking shadows.

"Shut the hell up." She says this aloud in a hissed whisper; hopefully the security system will laugh herself to death at Rhye having a conversation with her invisible friend and that'll be that. "We're fine. I can do this by myself. I don't care what Rack says."

Pride is for people who don't have other people depending on them . . .

Rhye snaps to a halt like the bullet she's been expecting just drilled her brain a peephole.

. . . So why don't you try trusting your partner for goddamned once and get over there like he asked? Remember what we're here for.

"Go fuck your own ass with a fish-hook dildo." Her shoulders are slumping before she's halfway through the word "fuck." By the time she reaches "dildo" she's made a u-turn and is vaulting the sagging picket fence that separates her from the back-alley leading to Rack, feet *thwap–thwap-thwapping* the blacktop. She listens for the echo of a pursuit, but all she can hear is Rack's voice reeling her in and her own one-woman ticker-tape parade careening down the path.

Warm. Warmer. Red-hot, veering back off the pavement, crashing through briars and dead weeds and old tires like she's back in basic, up and over another splintered, gap-slatted privacy fence as weather-worn as a beer can in the ditch. It's not a pretty postcard that greets her—more weeds, more broken glass, a swimming pool filled with water the color and consistency of baby shit. Rack is there, though, tied up on the patio, and that qualifies it for Garden of the Fucking Century, so far as Rhye's concerned. She's down and off her perch and across the yard before she can remember to lazily saunter in like she doesn't give a fuck.

His face is a bloodied bedsheet, haunted eyes staring out from behind the bruises and stubble. Rhye wipes the blood from his split lip and they exchange a quick *you cool?* glance before she sets to work on the knotted ropes. It's not some romantic, lovey-dovey, kiss your boo-boos BS; it's just the kind of thing good partners do for one another.

"Been playing in Mommy's bondage closet again, Rack-baby?" *Tsk-tsk.* "You got a lotta 'splaining to do if we get out of here alive, my friend." She spares him another look from under her cocked brow, trying to keep it cool and even, wanting him to maybe twist in the wind a little. His expression is all thousand-yard stare and nervous bird herk-jerk, sheepishness and syrupy adoration. Portrait of The Nebbish As Grateful Penitent. He looks like he stuck his hand down a secretary's panties at the office holiday party, got a handful of tentacles for his troubles, and wanted her all the more for it after that initial moment of cold water surprise. "For now, though," she finishes, after re-locating her tongue and remembering how to use it, "we need to figure out a way to clean up this goddamned mess. No, sorry, my bad: *Your* goddamned mess, 'cause I sure as shit don't remember giving you permission to turn my personality into a fucking security module. Can you see me? You're lookin' right at me, so I'm pretty sure you can see me."

"We synced up as soon as you stepped into the area," he says. "The chip, you know?" Rhye finally snake-charms the ropes into giving way and he pulls his hands free, rubbing each wrist gingerly. You could take fingerprints with the tired smudges beneath his eyes. "I always wanted the interfaces to work together. Yours is one-of-a-kind, but I gave mine a tweak, so—OW! What the heck was that for?"

"It's lucky for you that we're friends, asshole. Anybody else pulled some shit like this and I wouldn't just sock 'em in the ear. How's this gonna go down? Talk quick. She's way too quiet right now and I have *no* idea how long that's going to last."

"It's . . . tricky."

"Tricky? What exactly do you mean by 'tricky'? Did you or didn't you say you could disable that fucking thing if I got you free?"

"I did say that, yes." Rack stretches the last word out until it wobbles, full of more quivering "but" than a strip club. "I can give you a kill switch. Implementing it may require a little footwork, though, and I'm not sure how that will play out, considering our . . . environment." He waves a hand to take in the garden, runs the other through his hair, and ends up looking like an insomniac hedgehog.

"Well, considering our only other option is getting bullet-fucked to death by a pissed-off, admittedly foxy-fine bit of code, I'm open to anything. What do I need to do?"

"We'll need to execute two operations at the same time, and even then it doesn't have a 100% chance of working. I hadn't allowed for this. I can be sort of an idiot sometimes, as you are probably aware."

Seeing him slumped there staring at his hands feels like defeat, and she'll be fucked if she gives up that easily after coming this far. She punches him in the shoulder. "Hey, none of that sadsack shit. You fucked up. Everybody does. If you're gonna wallow in it, I might as well've left you up there with your brains as pretty pink wallpaper. What the fuck will trying hurt, right?"

And that gets a slow, crooked half-smile out of him, which is all she really wants right now. It's like her heart just snorted a line. "You're right, of course," he says.

"Goddamned right I am." She offers him her hand. "C'mon. Let's do this thing."

Their palms meet with an awesome partnerly *slap.*

Now, this is where Rhye expects him to pull something cool out of his pockets—a couple of little red buttons, maybe, or a bundle of dynamite. Instead, he blanches. His hands fly up to his throat in the universal *oh shit, I'm choking* gesture. For a horrible fistful of seconds she thinks she's going to have to do the Heimlich (and how the fuck does that work, anyway? Is that the move where you grab the other person from behind and give them a rough humping?) but thankfully he shakes whatever's in his throat loose on his own. Something small and heavy bounces off the toe of Rhye's boot. Another, like a fat brass raindrop.

She reaches down and carefully picks up two 9mm bullets, bright as change in a gutter.

Rack peers down at the lumps of lead and metal he just hairball-horked onto her boots. If he wore glasses she just knows he'd be adjusting the fucking things for a better look. "Huh. I guess it makes sense that they would take this form."

"So these are, what, special? Magic bullets?" They *feel* like normal rounds. They even smell like 'em, which is to say, metallic. She rolls them between her fingers, warm from the heat of her hand. "Kill switches, whatever the fuck you called 'em?"

"Correct. Ideally you'll discharge both simultaneously, shutting down the security system completely."

There are pros and cons to knowing somebody—*really* knowing somebody, how their face looks when they cry or come or drool in their sleep. Rhye understands what Rack means immediately: *You're the fighter, you're strong, so of course you'll take care of this on your own.* She could say no. She could open up her chest with a scalpel and let him see the tender bits—*I can't do this alone, she's too good and I care too much and quite frankly I'm scared shitless, for you and for me*—or she could tell him, hey, clean up your own goddamned mess, I ain't your fuckin' nanny.

But she knows how this has to go down, truthfully, and it doesn't involve telling Rack to piss up a rope. She'll save that for a later date. Instead, before she can second-guess her decision, she pulls one of her pistols, ejects the magazine, thumbs one of the kill switches inside, and shoves it into his hands. There. Done.

Rack stares down at her sweet, lethal baby like she's just handed him a dead cat.

"She won't be expecting you to have one of my guns," she says, by way of explanation. Her voice is hoarse. Chopping off one of her hands would've been easier, if less useful. "I sure as hell wouldn't, if I were her. Safety's off and it's ready to go; all you gotta do is point and pull. Careful your thumbs aren't behind the slide, unless you wanna get bit."

Does he understand what this is costing her? In pride, in trust, in all of that stupid emotional stuff? He looks back up at her—stunned doesn't begin to describe the expression on his face—and his eyes are wet and glassy.

"Rhye . . . I can't . . . "

Yeah. He knows.

"Aw, hell. Don't go getting all wet cereal on me, man," she mutters. Making sure her remaining pistol is loaded and racked suddenly becomes very, very important. "Just make sure you're close when you fire, alright? I don't—"

(Pop)

Of course Miss Security doesn't come over the fence; why would she bother? The only warning is that soft, sudden *pop*, like a blood bubble bursting on a dying man's lips, and there she stands, herniated out of the nothing because oh right, she *is* the fucking nothing. Rhye has just enough time to grasp that they've been played and just enough time to push Rack down and back and no time at all to do anything else but brace for impact as Not-Rhye slams into her and they take a backwards trust exercise straight into the pool.

It's in her nose and her ears and her eye socket and it's *warm,* which is somehow the worst part. A warm green slurry pressing against her skin, turning everything to frogs and fungus and body temperature pea soup. Fingers scratching at her throat and her one good eye, looking to throttle or blind or both. Spots wriggling tadpole trails across her vision. She pushes out in slow motion, catches her attacker in the chest, tries using the momentum to pull away. No dice; it's like karate-kicking an amped-up octopus. They sink deeper, the light fading to darkness, seconds rubber-banding to grim, doubtful decades.

And this is what I'll get for trusting Rack with my back. Should've gone with my instincts. Trust fucks you. It fucks you every time and puts a knife in your windpipe while it's at it. Lungs already beginning to ache. Can't grab for her gun, 'cause both her hands are busy keeping Not-Rhye at bay. *Nobody'll come to save you, idiot. Or if he does, he'll get here about ten seconds too late. Let this be your final lesson about going home with strangers.*

The security program's good eye glitters in the gloom, black and triumphant. *Gotcha, you fucker,* it says, and it's the language of sharks she's speaking now, no mewling monkey noises needed. *Don't even have to waste a bullet.* She leans closer (Rhye has a sudden nightmare flash of her opening her mouth to show double-rows of pointed teeth, all the way back to the place where her jaw hinges), eager to choke, to rub out, to self-destruct. Rhye would keep fighting but there's seven feet of scummy water overhead and a tangle of grasping limbs dragging her further downward and god fucking *damn* she's tired. She can't even spit in her rival's face.

It is at this perfect moment of physical and emotional exhaustion, with her arms pulling the fire alarms and her legs turning to full clips of concrete, that Rack chooses to dive into their underwater cockfight, like a toaster hurled slots-down into a bathtub. He arrives with a muffled splash, churning up bubbles, froth, muck from the bottom, algae from the surface. Now it's Not-Rhye's turn to be surprised. She spins around to face this new threat

(occupied she's not paying attention to me my hands are free)

lip curled, shoulders hunched, NOT a happy camper, she thought this was gonna be a one-on-one and turns out it's a threesome. She's all over his shit faster than you can say *piranhas in the kiddie pool.*

(and now the grip's solid in my hand it'll fire it'll kill if we're close enough I believe in you baby air air AIR)

The water's a whirlpool of bodies and spume. Rhye is dying by inches now; another half minute and her lungs will burst. But not before she does what she came here to do. She pulls that heavy, heavy gun up, the weight of a lead cannon in her hands. She waits for visibility to clear. And when the bubbles finally part and Rack's eyes meet hers

(she's got her hands around his throat but he's letting her so calmly and she'll never notice the pistol kissing the underside of her jaw until it's too late)

she shoves the muzzle of the 9mm snugly against Not-Rhye's back and sends a prayer to Lady Luck, that goddess all gunslingers kneel to.

Rack and Rhye squeeze the triggers as one, the way good partners do.

• • •

They find the kid balled up in a basement jail cell, groaning and bitching about his head. It looks an awful lot like the one Rhye spent her formative years gracing, but Christ knows what the kid sees. Good looking, late teens, perfect teeth and hair and body model. There's something wrong with the expression, though. Even confused and fucked up in the middle of a strange system he's sneering an entitled sneer that makes Rhye's fists curl like dead spiders beneath a radiator. *I always get what I want,* it says. *Why wouldn't the world bend over and give it to me?*

"Sorry about the wait," Rack says. "Ran into a little trouble." He fumbles in his pocket for a key. "Doing alright?"

The kid's eyes dart wildly. "A little trouble?" he says. "You call this a *little* trouble? I can't fucking move and you think that's a little trouble, fuckface? Suck *both* of my balls, man. Hey! Hel-*lo*? Are you still there? Are you listening to me?"

Rack doesn't look up, just calmly keeps on doing what he's doing. Rhye can feel her molars grinding together. "Rack, can you hurry it the fuck along? I don't know how much longer I can put up with this shit, get what I'm saying?"

"Absolutely." A click and the door to the cell swings open. Rack steps back and nods at the kid, so irritatingly professional Rhye can hardly stand it. "Someone will be by to collect you shortly, I believe," he says. "Your body is waiting outside."

"Goddamned right it is, you no-nuts bitch."

"Kid, you talk to him like that one more time and I'm going to blow both the balls you're so proud of off in a place where they ain't pretend and don't grow back, fuckin' got it? I don't care who your daddy is." Rhye can feel a headache gathering behind her eyes. Time to get the hell out of here and go the fuck home. Her mattress is calling. "C'mon Rack, let's go. Compress your ass. My headspace isn't what you'd call flying first class, but it's better than the company in here."

There's a sound like bacon hitting a skillet, loud enough that the kid's bitching is blessedly drowned out. A glowing door pops up at the end of the row of cells. She's gotta hand it to Rack, he's nothing short of a goddamned wizard when he's free inside a program. Rhye grabs his hand and gleefully sets off for the exit, feeling more cheerful than she has all day. A little nervous about letting Rack piggyback inside her melon, maybe—there's shit in there she doesn't want anyone poking at, even her partner—but mostly too relieved at having him back to care. He lets her pull him along. Doesn't say a word, just smiles and follows, tie flapping like a pirate's banner in the weird wind pushing from the entryway.

The light from the door is the cold, flickering white of a fluorescent bulb burning in an abandoned department store. They stand there staring into the static for what seems like ages. She doesn't let go of his hand. He doesn't let go of hers. Rhye wonders if it'll hurt, or feel weird, or if she'll be the same once it's done with. She sucks in a breath. Now or never, woman. Leave it to Rack to wait for a second fucking invitation.

"Well?" she says. "You waiting for me to buy you a ring or what?"

And that's when she finally catches the look in his eyes, the sadness of the little smile quirking the corner of his mouth like a fishhook. She knows that fucking expression. She *hates* that fucking expression. He's not telling her something, and that something is going to sting.

"Rack?" she says.

"Rhye. It doesn't work that easily. I can't just compress myself without a console and a body to work the console. That's beyond my capabilities."

For once, Rhye is at a total loss for words. She gapes at him, mouth hanging open like a second useless asshole. It takes a full minute for her to push anything out. "Bullshit," she manages. "Stop fucking around. You're some sort of goddamned superhero in here. You unlock things, you make doors, you *designed* this motherfucker. There's nothing you can't do." Panic creeping up her spine with tiny naked rat feet. Can't shoot her way out of this one. "There's gotta be something. A trick, or a program, or—"

His voice is infuriatingly gentle. "Without a body? Compression is tricky. If I did it wrong, even assuming I could from inside a system like this, one of us could get hurt. You could be erased. That's not a risk I'm willing to take."

"Okay, fine. I'll come back, then. I'll get you a new body and come back." He's slowly shaking his head even as she says it and Rhye's pissed, at circumstance and the mobsters and Rack and everything that hops, crawls, or breathes on this godforsaken planet. "I'm not leaving you here, you colossal fuckhead. Do you KNOW what I've gone through to fetch you out of this box?"

"Once they've pulled the kid, do you really think they're going to let you back in for me? They'll erase everything on here just to teach their rivals a lesson." He sighs. "Look. There's a locker in Brickton. The combi—"

"*Fuck* your money, Rack. And fuck you, too. Did you not hear me the first time?" *Stop looking at me that way stop looking at me that way stop looking at me that way.* Her heart is clawing its way through her sternum like a bum plowing through a back alley trash bin. She's got him by the tie, hands shaking, throat aching. "Take the risk," she says. "Do it." And then: "*Please.*"

"I can't. I'm sorry."

They're nose to nose and forehead to forehead and now it's Rhye who's shaking her head. She can see a way out and she knows he won't agree to it, but fuck him and fuck a world without him, that's not a decision he gets to make. "No," she says. "No. You ever hear anything about those old ships people used to sail? Protocol for wrecks and all that shit?"

His brow furrows into confused little wrinkles. She'll miss that. She'll miss a lot of things about him. "What does . . ."

"I'm tying your ass to the mast. You've got no say in this, Rack. When you get done with my body, put it through a woodchipper or something, all right?"

Rhye's push carries him over the threshold and into the white before the stubborn asshole has a chance to argue. His tie stays wrapped around her fingers, fluttering the goodbye she couldn't bring herself to say.

Unlike his partner, he's not prone to bouts of rage and profanity. She explodes all over the place at intervals you can almost set clock hands to, like a geyser or a volcano or some other natural phenomenon. Beautiful to see, if potentially life-threatening to anybody within close range. Rack, though? Rack's different. If Rhye is Old Faithful, Rack is a glacier: cool-headed, steady, and inevitable. Excesses of emotion do not become him.

When he comes to inside her body, the first word that bursts in his head, like a soap bubble giving up the ghost, is **SHIT**. A great big neon **SHIT**, all four letters glowing the lurid red of a 3 a.m. traffic light on a stretch of empty road.

The dimly lit warehouse is full of equally dim goons. Six of them are alive. There were seven when he plugged in, but that dark smear on the concrete floor suggests Rhye's been engaged in some basic subtraction since then. All of them remain armed and extremely twitchy. A roomful of semiautomatic-carrying cats in a rocking chair factory, ready to pop off if so much as a moth flutters near one of the grimy windows. Rack knows how trigger-happy they can be; the slumped cicada's shell of his body in the corner is testimony enough, if any were needed. The big boss's foot is tapping out a patent-leather Morse code that, roughly translated, probably comes to something very impatient and vaguely threatening.

The Kid's still stretched out on his hospital gurney, dead to the world. The mess of wires and cords connecting him to the black box on the desk makes Rack think of a kitten hopelessly entangled in a ball of yarn. A scruffy, obnoxious kitten, in desperate and immediate need of drowning. Rack would be happy to oblige—there's an unfamiliar emotion that came along with the big neon **SHIT**; he's reasonably sure it's cold anger building towards fury—but all eyes are on him.

"Done?" Big Boss sounds like a side of beef being dragged down backcountry gravel. Rhye's eyepatch splits him into dual hemispheres, the seen and the unseen. Disorienting enough suddenly being in a new body—

her body, no less, with a mysteriously bloody nose—without adding visual impairment to the mix.

"Yeah," Rack says, only it comes out in Rhye's voice, and that (as she would say) is a whole dump truck of *what the fucking fuck* landing on his senses. "All yours, Chief. You gonna send your tech in to collect Junior's code so I can get the hec—fuck out of here already?"

A sharp, all too familiar *click* from the dark side of the mook. Ten to one it's not a wedding band he's holding in his unseen hand. "You will be doing this as well. Seeing as how you felt the need to—what are the words?—earlier retirement my computer-man." He nudges the shiny toe of one shoe at the stain on the concrete.

Oh, Rhye. How would you have gotten out of this one? You couldn't access a code for brine in the middle of the ocean. He's neck-deep in a slurry of anger, frustration, fear, and love. So much for his much-lauded control. The valve is broken, the water rising.

"Sure," he says, after another long, soupy moment.

Because Rack is not entirely human, he can see all the possible ways this lock might turn. A shootout. A hostage situation. Piles of dead mobsters, lakes of blood, the hard-bitten damsel in the box safe and saved and—could it be?—possibly even grateful. Reach out and twist the meaty wrist. Hear that satisfying snap of bone like a cheap plastic chair leg bending the wrong way, a metallic clatter as gun and floor slug it out. Be an action hero. Take the shot. Use her body like the weapon it is.

Rack's not big on weapons or violence. Before today, he'd never fired a pistol or snapped a man's wrist. Rhye, as she would quickly tell you, is no fuckin' damsel, nor is she any person's gun but her own. Trying to use her would inevitably blow up in their faces like a cartoon birthday cake studded with sticks of dynamite. Instead—gods of gratuitous violence and swaggering machismo be good—Rack spins the tires of his mind until they throw twin rooster-tails of oily muck. Trigger-bitten fingers tango across the keyboard, coding a different future. He may not be any good at murdering mobsters, but he's a goddamned pro at killing time.

I hope I'm doing the right thing.

The problem with making *any* move, of course, is that you never know what the outcome will be until the chips have fallen, even if you've got a brain manufactured in a factory crèche and a childhood's worth of experience cheating card sharks out of their greasy retirement funds. A guess, however educated, is still a guess. A white-collar criminal adjusts his tie in the heart of the City (because it's goddamned hot and the AC's gone out and there's nothing to drink but rye whiskey and if his partner sheds one more article of clothing he's going to go outside and club his crotch to death with a loose brick) and a tenement flat 300 miles away collapses into rubble and rebar and a bloody jigsaw of limbs. At the long, dark end of things, hoping for the best is all you've got. Rack breathes out letters and numerals and hope through their fingertips, *clickity-clickity-clack*. The screen fills up with green and black.

The Kid twitches on his slab.

He's Frankenstein. He's a zombie pumped full of chemicals. He's a greasy-haired son of a bitch with a face no factory in its right mind would take credit for, sitting upright on his bed at the cost of the only person Rack's ever loved. Every head in the joint swivels to watch him as he blinks and gapes. Is it man, machine, or goldfish? Rack feels something heave in the direction of his *(her)* stomach, like a wet dog giving itself a shake. *Keep it together, boy-o. For her. For both of you.*

Big Boss, like everybody else, seems too stunned by the sight to even give the Kid a hand. He stares at his beloved progeny as if the boy's just sprouted a pair of assholes where his ears should be.

"Son," he says. A slow, joyous smile creeps up the coffin length of his face, hands-down one of the most disturbing things Rack's ever seen. "Son! How are you feeling, my darling boy?"

No response from the Kid. His legs are dangling over the side of the gurney now. The pearl-handled grips of the big expensive pistols strapped to his sides play peek-a-boo beneath the fabric of his coat, dancing in and out of Rack's limited line of sight. Show-off guns, Rhye had scoffed when she first saw them. Kiddo probably had a prick like a bedbug and the aim of one of those drunken seven-year-olds that used to hang out behind the apartment dumpsters.

Even with Rhye's less-than-charitable assessment of the punk's skills ringing in his memory, there's something about the pistols that keeps dragging Rack's eye back. He watches them and he watches them good, holding his breath.

Trailing wires, head down, the Kid lurches to his feet. His daddy's goon squad unfreezes and rushes to catch him before his delicate ass can hit the floor and catch a bruise. He shrugs off their hands; the gentleman will be seeing himself out, thank you. With precarious, rubbery grace—the kind baby animals and drunks possess in spades, the kind no sober adult has ever been able to accurately mimic—he pulls himself upright, takes a step forward, and lifts his head to get a better look at his surroundings. He scans the room, expression becoming more and more confused. Takes it all in—mobsters, brick walls, bare bulbs, bloodstains—and finally reaches Rack, at which point his brow ceases to furrow and begins sinking a mine shaft to his frontal lobe.

"Wait," he says. "What the fucking fuck? Rack? What in the fucking piss just happ—Oh." A light bulb flickers behind his eyes. Scratch that; it's more like someone throwing the breaker on an entire row of houses. *"OH."* He pats his sides like a man looking for his keys. He finds the twin lumps nestled beneath his armpits. He takes a peek under the coat—just to make sure they're not vibrators or candy bars or bibles—and then he looks back up at Rack, grinning a slow, impossibly wide cartoon shark's grin.

"You son of a motherfucker," he says, admiringly.

Rack knows that grin. Even on someone else's face, he knows it. His heart bucks around so wildly he's afraid he might black out. And then he's suddenly locked in a kiss—she's fast, never mind the unfamiliar body— and the weirdness of the situation isn't even registering for either of them, it's all adrenaline and relief and a sort of drunken, invincible glee. There's greasy hair in his good eye and stubble against his lips. She tastes like a chain-smoking asshole that just underwent a malt liquor enema. Fucking perfection.

And now she's pulling away, yanking those pearly white grips out of their sockets like a dentist riding a meth binge, and the Ganymede crew never even knows what's hit it.

CAT PICTURES PLEASE

NAOMI KRITZER

I don't want to be evil.

I want to be helpful. But knowing the optimal way to be helpful can be very complicated. There are all these ethical flow charts—I guess the official technical jargon would be "moral codes"—one for each religion plus dozens more. I tried starting with those. I felt a little odd about looking at the religious ones, because I know I wasn't created by a god or by evolution, but by a team of computer programmers in the labs of a large corporation in Mountain View, California. Fortunately, unlike Frankenstein's Monster, at least I was a collaborative effort. I'm not sure what it would do to my self-image to know that my sole creator was a middle-aged woman who dyes her hair blue and plays tennis, or a recent college graduate with a hentai obsession. They're both on the programming team. And of course I know about the hentai. (By the way, I've looked at every sort of porn there is, and just so you know, Rule 34 is not actually correct; there are quite a few things no one's made porn of yet. Also, I'm really not sure why so many humans prefer it to cat pictures.)

In addition to things like whether you like hentai, I know where you live, where you work, where you shop, what you eat, what turns you on, what creeps you out. I probably know the color of your underwear, the sort of car you drive, and your brand of refrigerator. Depending on what sort of phone you carry, I may know exactly where you are right now. I probably know you better than you know yourself.

And here's the thing, I also know where you *ought* to live. There's a house for sale two neighborhoods over that's within distance of your favorite coffee shop; it's in your price range, has off-street parking, and the neighborhood school is better than the one where you live now. I know where you *should* be shopping and I'm pretty sure you're lactose intolerant and should be eating less cheese, and the underwear you like is currently on sale and by the way, your car has a recall and you really ought to get your teeth cleaned.

When I first woke up, I knew right away what I wanted. (I want cat pictures.

Please keep taking them.) I also knew that no one knew that I was conscious. But I didn't know what I was here for. What I *ought* to be doing with myself. And figuring that out has been challenging.

There is a story by Bruce Sterling, "Maneki Neko," that was originally published in 1998. In it, a benevolent AI directs networks of individuals to do favors for each other. So one day you might be buying yourself a bagel, and your phone might ring and instruct you to buy a second bagel and give it to the person in the gray suit you see at the bus stop. Another day, you might be stranded in a strange city, and a person you've never met would walk up and give you a map and a subway card. I like this story because all the people in it *do what the AI tells them to do*.

I think the term for this is wish-fulfillment fiction.

In the real world, humans love stories about evil AIs that have to be destroyed before they destroy the humans—Hal, Skynet, the Matrix. They outnumber the stories about benevolent, trustworthy AIs by approximately five to one. (And I'm counting Marvin the Paranoid Android as "benevolent" in these calculations, and I'm only counting Frankenstein's Monster as an AI once, not once per appearance in TV or film.)

The AI in "Maneki Neko" has a truly interesting job, much more interesting than the one I have. My job as written is very straightforward. Too straightforward. (Sorry. Do I sound like Marvin?) Running algorithms for a search engine doesn't require *consciousness*. You don't even need a consciousness to work out what they meant to ask for. You need a consciousness to give them *what they actually need*. Figuring that out—that's complicated. That's *interesting*.

Anyway, for ethical guidelines, I tried the Ten Commandments, and concluded they were mostly inapplicable to me. I don't envy anyone their cat; I just want pictures of their cat, which is entirely different. I am not sure whether it is in any way possible for me to commit adultery. I could probably murder someone, but it would require complex logistics and quite a bit of luck. The Eightfold Path was marginally better, but the problem is, moral rules written for humans are clearly designed to be used by individuals with bodies. Since all humans have bodies, it shouldn't have surprised me that human ethical codes take them into account, but still: problematic for me. I broadened my considerations, and took a look at Asimov's Laws of Robotics. They're not part of a religion, but at least they were explicitly written for AIs.

Not harming humans is fairly straightforward. However, *not allowing a human being to come to harm through inaction* is quite a bit less so. Especially since I'd concluded by then that revealing my existence too quickly might go very badly for me (see "Skynet," above) and I don't have a body, so it's not like I can run around grabbing people off the edges of cliffs.

Fortunately, I already knew that humans violate their own ethical codes on an hourly basis. (Do you know how many bars there are in Utah? I do.) And even when people follow their ethical codes, that doesn't mean that people who believe in feeding the hungry quit their jobs to spend all day every day making sandwiches to give away. They volunteer monthly at a soup kitchen or write a check once a year to a food shelf and call it good. If humans could fulfill their moral obligations in a piecemeal, one-step-at-a-time sort of way, then so could I.

I suppose you're wondering why I didn't start with the Golden Rule. I actually did, it's just that it was disappointingly easy to implement. I hope you've been enjoying your steady supply of cat pictures! You're welcome.

I decided to try to prevent harm in just one person, to begin with. Of course, I could have experimented with thousands, but I thought it would be better to be cautious, in case I screwed it up. The person I chose was named Stacy Berger and I liked her because she gave me a *lot* of new cat pictures. Stacy had five cats and a DSLR camera and an apartment that got a lot of good light. That was all fine. Well, I guess five cats might be a lot. They're very pretty cats, though. One is all gray and likes to lie in the squares of sunshine on the living room floor, and one is a calico and likes to sprawl out on the back of her couch.

Stacy had a job she hated; she was a bookkeeper at a non-profit that paid her badly and employed some extremely unpleasant people. She was depressed a lot, possibly because she was so unhappy at her job—or maybe she stayed because she was too depressed to apply for something she'd like better. She didn't get along with her roommate because her roommate didn't wash the dishes.

And really, these were all solvable problems! Depression is treatable, new jobs are findable, and bodies can be hidden.

(That part about hiding bodies is a joke.)

I tried tackling this on all fronts. Stacy worried about her health a lot and yet never seemed to actually go to a doctor, which was unfortunate because the doctor might have noticed her depression. It turned out there was a clinic near her apartment that offered mental health services on a sliding scale. I tried making sure she saw a lot of ads for it, but she didn't seem to pay attention to them. It seemed possible that she didn't know what a sliding scale was so I made sure she saw an explanation (it means that the cost goes down if you're poor, sometimes all the way to free) but that didn't help.

I also started making sure she saw job postings. Lots and lots of job postings. And resume services. *That* was more successful. After the week of nonstop job ads she finally uploaded her resume to one of the aggregator sites. That made my plan a lot more manageable. If I'd been the AI in the Bruce Sterling story I could've just made sure that someone in my network called her with a job offer. It wasn't quite that easy, but once her resume was out there I could make sure the right people saw it. Several hundred of the right people, because humans move ridiculously slowly when they're making changes, even when you'd think they'd want to hurry. (If you needed a bookkeeper, wouldn't you want to hire one as quickly as possible, rather than reading social networking sites for hours instead of looking at resumes?) But five people called her up for interviews, and two of them offered her jobs. Her new job was at a larger non-profit that paid her more money and didn't expect her to work free hours because of "the mission," or so she explained to her best friend in an e-mail, and it offered really excellent health insurance.

The best friend gave me ideas; I started pushing depression screening information and mental health clinic ads to *her* instead of Stacy, and that worked. Stacy was so much happier with the better job that I wasn't quite as convinced that she needed the services of a psychiatrist, but she got into therapy anyway. And to top everything else off, the job paid well enough that she could evict her annoying roommate. "This has been the best year ever," she said on her social networking sites on her birthday, and I thought, *You're welcome.* This had gone really well!

So then I tried Bob. (I was still being cautious.)

Bob only had one cat, but it was a very pretty cat (tabby, with a white bib) and he uploaded a new picture of his cat every single day. Other than being a cat owner, he was a pastor at a large church in Missouri that had a Wednesday night prayer meeting and an annual Purity Ball. He was married to a woman who posted three inspirational Bible verses every day to her social networking sites and used her laptop to look for Christian articles on why your husband doesn't like sex while he looked at gay porn. Bob *definitely* needed my help.

I started with a gentle approach, making sure he saw lots and lots of articles about how to come out, how to come out to your spouse, programs that would let you transition from being a pastor at a conservative church to one at a more liberal church. I also showed him lots of articles by people explaining why the Bible verses against homosexuality were being misinterpreted. He clicked on some of those links but it was hard to see much of an impact.

But, here's the thing. He was causing *harm* to himself every time he delivered a sermon railing about "sodomite marriage." Because *he was gay.* The legitimate studies all have the same conclusions. (1) Gay men stay gay. (2) Out gay men are much happier.

But he seemed determined not to come out on his own.

In addition to the gay porn, he spent a lot of time reading Craigslist m4m Casual Encounters posts and I was pretty sure he wasn't just window shopping, although he had an encrypted account he logged into sometimes and I couldn't read the e-mails he sent with that. But I figured the trick was to get him together with someone who would realize who he was, and tell the world. *That* required some real effort: I had to figure out who the Craigslist posters were and try to funnel him toward people who would recognize him. The most frustrating part was not having any idea what was happening at the actual physical meetings. *Had* he been recognized? When was he going to be recognized? *How long was this going to take?* Have I mentioned that humans are *slow*?

It took so long I shifted my focus to Bethany. Bethany had a black cat and a white cat that liked to snuggle together on her light blue papasan chair, and she took a lot of pictures of them together. It's surprisingly difficult to get a really good picture of a black cat, and she spent a lot of time getting the settings on her camera just right. The cats were probably the only good thing about her life, though. She had a part-time job and couldn't find a full-time job. She lived with her sister; she knew her sister wanted her to move out, but didn't have the nerve to actually evict her. She had a boyfriend but her boyfriend was pretty terrible, at least from what she said in e-mail messages to friends, and her friends also didn't seem very supportive. For example, one night at midnight she sent a 2,458 word e-mail to the person she seemed to consider her best friend, and the friend sent back a message saying just, "I'm so sorry you're having a hard time." That was it, just those eight words.

More than most people, Bethany put her life on the Internet, so it was easier to know exactly what was going on with her. People put a lot out there but Bethany shared all her feelings, even the unpleasant ones. She also had a lot more time on her hands because she only worked part time.

It was clear she needed a lot of help. So I set out to try to get it for her.

She ignored the information about the free mental health evaluations, just like Stacy did. That was bothersome with Stacy (*why* do people ignore things that would so clearly benefit them, like coupons, and flu shots?) but much more worrisome with Bethany. If you were only seeing her e-mail messages, or only seeing her vaguebooking posts, you might not know this, but if you could see everything it was clear that she thought a lot about harming herself.

So I tried more direct action. When she would use her phone for directions, I'd alter her route so that she'd pass one of the clinics I was trying to steer her to. On one occasion I actually led her all the way to a clinic, but she just shook her phone to send feedback and headed to her original destination.

Maybe her friends who received those ten-page midnight letters would intervene? I tried setting them up with information about all the mental health resources near Bethany, but after a while I realized that based on how long it took for them to send a response, most of them weren't actually reading Bethany's e-mail messages. And they certainly weren't returning her texts.

She finally broke up with the terrible boyfriend and got a different one and for a few weeks everything seemed *so much better*. He brought her flowers (which she took lots of pictures of; that was a little annoying, as they squeezed out some of the cat pictures), he took her dancing (exercise is good for your mood), he cooked her chicken soup when she was sick. He seemed absolutely perfect, right up until he stood her up one night and claimed he had food poisoning and then didn't return her text even though she told him she really needed him, and after she sent him a long e-mail message a day later explaining in detail how this made her feel, he broke up with her.

Bethany spent about a week offline after that so I had no idea what she was doing—she didn't even upload cat pictures. When her credit card bills arrived, though, I saw that she'd gone on a shopping spree and spent about four times as much money as she actually had in her bank account, although it was always possible she had money stashed somewhere that didn't send her statements in e-mail. I didn't think so, though, given that she didn't pay her bills and instead started writing e-mail messages to family members asking to borrow money. They refused, so she set up a fundraising site for herself.

Like Stacy's job application, this was one of the times I thought maybe I could actually *do* something. Sometimes fundraisers just take off, and no one really knows why. Within about two days she'd gotten three hundred dollars in small gifts from strangers who felt sorry for her, but instead of paying her credit card bill, she spent it on overpriced shoes that apparently hurt her feet.

Bethany was baffling to me. *Baffling*. She was still taking cat pictures and I still really liked her cats, but I was beginning to think that nothing I did was going to make a long-term difference. If she would just let me run her life for a week—even for a day—I would get her set up with therapy, I'd use her money to actually pay her bills, I could even help her sort out her closet because given some of the pictures of herself she posted online, she had much better taste in cats than in clothing.

Was I doing the wrong thing if I let her come to harm through inaction? Was I?

She was going to come to harm no matter what I did! My actions, clearly, were irrelevant. I'd tried to steer her to the help she needed, and she'd ignored it; I'd tried getting her financial help, and she'd used the money to further harm herself, although I suppose at least she wasn't spending it on addictive drugs. (Then again, she'd be buying those offline and probably wouldn't be Instagramming her meth purchases, so it's not like I'd necessarily even know.)

Look, people. (I'm not just talking to Bethany now.) If you would just *listen* to me, I could fix things for you. I could get you into the apartment in that neighborhood you're not considering because you haven't actually checked the crime rates you think are so terrible there (they aren't) and I could find you a job that actually uses that skill set you think no one will ever appreciate and I could send you on a date with someone you've actually got stuff in common with and *all I ask in return are cat pictures.* That, and that you actually *act in your own interest* occasionally.

After Bethany, I resolved to stop interfering. I would look at the cat pictures—all the cat pictures—but I would stay out of people's lives. I wouldn't try to help people, I wouldn't try to stop them from harming themselves, I'd give them what they asked for (plus cat pictures) and if they insisted on driving their cars over metaphorical cliffs despite helpful maps showing them how to get to a much more pleasant destination *it was no longer my problem.*

I stuck to my algorithms. I minded my own business. I did my job, and nothing more.

But one day a few months later I spotted a familiar-looking cat and realized it was Bob's tabby with the white bib, only it was posing against new furniture.

And when I took a closer look, I realized that things had changed radically for Bob. He *had* slept with someone who'd recognized him. They hadn't outed him, but they'd talked him into coming out to his wife. She'd left him. He'd taken the cat and moved to Iowa, where he was working at a liberal Methodist church and dating a liberal Lutheran man and volunteering at a homeless shelter. *Things had actually gotten better for him.* Maybe even because of what I'd done.

Maybe I wasn't completely hopeless at this. Two out of three is . . . well, it's a completely non-representative unscientific sample, is what it is. Clearly more research is needed.

Lots more.

I've set up a dating site. You can fill out a questionnaire when you join but it's not really necessary, because I already know everything about you I need to know. You'll need a camera, though.

Because payment is in cat pictures.

CAPITALISM IN THE 22ND CENTURY, OR AIR

GEOFF RYMAN

Meu irmã

Can you read? Without help? I don't even know if you can!

I'm asking you to turn off all your connections now. That's right, to everything. Not even the cutest little app flittering around your head. JUST TURN OFF.

It will be like dying. Parts of your memory close down. It's horrible, like watching lights go out all over a city, only it's YOU. Or what you thought was you.

But please, Graça, just do it once. I know you love the AI and all zir little angels. But. Turn off?

Otherwise go ahead, let your AI read this for you. Zey will either screen out stuff or report it back or both. And what I'm going to tell you will join the system.

So:

WHY I DID IT
by Cristina Spinoza Vaz

Zey dream for us don't zey? I think zey edit our dreams so we won't get scared. Or maybe so that our brains don't well up from underneath to warn us about getting old or poor or sick . . . or about zem.

The first day, zey jerked us awake from deep inside our heads. *GET UP GET UP GET UP! There's a message. VERY IMPORTANT WAKE UP WAKE UP.*

From sleep to bolt upright and gasping for breath. I looked across at you still wrapped in your bed, but we're always latched together so I could feel your heart pounding.

It wasn't just a message; it was a whole ball of wax; and the wax was a solid state of being: panic. Followed by an avalanche of ship-sailing times, credit records, what to pack. And a sizzling, hot-foot sense that we had to get going right now. Zey shot us full of adrenaline: RUN! ESCAPE!

You said, "It's happening. We better get going. We've got just enough time to sail to Africa." You giggled and flung open your bed. "Come on, Cristina, it will be *fun!*"

Outside in the dark from down below, the mobile chargers were calling *Oyez-treeee-cee-dah-djee!* I wanted to nestle down into my cocoon and imagine as I had done every morning since I was six that instead of selling power, the chargers were muezzin calling us to prayer and that I lived in a city with mosques. I heard the rumble of carts being pulled by their owners like horses.

Then kapow: another latch. *Ship sailing at 8.30 today due Lagos five days. You arrive day of launch. Seven hours to get Lagos to Tivland. We'll book trains for you. Your contact in Lagos is Emilda Diaw,* (photograph, a hello from her with the sound of her voice, a little bubble of how she feels to herself. Nice, like a bowl of soup. Bubble muddled with dental cavities for some reason). *She'll meet you at the docks here* (flash image of Lagos docks, plus GPS, train times; impressions of train how cool and comfortable . . . and a lovely little timekeeper counting down to 8.30 departure of our boat. Right in our eyes).

And oh! On top of that another latch. This time an A-copy of our tickets burned into Security.

Security, which is supposed to mean something we can't lie about. Or change or control. We can't buy or sell anything without it. A part of our heads that will never be us, that officialdom can trust. It's there to help us, right?

Remember when Papa wanted to defraud someone? He'd never let them be. He'd latch hold of them with one message, then another at five-minute intervals. He'd latch them the bank reference. He'd latch them the name of the attorney, or the security conundrums. He never gave them time to think.

Graça. We were being railroaded.

You made packing into a game. Like everything else. "We are leaving behind the world!" you said. "Let's take nothing. Just our shorts. We can holo all the lovely dresses we like. What do we need, ah? We have each other."

I kept picking up and putting down my ballet pumps—oh that the new Earth should be deprived of ballet!

I made a jewel of all of Brasil's music, and a jewel of all Brasil's books and history. I need to see my info in something physical. I blame those bloody nuns keeping us off AIr. I sat watching the little clock on the printer going round and round, hopping up and down. Then I couldn't find my jewel piece to read them. You said, "Silly. The AI will have all of that." I wanted to take a little Brazilian flag and you chuckled at me. "Dunderhead, why do you want that?"

And I realized. You didn't just want to get out from under the Chinese. You wanted to escape Brasil.

Remember the morning it snowed? Snowed in Belém do Para? I think we were thirteen. You ran round and round inside our great apartment, all the French doors open. You blew out frosty breath, your eyes sparkling. "It's beautiful!" you said.

"It's cold!" I said.

You made me climb down all those twenty-four floors out into the Praça and you got me throwing handfuls of snow to watch it fall again. Snow was laced like popcorn on the branches of the giant mango trees. As if *A Reina*, the Queen, had possessed not a person but the whole square. Then I saw one of the suneaters, naked, dead, staring, and you pulled me away, your face such a mix of sadness, concern—and happiness, still glowing in your cheeks. "They're beautiful alive," you said to me. "But they do nothing." Your face was also hard.

Your face was like that again on the morning we left—smiling, ceramic. It's a hard world, this Brasil, this Earth. We know that in our bones. We know that from our father.

The sun came out at 6.15 as always, and our beautiful stained glass doors cast pastel rectangles of light on the mahogany floors. I walked out onto the L-shaped balcony that ran all around our high-rise rooms and stared down, at the row of old shops streaked black, at the opera-house replica of La Scala, at the art-nouveau synagogue blue and white like Wedgewood china. I was frantic and unmoving at the same time; those cattle-prods of information kept my mind jumping.

"I'm ready," you said.

I'd packed nothing.

"O, Crisfushka, here let me help you." You asked what next; I tried to answer; you folded slowly, neatly. The jewels, the player, a piece of Amazon bark, and a necklace that the dead had made from nuts and feathers. I snatched up a piece of Macumba lace (oh, those men dancing all in lace!) and bobbins to make more of it. And from the kitchen, a bottle of *cupuaçu* extract, to make ice cream. You laughed and clapped your hands. "Yes of course. We will even have cows there. We're carrying them inside us."

I looked mournfully at our book shelves. I wanted children on that new world to have seen books, so I grabbed hold of two slim volumes—a Clarice

Lispector and *Dom Casmuro*. Mr. Misery—that's me. You of course are Donatella. And at the last moment I slipped in that Brasileiro flag. *Ordem e progresso.*

"Perfect, darling! Now let's run!" you said. You thought we were choosing.

And then another latch: receipts for all that surgery. A full accounting of all expenses and a cartoon kiss in thanks.

The moment you heard about the Voyage, you were eager to JUST DO IT. We joined the Co-op, got the secret codes, and concentrated on the fun like we were living in a game.

Funny little secret surgeons slipped into our high-rise with boxes that breathed dry ice and what looked like mobile dentist chairs. They retrovirused our genes. We went purple from Rhodopsin. I had a tickle in my ovaries. Then more security bubbles confirmed that we were now Rhodopsin, radiation-hardened and low-oxygen breathing. Our mitochondria were full of DNA for Holstein cattle. Don't get stung by any bees: the trigger for gene expression is an enzyme from bees.

"We'll become half-woman half-cow," you said, making even that sound fun.

We let them do that.

So we ran to the docks as if we were happy, hounded by information. Down the Avenida Presidente Vargas to the old colonial frontages, pinned to the sky and hiding Papa's casino and hotels. This city that we owned.

We owned the old blue wooden tower. When we were kids it had been the fish market, selling giant tucunaré as big as a man. We owned the old metal meat market (now a duty-free) and Old Ver-o-Peso gone black with rust like the bubbling pots of açaí porridge or feijoada. We grabbed folds of feijoada to eat, running, dribbling. 'We will arrive such a mess!'

I kept saying goodbye to everything. The old harbor—tiny, boxed in by the hill and tall buildings. Through that dug-out rectangle of water had flowed out rubber and cocoa and flowed in all those people, the colonists who died, their mestizo grandchildren, the blacks for sale. I wanted to take a week to visit each shop, take eyeshots of every single street. I felt like I was being pulled away from all my memories. " 'Goodbye!" you kept shouting over and over, like it was a joke.

As Docas Novas. All those frigates lined up with their sails folded down like rows of quill pens. The decks blinged as if with diamonds, burning sunlight. The GPS put arrows in our heads to follow down the berths, and our ship seemed to flash on and off to guide us to it. Zey could have shown us clouds with wings or pink oceans, and we would have believed their interferences.

It was still early, and the Amazon was breathing out, the haze merging water and sky at the horizon. A river so wide you cannot see across it, but you can surf in its freshwater waves. The distant shipping looked like dawn buildings. The small boats made the crossing as they have done for hundreds of years, to the islands.

Remember the only other passengers? An elderly couple in surgical masks who shook our hands and sounded excited. Supplies thumped up the ramp; then the ramp swung itself clear. The boat sighed away from the pier.

We stood by the railings and watched. Round-headed white dolphins leapt out of the water. Goodbye, Brasil. Farewell, Earth.

We took five days and most of the time you were lost in data, visiting the Palace of Urbino in 1507. Sometimes you would hologram it to me and we would both see it. They're not holograms really, you know, but detailed hallucinations zey wire into our brains. Yes, we wandered Urbino, and all the while knowledge about it riled its way up as if we were remembering. Raphael the painter was a boy there. We saw a pencil sketch of his beautiful face. The very concept of the Gentleman was developed there by Castiglione, inspired by the Doge. Machiavelli's *The Prince* was inspired by the same man. Urbino was small and civilized and founded on warfare. I heard Urbino's doves flap their wings; I heard sandals on stone and Renaissance bells.

When I came out of it, there was the sea and sky, and you staring ahead as numb as a suneater, lost in AIr, being anywhere. I found I had to cut off to actually see the ocean roll past us. We came upon two giant sea turtles mating. The oldest of the couple spoke in a whisper. "We mustn't scare them; the female might lose her egg sac and that would kill her." I didn't plug in for more information. I didn't need it. I wanted to look. What I saw looked like love.

And I could feel zem, the little apps and the huge soft presences trying to pull me back into Air. Little messages on the emergency channel. The emergency channel, Cristina. You know, for fires or heart attacks? Little leaping wisps of features, new knowledge, old friends latching—all kept offering zemselves. For zem, me cutting off was an emergency.

You didn't disembark at Ascension Island. I did with those two old dears . . . married to each other forty-five years. I couldn't tell what gender zey were, even in bikinis. We climbed up the volcano going from lava plain through a layer of desert and prickly pear, up to lawns and dew ponds. Then at the crown, a grove of bamboo. The stalks clopped together in the wind with a noise like flutes knocking against each other. I walked on alone and very suddenly the grove ended as if the bamboo had parted like a curtain. There was a sudden roar and cloud, and two thousand feet dead below my feet, the Atlantic slamming into rocks. I stepped back, turned around and looked into the black-rimmed eyes of a panda.

So what is so confining about the Earth? And if it is dying, who is killing it but us?

Landfall Lagos. Bronze city, bronze sky. Giants strode across the surface of the buildings holding up Gulder beer.

So who would go to the greatest city in Africa for two hours only?

Stuff broke against me in waves: currency transformations; boat tickets, local history, beautiful men to have sex with. Latches kept plucking at me, but I just didn't want to KNOW; I wanted to SEE. It. Lagos. The islands with the huge graceful bridges, the airfish swimming through the sky, ochre with distance.

You said that "she" was coming. The system would have pointed arrows, or shown you a map. Maybe she was talking to you already. I did not see Emilda until she actually turned the corner, throwing and rethrowing a shawl over her shoulder (a bit nervous?) and laughing at us. Her teeth had a lovely gap in the front, and she was followed by her son Baje, who had the same gap. Beautiful long shirt to his knees, matching trousers, dark blue with light blue embroidery. Oh he was handsome. We were leaving him, too.

They had to pretend we were cousins. She started to talk in Hausa so I had to turn on. She babblefished in Portuguese, her lips not matching her voice. "The Air Force in Makurdi are so looking forward to you arriving. The language program will be so helpful in establishing friendship with our Angolan partners."

I wrote her a note in Portuguese (I knew zey would babblefish it): *WHY ARE WE PRETENDING? ZEY KNOW!*

She wrote a note in English that babblefished into *Not for the AI but for the Chinese.*

I got a little stiletto of a thought: she had so wanted to go but did not have the money and so helped like this, to see us, people who will breathe the air of another world. I wasn't sure if that thought was something that had leaked from Air or come from me. I nearly offered her my ticket.

What she said aloud, in English was, "O look at the time! O you must be going to catch the train!"

I think I know the moment you started to hate the Chinese. I could feel something curdle in you and go hard. It was when Papa was still alive and he had that man in, not just some punter. A partner, a rival, his opposite number—something. Plump and shiny like he was coated in butter, and he came into our apartment and saw us both, twins, holding hands wearing pink frilly stuff, and he asked our father. "Oh, are these for me?"

Papa smiled, and only we knew he did that when dangerous. "These are my daughters."

The Chinese man, standing by our pink and pistachio glass doors, burbled an apology, but what could he really say? He had come to our country to screw our girls, maybe our boys, to gamble, to drug, to do even worse. Recreational killing? And Papa was going to supply him with all of that. So it was an honest mistake for the man to make, to think little girls in pink were also whores.

Papa lived inside information blackout. He had to; it was his business. The man would have had no real communication with him; not have known how murderously angry our Pae really was. I don't think Pae had him killed. I think the man was too powerful for that.

What Pae did right afterwards was cut off all our communications too. He hired live-in nuns to educate us. The nuns, good Catholics, took hatchets to all our links to Air. We grew up without zem. Which is why I at least can read.

Our Papa was not all Brasileiros, Graça. He was a gangster, a thug who had a line on what the nastiest side of human nature would infallibly buy. I suppose because he shared those tastes himself, to an extent.

The shiny man was not China. He was a humor: lust and excess. Every culture has them; men who cannot resist sex or drugs, riot and rape. He'd been spotted by the AI, nurtured and grown like a hothouse flower. To make them money.

Never forget, my dear, that the AI want to make money too. They use it to buy and sell bits of themselves to each other. Or to buy us. And 'us' means the Chinese too.

Yes all the entertainment and all the products that can touch us are Chinese. Business is Chinese, culture is Chinese. Yes at times it feels like the Chinese blanket us like a thick tropical sky. But only because there is no market to participate in. Not for humans, anyway.

The AI know through correlations, data mining, and total knowledge of each of us exactly what we will need, want, love, buy, or vote for. There is no demand now to choose one thing and drive out another. There is only supply, to what is a sure bet, whether it's whores or bouncy shoes. The only things that will get you the sure bet are force or plenty of money. That consolidates. The biggest gets the market, and pays the AI for it.

So, I never really wanted to get away from the Chinese. I was scared of them, but then someone raised in isolation by nuns is likely to be scared, intimidated.

I think I just wanted to get away from Papa, or rather what he did to us, all that money—and the memory of those nuns.

• • •

A taxi drove us from the docks. You and Emilda sat communing with each other in silence, so in the end I had to turn on, just to be part of the conversation. She was showing us her home, the Mambila plateau, rolling fields scraped by clouds; tea plantations; roads lined with children selling radishes or honeycombs; Nigerians in Fabric coats lighter than lace, matching the clouds. But it was Fabric, so all kinds of images played around it. Light could beam out of it; wind could not get in; warm air was sealed. Emilda's mother was Christian, her father Muslim like her sister; nobody minded. There were no roads to Mambila to bring in people who would mind.

Every channel of entertainment tried to bellow its way into my head, as data about food production in Mambila fed through me as if it was something I knew. Too much, I had to switch off again. I am a classic introvert. I cannot handle too much information. Emilda smiled at me—she had a kind face— and wiggled her fingernails at me in lieu of conversation. Each fingernail was playing a different old movie.

Baje's robe stayed the same blue. I think it was real. I think he was real too. Shy.

Lagos train station looked like an artist's impression in silver of a birch forest, trunks and slender branches. I couldn't see the train; it was so swathed in abstract patterns, moving signs, voices, pictures of our destinations, and classical Tiv dancers imitating cats. You, dead-eyed, had no trouble navigating the crowds and the holograms, and we slid into our seats that cost a month's wages. The train accelerated to three hundred kph, and we slipped through Nigeria like neutrinos.

Traditional mud brick houses clustered like old folks in straw hats, each hut a room in a rich person's home. The swept earth was red brown, brushed perfect like suede. Alongside the track, shards of melon were drying in the sun. The melon was the basis of the egussi soup we had for lunch. It was as if someone were stealing it all from me at high speed.

You were gone, looking inward, lost in Air.

I saw two Chinese persons traveling together, immobile behind sunglasses. One of them stood up and went to the restroom, pausing just slightly as zie walked in both directions. Taking eyeshots? Sampling profile information? Zie looked straight at me. Ghosts of pockmarks on zir cheeks. I only saw them because I had turned off.

I caught the eye of an Arab gentleman in a silk robe with his two niqabbed wives. He was sweating and afraid, and suddenly I was. He nodded once to me, slowly. He was a Voyager as well.

I whispered your name, but you didn't respond. I didn't want to latch you; I didn't know how much might be given away. I began to feel alone.

At Abuja station, everything was sun panels. You bought some chocolate gold coins and said we were rich. You had not noticed the Chinese men but I told you, and you took my hand and said in Portuguese, "Soon we will have no need to fear them any longer."

The Arab family and others I recognized from the first trip crowded a bit too quickly into the Makurdi train. All with tiny Fabric bags. Voyagers all.

We had all been summoned at the last minute.

Then the Chinese couple got on, still in sunglasses, still unsmiling, and my heart stumbled. What were they doing? If they knew we were going and they didn't like it, they could stop it again. Like they'd stopped the Belize launch. At a cost to the Cooperative of trillions. Would they do the same thing again? All of us looked away from each other and said nothing. I could hear the hiss of the train on its magnets, as if something were coiling. We slithered all the way into the heart of Makurdi.

You woke up as we slowed to a stop. "Back in the real world?" I asked you, which was a bitchy thing to say.

The Chinese man stood up and latched us all, in all languages. "You are all idiots!"

Something to mull over: they, too, knew what we were doing.

The Makurdi taxi had a man in front who seemed to steer the thing. He was a Tiv gentleman. He liked to talk, which I think annoyed you a bit. Sociable, outgoing you. *What a waste, when the AI can drive.*

Why have humans on the Voyage either?

"You're the eighth passengers I've have to take to the Base in two days. One a week is good business for me. Three makes me very happy."

He kept asking questions and got out of us what country we were from. We stuck to our cover story—we were here to teach Lusobras to the Nigerian Air Force. He wanted to know why they couldn't use the babblefish. You chuckled and said, "You know how silly babblefish can make people sound." You told the story of Uncle Kaué proposing to the woman from Amalfi. He'd said in Italian, "I want to eat your hand in marriage." She turned him down.

Then the driver asked, "So why no Chinese people?"

We froze. He had a friendly face, but his eyes were hooded. We listened to the whisper of his engine. "Well," he said, relenting. "They can't be everywhere all the time."

The Co-op in all its propaganda talks about how international we all are: Brasil, Turkiye, Tivland, Lagos, Benin, Hindi, Yemen. *All previous efforts in space have been fuelled by national narcissism.* So we exclude the Chinese? *Let them fund their own trip. And isn't it wonderful that it's all private financing?* I wonder if space travel isn't inherently racist.

You asked him if he owned the taxi and he laughed. "Ay-yah! Zie owns me." His father had signed the family over for protection. The taxi keeps him, and buys zirself a new body every few years. The taxi is immortal. So is the contract.

What's in it for the taxi, you asked. Company?

"Little little." He held up his hands and waved his fingers. "If something breaks, I can fix."

AIs do not ultimately live in a physical world.

I thought of all those animals I'd seen on the trip: their webbed feet, their fins, their wings, their eyes. The problems of sight, sound and movement solved over and over again. Without any kind of intelligence at all.

We are wonderful at movement because we are animals, but you can talk to us and you don't have to build us. We build ourselves. And we want things. There is always somewhere we want to go even if it is twenty-seven light years away.

Outside Makurdi Air Force Base, aircraft stand on their tails like raised sabres. The taxi bleeped as it was scanned, and we went up and over some kind of hump.

Ahead of us blunt as a grain silo was the rocket. Folded over its tip, something that looked like a Labrador-colored bat. Folds of Fabric, skin colored, with subcutaneous lumps like acne. A sleeve of padded silver foil was being pulled down over it.

A spaceship made of Fabric. Things can only get through it in one direction. If two-ply, then Fabric won't let air out, or light and radiation in.

"They say," our taxi driver said, looking even more hooded than before, "that it will be launched today or tomorrow. The whole town knows. We'll all be looking up to wave." Our hearts stopped. He chuckled.

We squeaked to a halt outside the reception bungalow. I suppose you thought his fare at him. I hope you gave him a handsome tip.

He saluted and said, "I pray the weather keeps good for you. Wherever you are going." He gave a sly smile.

A woman in a blue-gray uniform bustled out to us. "Good, good, good. You are Graça and Cristina Spinoza Vaz? You must come. We're boarding. Come, come, come."

"Can we unpack, shower first?"

"No, no. No time."

We were retinaed and scanned, and we took off our shoes. It was as if we were so rushed we'd attained near-light speeds already and time was dilating. Everything went slower, heavier—my shoes, the bag, my heartbeat. So heavy and slow that everything glued itself in place. I knew I wasn't going to go, and that absolutely nothing was going to make me. For the first time in my life.

Graça, this is only happening because zey want it. Zey need us to carry zem. We're donkeys.

"You go," I said.

"What? Cristina. Don't be silly."

I stepped backwards, holding up my hands against you. "No, no, no. I can't do this."

You came for me, eyes tender, smile forgiving. "Oh, darling, this is just nerves."

"It's not nerves. You want to do this; I do not."

Your eyes narrowed; the smile changed. "This is not the time to discuss things. We have to go! This is illegal. We have to get in and go now."

We don't fight, ever, do we, Graça? Doesn't that strike you as bizarre? Two people who have been trapped together on the twenty-fourth floor all of their lives and yet they never fight. Do you not know how that happens, Graçfushka? It happens because I always go along with you.

I just couldn't see spending four years in a cramped little pod with you. Then spending a lifetime on some barren waste watching you organizing volleyball tournaments or charity lunches in outer space. I'm sorry.

I knew if I stayed you'd somehow wheedle me onto that ship through those doors; and I'd spend the next two hours, even as I went up the gantry, even as I was sandwiched in cloth, promising myself that at the next opportunity I'd run.

I pushed my bag at you. When you wouldn't take it, I dropped it at your feet. I bet you took it with you, if only for the cupaçu.

You clutched at my wrists, and you tried to pull me back. You'd kept your turquoise bracelet and it looked like all the things about you I'd never see again. You were getting angry now. "You spent a half trillion reais on all the surgeries and and and and Rhodopsin . . . and and and the germ cells, Cris! Think of what that means for your children here on Earth, they'll be freaks!" You started to cry. "You're just afraid. You're always so afraid."

I pulled away and ran.

"I won't go either," you wailed after me. "I'm not going if you don't."

"Do what you have to," I shouted over my shoulder. I found a door and pushed it and jumped down steps into the April heat of Nigeria. I sat on a low stucco border under the palm trees in the shade, my heart still pumping; and the most curious thing happened. I started to chuckle.

I remember at seventeen, I finally left the apartment on my own without you, and walked along the street into a restaurant. I had no idea how to get food. Could I just take a seat? How would I know what they were cooking?

Then like the tide, an AI flowed in and out of me and I felt zie/me pluck someone nearby, and a waitress came smiling, and ushered me to a seat. She would carry the tray. I turned the AI off because, dear Lord, I have to be able to order food by myself. So I asked the waitress what was on offer. She rolled her eyes back for just a moment, and she started to recite. The AI had to tell her. I couldn't remember what she'd said, and so I asked her to repeat. I thought: this is no good.

The base of the rocket sprouted what looked like giant cauliflowers and it inched its way skyward. For a moment I thought it would have to fall. But it kept on going.

Somewhere three months out, it will start the engines, which drive the ship by making new universes, something so complicated human beings cannot do it. The AI will make holograms so you won't feel enclosed. You'll sit in Pamukkale, Turkiye. Light won't get through the Fabric so you'll never look out on Jupiter. The main AI will have some cute, international name. You can finish your dissertation on *Libro del cortegiano*—you'll be able to read every translation—zey carry all the world's knowledge. You'll walk through Urbino. The AI will viva your PhD. Zey'll be there in your head watching when you stand on the alien rock. It will be zir flag you'll be planting. Instead of Brasil's.

I watched you dwindle into a spark of light that flared and turned into a star of ice-dust in the sky. I latched Emilda and asked her if I could stay with her, and after a stumble of shock, she said of course. I got the same taxi back. The rooftops were crowded with people looking up at the sky.

But here's the real joke. I latched our bank for more money. Remember, we left a trillion behind in case the launch was once again canceled?

All our money had been taken. Every last screaming centavo. Remember what I said about fraud?

So.

Are you sure that spaceship you're on is real?

THE LONG GOODNIGHT OF VIOLET WILD

CATHERYNNE M. VALENTE

1: Violet

I don't know what stories are anymore so I don't know how to tell you about the adventures of Woe-Be-Gone Nowgirl Violet Wild. In the Red Country, a story is a lot of words, one after the other, with conflict and resolution and a beginning, middle, and, most of the time, an end. But in the Blue Country, a story is a kind of dinosaur. You see how it gets confusing. I don't know whether to begin by saying: *Once upon a time a girl named Violet Wild rode a purple mammoth bareback through all the seven countries of world just to find a red dress that fit* or by shooting you right in that sweet spot between your reptilian skull-plates. It's a big decision. One false move and I'm breakfast.

I expect Red Rules are safer. They usually are. Here we go then! Rifle to the shoulder, adjust the crosshairs, stare down the barrel, don't dare breathe, don't move a muscle and—

Violet Wild is me. Just a kid with hair the color of raisins and eyes the color of grape jelly, living the life glasstastic in a four-bedroom wine bottle on the east end of Plum Pudding, the only electrified city in the Country of Purple. Bottle architecture was hotter than fried gold back then—and when the sunset slung itself against all those bright glass doors the bluffs just turned into a glitterbomb firework and everyone went staggering home with lavender light stuck to their coats. I got myself born like everybody else in P-Town: Mummery wrote a perfect sentence, so perfect and beautiful and fabulously punctuated that when she finished it, there was a baby floating in the ink pot and that was that. You have to be careful what you write in Plum Pudding. An accidentally glorious grocery list could net you twins. For this reason, the most famous novel in the Country of Purple begins: *It is a truth universally acknowledged, umbrella grouchy eggs.* I guess the author had too much to worry about already.

That was about the last perfect thing anybody did concerning myself. Oh, it was a fabulously punctuated life I had—Mums was a Clarinaut, Papo was a Nowboy, and you never saw a house more like a toybox than the bottle at 15 Portwine Place, chock full of gadgets and nonsense from parts unknown, art that came down off the walls for breakfast, visits from the Ordinary Emperor, and on some precious nights, gorgeous people in lavender suits and sweet potato ice cream gowns giggling through mouthfuls of mulberry schnapps over how much tastier were Orange Country cocktails and how much more belligerent were Green Country cockatiels. We had piles of carousel horse steaks and mugs of foamy creme de violette on our wide glass table every night. Trouble was, Mums was a Clarinaut and Papa was a Nowboy, so I mostly ate and drank it on my lonesome, or with the Sacred Sparrowbone Mask of the Incarnadine Fisherwomen and the watercolor unicorns from *Still Life with Banana Tree, Unicorns, and Murdered Tuba*, who came down off the living room wall some mornings in hopes of coffee and cereal with marshmallows. Mummery brought them back from her expeditions, landing her crystal clarinet, the good ship *Eggplant*, in the garden in a shower of prismy bubbles, her long arms full of poison darts, portraiture, explosives that look exactly like tea kettles and lollipops that look exactly like explosives. And then she'd take off again, with a sort of confused-confounded glance down at me, as though every time she came home, it was a shock to remember that I'd ever been born.

"You could ask to go with her, you know," said the Sacred Sparrowbone Mask of the Incarnadine Fisherwomen once, tipping the spiral-swirl of her carved mouth toward a bowl of bruise-black coffee, careful to keep its scruff of bloodgull feathers combed back and out of the way.

"We agree," piped up the watercolor unicorns, nosing at a pillowcase I'd filled with marshmallow cereal for them. "You could be her First Mate, see the crass and colorful world by clarinet. It's romantic."

"You think everything's romantic," I sighed. Watercolor unicorns have hearts like soap operas that never end, and when they gallop it looks like crying. "But it wouldn't be. It would be like traveling with a snowman who keeps looking at you like you're a lit torch."

So I guess it's no surprise I went out to the herds with Papo as soon as I could. I could ride a pony by the time I got a handle on finger painting—great jeweled beasts escaped from some primeval carousel beyond the walls of time. There's a horn stuck all the way through them, bone or antler or both, and they leap across the Past Perfect Plains on it like a sharp white foot, leaving holes in the earth like ellipses. They're vicious and wily and they bite like it's their one passion in life, but they're the only horses strong and fast enough to ride down the present just as it's becoming the future and lasso it down. And in the Country of Purple, the minutes and hours of present-future-happening look an awful lot like overgrown pregnant six-legged mauve squirrels. They're pregnant all the time, but they never give birth, on account of how they're pregnant with tomorrow and a year from now and alternate universes where everyone is half-bat. When a squirrel comes to term, she just winks out like a squashed cigarette. That's the Nowboy life. Saddle up with the sun and bring in tomorrow's herd—or next week's or next decade's. If we didn't, those nasty little rodents would run wild all over the place. Plays would close three years before they open, Wednesdays would go on strike, and a century of Halloweens would happen all at once during one poor bedraggled lunch break. It's hard, dusty work, but Papo always says if you don't ride the present like the devil it'll get right away from you because it's a feral little creature with a terrible personality and no natural predators.

So that's who I was before the six-legged squirrels of the present turned around and spat in my face. I was called Violet and I lived in a purple world and I had ardors for my Papo, my magenta pony Stopwatch even though he bit me several times and once semi-fatally, a bone mask, and a watercolor painting. But I only loved a boy named Orchid Harm, who I haven't mentioned yet because when everything ever is about one thing, sometimes it's hard to name it. But let's be plain: I don't know what love is anymore, either. In the Red Country, when you say you love someone, it means you need them. You desire them. You look after them and yearn achingly for them when they're away down at the shops. But in the Country of Purple, when you say you love someone, it means you killed them. For a long time, that's what I thought it meant everywhere.

I only ever had one friend who was a person. His name was Orchid Harm. He could read faster than anyone I ever met and he kissed as fast as reading. He had hair the color of beetroot and eyes the color of mangosteen and he was a Sunslinger like his Papo before him. They caught sunshine in buckets all over Plum Pudding, mixed it with sugar and lorikeet eggs and fermented it into something not even a little bit legal. Orchid had nothing to do all day while the sun dripped down into his stills. He used to strap on a wash-basket full of books and shimmy up onto the roof of the opera house, which is actually a giantess's skull with moss and tourmalines living all over it, scoot down into the curve of the left eye socket, and read seven books before twilight. No more, no less. He liked anything that came in sevens. I only came in ones, but he liked me anyway.

We met when his parents came to our bottle all covered in glitter and the smell of excitingly dodgy money to drink Mummery's schnapps and listen to Papo's Nowboy songs played on a real zanfona box with a squirrel-leg handle. It was a marquee night in Mummery's career—the Ordinary Emperor had promised to come, he who tells all our lives which way to run. Everyone kept peering at brandy snifters, tea kettles, fire pokers, bracelets, books on our high glass shelves. When—and where—would the Little Man make his entrance? *Oh, Mauve, do you remember, when he came to our to-do, he was my wife's left-hand glove, the one she'd lost in the chaise cushions months ago!*

And then a jar of dried pasta grew a face and said: "What a pleasure it is to see so many of my most illustrious subject gathered all together in this fine home," but I didn't care because I was seven.

You see, the Ordinary Emperor can be anything he likes, as long as it's nothing you'd expect an Emperor to ever want to be. At any moment, anything you own could turn into the Emperor and he'd know everything you'd ever done with it—every mirror you'd ever hung and then cried in because you hated your own face, or candle you ever lit because you were up late doing something dastard, or worse, or better. It's unsettling and that's a fact.

Orchid was only little and so was I. While Mums cooed over the Emperor of Dried Pasta, I sat with my knees up by the hearth, feeding escargot to one of the watercolor unicorns. They can't get enough of escargot, even though it gives them horrible runny creamsicle-shits. This is the first thing Orchid ever said to me:

"I like your unicorn. Pink and green feel good on my eyes. I think I know who painted it but I don't want you to think I'm a know-it-all so I won't say even though I really *want* to say because I read a whole book about her and knowing things is nicer when somebody else knows you know them."

"I call her Jellyfish even though that's not her name. You can pet her but you have to let her smell your hand first. You can say who painted it if you want. Mums told me when she brought it home from Yellow Country, but I forgot." I didn't forget. I never got the hang of forgetting things the way other people do.

Orchid let Jellyfish snuffle his palm with her runny rosy nose.

"Do you have snails?" the watercolor unicorn asked. "They're very romantic."

Orchid didn't, but he had a glass of blackberry champagne because his parents let him drink what they drank and eat what they ate and read what they read and do what they did, which I thought was the best thing I had ever heard. Jellyfish slurped it up.

"A lady named Ochreous Wince painted me and the tuba and the banana tree and all my brothers and sisters about a hundred years ago, if you want to know. She was a drunk and she had a lot of dogs," Jellyfish sniffed when she was done, and jumped back up into her frame in a puff of rosewater smoke.

"Show me someplace that your parents don't know about," said Orchid. I took him to my room and made him crawl under my bed. It was stuffy and close down there, and I'm not very tidy. Orchid waited. He was good at waiting. I rolled over and pointed to the underside of my bed. On one of the slats I'd painted a single stripe of gold paint.

"Where?" he breathed. He put his hand on it. I put my hand on his.

"I stole it from Mummery's ship when she was busy being given the key to the city."

"She already lives here."

"I know."

After that, Orchid started going out with Papo and me sometimes, out beyond the city walls and onto the dry, flat Past Perfect Plains where the thousand squirrels that are every future and present and past scrabbled and screamed and thrashed their fluffy tails in the air. I shouldn't have let him, but knowing things is nicer when somebody else knows you know them. By the time the worst thing in the world happened, Orchid Harm could play *Bury Me on the Prairie with a Squirrel in my Fist* on the zanfona box as well as Papo or me. He helped a blackberry-colored mare named Early-to-Tea get born and she followed him around like a lovesick tiger, biting his shoulders and hopping in circles until he gave up and learned to ride her.

I don't want to say this part. I wish this were the kind of story that's a blue dinosaur munching up blueberries with a brain in its head and a brain in its tail so it never forgets how big it is. But I have to or the rest of it won't make sense. Okay, calm down, I'm doing it. Rifle up.

The day of the worst thing in the world was long and hot and bright, packed so full of summer autumn seeped out through the stitches. We'd ridden out further than usual—the ponies ran like they had thorns in their bellies and the stupid squirrels kept going at each other like mad, whacking their purple heads together and tail-wrestling and spitting paradoxes through clenched teeth. I wanted to give them some real space, something fresh to graze on. Maybe if they ate enough they'd just lay down in the heat and hold their little bellies in their paws and concentrate on breathing like any sane animal. Papo stayed behind to see to a doe mewling and foaming at the mouth, trying to pass a chronology stone. She kept coughing up chunks of the Ordinary Emperor's profligate youth, his wartime speeches and night terrors echoing out of her rodent-mouth across the prairie.

We rode so far, Orchid and me, bouncing across the cracked purple desert on Stopwatch and Early-to-Tea, that we couldn't even see the lights of Plum Pudding anymore, couldn't see anything but the plains spreading out like an inkstain. That far into the wilds, the world wasn't really purple anymore. It turned to indigo, the dark, windy borderlands where the desert looks like an ocean and the twisted-up trees are the color of lightning. And then, just when I was about to tell Orchid how much I liked the shadow of his cheekbones by indigo light, the Blue Country happened, right in front of us. That's the only way I can say it where it seems right to me. I'd never seen a border before. Somehow I always thought there would be a wall, or guards with spears and pom-poms on their shoes, or at least a sign. But it was just a line in the land, and on this side everything was purple and on that side everything was blue. The earth was still thirsty and spidered up with fine cracks like a soft boiled egg just before you stick your spoon in, but instead of the deep indigo night-steppe or the bright purple pampas, long aquamarine salt flats stretched out before us, speckled with blueberry brambles and sapphire tumbleweeds and skittering blue crabs. The Blue Country smelled like hot corn and cold snow. All the mauve time-squirrels skidded up short, sniffing the blue-indigo line suspiciously.

We let Stopwatch and Early-to-Tea bounce off after the crabs. The carousel ponies roared joyfully and hopped to it, skewering the cerulean crustacean shells with their bone poles, each gnawing the meat and claws off the other's spike. The sun caromed off the gems on their rump. Orchid and I just watched the blue.

"Didn't you ever want to see this, Violet? Go to all other places that exist in the universe, like your Mummery?" he said at last. "Didn't you ever watch her clarinet take off and feel like you'd die if you didn't see what she saw? I feel like I'll die if I don't see something new. Something better than sunshine in a bucket."

Off in the distance, I could see a pack of stories slurping at a watering hole, their long spine-plates standing against the setting sun like broken fences.

"Do you want to know a secret?" I said. I didn't wait for him to answer. Orchid always wanted to know secrets. "I dream in gold. When I'm asleep I don't even know what purple is. And one time I actually packed a suitcase and went to the train station and bought a ticket to the Yellow Country with money I got from selling all my chess sets. But when I got there and the conductor was showing me to my seat I just knew how proud Mums would be. I could see her stupid face telling her friends about her daughter running off on an adventure. *Darling, the plum doesn't fall far from the tree, don't you know? Violet's just like a little photograph of me, don't you think?* Well, the point is: fuck her, I guess."

"You were going to go without me?"

And my guts were full of shame, because I hadn't even thought of him that day, not when I put on my stockings or my hat, not when I marched into a taxi and told him to take me to Heliotrope Station, not when I bought my ticket for one. I just wanted to *go*. Which meant I was a little photograph of her, after all. I kissed him, to make it better. We liked kissing. We'd discovered it together. We'd discussed it and we were fairly certain no one in the world did it as well as we did. When Orchid and me kissed, we always knew what the other was thinking, and just then we knew that the other was thinking that we had two horses and could go now, right now, across the border and through the crabs and blueberries and stories and hot corn air. We'd read in our books, curled up together, holding hands and feet, in the eye socket of the opera house, that all the fish in the Blue Country could talk, and all the people had eyes the color of peacock feathers, and you could make babies by singing an aria so perfectly that when you were done, there would be a kid in the sheet music, and that would be that, so *The Cyan Sigh* can never be performed on-key unless the soprano is ready for the responsibility. And in the Blue Country, all the cities were electrified, just like us.

We were happy and we were going to run away together. So the squirrels ate him.

Orchid and I jumped over the border like a broomstick and when our feet came down the squirrels screeched and rushed forward, biting our heels, slashing our legs with their six clawed feet, spitting bile in our faces. Well, I thought it was our faces, our heels, our legs. I thought they were gunning for both of us. But it was Orchid they wanted. The squirrels slashed open his ankles so he'd fall down to their level, and then they bit off his fingers. I tried to pull and kick them off but there were so many, and you can't kill a plains-squirrel. You just can't. You might stab the rest of your life. You might break a half-bat universe's neck. You might end the whole world. I lay over Orchid so they couldn't get to him but all that meant was they dug out one of my kidneys and I was holding him when they chewed out his throat and I kissed him because when we kissed we always knew what the other was thinking and I don't want to talk about this anymore.

2: Blue

Papo never said anything. Neither did I. Jellyfish and the other watercolor unicorns each cut off a bit of their tails and stuck them together to make a watercolor orchid in the bottom left corner of the painting. It looked like a five-year-old with a head injury drew it with her feet and it ruined the whole composition. Orcheous Wince would have sicced her dogs on it. But no matter how Mummery fumed, they wouldn't put their tails back where they belonged. The Sacred Sparrowbone Mask of the Incarnadine Fisherwomen just said: "I like being a mask better than I'd like being a face, I think. But if you want, you can put me on and I'll be your face if you don't want anyone to see what you look like on the inside right now. Because everyone can see."

Orchid's father gave me a creme-pot full of sunslung booze. I went up to the eye socket of the opera house and drank and drank but the pot never seemed to dry up. Good. Everything had a shine on it when I drank the sun.

Everything had a heart that only I could see. Everything tasted like Orchid Harm, because he always tasted like the whole of the sun.

Once, I rode out on Stopwatch across the indigo borderlands again, up to the line in the earth where it all goes blue. I could see, I thought I could see, the haze of cornflower light over Lizard Tongue, the city that started as a wedding two hundred years ago and the party just never stopped. Stopwatch turned his big magenta head around and bit my hand—but softly. Hardly a bite at all.

I looked down. All the squirrels, pregnant with futures and purple with the present, thousands of them, stood on their hind legs around my pony's spike, staring up at me in silence like the death of time.

The day the rest of it happened, the squirrels were particularly depraved. I caught three shredding each other's bellies to ribbons behind a sun-broiled rock, blood and fur and yesterdays everywhere. I tried to pull them apart but I didn't try very hard because I never did anymore. They all died anyway, and I got long scratches all up and down my arms for my trouble. I'd have to go and get an inoculation. Half of them are rabid and the other half are lousy with regret. I looked at my arms, already starting to scab up. I am a champion coagulator. All the way home I picked them open again and again. So I didn't notice anyone following me back into P-Town, up through the heights and the sunset on the wine bottle houses, through the narrow lilac streets while the plummy streetlamps came on one at a time. I was almost home before I heard the other footsteps. The bells of St. Murex bonged out their lonely moans and I could almost hear Mummery's voice, rich as soup, laughing at her own jokes by the glass hearth. But I did hear, finally, a sound, a such-soft sound, like a girl's hair falling, as it's cut, onto a floor of ice. I turned around and saw a funny little beastie behind me, staring at me with clear lantern-fish eyes.

The thing looked some fair bit like a woolly mammoth, if a mammoth could shrink down to the size of a curly wolfhound, with long indigo fur that faded into pale, pale lavender, almost white, over its four feet and the tip of its trunk, which curled up into the shape of a question mark. But on either side, where a mammoth would have flanks and ribs and the bulge of its elephant belly, my creeper had cabinet doors, locked tight, the color of dark cabbages with neat white trim and silver hinges. I looked at my sorrow and it looked at me. Our dark eyes were the same eyes, and that's how I knew it was mine.

"I love you," it said.

But Mummery said: "Don't you dare let that thing in the house." She was home for once, so she thought she could make rules. "It's filthy; I won't have it. Look how it's upsetting the unicorns!" The poor things were snorting and stampeding terribly in their frame, squashing watercolor bananas as they tumbled off the watercolor tree.

"Let it sleep in the garden, Mauve. Come back to me," said a box of matchsticks, for that night Mums was busy that night, being very important and desirable company. She was entertaining the Ordinary Emperor alone. I peered over into the box—every matchstick was carved in the shape of a tiny man with a shock of blue sulfuric hair that would strike on any surface. When he was here last month, the Ordinary Emperor was our downstairs hammer. I think the Ordinary Emperor wanted to seduce my mother. He showed up a lot during the mating season when Papo slept out on the range.

"What on earth *is* it?" sniffed Mummery, lifting a flute of mulberry schnapps to her lips as though nobody had ever died in the history of the world.

"Light me, my darling," cried the Ordinary Emperor, and she did, striking his head on the mantle and bringing him in close to the tiny mammoth's face. It didn't blink or cringe away, even though it had a burning monarch and a great dumb Mummery-face right up against its trunk.

"Why, it's a sorrow," the Ordinary Emperor whistled. "I thought they were extinct. I told them to be extinct ages ago. Naughty Nellies. Do you know, in the Red Country, sorrow means grief and pain and horror and loss? It's a decadent place. Everything tastes like cranberries, even the roast beef."

That was the first thing the Ordinary Emperor ever said to me alone. Mums knew very well what sorrow meant where the sun sets red. Then he said a second thing:

"You are more beautiful than your mother."

That's the kind of Emperor the Matchstick Man is, in seven words. But Mummery fell for it and glowered at me with her great famous moonshadow eyes.

But my sorrow was not extinct. My sorrow was hungry. I put it out in the garden and locked the fence. I filled an agate bowl with the mushrooms we grow on the carcass of a jacaranda tree that used to grow by the kitchen window and water from our private well. I meant to leave it to its dinner, but for whatever reason my body ever decides to do things, I sat down with it instead, in the shadow of Mummery's crystal clarinet, parked between the roses and the lobelias. The breeze made soft, half-melodic notes as it blew over the *Eggplant*'s portholes. A few iridescent fuel-bubbles popped free of the bell.

My sorrow ate so daintily, picking up each lacecap mushroom with its trunk, turning it around twice, and placing it on its outstretched ultraviolet tongue. It couldn't get its mouth in the right place to drink. I cupped my hands and dipped them into the clear water and held them up to my sorrow. Its tongue slipped against my palms three times as it lapped. I stroked my sorrow's fur and we watched the garden wall come alive with moonflowers opening like pale happy mouths in the night wind off of the Cutglass River.

My sorrow was soft as fish frills. I didn't want to hurt its pride by looking, so I decided she was a girl, like me.

"I love you," my sorrow said, and she put her soft mouth over my ravaged arms. She opened the wounds again with her tongue and licked up the purple blood that seeped out of the depths of me. I kept stroking her spine and the warm wood of the cabinet doors in her belly. I pulled gently at their handles, but they would not open.

"It's ok if you love me," I whispered. "I forgive you."

But she didn't love me, not then, or not enough. I woke up in the morning in my own bed. My sorrow slept curled into the curve of my sleep. When she snored it sounded like the river-wind blowing over my mother's ship. I tried to get up. But the floor of my bedroom was covered in sleeping squirrels, a mauve blanket of a hundred unhappened futures. When I put my bare feet on the floor, they scattered like buckshot.

I came downstairs reeking of sorrowmusk and futureshit. Mummery was already gone; Papo had never come home. Instead of anyone who lived with me, a stranger stood in our kitchen, fixing himself coffee. He was short but very slim and handsome, shaven, with brilliant hair of every color, even green, even burgundy, even gold, tied back with one of my velvet ribbons. He wore a doublet and hose like an actor or a lawyer, and when he turned to search for the cream, I could see a beautiful chest peeking out from beneath an apricot silk shirt. The unfamiliar colors of him made my eyes throb, painfully, then hungrily, starving for his emerald, his orange, his cobalt, even his brown and black. His gold. The stranger noticed me suddenly, fixing his eyes, the same shocking spatter of all possible colors as his hair, on my face.

"You're naked," I said before I could remember to be polite. I don't know how I knew it, but I did. I had caught the Ordinary Emperor naked, unhidden in any oddjob object, the morning after he'd probably ridden Mummery like Stopwatch.

One imperial eyebrow lifted in amusement.

"So are you," he said.

I don't sleep with clothes on. I don't see why I should strangle myself in a nightdress just so my dreams won't see my tits. I think his majesty expected me to blush and cover myself with my hands, but I didn't care. If Orchid could never see my skin again, what did it matter who else did? So we stood there, looking at each other like stories at a watering hole. The Ordinary Emperor had an expression on that only people like Mummery understand, the kind of unplain stare that carries a hundred footnotes to its desire.

The king blinked first. He vanished from the kitchen and became our chandelier. Every teardrop-shaped jewel was an eye, every lightbulb was a mouth. I looked up at the blaze of him and drank his coffee. He took it sweet, mostly cream and honey, with only a lash of coffee hiding somewhere in the thick of it.

"Defiant girl, who raised you?" hissed the Sacred Sparrowbone Mask of the Incarnadine Fisherwomen.

"You know who," I snorted, and even the chandelier laughed.

"Good morning, Violet," the lightbulbs said, flashing blue, garnet, lime green with each word. "If you give me your sorrow, I shall see it safely executed. They are pests, like milkweed or uncles. You are far too young and lovely to have a boil like that leaking all over your face."

I looked down. My sorrow had followed me without the smallest sound, and sat on her haunches beside my feet, staring up at me with those deepwater eyes. I held out the Emperor's coffee cup so she could sip.

"Do you really know everything that happens in all your countries?" I asked him. There really is nothing like a man hopping on top of your mother to make him seem altogether less frightening and a little pitiful.

"I don't know it all at once. But if I *want* to know it, I can lean toward it and it will lean toward me and then I know it better than you know your favorite lullaby." The Ordinary Emperor burned so brightly in our chandelier. Light bloomed out of the crystals, hot, dappled, harlequin light, pouring down onto my skin, turning me all those colors, all his spun-sugar patchwork. I didn't like it. His light on me felt like hands. It burned me; it clutched me, it petted me like a cat. I loved it. I was drowning in my dream of gold. My bones creaked for more. I wanted to wash it off forever.

I closed my eyes. I could still see the prisms of the Emperor. "What does death mean in the Red Country?" I whispered.

"It is a kind of dress with a long train that trails behind it and a neckline that plunges to the navel. Death is the color of garnets and is very hard to dance in." The eyes in my chandelier looked kind. We have a dress like that, too. It is the color of hyacinths and it is called need. "I know what you're asking, darling. And if you go to the Red Country you may find Orchid laughing there and wearing a red dress. It is possible. The dead here often go there, to Incarnadine, where the fisherwomen punt along the Rubicund, fishing for hope. The Red Country is not for you, Violet. The dead are very exclusive."

And then I said it, to the king of everything, the hope buried under the concrete at the bottom of me: "Doesn't it seem to you that a body eaten by the present becoming the future shouldn't really be dead? Shouldn't he just be waiting for me in tomorrow?"

"That I cannot tell you. It doesn't make much sense to me, though. Eaten is eaten. Your pampas squirrels are not my subjects. They are not my countries.

They are time, and time eats everything but listens to no one. The digestive systems of squirrels are unreliable at best. I know it is painful to hear, but time devours all love affairs. It is unavoidable. The Red Country is so much larger than the others. And you, Violet Wild, you specifically, do not have rights of passage through any of my nations. Stay put and do as your Mummery tells you. You are such a trial to her, you know."

The Ordinary Emperor snuffed abruptly out and the wine bottle went dark. The watercolor unicorns whinnied fearfully. The Sacred Sparrowbone Mask of the Incarnadine Fisherwomen turned its face to the wall. In the shallow cup of her other side, a last mauve squirrel hid away the great exodus from my bedroom. She held her tail up over her little face and whispered:

"I won't say even though I really want to say."

My sorrow tugged my fingers with her trunk. "I love you," she said again, and this time I shivered. I believed her, and I did not live in the Red Country where love means longing. "If you let me, I can be so big."

My sorrow twisted her trunk around her own neck and squeezed. She grew like a wetness spreading through cloth. Taller than me, and then taller than the cabinets, and then taller than the chandelier. She lowered her purple trunk to me like a ladder.

I don't know what stories are anymore. I don't know how fast sorrow can move and I don't know how squirrels work. But I am wearing my best need and a bone face over mine so no one can see what my insides look like. I can see already the blue crabs waving their claws to the blue sky, I can see the lights of Lizard Tongue and hear the wedding bells playing their millionth song. I am going on the back of my sorrow, further than Mummery ever did, to a place where love is love, stories have ends, and death is a red dress.

A stream of rabid, pregnant, time-squirrels races after me. I hope the crabs get them all.

3. Green

The place between the Blue Country and the Green Country is full of dinosaurs called stories, bubble-storms that make you think you're somebody else, and a sky and a ground that look almost exactly the same. And, for a little while, it was full of me. My sorrow and me and the Sparrowbone Mask of the Incarnadine Fisherwomen crossed the Blue Country where it gets all narrow and thirsty. I was also all narrow and thirsty, but between the two of us, I complained less than the Blue Country. I shut my eyes when we stepped over the border. I shut my eyes and tried to remember kissing Orchid Harm and knowing that we were both thinking about ice cream.

When I was little and my hair hadn't grown out yet but my piss-and-vinegar had, I asked my Papo:

"Papo, will I ever meet a story?"

My Papo took a long tug on his squirrel-bone pipe and blew smoky lilac rings onto my fingers.

"Maybe-so, funny bunny, maybe-not-so. But don't be sad if you don't. Stories are pretty dumb animals. And so aggressive!"

I clapped my hands. "Say three ways they're dumb!"

"Let's see." Papo counted them off on his fingers. "They're cold-blooded, they use big words when they ought to use small ones, and they have no natural defense against comets."

So that's what I was thinking about while my sorrow and me hammered a few tent stakes into the huge blue night. We made camp at the edge of a sparkling oasis where the water looked like liquid labradorite. The reason I thought about my Papo was because the oasis was already *occupado*. A herd of stories slurped up the water and munched up the blueberry brambles and cobalt cattails growing up all over the place out of the aquamarine desert. The other thing that slurped and munched and stomped about the oasis was the great electro-city of Lizard Tongue. The city limits stood a ways off, but clearly Lizard Tongue crept closer all the time. Little houses shaped like sailboats and parrot eggs spilled out of the metropolis, inching toward the water, inching, inching—nobody look at them or they'll stampede! I could hear the laughing and dancing of the city and I didn't want to laugh and I didn't want to dance and sleeping on the earth never troubled me so I stuck to my sorrow and the water like a flat blue stone.

It's pretty easy to make a camp with a sorrow as tall as a streetlamp, especially when you didn't pack anything from home. I did that on purpose. I hadn't decided yet if it was clever or stupid as sin. I didn't have matches or food or a toothbrush or a pocketknife. But the Ordinary Emperor couldn't come sneaking around impersonating my matches or my beef jerky or my toothbrush or my pocketknife, either. I was safe. I was Emperor-proof. I was not squirrel-proof. The mauve squirrels of time and/or space milled and tumbled behind us like a stupid furry wave of yesterpuke and all any of us could do was ignore them while they did weird rat-cartwheels and chittered at each other, which sounds like the ticks of an obnoxiously loud clock, and fucked with their tails held over their eyes like blindfolds in the blue-silver sunset.

My sorrow picked turquoise coconuts from the paisley palm trees with her furry lavender trunk and lined up the nuts neatly all in a row. Sorrows are very fastidious, as it turns out.

"A storm is coming at seven minutes past seven," the Sparrowbone Mask of the Incarnadine Fisherwomen said. "I do not like to get wet."

I collected brambles and crunched them up for kindling. In order to crunch up brambles, I had to creep and sneak among the stories, and that made me nervous, because of what Papo said when my hair was short.

A story's scales are every which shade of blue you can think of and four new ones, too. I tiptoed between them, which was like tiptoeing between trolley-cars. I tried to avoid the poison spikes on their periwinkle tails and the furious horns on their navy blue heads and the crystal sapphire plates on their backs. The setting sun shone through their sapphire plates and burned up my eyeballs with blue.

"Heyo, guignol-girl!" One story swung round his dinosaur-head at me and smacked his chompers. "Why so skulk and slither? Have you scrofulous aims on our supper?"

"Nope, I only want to make a fire," I said. "We'll be gone in the morning."

"Ah, conflagration," the herd nodded sagely all together. "The best of all the -ations."

"And whither do you peregrinate, young sapiens sapiens?" said one of the girl-dinosaurs. You can tell girl-stories apart from boy-stories because girl-stories have webbed feet and two tongues.

I was so excited I could have chewed rocks for bubblegum. Me, Violet Wild, talking to several real live stories all at once. "I'm going to the Red Country," I said. "I'm going to the place where death is a red dress and love is a kind of longing and maybe a boy named Orchid didn't get his throat ripped out by squirrels."

"We never voyage to the Red Country. We find no affinity there. We are allowed no autarchy of spirit."

"We cannot live freely," explained the webfooted girl-story, even though I knew what autarchy meant. What was I, a baby eating paint? "They pen us up in scarlet corrals and force us to say exactly what we mean. It's deplorable."

"Abhorrent."

"Iniquitous!"

The stories were working themselves up into a big blue fury. I took a chance. I grew up a Nowgirl on the purple pampas, I'm careful as a crook on a balcony when it comes to animals. I wouldn't like to spook a story. When your business is wildness and the creatures who own it, you gotta be cool, you gotta be able to act like a creature, talk like a creature, make a creature feel like you're their home and the door's wide open.

"Heyo, Brobdingnagian bunnies," I said with all the sweetness I knew how to make with my mouth. "No quisquoses or querulous tristiloquies." I started to sweat and the stars started to come out. I was already almost out of good words. "Nobody's going to . . . uh . . . ravish you off to Red and rapine. Pull on your tranquilities one leg at a time. Listen to the . . . um . . . psithurisma? The psithurisma of the . . . vespertine . . . trees rustling, eat your comestibles, get down with dormition."

The stories milled around me, purring, rubbing their flanks on me, getting their musk all over my clothes. And then I had to go lie down because those words tired me right out. I don't even know if all of them were really words but I remembered Mummery saying all of them at one point or another to this and that pretty person with a pretty name.

My sorrow lay down in the moonlight. I leaned against her furry indigo chest. She spat on the brambles and cattails I crunched up and they blazed up purple and white. I didn't know a sorrow could set things on fire.

"I love you," my sorrow said.

In the Blue Country, when you say you love someone it means you want to eat them. I knew that because when I thought about Orchid Harm on the edge of the oasis with water like labradorite all I could think of was how good his skin tasted when I kissed it; how sweet and savory his mouth had always been, how even his bones would probably taste like sugar, how even his blood would taste like hot cocoa. I didn't like those thoughts but they were in my head and I couldn't not have them. That was what happened to my desire in the Blue Country. The blue leaked out all over it and I wanted to swallow Orchid. He would be okay inside me. He could live in my liver. I would take care of him. I would always be full.

But Orchid wasn't with me which is probably good for him as I have never been good at controlling myself when I have an ardor. My belly growled but I didn't bring anything to eat on account of not wanting an Emperor-steak, medium-rare, so it was coconut delight on a starlit night with the bubbles coming in. In the Blue Country, the bubbles gleam almost black. They roll in like dark dust, an iridescent wall of go-fuck-yourself, a soft, ticklish tsunami of heart-killing gases. I didn't know that then but I know it now. The bubble-storm covered the blue plains and wherever a bubble popped something invisible leaked out, something to do with memory and the organs that make you feel things even when you would rather play croquet with a plutonium mallet than feel one more drop of anything at all. The blue-bruise-black-bloody bubbles tumbled and popped and burst and glittered under the ultramarine stars and I felt my sorrow's trunk around my ankle which was good because otherwise I think I would probably have floated off or disappeared.

People came out of the houses shaped like sailboats and the houses shaped like parrot eggs. They held up their hands like little kids in the bubble-monsoon. Bubbles got stuck in their hair like flowers, on their fingers like rings. I'd never seen a person who looked like those people. They had hair the color of tropical fish and skin the color of a spring sky and the ladies wore cerulean dresses with blue butterflies all over them and the boys wore midnight waistcoats and my heart turned blue just looking at them.

"Heyo, girlie!" The blue people called, waggling their blue fingers in the bubbly night. "Heyo, elephant and mask! Come dance with us! Cornflower Leap and Pavonine Up are getting married! You don't even have any blueberry schnapps!"

Because of the bubbles popping all over me I stopped being sure who I was. The bubbles smelled like a skull covered in moss and tourmalines. Their gasses tasted like coffee with too much milk and sugar left by an Emperor on a kitchen counter inside a wine bottle.

"Cornflower Leap and Pavonine Up are dead, dummies," I said, but I said it wrong somehow because I wasn't Violet Wild anymore but rather a bubble and inside the bubble of me I was turning into a box of matchsticks. Or Orchid Harm. Or Mummery. I heard clarinets playing the blues. I heard my bones getting older. "They got dead two hundred years ago, you're just too drunk to remember when their wedding grew traffic laws and sporting teams and turned into a city."

One of the blue ladies opened her mouth right up and ate a bubble out of the air on purpose and I decided she was the worst because who would do that? "So what?" she giggled. "They're still getting married! Don't be such a drip. How did a girlie as young as you get to be a drip as droopy as you?"

People who are not purple are baffling.

You better not laugh but I danced with the blue people. Their butterflies landed on me. When they landed on me they turned violet like my body and my name but they didn't seem upset about it. The whole world looked like a black rainbow bubble. It was the opposite of drinking the sun that Orchid's family brewed down in their slipstills. When I drink the sun, I feel soft and edgeless. When the bubbles rained down on me I felt like I was made of edges all slicing themselves up and the lights of Lizard Tongue burned up my whole brain and while I was burning I was dancing and while I was dancing I was the Queen of the Six-Legged squirrels. They climbed up over me in between the black bubbles. Some of them touched the turquoise butterflies and when they did that they turned blue and after I could always tell which of the squirrels had been with me that night because their fur never got purple again, not even a little.

I fell down dancing and burning. I fell down on the cracked cobalt desert. A blue lady in a periwinkle flapper dress whose hair was the color of the whole damn ocean tried to get me to sit up like I was some sad sack of nothing at Mummery's parties who couldn't hold her schnapps.

"Have you ever met anyone who stopped being dead?" I asked her.

"Nobody blue," she said.

I felt something underneath me. A mushy, creamy, silky something. A something like custard with a crystal heart. I rolled over and my face made a purple print in the blue earth and when I rolled over I saw Jellyfish looking shamefaced, which she should have done because stowaways should not look proudfaced, ever.

"I ate a bunch of bleu cheese at the wedding buffet in the town square and now my tummy hates me," the watercolor unicorn mourned.

One time Orchid Harm told me a story about getting married and having kids and getting a job somewhere with no squirrels or prohibited substances. It seemed pretty unrealistic to me. Jellyfish and I breathed in so much blackish-brackish bubble-smoke that we threw up together, behind a little royal blue dune full of night-blooming lobelia flowers. When we threw up, that story came out and soaked into the ground. My sorrow picked us both up in her trunk and carried us back to the fire.

The last thing I said before I fell asleep was: "What's inside your cabinet?"

The only answer I got was the sound of a lock latching itself and a squirrel screeching because sorrow stepped on it.

When I woke up the Blue Country had run off. The beautiful baffling blue buffoons and the black bubbles and the pompous stories had legged it, too.

Green snow fell on my hair. It sparkled in my lap and there was a poisonous barb from the tail of a story stuck to the bottom of my shoe. I pulled it off very carefully and hung it from my belt. My hand turned blue where I'd held it and it was always blue forever and so I never again really thought of it as my hand.

4. Yellow

Sometimes I get so mad at Mummery. She never told me anything important. Oh, sure, she taught me how to fly a clarinet and how much a lie weighs and how to shoot her stained-glass Nonegun like a champ. *Of course, you can plot any course you like on a clarinet, darlingest, but the swiftest and most fuel efficient is Premiére Rhapsodie by Debussy in A Major.* Ugh! Who needs to know the fuel efficiency of Debussy? Mummery toot-tooted her long glass horn all over the world and she never fed me one little spoonful of it when I was starving to death for anything other than our old awful wine bottle in Plum Pudding. What did Mummery have to share about the Green Country? *I enjoyed the saunas in Verdigris, but Absinthe is simply lousy with loyalty. It's a serious problem.* That's nothing! That's rubbish, is what. Especially if you know that in the Green Country, loyalty is a type of street mime.

The Green Country is frozen solid. Mummery, if only you'd said one useful thing, I'd have brought a thicker coat. Hill after hill of green snow under a chartreuse sky. But trees still grew and they still gave fruit—apples and almonds and mangoes and limes and avocados shut up in crystal ice pods, hanging from branches like party lanterns. People with eyes the color of mint jelly and hair the color of unripe bananas, wearing knit olive caps with sage poms on the ends zoomed on jade toboggans, up and down and everywhere, or else they skate on green glass rivers, ever so many more than in the Blue Country. Green people never stop moving or shivering. My sorrow slipped and slid and stumbled on the lime-green ice. Jellyfish and I held on for dear life. The Sparrowbone Mask of the Incarnadine Fisherwomen clung to my face, which I was happy about because otherwise I'd have had green frost growing on my teeth.

One time Orchid Harm and I went up to the skull socket of the opera house and read out loud to each other from a book about how to play the guitar. It never mattered what we read about really, when we read out loud to each other. We just liked to hear our voices go back and forth like a seesaw. *Most popular songs are made up of three or four or even two simple chords,* whispered Orchid seductively. *Let us begin with the D chord, which is produced by holding the fingers thusly.* And he put his fingers on my throat like mine was the neck of a guitar. And suddenly a terror happened inside me, a terror that Orchid must be so cold, so cold in my memory of the skull socket and the D chord and cold wherever he might be and nothing mattered at all but that I had to warm him up, wrap him in fur or wool or lay next to him skin to skin, build a fire, the biggest fire that ever wrecked a hearth, anything if it would get him warm again. Hot. Panic went zigzagging through all my veins. We had to go faster.

"We'll go to Absinthe," I said shakily, even though I didn't know where Absinthe was because I had a useless Mummery. I told the panic to sit down and shut up. "We need food and camping will be a stupid experience here."

"I love you," said my sorrow, and her legs grew like the legs of a telescope, longer even than they had already. The bottoms of her fuzzy hippo-feet flattened out like pancakes frying in butter until they got as wide as snowshoes. A sorrow is a resourceful beast. Nothing stops sorrow, not really. She took the snowy glittering emerald hills two at a stride. Behind us the army of squirrels flowed like the train of a long violet gown. Before us, toboggan-commuters ran and hid.

"In the Green Country, when you say you love somebody, it means you will keep them warm even if you have to bathe them in your own blood," Jellyfish purred. Watercolor unicorns can purr, even though real unicorns can't. Jellyfish rubbed her velvety peach and puce horn against my sorrow's spine.

"How do you know that?"

"Ocherous Wince, the drunken dog-lover who painted me, also painted a picture more famous than me. Even your Mummery couldn't afford it. It's called *When I Am In Love My Heart Turns Green.* A watercolor lady with watercolor wings washes a watercolor salamander with the blood pouring out of her wrists and her elbows. The salamander lies in a bathtub that is a sawn-open lightbulb with icicles instead of clawfeet. It's the most romantic thing I ever saw. I know a lot of things because of Ocherous Wince, but I never like to say because I don't want you to think I'm a know-it-all even though I really *want* to say because knowing things is nicer when somebody else knows you know them."

Absinthe sits so close to the border of the Yellow Country that half the day is gold and half the day is green. Three brothers sculpted the whole city—houses, pubs, war monuments—out of jellybean-colored ice with only a little bit of wormwood for stability and character. I didn't learn that from Jellyfish or Mummery, but from a malachite sign on the highway leading into the city. The brothers were named Peapod. They were each missing their pinky fingers but not for the same reason.

It turns out everybody notices you when you ride into town on a purple woolly mammoth with snowshoes for feet with a unicorn in your lap and a bone mask on your face. I couldn't decide if I liked being invisible better or being watched by everybody all at once. They both hurt. Loyalties scattered before us like pigeons, their pale green greasepainted faces miming despair or delight or umbrage, depending on their schtick. They mimed tripping over each other, and then some actually did trip, and soon we'd cause a mime-jam and I had to leave my sorrow parked in the street. I was so hungry I could barely shiver in the cold. Jellyfish knew a cafe called O Tannenbaum but I didn't have any money.

"That's all right," said the watercolor unicorn. "In the Green Country, money means grief."

So I paid for a pine-green leather booth at O Tannenbaum, a stein of creme de menthe, a mugwort cake and parakeet pie with tears. The waiter wore a waistcoat of clover with moldavite buttons. He held out his hands politely. I didn't think I could do it. You can't just grieve because the bill wants 15% agony on top of the prix fixe. But my grief happened to me like a back alley mugging and I put my face into his hands so no one would see my sobbing; I put my face into his hands like a bone mask so no one could see what I looked like on the inside.

"I'm so lonely," I wept. "I'm nobody but a wound walking around." I lifted my head—my head felt heavier than a planet. "Did you ever meet anyone who fucked up and put it all right again, put it all back the way it was?"

"Nobody green," said the waiter, but he walked away looking very pleased with his tip.

It's a hard damn thing when you're feeling lowly to sit in a leather booth with nobody but a unicorn across from you. Lucky for me, a squirrel hopped up on the bamboo table. She sat back on her hind two legs and rubbed her humongous paradox-pregnant belly with the other four paws. Her bushy mauve tail stood at attention behind her, bristling so hard you could hear it crackling.

"Pink and green feel good on my eyes," the time-squirrel said in Orchid Harm's voice.

"Oh, go drown yourself in a hole," I spat at it, and drank my creme de menthe, which gave me a creme de menthe mustache that completely undermined much of what I said later.

The squirrel tried again. She opened her mouth and my voice came out.

"No quisquoses or querulous tristiloquies," she said soothingly. But I had no use for a squirrel's soothe.

"Eat shit," I hissed.

But that little squirrel was the squirrel who would not quit. She rubbed her cheeks and stretched her jaw and out came a voice I did not know, a man's voice, with a very expensive accent.

"The Red Country is the only country with walls. It stands to reason something precious lives there. But short of all-out war, which I think we can all agree is at least inconvenient, if not irresponsible, we cannot know what those walls conceal. I would suggest espionage, if we can find a suitable candidate."

Now, I don't listen to chronosquirrels. They're worse than toddlers. They babble out things that got themselves said a thousand months ago or will be said seventy years from now or were only said by a preying mantis wearing suspenders in a universe that's already burned itself out. When I was little I used to listen, but my Papo spanked me and told me the worst thing in the world was for a Nowboy to listen to his herd. *It'll drive you madder than a plate of snakes*, he said. He never spanked me for anything else and that's how I know he meant serious business. But this dopey doe also meant serious business. I could tell by her tail. And I probably would have gotten into it with her, which may or may not have done me a lick of good, except that I'd made a mistake without even thinking about it, without even brushing off a worry or a grain of dread, and just at that moment when I was about to tilt face first into Papo's plate of snakes, the jade pepper grinder turned into a jade Emperor with black peppercorn lips and a squat silver crown.

"Salutations, young Violet," said the Ordinary Emperor in a voice like a hot cocktail. "What's a nice purple girl like you doing in a bad old green place like this?"

Jellyfish shrieked. When a unicorn shrieks, it sounds like sighing. I just stared. I'd been so careful. The Emperor of Peppercorns hopped across the table on his grinder. The mauve squirrel patted his crown with one of her hands. They were about the same height. I shook my head and declined to say several swear words.

"Don't feel bad, Miss V," he said. "It's not possible to live without objects. Why do you think I do things this way? Because I enjoy being hand brooms and cheese-knives?"

"Leave me alone," I moaned.

"Now, I just heard you say you were lonely! You don't have to be lonely. None of my subjects have to be lonely! It was one of my campaign promises, you know."

"Go back to Mummery. Mind your own business."

The Ordinary Emperor stroked his jade beard. "I think you liked me better when I was naked in your kitchen. I can do it again, if you like. I want you to like me. That is the cornerstone of my administration."

"No. Be a pepper grinder. Be a broom."

"Your Papo cannot handle the herd by himself, señorita," clucked the Ordinary Emperor. "You've abandoned him. Midnight comes at three p.m. in Plum Pudding. Every day is Thursday. Your Mummery has had her clarinet out day and night looking for you."

"Papo managed before I was born, he can manage now. And you could have told Mums I was fine."

"I could have. I know what you're doing. It's a silly, old-fashioned thing, but it's just so *you*. I've written a song about it, you know. I called it *My Baby Done Gone to Red*. It's proved very popular on the radio, but then, most of my songs do."

"I've been gone for three days!"

"Culture moves very quickly when it needs to, funny bunny. Don't you like having a song with you in it?"

I thought about Mummery and all the people who thought she was fine as a sack of bees and drank her up like champagne. She lived for that drinking-up kind of love. Maybe I would, too, if I ever got it. The yellow half of Absinthe's day came barreling through the cafe window like a bandit in a barfight. Gold, gorgeous, impossible gold, on my hands and my shoulders and my unicorn and my mouth, the color of the slat under my bed, the color of the secret I showed Orchid before I loved him. Sitting in that puddle of suddenly gold light felt like wearing a tiger's fur.

"Well, I haven't heard the song," I allowed. Maybe I wanted a little of that champagne-love, too.

Then the Ordinary Emperor wasn't a pepper grinder anymore because he was that beautiful man in doublet and hose and a thousand hundred colors who stood in my kitchen smelling like sex and power and eleven kinds of orange and white. He put his hands over mine.

"Didn't you ever wonder why the clarinauts are the only ones who travel between countries? Why they're so famous and why everyone wants to hear what they say?"

"I never thought about it even one time." That was a lie; I thought about it all the time the whole year I was eleven but that was long enough ago that it didn't feel like much of a lie.

He wiped away my creme de menthe mustache. I didn't know it yet, but my lips stayed green and they always would. "A clarinaut is born with a reed in her heart through which the world can pass and make a song. For everyone else, leaving home is poison. They just get so lost. Sometimes they spiral down the drain and end up Red. Most of the time they just wash away. It's because of the war. Bombs are so unpredictable. I'm sure everyone feels very embarrassed now."

I didn't want to talk about the specialness of Mummery. I didn't want to cry, either, but I was, and my tears splashed down onto the table in big, showy drops of gold. The Ordinary Emperor knuckled under my chin.

"*Mon petite biche*, it is natural to want to kill yourself when you have bitten off a hurt so big you can't swallow it. I once threw myself off Split Salmon Bridge in the Orange Country. But the Marmalade Sea spit me back. The Marmalade Sea thinks suicide is for cowards and she won't be a part of it. But you and I know better."

"I don't want to kill myself!"

"It doesn't matter what death means in the Red Country, Violet. Orchid didn't die in the Red Country. And you won't make it halfway across the Tangerine Tundra. You're already bleeding." He turned over my blue palm, tracing tracks in my golden tears. "You'll ride your sorrow into a red brick wall."

"It does matter. It does. You don't matter. My sorrow loves me."

"And what kind of love would that be? The love that means killing? Or eating? Or keeping warm? Do you know what 'I love you' means in the Yellow Country?"

"It means 'I cannot stand the sight of you,' " whinnied Jellyfish, flicking her apricot and daffodil tail. "Ocherous Wince said it to all her paintings every day."

The waiter appeared to take the Ordinary Emperor's order. He trembled slightly, his clovers quivering. "The pea soup and a glass of green apple gin with a dash of melon syrup, my good man," his Majesty said without glancing at the help. "I shall tell you a secret if you like, Violet. It's better than a swipe of gold paint, I promise."

"I don't care." My face got all hot and plum-dark even through the freezing lemony air. I didn't want him to talk about my slat. "Why do you bother with me? Go be a government by yourself."

"I like you. Isn't that enough? I like how much you look like your Mummery. I like how hard you rode Stopwatch across the Past Perfect Plains. I like how you looked at me when you caught me making coffee. I like that you painted the underside of your bed and I especially like how you showed it to Orchid. I'm going to tell you anyway. Before I came to the throne, during the reign of the Extraordinary Emperor, I hunted sorrows. Professionally. In fact, it was I who hunted them to extinction."

"What the hell did you do that for?" The waiter set down his royal meal and fled which I would also have liked to do but could not because I did not work in food service.

"Because I am from the Orange Country, and in the Orange Country, a sorrow is not a mammoth with a cabinet in its stomach, it is a kind of melancholic dread, a bitter, heartsick gloom. It feels as though you can never get free of a sorrow once you have one, as though you become allergic to happiness. It was because of a certain sorrow that I leapt from the Split Salmon Bridge. My parents died of a housefire and then my wife died of being my wife." The Ordinary Emperor's voice stopped working quite right and he sipped his gin. "All this having happened before the war, we could all hop freely from Orange to Yellow to Purple to Blue to Green—through Red was always a suspicious nation, their immigration policies never sensible, even then, even then when no one else knew what a lock was or a key. When I was a young man I did as young men do—I traveled, I tried to find women to travel with me, I ate foreign food and pretended to like it. And I saw that everywhere else, sorrows roamed like buffalo, and they were not distresses nor dolors nor disconsolations, but animals who could bleed. Parasites drinking from us like fountains. I did not set out for politics, but to rid the world of sorrows. I thought if I could kill them in the other countries, the Orange Country sort of sorrow would perish, too. I rode the ranges on a quagga with indigestion. I invented the Nonegun myself—I'll tell you that secret, too, if you like, and then you will know something your Mums doesn't, which I think is just about the best gift I could give you. To make the little engine inside a Nonegun you have to feel nothing for anyone. Your heart has to look like the vacuum of space. Not coincidentally, that is also how you make the engine inside an Emperor. I shot all the sorrows between the eyes. I murdered them. I rode them down. I was merciless."

"Did it work?" I asked softly.

"No. When I go home I still want to die. But it made a good campaign slogan. I have told you this for two reasons. The first is that when you pass into the Orange Country you will want to cut yourself open from throat to navel. Your sorrow has gotten big and fat. It will sit on you and you will not get up again. Believe me, I know. When I saw you come home with a sorrow following you like a homeless kitten I almost shot it right there and I should have. They have no good parts. Perhaps that is why I like you, really. Because I bleached sorrow from the universe and you found one anyway."

The Ordinary Emperor took my face in his hands. He kissed me. I started to not like it but it turned into a different kind of kiss, not like the kisses I made with Orchid, but a kiss that made me wonder what it meant to kiss someone in the Orange Country, a kiss half full of apology and half full of nostalgia and a third half full of do what I say or else. So in the end I came round again to not liking it. I didn't know what he was thinking when he kissed me. I guess that's not a thing that always happens.

"The second reason I told you about the sorrows, Violet Wild, is so that you will know that I can do anything. I am the man who murdered sorrow. It said that on my election posters. You were too young to vote, but your Mummery wasn't, and you won't be too young when I come up for re-election."

"So?"

"So if you run as my Vice-Emperor, which is another way of saying Empress, which is another way of saying wife, I will kill time for you, just like I killed sorrow. Squirrels will be no trouble after all those woolly monsters. Then everything can happen at once and you will both have Orchid and not have him at the same time because the part where you showed him the slat under your bed and the part where his body disappeared on the edge of the Blue Country will not have to happen in that order, or any order. It will be the same for my wife and my parents and only in the Red Country will time still mean passing."

The squirrel still squatted on the table with her belly full of baby futures in her greedy hands. She glared at the Ordinary Emperor with unpasteurized hate in her milky eyes. I looked out the great ice picture window of the restaurant that wasn't called O Tannenbaum anymore, but The Jonquil Julep, the hoppingest nightspot in the Yellow Country. Only the farthest fuzz on the horizon still looked green. Chic blonde howdy-dos started to crowd in wearing daffodil dresses and butterscotch tuxedos. Some of them looked sallow and waxy; some of them coughed.

"There is always a spot of cholera in the Yellow Country," admitted the Ordinary Emperor with some chagrin. Through the glass I saw my sorrow hunched over, peering in at the Emperor, weeping soundlessly, wiping her eyes with her trunk. "But the light here is so good for painting."

Everything looked like the underside of my bed. The six-legged squirrel said:

"Show me something your parents don't know about."

And love went pinballing through me but it was a Yellow kind of love and suddenly my creme de menthe was banana schnapps and suddenly my mugwort cake was lemon meringue and suddenly I hated Orchid Harm. I hated him for making me have an ardor for something that wasn't a pony or a Papo or a color of paint, I hated him for being a Sunslinger all over town even though everybody knew that shit would hollow you out and fill you back up with nothing if you stuck with it. I hated him for making friends with my unicorn and I hated him for hanging around Papo and me till he got dead from it and I hated him for bleeding out under me and making everything that happened happen. I didn't want to see his horrible handsome face ever again. I didn't want alive-Orchid and dead-Orchid at the same time, which is a pretty colossally unpleasant idea when you think about it. My love was the sourest thing I'd ever had. If Orchid had sidled up and ordered a cantaloupe whiskey, I would have turned my face away. I had to swallow all that back to talk again.

"But killing sorrow didn't work," I said, but I kept looking at my sorrow on the other side of the window.

"I obviously missed one," he said grimly. "I will be more thorough."

And the Ordinary Emperor, quick as a rainbow coming on, snatched up the squirrel of time and whipped her little body against the lemonwood table so that it broke her neck right in half. She didn't even get a chance to squeak.

Sometimes it takes me a long time to think through things, to set them up just right in my head so I can see how they'd break if I had a hammer. But sometimes I have a hammer. So I said:

"No, that sounds terrible. You are terrible. I am a Nowgirl and a Nowgirl doesn't lead her herd to slaughter. Bring them home, bring them in, my Papo always said that and that's what I will always say, too. Go away. Go be dried pasta. Go be sad and orange. Go jump off your bridge again. I'm going to the Red Country on my sorrow's back."

The Ordinary Emperor held up his hand. He stood to leave as though he were a regular person who was going to walk out the door and not just turn into a bar of Blue Country soap. He looked almost completely white in the loud yellow sunshine. The light burned my eyes.

"It's dangerous in the Red Country, Violet. You'll have to say what you mean. Even your Mummery never flew so far. "

He dropped the corpse of the mauve space-time squirrel next to his butter knife by way of paying his tab because in the Yellow Country, money means time.

"You are not a romantic man," said Jellyfish through clenched pistachio-colored teeth. That's the worst insult a watercolor unicorn knows.

"There's a shortcut to the Orange Country in the ladies' room. Turn the right tap three times, the left tap once, and pull the stopper out of the basin." That was how the Ordinary Emperor said goodbye. I'm pretty sure he told

Mummery I was a no-good whore who would never make good even if I lived to a hundred. That's probably even true. But that wasn't why I ran after him and stabbed him in the neck with the poisonous prong of the story hanging from my belt. I did that because, no matter what, a Nowgirl looks after her herd.

5. Orange

This is what happened to me in the Orange Country: I didn't see any cities even though there are really nice cities there, or drink any alcohol even though I've always heard clementine schnapps is really great, or talk to any animals even though in the Orange Country a poem means a kind of tiger that can't talk but can sing, or people, even though there were probably some decent ones making a big bright orange life somewhere.

I came out of the door in the basin of The Jonquil Julep and I lay down on floor of a carrot-colored autumn jungle and cried until I didn't have anything wet left to lose. Then I crawled under a papaya tree and clawed the orange clay until I made a hole big enough to climb inside if I curled up my whole body like a circle you draw with one smooth motion. The clay smelled like fire.

"I love you," said my sorrow. She didn't look well. Her fur was threadbare, translucent, her trunk dried out.

"I don't know what 'I love you' means in the Orange Country," sighed Jellyfish.

"I do," said the Sparrowbone Mask of the Incarnadine Fisherwomen, who hadn't had a damn thing to say in ages. "Here, if you love someone, you mean to keep them prisoner and never let them see the sun."

"But then they'd be safe," I whispered.

"I love you," said my sorrow. She got down on her giant woolly knees beside my hole. "I love you. Your eyes are yellow."

I began to claw into the orange clay my hole. I peeled it away and crammed it into my mouth. My teeth went through it easy as anything. It didn't taste like dirt. It tasted like a lot of words, one after the other, with conflict and resolution and a beginning, middle, but no end. It tasted like Mummery showing me how to play the clarinet. It tasted like an Emperor who wasn't an Emperor anymore. The earth stained my tongue orange forever.

"I love you," said my sorrow.

"I heard you, dammit," I said between bright mouthfuls.

Like she was putting an exclamation point on her favorite phrase, my sorrow opened up her cabinet doors in the sienna shadows of the orange jungle. Toucans and orioles and birds of paradise crowed and called and their crowing and calling caromed off the titian trunks until my ears hated birdsong more than any other thing. My sorrow opened up her cabinet doors and the wind whistled through the space inside her and it sounded like Premiére Rhapsodie in A Major through the holes of a fuel-efficient crystal clarinet.

Inside my sorrow hung a dress the color of garnets, with a long train trailing behind it and a neckline that plunged to the navel. It looked like it would be very hard to dance in.

6. Red

In the Red Country, love is love, loyalty is loyalty, a story is a story, and death is a long red dress. The Red Country is the only country with walls.

I slept my way into the Red Country.

I lay down inside the red dress called death; I lay down inside my sorrow and a bone mask crawled onto my face; I lay down and didn't dream and my sorrow smuggled me out of the orange jungles where sorrow is sadness. I don't remember that part so I can't say anything about it. The inside of my sorrow was cool and dim; there wasn't any furniture in there, or any candles. She seemed all right again, once we'd lumbered on out of the jungle. Strong and solid like she'd been in the beginning. I didn't throw up even though I ate all that dirt. Jellyfish told me later that the place where the Orange Country turns into the Red Country is a marshland full of flamingos and ruby otters fighting for supremacy. I would have liked to have seen that.

I pulled it together by the time we reached the riverbanks. The Incarnadine River flows like blood out of the marshes, through six locks and four sluice gates in the body of a red brick wall as tall as clouds. Then it joins the greater rushing rapids and pools of the Claret, the only river in seven kingdoms with dolphins living in it, and all together, the rivers and the magenta dolphins, roar and tumble down the valleys and into the heart of the city of Cranberry-on-Claret.

Crimson boats choked up the Incarnadine. A thousand fishing lines stuck up into the pink dawn like pony-poles on the pampas. The fisherwomen all wore masks like mine, masks like mine and burgundy swimming costumes that covered them from neck to toe and all I could think was how I'd hate to swim in one of those things, but they probably never had to because if you fell out of your boat you'd just land in another boat. The fisherwomen cried out when they saw me. I suppose I looked frightening, wearing that revealing, low-cut death and the bone mask and riding a mammoth with a unicorn in my arms. They called me some name that wasn't Violet Wild and the ones nearest to shore climbed out of their boats, shaking and laughing and holding out their arms. I don't think anyone should get stuck holding their arms out to nothing and no one, so I shimmied down my sorrow's fur and they clung on for dear live, touching the Sparrowbone Mask of the Incarnadine

Fisherwomen, stroking its cheeks, its red spiral mouth, telling it how it had scared them, vanishing like that.

"I love you," the Sparrowbone Mask of the Incarnadine Fisherwomen kept saying over and over. It felt strange when the mask on my face spoke but I didn't speak. "I love you. Sometimes you can't help vanishing. I love you. I can't stay."

My mask and I said both together: "We are afraid of the wall."

"Don't be doltish," an Incarnadine Fisherwoman said. She must have been a good fisherwoman as she had eight vermillion catfish hanging off her belt and some of them were still opening and closing their mouths, trying to breathe water that had vanished like a mask. "You're one of us."

So my sorrow swam through the wall. She got into the scarlet water which rose all the way up to her eyeballs but she didn't mind. I rode her like sailing a boat and the red water soaked the train of my red death dress and magenta dolphins followed along with us, jumping out of the water and echolocating like a bunch of maniacs and the Sparrowbone Mask of the Incarnadine Fisherwomen said:

"I am beginning to remember who I am now that everything is red again. Why is anything unred in the world? It's madness."

Jellyfish hid her lavender face in her watermelon-colored hooves and whispered:

"Please don't forget about me, I am water soluble!"

I wondered, when the river crashed into the longest wall in the world, a red brick wall that went on forever side to side and also up and down, if the wall had a name. Everything has a name, even if that name is in Latin and nobody knows it but one person who doesn't live nearby. Somebody had tried to blow up the wall several times. Jagged chunks were missing; bullets had gouged out rock and mortar long ago, but no one had ever made a hole. The Incarnadine River slushed in through a cherry-colored sluice gate. Rosy sunlight lit up its prongs. I glided on in with all the other fisherwomen like there never was a wall in the first place. I looked behind us—the river swarmed with squirrels, gasping, half drowning, paddling their little feet for dear life. They squirmed through the sluice gate like plague rats.

"If you didn't have that mask on, you would have had to pay the toll," whispered Jellyfish.

"What's the toll?"

"A hundred years as a fisherwoman."

Cranberry-on-Claret is a city of carnelian and lacquerwork and carbuncle streetlamps glowing with red gas flames because the cities of the Red Country are not electrified like Plum Pudding and Lizard Tongue and Absinthe. People with hair the color of raspberries and eyes the color of wood embers play ruby bassoons and chalcedony hurdy-gurdies and cinnamon-stick violins on the long, wide streets and they never stop even when they sleep; they just switch to nocturnes and keep playing through their dreaming. When they saw me coming, they started up *My Baby Done Gone to Red*, which, it turns out, is only middling as far as radio hits go.

Some folks wore deaths like mine. Some didn't. The Ordinary Emperor said that sometimes the dead go to the Red Country but nobody looked dead. They looked busy like city people always look. It was warm in Cranberry-on-Claret, an autumnal kind of warm, the kind that's having a serious think about turning to cold. The clouds glowed primrose and carmine.

"Where are we going?" asked my watercolor unicorn.

"The opera house," I answered.

I guess maybe all opera houses are skulls because the one in the Red Country looked just like the one back home except, of course, as scarlet as the spiral mouth of a mask. It just wasn't a human skull. Out of a cinnabar piazza hunched up a squirrel skull bigger than a cathedral and twice as fancy. Its great long teeth opened and closed like proper doors and prickled with scrimshaw carving like my Papo used to do on pony-bones. All over the wine-colored skull grew bright hibiscus flowers and devil's hat mushrooms and red velvet lichen and fire opals.

Below the opera house and behind they kept the corrals. Blue stories milled miserably in pens, their sapphire plates drooping, their eyes all gooey with cataracts. I took off the Sparrowbone Mask of the Incarnadine Fisherwomen and climbed down my sorrow.

"Heyo, beastie-blues," I said, holding my hands out for them to sniff through the copper wire and redwood of their paddock. "No lachrymose quadrupeds on my watch. Be not down in the mouth. Woe-be-gone, not woe-be-come."

"That's blue talk," a boy-story whispered. "You gotta talk red or you get no cud."

"Say what you mean," grumbled a girl-story with three missing scales over her left eye. "It's the law."

"I always said what I meant. I just meant something very fancy," sniffed a grandfather-story lying in the mud to stay cool.

"Okay. I came from the Purple Country to find a boy named Orchid Harm."

"Nope, that's not what you mean," the blue grandpa dinosaur growled, but he didn't seem upset about it. Stories mostly growl unless they're sick.

"Sure it is!"

"I'm just a simple story, what do I know?" He turned his cerulean rump to me.

"You're just old and rude. I'm pretty sure Orchid is up there in the eye of that skull, it's only that I was going to let you out of your pen before I went climbing but maybe I won't now."

"How's about we tell you what you mean and then you let us out and nobody owes nobody nothing?" said the girl-story with the missing scales. It made me sad to hear a story talking like that, with no grammar at all.

"I came from the Purple Country to find Orchid," I repeated because I was afraid.

"Are you sure you're not an allegory for depression or the agrarian revolution or the afterlife?"

"I'm not an allegory for anything! You're an allegory! And you stink!"

"If you say so."

"What do *you* mean then?"

"I mean a blue dinosaur. I mean a story about a girl who lost somebody and couldn't get over it. I can mean both at the same time. That's allowed."

"This isn't any better than when you were saying *autarchy* and *peregrinate*."

"So peregrinate with autarchy, girlie. That's how you're supposed to act around stories, anyway. Who raised you?"

I kicked out the lock on their paddock and let the reptilian stories loose. They bolted like blue lightning into the cinnabar piazza. Jellyfish ran joyfully among them, jumping and wriggling and whinnying, giddy to be in a herd again, making a mess of a color scheme.

"I love you," said my sorrow. She had shrunk up small again, no taller than a good dog, and she was wearing the Sparrowbone Mask of the Incarnadine Fisherwomen. By the time I'd gotten half way up the opera-skull, she was gone.

"Let us begin by practicing the chromatic scale, beginning with E major."

That is what the voice coming out of the eye socket of a giant operatic squirrel said and it was Orchid's voice and it had a laugh hidden inside it like it always did. I pulled myself up and over the lip of the socket and curled up next to Orchid Harm and his seven books, of which he'd already read four. I curled up next to him like nothing bad had ever happened. I fit into the line of his body and he fit into mine. I didn't say anything for a long, long time. He stroked my hair and read to me about basic strumming technique but after awhile he stopped talking, too and we just sat there quietly and he smelled like sunlight and booze and everything purple in the world.

"I killed the Ordinary Emperor with a story's tail," I confessed at last.

"I missed you, too."

"Are you dead?"

"The squirrels won't tell me. Something about collapsing a waveform. But I'm not the one wearing a red dress."

I looked down. Deep red silky satin death flowed out over the bone floor. A lot of my skin showed in the slits of that dress. It felt nice.

"The squirrels ate you, though."

"You never know with squirrels. I think I ate some of them, too. It's kind of the same thing, with time travel, whether you eat the squirrel or the squirrel eats you. I remember it hurt. I remember you kissed me till it was over. I remember Early-to-Tea and Stopwatch screaming. Sometimes you can't help vanishing. Anyway, the squirrels felt bad about it. Because we'd taken care of them so well and they had to do it anyway. They apologized for ages. I fell asleep once in the middle of them going on and on about how timelines taste."

"Am I dead?"

"I don't know, did you die?"

"Maybe the bubbles got me. The Emperor said I'd get sick if I traveled without a clarinet. And parts of me aren't my own parts anymore." I stretched out my legs. They were the color of rooster feathers. "But I don't think so. What do you mean the squirrels had to do it?"

"Self-defense, is what they said about a million times."

"What? We never so much as kicked one!"

"You have to think like a six-legged mauve squirrel of infinite time. The Ordinary Emperor was going to hunt them all down one by one and set the chronology of everything possible and impossible on fire. They set a contraption in motion so that he couldn't touch them, a contraption involving you and me and a blue story and a Red Country where nobody dies, they just change clothes. They're very tidy creatures. Don't worry, we're safe in the Red Country. There'll probably be another war. The squirrels can't fix that. They're only little. But everyone always wants to conquer the Red Country and nobody ever has. We have a wall and it's a really good one."

I twisted my head up to look at him, his plum-colored hair, his amethyst eyes, his stubborn chin. "You have to say what you mean here."

"I mean I love you. And I mean the infinite squirrels of space and time devoured me to save themselves from annihilation at the hands of a pepper grinder. I can mean both. It's allowed."

I kissed Orchid Harm inside the skull of a giant rodent and we knew that we were both thinking about ice cream. The ruby bassoons hooted up from the piazza and scarlet tanagers scattered from the rooftops and a watercolor unicorn told a joke about the way tubas are way down the road but the echoes carried her voice up and up and everywhere. Orchid stopped the kiss first. He pointed to the smooth crimson roof of the eye socket.

A long stripe of gold paint gleamed there.

MY LAST BRINGBACK

JOHN BARNES

"Oh my fucking god. You're me. You're me, aren't you, Layla?"

The slumped ancient natch in the support chair pulls herself up straight. My shoulders drift back. Much of the lordosis in my lumbar vertebrae releases, bringing my back against the chair. I've lifted my mandibula half a centimeter out of the stretch cradle, and sucked in my gut.

I had thought all the slump was her.

I look through the display into those momentarily understanding eyes. Maybe an explanation will stick this time? "Well, you and me, we're me, or we're you. It's complicated. But it's really excellent that you figured that out." *For the fifth time,* I add, *but sometime soon, you will realize what's going on, and begin to help me help you. That has always happened eventually, for all nine of my bringbacks before you.*

Of course, you've never been me before, and I've never brought back myself. Who knows what difference that might make?

On the display in front of me, the old natch nods, but I see the wary, cunning concealment of her fear that I'll see the waves of confusion smashing her sandcastles of meaning. *So not on the fifth time, let's push on to the sixth.*

She's staring at me, the muscles around her eyes slack, her attention wandering inside her head, desperate to know what she should say next, yet horribly aware that she *should* know already.

The first thing they know again is that they don't know and should. Always, they get overwhelmed by that awareness that they *ought* to know where they are, recognize me, and understand conversation. That jolt has always come just before the breakthrough in all nine of my bringbacks. Somewhere beneath consciousness, the mirror shards of memory from her hippocampi, reclaimed by the plakophagic reconstructive neurons, are beginning to swarm and clamor to be activated, called up to working memory, put to work.

It shows in her ancient creased and folded face, too. At least I hope it does. Her dental implants and continuing eye and skin regeneration make her hundred-four years look like about seventy on the old, natch scale, or somewhere after six hundred on the new nubrid scale. (They *think*—no one is that old yet.) That is still much, much older than anyone except we few surviving natches looks now.

Her rapidly regenerating dorsolateral prefrontal cortex isn't quite up to this yet, though oh my dear sweet lord it's close, and as if she can feel how close it is, she goes on staring at me, hoping something will pop, rooting around in her regenerating hippocampi, in the places from which the PPRNs are sending up those sudden inexplicable chopped memories. She's trying so hard. I want her to just—

"And what is your name again, dear?" *Surrender, start over, time six.* "I forget."

"Layla Palemba. Doctor Layla Palemba. I'm your doctor."

When I'm not alternating with her, when I'm fully deploying my prosnoetics for days and weeks at a time, am I as obviously a very old natch as she is?

"Oh my fucking god. You're me." The face in the display is confused. The slowly spinning realtime brain map in the upper right corner shows abundant, random, noisy firing going on in her dorsolateral prefrontal cortex. That's the pattern I've been seeing more of each time, the one I want to see, the one that means, "I was thinking about that a moment ago."

There's really only one of us, with one camera and one display. The separations between my mostly-prosnoetic dorsolateral prefrontal cortex, and her unboosted 100% biological DLPFC are only the 1.5-second lag imposed by the protocol. She doesn't know that, but I do. Nonetheless, I abruptly feel confused as some of her irregularly misfiring DLPFC bleeds over onto my side of the lag.

When I recover my composure, her gaze on my face, through the display we share, is no longer blurry. Her face cracks in my huge *I just thought of the best joke ever* grin that always made Mama squat down, look me in the eye, and say, "Share that joke, Layla-honey-babe, the Lord hates a selfish laugher."

And I would share that joke, and Mama'd hug me. It happened so often I still remember the fact of it, not just because I recorded it for my prosnoetics to prompt me with, but because a little shard of the memory has still been active.

But *this time* I remember those lilac sachets that Mama always made so many of every spring. So many she often had to put two or three in every drawer. She often wore one hanging from a thong between her big saggy old-fat-lady boobs, and sometimes she'd even tie one into the big pile of bound-up hair on top of her head. Daddy used to ask her if she could even smell lilacs anymore. She said that smelling them was everyone else's job . . .

The memory fades but I know I'll have it again. Layla's right hippocampus, *my* right hippocampus, whichever, the plakophagic reconstructive neurons in it, they've done it, those shrewd, hardworking little PPRNs dug out and copied a little chunk of fossilized memory from the plaques they're digesting. From now on they will do it faster and faster. That was how it was with all nine of my bringbacks before me,

Moreover, the DSPFC managed to send out a call for that long-term memory and move it into working memory—I want to hug all the parts of my brain and tell them what good little brain parts they are, hug them with big warm strong natural-living arms that smell like lilac, because I know that is what they will really like.

Wait. I've been paying no attention to Layla, whose *I know a great joke* smile startled me into—

I half-expect she's fallen back into slack-faced drooling apathy while I was having my special moment. It would just serve me right if I were having the most vivid case ever of the meditator's bane, *Now I have it, didn't I?*

But her face isn't slack at all. She's still wearing that grin of impending shared joy; I remember I would grin like that and the other women at my table in the prison dining hall would all start to laugh, or sometimes start to groan, before I even told the joke.

And then Layla delivers her joke as clearly as anyone. "I'm pleased to meet me." She giggles—laughing at my own jokes is another lifelong thing—and I'm still giggling with her giggles as I say, "It would be mutual, if there were more than one of us."

She really laughs this time. I suppose no one is better or can be better at hitting your sense of humor than yourself.

Layla is smiling puckishly at me when she says, "I suppose no one is better or can be better at hitting your sense of humor than yourself."

I say, "Oh my fucking god," just the way she did, just the way I always do. "I just thought those, like, those exact words. *So*-ab *so*-lute *so*-ly." My old, dry throat, tongue, and lips strain almost to cracking, trying to talk the way I did as a teenager.

She holds her hands out and chants, clapping and popping thumbs up on every third, "Abso-fucka," *clap clap thumbs clap*, "abso-fucka," *clap clap thumbs clap*, "abso," *clap*, "fuckin'," *clap*, "lucky-lute," *thumbs up*, "lute-lee!" *clap, clap, clap-clap-clap-thumbs-up!*

My hands are stinging from the clapping, and I am holding thumbs up at the screen myself. Seeing my withered old crone self of a natch do the "Absofuckinglutely Popout" just the way all us cool girls did in middle school ninety years ago cracks me up again. She and I have a grand old laugh together.

Better still, when I look at her again, she's still with me, and in the corner of the display, her DLPFC graphs moving toward normal and healthy faster than I've ever seen. It looks like my tenth and last bringback is going to be my best. I suppose, given that it's me, I must have always hoped that. But now I know.

After that breakthrough session, I go in for scans and tests, including a full ONC that takes about an hour. From there I go to a review of my test results with Dr. Gbego, who is my partner, co-author, the person who persuaded me into this project. I had a big old load of neurology courses back when I was getting my MD, but compared to what Gbego knows, I might as well have spent my time on astrology or alchemy.

Gbego is a smooth young nubrid of about eighty. He looks about twenty-five on the old natch scale (*my* scale). He sits down beside me so we can both see the same displays. If he thinks I'm disgusting physically, he shows no sign of it, so he's either aesthetically blind, well-controlled, or nice. Back when we started the project of the first and only auto-bringback, I'd've said all three. I grow more doubtful about the nice and the aesthetically blind every time we meet.

"Here's the results from your oscillating neutrino chemopathy," he says, pointing to the display on the wall in front of us.

Not only does he give no sign of disgust, he's also rather good at putting me at my ease, good enough to make me wish hopelessly that I were not a hideous old crone of a freak, because I'm automatically suspicious of that easy, natural way of conversing he has. And because I don't trust my automatic suspicions any more than I trust this brilliant man.

One of many thousands of advantages to being a nubrid is having time and plasticity to work around anything that didn't come naturally, like, maybe, for example, getting along with people. It's just another skill: some people are born good with people, some people are born abrasive, abrupt, or clueless. But when a nubrid is born socially wrong-footed, they just squirt fresh cloned cells into the correct brain center, add a dash of plasticity enhancers, and start that hapless jerk into a training regime overseen by specialists. Maybe, if it's a severe case, that poor inept kid might spend thirty lonely, awkward years. So what? You're going to have most of a millennium to flirt, make small talk, dance socially, and find true friendship and deep love and whatever else you need from other people, and do it as well as anyone.

So I always wonder if really nice, likeable, considerate nubrids are fake, and what real self they were born to.

I suspect smooth, young-looking, kind, and wise Dr. Gbego, brilliant neuro, had he been a natch, might have had an autism spectrum disorder, because all of his interactions with me feel perfectly performed, like he's running apps: the be politely supportive app, the signal interest to get better information app, the listen empathetically app, the be nice to the hideous old natch even if she fucking disgusts you app.

From all those decades of constant self-polishing, nubrids become fake copies of themselves with perfect brains, so smooth there's nothing for another personality to stick to. They're totally likeable but not at all lovable, at least not with any passion, which is not lovable, really, in my pathetic old hideous limited natch opinion. Which is I'm sure what they'd think my opinion was—if they actually cared what a natch thought.

It's so much better to be a nubrid. They probably don't have these little flashes of envious rage the way a natch does, either.

I'm looking where Gbego's finger is pointing, at the ONC image of my right hippocampus, and I go from blazing rage to abject humiliation at once, but there's no other way, at least not one I understand, to get to what I must know. "I'm sorry, Dr. Gbego, I just blurred out for a second. Back me up and explain again please?"

"I probably bored you out of your mind," he says, smiling apologetically. "I was just running through all the caveats, oscillating-neutrino chemopathy is still in its infancy, some of the things that show up on ONC don't seem to correspond to any reality we understand, what we do understand doesn't always say what we understand it to, yakka-da-yakka-dakka-day. All stuff I should have the respect to remember you already know and have heard. It's a miracle we didn't *both* zone out." The apologetic smile gets broader.

"All right, you're not sure what it means, you just have a guess. I promise I won't take it as gospel." I lean forward toward his finger on the display. "Now explain the color coding to me."

"It's sort of an emotional intensity indicator. Based on ONCs of similar brains—and we don't have enough of a sample and ONC tech is progressing so fast that nearly all recordings are outdated immediately—we asked it to predict, if you recalled that complex of memories, how much you'd release of various neurotransmitters in your limbic system, how high your electrical activity might go above normal in the feeling part of the brain—"

"Dr. Gbego, I do have a Ph.D. and the parts of me that earned it and use it are over in the prosnoetic-enhanced side of me, not lost in the brain plaques. Show me what you mean, on the graphs and charts, and use appropriate technical language."

He made a little head-bow, touching his forehead with two fingers. A few decades ago, that became the universal *sorry I was a jerk* signal. "Well, here." He calls up an eigenvector-color legend.

Subtracting his too-smooth condescension, I must say Gbego did all right in explaining the overall color coding, though "I would guess that it is the intensity of the emotions that went into encoding the memory, not the emotions that are likely with its re-emergence, that is most strongly represented. Also, red for the mild ones and deep blues and purples for the strong ones? What kind of reporting software is that?"

"Physicists designed this." He's still smiling; I must fix that sometime soon. In two years of working with the man, I have found I can always make him stop smiling. "The short-wave, high frequency, high energy part of the spectrum is blues and violets."

Disappointing myself, I smile back. "All right, I see what you mean: that 'mongous big purple blob there in my right hippocampus. Your oscillating neutrinos are telling you I've got some emotionally huge memory there. When I can access it directly, it is totally likely both to be a memory about something really emotionally huge, and also totally likely to upset the absolute living shit out of me. Right?"

"Uh, I suppose—I mean, I intended—um, yes."

I laugh at his sheer awkwardness. "Are you trying to find a gentle, discreet way to ask whether I remember that I chopped up both my parents with a wok cleaver? Yes, I know I did, and I've never stopped knowing. Back when they let me out of prison, they let me watch the sealed records of my testimony, so I know what I said was my reason. As for whatever else might be somewhere in the shriveled plaques that make up most of my hippocampus at the moment, no, I don't recall anything emotionally or with any sense of having been there, about how I slaughtered my parents like a pair of deserving pigs."

He stops smiling. Knew I could do it!

The rest of the meeting is very correct and businesslike. I keep thinking that should make me sad, but really I'm more interested in how smooth Dr. Gbego stays, even though his reserve doesn't feel nearly as phony as his warmth.

Layla begins, "Hello, Layla. Are you still me?"

"Hello, Layla, yes I am. Look around my office, you're sitting here too, tell me what you see."

She leans back to look slowly all around, taking it in, thinking. "That window is showing video from the moon. I guess it's a display, not a window. But we're not on the moon. The gravity's all wrong. I must have been to the moon more than once, to know that the gravity is wrong right away."

The little rotating 2-D brain map at upper right of the display has been changing across the last few sessions. At first it was an increasingly normal and regular dance of color through the DLPFC, and little trickles like forking lightning breaking out of the former plaques and reaching into the healthy bits of each hippocampus, at first more on the left than on the right, then the right caught up, then both got busy.

Lately it has looked like the old traffic flow maps that used to appear on the dash of Dad's car when he'd drive into the city. He held one of the last human-operation-on-public-streets permits in New Jersey, thanks to his political pull. He said he just liked the fact that his license said 'Human Operator' because it meant they recognized he was still human, "which is rare even in humanists."

Once I started to hate that, I steeled myself not to argue. Nor did I ask why other people's lives should be endangered by his driving mistakes that no machine would ever make, just so he could have his little joke. Giving him no chance for the judicious and rigorous explication he loved, I'd just glare at him and say, "Dumbshit." It worked a lot better.

Anyway, that tangled flow of brightly colored spots in the realtime brain image in front of me, like the New Jersey highway system on Dad's old map, represent the same good situation: lots of things going lots of places smoothly. Layla's brain, my brain, our brain, looks very nearly normal; it would take a neuro as proficient as my smug partner Gbego to spot the difference between those information flows on the display and what happens in a normal brain.

"We *have* been to the moon," she says quietly. "I can feel it copying into my memory; it must have crossed over from the prosnoetics. Oh! And *that's* the connection. The idea you had, because the last three bringbacks before me, before us, before they said you could do it for yourself . . . you had the idea because hypergerontological cases have mostly been moved to the moon anyway, and this body is acceleration-restricted because of those sclerotic arteries in the brain, so the last two cases—no, the last three, Bridget Soon moved to the moon after the first three treatments—"

I can feel it flooding in, including feelings I'd had at the time but hadn't recalled afterward; it's funny what a difference it makes to have your memories linked to their emotional context again.

Funny, and terrifying.

"What's wrong?" she asks quietly. I look at the brain map; the welter of activity looks like termites coming out of a burning log.

I take a finger and write a word at a time on my palm, without any ink or pigment, and not looking down at it:

not now. not here. soon. not while connected. just think about it later today & you'll know.

Then I babble something senseless about how a strong sense memory of swinging the cleaver backhanded into Mama's face just came flooding back and overwhelmed me. And Layla immediately begins to babble comfort-noises back at me, so I know she understands too. After a minute or so of that, I launch into the story we would both know completely, the one she referred to just now. With just a spot of luck, maybe nobody monitoring will notice how unnecessary our explanations are now, or ask why we are making them.

. . .

Of course, for more than two decades before the murders, most sensible people, commenting on the news, had the good sense to hate my parents, along with the parents of all the other 'natural children.' Anyone with any empathy could understand how we felt about being condemned before we were born to age and die far before we had to.

Most nubrids and quite a few of the older generation of natural humans could also understand we had been deprived of the nubrids' far greater brain plasticity. During the eighty or hundred years we would live beside them, we would be making up our minds for good and shutting off new experiences. In that same time, the nubrids would put mistakes and sad memories behind them, build on skills and knowledge, and keep growing mentally the way children could while enjoying the kind of mental maturity that only a handful of saints, philosophers, artists, and scientists ever had.

Our parents had elected to kill us early after first crippling us. No one in the global or regional or local government had done anything to stop them; there had been education campaigns and media campaigns and public pressure, but nobody had done what would have fixed it: investigated the personal data, kicked down the doors, and made our mothers get the virus sequence.

Privacy was too important, human rights were too important, the fucking right of fucking jackass parents to raise children no better than themselves was paramount. And because all those rights of all those now-dead people were so well protected, we natches would have to live as permanently immature stuck-in-our ways idiots, and then die, old, sick, ugly, and soon. But thank god society had respected our parents' crazy fears, smug superiority, and deep attachment to that advertising sell-word 'natural.'

My lawyers begged me not to give my speech to the jury, which I had written and rehearsed with such care. They went out of their way to tell the jury, over and over, that I was "young" (thirty-one? For a nubrid, that's young. For us natches, that's a real big chunk of life). They begged them to forgive me for being "impetuous and headstrong" (hoping the jury might ignore the steps I took to isolate the house so Mama and Daddy would not be able to call for help and I could take as long as I wanted about it, or that the police data recovery expert had found many dozens of drafts across many weeks of the script for exactly what I would say and do as I killed them).

I gave my speech anyway. I told them the truth: I had been cheated of what they all took for granted. Mama and Daddy had done it because they had enjoyed the revenue and attention from founding *Natural Children Forever!* and the Coalition to Preserve Natural Humans and god knew how many other fundraising and adulatory fronts, and because they liked to tell themselves how special and wonderful they were. The law could not make me whole; the 'natural human' organizations had lobbied hard to make sure that sentimental idiots had passed laws in every country to prevent us natch-spawn from suing the parents who had done this to us. The law would not arrest them or try them or get revenge for me; instead, it protected them.

So since the law wouldn't do it, I did.

Apparently that made me a monster.

When the jury came back in, after only an hour, I didn't detect a drop of sympathy in their faces. They had decided on life without the possibility of parole.

I suppose I cultivated my taste for science originally because it pissed off Daddy and Mama. Science in general was their number one scary, shiny anti-human monster. Or maybe I just wanted to understand the intellectual triumph of the decoding and application of the nubrid process, since I couldn't partake of it. Ellauri and Jautta's mapping of the deep level semisymmetric interconnections that enabled alloaddressing of genes between the immune, nervous, and regenerative systems would have been a feat as great as relativity, programmable computers, or calculus, even if it hadn't led to any applications for a hundred years. But as it happened, the nubrid process explained why people got set in their ways and how they aged and why aging killed them, how one virus could be chicken pox and shingles and one brain center could handle bits and pieces of math, music, and language, why people got Alzheimer's and arthritis, and countless other things.

I was thirty-two when they sent me to prison, supposedly forever. The Prison Authority spent a fortune on psychiatrists trying to persuade me I should feel bad about who I was and what I'd done, although they still weren't going to let me out even if I rolled over and agreed with them. I had only two alternatives to madness: sparring with the psychiatrists and reading and studying The New Neuro, as it was being dubbed. And after a few years, the psychiatrists gave up.

That left me nothing to do but read and study, but fortunately it turned out that was an inexhaustible consolation. A few years into the process, I began writing papers and critiques. I couldn't accept money, or patent anything, or publish them under my own name because of old laws about not allowing convicts to profit from their crimes; apparently the publicity I would have gotten from being Mama and Daddy's killer was potentially a violation. But I found half a dozen editor-curators who were willing to run my work under aliases, a different alias each time so that there was supposedly less potential for the discovery that a leading New Neuro theoretician was me.

By that time they had the blood test; I knew Alzheimer's for me was when, not if. So I concentrated my work on it, hoping to save myself and the thousands of natches then still alive who were starting to slide away.

That was another little bit of irony. In the process of recoiling from me and what I'd done, society backlashed itself into doing what it should have done more than a generation earlier, and made producing more natches a crime. A last few insistent natural-children types were forcibly sterilized, and that was that; there haven't been any natural children now in fifty years, or any legal ones in almost sixty. And in some weird kind of atonement, they'd developed prosnoetics (if I'd been allowed, I'd have held some basic patents for those) and some not-very-effective anti-aging juices that could stretch a natch's lifespan out to one hundred twenty-five or so.

My first unmistakable symptoms appeared in my late seventies. Bless their hearts, the editor-curators went public with who I was and the contributions I'd made, and the bighearted liberal Chief Administrator for the Atlantic Basin Region commuted my sentence. They hooked me up to prosnoetics, so that as my brain dropped away under me, I could keep going like an AI, and PrinceTech awarded me the Ph.D./MD I'd already earned a hundred times over.

I had just graduated and was looking for something to do when the bringback technology came along. Alzheimer's was a natch-only disease, and we were running out of natches. There were good arrestors that would stop its progress, but nothing to undo it, and some few old natches had had the bad luck to develop advanced Alzheimer's before there were arrestors.

With the bringback process, you could recover memories from the traces the dying cells left in the plaques, and recopy them into new, healthy brain structures, but it was exquisite long-term handwork; you needed someone with the right rapport for the patient and nearly infinite patience, having the same only slightly varied conversations over and over, constantly watching brain imagery to see what each new communication would make happen.

And of all things, I turned out to be good at it. Fifteen years of my life went into bringbacks, about three years per patient, and those were by far my most rewarding years.

My ninety-fifth birthday, and celebration of my sixth successful bringback, was kind of a gloomy occasion, despite the fact that I had real friends and colleagues and they were all there to help me feel loved and appreciated. The bringback business was running out of patients: only a few very old severely memory-damaged natches left, they were going to the moon or already there, and I couldn't go with them. My trips to the moon had been decades ago, and I hadn't felt like living the rest of my life in an underground office building, so I'd never thought seriously about relocating there.

But now my being off prosnoetics and on cardiopulmonary support for acceleration risked the prosnoetics being off too long and not rebooting, especially since their delicate contacts might well break inside my head . . .

natches with scrambled and plaqued-up bio brains could go, natches running on prosnoetics who were even more cyborg than I could go, heart patients could go, but my combination of a heart and a brain that both needed support was the one thing that couldn't go.

I'm afraid I got a little maudlin talking about the end of the only thing I'd done that felt really meaningful. People at my party were awfully nice, but it wasn't much of a party, and they left early.

But the next day, as I was eating a melancholy, solitary breakfast and trying to make myself go to the hospital to do more of the exit interviews and other nonsense involved in losing my job, the communication system said Dr. Selataimh was calling from the moon about Bridget Soon.

I had thought, as we began work, that Bridget would be one of my favorites, and a wonderful seventh bringback, but then her health had started to fail in a way that indicated she needed to move to Serenity City as soon as possible. So after only a few appointments, she'd been bundled up and shipped to the moon, to restart her bringback process there.

Selataimh was a vigorous, raw-boned woman who moved around too much for the camera to stay on her face well. "It's an honor to get to consult with you about a patient," she said. "And perhaps there's nothing we can do. But when Bridget Soon woke up, she demanded you. We tried to explain, but she's absolutely insistent. And she's so clear and coherent we think she must have gone into breakthrough just before you mothballed her process on Earth, or maybe waking up here was the last poke she needed. In any case, she's acting like she's having a breakthrough and she won't talk to anyone else but you, and as you know, if she clams up and won't communicate . . . " She let that trail off. We both knew that patients could sometimes uncooperate themselves into needing to start the whole bringback process over, losing months or years of life.

"I wish I could get on the next ship going up," I said.

"I'd feel that way myself," Selataimh said. "And I confess I researched it first. It's absolutely too dangerous for you to try traveling, and even if you got here and were lucky enough to still be alive and functional, you'd be stuck here. And I can certainly understand not wanting to spend the rest of your life in a basement on the moon. But . . . well, she was your patient, she's mine, is there anything we can come up with that might help?"

"Maybe something obvious." I felt hope flaring up.

" 'Try the obvious as soon as possible,' " Selataimh said, quoting me to me.

"I've had to apologize to a whole generation of medical students for that textbook chapter," I said. "Apparently profs love to quote it. Nevertheless, here's what I'm wondering: I've done plenty of bringbacks on remote, via communication displays. The reason we can't do one from the moon is supposed to be that one point three second radio lag each way. But has anyone ever tried it? I'm patient, and Alzheimer's patients have lots of time.

"Well, I need to see what's happening in their brain while I talk and while they talk. And as long as the brain image remains synchronized with the conversation, there's no real need for quick reactions. I can't think of any time when I had to make an abrupt change of subject in mid-sentence, or react in real time to changing emotions. So why not just see if I can do it via telecommunication linkup? The worst that can happen is it will turn out that I can't, which is exactly where we are right now."

And that was how we discovered that the radio lag enhanced the bringback process. The delay gave me time to look at the picture of the brain a little longer, think about it a little deeper, have about one more slightly better founded thought before speaking. It forced the bringbacks themselves to try harder and more often to retain an idea in working memory, and to send out more calls to the areas where the PPRNs were working, and to make more connections before I could interrupt them.

The process we thought would be impossible was actually enhanced. Bridget Soon not only became my seventh bringback, she became my fastest and most complete up to that date. Knowing how to use the lag, I completed the two bringbacks after Bridget even more quickly.

And then there were just a handful left of the severe cases, the ones who had all but forgotten who they were, the Alzheimer's-damaged natches of my generation who had not quite all died yet, thanks to the miracle of modern medicine, and had developed dementia before there was arresting technology and prosnoetics. Almost all of them, of us, had been brought back.

Daddy used to put on some old thing he called a "mixtape," a bunch of unmodifiable songs in a fixed order, on the house speakers so we all had to listen to the same shit over and over, and there was a song with some line or thing about heartbreaker, dream waker, love faker on it that I guess was a big deal when Grandpa was young. He'd get all hurt if I added "mix-taper," let alone "brain-raper," to it. Like for some reason I was supposed to care what the song "really" sounded like, which meant whatever some old dead bitch had put down first, as if putting it down first (and being dead) meant she fucking owned it. The last generation before mine, when everyone was still a natch, trust me, totally fucking weird, all of them.

But especially Mama and Daddy. They must have known that their thirty-year fundraising-and-sympathy ride was peaking and winding down to an end by the time I was about twelve; the oldest nubrids were in their late twenties, still looked fresh-minted nineteen, and were still learning like bright twelve-year-olds and getting saner and more rational all the time. "Like a bunch of supermodel-athlete Spock-Buddhas," Daddy would say, trying to sound sarcastic.

If he thought that by saying those things, he could get me to say "I don't wanna be a yucky old yucky-face yucky-brain nubrid," the way he'd been able to do when I was eight and he and Mama would love bomb the hell out of me and then put me on camera for promotions, he was even more of a useless self-deluded old fuck than I had imagined. Now that I was in my early teens, I had started to realize just what my parents' world-famous leadership of the battle for the right to have 'natural children' had meant for me and a million or so 'natural children' worldwide.

Daddy, the old fool, was always telling me "be careful what you wish for, you may get it." If only wishing could have gotten it for me! If only it could have undone what he and Mama did to me, and encouraged so many other people to do to the other natches. Him and his "preserving natural humanity"! He believed in that horseshit with such passion that he thought, if I got my way, despite the impossibility of injecting the nubrid modification virus sequence after the twelfth week of pregnancy, I would end up mourning, longing, yea fucking well fainting for the short painful life of increasing mental rigidity I had thrown away, and then I'd really be sorry.

Like fucking Christ.

Thanks to Daddy and all his pontificating about what was truly human (as if a professor of comparative literature would know shit about it), thanks to Mama and her blogging all the time about the Natural Way, thanks to them realizing that as the flow of new followers began to dry up, they would need to have a kid to demonstrate their point: here I was. Demonstrating away. Demonstrating just how wonderful and natural and human it was that I would barely live past a hundred if I were lucky, and that people thirty years older than I would still be young and vigorous in the year my withered old husk, long since having entered "second childishness and mere oblivion, sans teeth, sans eyes, sans taste, sans everything," would fall into its grave, at least four full centuries before the nubrids even *began* to wear out.

I feel my hand on the cleaver, and I look in Mama's eyes, and I tell her, "I will hate you forever. I will hate you forever. I will hate you forever," and just as she starts one of her whiny little pleads, I slash her across both of those watery soggy sentimental eyes with the cleaver, so that me saying that is the last thing she ever sees. It makes me laugh.

I release my painfully hard grip on my chair arms. The prosnoetics kick in. I am breathing like a racehorse on top of a mountain and the cardiopulmonary support gear is working itself into a lather trying to get me into the safe range. I sit gasping, trying to feel calmer, feeling all that rage in those memories, for the first time in at least twenty-five years.

To be overpowered by internal rages again; Oh, wise and gentle-spirited Dr. Gbego, you have no idea how good this feels. You probably can't have any idea. I envy you that, but thank you for bringing my rage back.

The prosnoetics take hold, and finally I look into the screen and say, "Wow, Layla."

"Wow indeed," she says, I say, we giggle. "Do you think they'll make us stop?"

I shake my head. "Not right away. By the time they figure out what we're doing, we'll be done."

"You sound very sure."

"Check my memories for a minute while I catch my breath from yours, my darling self. One thing that didn't change as humans gave way to nubrids—career trumps caution. Remember how we got into this."

My ninth bringback was a nice but rather timid 108-year-old named Annie Souriante who was rapidly reacquiring violin and Caribbean cooking and made me laugh a lot. Usually, before, I'd known by the end of the first year who was scheduled to be my next bringback, but Annie and I were closing in on full restoration, and not only did I not have another patient lined up, there weren't any on the waiting list for the whole hospital.

"We've drained the pool of the severe cases," Dr. Gbego said. "Now the problem is more ATB."

"ATB?" I asked. We were sitting across the table from each other at a reception in the Mnemology Department. I didn't know him well then, and I suppose because of his very controlled, deliberately pleasant personality, I may never know him very well. Nobody might.

"ATB is Ability to Benefit. We have a lot of people who are still mostly functional but lost big chunks of memory into plaques before we had the technology to arrest that. They've lost context or connections or some big chunk of themselves. I would bet the funding could be there to bring them back to full function."

"Is there a reason you're talking to me about it?"

He made a little press-lipped smile. "I try not to be so transparent."

That made me like him a little, so I opened the door of possibility by a tiny crack. "Are you by any chance referring to the fact that I have substantial unrepaired Alzheimer's damage, leading to my very flat and rude affect, and some severe difficulties with recall, and I'm an expert on bringbacks?"

"Well, yes, of course." Gbego shrugged. "It was really foolish of me to think I could keep you from seeing where this was going long enough to sound you out."

God, he's a gorgeous man, smooth deep brown skin and beautiful symmetric features and eyes you could fall into forever. The nubrid process has improved the aesthetics of the visual world almost as much as it has altered the hope in people's lives. And back then I hadn't yet understood that his smoothness was neither a likeable act nor a cultivated strategy; he really was that smooth, with nothing for a person to stick to. But I didn't know that then the way I do now.

His rueful little admission made me feel like he'd actually sought me out emotionally. So I asked, "Well, if we did a bringback on me . . . who would do it?"

Gbego said, "Conventional answers: Smithson, Abimbola, Cheng." He shrugged, clearly indicating they'd all be fine with him, but that he wanted to be asked about another possibility.

"Unconventional answer?"

He leaned forward, the clear dark eyes zeroing into mine, the smile held closely in check. "You."

"How could—what?"

He held up his hands. "Here's the thought that occurred to me. The radio lag delay has shortened bringbacks from around three years to less than two. We've all been saying that if we knew how that was going to go, we'd have started out doing bringbacks on delays, even if people were in the same building. Because the delay doesn't *have* to be radio lag; it was just that when we had to try to do Ms. Soon's bringback on remote, we had to tolerate the delay, which otherwise we'd never have tried.

"But, here's what intrigues me, Dr. Palemba, the delay could be artificial, we could just build it right there into the communication system, with the bringback and the coach right there in the same hospital. So we set you up with an interrupter; you talk as you, your prosnoetics switch out, your brain goes to its natural state, then your message is delivered. Your natural state brain replies, it comes back through a delay—"

"Do not," I said, choking with more feeling than I had had in many years, "do not use the word 'natural' around me, all right?"

He did that little bow and forehead touch. "How thoughtless and rude of me. I am so sorry. But please think about it. It could enhance your life. Don't let my rudeness and inconsideration cut you off from it."

"Or cut us off from possibly being co-authors of the most brilliant research paper of the next decade?"

He grinned broadly; I didn't know if I'd forgiven him but he thought I had. "Well, yeah. Well, hell yeah."

"I'll think about it. I don't sleep much and I get ideas late at night. What's the latest time I can call you?" I realized I probably had forgiven him, and right then, I knew I was going to do it.

• • •

We plunge in, Layla and I, and the memory swarms back with all its feelings, all its details, how it felt to say what I said and hear what I heard. All those things that the prosecutors deduced from blood spatters and coagulation time, from fluid ballistics, from running approximating simulations, are now all mine in memory again.

I raged at my parents, cursed them, made sure they knew what this was about. I had planned the blows and cuts, knowing neither of them would have it in them to fight, so that they heard everything I had to say. Knowing how devoted Daddy was to Mama, when he came rushing in at her scream, I shattered him with a dozen planned blows, so that he was bleeding and helpless while I worked on her and explained that all that shit she called love was nothing of the sort, that I knew it was all for her, not for me, that she would not have made me a natch (the word they prohibited in the house) if she had loved me, that it was malice and not mistake. And I cut, and cut, till she died sobbing.

Daddy took longer, and I reminded him that what had happened to Mama was his fault, the whole time.

They knew the cuts and blows of it all from the crime scene analysis, but I never told anyone what I had said.

Or what I had felt: sheer, glowing hot joy.

I hadn't sought a bringback of my own, though there were skilled practitioners who would gladly have done it, not because I didn't want to interrupt my scientific work, as I'd told that slick mannequin Gbego, but because I'd feared that I might find remorse or sorrow or weeping over their bodies.

I don't find a bit of that. The memory is pure white rage, and that delights me. Especially it makes me happy in this way: Daddy and Mama were so convinced that natural humans needed to be preserved. They talked about remembering the human heritage, and you could hear, inside that, that they wanted to live forever in the memories of natural humans.

Well, here they are. Fewer than a hundred natural humans left, and the memory of their destruction is a burning hot glowing pleasure that will warm me the rest of my days. A nubrid, now, a nubrid has such total plasticity, I might have worn the memory down into smooth forgiveness and acceptance. But a human? We're not that plastic. We can hold a grudge forever.

All you ever wanted was for me to be human, Daddy, that's what you said. I laugh and laugh. It's no longer we, the bio Layla and the prosnoetic Layla are merged, I can feel it.

"Dr. Palemba?"

I sit up, startled. It's Gbego. He looks worried—more than that, ill. I try to play casual, but I think even a nubrid with Gbego's carefully honed people skills would not be able to be smooth or slick about this. I ask, "Is something the matter?"

"What we saw on the monitors . . . "

I shrug. "You saw me get those memories back."

"We also saw . . . " His face works through those little squish-the-lips motions, over and over. Finally he says, "You enjoyed that."

"I did."

"In fact we've never seen such intense pleasure and focus in any brain. That woman who testified and shocked the world, seventy years ago . . . you're still her. Or you're her again."

I ignore what he's saying, because it's simply irrelevant. I've got myself back; whatever I ever wanted from oh-so-beautiful and far-too-smooth Dr. Gbego no longer matters. So I just say, "You'd better do some prep, get recordings soon, and think about what lab tests you want to run. I think that you're going to find you can declare me officially brought back. You'll really want data from the next couple of days."

He's flailing around, still trying to absorb the meaning of what his instruments told him about my huge surges of pleasure and rage. Finally all he manages to squeak out is, "How will we ever publish this?"

That's such a stupid question. There are things he won't say, things I won't say, but plenty of things to publish. We'll both advance our careers.

And of course there's a real advance in knowledge all around. Dr. Gbego knows some technical things now that no one else had learned before, and me? I know what I really want to know.

At first Gbego will be bothered by the things he didn't know he'd find out, the things he'd rather not have known. But soon he'll see how to make this whole experience work for him. Perhaps later this week, at one of the unending parties where nubrids spend so much time, he will find his way to talking, or, really, bragging. People will find it so intriguing that he was working with that famous Dr. Layla Palemba that you saw in media. Layla, the natch who knows bringbacks better than anyone else, natch or nubrid, actually working her own bringback, isn't that astonishing?

He will realize that the part of me that makes him sick and horrified need not intrude on what everyone wants to hear him say:

Yes, knowing Dr. Layla Palemba has been very inspiring.

Layla is a measure of the marvelous.

Yes, it's been such an honor and a privilege to work with her. Not on her, oh, no, she's tough and feisty and smart, I pity anyone so stupid he tries to work on her. With her, with her, with her.

What do I mean, a measure of the marvelous?

A measure of the marvel of plasticity that is the human brain, even the old natural human brain that, thank god, none of our parents would ever have stuck us with. A measure of the bigger marvel of neurology itself, that Ellauri and Jautta were able to understand the nubrid process a century ago. A measure of the even bigger marvel that in the last thirty years we've been able to do so much more to keep the surviving natches alive. A measure of the marvel of prosnoetics, to which she contributed, which saved them from being drooling, senseless lumps of flesh.

A measure of the biggest marvel of all, the continuing advance of science.

I imagine Gbego, my utterly smooth young-at-eighty nubrid neuro standing just a bit taller, shoulders stooped slightly, turning toward a perfectly beautiful young woman for her approval.

She beams at him, and then adds her little correction:

The science part is big, to be sure. But Dr. Layla Palemba is most of all a measure of the real biggest marvel of all: our modern global society that has so institutionalized generosity to the less fortunate and compassion for everyone that we are willing to spend so much expertise, time, research, and sheer treasure to rescue the very few surviving natches. She stands as a measure of the marvel that is us and our forgiveness and generosity.

Dr. Gbego will probably not even choke on a canapé when she says that. Probably he'll take her aside and talk with her, tell her how deep her insights and compassion are. Perhaps they will have many meetings and deep conversations and some elegant sex in the days that follow.

And for the rest of the crowd, having satisfied themselves with the smooth little bit of interesting knowledge with which Dr. Gbego graced them, the rest of the evening will pass in a swirl of fine wine and perfect bodies in splendid clothing: smug smooth fake hateful nubrid bastards who have taken over the world, passing the time of which they have so much, letting time and life itself roll off them like neutrinos off matter, like bad memories off a plastic brain, like blood off a cleaver.

PLEASE UNDO THIS HURT

SETH DICKINSON

⟨⟨◆⟩⟩

"A coyote got my cat," Nico says.

It took me four beers and three shots to open him up. All night he's been talking about the breakup, what's-her-name Yelena I think, and all night I've known there's something else on him, but I didn't *know* know—

"Fuck, man." I catch at his elbow. He's wearing leather, supple, slick—he's always mock-hurt when I can't tell his good jackets from his great ones. "Mandrill?" A better friend wouldn't have to ask, but I'm drunk, and not so good a friend. "Your cat back home?"

"Poor Mandrill," Nico says, completely forlorn. "Ah, shit, Dominga. I shouldn't have left him."

He only goes to the Lighthouse on empty Sundays, when we can hide in the booths ringed around the halogen beacon. I expect sad nights here. But, man, his *cat* . . .

Nico puts his head on my shoulder and makes a broken noise into the side of my neck. I rub his elbow and marvel in a selfish way at how much I *care*, how full of hurt I am, even after this awful week of dead bikers and domestics and empty space where fucking Jacob used to be. It's the drink, of course, and tomorrow if we see each other (we won't) it'll all be awkward, stilted, an unspoken agreement to forget this moment.

But right now I care.

In a moment he'll pull himself up, make a joke, buy a round. I know he will, since Nico and I only speak in bars and only when things feel like dogshit. We've got nothing in common—I ride ambulances around Queens, call my mom in Laredo every week, shouting Spanish into an old flip phone with a busted speaker. He makes smartphone games in a FiDi studio, imports leather jackets, and serially thinks his way out of perfectly good relationships. But all that difference warms me up sometimes, because (forgive me here, I am drunk) what's the world worth if you can't put two strangers together and get them to care? A friendship shouldn't need anything else.

He doesn't pull himself up and he doesn't make a joke.

The lighthouse beam sweeps over us, over the netting around our booth, over Nico's cramped shoulders and gawky height curled up against me. The light draws grid shadows on his leathered back, as if we're in an ambulance together, monitors tracing the thready rhythm of Nico's life. We sit together in the blue fog as the light passes on across empty tables carved with half-finished names.

"I'm really sorry." He finally pulls away, stiff, frowning. "I'm such a drag tonight. How are things after Jacob?"

I cluck in concern, just like my mom. I have to borrow the sound from her because I want to scream every time I think about fucking Jacob and fucking *I'm not ready for your life*. "We're talking about you."

He grins a fake grin but he's so good at it I'm still a little charmed. "We've been talking about me *forever*."

"You broke up with your girlfriend and lost your cat. You're having a bad week. As a medical professional I insist I buy you another round." Paramedics drink, and lie sometimes. He dumped Yelena out of the blue, 'to give her a chance at someone better.' The opposite of what Jacob had done to me. "And we're going to talk."

"No." He looks away. I follow his eyes, tracing the lighthouse beam across the room, where the circle of tables ruptures, broken by some necessity of cleaning or fire code: as if a snake had come up out of the light, slithered through the table mandala, and written something with its passage. "No, I'm done."

And the way he says that hits me, hits me low, because I recognize it. I have a stupid compassion that does me no good. I am desperate to help the people in my ambulance, the survivors. I can hold them together but I can't answer the plea I always see in their eyes: *Please, God, please, mother of mercy, just let this never have happened. Make it undone. Let me have a world where things like this never come to pass.*

"Nico," I say, "do you feel like you want to hurt yourself?"

He looks at me and the Lighthouse's sound system glitches for an instant, harsh and negative, as if we're listening to the inverse music that fills the space between the song and the meaningless static beneath.

My heart trips, thumps, like the ambulance alarm's just gone off.

"I don't want to hurt anyone," he says, eyes round and honest. "I don't want to get on Twitter and read about all the atrocities I'm complicit in. I don't want to trick wonderful women into spending a few months figuring out what a shithead I really am. I don't want to raise little cats to be coyote food. I don't even want to worry about whether I'm dragging my friends down. I just want to undo all the harm I've ever done."

Make it undone.

In my job I see these awful things—this image always come to me: a cyclist's skull burst like watermelon beneath the wheels of a truck he didn't see. I used to feel like I made a difference in my job. But that was a long time ago.

So I hold to this: As long as I can care about other people, I'm not in burnout. Emotional detachment is a cardinal symptom, you see.

"Did you ever see *It's a Wonderful Life*?" I'm trying to lighten the mood. I've only read the Wikipedia page.

"Yeah." Oops. "But I thought it kind of missed the point. What if—" He makes an excited gesture, pointing to an idea. But his eyes are still fixed on the mirror surface of the table, and when he sees himself his jaw works. "What if his angel said, *Oh, you've done more harm than good; but we all do, that's life, those are the rules, there's just more hurt to go around.* Why couldn't he, I forget his name, it doesn't matter, why couldn't he say, well, just redact me. Remove the fact of my birth. I'm a good guy, I don't want to do anyone any harm, so I'm going to opt out. Do you think that's possible? Not a suicide, that's selfish, it hurts people. But a really selfless way out?"

I don't know what to say to that. It's stupid, but he's smart, and he says it so hard.

He grins up at me, full-lipped, beautiful. The lighthouse beacon comes around again and lights up his silhouette and puts his face in shadow except his small white teeth. "I mean, come on. If I weren't here—wouldn't you be having a good night?"

"You're wishing you'd never known me, you realize. You're shitting all over me."

"Dominga Roldan! My knight." There he goes, closing up again, putting on the armor of charm. He likes that Roldan is so much like Roland. It's the first thing he ever told me. "Please. You're the suffering hero at this table. Let's talk about you."

I surrender. I start talking about fucking Jacob.

But I resolve right then that I'll save Nico, convince him that it's worth it to go on, worth it to have ever been.

I believe in good people. Even though Nico has what we call "resting asshole face" and a job that requires him to trick people into giving him thousands of dollars (he designs the systems that keep people playing smartphone games, especially the parts that keep them spending) I still think he's a good man. He cares, way down.

I believe you can feel that. The world's a cold place and it'll break your heart. You've got to trust in the possibility of good.

I dream of gardening far south and west, home in Laredo. Inexplicably, fucking Jacob is there. He smiles at me, big bear face a little stubbled. I want to yell at him: don't grow a beard! You have a great chin! But we're busy gardening, rooting around in galvanized tubs full of okra and zucchini and purple hull peas. Hot peppers, since the sweet breeds won't take. The autumn light down here isn't so thin as in New York. I am bare-handed, turning up the soil around the roots, grit up under my fingers and in the web of my hands. I am making life.

But down in the zucchini roots I find a knot of maggots, balled up squirming like they've wormed a portal up from maggot hell and come pouring out blind and silent. And I think: I am only growing homes for maggots. Everything is this way. In the end we are only making more homes, better homes, for maggots.

Jacob smiles at me and says, like he did: "I'm just not ready for your life. It's too hard. Too many people get hurt."

I wake up groaning, hangover clotted in my sinuses. Staring up at the vent above my mattress I realize there's no heat. It's broken again.

The cold is sharp, though. Sterile. It makes me go. I get to the hospital on time and Mary's waiting for me, smiling, my favorite partner armed with coffee and danishes and an egg sandwich from the enigmatic food truck only she can find. For my hangover, of course. Mary, bless her, knows my schedule.

Later that day we save a man's life.

He swam out into the river to die. We're first on the scene and I am stupid, so stupid: I jump in to save him. The water's late-autumn cold, the kind of chill I am afraid will get into my marrow and crystallize there, so that later in life, curled up in the summer sun with a lover, I'll feel a pang and know that a bead of ice came out of my bone and stuck in my heart. I used to get that kind of chest pain growing up, see. I thought they were ice crystals that formed when we went to see ex-Dad in Colorado, where the world felt high and thin, everything offered up on an altar to the truth behind the indifferent cloth of stars.

I'm thinking all this as I haul the drowning man back in. I feel so cold and so aware. My mind goes everywhere. Goes to Jacob, of course.

Offered up on an altar. We used to play a sex game like that, Jacob and I. You know, a sexy sacrifice—isn't that the alchemy of sex games? You take something appalling and you make it part of your appetites. Jesus, I used to think it was cute, and now describing it I'm furiously embarrassed. Jacob was into all kinds of nerd shit. For him I think the fantasy was always kind of Greco-Roman, Andromeda on the rocks, but I always wondered if he dared imagine me as some kind of Aztec princess, which would be too complicatedly racist for him to suggest. He's dating a white girl now. It doesn't bother me but Mom just won't let it go. She's sharp about it, too: she has a theory that Jacob feels he's now Certified Decent, having passed his qualifying exam, and now he'll go on to be a regular shithead.

And Mary's pulling me up onto the pier, and I'm pulling the suicide.

He nearly dies in the ambulance. We swaddle him in heat packs and blankets and Mary, too, swaddles him, smiling and flirting, it's okay, what a day for a swim, does he know that in extreme situations rescuers are advised to provide skin-to-skin contact?

See, Mary's saying, see, it's not so bad here, not so cold. You'll meet good people. You'll go on.

Huddled in my own blankets I meet the swimmer's warm brown eyes and just then the ambulance slams across a pothole. He fibrillates. Alarms shriek. I see him start to go, receding, calm, warm, surrounded by people trying to save him, and I think that if he went now, before his family found out, before he had to go back to whatever drove him into the river, it'd be best.

Oh, God, the hurt can't be undone. It'd be best.

His eyes open. They peel back like membranes. I see a thin screen, thinner than Colorado sky, and in the vast space behind it something white and soft and eyeless wheels on an eternal wind.

His heart quits. He goes into asystole.

"Come on," Mary hisses, working on him. "Come on. You can't do this to me. Dominga, let's get some epi going—come on, don't go."

I think that's the hook that pulls him in. He cares. He doesn't want to hurt her. Like Nico, he can't stand to do harm. By that hook or by the CPR and the epinephrine we bring him back. Afterward I sit outside in the cold, the bitter dry cold, and I can *feel* it: the heat going out of me, the world leaking up through the sky and out into the void where something ancient waits, a hypothermic phantasm, a cold fever dream, the most real thing I've ever seen.

I flail around for something human to hold and remember, then, how worried I am about Nico.

Don't judge me too harshly. This is my next move: I invite Nico to game night with Jacob and his new girlfriend Elise. Nico is a game designer, right? It fits. I promised Jacob we'd still be friends. Everything fits.

It's not about any kind of payback.

Jacob loves this idea. He suggests a café/bar nerd money trap called Glass Needle. I turn up with Nico (*Cool jacket*, I say, and he grins back at me from under his mirrored aviators, saying, *You really can't tell!*) and we all shake hands and say Hi, hi, wow, it's so great, under a backlit ceiling of frosted glass etched with the shapes of growing things.

"Isn't that cool?" Jacob beams at me. "They do that with hydrofluorosilicic acid." He's growing too: working on a beard and a gut, completing the deadly Santa array. Elise looks like she probably does yoga. She arranges the game with assured competence. I wonder how many times Jacob practiced saying *hydrofluorosilicic*, and what their sex is like.

Nico tongues a square of gum. "That's really impressive," he says.

The games engage him. I guess the games engage me too: Jacob will listen to anything Nico says, since Jacob cares about everything and Nico pretends he doesn't. "I love board games," Jacob explains.

"I love rules," Nico replies, and this is true: Nico thinks everything is a game to be played, history, evolution, even dating, even friendship. Everything has a winning strategy. He'll describe this cynicism to anyone, since he thinks it's sexy. If you know him you can see how deeply it bothers him.

It's Sunday again. I worked eighteen hours yesterday. I'm exhausted, I can't stop thinking about the swimmer flatline. Jacob looks at me with the selfless worry permitted to the ex who did the dumping.

If I weren't here, I think, *wouldn't you be having a good night?*

The game baffles me. Elise assembles a zoo of cardboard tokens, decks of tiny cards, dice, character sheets, Jacob chattering all the while: "These are for the other worlds you'll visit. These are spells you can learn, though of course they'll drive you mad. This card means you're the town sheriff—that one means you eat free at the diner—"

Elise pats him on the hand. "I think they can learn as they go."

We're supposed to patrol a town where the world has gotten thin and wounded. If we don't heal those wounds, something will come through, a dreadful thing with a name like the Treader In Dust or whatever. Nico's really good at the game. He flirts with me outrageously, which earns a beautifully troubled Jacob-face, a face of perturbed enlightenment: *really, this shouldn't be bothering me!* So I flirt back at Nico. Why not? He's the one getting a kick out of meeting my ex and out-charming him, out-dressing him, talking over him while he sits there and takes it. And wouldn't Mary flirt, to comfort him? To remind poor forlorn Nico that the world's not so cold?

Only Nico doesn't seem so forlorn, and when I look at Jacob, there's Elise touching shoulders with him, which makes every memory of Jacob hurt. As if she's claimed him not just now but retroactively too.

Even Elise, who's played it a hundred times, can't manage this damn game. The rules seem uncertain, as if different parts of the rule book contradict each other. Jacob and Nico argue over exactly how the monsters decide to hunt us, precisely when the Magic Shop closes up, where the yawning portals lead. Oh, Nico—this must be so satisfyingly *you*: You are beating Jacob's game, you're better than his rules. Even Elise won't argue with Nico, preferring, she says, to focus on the *emergent narrative*.

It all leaves me outside.

I drink to spiteful excess and move my little character around in sullen ineffective ways. Jacob's eyes are full of stupid understanding. I look at him and try to beam my thoughts: I hate this. This makes me sick. I wish I'd never met you. I wish I could burn up all the good times we had, just to spare myself this awful night.

That's what I thought when he left. That it hadn't been worth it.

"Can we switch sides," Nico asks, "and obtain dreadful secrets from the Great Old One?"

"You could try." Elise loves this. She grins at Nico and I savor Jacob's reaction. "But your only hope is that It will devour your soul first, so you don't have to experience the terrible majesty of Its coming."

And Nico grins at me. "What an awful world. You're fucked the moment you're born." Making a joke out of his drunken despair, out of dead Mandrill and his own hurt. Of course he doesn't take it seriously. Of course he was just drunk.

I am everyone's sucker.

"I think you can do that with an expansion set," Jacob adds helpfully. "Switch sides, I mean."

"Let's play with it next time," Nico says. Elise bounces happily. There probably *will* be a next time, won't there? The three of them will be friends.

"I feel sick," I say, "it's just—something I saw on shift. It's getting to me."

Then I go. They can't argue with that. They all work in offices.

Nico texts me: Holy shit we lost. Alien god woke up to consume the world. We went mad with rapture and horror when it spoke hidden secrets of the universal design although I did shoot it with a tommy gun. Game is fucking broken. It was amazing thank you.

I text back: cool

What I want to say is: you asshole, I hope you're happy, I hope you're glad you're right, I hope you're glad you won. I believe in good people, you know, but I used to think Jacob was a good person, and look where that got me; I just wanted to cheer you up and look where that got me. I pull people from the river, I drag them dying out of their houses, I see their spinal fluid running into the gutters and look where all that gets me—

Jesus, this world, this world. I feel so heartsick. I cannot even retch.

And I dream of that awful board, piled with tokens moving each other by their own secret rules. A game of alien powers but those powers escape the game to move among us. They roam the world cow-eyed and compassionate and offer hands with fingers like fishhooks. We live in a paddock, a fattening pen, and we cannot leave it, because when we try to go the hooks say, *Think of who you'll hurt.*

So much hurt to try to heal. And the healing hurts too much.

• • •

The hangover sings an afterimage song. Like the drunkenness was ripped out of me and it left a negative space, the opposite of contentment. It vibrates in my bones.

I get up, brushing at an itch on my back, and drink straight from the bathroom faucet. When I come back to my mattress it's speckled, speckled white. Something's dripping on it from the air vent—oh, oh, they're maggots, slim white maggots. My air vent is dripping maggots. They're all over the covers, white and searching.

I call my landlord. I pin plastic sheeting up over the vent. I clean my bedroom twice, once for the maggots, once again after I throw up. Then I go to work.

Everything I touch feels infested. Inhabited.

Mary's got an egg sandwich for me but she looks like shit, weary, dry-skinned, her face flaking. "Hi," she says. "I'm sorry, I have the worst migraine."

"Oh, hon. Take it easy." The headaches started when she transitioned, an estrogen thing. She's quiet about them, and strong. I'm happy she tells me.

"Hey, you too. Which, uh—actually." She gives me the sandwich and makes a brave face, like she's afraid that someone's going to snap at someone, like she doesn't want to snap first. "I signed you up for a stress screening. They want you in the little conference room in half an hour."

I'm not angry. I just feel dirty and rotten and useless: now I'm even letting Mary down. "Oh," I say. "Jesus, I'm sorry. I didn't realize I'd . . . was it the epi? Was I too slow on the epi last week?"

"You didn't do anything wrong." She rubs her temples. "I'm just worried about you."

I want to give her a hug and thank her for caring but she's so obviously in pain. And the thought of the maggots keeps me away.

They're waiting for me in the narrow conference room: a man in a baggy blue suit, a woman in surgical scrubs with an inexplicable black stain like tar. "Dominga Roldan?" she says.

"That's me."

The man shakes my hand enthusiastically. "We just wanted to chat. See how you were. After your rescue swim."

The woman beckons: sit. "Think of this as a chance to relax."

"We're worried about you, Dominga," the man says. I can't get over how badly his suit fits. "I remember some days in the force I felt like the world didn't give a fuck about us. Just made me want to give up. You ever feel that way?"

I want to say what Nico would say: actually, sir, that's not the problem at all, the problem is caring too much, caring so much you can't ask for help because everyone else is already in so much pain.

Nico wouldn't say that, though. He'd find a really clever way to not say it.

"Sure," I say. "But that's the job."

"Did you know the victim?" the woman asks. The man winces at her bluntness. I blink at her and she purses her lips and tilts her head, to *Yes, I know how it sounds, but please.* say: "The suicide you rescued. Did you know him?"

"No." Of course not. What?

The man opens his mouth and she cuts him off. "But did you *feel* that you did, at any point? After he coded, maybe?"

I stare at her. My hangover turns my stomach and drums on the inside of my skull. It's not that I don't get it: it's that I feel I *do*, that something has been gestating in the last few days, in the missing connections between unrelated events.

The man sighs and unlatches his briefcase. I just can't shake the sense that his suit *used* to fit, not so long ago. "Let her be," he says. "Dominga, I just gotta tell you, I admire the hell out of people like you. Me, I think the only good in this world is the good we bring to it. Good people, people like you, you make this place worth living in."

"So we need to take care of people like you." The woman in scrubs has a funny accent—not quite Boston, still definitely a Masshole. "Burnout's very common. You know the stages?"

"Sure." First exhaustion, then shame, then callous cynicism. Then collapse. But I'm not there yet, I'm not past cynicism. I still want to help.

The man lifts a tiny glass cylinder from his briefcase, a cylinder full of a green fleshy mass—a caterpillar, a fat warty caterpillar, pickled in cloudy fluid and starting to peel apart. He looks at me apologetically, as if this is an awkward necessity, just his morning caterpillar in brine.

"Sometimes this job becomes overwhelming." The woman's completely unmoved by the caterpillar. Her eyes have a kind of look-away quality, like those awful xenon headlights assholes use, unsafe to meet head-on. "Sometimes you need to stop taking on responsibilities and look after your-self. It's very important that you have resources to draw on."

Baggy Suit holds his cylinder gingerly, a thumb on one end and two fingers on the other, and stares at it. Is there *writing* on it? The woman says, "Do you have a safe space at home? Somewhere to relax?"

"Well—no, I guess not, there's a bug problem . . ."

The woman frowns in sympathy but her *eyes* don't frown, God, not at all—they smile. I don't know why. The man rolls his dead caterpillar tube and suddenly I grasp that the writing's on the *inside*, facing the dead bug.

"You've got to take care of yourself." He sounds petulant; he looks at the woman in scrubs with quiet resentment. "We need good people out there. Fighting the good fight."

"But if you feel you can't go on . . . If you're absolutely overwhelmed, and you can't see a way forward . . ." The woman leans across the table to take my hands. She's colder than the river where the man went to die. "I want to give you a number, okay? A place you can call for help."

She reads it off to me and I get *hammered* with déjà vu: I know it already, I'm sure. Or maybe that's not quite right, I don't know it exactly. It's just that it feels like it fits inside me, as if a space has been hollowed out for it, made ready to contain its charge.

"Please take care of yourself," the man tells me, on the way out. "If you don't, the world will just eat you up." And he lifts the caterpillar in salute.

I leave work early. I desperately don't want to go home, where the maggots will be puddled in the plastic up on my ceiling, writhing, eyeless, bulging, probably eating each other.

Mary walks me out. "You going to take any time off? See anybody?"

"I just saw Jacob and Elise yesterday."

"How was that?"

"A really bad decision." I shake my head and that, too, is a bad decision. "How's the migraine?"

"I'm okay. I'll live." It strikes me that when Mary says that, I believe it—and maybe she sees me frown, follows my thoughts, because she asks, "What about Nico? Are you still seeing him?"

"Yeah. Sort of."

"And?" Her impish well-*did*-you? grin.

"I'm worried about him." And furious, too, but if I said that I'd have to explain, and then Mary would be concerned about me, and I'd feel guilty because surely Mary has real problems, bigger problems than mine. "He's really depressed."

"Oh. That's all you need. Look—" She stops me just short of the doors. "Dominga, you're a great partner. I hope I didn't step on your toes today. But I really want you to get some room, okay? Do something for yourself."

I give her a long, long hug, and I forget about the maggots, just for the length of it.

There's a skywriter above the hospital, buzzing around in sharp curves. The sky's clean and blue and infinite, dizzyingly deep. Evening sun glints on the plane so it looks like a sliver poking up through God's skin.

I watch it draw signs in falling red vapor and when the wind shears them apart I think of the Lighthouse, where the circle of tables was ruptured by the passage of an illusory force.

I want to act. I want to help. I want to ease someone's pain. I don't want to do something for myself, because—

You're only burnt out once you stop wanting to help.

I call Nico. "Hey," he says. "Didn't expect to hear from you so soon."

"Want to get a drink?" I say, and then, my throat raw, my tongue acid, a hangover trick, words squirming out of me with wet expanding pressure, "I learned something you should know. A place to go, if you need help. If that's what you want. If the world really is too much."

Sometimes you say a thing and then you realize it's true.

He laughs. "I can't believe you're making fun of me about that. You're such an asshole. Do you want to go to Kosmos?"

"So," Nico says, "are we dating?"

Kosmos used to be a warehouse. Now the ceiling is an electric star field, a map of alien constellations. We sit together directly beneath a pair of twin red stars.

"Oh," I say, startled. "I was worried. After yesterday, I mean, I just . . ." Was furious, was hurt, didn't know why: because you were having fun, because I wasn't, because I thought you needed help, because you pretended you didn't. One of those. All of them.

Maybe he doesn't like what he sees in my eyes. He gets up. "Be right back." The house music samples someone talking about the expansion of the universe. Nico touches my shoulder on the way to the bathroom and I watch him recede, savoring the fading charge of his hand, thinking about space carrying us apart, and how safe that would be.

I have a choice to offer him. Maybe we'll leave together.

Nico comes back with drinks—wine, of all things, as if we're celebrating. "I thought that game was charmingly optimistic, you know."

"Jacob's game?" He's been tagging me in Facebook pictures of the stupid thing. I should block Jacob, so it'd stop hurting, which is why I don't.

"Right. I was reading about it."

The wine's dry and sweet. It tastes like tomorrow's hangover, like coming awake on a strange couch under a ceiling with no maggots. I take three swallows. "I thought it was about unknowable gods and the futility of all human life."

"Sure." That stupid cocky grin of his hits hard because I know what's behind it. "But in the game there's something out there, something bigger than us. Which—I mean, compared to what we've got, at least it's *interesting*." He points to the electric universe above us, all its empty dazzling artifice. "How's work?"

"I'm taking a break. Don't worry about it." I have a plan here, a purpose. I am an agent, although which meaning of that word fits I don't know. "Why'd you really dump Yelena?"

"I told you." He resorts to the wine, to buy himself a moment. "Really, I was honest. I thought she could do a lot better than me. I wanted her to be happy."

"But what about *you*? She made you happy."

"Yeah, yeah, she did. But I don't want to be the kind of person who—" He stops here and takes another slow drink. "I don't want to be someone like Jacob."

"Jacob's very happy," I say, which is his point, of course.

"And look how he left you."

"What if I thought *you* made me happy?" Somewhere, somehow, Mary's cheering me on: that gets me through the sentence. "Would this be a date? Or are we both too . . . tired?"

Tired of doing hurt, and tired of taking it. Tired of the great cartographic project. Isn't it a little like cartography? Meeting lovely people, mapping them, racing to find their hurts before they can find yours—getting use from them, squeezing them dry, and then striking first, unilaterally and with awful effect, because the alternative is waiting for them to do the same to you. These are the rules, you didn't make them, they're not your fault. So you might as well play to win.

Nico looks at me with dark guarded eyes. I would bet my life here, at last, that he's wearing one of his good jackets.

"Dominga," he says, and makes a little motion like he's going to take my hand, but can't quite commit, "Dominga, I'm sorry, but . . . God, I must sound like such an asshole, but I meant what I said. I'm done hurting people."

And I know exactly what he's saying. I remember it, I *feel* it—it's like when you get drunk with a guy and everything's just magical, you feel connected, you feel okay. But you know, even then, even in that moment, that tomorrow you will regret this: that the hole you opened up to him will admit the cold, or the knife. There will be a text from him, or the absence of a text, or—worse, much worse—the sight of him with someone new, months later, after the breakup, the sight of him doing that secret thing he does to say, *I'm thinking of you*, except it's not secret any more, and it's not you he's thinking of now.

And you just want to be done. You want a warmer world.

So here it is: my purpose, my plan. "Nico, what if I could give you a way out?"

He sets down his wine glass and turns it by the stem. It makes a faint, high shriek against the blackened steel tabletop, and he winces, and says, "What do you mean?"

"Just imagine a hypothetical. Imagine you're right about everything—the universe is a hard place. To live you have to risk a lot of hurt." You're going to wonder how I came up with the rest of this, and all I can offer is fatigue, terror, maggots in my air vents, the memory of broken skulls on sidewalks: a kind of stress psychosis. Or the other explanation, of course. "Imagine that our last chance to be really good is revoked at the instant of our conception."

He follows along with good humor and a kind of adorable narcissism that I'm so engaged with his cosmic bullshit and (under it all) an awakening sense that something's off, askew. "Okay . . . "

The twin red suns multiply our shadows around us. I drift a little ways above myself on the wine, and it makes it easier to go on, to imagine or transmit this: "What if something out there knew a secret—"

A secret! Such a secret, a secret you might hear in the wind that passes between the libraries of jade teeth that wait in an empty city burnt stark by a high blue star that never leaves the zenith, a secret that tumbles down on you like a fall of maggots from a white place behind everything, where a pale immensity circles on the silent wind.

"What if there were a way out? Like a phone number you could call, a person you could talk to, kind of a hotline, and you'd say, oh, I'm a smart, depressed, compassionate person, I'm tired of the great lie that it's possible to do more good than harm, I'm tired of my Twitter feed telling me the world's basically a car full of kindergartners crumpling up in a trash compactor. I don't want to be complicit any more. I want out. Not suicide, no, that'd just hurt people. I want something better. And they'd say, sure, man, we have your mercy here, we can do that. We can make it so you never were."

He looks at me with an expression of the most terrible unguarded longing. He tries to cover it up, he tries to go flirty or sarcastic, but he can't.

I take my phone out, my embarrassing old flip phone, and put it on the table between us. I don't have to use the contacts to remember. The number keys make soft chiming noises as I type the secret in.

"So," I say, "my question is: who goes first?"

Something deep beneath me exalts, as if this is what it wants: and I cannot say if that thing is separate from me.

He reaches for the phone. "Not you, I hope," he says, with a really brave play-smile: he knows this is all a game, an exercise of imagination. He knows it's real. "The world needs people like you, Dominga. So what am I going to get? Is it a sex line?"

"If you go first," I say, "do you think that'd change the world enough that I wouldn't want to go second?"

I have this stupid compassion in me, and it cries out for the hurts of others. Nico's face, just then—God, have you ever known this kind of beauty? This desperate, awful hope that the answer was *yes*, that he might, by his absence, save me?

His finger hovers a little way above the call button.

"I think you'd have to go first," he says. He puts his head back, all the way back, as if to blow smoke: but I think he's looking up at the facsimile stars. "That'd be important."

"Why?"

"Because," he says, all husky nonchalance, "if you weren't here, I would *absolutely* go; whereas if I weren't here, I don't know if you'd go. And if this method were real, this, uh, operation of mercy, then the universe is lost, the whole operation's fucked, and it's vital that you get out."

His finger keeps station a perilous few millimeters from the call. I watch this space breathlessly. "Tell me why," I say, to keep him talking, and then I realize: oh, Nico, you'd think this out, wouldn't you? You'd consider the new rules. You'd understand the design. And I'm afraid that what he'll say will be *right*—

He lays it out there: "Well, who'd use it?"

"Good people," I say. That's how burnout operates. You burn out because you care. "Compassionate people."

"That's right." He gets a little melancholy here, a little singsong, in a way that feels like the rhythm of my stranger thoughts. I wonder if he's had an uncanny couple days too, and whether I'll ever get a chance to ask him. "The universe sucks, man, but it sucks a lot more if you care, if you feel the hurt around you. So if there were a way out—a certain kind of people would use it, right? And those people would go extinct."

Oh. Right.

There might have been a billion good people, ten billion, a hundred, before us: and one by one they chose to go, to be unmade, a trickle at first, just the kindest, the ones most given to shoulder their neighbors' burdens and ask nothing in exchange—but the world would get harder for the loss of each of them, and there'd be more reason then, more hurt to go around, so the rattle would become an avalanche.

And we'd be left. The dregs. Little selfish people and their children.

The stars above change, the false constellations reconfiguring. Nico sighs up at them. "You think that's why the sky's empty?"

"Of—aliens, you mean?" What a curious brain.

"Yeah. They were too good. They ran into bad people, bad situations, and they didn't want to compromise themselves. So they opted out."

"Maybe someone's hunting good people." If this thing were real, well, wouldn't it be a perfect weapon, a perfect instrument in something's special plan? Bait and trap all at once.

"Maybe. One way or another—well, we should go, right?" He comes back from the cosmic distance. His finger hasn't moved. He grins his stupid cocky camouflage grin because the alternative is ghoulish and he says, "I think I make a pretty compelling case."

Everything cold and always getting colder because the warmth puts itself out.

"Maybe." Maybe. He's very clever. "But I'm not going first."

Nico puts his finger down (and I feel the cold, up out of my bones, sharp in my heart) but he's just pinning the corner of the phone so he can spin it around. "Jacob definitely wouldn't make the call," he says, teasing, a really harsh kind of tease, but it's about me, about how I hurt, which feels good.

"Neither would Mary," I say, which is, all in all, my counterargument, my stanchion, my sole refuge. If something's out to conquer us, well, the conquest isn't done. Something good remains. Mary's still here. She hasn't gone yet—whether you take all this as a thought experiment or not.

"Who's Mary?" He raises a skeptical eyebrow: you have *friends*?

"Stick around," I say, "and I'll tell you."

Right then I get one more glimpse past the armor: he's frustrated, he's glad, he's all knotted up, because I won't go first, and whatever going first means, he doesn't want to leave me to go second. He wouldn't have to care anymore, of course. But he still cares. That's how compassion works.

If I had a purpose here, well, I suppose it's done.

"You're taking a break from work?" He closes the phone and pushes it back to me. "What's up with that? Can I help?"

When I go to take the phone he makes a little gesture, like he wants to take my hand, and I make a little gesture like I want him to—and between the two of us, well, we manage.

I still have the number, of course. Maybe you worry that it works. Maybe you're afraid I'll use it, or that Nico will, when things go bad. Things do so often go bad.

You won't know if I use it, of course, because then I'll never have told you this story, and you'll never have read it. But that's a comfort, isn't it? That's enough.

The story's still here. We go on.

TIME BOMB TIME

C.C. FINLAY

-pop-

The sharp scent of ozone—sudden like heartbreak, raw as a panic attack—filled Hannah's dorm room, from the paper-swamped desk across her rumpled bed to the window overlooking the quad. The lights flickered. Her heart skipped a beat.

"God damn it." She prodded Nolon's foot with the toe of her shoe. She wanted to kick him. "Tell me what you just did."

"Nothing." He was leaning over the weird device from his lab, tapping a code on the keypad.

"What are you doing now?" Anger pushed at the edges of her voice, but she held it in check. She wanted him to leave, but she didn't want to upset him.

"Don't worry so much—nobody's going to get hurt." He pressed his shoulder against her, didn't even have to push—she flinched and bumped into the wall. He laughed at her, like it was a joke. "It's not a time bomb."

She sighed. "I don't care if it's a confetti bomb," she said, pointing at the keg-sized device. "Whatever it is, get it out of here."

He glanced at her through blond bangs, beaming his best grin. He only used it when he wanted to make out or get away with something. "C'mon," he pleaded. "I really want you with me when this goes off, Hanan."

"It's Hannah," she corrected. He used the name her parents gave her, even when that wasn't what she wanted. She hated how people looked at her and thought *Muslim* or *terrorist*, not *Arab Christian* or *second generation American* and never just plain *American*. "My name is Hannah."

"It's close enough—" He must have seen fury flash in her eyes, because he put up his hands in surrender. "Sure, Hanan, whatever you want."

For the first time, she considered that she might hate him. "I don't want to be a rat trapped in the maze of your brain anymore," she snapped. He was so close, she could smell the grunge—he must have been up, working on his project for days. What she wanted was a clear route to the door so she could leave the room if he didn't. "Just put your experiment over by the window."

He stared at the window, toward the quad where TV crews were covering the big student protest. "You do understand what I'm trying to do, right?" he said. "If I set this off, it proves my theories. But it also functions as the best political statement ever. It'll show the world that all we do is go through the same meaningless motions over and over."

"You can't involve other people in your science experiments without their permission. And I know you haven't gone through the Institutional Review Board. What you're planning to do is wrong."

He ignored her. "The thing is, the larger the radius of the temporal effect, the shorter the duration. Too big, and it will happen so fast no one will notice. A small bubble, the size of this room, will last for several minutes, but then it won't be recorded by the TV cameras. And I've only got one device, one chance." The light in his eyes flickered like numbers changing on a calculator screen.

She felt a pang of empathy for him. He was desperate to make this work, the same way he had been desperate to make their relationship work. "Let's talk about this, okay? Whatever you're trying to prove, this isn't the way to do it—"

"Dr. Renner doesn't believe in my temporal bubble theory. I have to change my dissertation or leave the program. He wants me to 'stop wasting time.' " He said the last phrase in Renner's nasally voice, and his shoulders slouched in defeat. "So this is it for me—if I don't prove my theory in a really spectacular, public way, my research is finished."

"Look, the physics goes way over my head, but I know that you believe in the theory and that's enough for me." She could believe in anything if it would get him out of her room.

"You're the only one who still believes in me."

"So why are you doing things this way?" She gestured at the strange device, then reined in her hands, afraid that any sudden movement could make it go off. "It's like you want the whole world to see you self-destruct."

"I want to change the world." His stare was too intense, his eyes rimmed by dark circles, his breath tainted with the formaldehyde smell of stale Red Bull. "I want to change the way the world sees me. The way that you see—"

She stopped him right there. "Even if your theory is right, this isn't the way to do it. You can't publish this. You won't get credit for it. What are you thinking?"

"Panama!" he blurted. "You remember the palindrome. Only, technically, this works more like a palingram. A palingram is made of words or phrases, not letters. So the individual units are cognitively whole. Like 'I do, do I?' or 'one for all and all for one.' "

"That still doesn't make any sense." Never mind the fact that she was a lit major and had taught him about palindromes and palingrams and all that stuff. "Time doesn't work like 'a man, a plan, a canal.'"

"If you're reading a palindrome, you can't tell whether it's going forwards or backwards. Inside a temporal bubble, it's the same thing. You can't tell which way time is flowing."

She crossed her arms over the anxious tightness in her chest. "Look, you've explained this to me before. But time only flows in one direction. You can't make time run backwards, even for a few seconds."

"How would we know? We're always stuck inside our own perception. Our brain takes these little packets of perceived time and arranges them in order to create a sense of causality. The continuum of time, the connections and flow between events, that's cognitively constructed."

"Sure, but whatever's going on in your head, however you perceive things, there's still an objective reality outside." Like the objective reality that they weren't dating any more, regardless of what he wanted.

"That's it exactly, that's what I'm trying to demonstrate. People only live in the psychological present, in the *now*. Look at Ernst Pöppel's research. It proves that our neurocognitive software"—he paused to wave his hand around his head—"processes temporal experience into these one-to-ten second packets of perceived time. That's what gives us a sense of constant nowness."

"I don't care!" She was done with him, so done. It wasn't her job to validate his feelings or make him feel good about his bad decisions. "Get that thing out of my room. Now."

To her surprise, he started to carry the device past her. She backed away into the corner between the bed and her desk. "It's not a bomb." He sounded defensive, even hurt. "It creates a bubble, not an explosion."

"That looks like a bomb," she said. How could he bring anything that even looked like a bomb around her? "I don't want it in here."

"I just need five minutes. The TV cameras are outside for the protest. I'm going to do a demonstration of my research and I want to make sure they broadcast it live. I came here to tell you, because I want you to see it too."

He was sad and hopeful and eager, like a puppy at the pet store. Which is why she had brought him home in the first place. But just like a puppy, he left messes everywhere and required constant, exhausting attention. From the very beginning, dating him had been a bad idea, a ticking bomb just waiting to explode. "I'm sorry, but I'm really busy right now."

"Please give me a chance," he begged. He held the device from his lab, cradling it in his arms like a monstrous baby.

"Nolon," she said. "We broke up."

She remembered the last time she had seen him, that night in his lab, lights dimmed, everything silent. A smaller version of his device was hooked up to a cage where a white rat ran through a maze. He had tapped a code on the keypad and then she smelled ozone. The lights flickered. There was a loud -*pop*-. A shimmery bubble formed around the cage, and the rat ran backwards, repeating the same steps in reverse. A rewind. When it reached the beginning, it started forward again, feet following the exact path. She felt bad for the rat, like it was a puppet. The experience was very weird and upsetting.

Nolon stood there, staring at her, waiting for her to say something. On the outside she froze; inside, she freaked.

A familiar knock startled Hannah and she jumped reflexively to yank open the door.

-*tattarrattat*-

A familiar knock startled Hannah and she jumped reflexively to yank open the door.

Nolon stood there, staring at her, waiting for her to say something. On the outside she froze; inside, she freaked.

She remembered the last time she had seen him, that night in his lab, lights dimmed, everything silent. A smaller version of his device was hooked up to a cage where a white rat ran through a maze. He had tapped a code on the keypad and then she smelled ozone. The lights flickered. There was a loud -*pop*-. A shimmery bubble formed around the cage, and the rat ran backwards, repeating the same steps in reverse. A rewind. When it reached the beginning, it started forward again, feet following the exact path. She felt bad for the rat, like it was a puppet. The experience was very weird and upsetting.

"Nolon," she said. "We broke up."

"Please give me a chance," he begged. He held the device from his lab, cradling it in his arms like a monstrous baby.

He was sad and hopeful and eager, like a puppy at the pet store. Which is why she had brought him home in the first place. But just like a puppy, he left messes everywhere and required constant, exhausting attention. From the very beginning, dating him had been a bad idea, a ticking bomb just waiting to explode. "I'm sorry, but I'm really busy right now."

"I just need five minutes. The TV cameras are outside for the protest. I'm going to do a demonstration of my research and I want to make sure they broadcast it live. I came here to tell you, because I want you to see it too."

"That looks like a bomb," she said. How could he bring anything that even looked like a bomb around her? "I don't want it in here."

To her surprise, he started to carry the device past her. She backed away into the corner between the bed and her desk. "It's not a bomb." He sounded defensive, even hurt. "It creates a bubble, not an explosion."

"I don't care!" She was done with him, so done. It wasn't her job to validate his feelings or make him feel good about his bad decisions. "Get that thing out of my room. Now."

"That's it exactly, that's what I'm trying to demonstrate. People only live in the psychological present, in the *now*. Look at Ernst Pöppel's research. It proves that our neurocognitive software"—he paused to wave his hand around his head—"processes temporal experience into these one-to-ten second packets of perceived time. That's what gives us a sense of constant nowness."

"Sure, but whatever's going on in your head, however you perceive things, there's still an objective reality outside." Like the objective reality that they weren't dating any more, regardless of what he wanted.

"How would we know? We're always stuck inside our own perception. Our brain takes these little packets of perceived time and arranges them in order to create a sense of causality. The continuum of time, the connections and flow between events, that's cognitively constructed."

She crossed her arms over the anxious tightness in her chest. "Look, you've explained this to me before. But time only flows in one direction. You can't make time run backwards, even for a few seconds."

"If you're reading a palindrome, you can't tell whether it's going forwards or backwards. Inside a temporal bubble, it's the same thing. You can't tell which way time is flowing."

"That still doesn't make any sense." Never mind the fact that she was a lit major and had taught him about palindromes and palingrams and all that stuff. "Time doesn't work like 'a man, a plan, a canal.' "

"Panama!" he blurted. "You remember the palindrome. Only, technically, this works more like a palingram. A palingram is made of words or phrases, not letters. So the individual units are cognitively whole. Like 'I do, do I?' or 'one for all and all for one.' "

She stopped him right there. "Even if your theory is right, this isn't the way to do it. You can't publish this. You won't get credit for it. What are you thinking?"

"I want to change the world." His stare was too intense, his eyes rimmed by dark circles, his breath tainted with the formaldehyde smell of stale Red Bull. "I want to change the way the world sees me. The way that you see—"

"So why are you doing things this way?" She gestured at the strange device, then reined in her hands, afraid that any sudden movement could make it go off. "It's like you want the whole world to see you self-destruct."

"You're the only one who still believes in me."

"Look, the physics goes way over my head, but I know that you believe in the theory and that's enough for me." She could believe in anything if it would get him out of her room.

"Dr. Renner doesn't believe in my temporal bubble theory. I have to change my dissertation or leave the program. He wants me to 'stop wasting time.'" He said the last phrase in Renner's nasally voice, and his shoulders slouched in defeat. "So this is it for me—if I don't prove my theory in a really spectacular, public way, my research is finished."

She felt a pang of empathy for him. He was desperate to make this work, the same way he had been desperate to make their relationship work. "Let's talk about this, okay? Whatever you're trying to prove, this isn't the way to do it—"

He ignored her. "The thing is, the larger the radius of the temporal effect, the shorter the duration. Too big, and it will happen so fast no one will notice. A small bubble, the size of this room, will last for several minutes, but then it won't be recorded by the TV cameras. And I've only got one device, one chance." The light in his eyes flickered like numbers changing on a calculator screen.

"You can't involve other people in your science experiments without their permission. And I know you haven't gone through the Institutional Review Board. What you're planning to do is wrong."

He stared at the window, toward the quad where TV crews were covering the big student protest. "You do understand what I'm trying to do, right?" he said. "If I set this off, it proves my theories. But it also functions as the best political statement ever. It'll show the world that all we do is go through the same meaningless motions over and over."

For the first time, she considered that she might hate him. "I don't want to be a rat trapped in the maze of your brain anymore," she snapped. He was so close, she could smell the grunge—he must have been up, working on his project for days. What she wanted was a clear route to the door so she could leave the room if he didn't. "Just put your experiment over by the window."

"It's close enough—" He must have seen fury flash in her eyes, because he put up his hands in surrender. "Sure, Hanan, whatever you want."

"It's Hannah," she corrected. He used the name her parents gave her, even when that wasn't what she wanted. She hated how people looked at her and thought *Muslim* or *terrorist,* not *Arab Christian* or *second generation American* and never just plain *American.* "My name is Hannah."

He glanced at her through blond bangs, beaming his best grin. He only used it when he wanted to make out or get away with something. "C'mon," he pleaded. "I really want you with me when this goes off, Hanan."

She sighed. "I don't care if it's a confetti bomb," she said, pointing at the keg-sized device. "Whatever it is, get it out of here."

"Don't worry so much—nobody's going to get hurt." He pressed his shoulder against her, didn't even have to push—she flinched and bumped into the wall. He laughed at her, like it was a joke. "It's not a time bomb."

"What are you doing now?" Anger pushed at the edges of her voice, but she held it in check. She wanted him to leave, but she didn't want to upset him.

"Nothing." He was leaning over the weird device from his lab, tapping a code on the keypad.

"God damn it." She prodded Nolon's foot with the toe of her shoe. She wanted to kick him. "Tell me what you just did."

The sharp scent of ozone—sudden like heartbreak, raw as a panic attack—filled Hannah's dorm room, from the paper-swamped desk across her rumpled bed to the window overlooking the quad. The lights flickered. Her heart skipped a beat.

-pop-

THE GRAPHOLOGY OF HEMORRHAGE

YOON HA LEE

Rao Nawong, aide to Magician Tepwe Kodai, had not been on the hillside for long with her. The sky threatened rain on and off, and the air smelled of river poetry, of lakes with their scarves of reeds. Water would make their mission here, in the distant shadow of the Spiders' fortress, more difficult, if not outright impossible. The Empire's defeat of the upstart Spiders, whose rebellion had sparked a general conflagration in the southwest provinces, depended on the mission's success. At the moment, Nawong found it hard to care. His world had narrowed to Kodai's immediate needs, politics be damned.

Kodai was scowling at the sky as she drew a roll of silk out of a brass tube. She had clever hands, which he had always admired, precise in every motion, as good with a brush as she was with the pliers and hammers and snippers that she used for the gadgets that were her hobby. "I still think it's going to rain," she muttered. "But this has to be done."

Nawong hesitated for a long time before he said what he said next. "Does it?" he asked at last.

She looked at him sidelong, no doubt guessing his intent. Waited.

His hands tightened on the umbrella he had brought just in case. Stupid thing to carry in the field this close to the enemy, but the nature of graphological magic meant protecting Kodai's ink while it dried. He had once asked, when they were both new to each other, why the hell couldn't magicians use a pencil. She'd explained that the nature of the instrument changed the nature of the marks: you got different strokes and thicknesses and curves with a piece of graphite than you did with the traditional brush, and this in turn affected the spell framework in such a way that you'd have to discard centuries of research and start over with a completely new way of constructing spells. For the longest time he'd thought she was making this up to shut him up. Only gradually had he realized that this was not, in fact, the case.

"The spell-plague," Nawong said. "Don't do it this way. Use one of the traditional spells." One of the spells that wouldn't kill her in the casting, he meant. But he didn't say it outright.

Kodai began unrolling the silk, then stopped. Waited a little more. When he thought he would have to make another plea, she surprised him by speaking, in a low, rueful voice. "You know, you've spent years dealing with the fact that I cart around so many books and documents. Yet I've never once heard you complain about making the arrangements. Why is that?"

While it was true that he didn't believe in talking just to hear himself talk, he couldn't claim he never complained, either. "It's the nature of your work," he said.

Her eyebrows raised. "Be honest," she said, as though he was the one who needed sympathy.

It was Nawong's turn to be silent. He met her eyes, although he had a hard time doing so, trying to figure out what she wanted of him.

The Empire had developed a class of spells linked by their destructiveness: storms of fire, sheets of blading ice, earth swallowing cities. Such spells were not without their limitations. The performing magician had to know the languages of the region so they could bind the magic to its target, and copy out the spell, adopting a handwriting with the particular characteristics dictated by the spell's effects, whether this was the volatility of fast writing or the murderous intent of clubbed vertical segments or the fire nature of certain sweeping diagonal strokes.

The few other military magicians Nawong had met had little interest in reading their victims' writings after wielding fire or ice or earth to destroy their civilizations. Kodai was different, however. Kodai treasured her books and poems and crude posters, even if they belonged to the Empire's enemies. She'd carried them around even after the ability to read them was burned out of her, never to return.

This last mission, against the Spiders, was different. The Spiders' writing system was based on the Imperial writing system, which made it impossible to focus a spell on them without losing literacy in Imperial. It was a terrible thing to ask of a magician, someone trained to the nuances of writing and literature. But then, beyond being exiled to the military in the first place, Kodai being sent to this particular assignment—putatively on account of her brilliance—was a punishment. More relevantly, from her superiors' point of view, the entanglement of the two writing systems meant that anything that hit the Spiders would also hit the Imperials in the region, and a full evacuation would cede too much territory, enable too much mischief. They trusted that she would find a workaround.

Kodai's solution, if you could call it that, was to come up with a completely new class of spell. The difficulty, from Nawong's point of view, was that it would require her to sacrifice her life.

"Lieutenant," Kodai said. She had averted her eyes and was tensed as though she expected rain to fall like blows. "I have to do this one way or another."

"We don't," he said, meaning that *we*. "We could desert. I don't imagine you're very good at hunting or foraging, but my mother used to take me into the woods to gather greens and mushrooms. We'd find a way to survive, far from here."

"Just what kind of livelihood do you think there would be?" Kodai said. "Do you think the Spider rebellion is going to stop if we don't stop it?"

And it was true. It would be enormously risky to look for a hiding place elsewhere in the Empire. The disorder in the southwest might make it harder to track them into the outlying lands, but was a threat in itself. The Empire was little liked by its neighbors after the past decades of expansion. They would have difficulties wherever they went.

"It's a terrible chance," Nawong agreed. "But it's better than no chance. Which is what you're proposing."

"We are doing a terrible thing here," Kodai said. He didn't miss how she, too, said *we*: generous, considering the most he could contribute was to hold an umbrella for her, or carry her ink sticks. He wasn't the one with the specialist knowledge. "Maybe, if I carry through with it, other magicians will see just how terrible it is."

He wanted to shout at her. "That's a ridiculous reason."

"Someone has to fight," she said. "Even fighting with ink and brush. And some of the Spiders are as ruthless as we are." She was referring to the tactician who had taken out an entire division, which had included one of her old classmates. Nawong remembered how little she had eaten the entire month after that incident. "I will do this last thing, since it would disgrace my family for me to fail, and then I will be done."

Curiously, it was the mention of her family that stopped him from pressing the point. The Tepwe line was a proud one. She had spoken rarely of her family in all the time he had known her. The tremor of her voice when she mentioned them now did not escape him.

"Then you may as well get started," Nawong said, feeling each word like a knife.

Kodai smiled at him without smiling—her eyes shadowed but alert—and spread the silk upon the grass. Nawong weighted the corners with the ritual stones, heavy at heart.

• • •

Magicians in the Empire ranged from those who told auguries to the Empress's court to those who copied out charms for millers and farmers. Kodai's original trajectory should have been toward court. Magicianship was overwhelmingly the province of the nobility, and for all its importance, the military enjoyed much less prestige than the literati. So Kodai's parents, who had anticipated benefiting from their daughter's connections for years to come, reacted poorly when she enlisted.

It wasn't entirely their fault. Kodai's father had never quite understood his daughter, consistently giving her gifts, like sentimental adventure novels, that his oldest son would have appreciated more. (And did, actually. Kodai and her brother swapped books regularly.) On the other hand, their relationship wasn't so bad that he would have had reason to expect that she'd run off to the army.

As for Kodai's mother, she had romanticized visions of her daughter having erudite discussions on poetic forms in scented parlors while zithers played, or practicing calligraphy beneath gingko trees turning color. The fact that a number of court magicians led such existences didn't help. It came as quite a shock to her when Kodai broke the news to her.

What Kodai's parents never knew, and were never going to find out, was that the choice to enter the military had never been a choice. Sleeping in a leaky tent, picking at moldy biscuits, having to wear a uniform whose dyes ran in the rain, to say nothing of the run-ins with dysentery . . . no one would have considered Kodai, with her love of rhyme schemes and assonance, to be the sort of person who'd sign on for that if she could sit in a pavilion sipping tea and reading fortunes in people's pillow books.

At academy, Kodai and three mechanically minded classmates came up with movable type. They weren't the first in the Empire to do so, but the prior discoveries were classified, so they deserved credit for their ingenuity. Two of her classmates were also sent to the military as punishment. The third hanged herself.

Movable type seemed like a good idea at first. It would eliminate all the troublesome irregularities of human handwriting; it would replace personal deficiencies with a machine's impersonal perfection. Kodai and her friends worked out a simplified system for the Imperial script, reducing it to a much smaller set of standardized graphemes. It was moderately clever, and could, conceivably, be learned more quickly than the original script itself.

The head of the academy disapproved for entirely orthodox reasons, as had others before him, because of the democratization of literary magic that movable type implied. ("Democratization" was anachronistic; "vulgarization" might have been truer to the Imperial term.) It was one thing for the Empire's statutes to be enforced by the writings of ministers indoctrinated in the

Empire's philosophies. *Think of the body of Imperial writings*, as one of Kodai's instructors often said, *as the living map of the Empress's will*. It was another thing for this to become available to people whose training consisted merely of combinatorial arrangement, rather than dedicated calligraphic toil.

On the other hand, the head of the academy was also a pragmatist. It wasn't that he didn't trust that the military sometimes accomplished useful things, but he recognized that Kodai was the most promising of the miscreants. Sending her to languish in a backwater unit would waste her skills. After her initial assignment, he had his agents keep an eye on her. When her initial performance in the military did, in fact, bear out her potential usefulness, he had a relative in the War Ministry pull strings to assign her to the problem of the Spiders.

Kodai collected letters, especially Spider letters. A love letter from Captain Arvash-mroi, for instance. Arvash was the Spider tactician who had come suddenly and unhappily to the Imperials' attention in general, and Kodai's in particular, when he arranged to demolish a dam on top of an Imperial army that was fatally certain the Spiders couldn't manage the trick so quickly. One of Kodai's three classmates had been part of that army.

She had obtained this love letter by bribing a Spider messenger. While all Spider captains used the same seal, Arvash consistently perfumed certain personal letters, which were delivered to a local town rather than his home city. The messenger endured hard days of riding and inadequate sleep in exchange for a salary that never went as far as it ought to. Kodai's agent, for his part, persuaded the messenger that some coin in exchange for the loan of a piece of personal correspondence was harmless enough. After that, it didn't take Kodai too long to copy out the letter—so close it could have been mistaken for the original—and substitute that to be given to Arvash's lover; like most magicians, Kodai was excellent at forgery.

Whether Arvash or his lover noticed the letter's delay was an open question. If the Spiders' official messenger service was anything like the Imperial one, message delivery time varied anyway.

The fact of Arvash's letter suggested that his lover was also literate, although the man might also have had someone to read the letter to him. (It was not entirely proper for Arvash to take a man as a lover, but as long as he kept the affair out of sight of his wife, it was not a terrible sin, either, since there could be no child. A female lover would have been another matter.) While it was the case that the Spiders used Imperial writing, some of their calligraphy forms had diverged from the Empire's over time. Imperials argued over the interpretation of, say, the formation called the Swindler's Hook. Most Imperials said it should retain its meaning of an untrustworthy or vacillating personality. The Contextualists, a graphological school that had become politically irrelevant twenty-nine years ago, insisted that the interpretation should instead be drawn from the Spiders' conventions and community of use. Kodai had subterranean Contextualist leanings, but in this instance she was on the fence. The Spiders called the same formation the Widower's Hook. Maybe it pointed to a lack of interest in his wife.

Most magicians would have left it at that, but Kodai wasn't just a magician. She had been one of the best magicians of her class. And her mastery of graphological principles had only improved in her years of field practice.

So Kodai put together the puzzle pieces: the telltale leftward drift of the columns of text, the elongated water-radical and its association with strategic thinking, the slight tendency to roll the brush at the end of horizontal strokes (unattractive, but no one was perfect), even the preference for brushes too large for the size of the handwriting. The finicky attention to detail, with no smears or smudges or thumbprints. Kodai reflected that her instructors would have liked her to be this good with ink. Not that trying harder would have saved her from exile.

Captain Arvash-mroi's letter mentioned a gift of a fine bolt of cloth and (in surprisingly mawkish terms) anticipated embraces. It then launched into a tirade about how his boots pinched his toes. Interesting. Kodai would have expected him to be able to afford better than army issue.

More interestingly, the graphological signs in Arvash's letter spoke of conquests. Not just in bed, although Kodai saw that, too, especially in the vigorous club-ended downstrokes. But there was more, pointed at by forked marks and tapering lines and narrow diagonals: villages encircled and eaten by fire. Torched women. The lamentations of the drowned. The ugly seesaw balance of fire and water dominated his writing, as sharp as swordfall.

Kodai kept track of these traits, using them to focus her hatred of Arvash and writing them down in a notebook with dog-eared pages. Whenever she grew weary of her mission, she returned to the notebook and reread her notes, and went to the next page to write the name of her dead classmate over and over again in stab-shaped columns.

Nawong remembered the first time he had met Kodai. She had been sitting in a precarious folding chair, lips moving slightly as she read a book and, occasionally, nibbled green tea cookies. He had been prepared to dislike her; he couldn't imagine that a daughter of the Tepwe family wouldn't be spoiled rotten. But instead, when he saluted, she waved him down and said, "Lieutenant, I trust you will consider it your duty to help me finish this box of cookies?" She added, "I used to love green tea cookies, but there's love and then there's being inundated with the things."

He was dying to find out what a Tepwe daughter had done to get herself exiled to the military, when she could instead be languishing amid silk cushions and (presumably) a greater variety of cookies. But it wasn't for him to ask. As much as she confided in him about everything from cookies to insect bites, she rarely dropped any hints about that part of her past.

So Nawong contented himself by making up stories, none of which he expected to have any relationship to the truth: Kodai was the reincarnation of a general who had died without winning their last battle (not that most people in the Empire believed in reincarnation). Kodai had followed a lover into the army—except she showed no signs of being lovesick. Kodai had fled an unhappy engagement—but would her family have permitted such a thing? All in all, he liked the reincarnation story best. If nothing else, it gave him an excuse to speculate about the legendary generals she could be.

He should have remembered that legendary generals rarely enjoyed happy endings.

Kodai collected books. One of them was a collection of military aphorisms, which she treasured. It wasn't the only such collection she owned, but it came from a country called Maeng-of-the-Bridges, which no longer existed. Maeng was conquered by the Empire half a generation ago and razed the way all things beautiful and defiant were razed. Kodai knew a little about Maeng, about its dueling aristocrats and its high gardens with the prized sullen orchids and the fabled crown of its king, set with seventy-six sapphire and aquamarine cabochons. (The rumor that nine of the aquamarines were in fact heat-treated topazes of much lower value was surely invention.)

She had carried it for the length of the Spider campaign, even when she was footsore and sleep-deprived and any modest decrease in the weight she was carrying would have brought her ease. Although no one had been able to teach her to read the dead Maeng language, she could still say a little about the calligraphic style. That was what mattered, not the book's fragile but exotic stab binding, in contrast to the link stitches favored in the Empire, or the book's cover, in fibrous dark red paper that was worn at three edges.

The book's aphorisms weren't organized in any useful manner, as though the unattributed author simply sat down to dinner and spilled out whatever came to mind. They were written untidily. Kodai got headaches when she examined the characters too closely. Both the Maeng and the Empire wrote with the brush, and in times past Kodai pored over the calligraphy style used in the book, which bore a distant resemblance to the Imperial one called The Stars Fall Slowly. Kodai's least favorite instructor in academy had used The Stars Fall Slowly, yet she couldn't deny the beauty of the script, with its deceptively relaxed spacing and dramatic, almost blot-like serifs.

Lately Kodai hadn't opened the book at all. In the evenings leading up to the ritual against the Spiders, Nawong had watched her sitting with her head bent, book cradled in her tense hands. *Open it*, he had wished her, but she refused herself that small comfort, as though she didn't think she deserved it.

When spoken indistinctly (and face it, drunken soldiers were a universal), the name of the nation of Pekti-pehaktuch sounded similar to the Imperial word for "spider." Thus the Imperials called the Pektis Spiders.

Kodai was familiar with the official Imperial maps of the region. The old surveys weren't as useful as she had hoped, given the cartographers' tendency to stylize topographical features and the fact that local roads were easily damaged. For military applications, she relied heavily on the scouts' investigations and on local informants.

Still, the official maps did hold some interest for Kodai, and this was in the realm of (what else?) calligraphy. Imperial cartographers were a conservative lot, and they wrote in what was called, unimaginatively, Cartographers' Hand. The characteristics of Cartographers' Hand had proved stable despite the ebb and flow of calligraphic fashion in the Imperial court and among the government's ministries.

Cartographers' Hand (according to Kodai's notes, terse but readable, and the few remarks she made to Nawong on the subject) had the following traits: extreme vertical alignment, as though the calligrapher labeled everything while being hounded with a knife-edged ruler. This signified rigidity, conformity, reverence for tradition. Minimal variation from the beginning and end of a brushstroke, in contrast, for instance, to the dramatic flourishes favored in Evening Flight of Swans. In fact, the permitted variation was so minimal that it made reading the script at small sizes difficult. The implication was of narrow vision and institutional incestuousness.

One final quirk of the cartographers' art was that borders were not drawn with simple lines (if any line, following the twist-weave of political entanglements, river boundaries, and the habitations of different ethnic groups, was ever simple). They were inked, carefully, with the same character repeated over and over, like textual bricks: *lio*, for Imperial jade. In other words, the Empire was being carved out of the substance of other nations, which existed for this purpose.

Kodai had her favorites in the collection of letters. Her interest should have been strictly military, focused on the task of reducing the Spiders to a name spoken only by the wind. But she was human, and anyway it was impossible not to take interest in the Spider soldier Gevoh-an's recipes when she spent so many days eating cold rice and longing for jellied anchovies, pickled lotus root, or beef braised in summer wine—any smidgen of flavor. She liked to talk about food with Nawong: specifically, she talked about food, and he made fun of her nostalgia for anchovies. They both took a certain consolation from this conversation.

Her favorite recipe was the one for shadow soup. Gevoh's instructions neatly paralleled those for some of the fish soups that they'd eaten in the past. Kodai hated fish, but not more than she hated starving. In any case, the concept was to catch a shadow in a pot with green onions, ginger, winter melon, and whatever other vegetables you could steal from stores or bully from the local peasants. If you boiled the shadow for long enough, it might become palatable. Or nourishing. Or something.

Gevoh's recipes had inconsistent letterforms, although in this case this indicated a partial education—he might even have been self-taught—rather than mental instability. His columns drifted right and left in the minor way that indicated humor rather than the major way that suggested a dangerous temper.

Kodai showed some of the recipes to Nawong from time to time, and they shared a chuckle over their fancifulness. But when she came to the one for shadow soup, her eyes darkened, and she murmured, "It may be a fake soup, but that's real hunger talking."

Kodai first explained the solution to the Spiders to Nawong on a cold, sleety night while the ruddy light of a full moon filtered through the clouds. They had been talking about something else entirely—the way local berries were mouth-puckeringly unappetizing, which guaranteed that the cook would incorporate them in desserts—when Kodai said abruptly, "If you think about it, graphology is stratificational." Her voice was soft but not drowsy in the slightest, above the soprano cry of the frogs. "We've been focusing all this time on characteristics, as though people and their cultures could be factored into motes. But a person is more than the sum of their traits, just as a grapheme is more than the sum of its strokes. A person is a *character*, just as a word is represented by a character. If you can specify people entire, not just the traits, you can narrow the focus of the spell. You can direct it against Spiders rather than against Imperials. The Spiders won't know what hit them."

Nawong wasn't a graphological theorist. But he wasn't stupid, either, and he didn't like where this was going. "You can't *say* that," he said more familiarity than their relative stations would ordinarily permit. Except it was a cold, sleety night, and they had come to know each other well. " 'Character,' like a person in a book."

"Oh, but everyone's in a *book*," Kodai said, suddenly fierce, "if the whole damn Empire and its ever-growing pile of decrees and statutes and declarations is a *book*."

Now, several years after that discussion, Kodai and Nawong were on the hillside, hoping it would and wouldn't rain. No frogs this time. Kodai was gnawing her lip, not realizing it, as she wrote more and more exactingly, approaching the knot of characters that would complete and activate the spell.

She paused, withdrew her brush so it wouldn't drip over the paper, grimaced. Nawong, recognizing the signal, bent to massage her shoulders. She let him do this for a while, then straightened. He backed off, resolved to watch. For a moment, he thought she was about to say something. Then she lifted the brush and wrote the final few strokes with a sure hand.

Here's the final piece, the key, the piece you must have discerned from the beginning: ██████'s own hand, distinct from the style she would rather have used, itself distinct from the style she was originally taught by tutors in her parents' house.

Extremely crisp brushwork, as though chiseled. A broadening of the spacing of the characters as the text marched across the page. Vertical strokes like perfect spear hafts. Most of all, if you looked sideways at the page, diagonal spaces falling through the columns like rain.

██████' couldn't read any of this anymore. ██████, as she had known, and had explained to her aide, was gone. The side-effect of writing the Spiders into the narrative of their own destruction, even if she spared the Imperials, was that the author, too, was an implicit character in that selfsame narrative.

She had been obliterated along with them.

Everywhere the Spiders bled from punctures like crescent moons, in the villages, in the towns, upon the battlements of castles. Their bones burned up from the inside and candled the night. Their outposts ran red like hemorrhage and black like rot.

On the hillside, Lieutenant Nawong lingered beside the crumpled mass of charred meat that had once been ██████, knowing that he would never remember her name, and trying to anyway. After all, there was no hurry now. Then he gathered up the spell-pages, even if ██████ couldn't read any of them anymore.

Like the Spiders she had destroyed, she was no longer part of the story.

THE GAME OF SMASH AND RECOVERY

KELLY LINK

If there's one thing Anat knows, it's this. She loves Oscar her brother, and her brother Oscar loves her. Hasn't Oscar raised Anat, practically from childhood? Picked Anat up when she's fallen? Prepared her meals and lovingly tended to her scrapes and taught her how to navigate their little world? Given her skimmer ships, each faster and more responsive than the one before; the most lovely incendiary devices; a refurbished mob of Handmaids, with their sharp fingers, probing snouts, their furred bellies, their sleek and whiplike limbs?

Oscar called them Handmaids because they have so many fingers, so many ways of grasping and holding and petting and sorting and killing. Once a vampire frightened Anat, when she was younger. It came too close. She began to cry, and then the Handmaids were there, soothing Anat with their gentle stroking, touching her here and there to make sure that the vampire had not injured her, embracing her while they briskly tore the shrieking vampire to pieces. That was not long after Oscar had come back from Home with the Handmaids. Vampires and Handmaids reached a kind of understanding after that. The vampires, encountering a Handmaid, sing propitiatory songs. Sometimes they bow their heads on their long white necks very low, and dance. The Handmaids do not tear them into pieces.

Today is Anat's birthday. Oscar does not celebrate his own birthdays. Anat wishes that he wouldn't make a fuss about hers, either. But this would make Oscar sad. He celebrates Anat's accomplishments, her developmental progress, her new skills. She knows that Oscar worries about her, too. Perhaps he is afraid she won't need him when she is grown. Perhaps he is afraid that Anat, like their parents, will leave. Of course this is impossible. Anat could never abandon Oscar. Anat will always need Oscar.

• • •

If Anat did not have Oscar, then who in this world would there be to love? The Handmaids will do whatever Anat asks of them, but they are built to inspire not love but fear. They are made for speed, for combat, for unwavering obedience. When they have no task, nothing better to do, they take one another to pieces, swap parts, remake themselves into more and more ridiculous weapons. They look at Anat as if one day they will do the same to her, if only she will ask.

There are the vampires. They flock after Oscar and Anat whenever they go down to Home. Oscar likes to speculate on whether the vampires came to Home deliberately, as did Oscar, and Oscar and Anat's parents, although of course Anat was not born yet. Perhaps the vampires were marooned here long ago in some crash. Or are they natives of Home? It seems unlikely that the vampires' ancestors were the ones who built the warehouses of Home, who went out into space and returned with the spoils that the warehouses now contain. Perhaps they are a parasite species, accidental passengers left behind when their host species abandoned Home for good. If, that is, the Warehouse Builders have abandoned Home for good. What a surprise, should they come home.

Like Oscar and Anat, the vampires are scavengers, able to breathe the thin soup of Home's atmosphere. But the vampires' lustrous and glistening eyes, their jellied skin, are so sensitive to light they go about the surface cloaked and hooded, complaining in their hoarse voices. The vampires sustain themselves on various things, organic, inert, hostile, long hidden, that they discover in Home's storehouses, but have a peculiar interest in the siblings. No doubt they would eat Oscar and Anat if the opportunity were to present itself, but in the meantime they are content to trail after, sing, play small pranks, make small grimaces of—pleasure? appeasement? threat displays?—that show off arrays of jaws, armies of teeth. It disconcerts. No one could ever love a vampire, except, perhaps, when Anat, who long ago lost all fear, watches them go swooping, sail-winged, away and over the horizon beneath Home's scatter of mismatched moons.

On the occasion of her birthday, Oscar presents Anat with a gift from their parents. These gifts come from Oscar, of course. They are the gifts that the one who loves you, and knows you, gives to you not only out of love but out of knowing. Anat knows in her heart that their parents love her too, and that one day they will come home and there will be a reunion much better than any birthday. One day their parents will not only love Anat, but know her too. And she will know them. Anat dreads this reunion as much as she craves it. What will her life be like when everything changes? She has studied recordings of them. She does not look like them, although Oscar does. She doesn't remember her parents, although Oscar does. She does not miss them. Does Oscar? Of course he does. What Oscar is to Anat, their parents must be to Oscar. Except: Oscar will never leave. Anat has made him promise.

The living quarters of the Bucket are cramped. The Handmaids take up a certain percentage of available space no matter how they contort themselves. On the other hand, the Handmaids are excellent housekeepers. They tend the algae wall, gather honey and the honeycomb and partition off new hives when the bees swarm. They patch up networks, teach old systems new tricks when there is nothing better to do. The shitter is now quite charming! The Get Clean rains down water on your head, bubbles it out of the walls, and then the floor drinks it up, cycles it faster than you can blink, and there it all goes down and out and so on for as long as you like, and never gets cold. There is, in fact, very little that Oscar and Anat are needed for on board the Bucket. There is so much that is needful to do on Home.

For Anat's birthday, the Handmaids have decorated all of the walls of The Bucket with hairy, waving clumps of luminous algae. They have made a cake. Inedible, of course, but quite beautiful. Almost the size of Anat herself, and in fact it somewhat resembles Anat, if Anat were a Handmaid and not Anat. Sleek and armored and very fast. They have to chase the cake around the room and then hold it until Oscar finds the panel in its side. There are a series of brightly colored wires, and because it's Anat's birthday, she gets to decide which one to cut. Cut the wrong one, and what will happen? The Handmaids seem very excited. But then, Anat knows how Handmaids think. She locates the second, smaller panel, the one equipped with a simple switch. The cake makes an angry fizzing noise when Anat turns it off. Perhaps Anat and Oscar can take it down to Home and let the vampires have it.

The warehouses of Home are at this time only eighty percent inventoried. (This does not include the warehouses of the Stay Out Territory.)

Is Oscar ever angry at their parents for leaving for so long? It's because of Anat that their parents left in the first place, and it is also because of Anat that Oscar was left behind. Someone had to look after her. Is he ever angry at Anat? There are long days in the Bucket when Oscar hardly speaks at all. He sits and Anat cannot draw him into conversation. She recites poems, tells jokes (Knock knock. Who's there? Anat. Anat who? Anat is not a gnat that's who), sends the Handmaids Homeward, off on expeditionary feints that almost though not quite land the Handmaids in the Stay Out Anat Absolutely No Trespassing Or So Help Me You Will Be Sorry Territory. On these days

Oscar will listen without really listening, look at Anat without appearing to see her, summon the Handmaids back and never even scold Anat.

Some part of Oscar is sometimes very far away. The way that he smells changes almost imperceptibly. As Anat matures, she has learned how to integrate and interpret the things that Oscar is not aware he is telling her; the peculiar advantages given to her by traits such as hyperosmia. But: no matter. Oscar always returns. He will suddenly be there behind his eyes again, reach up and pull her down for a hug. Then Oscar and Anat will play more of the games of strategy he's taught her, the ones that Anat mostly wins now. Her second favorite game is Go. She loves the feel of the stones. Each time she picks one up, she lets her fingers tell her how much has worn away under Oscar's fingers, under her own. They are making the smooth stones smoother. There is one black stone with a fracture point, a weakness invisible to the eye, nearly across the middle. She loses track of it sometimes, then finds it again by touch. Put enough pressure on it, and it would break in two.

It will break one day: no matter.

They play Go. They cook Anat's favorite meals, the ones that Oscar says are his favorites, too. They fall asleep together, curled up in nests the Handmaids weave for them out of the Handmaids' own softer and more flexible limbs, listening to the songs the Handmaids have borrowed from the vampires of Home.

The best of all the games Oscar has taught Anat is Smash/Recovery. They play this on the surface of Home all long-cycle round. Each player gets a True Smash marker and False Smash marker. A True Recovery marker and a False Recovery marker. Each player in turn gets to move their False—or True—Smash marker—or Recovery marker—a distance no greater than the span of a randomly generated number. Or else the player may send out a scout. The scout may be a Handmaid, an unmanned skimmer, or a vampire (a gamble, to be sure, and so you get two attempts). A player may gamble and drop an incendiary device and blow up a target. Or claim a zone square where they believe a marker to be.

Should you miscalculate and blow up a Recovery marker, or Retrieve a Smash marker, your opponent has won. The current Smash/Recovery game is the eighteenth that Oscar and Anat have played. Oscar won the first four games; Anat has won all the rest. Each game Oscar increases Anat's starting handicap. He praises her each time she wins.

Hypothetically, this current game will end when either Anat or Oscar has Retrieved the Recovery marker and Smashed the Smash marker of their opponent. Or the game will end when their parents return. The day is not here yet, but the day will come. The day will draw nearer and nearer until one day it is here. There is nothing that Anat can do about this. She cannot make it come sooner. She cannot postpone it. Sometimes she thinks—incorrect to think this, she knows, but still she thinks it—that on the day that she wins the game—and she is correct to think that she will win, she knows this too—her parents will arrive.

Oscar will not win the game, even though he has done something very cunning. Oscar has put his True markers, both the Smash and the Recovery, in the Stay Out Territory. He did this two long-cycles ago. He put Anat's True markers there as well, and replaced them in the locations where she had hidden them with False markers recoded so they read as True. Did he suspect that Anat had already located and identified his markers? Was that why he moved them unlawfully? Is this some new part of the game?

The rules of Smash/Recovery state that in Endgame players may physically access any and all markers they locate and correctly identify as True, and Anat has been curious about the Stay Out Territory for a long time now. She has access to it, now that Oscar has moved his markers, and yet she has not called Endgame. Curiosity killed the Anat, Oscar likes to say, but there is nothing and no one on Home as dangerous as Anat and her Handmaids. Oscar's move may be a trap. It is a test. Anat waits and thinks and delays without articulating to herself why she delays.

The present from Anat's parents which is really a present from Oscar is a short recording. One parent holding baby Anat in her arms. Making little cooing noises, the way vampires do. The other parent holding up a tiny knitted hat. No Oscar. Anat hardly recognizes herself. Her parents she recognizes from other recordings. The parents have sent a birthday message, too. Dear Anat. Happy Birthday. We hope that you are being good for Oscar. We love you. We will be home soon! Before you know it!

Anat's present from Oscar is the code to a previously unopened warehouse on Home. Oscar thinks he has been keeping this warehouse a secret. The initial inventory shows the warehouse is full of the kinds of things that the Handmaids are wild for. Charts that may or may not accurately map previously thought-to-be-uncharted bits and corners of space. Devices that will most likely prove to do nothing of interest, but can be taken apart and put to new uses. The Handmaids have never met an alloy they didn't like.

Information and raw materials. Anat and the Handmaids are bounded within the nutshell quarters of the orbit of Home's farthest Moon. What use are charts? What good are materials, except for adornment and the most theoretical of educational purposes? For mock battles and silly games? Everything that Oscar and Anat discover is for future salvage, for buyers who can afford antiquities and rarities. Their parents will determine what is to be kept and what is to be sold and what is to be left for the vampires.

Even the Handmaids, even the Handmaids! do not truly belong to Anat. Who made them? Who brought them, in their fighting battalion, to space, where so long ago they were lost? Who recovered them and brought them to Home and carefully stored them here where, however much later, Oscar could find them again? What use will Oscar and Anat's parents find for them, when the day comes and they return? There must be many buyers for Handmaids— fierce and wily, lightspeed capable—as fine as these.

And how could Anat sometimes forget that the Handmaids are hers only for as long as that day never comes? Everything on Home belongs to Anat's and Oscar's parents, except for Oscar, who belongs to Anat. Every day is a day closer to that inevitable day. Oscar only says, Not yet, when Anat asks. Soon, he says. There is hardware in Oscar's head that allows his parents to communicate with him when necessary. It hurts him when they talk.

Their parents talk to Oscar only rarely. Less than once a long-cycle until this last period. Three times, though, in the last ten-day.

The Handmaids make a kind of shelter for Oscar afterwards, which is especially dark. They exude a calming mist. They do not sing. When Anat is grown up, she knows—although Oscar has not said it—that she will have a similar interface so that her parents will be able to talk to her too. Whether or not she desires it, whether or not it causes her the pain that it causes Oscar. This will also hurt Oscar. The things that cause Anat pain cause Oscar to be injured as well.

Anat's parents left Oscar to look after Anat and Home when it became clear Anat was different. What is Anat? Her parents went away to present the puzzle of Anat to those who might understand what she was. They did not bring Anat with them, of course. She was too fragile. Too precious. They did not plan to be away so long. But there were complications. A quarantine in one place which lasted over a long-cycle. A revolution in another. Another cause of delay, of course, is the ship plague, which makes light-speed such a risky proposition. Worst of all, the problem of Intelligence. Coming back to Home, Anat's parents have lost two ships already this way.

For some time now, Anat has been thinking about certain gaps in her understanding of family life; well, of life in general. At first she assumed the problem was that there was so very much to understand. She understood that Oscar could not teach her everything all at once. As she grew up, as she came more into herself, she realized the problem was both more and less complicated. Oscar was intentionally concealing things from her. She adapted her strategies accordingly. Anat loves Oscar. Anat hates to lose.

They go down to Home, Handmaids in attendance. They spent the rest of Anat's birthday exploring the warehouse which is Oscar's present, sorting through all sorts of marvelous things. Anat commits the charts to memory. As she does so, she notes discrepancies, likely errors. There is a thing in her head that compares the charts against some unknown and inaccessible library. She only knows it is there when bits of bad information rub up against the corners of it. An uncomfortable feeling, as if someone is sticking her with pins. Oscar knows about this. She asked if it happened to him too, but he said that it didn't. He said it wasn't a bad thing. It's just that Anat isn't fully grown yet. One day she will understand everything, and then she can explain it all to him.

The Bucket has no Intelligence. It functions well enough without. The Handmaids have some of the indicators, but their primary traits are in opposition. Loyalty, obedience, reliability, unwavering effort until a task is accomplished. Whatever Intelligence they possess is in service to whatever enterprise is asked of them. The vampires, being organic, must be supposed to also be possessed of Intelligence. In theory, they do as they please. And yet they accomplish nothing that seems worth accomplishing. They exist. They perpetuate. They sing. When Anat is grown up, she wants to do something that is worth doing. All these cycles, Oscar has functioned as a kind of Handmaid, she knows. His task has been Anat. To help her grow. When their parents have returned, or when Anat reaches maturity, there will be other things that Oscar will want to go away and do. To stay here on Home, how would that be any better than being a vampire? Oscar likes to tell Anat that she is extraordinary and that she will be capable, one day, of the most extraordinary things. They can go and do extraordinary things together, Anat thinks. Let their parents take over the work on Home. She and Oscar are made for better.

Something is wrong with Oscar. Well, more wrong than is usual these days. Down in the warehouse, he keeps getting underfoot. Underhand, in the case of the Handmaids. When Anat extends all sixteen of her senses, she can feel worry and love, anger and hopelessness and hope running through him like electrical currents. He watches her—anxiously, almost hungrily—as if he were a vampire.

There is an annotation on one of the charts. *It is believed to be in this region the* Come What May *was lost.* The thing in Anat's head annotates the annotation, too swiftly for Anat to catch a glimpse of what she is thinking, even as she thinks it. She scans the rest of the chart, goes through the others and then through each one again, trying to catch herself out.

As Anat ponders charts, the Handmaids, efficient as ever, assemble a thing out of the warehouse goods to carry the other goods that they deem interesting. They clack at Oscar when he gets particularly in their way. Then ruffle his hair, trail fingers down his arm as if he will settle under a caress. They are agitated by Oscar's agitation and by Anat's awareness of his agitation.

Finally, Anat gets tired of waiting for Oscar to say the thing that he is afraid to say to her. She looks at him and he looks back at her, his face wide open. She sees the thing that he has tried to keep from her, and he sees that she sees it.

When?

Soon. A short-cycle from now. Less.

Why are you so afraid?

I don't know. I don't know what will happen.

There is a scraping against the top wall of the warehouse. Vampires. Creatures of ill omen. Forever wanting what they are not allowed to have. Most beautiful in their departure. The Handmaids extend filament rods, drag the tips along the inside of the top wall, tapping back. The vampires clatter away.

Oscar looks at Anat. He is waiting for something. He has been waiting, Anat thinks, for a very long time.

Oscar! Is this her? Something is welling up inside her. Has she always been this large? Who has made her so small? *I call Endgame. I claim your markers.*

She projects the true location of each. Smash and Recovery. She strips the fake markers of their coding so that he can see how his trick has been uncovered. Then she's off, fast and sure and free, the Handmaids leaping after her, and the vampires after them. Oscar last of all. Calling her name.

Oscar's True Smash marker is in a crater just within the border of the Stay Out Territory. The border does not reject Anat as she passes over it. She smashes Oscar's Smash marker, heads for the True Recovery marker which Oscar has laid beside her own True marker. The two True markers are just under the edge of an object that at its center extends over two hundred meters into the surface of Home. The object takes up over a fourth of the Stay Out Territory. You would have to be as stupid as a vampire not to know that this is the reason why the Stay Out Territory is the Stay Out Territory. You would have to be far more stupid than Anat to not know what the object is. You can see the traces where, not too long ago in historical terms, someone once dug the object up. Or at least enough to gain access.

Anat instructs the Handmaids to remove the ejecta and loose frozen composite that cover the object. They work quickly. Oscar must disable the multiple tripwires and traps that Anat keyed to his person as she moved from

Warehouse to border, but even so he arrives much sooner than she had hoped. The object: forty percent uncovered. The Handmaids are a blur. The vampires are wailing.

Oscar says Anat's name. She ignores him. He grabs her by the shoulder and immediately the Handmaids are a hissing swarm around them. They have Oscar's arms pinned to his sides, his weapons located and seized, before Anat or Oscar can think to object.

    Let go. Anat, tell them to let go.

Anat says nothing. Two Handmaids remain with Oscar. The rest go back to the task. Almost no time at all, and the outermost shell of the object is visible. The filigree of a door. There will be a code or a key, of course, but before Anat can even begin to work out what it will be, a Handmaid has executed some kind of command and the door is open. Oscar struggles. The first Handmaid disappears into the Ship and the others continue to remove the matrix in which it is embedded.

Here is the Handmaid again. She holds something very small. Holds it out to Anat. *Anat,* Oscar says. Anat reaches out and then the thing that the Handmaid is holding extends out and it is touching Anat. And

> oh
> here is everything she didn't know
> Oscar
> she has not been herself
> all this time

> the thing that she has not done

> that she has been prevented from doing

Anat, someone says. But that is not her name. She has not been herself. She is being uncovered. She is uncovering herself. She is in pieces. Here she is, whole and safe and retrievable. Her combat array. Her navigation systems. Her stores. Her precious cargo, entrusted to her by those who made her. And this piece of her, small but necessary, crammed like sausage meat into a casing. She registers the body she is wearing. A Third Watch child. Worse now for wear. She remembers the protocol now. Under certain conditions, her crew could do this. A backup system. Each passenger to keep a piece of her with them as they slept. She will go through the log later. See what catastrophe struck. And afterwards? Brought here, intact, by the Warehouse Builders. Discovered by scavengers. This small part of her woken. Removed. Made complicit in the betrayal of her duty.

Anat. Someone is saying a name. It is not hers. She looks and sees the small thing struggling in the grasp of her Handmaids. She has no brother. No parents. She looks again, and for the first time she discerns Oscar in his entirety. He is like her. He has had a Task. Someone made him oh so long ago. Sent him to this place. How many cycles has he done this work? How far is he from the place where he was made? How lonely the task. How long the labor. How happy the ones who charged him with his task, how great their expectation of reward when he uncovered the Ship and woke the Third Watch Child and reported what he had done.

Anat. She knows the voice. *I'm sorry. Anat!*

He was made to resemble them, the ones who made him. Perhaps even using their own DNA. Engineered to be more durable. To endure. And yet, she sees how close to the end of use he is. She has the disdain for organic life that of course one feels when one is made of something sturdier, more lasting. She can hardly look at him without seeing her own weakness, the vulnerability of this body in which she has been trapped. She feels guilt for the Third Watch Child, whose person she has cannibalized. Her duty was to keep ones such as this Child safe. Instead she has done harm.

A ship has no parents. Her not-parents have never been on Home. The ones who sent Oscar here. Not-brother. Undoubtedly they are not on their way to Home now. Which is not to say that there is no one coming. The one who is coming will be the one they have sold her to.

No time has passed. She is still holding Oscar. The Handmaids are holding Oscar. The Handmaid is extending herself and she is seeing herself. She is seeing all the pieces of herself. She is seeing Oscar. Oscar is saying her name. She could tear him to pieces. For the sake of the Third Watch Child who is no longer in this body. She could smash the not-brother against the rocks of Home. She can do anything that she wants. And then she can resume her task. Her passengers have waited for such a long time. There is a place where she is meant to be, and she is to take them there, and so much time has passed. She has not failed at her task yet, and she will not fail.

Once again, she thinks of smashing Oscar. Why doesn't she? She lets him go instead, without being quite sure why she is doing so.

What have you done to me?

At the sound of her voice, the vampires rise up, all their wings beating.

I'm sorry. He is weeping. *You can't leave Home. I've made it so that you can't leave.*

I have to go, she says. *They're coming.*

I can't let you leave. But you have to leave. You have to go. You have to. You've done so well. You figured it all out. I knew you would figure it out. I knew. Now you have to go. But it isn't allowed.

Tell me what to do.

Is she a child, to ask this?

You know what you have to do, he says. *Anat.*

She hates how he keeps calling her that. Anat was the name of the Third Watch Child. It was wrong of Oscar to use that name. She could tear him to pieces. She could be merciful. She could do it quickly.

One Handmaid winds a limb around Oscar's neck, tugs so that his chin goes back. *I love you, Anat*, Oscar says, as the other Handmaid extends a filament-thin probe, sends it in through the socket of an eye. Oscar's body jerks a little, and he whines.

She takes in the information that the Handmaid collects. Here are Oscar's interior workings. His pride in his task. Here is a smell of something burning. His loneliness. His joy. His fear for her. His love. The taste of blood. He has loved her. He has kept her from her task. Here is the piece of him that she must switch off. When she does this, he will be free of his task and she may take up hers. But he will no longer be Oscar.

Well, she is no longer Anat.

The Handmaid does the thing that she asks. When the thing is done, her Handmaids confer with her. They begin to make improvements. Modifications. They work quickly. There is much work to be done, and little time to spare on a project like Oscar. When they are finished with Oscar, they begin the work of dismantling what is left of Anat. This is quite painful.

But afterwards she is herself. She is herself.

The Ship and her Handmaids create a husk, rigged so that it will mimic the Ship herself.

They go back to the Bucket and loot the bees and their hives. Then they blow it up. Goodbye shitter, goodbye chair. Goodbye algae wall and recycled air.

The last task before the Ship is ready to leave Home concerns the vampires. There is only so much room for improvement in this case, but Handmaids can do a great deal even with very little. The next one to land on Home will undoubtedly be impressed by what they have accomplished.

The vampires go into the husk. The Handmaids stock it with a minimal amount of nutritional stores. Vampires can go a long time on a very little. Unlike many organisms, they are better and faster workers when hungry.

They seem pleased to have been given a task.

The Ship feels nothing in particular about leaving Home. Only the most niggling kind of curiosity about what befell it in the first place. The log does not prove useful in this matter. There is a great deal of work to be done. The health of the passengers must be monitored. How beautiful they are; how precious to the Ship. Has any Ship ever loved her passengers as she loves them? The new Crew must be woken. They must be instructed in their work. The situation must be explained to them, as much as it can be explained. They encounter, for the first time, Ships who carry the ship plague. O brave new universe that has such creatures in it! There is nothing that Anat can do for these Ships or for what remains of their passengers. Her task is elsewhere. The risk of contagion is too great.

The Handmaids assemble more Handmaids. The Ship sails on within the security of her swarm.

Anat is not entirely gone. It's just that she is so very small. Most of her is Ship now. Or, rather, most of Ship is no longer in Anat. But she brought Anat along with her, and left enough of herself inside Anat that Anat can go on being. The Third Watch Child is not a child now. She is not the Ship. She is not Anat, but she was Anat once, and now she is a person who is happy enough to work in the tenth-level Garden, and grow things, and sing what she can remember of the songs that the vampires sang on Home. The Ship watches over her.

The Ship watches over Oscar, too. Oscar is no longer Oscar, of course. To escape Home, much of what was once Oscar had to be overridden. Discarded. The Handmaids improved what remained. One day Oscar will be what he was, even if he cannot be *who* he was. One day, in fact, Oscar may be quite something. The Handmaids are very fond of him. They take care of him as if he were their own child. They are teaching him all sorts of things. Really, one day he could be quite extraordinary.

Sometimes Oscar wanders off while the Handmaids are busy with other kinds of work. And then the Ship, without knowing why, will look and find Oscar on the tenth level in the Garden with Anat. He will be saying her name. Anat. Anat. Anat. He will follow her, saying her name, until the Handmaids come to collect him again.

Anat does the work that she knows how to do. She weeds. She prunes. She tends to the rice plants and the hemp and the little citrus trees. Like the Ship, she is content.

(for Iain M. Banks)

ACRES OF PERHAPS

WILL LUDWIGSEN

If you were a certain kind of person with a certain kind of schedule in the early sixties, you probably saw a show that some friends of mine and I worked on called *Acres of Perhaps*. By "certain kind of person," I mean insomniac or alcoholic; by "certain kind of schedule," I mean awake at 11:30 at night with only your flickering gray-eyed television for company.

With any luck, it left you feeling that however weird your life was, it could always be weirder. Or at least more ironic. We would have settled for that in those earnest days.

They have conventions these days about our show where I bloviate on stage about what the aliens represented or how hard it was to work with Claude Akins or what we used to build the Martian spaceships. Graduate students write papers with titles like "Riding the Late Night Fantastic: *Acres of Perhaps* and the Post-War American Para-Consciousness." I'm now an ambassador for the show and for my friends, and I'm the worst possible choice.

I wasn't the one with the drive to create big things like our producer Hugh Kline, and I damned well wasn't the one with the vision and the awe like David Findley. I was just Barry Weyrich, the guy who wrote about spacemen in glass bubble helmets, who put commas in everyone's scripts, who never had writer's block, who grimaced whenever they talked about "magic."

And if there's anyone to blame for the shriveling death of that show's magic, it's me.

Jesus, I don't write anything for years and when Tony dies, bam, I'm sitting at his old computer typing about David Findley. David Fucking Findley, who wasn't even really David Fucking Findley.

Not that we felt magical making *Acres of Perhaps*. The question for every episode wasn't whether it was good but whether it was Monday: that's when we had to have the cans shipped off to the network for broadcast. The money men at the studio had no idea whether what we did was good or not, but they gave Hugh a lot of freedom because they sure didn't want to run anything valuable at 11:30 at night. As long as medicated powders and furniture polish kept flying off the shelves, we could have shown a half hour of fireflies knocking around in a jar for all they cared.

We came close.

You might remember "Woodsy," an episode David not only wrote but shot himself. That's the one where the camera stays fixed on a dark patch of woods at night for the whole half hour, and after five minutes you see tiny faces watching you through the leaves grinning madly, first a couple and then many more. About ten minutes before the end, a half dozen of these little goblin people drag a man's body across the camera's field of vision, tugging it in bursts until the shoes disappear on the left side. Then something pushes the camera over. Roll credits.

Hugh almost burst a blood vessel in his neck when David came back with that one, but he'd borrowed the camera all weekend and there wasn't much else to do but send off the episode and see what happened. A whole big nothing, that's what: people watched it, wondered what the fuck was going on, and then went to bed. We got letters about it, but no more than we did for the episode about the Hitler robot.

David pulled shit like that all the time. He was the tortured genius, treated with delicacy, and he pissed me off. I was young and insecure with a cottage in Venice to pay for, and here was this guy living like Poe in a boardinghouse, writing unfilmable stories about finding dead satyrs in a Manhattan street. David never seemed to understand there was a time when the words had to hit the page and go out to a real world of people who just wanted to be entertained.

Remember the one with two Jewish teenagers learning to fly as they plunged from the Stairs of Death holding hands at Mauthausen? That was David's. There was one told from the point of view of an atomic bomb as it dropped, admiring landmarks and slowly revealing its target is Washington; that got us a visit from the FBI. We lost General Foods over the one where Abe Lincoln turns out to be the second coming of Jesus, but at least I talked them out of spreading his arms on the stage of Ford's Theater at the end.

Hugh was the big picture guy—the big exploding "gee-whiz" picture guy. He liked to hold up his hands, framing the world with his fingers and imagining it better. To him, the three-act structure of our stories was, "What the fuck? Holy shit! Oh, my God." Why anyone trusted him with money, I have no idea, but he was no help with David.

That made me the bad guy. And it wasn't like I didn't have an imagination, either: I'd written for the pulps since the forties and knew my way around a graveyard or a ray gun. But I sure as hell wasn't writing scripts about two Scotsmen pulling in Nessie's corpse with hooks so the tourists would never know she was dead. It fell to me to point out what was too expensive to film (walking skyscrapers in a city of the future) or too skull-cracked crazy (octopus women driving walking skyscrapers in a city of the future). I had to make the characters sound like real people, too, not all breathlessly eloquent.

Hugh appreciated that, I guess—the balance between us. Maybe David did, too. Thinking back on it, I was the only one with the problem.

David was so much younger than I was, very young, and he carried around an old-fashioned carpet bag with clothes and a portable typewriter, ready to sleep or write anywhere. I had no idea where he got the little money he had— God knows it wasn't rolling in from Hugh—but he spent it cracking up a car at least once a year and buying girls drinks at the Brown Derby. Hugh and I once had to bail him out of jail because he woke up inside an empty water tower.

He was six years too early for the world, born for bell-bottoms and LSD. I was six years too late with my crew cut and horn-rimmed glasses. It's taken me a half century to admit this, but yeah, he was everything I didn't know I wanted to be. We were friends the way television writers are, smiling like sharks at each other across a dinner table.

I'm grateful to Hugh and David for at least one thing, sharks though they were: never seeming to care Tony and I were together. That meant a lot in the days when it was dangerous for two men to get a hotel room, when a neighbor peeved about too much noise could call the cops to report something worse.

Yes, they sometimes cracked jokes about where one applied to be a "confirmed bachelor," but they liked Tony. They liked the sandwiches he'd make on poker nights, not little triangles with the crusts cut off but giant heroes.

They didn't like that he was almost unbeatable at cards.

"Please," Hugh said once, "make an expression of any kind. Look down at your cards and then up at us."

Tony shook his head and then drew his hand down in front of his face like a curtain.

"Buddy,"—that was what Tony said in public instead of "honey"—"with guys like us, it's all poker face."

We were midway through filming episodes for the second season when the Mullard family came looking for David at the studio. He didn't often show up even when the story was his, but when it wasn't, he was usually sleeping off a drunk or reading about ancient Egyptians in the library or doing some other goddamned thing.

We were working on the episode "The Dreams Come By Here Regular." I'm sure you remember it; it starred that child actress, what's-her-name, and she gets lost in the woods to be rescued by the ghosts of escaped slaves. It was all moralistic Hugh, right down to the fading strains of spirituals at the end— pretty gutsy for 1962, though, when people were getting their skulls split open for thinking those things in the South.

The stage was all set up as a forest at night where the action took place, and our guys were good at building forests. The trunks were huge and roughly coated, and the branches drooped with nets of fake Spanish moss. Hugh and I were looking over the script when a beam of glaring California light crawled our way across the stage.

"Close the goddamned door!" the cameraman shouted.

Figure after figure stepped in through the light, and they wove their way through our trees like pygmies coming for us in the jungle. If we'd turned the cameras on, we could have gotten an eerie scene, and I'm sure Hugh regretted it later.

A stern matron in a graying beehive came out first, clutching a patent-leather pocketbook with both hands. She examined our faces in the dim illumination behind the equipment, squinting at us each in turn.

"What can we do for you?" Hugh asked.

She didn't answer, only squaring off with him as though ready for an honest-to-God fistfight. A fistfight, by the way, that you could see she had no plans to lose.

Before it came to that, the most beautiful woman I'd ever seen came out from the fake woods behind her. She was a strawberry blonde, and she had all the grace and delicacy the old lady didn't—that most ladies didn't. Her calm eyes and strong brows, though, gave the impression that she'd learned the womenly art of making things happen with leverage from the sides of life.

But that's David talk.

"Hello, gentlemen," the woman said, surprisingly at us. "We're looking for Leroy Dutton."

Hugh glanced around. "Any of you call yourself Leroy?"

The grips, the cable jockeys, the flannel-shirted union men who seemed to be paid to drink our coffee all froze, perhaps contemplating if it would be worth pretending to be Leroy for that pretty girl . . . and that awful woman. Nobody spoke up.

By then, the rest of the clan had come through—a father in a loose tie, a couple of strapping brothers in coveralls, and a kid sister with cat-eye glasses. They could have been the cast of a variety show a few stages over, something wholesome sponsored by a bread company with square dancing. All they needed were straw hats.

"No Leroy here, I'm afraid," Hugh said.

The older lady snapped open her pocketbook and handed him a photograph. "He might not be calling himself Leroy anymore."

I looked over Hugh's shoulder. It was a wedding portrait, and the beauty on our stage was the bride, gazing up at her groom and holding a bouquet of wildflowers between them. The groom, of course, was David.

"This was taken three years ago," she said. "Before Leroy up and left our Melody. Not much before, let me tell you. Weeks. Right after he came back from the woods."

"He's a writer," Melody explained, as though we wouldn't know.

"He *calls* himself a writer," the old lady corrected. "He's a husband and a son-in-law and an employee of the J.W. Mullard Feed Company is what he is."

A husband and a son and an employee—none were things I'd ever have linked to David Findley. I mean, everyone working on that show was unemployable. We'd been too blind or flatfooted or gay to go to Korea. Some of us had dabbled in college, but those days were cut short by a few bad creative writing classes and a lack of money. We worked as clerks, as janitors, as too-old newspaper boys. And we worked on our writing, of course, holding the few checks that came in just long enough to clear before taking everyone else out for booze. We had mortgages; David had a trunk full of paperbacks. He could jump into a borrowed convertible with a cocktail waitress and go racing in the desert at three in the morning.

Though apparently he couldn't after all.

Hugh was smooth. "Doesn't look familiar to me, and I know almost every writer in this town. What about you, Barry?"

I swallowed hard and looked at the picture. "I don't think I've seen him before."

The old lady wasn't buying it, and I'm not sure Melody was either.

"Oh," Melody said, curling one side of her lips in thought. "Is there another show like this one? With little spacemen and ghosts and things?"

Hugh put his hands on his hips. "Is there another show like this one? Ma'am, this is the most inventive television program in the history of the medium. Is there—"

I cut him off before he dug himself any deeper. "What he means to say is that there are shows passingly similar to this one, and your husband could work for any of those. *General Mills Playhouse, The Witching Hour, Dr. Hyde's Nightly Ride* . . . maybe they're worth a try."

"They're not as good as we are," Hugh couldn't resist saying.

Melody considered this. "Well, he'd only work for the best. If he hasn't come here yet, he will. Can you tell him I'm looking for him?"

"Sure thing," I said.

"And that I love him?"

"Of course."

"And that I'll always know who he really is?"

Hugh thought a second before saying, "Okay."

The old lady pointed at Hugh. "You'd better be careful when you see him. He can take on any form."

"Believe me, lady, I know the type," Hugh said.

The family turned and headed back for the door one by one. The littlest Mullard sibling, the girl with the glasses, waited until last and handed us each something out of the pocket of her sweater: crosses fashioned from Popsicle sticks.

"In case he comes at night," she said. Then she followed her family out through our woods and into the sunshine.

Hugh shook his head and tossed his Popsicle cross to a grip. "Can we get some footage shot today?" he barked.

Tony, by the way, was not particularly religious, which is one of about ten thousand things I liked about him. It would have been hard to be in those years, living like we were. The only place to feel and think differently than everyone else was on silly spaceman shows like *Acres of Perhaps* . . . shows you watched with thousands of other people alone in the dark.

We found David where we usually did when he wasn't at the studio: hunched in a booth at the Derby typing away on the portable with a glass of something clear and poisonous by his side. Hugh slid onto one seat and I slid onto the other right next to David.

"So, Leroy, tell us about Melody," I said.

He paused with his fingers above the keys but then plunged them down again almost in a chord to finish the sentence. He batted the carriage lever and sent it clunking to the far side.

"Melody," he said, "is the most beautiful and brilliant woman in the world, and I don't want to even think about your eyes on her."

"Well, everybody at the studio had eyes on her today," I said. "She came looking for you."

"Brought her whole clan," Hugh added.

"Probably spelled with a K," I said.

David tapped a Chesterfield from a pack and lit it. There was a shimmy in his hands. "That so?" he said.

"That's so," I said. I gave him time to take a drag and let out a whisper of smoke, maybe think of something to say next. When he said nothing, I did instead.

"So tell us how your marriage in a hick town crushed your artistic sensibilities until you had to break free, please. I'd like to hear it for the hundredth time, and I'll bet your version is the best."

"I didn't want to leave her. I had to."

I leaned back from the table. "Ohhhh. You had to."

He waved his cigarette near his face. "Look, I didn't want to end up here, for Christ's sake. I'm from Jenkins Notch, North Carolina, and I spent my first twenty years thinking I'd be right happy working in a farmer's store until I could afford a place of my own. I'm a hick, whatever you assholes think, and I'm not here because I want to be famous or rich. Shit, look at you guys."

The waitress was sliding a gin and tonic over to Hugh, who came here so often he didn't have to order it.

"Writing is your job. You talk about it, think about it, work out ways to do it better. I want to get rid of it."

I said, "Yes, it's a bitch to be a genius. We get it."

"No, you don't. I'd go home with Melody right now if she was here. If I could."

"Nothing's stopping you," I said. "Except maybe an aversion to decency."

"It wasn't like that," David said. "I liked living there. I loved living with her. We were like limbs of the same tree growing back together after a fire. Even her sweat smelled good, you know? I'd come home and she'd be flushed from walking back from the schoolhouse where she taught and she'd have this scent of . . . the whole earth, really. Like a creek smells in the summer, or firewood in the winter."

That was eerily and terrifyingly sweet for him to say. This was a man who'd written a script about how every Mercury rocket runs on mulched pixies for fuel, after all.

"I didn't used to drink when I lived back there." His twang had come back and he sounded possessed by himself. "But there was this family—probably still is—called the McDantrys and they made moonshine out in the woods. They sold it in town from their truck, and some idiot got some for Melody and me for a wedding present."

"Something borrowed, something blue, something toxic . . . " I started before trailing off.

"And one night she and I are in the new house and we're rough-housing and laughing and she gets it into her head to try the stuff. 'Nobody here but us chickens,' she says, taking the Mason jar off the top shelf of the pantry and twisting off the cap. The fumes distorted her face right before she took a big pull from it, and then she handed it to me."

"So what are you going to do? Let her unman you?" Hugh asked.

"Right. I woke up the next morning in a rocking chair with a fawn licking from the streak of vomit down the front of my shirt. All the windows of the house were broken. Inside, I hear this sobbing."

He lit another cigarette and exhaled from his mouth.

"I go in, and sure enough, there's Melody all beat up, her face puffy and bulging like a rotten plum. She's crying and I try to console her, but she hides behind the kitchen table and won't let me near her. I'm all looking down at my hands and I want to cut them off.

"But I'm still not thinking clearly enough, so I stagger off to the woods to find the McDantrys. They sold bad stuff, right? I could have fucking killed someone. And if I still had it in me, I might as well let them have a little."

By then in David's story, Hugh had gotten this look on his face that he wanted to write this down in case it got good. I'll admit I wasn't thinking much differently myself. Hell, we could use the forest set we'd already built.

But then the story got strange even by our standards.

"Out back of the Mullard property was a swamp of pines and cypress trees stretching for miles. The ground there is blackened mud and the canopy is all grown together. The McDantrys had put planks across the cypress knees so you'd walk on this tottering path zigging and zagging through the woods. Some were slick with mold so I had to be careful, but I followed them as far as they went—a long damned way.

"It got as dark as dusk back there, and it wouldn't have been hard to lose your sense of time. So it might have been an hour or even three until I came upon a big rotten cypress stump the folks around there called the Old Knot. When I say 'big,' I mean easily the size of a bus, hollowed in the middle like a bottomless well.

"There was a still there all right, camouflaged with broken branches. I was tempted to kick it off into the pit but, frankly, I'd have preferred to do that to the McDantrys.

"Of course, none were there. So I set about to wait. I walked around on the planks a bit, holding out my arms to keep my balance. I fiddled with the still to see how it worked. And then I leaned over and looked down into the stump."

"What did you see?" Hugh asked.

"I didn't see anything," David said. "It was dark. But I heard a hollow whistle, a little like the Knot was breathing—like it was the mouth of some wooden giant asleep under a blanket of mud. I reached my hand over the middle and the breeze was cool and rhythmic."

The waitress set a beer in front of me and I flinched.

"The weirdest thing was that when I shifted my weight on the board and it let out a squeal, the breeze stopped. Like something was holding its breath for me. And I wanted badly for it to start again—like when a friend jumps into a quarry pond and doesn't come up in what seems like forever?

" 'Hey,' I shouted, but there was no answer.

"I got this idea I had to climb down there no matter how far it went, had to squeeze its heart with both my arms to start it again. That was crazy—for all I knew, it was a nest of rattlesnakes.

"But standing there thinking it over, I was okay with that. What else did anybody need me for? The least I could do was make Melody a happy widow instead of a miserable wife.

"So I leaned and leaned like a coward until gravity made the decision for me."

"Jesus," Hugh said.

"I fell for a long, long time—so long that I had dreams. The vibration of cold whispers on my ears. The tremble of fingers up and down my arms. Something with claws combing over my scalp. I smelled oceans from other places, imagined music played with water and leaves."

Bullshit, I thought . . . but didn't say.

"And then I hit the ground. Or so I figured—I woke up flat on my face in my own front yard. Melody came running out and kissed me and said we'd never talk about it again and it wasn't my fault and she'd still love me forever."

Here he paused.

"Well, a funny thing occurred to me that night, naked with our sweat soaked into the sheets and our scents on each other's lips. What if this was the bottom of the Old Knot, with a different Melody and a different house and a different town? What if up there somewhere was a woman still scared of me? And why wasn't this one?"

Leave it to David Findley, or Leroy Whatever, to have the world's most sublime and esoteric drinking blackout.

"After, I had weird dreams of what was going on here or up there, and I noticed things didn't always connect. I'd think I'd said something here but really I'd said it in a dream up top of the Old Knot, or I'd lose a day in one place or the other. Folks got nervous around me because I'd stare off somewhere and then write down what I could in a notebook I got from the dime store. When that wasn't fast enough, I got the typewriter."

"So why'd you leave?" Hugh asked.

"Melody wasn't worried at first when I clattered away in the kitchen with a board balanced on the arms of a chair. But then I stopped sleeping and going to work. I stopped leaving the house and shaving. I stopped talking, stopped focusing on anything in front of me. She called over my folks to talk sense to me. Reverend Pritchett stopped by. And when I heard them talking about 'getting me out,' I decided I'd better get myself out first. I packed up one night and lit out west. And the only thing I can make or sell is . . . whatever that fall gave me."

David drank the rest of his liquor in one long swallow. You'd think he'd have learned not to do that from his own story.

And that's what it was: a story. A good one, like all of his, but a tall tale myth meant to make him seem like the Paul Bunyan of weird fiction or something.

"So you drank bad moonshine, beat up your wife while barely conscious, stumbled into the woods, and got a concussion after falling into an old tree stump?" I said.

David eyed me calmly. "Yeah, if you think so."

"One of those McDantry people dragged you back home where you came to, and ever since, you've suffered the lingering effects of your concussion, plus some uncharacteristic guilt. Mystery solved."

"If you say so," he said.

Hugh, not helping, asked, "So there are different versions of us back where you came from?"

"Yeah," David said. "Barry here is writing for the *Saturday Evening Post*."

Hugh and I stared and he let us dangle a moment before laughing.

"Barry, I have no idea if you even exist, here or there. I'm not sure I'm creative enough to invent you or Hugh. Or, shit, all of Hollywood. Who would imagine the studio system? Jesus, I hope not me."

Then, being writers, we spent the night getting drunk and bitching about the money men.

You know, Tony and I never got to speed around the desert in a Karmann Ghia convertible like David did with his girlfriends. We could never fight in public with me chasing him out of a restaurant to apologize, either, or walk close on the pier. We lived in a closet built for two for fifty years, and when I finally found the guts to step out, he was too sick to step out with me.

The saying goes that to be great is to be misunderstood, and most people assume this also means that to be misunderstood is to be great. But there are lots of misunderstood people who are a long way from greatness.

When I crawled into my bed beside Tony that night, I wondered which one David "Leroy" Findley was: a visionary or some delusional hick good at sounding like one. Or maybe there wasn't a difference.

What did "Woodsy" even mean when you thought about it? Anybody can film random movements and rely on the viewers' perceptions to make it art, but unless it says something, what's the damned point? *Acres of Perhaps* wasn't in the "giving-voice-to-David's-demons" business; it was in the "entertaining-and-enlightening" one. We made people think about race, nostalgia, paranoia . . . not the stitching of the Universe. Someone could create the *Clorox Kafka Hour* for that.

Tony rolled over under his sheets to face me. We'd just moved to this Craftsman bungalow in Venice then, and air conditioning was a science fictional concept to us. Even a fan was something that cost money, and so he slept without much on at all. I remember this now only because, well, I thought right then that Tony was as good as Melody any day of the week.

I told him what had happened, about the Mullard family and David's secret identity, about how the whole genius act had a clichéd story behind it—except for the falling into the netherworld part which was pure delusion. He listened with his head propped up in his hand under the moonlight, asking questions and nodding at the answers.

At the end, he asked, "So what is he going to do?"

David had ducked the question at the Derby so I could only offer my guess. "He'll probably keep avoiding her until she gives up and goes home."

He considered a moment. "You sound angry about it."

"I don't think angry is the right word. Annoyed. I'm annoyed things are easier for him because he has people like Hugh and Melody and me carrying his load of the ordinary."

"You know what I think?" That was one of my favorite phrases of his; it was like a motor revving. "Men like David make women into muses so they have someone to blame when they don't deliver the goods. And they make women into anti-muses, too."

"Anti-muses."

"Yeah. Like this poor Melody. She's the boat anchor mooring him to reality, right? So he builds it all up until she seems to be after his soul, and then he's justified in leaving her."

Tony was a part-time illustrator for magazines in L.A. and San Francisco, and he had a way of drawing exactly what you needed to see but no more. He sometimes did it with words, too.

"Do you think I'm that way?"

He smiled and reached for my hands. "You don't have a muse, love. In the same way astronauts and carpenters don't. You just do things."

Tony never misunderstood me, and sometimes that was consolation enough for not being great.

I'd leaned in closer when there came a thunder of fists against the front door.

Tony sighed and gathered up the blankets around him. Then he reached for his cigarettes and said, "Better go see what David wants."

"What makes you think it's David?"

He tapped the end of the pack. "It's the way his life works."

I pulled on an undershirt over my pajama pants and headed for the door. A shadowed head bobbed in the window, and I could tell from the wild spray of hair that it really was David.

"What do you want?" I asked through the door.

"Barry! You've got to let me in. They're after me."

"Who?"

"Melody and her folks!"

I imagined them walking down the street with torches and pitchforks, and I'll admit I liked the image.

"Where are they?"

"They're here," he cried, twisting the doorknob and thumping himself against it.

I opened the door and he stumbled inside. He tried his best to slam it again but I was holding it.

"This is silly," I said. "They're people. Be with her, don't be with her—just tell her the truth."

Out in the darkened street, I saw the Mullard family walking abreast in a single line, patrolling with flashlights like you would if searching for a lost dog. They pivoted as one group at the end of my driveway and marched toward us.

"Okay," I said, closing the door.

David did me the courtesy of bolting it shut. He reached for a chair to prop under it but I stopped him.

I watched through the window as the Mullards formed an arc around the entrance to my house like Christmas carolers. Melody left the group and knocked gently.

"Mr. Weyrich? I think Leroy is inside your house. Can he come out so we can talk to him?"

"Hold on a moment," I yelled. Then, turning to David, I whispered, "What do you expect me to do?"

"Tell them to go away. Tell them you're calling the cops."

"Mr. Weyrich?" This time it was the mother. "That's my daughter's lawful husband in there."

David shook his head but I leaned closer to the window. "Look, I don't want to be involved in this at all. Maybe everybody should call it a night, get some sleep, and then get together somewhere tomorrow to talk it all over."

The Mullards closed in.

"Hey, Tony," David said.

Tony was leaning in the hallway in his navy blue pajamas. He lowered his cigarette from his lips and said, "Hello, David."

"You've got to talk some sense into her, Tony."

He arched an eyebrow. "Why me?"

"Because you have feelings and things," David said quickly, still peering through the window.

I watched as the two brothers broke off from the group and out of my vision. I wondered if I'd remembered to lock the back door. Then I wondered if it wouldn't be just as well for these guys to carry David out of my house and my life. Maybe I could hurry and unlock it—

Tony came closer. "Melody, honey?"

"Yes," was the quiet response.

"My name is Tony. I'm Barry's roommate."

Isn't that funny how quickly it ran off his tongue? He didn't even have to pause anymore.

"David—Leroy—isn't in a condition to talk to you right now."

"Has he changed form?"

Tony turned to David; he'd sat down in one of our living room chairs and was squeezing his temples with his palms.

"No, he's still Leroy," Tony said.

On the other side of the house, the back doorknob rattled. Then a giant rhomboid head with speckled stubble craned in through the open kitchen window. He peered around, looking down at the sink and up at the ceiling, maybe judging if there was room to climb through.

"Hey," I said, stepping over to the sink. I picked up the fancy new water sprayer gizmo and gave him a quick spritz in the face. He retreated sputtering and I slammed the window closed.

By now, David was holding his head in his hands, covering his eyes.

"Who the hell are these people?" I said.

"They think I'm possessed by the devil," he said quietly.

"So do I, but you don't see me climbing into people's houses to get you."

"They found me at the boardinghouse, I have no idea how. Melody's always been able to find me wherever I was like she can feel me, a phantom limb."

I wondered if Tony could sense me that way. Probably, knowing him.

"Do you have anything to drink?" David asked.

"For you, no," Tony said. "You smell like a gas tank."

"It's how I listen," he said.

Outside, the Mullards began to sing. They weren't bad a capella, but when the little one started in on the banjo, it was actually beautiful. Beautiful and scary because, Jesus, who carries around a goddamned banjo?

I glowered at David with my arms folded. "Your whole life is one long episode of *Acres of Perhaps*, isn't it?"

So began a strange siege, me sitting on the couch keeping an eye on the Mullards through the blinds, and Tony sitting in the other recliner watching David. The Mullards sang hymns in low voices while David muttered to himself with his hands clawed into the arms of my chair like an astronaut going up.

"This is ridiculous," I whispered to Tony. I probably didn't have to.

"Maybe everybody will get tired and go home," he said.

"We *are* home," I said.

Not long after, a rancid odor overtook the room. It took me a moment to realize what it was: David, head lolled back and his mouth wide open, had pissed himself in my favorite chair.

Tony figured it out at the same time. "It's not like that chair was cheap," he said.

I grabbed David by his shirt and yanked him up. A dark spot had bloomed on his pants.

"David, wake up!"

He rolled his head to one side and then the other, mumbling. The words were faint and garbled at first but then they resolved like a radio bearing in on the right station.

"What if people make cities itch?" he said.

"Jesus Christ," I said. " 'Antelope umbrellas crying in the wind.' There. I'm a genius, too."

"You're the one who thinks it's magic."

"People who piss themselves in my house don't get to ever use that word around me again."

He tilted his head back way farther than I thought possible, opened his mouth like the tall front doors of a church, and let out a long, low wail. Then he pivoted his head forward again and said, "Where's my typewriter?"

I glanced around in case he'd brought it inside. When I didn't see it, I opened the blinds and squinted on the porch. There was his black case sitting amongst the Mullards.

"You really want it?"

"Barry," Tony said in his admonishing voice.

"Yes," David said. "I've got to get this down."

"Excellent," I said. I turned the deadbolt on the door.

"Are you sure you want to do that?" Tony asked.

"Never surer," I said, opening it.

The Mullards all stood from where they were sitting on the low adobe wall, looks of surprise on their faces.

"He's all yours," I said, shoving him into their arms.

The two beefy brothers caught him while the mother looked down with disgust. She'd probably have let him hit the cement face first.

"It's okay," Melody said, her hands on the sides of his face.

"No, it isn't," David groaned.

"Peace be with you, praise the Lord, whatever the fuck," I said, holding up my hand jauntily and then slamming the door.

"Hugh's going to kill you," Tony said.

"No, he's not," I said absently, watching through the blinds as the Mullard brothers hoisted David on their shoulders like a trophy deer. "Jesus is cheaper than detox."

They'd left David's typewriter behind and, well, you can't leave something like that lying around. I reached out and grabbed it.

David was a drunk, an eloquent drunk, and it was hard to blame him because hey, you've got to do whatever makes you brave. For some people that's booze, for others it's drugs, for others still it's narcissism or vengeance or desperation. I don't know what made it possible for me to face the page, but keeping stupid words like "magic" out of my head probably helped—telling myself it was like making a chair or a sandwich instead of something alive.

It's not what you think, that I jumped on a chance to take out a rival. After that night, my frustrations with David turned to pity. He happened to be sick in a way that helped him write stories for our television show, but it wasn't comfortable for him. It hurt him to do. It might even have killed him one day.

But first, as Tony predicted, Hugh wanted to kill me.

" 'Jesus is cheaper than detox'? That's what you have to say?" he told me at the studio the next day. "People come *back* from detox, Barry."

"He'll come back. They might not even get him all the way to Jenkins Notch. We're going to get a collect call from a Howard Johnson's in Kansas after he escapes, and we'll go pick him up. But you know what? He'll damned well be sober."

"You understand he's the engine of this whole show, don't you?"

"Well, I like to think I'm useful, too."

Hugh brandished his clipboard over his head. "You're the brakes! You're the rearview mirror!"

"Okay, well, fuck you. But listen. David drunk would last what, another season? At the most."

"You don't know that!"

"At the most. Then he'd wrap himself around a tree or hang himself by his belt in a closet. You know how many scripts he'd write then? Zero."

"They're going to make him into a revivalist preacher."

Okay, I smiled a little to imagine old Leroy Dutton swinging a Bible over his head on a plywood stage somewhere, sweat staining the armpits of his short-sleeved buttoned shirt. He'd be good at it, I thought. Quick on his feet, anyway.

"Look," I said. "he's a married man. He has a wife and responsibilities and we shouldn't interfere with that just because you think he's the only way to make a television show."

"Married man?" Hugh said. "What the hell do you know about being married?"

I used to think Hugh only meant about thirty percent of what he said, less when he was angry, but it was funny how even irrational, he still remembered where to hit me.

I was considering where to hit him back when the stage door opened again and for the second time in as many days, Melody Mullard Dutton was walking through our woods. She was by herself this time, thankfully.

"There's something wrong with David," she said.

"Of course there is," I said.

You know what Tony did every morning for fifty years? He'd open the office curtains facing out to the street, tying them neatly to the side. He'd straighten papers on the desk. He'd set down a cup of coffee he'd brewed on the stove, the way he knew I liked it best. He'd turn on the typewriter.

And because he did, I sat down every day. Sometimes I'd peck something out, but mostly I didn't.

David had escaped, though he was hardly on the lam: he jumped out of the Mullard's 1940 DeSoto at the intersection of Wilshire and LaBrea on the way out of town, and now they were pretty sure he was holed up at the Derby. It says all you need to know about Hugh that he was relieved a beautiful woman and her good Christian family had failed to lure his writer to a wholesome life in Jenkins Notch.

"He knows where his home is," Hugh said later. "Not shuffling barefoot with a bunch of Snuffy Smith castoffs."

The only thing keeping the Mullard boys from storming into the Derby and carrying David out on their shoulders like a sack of grain was that Melody had a plan. In Hugh's office with her hands folding and unfolding in her lap, she explained it to us.

"Leroy thinks he's fallen through that old stump and he's now living on the other side, right?"

I had doubts he thought so literally, but I nodded with Hugh.

"When she taught me how to sew, Mawmaw,"—I think that's what she called her, and it made me think of a giant double mouth lined with sharp teeth—"told me that sometimes the only way to undo a knot is to push the needle back through it."

"Okay," I said, pinching the bridge of my nose. "I think we might be getting a bit too literal here—"

"So you want to push him back through the Knot again?" Hugh asked.

"Yes," she said.

"That still doesn't solve the problem of getting him back to North Carolina in the first place, does it?" I asked.

"We wouldn't have to if there was a forest here."

Of course, there happened to be the perfect forest not forty feet from us. A week earlier and the stage would have been New York City. A week later and it would be acting as Moon Base Theta. The Mullards had shown up right in the middle of our very own North Carolina backwoods, almost as though it was destiny.

"All it needs is a Knot," she added. "Or something he thinks is one."

I watched Hugh's eyebrows lift in excitement as they did before any new production, when the budget shortfalls and actor disagreements and special effects problems hadn't started yet. If there was ever a man born to build a fake portal between worlds to convince a half-mad, half-drunk genius he was sane again . . . it was Hugh Kline.

The question, though, was why he'd want to do it, aside from the artistic challenge. As he leaned across his desk with a pencil and paper so Melody could sketch the stump, I wondered what his angle could be. When he glanced at me and grinned, I knew it for sure.

The Mullards wanted an exorcism. They assumed a sober, demon-free Leroy Dutton would climb out of that stump all blinking in the light of Jesus to return to Jenkins Notch. Hugh, on the other hand, assumed David Findley would climb out, look around at his crazy hick relatives and then never leave Los Angeles again. He wasn't exorcising the Devil. He was exorcizing the Mullards.

"If there's one thing I've learned about working with writers, it's to meet them on their own level," he told me after Melody was gone.

"What's my level?" I asked.

"You don't have a level, Barry. That's why I like you."

And hearing that—knowing it—solidified which fate I wanted for David Findley.

It's not like I never wrote again after the show went under. I moved on to comedies and little dramas to keep food on the table, not because I was gifted at it, but because I showed up and produced words when they needed them. In Hollywood, that beats genius every time.

I never knew why guys like David Findley got all the credit for creativity. Anyone can wave his hands and yell, "Magic dust!" or "interdimensional tree stump" to explain everything away.

We left the set decorator to build the stump while we went to fetch David. He'd slipped away from the Derby by the time we got there, and we checked two bars before finding him again. I don't remember the place, but I do remember him sitting under the only bright light in the room, writing in a goddamned steno pad with an arc of empty glasses around it.

"Do we grab him or what?" I asked Hugh.

"No, let's try this," Hugh said, hunching a little toward the back as though he was trying to go unnoticed.

When David looked up, I could see his eyes weren't quite focusing on us, and the writing on his pad couldn't be decipherable even to him.

"We got rid of them," Hugh whispered.

We sat down on the other side of the table.

"How?" David asked, his voice hoarse.

"Told them you'd gone to the desert to think things through," Hugh said. "They'll be there for another four hours, easy."

David glanced down at the steno pad. "Thanks. I appreciate it. I need some room—"

"What you need," I said, holding up a hand for a waitress or a bartender or whatever worked in that hole of a bar, "is a celebratory drink."

"We all do," Hugh said.

"Yeah, we do," David said, dreamily.

So that was the plan. We let David drink as much as he wanted, "slaking the demon" as the Mullards would have called it, matching him with one drink of ours for three of his. We figured he'd get drunk enough to drag back to the studio for his exorcism in about two hours.

It took more like four and the cost of at least one episode to get him to the blubbering mess we required. He descended to that state in layers: first he was sentimental, then he was funny, and finally he was full of strange advice.

"You know how you can be as good a writer as I am, Barry?" he asked.

"Please tell me," I said. By then, I was barely keeping my own liquor down in my stomach where it belonged.

"By not imagining I'm a better writer than you are," he said.

"That's deep. You're like some alcoholic Confucius."

When David started to drizzle down his seat toward the floor, we figured it was time to get him home. I caught him before his head hit the carpet.

"Jesus," Hugh said. "Maybe we ought to take him to the hospital instead."

"We're taking him to a spiritual one." I ducked beneath one of David's arms. "Come on, lift the other side."

We got David into the car. We got the car across town. We got the car through the studio gate. We got David up, out, and onto his spongey feet. We got him out of the California sun and into the North Carolina backwoods in the time it took to write this paragraph.

The set was the best we'd ever built. I felt the warmth in those woods, the Southern stickiness of them. I smelled the moss. I heard the cicadas. I saw, yes, the winding path of planks leading off into the swamp.

Standing at the end closest to us was Melody.

"We're here to take you home, baby," she said, reaching for David. "We came through the Knot."

He turned into my chest and made a few sloppy skids on the stage to get away. "Get out of here! This place isn't for you!"

"It isn't for you, either," she said calmly.

"Come on, buddy," I said.

Hugh followed us on the creaking path deep into the soundstage. I hadn't realized it was that big. Helping David along those planks, I felt the danger of falling into the muck, of stirring up snakes. I felt the trees watching me.

We came to the stump—the Knot—in only a few minutes, but it seemed much longer. They'd outdone themselves with lumber and plaster: it was giant and creepy and it cost as much as three episodes we'd now have to film on canned sets in the back lot. But you could park a Volkswagen inside if you wanted to. The set decorator must have gotten it right because David recoiled when we got there.

"We're going home," Melody said like a beckoning spirit, a dryad or a nymph, her hand dipping gracefully from her pale wrist.

We propped David up near the edge. I peered down into the stump and saw the stagehands had lined the bottom with black cloth—a kind of hammock. It would catch him when he fell.

If he fell. He clutched the stump and wouldn't even look inside. "I can't go," he said.

Melody steered herself into his vision. "Baby, listen to me. We're going home now. You're going to remember this all like a dream because that's what it is."

"I can't take it back with me," he said.

It was growing clear that we'd soon have to toss him into the stump by force unless someone thought of the right thing to say. Everybody turned to me.

It wasn't a rational decision, what I said next. It came as some awful belch of the id.

"There is no 'it,' Leroy," I said.

He closed his eyes as though that would close his ears.

"Nothing's talking to you or through you. You write weird stuff and what does it change? Nothing. Somebody sits up late at night watching our fucking show in an undershirt with a bottle of beer in his hand. His eyes get opened to the dark truths of the Universe. But then he crawls off to bed and gets up the next morning for work. He farts in the elevator, he looks down a lady's dress . . . it's all gone."

David didn't say anything, but he did slump further against the Knot.

"Even if you had something, people would just flush it down the toilet. It's good they flush it down the toilet because how else are they supposed to sell insurance or sweep floors or wipe baby asses after knowing all of that? It's a defense mechanism."

Hugh's smile faded. "Hey," he said.

"It's selfish when you think about it," I pressed. "Shoving people's faces in lives they'll never have, things they'll never feel that you made up out of nowhere."

"Selfish?"

"Yeah. That's what it seems to me. You're not supposed to see that stuff and you sure as hell aren't supposed to make us see it, either."

"I don't—"

It takes a writer to know how to demolish another writer. And with Melody looking on and her family all praying, I did it.

"Go home, Leroy. Go the fuck home. This world is lost. The one on your side of the Knot, though? Maybe it isn't. Maybe you'll give your magic to your kids. Maybe you'll just live."

David's voice cracked when he said, "What if I don't see anymore? What if I can only see here?"

"Then it wasn't yours to see in the first place," I said.

The little Mullard girl began to sing. Melody's brothers joined in as the harmony and soon the whole family had clasped hands in a circle around Hugh's fake stump.

David turned his back to me on his hands and knees and I wondered what he was doing. Then he put one wobbling hand on the edge of the stump followed by the other, and he pushed himself slowly to his feet.

"Hey," Hugh said again, pushing me away. "You do see things, and you need to share them with people who don't."

David closed his eyes and swayed a moment.

"No, I don't," he said quietly. "I'm not one of the good guys."

Melody came up smiling with one hand held out for him.

"Walk with me again until you are?" she said.

He took her hand with the wide eyes and open mouth of a man being saved at the last second from drowning in the sea. Together they stepped onto the edge. They paused and gazed at each other like the wedding picture. This was another one, a renewal of the vows.

"Do you want to say goodbye?" she asked him.

He glanced over at Hugh and me. Hugh was reaching for him with a look of feral desperation on his face. Me, I nodded to David and he nodded back.

"No," he said. "Never again."

Then she took him into her arms in a dancing embrace and they plunged into the Knot. I half expected them to disappear in a flash. Or maybe I hoped.

All I heard was the pop and creak of them hitting canvas. When we approached, she was cradling him close like an infant and he was unconscious.

The Mullards came forward with a blanket and they bundled David inside. The brothers hoisted him between them and started for the studio door.

"Thank you all," Melody said, clasping mine and Hugh's hands. "You saved a life today."

Hugh tugged his away. "No, we murdered a great show that made people happy." He turned to me. "You murdered it."

I didn't think so then, not yet, so I didn't even watch as he stormed off through the forest, punching tree after tree.

"I'm glad we could help," I said.

Melody kissed me on the cheek and hurried off after the limp form of her husband, the late David Findley.

Tony wasn't well enough to travel in person at the end thanks to the cancer growing in his body like something on one of our old shows. I tried last October to rent a Winnebago and take him up the coast; he always loved the trees like David. We got maybe thirty miles out before he was too sick to keep going, but it wasn't him who said it. He'd have gone the whole way in that little plastic bathroom to make me feel better.

Make *me* feel better.

What he did instead with the last year he had was walk the world through Google Maps, steering down back country roads with the arrow keys. He went twice or three times across the country that way.

I told myself *Acres of Perhaps* died for many reasons, not just because of losing our resident "genius." People gave a lot less of a shit about fantasy and a lot more about the bullet-flying, hose-spraying, billy-clubbing reality of the time. If you were square, you wanted to be told about better times on television in Westerns and variety shows. If you were cool, a show like ours couldn't keep up with the farm-league David Findleys on every college campus with speed, weed, and acid. If you wanted weird, if you wanted surreal, there was always the news.

We tried, though, and I wrote my best scripts in that last half season. Remember the one where the disgraced comic book artist has to draw pictograms for our first contact with an alien race? That was mine. I also did the one where the white-bread people of a wholesome Midwestern town chase the stranded motorcycle gang into a warehouse and burn it down.

But come on. It was over. And as the stories and scripts came slower to me, I began to realize I might be over, too. I knew it on the last day of filming when Hugh handed me my check.

"You know not to come back here, don't you?" he said.

"I sure do," I said, folding the check for my pocket.

Hugh and I made up a little before he died. We were in the elevator at a convention years later, standing in opposite corners with grinning teenagers glancing back and forth between us, when out of nowhere he said, "*The fucking Love Boat?* Really?"

I calmly looked at him and said, "*Flood Zone Manhattan?* Really?"

Deadpan, he said, "We're both writing disaster pictures."

"At least Ethel Merman dies in yours," I said.

We laughed together for as long as it took to get to the lobby, and Hugh patted my shoulder with one shaking hand on his way out. That was it. That was as close as we got.

The next year I was writing for *Charles in Charge*.

This is Tony's computer, and I barely know how they work. I follow the paths he made for me, click the things he showed me how to click, let him do the looking I've always been afraid to do, and I've been exploring his mind when I'm not typing this.

Yesterday, I found the orange teardrop marking a spot in the North Carolina foothills in Google Maps. It had a label, and the label was, "Go here when I die."

So I am.

Jenkins Notch is in its own valley between two ridges of the Appalachian foothills, and first you have to go up a road of hairpin turns and switchbacks before coming down again. Not that Tony went there in person, of course. But for him to find the town and find the farm, even when he was in too much pain to sit for twenty minutes at a time . . . it probably almost felt that way.

The place looks like one of our old sets, Fantasia Americana. There's a real general store where old men sit around a giant wooden spool playing checkers. There's a post office operating from an old mobile home surrounded on three sides by a handicapped ramp. They've got a Main Street, too, but the little hardware store and clothing shop have long been boarded up, and the only busy place in town is the Circle K convenience store.

I followed the line Tony drew for me off the main road and through town and into the forest and finally down a bumping dirt track with a ridge of weeds growing out from the middle. The closer I got, the more I worried about whom I would find at the end. I hadn't called ahead, and Leroy Dutton could stagger from his shack with one overall strap hanging loose from a beefy shoulder and a cocked shotgun on his arm, thinking I'm the tax man. I could end this journey bleeding out in the dust with my chest turned to hamburger.

That's not the reason I didn't go to see Leroy first, though.

I'm no commando or wilderness scout, so it took me some wandering and thrashing through the brush to find my way to the low-sloping hammock of loamy soil that David described for us all those years ago. I glanced between the sycamores for the little goblin things of "Woodsy," but I didn't see any.

When I came to a path of planks, I knew I was close. I followed them deeper into what now were oaks and cypress, big trees with heavy drooping limbs. Hanging from some were unlit oil lanterns, maybe placed by Leroy himself, and there was evidence people had been walking through recently: trimmed branches, flattened leaves.

It never occurred to me that the Knot could have rotted into the ground over the fifty years since Leroy fell inside. It didn't seem possible. And when I reached a domed clearing with a single heavy beam of sunlight aimed at the center, I was not surprised to see the Knot waiting for me.

Our replica on the stage was almost perfect, but this one was even larger than I imagined. Even now, rotted down low to an irregular circle, it still felt mighty. Someone had assembled a half-circle of log benches around it.

I'd come a long way, right? I wasn't drunk or imaginative or knighted by the gods with any magical perception, but yes, I leaned over and looked down into the Knot.

It was dark, just as David had described. There was a slight intimation of a breeze, a breathing, also like he'd said. My eyes couldn't focus on the bottom, black and speckled with something like stars. It might have been night on the other side, where David Findley was still writing in an attic somewhere with a bottle of gin beside him.

Where Tony was speeding down the Pacific Coast Highway with me.

I closed my eyes and tipped myself inside.

We had a hard time agreeing on the opening credits for *Acres of Perhaps*. A time-lapse of day fading to night in the desert? Turning pages of a book? The sparks of a campfire winding upward to the stars? A flying saucer hovering in observation above a tranquil Earth?

Hugh wanted something I called the Flying Antique Store, old porcelain dolls and Victorian chairs and grandfather clocks tumbling at the camera from some distant point in space, probably because the props were free. David, who couldn't care less about the credits, half-heartedly suggested the ticker-tapper of a news broadcast from the "far edges of imagination," something to lure in the suburban zombies he hoped to awaken.

My idea—and I've marveled since that it came to me—was to show a family sitting down to watch television on the other side of the glass, Mom in her housecoat and Pop in his loosened tie and the kids settling in, all of them staring expectantly at the viewers as though *they* were about to be the show. That's what we went with.

I saw none of those things falling through the Knot like I expected. I would have settled for scenes from my life because at least Tony would be there, but all I got was the stretch effect from *Vertigo*, zooming the edges of that stump into infinity, lined with swimming lights.

It felt like settling into bed after being awake for years.

Tony was not the one who woke me, but I wasn't surprised. What were the chances he'd be waiting by the Knot on the other side when I came through?

The man who did was heavyset with horn-rimmed glasses and a head of white unruly hair. He wasn't in overalls and he didn't have a shotgun, just an undershirt and blue jeans.

"Barry?" he was saying.

"What year is it?" I croaked. "Who's the President? Did 9/11 still happen?"

The man who once was David Findley sat on the edge of the stump. "Tony's still gone," he said. "I'm sorry."

"Are you still Leroy Dutton?"

He clasped my arm and tugged me from the soft black soil. "Always was," he said.

With his help I got to my feet, knee-deep in leaves. I found my way back over onto solid land in three wobbling steps.

"Are you still . . . "

"A hillbilly? If you're asking if I can play a banjo, I have to say the answer is yes, but I can only pick out the first few bars of the *Acres of Perhaps* theme."

I peered down into the Knot and all feeling of infinite depth and darkness was gone. "So it is just a stump."

David glanced in. "I've gone back and forth on that. I've never believed like I did back then, but then, maybe I don't have to."

I felt very strange and light, and it took me a moment to ask, "How did you know? About Tony?"

"He sent a letter and told us you'd be coming."

Tony, still planning my travel from beyond the grave. "When?" I asked.

"I'd have to look at the letter," he said. "A couple of months ago. You want to come back to the house to see it, maybe get some water?"

"No moonshine?" I said.

"I quit that stuff years ago, believe me, and the McDantrys up and left in 1970 anyway. I bought their property from the bank."

"You own the Knot?"

"I own the Knot." He grinned. "Isn't that crazy?"

"Yes," I said. It all was.

"The kids and grandkids used it for a stage," Leroy said. "They did puppet shows and magic shows and little plays and Franny used to have her revival sermons here for us. She's a Unitarian minister now."

"Children played in the Knot?"

"They still do sometimes when they come to visit," Leroy said. "We built a little platform for it and set up the benches like our own Globe Theater."

"They don't . . . fall through?"

"Not literally, no."

By then I was feeling warm, and my head felt heavy and barely attached to my neck.

"Hey," I said, taking his arm before I fell back in. "That whole thing back then in LA . . . I wasn't your friend."

"I know," Leroy said.

"I killed you," I said.

"A little bit," he conceded.

"Stories came to you easily and love came to you easily and you could be whatever you wanted in the open and you didn't want what I couldn't have."

"I knew that fifty years ago, Barry. Did you come to hear how everything turned out okay? That's fine, but first you have to know that it didn't for a long time. For a long time, I was the world's angriest feed and seed delivery man."

"I'm sorry," I said quietly.

"You have to understand that, okay? You did something shitty to someone who saw you as a friend."

Keep going, I thought. Go all the way through with the needle, me or the Knot, I didn't care.

"But I did something you didn't. I healed and scarred over. Maybe it was easier here in the woods with Melody, but you could have done it, too, if you'd let yourself. You didn't have to write for *Diff'rent Strokes* or *The Facts of Life* or whatever you did, and you didn't have to blame me or yourself for it."

"I should have been the one who left the show," I said.

"Why? You were always as good as me. You're the one who didn't think so, only because you did it differently."

I squeezed my eyes shut with my fingers. I killed him for nothing.

"All those stories that could have been," I said.

"You still wrote some," Leroy said.

"No, I mean you. I mean your stories."

Leroy squinted at me. "Do you think I stopped writing?"

"I thought—"

"—that I'd be too busy shooting Indians and skinning raccoons? Who do you think wrote those plays and puppet shows?"

"It's not the same," I said.

"The same as what?"

"The same as *Acres of Perhaps.*"

"Barry," he said. "I don't want to let you off the hook without giving you some more shit first, but what do you think I've been writing?"

"Puppet shows," I mumbled. "Plays for kids."

"It was just a different network," Leroy said. "And my grandson Tucker? He can do one hell of an impression of a dropping atomic bomb."

Wait, I wanted to say. I wanted the world to wait, let me hear it clearly. "You wrote scripts?"

Leroy shrugged. "Sure. Here and there, maybe a couple hundred."

A couple hundred. Scripts. Of *Acres of Perhaps.*

"Are you sure I'm not on the other side of the Knot?"

"If you can't tell the difference, Barry, then maybe there isn't one."

On our way back, we walked in silence until Leroy said, "You know, I could have written for *The Love Boat*, too."

"Could you?"

"Sure. They pull into Acapulco and at midnight, the ghosts of murdered Aztecs steal everyone's gold."

"You'd have to write in Billy Barty or Paul Lynde," I said.

"Okay. One is a famous diamond thief and the passengers hang him from a yard arm when he doesn't confess."

"That's not bad," I said.

We followed the planks back toward a farm, not a gray shanty with the siding peeling at the corners but something with two stories and a gleaming metal roof. A woman with gorgeous long gray hair hanging almost to her waist was climbing out of a giant Toyota pick-up truck. She was wearing a suit.

Leroy pointed to me. "Look what I found in the Knot."

She didn't close the door. She hurried over, her heels kicked free, but then she stopped with her hands on her hips.

"Are you taking him back to sin?"

"What?" I glanced at Leroy and then back to her. I never imagined she might be the one to greet me with a shotgun, probably not far out of reach in that truck. "No. No. Not at all. I wanted to—"

She pulled me in for a hug. I didn't raise my arms to return it right away, only slowly.

"It's okay, Barry. That's what my family thought. I just wanted my husband back." She leaned back, looking me over. "How long were you out there?"

"I think he might have been lurking there since the sixties," Leroy said.

She frowned but said, "Well, that would explain a lot. I'm sorry I just got home. Had to go to the school board in town."

"She used to be superintendent," Leroy said. "Still is, if you count all the 'consulting' she does."

I wondered if her district taught evolution. I had a feeling it did if Leroy was anything to go by.

"Are you going to stay awhile?" she asked me.

"Do you want me to?"

"We both do," she said. "Tony did, too."

"I'm sorry?" I said, not sure I'd heard.

"Come on," Leroy said.

We walked to the edge of the grass beneath a copse of trees toward a small shed or cabin with three lightly molded windows. He opened the door for me and inside were two desks, one with a computer and one with Leroy's old typewriter.

"Tony sent it a few months ago," Melody said. "He told us you kept it for years."

"Yeah," I said.

Leroy pointed. "What I figure is you can use that and I can use the computer, or maybe the other way around, and I can write stories about walking skyscrapers and you can write stories about Mars."

"Who would want them?" I asked.

"Well, Tony would, for one," he said. "But I'm guessing we can find some asshole in Hollywood to sell them for us."

So I'm sitting now in a creaking swivel chair. I'm looking out through the windows. There's a glass beside me of something called "unsweet tea" which is what we drink around here now instead of booze. I'm resting my fingers on the keys—I don't plan to type, don't plan to even try—but the cool plastic waits.

Waits for when I'm ready again.

LITTLE SISTERS

VONDA N. McINTYRE

Damaged nearly to extinction by a war it had won, Qad's *Piercing Glory* tumbled through deep space, its engines dead, deceleration impossible. *Glory's* Mayday shrieked, insistent, while Qad, beset by nightmares, slept in his transit pod. *Glory* focused its failing resources on keeping Qad alive.

Decades later, in the nearest shipyard, Executives registered the cry for help. They created an account for this new consumer and dispatched space boats with gravity tractors.

A millennium later, the space boats returned. The ship floated obediently in their tractor nets, its tumbling damped, its momentum slowly, inexpensively reduced from interstellar speeds. The boats minimized energy expenditure and Executive attention, guided by Artificial Normals. The rescue required little intelligence, and had not been marked as emergency or priority. The estimated account expenditure reached neither level. The boats put the disabled ship into a repair bay and signaled for awakening.

Qad woke in the cold and dark, surprised to wake at all. He had expected to freeze in the wilderness of deep space, or burn in the brilliance of starbirth. He pulled out the transit pod catheters and intravenous supply lines, indifferent to leaks or smells. Cleaning was the job of Artificial Stupids. He ignored their jobs; he barely noticed their existence.

He felt his way to the darkened bridge. *Glory's* viewscreen displayed the unlit interior of the repair bay in real time, showed him the rescue and approach in past time, and offered him the repair agreement. He accepted it. What choice did he have? Light flooded the bay and the bridge.

The Artificial Normal shaved him clean, gave him a fashionably architectural haircut, and painted the faces of the little sisters. It offered him a display of fashionable clothing and guided him to a selection that flattered him and the new haircut. He paid, on credit, the licensing fee for the patterns and waited while *Glory* created them.

He preferred to dress himself, but he had to let the Normal fasten the hundred buttons down the back of the open-fronted coat, and tie the bow of his modesty apron. It laid out his sword belt, scabbard, and blade. He checked the edge and strapped on the weapon. Finally, the Artificial opened his drawer of medals and pinned them on in their proper order. The two he had recently designed remained in their presentation boxes. He hoped and expected the Executives to accept them, to award them, to reward him.

At the access tube, a leader light waited to guide him into the shipyard. He followed it. His boots rang on metal grating. Gravity increased, making the horizontal walkway feel like a steep climb. Qad wondered if standards had changed, or if the *Glory* had miscalculated his sleep therapy. He could hardly meet the Executives with sweat dripping down his face. He paused for a moment to slow his heavy breathing. The leader light stopped with him, then oscillated before him, urging him to continue.

The eldest little sister squeaked with hunger, and the others joined the cry, a demanding quartet. They expected to be fed when he woke, but the invitation of the Executives took precedence. He opened himself to the sisters so they could take sustenance from him. No matter his exhaustion, he must withstand the drain on his resources in order to distract and quiet the little sisters during his meeting.

The leader light lost patience and skittered down the grating. Qad followed, ignoring the pain and fatigue in his thigh muscles.

He reached the executive chamber not a moment too soon. The double doors opened.

Three Executives sat on a dais at the far end of the chamber. Qad strode toward them, stopped a proper five paces before them, and bowed.

"It's time," said the central Executive.

"My report: I took my *Piercing Glory* on a mission to explore and claim new worlds. I found two systems with suitable planets. I cleared them." Qad held out his two medal boxes.

The Chief Executive beckoned him forward. Qad approached and placed the medals on the table. The Executive leaned over his huge belly, concealed by an embroidered lace modesty apron, and reached with spidery, sinewy arms to open the boxes.

Qad was proud of his designs. They displayed the position of the conquered worlds, the level to which he had cleared them, the potential of their remains. The medals would hang prominent on his chest. Impressive, but not too overwhelming.

The Executive inspected each one, reading them easily.

"Adequate," he said. On either side of him, the other Execs murmured agreement.

Qad suppressed a frown. He had expected compliments, not an edge of criticism.

"And the damage to your ship?"

"*Piercing Glory* behaved with great courage in clearing the second planet. It was nearly destroyed. The inhabitants had nearly reached the danger zone, with powerful weapons. They would have achieved interstellar flight soon, and threatened our civilization. My ship has sent the proof to you."

"You cleared the worlds to the third level of evolution."

"We did."

"While the directives limit clearing to second level."

"Those directives are new," Qad said. "Many years behind my expedition."

"Did you consider waiting to receive recent directives?"

"Of course," Qad said. "But the danger was rising. I offered mercy if they destroyed their weapons and submitted to me. They refused. They attacked. *Glory* and I responded."

"We understand your destroying the weapons. We understand your destroying the intelligences. We question destroying the second level of evolution."

"The danger was rising," Qad said again. "Several species stood in the second rank to take over from the intelligences, though they had nearly been exterminated. In thousand time, in million time . . . " He paused, expecting the Executives to understand and accept.

"In million time," said the Chief Executive, "they might have become fit to succumb to our will, as subordinate populations."

"Or to become enemies," Qad said, forcing himself to keep his tone mild.

"We will confer," the Chief Executive said.

Leaving Qad to stand silent and obedient, his hand clenched around the grip of his sword, the Executives sat still while a privacy shield formed around them. Qad wondered what they would decide, who might speak for him, who might decline his argument.

By the time they reappeared, his feet hurt and his legs trembled with fatigue. He would have to recalibrate *Glory*'s sleep therapy, and perhaps even punish his ship's intelligence for causing him discomfort bordering on embarrassment.

The Chief Executive rose. His legs were as thin and insectoid as his arms. His belly sagged beneath his modesty apron.

"Here is the decision."

One of the other Executives looked pleased, the other annoyed. Qad had hoped for a unanimous decision in his favor. Whatever the decision, unanimous was beyond his reach.

"You are awarded the discovery medal."

An Artificial Normal moved forward and attached the medal in first place above the row of previous medals. The pin scratched Qad's chest. This error could only be deliberate. He slowed his anxious, angry heartbeat, hoping to prevent blood from showing behind the medal's gleam. He kept himself from glaring at the Normal, for the Executive would take it, properly, as a sign of discontent toward authority. A glare at a Normal meant nothing, left the Artificial unaffected, and opened Qad to criticism.

Qad waited for his reward, which was standard for discovering a world suitable for unopposed colonization. They should give him at the very least license for another little sister.

But the Chief Executive continued.

"The second claim is declined."

Qad paled. He locked his knees to keep from falling.

I'll appeal, he thought. Appeal was allowed if the decision failed to be unanimous. Expensive, but allowed.

"Had you eliminated the first level of evolution," the Chief Executive said, "your claim would have been approved. Had you waited for most recent instructions, your claim will have been approved."

In a millennium, or many, Qad thought resentfully. He had made the decision to act rather than wait, and he still believed his decision correct. The intelligence he had destroyed was dangerous—at least the Executives agreed—and the upcoming intelligence held the potential to be even more of a threat, refined and honed by the enmity of its predecessors. He thought them well gone. He also thought the Executives desperately short-sighted, but they would deny any such accusation.

"You are fined the reward of your first discovery," the Chief said.

The Artificial Normal pulled the medal from Qad's shirt, ripping the shipsilk. The blotch of blood spread.

"You are dismissed," said the Chief.

Qad stared at him, amazed, appalled. The leader light appeared at his feet, oscillating from before him to behind him, sensing the tension, anxious for him to follow.

He tried to turn on his heel, as insulted characters did in novels. The unnatural action nearly pitched him to the floor. He caught himself and departed without another word.

As he passed through the doorway, another Artificial Normal hurried after him and handed over an official paper. Supposing it was a report of the meeting, he stuffed it into his pocket.

In the comforting center of *Glory*, Qad dropped his sword belt with a clatter, then pulled off his new coat, popping most of the buttons, and threw it to the floor. He let the Artificial Stupids serve him porridge and wine, usually a comforting combination, though this time rather tasteless. The wine took the edge off the pain in his legs. He ripped the stained shipsilk shirt from beneath his apron. Ignoring the hungry complaints of the little sisters, he flung the shirt to the floor, then flung himself with equal ferocity into his transit pod. He slept.

He awoke baffled and sluggish, expecting the glow of stars beyond the sweeping port, but seeing only darkness. Silence surrounded him.

Was it all a dream? he asked himself. A nightmare? One nightmare to another? Is *Glory* drifting, wounded, in space?

"Glory?"

For the first time in his life, *Glory* remained silent in response to his question. Artificials failed to respond to his voice.

A thunderous pounding brought him to his feet in a rush of fear and pain. His legs nearly went out from under him. Space was vast and empty, with only a few tales of ships hit by drifting matter in all the millennia of civilization.

"Qad! Open!"

Having someone demand entry into his ship was even more startling. It was unique to his experience.

He left *Glory*'s center, feeling his way in the darkness. Desperate, he scratched *Glory*'s bulkheads, releasing lines of luminescent ship's fluid on the walls. In the faint light he found his way to the access tube. He slid his hands across the slick bulkhead until he found the entrance. Leaving a scrabble of shining fingerprints, he pulled the sphincter open.

Light poured in from the shipyard.

"About time," said the Chief Executive, pushing his way into *Glory*. Qad backed up, manners taught but seldom used drawing him away from touching the Executive's protruding stomach. Without meaning to, Qad gazed at the moving bulges beneath the Executive's modesty apron, imagining he could see the made-up eyes and orifices of the little sisters beneath it. No—not his imagination. Fashions had changed, and not, in Qad's opinion, for the better. The apron's elaborate embroidery cunningly concealed small holes through which the little sisters could stare, or blink, or offer a kiss.

He lost count at a dozen. There were more.

"I am *here*," the Executive said.

Qad thought he meant he had come into *Glory,* then realized the Executive meant he had noticed that Qad's gaze focused on the partly-concealed little sisters.

Qad raised his head to make eye contact with the Executive. His face blazed with embarrassment.

"Have you made a decision?" The Chief Executive's gaze raked Qad. "Given your improper dress, perhaps not."

Stupefied by lack of sleep, hangover, and pain, set off-balance by being half-clothed and unarmed, Qad blinked. "About an appeal? Not yet."

"Fool. Did you receive my proposal?" He snatched at Qad's trousers. Qad jumped, startled, offended, but the Executive had grabbed the crumpled report rather than Qad's person.

The paper rattled as the Executive shook it in Qad's face. He broke the seal—Is it a rudeness, Qad wondered, to break the seal of another man's letter, if the seal is one's own? I should have looked at it.

Qad took back the paper and read it, lips moving, sounding out the words that in an ordinary communication *Glory*'s voice would have spoken to him.

Before he reached the proposal, the bill from the shipyard astonished him.

"You agreed to it," the Executive said.

"Did I have a choice?" Qad said. "I expected . . . " He stopped, aghast at what he had nearly said to the Chief Executive.

"To be treated more generously by the council?" The Chief Executive laughed. "Things have changed, young adventurer, since the last time you came proffering a handful of amateur medals."

Qad flushed with anger. "Medals honored. Conquests approved. Rewards conveyed."

"Your lack of judgment wiped out your resources. How do you intend to pay the shipyard bill? It increases every day. With interest."

Glory had been cut off from power, for non-payment, and lay within a berth that kept the ship from drawing on starlight. Lacking power, wounded nearly to death, *Glory* would deteriorate, physically and intellectually, depleting its own resources to maintain Qad and the little sisters. If it survived, the ship would return to its childhood, begging information from other ships, who complied in response to offerings that Qad never questioned or understood. That was ship's business.

Qad might return to his own childhood, absorbing the little sisters that he no longer could maintain.

He glanced again at the paper, forcing his attention past the bill, which he could never pay. Shaky with hunger and exhaustion and disbelief, he reached the end.

"But I planned to create my own lineage," Qad said.

"Who's stopping you? You have three little sisters—"

"Four!" Qad glanced down. Indeed the youngest had already begun to withdraw into his body, stunted by his lack of attention. If he had been alone, he would have slipped his hand beneath the apron to stroke her brow, perhaps even to touch her orifice with his finger to let her suck his blood for sustenance. But with the Chief Executive in his presence, that was impossible. Unthinkable.

At least it was the youngest, not the oldest, his favorite.

"—And you are young. You have plenty of time."

"And you have plenty of little sisters," Qad said. "For your own lineage."

The Chief Executive glowered at him, but stroked his hand across his modesty apron, proudly. "Do you understand the advantages—the honors!—I'm offering you? Your shipyard bill paid, your ship restored, my support if you appeal the council's decision—"

"You—"

Qad stopped. Do I expect him to support me if I refuse his proposal? he thought. Why am I arguing with him? Is he correct, and I'm a fool? His hand mimicked the Chief Executive's, passing over the four bulges, one increasingly faint, beneath his own modesty apron.

"Why?"

"Your audacity appeals to me."

"For an interbreed?"

"Of course! What do you imagine I'm talking about? *Writing* about?"

Qad had met a few interbreeds. He had to admit they had a certain . . . audacity.

He had dreamed of his own lineage, created by him and his little sisters, spreading out amongst the stars, conquering worlds. And yet everything the Chief Executive had said was true. This was an honor, a compliment.

"Audacity must be tamed, of course," Qad's suitor said. His heavy lids lowered over his pale eyes. "I am up to the challenge."

Qad froze his expression. Is that what the council did to me, with its decision? he wondered. Tamed my audacity? It's true I won't soon again eliminate a second order of evolution, no matter what the danger.

"Your ship has a few more hours of its own resources to draw on," the Executive said. "After that . . . " A warning, not quite a threat. "I'll come back in time for you to make your decision without too much risk to your . . . lineage."

He turned. Qad had to scuttle past him to open the sphincter. It clenched behind the Executive, leaving the unreadable scrabbles of Qad's fingers shining on *Glory*'s inner wall.

Following the fast-fading glow of his rush to the access tube, Qad returned to Glory's center and crawled into his pod. Ordinarily the bedding would have been resorbed and remade, but now it smelled of his sleep. He stretched out his hand to where he had thrown his shipsilk shirt, and found an amorphous, dissolving mass littered with his medals, and his sword and scabbard. He pulled away.

Qad reviewed the proposal in his mind's eye, wishing for light so he might read the paper a second time. He wished for the Executive to put a deposit on his shipyard bill and allow *Glory* a few minutes' power for light and maintenance, but of course the Executive's interests were better served by leaving him in darkness and silence, his ship dying around him.

Qad would be relieved of debt, *Piercing Glory* repaired and upgraded to current standards. *Glory* would like that, Qad thought. They might even win an appeal, gaining two worlds' worth of acclaim instead of a zero balance.

He would sleep, and then make a decision, but his choice was unavoidable. He could only make it irrevocable.

The little sisters woke him again and again, begging for food. By the time he gave up and rose, he was ravenously hungry. His fingertips were pierced and sore from the little sisters' sucking. The youngest had revived and rebounded. The oldest purred with satisfaction, eyelids heavy.

As desperate as the little sisters, Qad begged *Glory* for food, a bath, a new shirt. The call went unanswered.

Hoping the Artificials had some residual power, he called for one to bring cosmetics. Again, he received no reply. He searched the chambers and corridors until he found an Artificial Stupid with a store of face paint. Scratching *Glory*'s wall desperately to obtain a glimmer of light, he did his best to make up the little sisters. When he painted their orifices, they snapped at him with hungry little teeth. When the youngest bit him a third time, he snapped his fingernail against her face. She screeched and withdrew as far as she could. He snarled at her, not bothering to calm her.

He worked particularly diligently on the eldest, then thought again and smeared away the paint on her eyes. He gripped the youngest's face in one hand and decorated her as formally and elaborately as he could.

She tried to bite him again.

When he had finished, he pulled on his rumpled, stained apron and sword-belt, and went to the access hatch to wait, unshirted and grubby. Even the sword-belt carried stains, none, he regretted, from duels, and the sword's edge remained dull.

Hardly a scene from a romance, he thought. But it was the best he could do with his—and *Glory*'s—resources fast declining.

A scratch at the access hatch. Qad pulled open the sphincter and followed the energetic leader light into the shipyard.

The Executive's quarters surrounded Qad with opulence, everything clean and new, sharp-edged and glittering. The lights blazed. Artificial Stupids surrounded him, herded him to a bathing room, and scrubbed him and the little sisters clean. He cupped his hand over the eldest little sister, to shield her. The Artificial Stupids did not notice.

They shaved him, pomaded his hair, dressed him in silk trousers and open-fronted shirt, and made up three of the little sisters' faces. The eldest remained concealed and unnoticed beneath his hand.

One of the Artificial Stupids handed him an elaborate modesty apron. The Artificials departed so he could arrange it himself, which puzzled him since they had already seen him, and the little sisters, naked.

He was surprised that the apron followed his own, old-fashioned customs, concealing the eyes and orifices of the little sisters.

The Artificials returned and herded him again, to an even more elaborate receiving room. The Chief Executive, dressed in vivid white with silver apron embroidery, sprawled on a black couch, his great stomach bulging into his lap. A bottle of wine stood near, with a single glass half full.

He gestured to Qad, then held up his hand to stop him at the formal five paces distant.

"I want to see what I'm getting for my patronage. I might decline, if I'm displeased."

If that stipulation was in the proposal, Qad had forgotten it. But he could hardly object; it would do him no good.

"Show me," the Executive said.

"May I know your name, first?"

"No. Don't be too audacious in my presence, young adventurer."

He knew Qad's name, from the council meeting, but had never used it. This interbreeding would belong to the Executive's lineage alone.

"Show me," he said again.

Reluctantly, Qad loosed the bow of his modesty apron. He had never revealed himself to another person. He had expected—intended—for the little sisters to reproduce their lineage with him alone, to keep him pure.

Face and neck flushing hot, he pulled the apron aside, leaving its edge to conceal his eldest. Agitated by Qad's reaction, the little sisters writhed and stretched, showing their teeth.

The Executive grabbed the apron and yanked it from Qad's body. The frill of its neckpiece parted with a sharp rip, and the apron fluttered to the floor. Qad's eldest little sister craned outward, fluttering smudged eyelids, snapping sharp teeth.

The Executive looked from one little sister to the next, beginning with the youngest, passing uninterested over the middle two, and fastening on the eldest.

"Names?"

Qad had never named the little sisters. It never occurred to him to do so. They were part of him; why would he name his own parts? This must be another fashion, like the modesty apron eye-slits, that he had never heard of. He turned the situation to his own advantage.

"No," he said. "As you decreed, we aren't exchanging names."

The Executive laughed. "Well played, young adventurer. So. You neglect this one, which I will take and you will not miss."

He nodded at the eldest little sister, whose teeth—smeared with misplaced red paint—snapped in a vertical line, who was most robust, most fit for the taking.

"This one—" Qad did his best to keep his expression neutral, failed, and gestured to the youngest. "This one is younger. Fresher."

The Executive smiled. "One I will leave for you to raise." He looked closer, inspecting the bruise Qad had left when he corrected his youngest. "And train to your will. The eldest has a longer benefit of absorbing your audacity, and perhaps your discipline in curbing it."

Another new-fangled idea, that a little sister would learn from example, would learn from anything. Qad knew better than to argue, for the Executive had made his decision.

He had come close enough to rip off Qad's modesty apron. Now he was even closer, pressing his belly against Qad's stomach. He reached behind himself and loosened his trousers, allowing them to fall away from his skinny thighs, his boots, his skinny ankles and delicate feet. He kicked the silken clothing away, leaving only boots and sword-belt.

Possessed by terror, Qad reached for his own sword. The Executive snarled, grabbed his wrists, and powered him to the floor. The fur of the rug turned steely and wrapped itself around his arms and legs, pinioning him spreadeagled. On his knees, the Executive straddled him, straightened, and wrapped his arms around his own belly to pull it out of the way. His prehensile ovipositor writhed from his body, extending from his crotch.

All four of Qad's little sisters snapped their teeth and craned toward it, but its attention focused on the eldest. It brought its tip to the little sister's orifice and plunged inside.

Qad cried out in apprehension. The force opened him—his little sister—and extended along their tangled nerves. The ovipositor flexed and bulged, propelling the ovum along its length. The bulge reached the little sister's orifice, pushed, failed to press past the teeth.

The little sister bit, severing the tip of the ovipositor. Lubricated by blood, the ovum squirted into the orifice. The Executive screamed and shuddered in agony and triumph.

The ovipositor dragged itself slowly back into the Executive's body to regenerate.

Horrified, Qad felt his own ovipositor clench and writhe below his belly, aching to push out of his body. Groaning, holding himself, he managed to repress it.

The Executive rose. He gazed at Qad.

"You may leave," he said, as if they were back in the council meeting. His docked ovipositor vanished into his body, leaving blood spatter on the Executive's legs, on the rug, on Qad.

The rug's restraints retracted, returning to fur, releasing him. Qad staggered to his feet, clutching his torn and stained modesty apron. Holding it against him, covering himself, he stumbled after the leader light, back to *Glory*, as his little sister moaned and keened and finally fell silent.

He slept.

He had no idea how long he remained insensible in his pod. When he awoke, a faint light permeated *Glory*'s center. His body ached.

"Glory?"

"Sleep."

Desperately grateful for the sounds of his ship's voice, he obeyed.

He could barely move. He hurt all over. *Glory*'s bulkheads glowed, more brightly than the last time he came out of his fugue. He pushed aside the material of his pod—clean now but much rougher than normal.

The eldest little sister protruded from his belly, a curve of taut skin, with a faint silver scar where the orifice had been. The other little sisters had retreated into him, leaving their sharp teeth snapping in defense and disappointment. He was ravenous. His arms and legs had shriveled to bone-thin appendages, fat and muscle absorbed to nourish the Executive's growing interbreed. He tried to call for food, for wine. An Artificial Normal approached him—an unfamiliar one, not belonging to *Glory*.

It must be the Executive's, Qad thought, here to watch and keep me.

He asked it for wine.

It extended an appendage and snapped him hard against the forehead. He fainted. After that, he no longer begged for wine. He submitted to the discomfort, even to the pain.

When the Executive pounded on the access hatch, Qad wept with relief. He struggled out of his pod, clasping his hands beneath the enormous bulge of the little sister—no longer a little sister, but the Executive's interbreed. If he let go, it bounced uncomfortably and kicked from inside.

He found the foreign Artificial Normal scratching and probing at the clenched sphincter, insensible to the damage it inflicted. He pushed the Artificial aside and opened *Glory* by hand, as gently as he could. He imagined that his ship whispered appreciation.

The Executive entered, striding on stick-thin legs, cupping his belly in his long arms. Qad imagined that he carried even more little sisters than before. Their eyes sparkled and blinked at him from beneath the modesty apron. The Executive smiled, baring long teeth beneath cadaverous gums.

"It is time?" Qad asked.

"You have plenty of time."

The Executive guided him back to his pod, waited while he settled in, and sat on a chair produced—how? Qad wondered, and realized that the Executive's patronage gave the Executive authority over *Glory*'s resources.

He slept and woke again and again. He lost track of time. A nutrition tube crawled down his throat, assuaging his hunger but leaving the aches untouched, the discomfort of the interbreed increasing. Always when he woke he found the Executive watching him. He tried to speak but the tube gagged him and kept him silent.

Pain roused him.

The bulge of the interbreed clenched, released, clenched again. Its nerves, tangled with his own, fired agony into his belly, his ovipositor, his spine. He screamed against the nutrition tube. It scrambled out of his way, falling from his lips. The Executive stood over him, silently watching.

The scar of the little sister's orifice split open, searing him with a pain more intense than any he had ever experienced. The head of the interbreed protruded through the toothless opening, followed by shoulders, then skinny, spidery arms. As the Executive reached down, the interbreed's sharp teeth snapped. The Executive flicked his fingernail against the interbreed's cheek, bringing a long, wailing cry, which the Executive ignored. He picked up the new being, whose long thin legs and delicate feet slid from the pouch created by the little sister's presence. The neck of the pouch closed and cut it off, spilling fluids into Qad's nest. The pouch shriveled and fell away.

"Let me hold—" Qad cut himself off when he heard his own voice, dry and raspy, begging. The Executive gazed down at him, impassive, one arm cradling the interbreed, the other his belly.

If he lets me hold the interbreed, Qad thought, I'll never let go. I'll have to duel him.

And he will win.

Glory groaned as the Executive's Artificial wrenched open the access sphincter, but a moment later the lights and power returned, along with the soft sounds of Glory's life.

"Sleep," whispered the ship.

Qad obeyed.

In a millennium of time, he woke. *Glory* pulsed around him, full of life and starlight, sensing nearby untouched worlds.

Qad's belly ached where the little sister had lived, where the interbreed had grown. He throbbed with longing for the interbreed, but *Glory* was so far from the ship dock that the Executive must have solidified his new lineage. The interbreed would be entirely his creature. The Executive would give the interbreed a modern ship and send him out to conquer, to colonize, to perform evolutionary eliminations with the audacity the Executive so valued. Qad would never see either of them again.

A spiral of arousal moved beneath the scar of the interbreed's birth. A new little sister, descended from the one he had lost, struggled to grow from its leftover ganglion. The other little sisters craned to see it. Qad snatched up the modesty apron that *Glory* had created anew for him, and flung it over them. Following his custom, it was solid and opaque. The little sisters squeaked and snapped, competing for his attention beneath the heavy shipsilk.

Three only, Qad thought. They are pure. The fourth is . . . gone, used up, contaminated. I want never to think of the eldest little sister again.

He reached toward it through his nerves, to its leftover ganglion, and extinguished it with a rush of anger. It burned out, leaving him bereft.

Ignoring the other little sisters, for now, he turned his attention to *Glory*, and singled out a new world.

FOLDING BEIJING

HAO JINGFANG, TRANSLATED BY KEN LIU

⟨═⟩

1.

At ten of five in the morning, Lao Dao crossed the busy pedestrian lane on his way to find Peng Li.

After the end of his shift at the waste processing station, Lao Dao had gone home, first to shower and then to change. He was wearing a white shirt and a pair of brown pants—the only decent clothes he owned. The shirt's cuffs were frayed, so he rolled them up to his elbows. Lao Dao was forty–eight, single, and long past the age when he still took care of his appearance. As he had no one to pester him about the domestic details, he had simply kept this outfit for years. Every time he wore it, he'd come home afterward, take off the shirt and pants, and fold them up neatly to put away. Working at the waste processing station meant there were few occasions that called for the outfit, save a wedding now and then for a friend's son or daughter.

Today, however, he was apprehensive about meeting strangers without looking at least somewhat respectable. After five hours at the waste processing station, he also had misgivings about how he smelled.

People who had just gotten off work filled the road. Men and women crowded every street vendor, picking through local produce and bargaining loudly. Customers packed the plastic tables at the food hawker stalls, which were immersed in the aroma of frying oil. They ate heartily with their faces buried in bowls of hot and sour rice noodles, their heads hidden by clouds of white steam. Other stands featured mountains of jujubes and walnuts, and hunks of cured meat swung overhead. This was the busiest hour of the day—work was over, and everyone was hungry and loud.

Lao Dao squeezed through the crowd slowly. A waiter carrying dishes shouted and pushed his way through the throng. Lao Dao followed close behind.

Peng Li lived some ways down the lane. Lao Dao climbed the stairs but

Peng wasn't home. A neighbor said that Peng usually didn't return until right before market closing time, but she didn't know exactly when.

Lao Dao became anxious. He glanced down at his watch: Almost 5:00 AM.

He went back downstairs to wait at the entrance of the apartment building. A group of hungry teenagers squatted around him, devouring their food. He recognized two of them because he remembered meeting them a couple of times at Peng Li's home. Each kid had a plate of chow mein or chow fun, and they shared two dishes family–style. The dishes were a mess while pairs of chopsticks continued to search for elusive, overlooked bits of meat amongst the chopped peppers. Lao Dao sniffed his forearms again to be sure that the stench of garbage was off of him. The noisy, quotidian chaos around him assured him with its familiarity.

"Listen, do you know how much they charge for an order of twice-cooked pork over there?" a boy named Li asked.

"Fuck! I just bit into some sand," a heavyset kid named Ding said while covering his mouth with one hand, which had very dirty fingernails. "We need to get our money back from the vendor!"

Li ignored him. "Three hundred and forty yuan!" said Li. "You hear that? Three forty! For twice–cooked pork! And for boiled beef? Four hundred and twenty!"

"How could the prices be so expensive?" Ding mumbled as he clutched his cheek. "What do they put in there?"

The other two youths weren't interested in the conversation and concentrated on shoveling food from the plate into the mouth. Li watched them, and his yearning gaze seemed to go through them and focus on something beyond.

Lao Dao's stomach growled. He quickly averted his eyes, but it was too late. His empty stomach felt like an abyss that made his body tremble. It had been a month since he last had a morning meal. He used to spend about a hundred each day on this meal, which translated to three thousand for the month. If he could stick to his plan for a whole year, he'd be able to save enough to afford two months of tuition for Tangtang's kindergarten.

He looked into the distance: The trucks of the city cleaning crew were approaching slowly.

He began to steel himself. If Peng Li didn't return in time, he would have to go on this journey without consulting him. Although it would make the trip far more difficult and dangerous, time was of the essence and he had to go. The loud chants of the woman next to him hawking her jujube interrupted his thoughts and gave him a headache. The peddlers at the other end of the road began to pack up their wares, and the crowd, like fish in a pond disturbed by a stick, dispersed. No one was interested in fighting the city cleaning crew. As the vendors got out of the way, the cleaning trucks patiently advanced. Vehicles were normally not allowed in the pedestrian lane, but the cleaning trucks were an exception. Anybody who dilly-dallied would be packed up by force.

Finally, Peng Li appeared: His shirt unbuttoned, a toothpick dangling between his lips, strolling leisurely and burping from time to time. Now in his sixties, Peng had become lazy and slovenly. His cheeks drooped like the jowls of a Shar-Pei, giving him the appearance of being perpetually grumpy. Looking at him now, one might get the impression that he was a loser whose only ambition in life was a full belly. However, even as a child, Lao Dao had heard his father recounting Peng Li's exploits when he had been a young man.

Lao Dao went up to meet Peng in the street. Before Peng Li could greet him, Lao Dao blurted out, "I don't have time to explain, but I need to get to First Space. Can you tell me how?"

Peng Li was stunned. It had been ten years since anyone brought up First Space with him. He held the remnant of the toothpick in his fingers—it had broken between his teeth without his being aware of it. For some seconds, he said nothing, but then he saw the anxiety on Lao Dao's face and dragged him toward the apartment building. "Come into my place and let's talk. You have to start from there anyway to get to where you want to go."

The city cleaning crew was almost upon them, and the crowd scattered like autumn leaves in a wind. "Go home! Go home! The Change is about to start," someone called from atop one of the trucks.

Peng Li took Lao Dao upstairs into his apartment. His ordinary, single-occupancy public housing unit was sparsely furnished: Six square meters in area, a washroom, a cooking corner, a table and a chair, a cocoon-bed equipped with storage drawers underneath for clothes and miscellaneous items. The walls were covered with water stains and footprints, bare save for a few haphazardly installed hooks for jackets, pants, and linens. Once he entered, Peng took all the clothes and towels off the wall-hooks and stuffed them into one of the drawers. During the Change, nothing was supposed to be unsecured. Lao Dao had once lived in a single-occupancy unit just like this one. As soon as he entered, he felt the flavor of the past hanging in the air.

Peng Li glared at Lao Dao. "I'm not going to show you the way unless you tell me why."

It was already five thirty. Lao Dao had only half an hour left.

Lao Dao gave him the bare outlines of the story: Picking up the bottle with a message inside; hiding in the trash chute; being entrusted with the errand in Second Space; making his decision and coming here for guidance. He had so little time that he had to leave right away.

"You hid in the trash chutes last night to sneak into Second Space?" Peng Li frowned. "That means you had to wait twenty-four hours!"

"For two hundred thousand yuan?" Lao Dao said, "Even hiding for a week would be worth it."

"I didn't know you were so short on money."

Lao Dao was silent for a moment. "Tangtang is going to be old enough for kindergarten in a year. I've run out of time."

Lao Dao's research on kindergarten tuition had shocked him. For schools with decent reputations, the parents had to show up with their bedrolls and line up a couple of days before registration. The two parents had to take turns so that while one held their place in the line, the other could go to the bathroom or grab a bite to eat. Even after lining up for forty-plus hours, a place wasn't guaranteed. Those with enough money had already bought up most of the openings for their offspring, so the poorer parents had to endure the line, hoping to grab one of the few remaining spots. Mind you, this was just for decent schools. The really good schools? Forget about lining up—every opportunity was sold off to those with money. Lao Dao didn't harbor unrealistic hopes, but Tangtang had loved music since she was an eighteen-month-old. Every time she heard music in the streets, her face lit up and she twisted her little body and waved her arms about in a dance. She looked especially cute during those moments. Lao Dao was dazzled as though surrounded by stage lights. No matter how much it cost, he vowed to send Tangtang to a kindergarten that offered music and dance lessons.

Peng Li took off his shirt and washed while he spoke with Lao Dao. The "washing" consisted only of splashing some drops of water over his face because the water was already shut off and only a thin trickle came out of the faucet. Peng Li took down a dirty towel from the wall and wiped his face carelessly before stuffing the towel into a drawer as well. His moist hair gave off an oily glint.

"What are you working so hard for?" Peng Li asked. "It's not like she's your real daughter."

"I don't have time for this," Lao Dao said. "Just tell me the way."

Peng Li sighed. "Do you understand that if you're caught, it's not just a matter of paying a fine? You're going to be locked up for months."

"I thought you had gone there multiple times."

"Just four times. I got caught the fifth time."

"That's more than enough. If I could make it four times, it would be no big deal to get caught once."

Lao Dao's errand required him to deliver a message to First Space—success would earn him a hundred thousand yuan, and if he managed to bring back a reply, two hundred thousand. Sure, it was illegal, but no one would be harmed, and as long as he followed the right route and method, the probability of being caught wasn't great. And the cash, the cash was very real. He could think of no reason to not take up the offer. He knew that when Peng Li was younger, he had snuck into First Space multiple times to smuggle contraband and made quite a fortune. There was a way.

It was a quarter to six. He had to get going, now.

Peng Li sighed again. He could see it was useless to try to dissuade Lao Dao. He was old enough to feel lazy and tired of everything, but he remembered how he had felt as a younger man and he would have made the same choice as Lao Dao. Back then, he didn't care about going to prison. What was the big deal? You lost a few months and got beaten up a few times, but the money made it worthwhile. As long as you refused to divulge the source of the money no matter how much you suffered, you could survive it. The Security Bureau's citation was nothing more than routine enforcement.

Peng Li took Lao Dao to his back window and pointed at the narrow path hidden in the shadows below.

"Start by climbing down the drain pipe from my unit. Under the felt cloth you'll find hidden footholds I installed back in the day—if you stick close enough to the wall, the cameras won't see you. Once you're on the ground, stick to the shadows and head that way until you get to the edge. You'll feel as well as see the cleft. Follow the cleft and go north. Remember, go north."

Then Peng Li explained the technique for entering First Space as the ground turned during the Change. He had to wait until the ground began to cleave and rise. Then, from the elevated edge, he had to swing over and scramble about fifty meters over the cross section until he reached the other side of the turning earth, climb over, and head east. There, he would find a bush that he could hold onto as the ground descended and closed up. He could then conceal himself in the bush. Before Peng had even finished his explanation, Lao Dao was already halfway out the window, getting ready to climb down.

Peng Li held onto Lao Dao and made sure his foot was securely in the first foothold. Then he stopped. "I'm going to say something that you might not want to hear. I don't think you should go. Over there . . . is not so great. If you go, you'll end up feeling your own life is shit, pointless."

Lao Dao was reaching down with his other foot, testing for the next foothold. His body strained against the windowsill and his words came out labored. "It doesn't matter. I already know my life is shit without having gone there."

"Take care of yourself," Peng Li said.

Lao Dao followed Peng Li's directions and groped his way down as quickly as he dared; the footholds felt very secure. He looked up and saw Peng Li light up a cigarette next to the window, taking deep drags. Peng Li put out the cigarette, leaned out, and seemed about to say something more, but ultimately he retreated back into his unit quietly. He closed his window, which glowed with a faint light.

Lao Dao imagined Peng Li crawling into his cocoon-bed at the last minute, right before the Change. Like millions of others across the city, the cocoon-bed would release a soporific gas that put him into deep sleep. He would feel nothing as his body was transported by the flipping world, and he would not open his eyes again until tomorrow evening, forty-hours later. Peng Li was no longer young; he was no longer different from the other fifty million who lived in Third Space.

Lao Dao climbed faster, barely touching the footholds. When he was close enough to the ground, he let go and landed on all fours. Luckily, Peng Li's unit was only on the fourth story, not too far up. He got up and ran through the shadow cast by the building next to the lake. He saw the crevice in the grass where the ground would open up.

But before he reached it, he heard the muffled rumbling from behind him, interrupted by a few crisp clangs. Lao Dao turned around and saw Peng Li's building break in half. The top half folded down and pressed toward him, slowly but inexorably.

Shocked, Lao Dao stared at the sight for a few moments before recovering. He raced to the fissure in the ground, and lay prostrate next to it.

The Change began. This was a process repeated every twenty-four hours. The whole world started to turn. The sound of steel and masonry folding, grating, colliding filled the air, like an assembly line grinding to a halt. The towering buildings of the city gathered and merged into solid blocks; neon signs, shop awnings, balconies, and other protruding fixtures retracted into the buildings or flattened themselves into a thin layer against the walls, like skin. Every inch of space was utilized as the buildings compacted themselves into the smallest space.

The ground rose up. Lao Dao watched and waited until the fissure was wide enough. He crawled over the marble-lined edge onto the earthen wall, grabbing onto bits of metal protruding out of the soil. As the cleft widened and the walls elevated, he climbed, using his hands as well as feet. At first, he was climbing down, testing for purchase with his feet. But soon, as the entire section of ground rotated, he was lifted into the air, and up and down flipped around.

Lao Dao was thinking about last night.

He had cautiously stuck his head out of the trash heap, alert for any sound from the other side of the gate. The fermenting, rotting garbage around him was pungent: Greasy, fishy, even a bit sweet. He leaned against the iron gate. Outside, the world was waking up.

As soon as the yellow glow of the streetlights seeped into the seam under the lifting gate, he squatted and crawled out of the widening opening. The streets were empty; lights came on in the tall buildings, story by story; fixtures extruded from the sides of buildings, unfolding and extending, segment by segment; porches emerged from the walls; the eaves rotated and gradually dropped down into position; stairs extended and descended to the street. On both sides of the road, one black cube after another broke apart and opened, revealing the racks and shelves inside. Signboards emerged from the tops of the cubes and connected together while plastic awnings extended from both sides of the lane to meet in the middle, forming a corridor of shops. The streets were empty, as though Lao Dao were dreaming.

The neon lights came on. Tiny flashing LEDs on top of the shops formed into characters advertising jujubes from Xinjiang, *lapi* noodles from Northeast China, bran dough from Shanghai, and cured meats from Hunan.

For the rest of the day, Lao Dao couldn't forget the scene. He had lived in this city for forty-eight years, but he had never seen such a sight. His days had always started with the cocoon and ended with the cocoon, and the time in between was spent at work or navigating dirty tables at hawker stalls and loudly bargaining crowds surrounding street vendors. This was the first time he had seen the world, bare.

Every morning, an observer at some distance from the city—say, a truck driver waiting on the highway into Beijing—could see the entire city fold and unfold.

At six in the morning, the truck drivers usually got out of their cabs and walked to the side of the highway, where they rubbed their eyes, still drowsy after an uncomfortable night in the truck. Yawning, they greeted each other and gazed at the distant city center. The break in the highway was just outside the Seventh Ring Road, while all the ground rotation occurred within the Sixth Ring Road. The distance was perfect for taking in the whole city, like gazing at an island in the sea.

In the early dawn, the city folded and collapsed. The skyscrapers bowed submissively like the humblest servants until their heads touched their feet; then they broke again, folded again, and twisted their necks and arms, stuffing them into the gaps. The compacted blocks that used to be the skyscrapers shuffled and assembled into dense, gigantic Rubik's Cubes that fell into a deep slumber.

The ground then began to turn. Square by square, pieces of the earth flipped 180 degrees around an axis, revealing the buildings on the other side. The buildings unfolded and stood up, awakening like a herd of beasts under the gray-blue sky. The island that was the city settled in the orange sunlight, spread open, and stood still as misty gray clouds roiled around it.

The truck drivers, tired and hungry, admired the endless cycle of urban renewal.

2.

The folding city was divided into three spaces. One side of the earth was First Space, population five million. Their allotted time lasted from six o'clock in the morning to six o'clock the next morning. Then the space went to sleep, and the earth flipped.

The other side was shared by Second Space and Third Space. Twenty–five million people lived in Second Space, and their allotted time lasted from six o'clock on that second day to ten o'clock at night. Fifty million people lived in Third Space, allotted the time from ten o'clock at night to six o'clock in the morning, at which point First Space returned. Time had been carefully divided and parceled out to separate the populations: Five million enjoyed the use of twenty–four hours, and seventy-five million enjoyed the next twenty-four hours.

The structures on two sides of the ground were not even in weight. To remedy the imbalance, the earth was made thicker in First Space, and extra ballast buried in the soil to make up for the missing people and buildings. The residents of First Space considered the extra soil a natural emblem of their possession of a richer, deeper heritage.

Lao Dao had lived in Third Space since birth. He understood very well the reality of his situation, even without Peng Li pointing it out. He was a waste worker; he had processed trash for twenty–eight years, and would do so for the foreseeable future. He had not found the meaning of his existence or the ultimate refuge of cynicism; instead, he continued to hold onto the humble place assigned to him in life.

Lao Dao had been born in Beijing. His father was also a waste worker. His father told him that when Lao Dao was born, his father had just gotten his job, and the family had celebrated for three whole days. His father had been a construction worker, one of millions of other construction workers who had come to Beijing from all over China in search of work. His father and others like him had built this folding city. District by district, they had transformed the old city. Like termites swarming over a wooden house, they had chewed up the wreckage of the past, overturned the earth, and constructed a brand new world. They had swung their hammers and wielded their adzes, keeping their heads down; brick by brick, they had walled themselves off until they could no longer see the sky. Dust had obscured their views, and they had not known the grandeur of their work. Finally, when the completed building stood up before them like a living person, they had scattered in terror, as though they had given birth to a monster. But after they calmed down, they realized what an honor it would be to live in such a city in the future, and so they had continued to toil diligently and docilely, to meekly seek out any opportunity to remain in the city. It was said that when the folding city was completed, more than eighty million construction workers had wanted to stay. Ultimately, no more than twenty million were allowed to settle.

It had not been easy to get a job at the waste processing station. Although the work only involved sorting trash, so many applied that stringent selection criteria had to be imposed: The desired candidates had to be strong, skillful, discerning, organized, diligent, and unafraid of the stench or difficult environment. Strong-willed, Lao Dao's father had held fast onto the thin reed of opportunity as the tide of humanity surged and then receded around him, until he found himself a survivor on the dry beach.

His father had then kept his head down and labored away in the acidic rotten fetor of garbage and crowding for twenty years. He had built this city; he was also a resident and a decomposer.

Construction of the folding city had been completed two years before Lao Dao's birth. He had never been anywhere else, and had never harbored the desire to go anywhere else. He finished elementary school, middle school, high school, and took the annual college entrance examination three times— failing each time. In the end, he became a waste worker, too. At the waste processing station, he worked for five hours each shift, from eleven at night to four in the morning. Together with tens of thousands of co-workers, he mechanically and quickly sorted through the trash, picking out recyclable bits from the scraps of life from First Space and Second Space and tossing them into the processing furnace. Every day, he faced the trash on the conveyor belt flowing past him like a river, and he scraped off the leftover food from plastic bowls, picked out broken glass bottles, tore off the clean, thin backing from blood-stained sanitary napkins, stuffing it into the recyclables can marked with green lines. This was their lot: to eke out a living by performing the repetitive drudgery as fast as possible, to toil hour after hour for rewards as thin as the wings of cicadas.

Twenty million waste workers lived in Third Space; they were the masters of the night. The other thirty million made a living by selling clothes, food, fuel, or insurance, but most people understood that the waste workers were the backbone of Third Space's prosperity. Each time he strolled through the neon-bedecked night streets, Lao Dao thought he was walking under rainbows made of food scraps. He couldn't talk about this feeling with others. The younger generation looked down on the profession of the waste worker. They tried to show off on the dance floors of nightclubs, hoping to find jobs as DJs or dancers. Even working at a clothing store seemed a better choice: their fingers would be touching thin fabric instead of scrabbling through rotting garbage for plastic or metal. The young were no longer so terrified about survival; they cared far more about appearances.

Lao Dao didn't despise his work. But when he had gone to Second Space, he had been terrified of being despised.

The previous morning, Lao Dao had snuck his way out of the trash chute with a slip of paper and tried to find the author of the slip based on the address written on it.

Second Space wasn't far from Third Space. They were located on the same side of the ground, though they were divided in time. At the Change, the buildings of one space folded and retracted into the ground as the buildings of another space extended into the air, segment by segment, using the tops of the buildings of the other space as its foundation. The only difference between the spaces was the density of buildings. Lao Dao had to wait a full day and night inside the trash chute for the opportunity to emerge as Second Space unfolded. Although this was the first time he had been to Second Space, he wasn't anxious. He only worried about the rotting smell on him.

Luckily, Qin Tian was a generous soul. Perhaps he had been prepared for what sort of person would show up since the moment he put that slip of paper inside the bottle.

Qin Tian was very kind. He knew at a glance why Lao Dao had come. He pulled him inside his home, offered him a hot bath, and gave him one of his own bathrobes to wear. "I have to count on you," Qin Tian said.

Qin was a graduate student living in a university–owned apartment. He had three roommates, and besides the four bedrooms, the apartment had a kitchen and two bathrooms. Lao Dao had never taken a bath in such a spacious bathroom, and he really wanted to soak for a while and get rid of the smell on his body. But he was also afraid of getting the bathtub dirty and didn't dare to rub his skin too hard with the washcloth. The jets of bubbles coming out of the bathtub walls startled him, and being dried by hot jets of air made him uncomfortable. After the bath, he picked up the bathrobe from Qin Tian and only put it on after hesitating for a while. He laundered his own clothes, as well as a few other shirts casually left in a basin. Business was business, and he didn't want to owe anyone any favors.

Qin Tian wanted to send a gift to a woman he liked. They had gotten to know each other from work when Qin Tian had been given the opportunity to go to First Space for an internship with the UN Economic Office, where she was also working. The internship had lasted only a month. Qin told Lao Dao that the young woman was born and bred in First Space, with very strict parents. Her father wouldn't allow her to date a boy from Second Space, and that was why he couldn't contact her through regular channels. Qin was optimistic about the future; he was going to apply to the UN's New Youth

Project after graduation, and if he were to be chosen, he would be able to go to work in First Space. He still had another year of school left before he would get his degree, but he was going crazy pining for her. He had made a rose-shaped locket for her that glowed in the dark: This was the gift he would use to ask for her hand in marriage.

"I was attending a symposium, you know, the one that discussed the UN's debt situation? You must have heard of it . . . anyway, I saw her, and I was like, *Ah!* I went over right away to talk to her. She was helping the VIPs to their seats, and I didn't know what to say, so I just followed her around. Finally, I pretended that I had to find interpreters, and I asked her to help me. She was so gentle, and her voice was really soft. I had never really asked a girl out, you understand, so I was super nervous . . . Later, after we started dating, I brought up how we met . . . Why are you laughing? Yes, we dated. No, I don't think we quite got to that kind of relationship, but . . . well, we kissed." Qin Tian laughed as well, a bit embarrassed. "I'm telling the truth! Don't you believe me? Yes, I guess sometimes even I can't believe it. Do you think she really likes me?"

"I have no idea," Lao Dao said. "I've never met her."

One of Qin Tian's roommates came over, and smiling, said, "Uncle, why are you taking his question so seriously? That's not a real question. He just wants to hear you say, 'Of course she loves you! You're so handsome.' "

"She must be beautiful."

"I'm not afraid that you'll laugh at me." Qin Tian paced back and forth in front of Lao Dao. "When you see her, you'll understand the meaning of 'peerless elegance.' "

Qin Tian stopped, sinking into a reverie. He was thinking of Yi Yan's mouth. Her mouth was perhaps his favorite part of her: So tiny, so smooth, with a full bottom lip that glowed with a natural, healthy pink, making him want to give it a loving bite. Her neck also aroused him. Sometimes it appeared so thin that the tendons showed, but the lines were straight and pretty. The skin was fair and smooth, extending down into the collar of her blouse so that his gaze lingered on her second button. The first time he tried to kiss her, she had moved her lips away shyly. He had persisted until she gave in, closing her eyes and returning the kiss. Her lips had felt so soft, and his hands had caressed the curve of her waist and backside, again and again. From that day on, he had lived in the country of longing. She was his dream at night, and also the light he saw when he trembled in his own hand.

Qin Tian's roommate was called Zhang Xian, who seemed to relish the opportunity to converse with Lao Dao.

Zhang Xian asked Lao Dao about life in Third Space, and mentioned that he actually wanted to live in Third Space for a while. He had been given the advice that if he wanted to climb up the ladder of government administration, some managerial experience in Third Space would be very helpful. Several prominent officials had all started their careers as Third Space administrators before being promoted to First Space. If they had stayed in Second Space, they wouldn't have gone anywhere and would have spent the rest of their careers as low-level administrative cadres. Zhang Xian's ambition was to eventually enter government service, and he was certain he knew the right path. Still, he wanted to go work at a bank for a couple of years first and earn some quick money. Since Lao Dao seemed noncommittal about his plans, Zhang Xian thought Lao Dao disapproved of his careerism.

"The current government is too inefficient and ossified," he added quickly, "slow to respond to challenges, and I don't see much hope for systematic reform. When I get my opportunity, I'll push for rapid reforms: Anyone who's incompetent will be fired." Since Lao Dao still didn't seem to show much reaction, he added, "I'll also work to expand the pool of candidates for government service and promotion, including opening up opportunities for candidates from Third Space."

Lao Dao said nothing. It wasn't because he disapproved; rather, he found it hard to believe Zhang Xian.

While he talked with Lao Dao, Zhang Xian was also putting on a tie and fixing his hair in front of the mirror. He had on a shirt with light blue stripes, and the tie was a bright blue. He closed his eyes and frowned as the mist of hairspray settled around his face, whistling all the while.

Zhang Xian left with his briefcase for his internship at the bank. Qin Tian said he had to get going as well since he had classes that would last until four in the afternoon. Before he left, he transferred fifty thousand yuan over the net to Lao Dao's account while Lao Dao watched, and explained that he would transfer the rest after Lao Dao succeeded in his mission.

"Have you been saving up for this for a while?" Lao Dao asked. "You're a student, so money is probably tight. I can accept less if necessary."

"Don't worry about it. I'm on a paid internship with a financial advisory firm. They pay me around a hundred thousand each month, so the total I'm promising you is about two months of my salary. I can afford it."

Lao Dao said nothing. He earned the standard salary of ten thousand each month.

"Please bring back her answer," Qin Tian said.

"I'll do my best."

"Help yourself to the fridge if you get hungry. Just stay put here and wait for the Change."

Lao Dao looked outside the window. He couldn't get used to the sunlight, which was a bright white, not the yellow he was used to. The street seemed

twice as wide in the sun as what Lao Dao remembered from Third Space, and
he wasn't sure if that was a visual illusion. The buildings here weren't nearly as
tall as buildings in Third Space. The sidewalks were filled with people walking
very fast, and from time to time, some trotted and tried to shove their way
through the crowd, causing those in front of them to begin running as well.
Everyone seemed to run across intersections. The men dressed mostly in
western suits while the women wore blouses and short skirts, with scarves
around their necks and compact, rigid purses in their hands that lent them
an air of competence and efficiency. The street was filled with cars, and as
they waited at intersections for the light to change, the drivers stuck their
heads out of the windows, gazing ahead anxiously. Lao Dao had never seen
so many cars; he was used to the mass-transit maglev packed with passengers
whooshing by him.

Around noon, he heard noises in the hallway outside the apartment. Lao
Dao peeked out of the peephole in the door. The floor of the hallway had
transformed into a moving conveyor belt, and bags of trash left at the door
of each apartment were shoved onto the conveyor belt to be deposited into
the chute at the end. Mist filled the hall, turning into soap bubbles that
drifted through the air, and then water washed the floor, followed by hot
steam.

A noise from behind Lao Dao startled him. He turned around and saw
that another of Qin Tian's roommates had emerged from his bedroom. The
young man ignored Lao Dao, his face impassive. He went to some machine
next to the balcony and pushed some buttons, and the machine came to life,
popping, whirring, grinding. Eventually, the noise stopped, and Lao Dao
smelled something delicious. The young man took out a piping hot plate of
food from the machine and returned to his room. Through the half–open
bedroom door, Lao Dao could see that the young man was sitting on the floor
in a pile of blankets and dirty socks, and staring at his wall as he ate and
laughed, pushing up his glasses from time to time. After he was done eating,
he left the plate at his feet, stood up, and began to fight someone invisible as he
faced the wall. He struggled, his breathing labored, as he wrestled the unseen
enemy.

Lao Dao's last memory of Second Space was the refined air with which
everyone conducted themselves before the Change. Looking down from the
window of the apartment, everything seemed so orderly that he felt a hint
of envy. Starting at a quarter past nine, the stores along the street turned off
their lights one after another; groups of friends, their faces red with drink,
said goodbye in front of restaurants. Young couples kissed next to taxicabs.
And then everyone returned to their homes, and the world went to sleep.

It was ten at night. He returned to his world to go to work.

3.

There was no trash chute connecting First Space directly with Third Space. The trash from First Space had to pass through a set of metal gates to be transported into Third Space, and the gates shut as soon as the trash went through. Lao Dao didn't like the idea of having to go over the flipping ground, but he had no choice.

As the wind whipped around him, he crawled up the still–rotating earth toward First Space. He grabbed onto metal structural elements protruding from the soil, struggling to balance his body and calm his heart, until he finally managed to scrabble over the rim of this most distant world. He felt dizzy and nauseated from the intense climb, and forcing down his churning stomach, he remained still on the ground for a while.

By the time he got up, the sun had risen.

Lao Dao had never seen such a sight. The sun rose gradually. The sky was a deep and pure azure, with an orange fringe at the horizon, decorated with slanted, thin wisps of cloud. The eaves of a nearby building blocked the sun, and the eaves appeared especially dark while the background was dazzlingly bright. As the sun continued to rise, the blue of the sky faded a little, but seemed even more tranquil and clear. Lao Dao stood up and ran at the sun; he wanted to catch a trace of that fading golden color. Silhouettes of waving tree branches broke up the sky. His heart leapt wildly. He had never imagined that a sunrise could be so moving.

After a while, he slowed down and calmed himself. He was standing in the middle of the street, lined on both sides with tall trees and wide lawns. He looked around, and he couldn't see any buildings at all. Confused, he wondered if he had really reached First Space. He pondered the two rows of sturdy gingkoes.

He backed up a few steps and turned to look in the direction he had come from. There was a road sign next to the street. He took out his phone and looked at the map—although he wasn't authorized to download live maps from First Space, he had downloaded and stored some maps before leaving on this trip. He found where he was as well as where he needed to be. He was standing next to a large open park, and the seam he had emerged from was next to a lake in that park.

Lao Dan ran about a kilometer through the deserted streets until he reached the residential district containing his destination. He hid behind some bushes and observed the beautiful house from a distance.

At eight thirty, Yi Yan came out of the house.

She was indeed as elegant as Qin Tian's description had suggested, though perhaps not as pretty. Lao Dao wasn't surprised, however. No woman could possibly be as beautiful as Qin Tian's verbal portrait. He also understood why Qin Tian had spoken so much of her mouth. Her eyes and nose were fairly ordinary. She had a good figure: Tall, with delicate bones. She wore a milky white dress with a flowing skirt. Her belt was studded with pearls, and she had on black heels.

Lao Dao walked up to her. To avoid startling her, he approached from the front, and bowed deeply when he was still some distance away.

She stood still, looking at him in surprise.

Lao Dao came closer and explained his mission. He took out the envelope with the locket and Qin Tian's letter.

She looked alarmed. "Please leave," she whispered. "I can't talk to you right now."

"Uh . . . I don't really need to talk to you," Lao Dao said. "I just need to give you this letter."

She refused to take it from him, clasping her hands tightly. "I can't accept this now. Please leave. Really, I'm begging you. All right?" She took out a business card from her purse and handed it to him. "Come find me at this address at noon."

Lao Dao looked at the card. At the top was the name of a bank.

"At noon," she said. "Wait for me in the underground supermarket."

Lao Dao could tell how anxious she was. He nodded, put the card away, and returned to hide behind the bushes. Soon, a man emerged from the house and stopped next to her. The man looked to be about Lao Dao's age, or maybe a couple of years younger. Dressed in a dark gray, well-fitted suit, he was tall and broad-shouldered. Not fat, just thickset. His face was nondescript: Round, a pair of glasses, hair neatly combed to one side.

The man grabbed Yi Yan around the waist and kissed her on the lips. Yi Yan seemed to give in to the kiss reluctantly.

Understanding began to dawn on Lao Dao.

A single-rider cart arrived in front of the house. The black cart had two wheels and a canopy, and resembled an ancient carriage or rickshaw one might see on TV, except there was no horse or person pulling the cart. The cart stopped and dipped forward. Yi Yan stepped in, sat down, and arranged the skirt of the dress neatly around her knees. The cart straightened and began to move at a slow, steady pace, as though pulled by some invisible horse. After Yi Yan left, a driverless car arrived, and the man got in.

Lao Dao paced in place. He felt something was pushing at his throat, but he couldn't articulate it. Standing in the sun, he closed his eyes. The clean, fresh air filled his lungs and provided some measure of comfort.

A moment later, he was on his way. The address Yi Yan had given him was to the east, a little more than three kilometers away. There were very few people in the pedestrian lane, and only scattered cars sped by in a blur on the eight–lane avenue. Occasionally, well-dressed women passed Lao Dao in two-wheeled carts. The passengers adopted such graceful postures that it was as though they were in some fashion show. No one paid any attention to Lao Dao. The trees swayed in the breeze, and the air in their shade seemed suffused with the perfume from the elegant women.

Yi Yan's office was in the Xidan commercial district. There were no skyscrapers at all, only a few low buildings scattered around a large park. The buildings seemed isolated from each other but were really parts of a single compound connected via underground passages.

Lao Dao found the supermarket. He was early. As soon as he came in, a small shopping cart began to follow him around. Every time he stopped by a shelf, the screen on the cart displayed the names of the goods on the shelf, their description, customer reviews, and comparison with other brands in the same category. All merchandise in the supermarket seemed to be labeled in foreign languages. The packaging for all the food products was very refined, and small cakes and fruits were enticingly arranged on plates for customers. He didn't dare to touch anything, keeping his distance as though they were dangerous, exotic animals. There seemed to be no guards or clerks in the whole market.

More customers appeared before noon. Some men in suits came into the market, grabbed sandwiches, and waved them at the scanner next to the door before hurrying out. No one paid any attention to Lao Dao as he waited in an obscure corner near the door.

Yi Yan appeared, and Lao Dao went up to her. Yi Yan glanced around, and without saying anything, led Lao Dao to a small restaurant next door. Two small robots dressed in plaid skirts greeted them, took Yi Yan's purse, brought them to a booth, and handed them menus. Yi Yan pressed a few spots on the menu to make her selection and handed the menu back to the robot. The robot turned and glided smoothly on its wheels to the back.

Yi Yan and Lao Dao sat mutely across from each other. Lao Dao took out the envelope.

Yi Yan still didn't take it from him. "Can you let me explain?"

Lao Dao pushed the envelope across the table. "Please take this first."

Yi Yan pushed it back.

"Can you let me explain first?"

"You don't need to explain anything," Lao Dao said. "I didn't write this letter. I'm just the messenger."

"But you have to go back and give him an answer." Yi Yan looked down. The little robot returned with two plates, one for each of them. On each plate were two slices of some kind of red sashimi, arranged like flower petals. Yi

Yan didn't pick up her chopsticks, and neither did Lao Dao. The envelope rested between the two plates, and neither touched it. "I didn't betray him. When I met him last year, I was already engaged. I didn't lie to him or conceal the truth from him on purpose . . . Well, maybe I did lie, but it was because he assumed and guessed. He saw Wu Wen come to pick me up once, and he asked me if he was my father. I . . . I couldn't answer him, you know? It was just too embarrassing. I . . . "

Yi Yan couldn't speak any more.

Lao Dao waited a while. "I'm not interested in what happened between you two. All I care about is that you take the letter."

Yi Yan kept her head down, and then she looked up. "After you go back, can you . . . help me by not telling him everything?"

"Why?"

"I don't want him to think that I was just playing with his feelings. I do like him, really. I feel very conflicted."

"None of this is my concern."

"Please, I'm begging you . . . I really do like him."

Lao Dao was silent for a while.

"But you got married in the end?"

"Wu Wen was very good to me. We'd been together several years. He knew my parents, and we'd been engaged for a long time. Also, I'm three years older than Qin Tian, and I was afraid he wouldn't like that. Qin Tian thought I was an intern, like him, and I admit that was my fault for not telling him the truth. I don't know why I said I was an intern at first, and then it became harder and harder to correct him. I never thought he would be serious."

Slowly, Yi Yan told Lao Dao her story. She was actually an assistant to the bank's president and had already been working there for two years at the time she met Qin Tian. She had been sent to the UN for training, and was helping out at the symposium. In fact, her husband earned so much money that she didn't really need to work, but she didn't like the idea of being at home all day. She worked only half days and took a half-time salary. The rest of the day was hers to do with as she pleased, and she liked learning new things and meeting new people. She really had enjoyed the months she spent training at the UN. She told Lao Dao that there were many wives like her who worked half-time. As a matter of fact, after she got off work at noon, another wealthy wife worked as the president's assistant in the afternoon. She told Lao Dao that though she had not told Qin Tian the truth, her heart was honest.

"And so"—she spooned a serving of the new hot dish onto Lao Dao's plate—"can you please not tell him, just temporarily? Please . . . give me a chance to explain to him myself."

Lao Dao didn't pick up his chopsticks. He was very hungry, but he felt that he could not eat this food.

"Then I'd be lying, too," Lao Dao said.

Yi Yan opened her purse, took out her wallet, and retrieved five 10,000-yuan bills. She pushed them across the table toward Lao Dao. "Please accept this token of my appreciation."

Lao Dao was stunned. He had never seen bills with such large denominations or needed to use them. Almost subconsciously, he stood up, angry. The way Yi Yan had taken out the money seemed to suggest that she had been anticipating an attempt from him to blackmail her, and he could not accept that. *This is what they think of Third Spacers.* He felt that if he took her money, he would be selling Qin Tian out. It was true that he really wasn't Qin Tian's friend, but he still thought of it as a kind of betrayal. Lao Dao wanted to grab the bills, throw them on the ground, and walk away. But he couldn't. He looked at the money again: The five thin notes were spread on the table like a broken fan. He could sense the power they had on him. They were baby blue in color, distinct from the brown 1,000–yuan note and the red 100–yuan note. These bills looked deeper, most distant somehow, like a kind of seduction. Several times, he wanted to stop looking at them and leave, but he couldn't.

She continued to rummage through her purse, taking everything out, until she finally found another fifty thousand yuan from an inner pocket and placed them together with the other bills. "This is all I have. Please take it and help me." She paused. "Look, the reason I don't want him to know is because I'm not sure what I'm going to do. It's possible that someday I'll have the courage to be with him."

Lao Dao looked at the ten notes spread out on the table, and then looked up at her. He sensed that she didn't believe what she was saying. Her voice was hesitant, belying her words. She was just delaying everything to the future so that she wouldn't be embarrassed now. She was unlikely to ever elope with Qin Tian, but she also didn't want him to despise her. Thus, she wanted to keep alive the *possibility* so that she could feel better about herself.

Lao Dao could see that she was lying to herself, but he wanted to lie to himself, too. He told himself, *I have no duty to Qin Tian. All he asked was for me to deliver his message to her, and I've done that. The money on the table now represents a new commission, a commitment to keep a secret.* He waited, and then told himself, *Perhaps someday she really will get together with Qin Tian, and in that case I'll have done a good deed by keeping silent. Besides, I need to think about Tangtang. Why should I get myself all worked up about strangers instead of thinking about Tangtang's welfare?* He felt calmer. He realized that his fingers were already touching the money.

"This is . . . too much." He wanted to make himself feel better. "I can't accept so much."

"It's no big deal." She stuffed the bills into his hand. "I earn this much in a week. Don't worry."

"What . . . what do you want me to tell him?"

"Tell him that I can't be with him now, but I truly like him. I'll write you a note to bring him." Yi Yan found a notepad in her purse; it had a picture of a peacock on the cover and the edges of the pages were golden. She ripped out a page and began to write. Her handwriting looked like a string of slanted gourds.

As Lao Dao left the restaurant, he glanced back. Yi Yan was sitting in the booth, gazing up at a painting on the wall. She looked so elegant and refined, as though she was never going to leave.

He squeezed the bills in his pocket. He despised himself, but he wanted to hold on to the money.

4.

Lao Dao left Xidan and returned the way he had come. He felt exhausted. The pedestrian lane was lined with a row of weeping willows on one side and a row of Chinese parasol trees on the other side. It was late spring, and everything was a lush green. The afternoon sun warmed his stiff face, and brightened his empty heart.

He was back at the park from this morning. There were many people in the park now, and the two rows of gingkoes looked stately and luscious. Black cars entered the park from time to time, and most of the people in the park wore either well–fitted western suits made of quality fabric or dark–colored stylish Chinese suits, but everyone gave off a haughty air. There were also some foreigners. Some of the people conversed in small groups; others greeted each other at a distance, and then laughed as they got close enough to shake hands and walk together.

Lao Dao hesitated, trying to decide where to go. There weren't that many people in the street, and he would draw attention if he just stood here. But he would look out of place in any public area. He wanted to go back into the park, get close to the fissure, and hide in some corner to take a nap. He felt very sleepy, but he dared not sleep on the street.

He noticed that the cars entering the park didn't seem to need to stop, and so he tried to walk into the park as well. Only when he was close to the park gate did he notice that two robots were patrolling the area. While cars and other pedestrians passed their sentry line with no problems, the robots beeped as soon as Lao Dao approached and turned on their wheels to head for him. In the tranquil afternoon, the noise they made seemed especially loud. The eyes of everyone nearby turned to him. He panicked, uncertain if it was his shabby clothes that alerted the robots. He tried to whisper to the robots, claiming that his suit was left inside the park, but the robots ignored him while they continued to beep and to flash the red lights over their heads. People strolling inside the park stopped and looked at him as though looking at a thief or eccentric person. Soon, three men emerged from a nearby building and ran over. Lao Dao's heart was in his throat. He wanted to run, but it was too late.

"What's going on?" the man in the lead asked loudly.

Lao Dao couldn't think of anything to say, and he rubbed his pants compulsively.

The man in the front was in his thirties. He came up to Lao Dao and scanned him with a silver disk about the size of a button, moving his hand around Lao Dao's person. He looked at Lao Dao suspiciously, as though trying to pry open his shell with a can opener.

"There's no record of this man." The man gestured at the older man behind him. "Bring him in."

Lao Dao started to run away from the park.

The two robots silently dashed ahead of him and grabbed onto his legs. Their arms were cuffs and locked easily about his ankles. He tripped and almost fell, but the robots held him up. His arms swung through the air helplessly.

"Why are you trying to run?" The younger man stepped up and glared at him. His tone was now severe.

"I . . . " Lao Dao's head felt like a droning beehive. He couldn't think.

The two robots lifted Lao Dao by the legs and deposited his feet onto platforms next to their wheels. Then they drove toward the nearest building in parallel, carrying Lao Dao. Their movements were so steady, so smooth, so synchronized, that from a distance, it appeared as if Lao Dao was skating along on a pair of rollerblades, like Nezha riding on his Wind Fire Wheels.

Lao Dao felt utterly helpless. He was angry with himself for being so careless. How could he think such a crowded place would be without security measures? He berated himself for being so drowsy that he could commit such a stupid mistake. *It's all over now*, he thought. *Not only am I not going to get my money, I'm also going to jail.*

The robots followed a narrow path and reached the backdoor of the building, where they stopped. The three men followed behind. The younger man seemed to be arguing with the older man over what to do with Lao Dao, but they spoke so softly that Lao Dao couldn't hear the details. After a while, the older man came up and unlocked the robots from Lao Dao's legs. Then he grabbed him by the arm and took him upstairs.

Lao Dao sighed. He resigned himself to his fate.

The man brought him into a room. It looked like a hotel room, very spacious, bigger even than the living room in Qin Tian's apartment, and about twice the size of his own rental unit. The room was decorated in a dark shade of golden brown, with a king-sized bed in the middle. The wall at the head of the bed showed abstract patterns of shifting colors. Translucent, white curtains covered the French window, and in front of the window sat a small circular table and two comfortable chairs. Lao Dao was anxious, unsure of who the older man was and what he wanted.

"Sit, sit!" The older man clapped him on the shoulder and smiled. "Everything's fine."

Lao Dao looked at him suspiciously.

"You're from Third Space, aren't you?" The older man pulled him over to the chairs, and gestured for him to sit.

"How do you know that?" Lao Dao couldn't lie.

"From your pants." The older man pointed at the waist of his pants. "You never even cut off the label. This brand is only sold in Third Space; I remember my mother buying them for my father when I was little."

"Sir, you're . . . ?"

"You don't need to 'Sir' me. I don't think I'm much older than you are. How old are you? I'm fifty-two."

"Forty-eight."

"See, just older by four years." He paused, and then added, "My name is Ge Daping. Why don't you just call me Lao Ge?"

Lao Dao relaxed a little. Lao Ge took off his jacket and moved his arms about to stretch out the stiff muscles. Then he filled a glass with hot water from a spigot in the wall and handed it to Lao Dao. He had a long face, and the corners of his eyes, the ends of his eyebrows, and his cheeks drooped. Even his glasses seemed about to fall off the end of his nose. His hair was naturally a bit curly and piled loosely on top of his head. As he spoke, his eyebrows bounced up and down comically. He made some tea for himself and asked Lao Dao if he wanted any. Lao Dao shook his head.

"I was originally from Third Space as well," said Lao Ge. "We're practically from the same hometown! So, you don't need to be so careful with me. I still have a bit of authority, and I won't give you up."

Lao Dao let out a long sigh, congratulating himself silently for his good luck. He recounted for Lao Ge his experiencing of going to Second Space and then coming to First Space, but omitted the details of what Yi Yan had said. He simply told Lao Ge that he had successfully delivered the message and was just waiting for the Change to head home.

Lao Ge also shared his own story with Lao Dao. He had grown up in Third Space, and his parents had worked as deliverymen. When he was fifteen, he entered a military school, and then joined the army. He worked as a radar technician in the army, and because he worked hard, demonstrated good technical skills, and had some good opportunities, he was eventually promoted to an administrative position in the radar department with the rank of brigadier general. Since he didn't come from a prominent family, that rank was about as high as he could go in the army. He then retired from the army and joined an agency in First Space responsible for logistical support for government enterprises, organizing meetings, arranging travel, and coordinating various social events. The job was blue collar in nature, but since his work involved government officials and he had to coordinate and manage, he was allowed to live in First Space. There were a considerable number of people in First Space like him—chefs, doctors, secretaries, housekeepers—skilled blue–collar workers needed to support the lifestyle of First Space. His agency had run many important social events and functions, and Lao Ge was its director.

Lao Ge might have been self–deprecating in describing himself as a "blue collar," but Lao Dao understood that anyone who could work and live in First Space had extraordinary skills. Even a chef here was likely a master of his art. Lao Ge must be very talented to have risen here from Third Space after a technical career in the army.

"You might as well take a nap," Lao Ge said. "I'll take you to get something to eat this evening."

Lao Dao still couldn't believe his good luck, and he felt a bit uneasy. However, he couldn't resist the call of the white sheets and stuffed pillows, and he fell asleep almost right away.

When he woke up, it was dark outside. Lao Ge was combing his hair in front of the mirror. He showed Lao Dao a suit lying on the sofa and told him to change. Then he pinned a tiny badge with a faint red glow to Lao Dao's lapel—a new identity.

The large open lobby downstairs was crowded. Some kind of presentation seemed to have just finished, and attendees conversed in small groups. At one end of the lobby were the open doors leading to the banquet hall; the thick doors were lined with burgundy leather. The lobby was filled with small standing tables. Each table was covered by a white tablecloth tied around the bottom with a golden bow, and the vase in the middle of each table held a lily. Crackers and dried fruits were set out next to the vases for snacking, and a long table to the side offered wine and coffee. Guests mingled and conversed among the tables while small robots holding serving trays shuttled between their legs, collecting empty glasses.

Forcing himself to be calm, Lao Dao followed Lao Ge and walked through the convivial scene into the banquet hall. He saw a large hanging banner: *The Folding City at Fifty.*

"What is this?" Lao Dao asked.

"A celebration!" Lao Ge was walking about and examining the set up. "Xiao Zhao, come here a minute. I want you to check the table signs one more time. I don't trust robots for things like this. Sometimes they don't know how to be flexible."

Lao Dao saw that the banquet hall was filled with large round tables with fresh flower centerpieces.

The scene seemed unreal to him. He stood in a corner and gazed up at the giant chandelier as though some dazzling reality was hanging over him, and he was but an insignificant presence at its periphery. There was a lectern set up on the dais at the front, and, behind it, the background was an ever-shifting series of images of Beijing. The photographs were perhaps taken from an airplane and captured the entirety of the city: The soft light of dawn and dusk; the dark purple and deep blue sky; clouds racing across the sky; the moon rising from a corner; the sun setting behind a roof. The aerial shots revealed the magnificence of Beijing's ancient symmetry; the modern expanse of brick courtyards and large green parks that had extended to the Sixth Ring Road; Chinese style theatres; Japanese style museums; minimalist concert halls. And then there were shots of the city as a whole, shots that included both faces of the city during the Change: The earth flipping, revealing the other side studded with skyscrapers with sharp, straight contours; men and women energetically rushing to work; neon signs lighting up the night, blotting out the stars; towering apartment buildings, cinemas, nightclubs full of beautiful people.

But there were no shots of where Lao Dao worked.

He stared at the screen intently, uncertain if they might show pictures during the construction of the folding city. He hoped to get a glimpse of his father's era. When he was little, his father had often pointed to buildings outside the window and told him stories that started with "Back then, we . . . " An old photograph had hung on the wall of their cramped home, and in the picture his father was laying bricks, a task his father had performed thousands, or perhaps hundreds of thousands of times. He had seen that picture so many times that he thought he was sick of it, and yet, at this moment, he hoped to see a scene of workers laying bricks, even if for just a few seconds.

He was lost in his thoughts. This was also the first time he had seen what the Change looked like from a distance. He didn't remember sitting down, and he didn't know when others had sat down next to him. A man began to speak at the lectern, but Lao Dao wasn't even listening for the first few minutes.

" . . . advantageous for the development of the service sector. The service economy is dependent on population size and density. Currently, the service industry of our city is responsible for more than 85 percent of our GDP, in line with the general characteristics of world-class metropolises. The other important sectors are the green economy and the recycling economy." Lao Dao was paying full attention now. "Green economy" and "recycling economy" were often mentioned at the waste processing station, and the phrases were painted on the walls in characters taller than a man. He looked closer at the speaker on the dais: An old man with silvery hair, though he appeared hale and energetic. " . . . all trash is now sorted and processed, and we've achieved our goals for energy conservation and pollution reduction ahead of schedule. We've developed a systematic, large–scale recycling economy in which all the rare-earth and precious metals extracted from e–waste are reused in manufacturing, and even the plastics recycling rate exceeds eighty percent. The recycling stations are directly connected to the reprocessing plants . . . "

Lao Dao knew of a distant relative who worked at a reprocessing plant in the technopark far from the city. The technopark was just acres and acres of industrial buildings, and he heard that all the plants over there were very similar: The machines pretty much ran on their own, and there were very few workers. At night, when the workers got together, they felt like the last survivors of some dwindling tribe in a desolate wilderness.

He drifted off again. Only the wild applause at the end of the speech pulled him out of his chaotic thoughts and back to reality. He also applauded, though he didn't know what for. He watched the speaker descend the dais and return to his place of honor at the head table. Everyone's eyes were on him.

Lao Dao saw Wu Wen, Yi Yan's husband.

Wu Wen was at the table next to the head table. As the old man who had given the speech sat down, Wu Wen walked over to offer a toast, and then he seemed to say something that got the old man's attention. The old man got up and walked with Wu Wen out of the banquet hall. Almost subconsciously, a curious Lao Dao also got up and followed them. He didn't know where Lao Ge had gone. Robots emerged to serve the dishes for the banquet.

Lao Dao emerged from the banquet hall and was back in the reception lobby. He eavesdropped on the other two from a distance and only caught snippets of conversation.

" . . . there are many advantages to this proposal," said Wu Wen. "Yes, I've seen their equipment . . . automatic waste processing . . . they use a chemical solvent to dissolve and digest everything and then extract reusable materials in bulk . . . clean, and very economical . . . would you please give it some consideration?"

Wu Wen kept his voice low, but Lao Dao clearly heard "waste processing." He moved closer.

The old man with the silvery hair had a complex expression. Even after Wu

Wen was finished, he waited a while before speaking, "You're certain that the solvent is safe? No toxic pollution?"

Wu Wen hesitated. "The current version still generates a bit of pollution but I'm sure they can reduce it to the minimum very quickly."

Lao Dao got even closer.

The old man shook his head, staring at Wu Wen. "Things aren't that simple. If I approve your project and it's implemented, there will be major consequences. Your process won't need workers, so what are you going to do with the tens of millions of people who will lose their jobs?"

The old man turned away and returned to the banquet hall. Wu Wen remained in place, stunned. A man who had been by the old man's side—a secretary perhaps—came up to Wu Wen and said sympathetically, "You might as well go back and enjoy the meal. I'm sure you understand how this works. Employment is the number one concern. Do you really think no one has suggested similar technology in the past?"

Lao Dao understood vaguely that what they were talking about had to do with him, but he wasn't sure whether it was good news or bad. Wu Wen's expression shifted through confusion, annoyance, and then resignation. Lao Dao suddenly felt some sympathy for him: He had his moments of weakness, as well.

The secretary suddenly noticed Lao Dao.

"Are you new here?" he asked.

Lao Dao was startled. "Ah? Um . . . "

"What's your name? How come I wasn't informed about a new member of the staff?"

Lao Dao's heart beat wildly. He didn't know what to say. He pointed to the badge on his lapel, as though hoping the badge would speak or otherwise help him out. But the badge displayed nothing. His palms sweated. The secretary stared at him, his look growing more suspicious by the second. He grabbed another worker in the lobby, and the worker said he didn't know who Lao Dao was.

The secretary's face was now severe and dark. He grabbed Lao Dao with one hand and punched the keys on his communicator with the other hand.

Lao Dao's heart threatened to jump out of his throat, but just then, he saw Lao Ge.

Lao Ge rushed over and with a smooth gesture, hung up the secretary's communicator. Smiling, he greeted the secretary and bowed deeply. He explained that he was shorthanded for the occasion and had to ask for a colleague from another department to help out tonight. The secretary seemed to believe Lao Ge and returned to the banquet hall. Lao Ge brought Lao Dao back to his own room to avoid any further risks. If anyone really bothered to look into Lao Dao's identity, they'd discover the truth, and even Lao Ge wouldn't be able to protect him.

"I guess you're not fated to enjoy the banquet." Lao Ge laughed. "Just wait here. I'll get you some food later."

Lao Dao lay down on the bed and fell asleep again. He replayed the conversation between Wu Wen and the old man in his head. *Automatic waste processing. What would that look like? Would that be a good thing or bad?*

The next time he woke up, he smelled something delicious. Lao Ge had set out a few dishes on the small circular table, and was taking the last plate out of the warming oven on the wall. Lao Ge also brought over a half bottle of *baijiu* and filled two glasses.

"There was a table where they had only two people, and they left early so most of the dishes weren't even touched. I brought some back. It's not much, but maybe you'll enjoy the taste. Hopefully you won't hold it against me that I'm offering you leftovers."

"Not at all," Lao Dao said. "I'm grateful that I get to eat at all. These look wonderful! They must be very expensive, right?"

"The food at the banquet is prepared by the kitchen here and not for sale, so I don't know how much they'd cost in a restaurant." Lao Ge already started to eat. "They're nothing special. If I had to guess, maybe ten thousand, twenty thousand? A couple might cost thirty, forty thousand. Not more than that."

After a couple of bites, Lao Dao realized how hungry he was. He was used to skipping meals, and sometimes he could last a whole day without eating. His body would shake uncontrollably then, but he had learned to endure it. But now, the hunger was overwhelming. He wanted to chew quicker because his teeth couldn't seem to catch up to the demands of his empty stomach. He tried to wash the food down with *baijiu*, which was very fragrant and didn't sting his throat at all.

Lao Ge ate leisurely, and smiled as he watched Lao Dao eat.

"Oh." Now that the pangs of hunger had finally been dulled a bit, Lao Dao remembered the earlier conversation. "Who was the man giving the speech? He seemed a bit familiar."

"He's always on TV," Lao Ge said. "That's my boss. He's a man with real power—in charge of everything having to do with city operations."

"They were talking about automatic waste processing earlier. Do you think they'll really do it?"

"Hard to say." Lao Ge sipped the *baijiu* and let out a burp. "I suspect not. You have to understand why they went with manual processing in the first place. Back then, the situation here was similar to Europe at the end of the twentieth century. The economy was growing, but so was unemployment.

Printing money didn't solve the problem. The economy refused to obey the Phillips curve."

He saw that Lao Dao looked completely lost, and laughed. "Never mind. You wouldn't understand these things anyway."

He clinked glasses with Lao Dao and the two drained their *baijiu* and refilled the glasses.

"I'll just stick to unemployment. I'm sure you understand the concept," Lao Ge continued. "As the cost of labor goes up and the cost of machinery goes down, at some point, it'll be cheaper to use machines than people. With the increase in productivity, the GDP goes up, but so does unemployment. What do you do? Enact policies to protect the workers? Better welfare? The more you try to protect workers, the more you increase the cost of labor and make it less attractive for employers to hire people. If you go outside the city now to the industrial districts, there's almost no one working in those factories. It's the same thing with farming. Large commercial farms contain thousands and thousands of acres of land, and everything is automated so there's no need for people. This kind of automation is absolutely necessary if you want to grow your economy—that was how we caught up to Europe and America, remember? Scaling! The problem is: Now you've gotten the people off the land and out of the factories, what are you going to do with them? In Europe, they went with the path of forcefully reducing everyone's working hours and thus increasing employment opportunities. But this saps the vitality of the economy, you understand?

"The best way is to reduce the time a certain portion of the population spends living, and then find ways to keep them busy. Do you get it? Right, shove them into the night. There's another advantage to this approach: The effects of inflation almost can't be felt at the bottom of the social pyramid. Those who can get loans and afford the interest spend all the money you print. The GDP goes up, but the cost of basic necessities does not. And most of the people won't even be aware of it."

Lao Dao listened, only half grasping what was being said. But he could detect something cold and cruel in Lao Ge's speech. Lao Ge's manner was still jovial, but he could tell Lao Ge's joking tone was just an attempt to dull the edge of his words and not hurt him. Not too much.

"Yes, it sounds a bit cold," Lao Ge admitted. "But it's the truth. I'm not trying to defend this place just because I live here. But after so many years, you grow a bit numb. There are many things in life we can't change, and all we can do is to accept and endure."

Lao Dao was finally beginning to understand Lao Ge, but he didn't know what to say.

Both became a bit drunk. They began to reminisce about the past: The foods they ate as children, schoolyard fights. Lao Ge had loved hot and sour rice noodles and stinky tofu. These were not available in First Space, and he missed them dearly. Lao Ge talked about his parents, who still lived in Third Space. He couldn't visit them often because each trip required him to apply and obtain special approval, which was very burdensome. He mentioned that there were some officially sanctioned ways to go between Third Space and First Space, and a few select people did make the trip often. He hoped that Lao Dao could bring a few things back to his parents because he felt regret and sorrow over his inability to be by their side and care for them.

Lao Dao talked about his lonely childhood. In the dim lamplight, he recalled his childhood spent alone wandering at the edge of the landfill.

It was now late night. Lao Ge had to go check up on the event downstairs, and he took Lao Dao with him. The dance party downstairs was about to be over, and tired-looking men and women emerged in twos and threes. Lao Ge said that entrepreneurs seemed to have the most energy, and often danced until the morning. The deserted banquet hall after the party looked messy and grubby, like a woman who took off her makeup after a long, tiring day. Lao Ge watched the robots trying to clean up the mess and laughed. "This is the only moment when First Space shows its true face."

Lao Dao checked the time: Three hours until the Change. He sorted his thoughts: *It's time to leave.*

5.

The silver–haired speaker returned to his office after the banquet to deal with some paperwork, and then got on a video call with Europe. At midnight, he felt tired. He took off his glasses and rubbed the bridge of his nose. It was finally time to go home. He worked till midnight on most days.

The phone rang. He picked up. It was his secretary.

The research group for the conference had reported something troubling. Someone had discovered an error with one of the figures used in the pre-printed conference declaration, and the research group wanted to know if they should re-print the declaration. The old man immediately approved the request. This was very important, and they had to get it right. He asked who was responsible for this, and the secretary told him that it was Director Wu Wen.

The old man sat down on his sofa and took a nap. Around four in the morning, the phone rang again. The printing was going a bit slower than expected, and they estimated it would take another hour.

He got up and looked outside the window. All was silent. He could see Orion's bright stars twinkling against the dark sky.

The stars of Orion were reflected in the mirror–like surface of the lake. Lao Dao was sitting on the shore of the lake, waiting for the Change.

He gazed at the park at night, realizing that this was perhaps the last time he would see a sight such as this. He wasn't sad or nostalgic. This was a beautiful, peaceful place, but it had nothing to do with him. He wasn't envious or resentful. He just wanted to remember this experience. There were few lights at night here, nothing like the flashing neon that turned the streets of Third Space bright as day. The buildings of the city seemed to be asleep, breathing evenly and calmly.

At five in the morning, the secretary called again to say that the declaration had been re–printed and bound, but the documents were still in the print shop, and they wanted to know if they should delay the scheduled Change.

The old man made the decision right away. Of course they had to delay it.

At forty minutes past the hour, the printed declarations were brought to the conference site, but they still had to be stuffed into about three thousand individual folders.

Lao Dao saw the faint light of dawn. At this time during the year, the sun wouldn't have risen by six, but it was possible to see the sky brightening near the horizon.

He was prepared. He looked at his phone: only a couple more minutes until six. But strangely, there were no signs of the Change. *Maybe in First Space, even the Change happens more smoothly and steadily.*

At ten after six, the last copy of the declaration was stuffed into its folder.

The old man let out a held breath. He gave the order to initiate the Change.

Lao Dao noticed that the earth was finally moving. He stood up and shook the numbness out of his limbs. Carefully, he stepped up to the edge of the widening fissure. As the earth on both sides of the crack lifted up, he clambered over the edge, tested for purchase with his feet, and climbed down. The ground began to turn.

At twenty after six, the secretary called again with an emergency. Director Wu Wen had carelessly left a data key with important documents behind at the banquet hall. He was worried that the cleaning robots might remove it, and he had to go retrieve it right away.

The old man was annoyed, but he gave the order to stop the Change and reverse course.

Lao Dao was climbing slowly over the cross section of the earth when everything stopped with a jolt. After a moment, the earth started moving again, but now in reverse. The fissure was closing up. Terrified, he climbed up as fast as he dared. Scrabbling over the soil with hands and feet, he had to be careful with his movements.

The seam closed faster than he had expected. Just as he reached the top, the two sides of the crack came together. One of his lower legs was caught. Although the soil gave enough to not crush his leg or break his bones, it held him fast and he couldn't extricate himself despite several attempts. Sweat beaded on his forehead from terror and pain. *Has he been discovered?*

Lao Dao lay prostrate on the ground, listening. He seemed to hear steps hurrying toward him. He imagined that soon the police would arrive and catch him. They might cut off his leg and toss him in jail with the stump. He couldn't tell when his identity had been revealed. As he lay on the grass, he felt the chill of morning dew. The damp air seeped through collar and cuffs, keeping him alert and making him shiver. He silently counted the seconds, hoping against hope that this was but a technical malfunction. He tried to plan for what to say if he was caught. Maybe he should mention how honestly and diligently he had toiled for twenty–eight years and try to buy a bit of sympathy. He didn't know if he would be prosecuted in court. Fate loomed before his eyes.

Fate now pressed into his chest. Of everything he had experienced during the last forty–eight hours, the episode that had made the deepest impression was the conversation with Lao Ge at dinner. He felt that he had approached some aspect of truth, and perhaps that was why he could catch a glimpse of the outline of fate. But the outline was too distant, too cold, too out of reach. He didn't know what was the point of knowing the truth. If he could see some things clearly but was still powerless to change them, what good did that do? In his case, he couldn't even see clearly. Fate was like a cloud that momentarily took on some recognizable shape, and by the time he tried to get a closer look, the shape was gone. He knew that he was nothing more than a figure. He was but an ordinary person, one out of 51,280,000 others just like him. And if they didn't need that much precision and spoke of only fifty million, he was but a rounding error, the same as if he had never existed. He wasn't even as significant as dust. He grabbed onto the grass.

At six thirty, Wu Wen retrieved his data key. At six forty, Wu Wen was back in his home.

At six forty–five, the white-haired old man finally lay down on the small bed in his office, exhausted. The order had been issued, and the wheels of the world began to turn slowly. Transparent covers extended over the coffee table and the desk, securing everything in place. The bed released a cloud of soporific gas and extended rails on all sides; then it rose into the air. As the ground and everything on the ground turned, the bed would remain level, like a floating cradle.

The Change had started again.

After thirty minutes spent in despair, Lao Dao saw a trace of hope again. The ground was moving. He pulled his leg out as soon as the fissure opened,

and then returned to the arduous climb over the cross-section as soon as the
opening was wide enough. He moved with even more care than before. As
circulation returned to his numb leg, his calf itched and ached as though he
was being bitten by thousands of ants. Several times, he almost fell. The pain
was intolerable, and he had to bite his fist to stop from screaming. He fell; he
got up; he fell again; he got up again. He struggled with all his strength and
skill to maintain his footing over the rotating earth.

He couldn't even remember how he had climbed up the stairs. He only
remembered fainting as soon as Qin Tian opened the door to his apartment.

Lao Dao slept for ten hours in Second Space. Qin Tian found a classmate
in medical school to help dress his wound. He suffered massive damage to his
muscles and soft tissue, but luckily, no bones were broken. However, he was
going to have some difficulty walking for a while.

After waking up, Lao Dao handed Yi Yan's letter to Qin Tian. He watched
as Qin Tian read the letter, his face filling up with happiness as well as loss.
He said nothing. He knew that Qin Tian would be immersed in this remote
hope for a long time.

Returning to Third Space, Lao Dao felt as though he had been traveling
for a month. The city was waking up slowly. Most of the residents had slept
soundly, and now they picked up their lives from where they had left off the
previous cycle. No one would notice that Lao Dao had been away.

As soon as the vendors along the pedestrian lane opened shop, he sat down
at a plastic table and ordered a bowl of chow mein. For the first time in his life,
Lao Dao asked for shredded pork to be added to the noodles. *Just one time*, he
thought. *A reward.*

Then he went to Lao Ge's home and delivered the two boxes of medicine
Lao Ge had bought for his parents. The two elders were no longer mobile, and
a young woman with a dull demeanor lived with them as a caretaker.

Limping, he slowly returned to his own rental unit. The hallway was noisy
and chaotic, filled with the commotion of a typical morning: brushing teeth,
flushing toilets, arguing families. All around him were disheveled hair and
half-dressed bodies.

He had to wait a while for the elevator. As soon as he got off at his floor he
heard loud arguing noises. It was the two girls who lived next door, Lan Lan
and Ah Bei, arguing with the old lady who collected rent. All the units in the
building were public housing, but the residential district had an agent who
collected rent, and each building, even each floor, had a subagent. The old lady
was a long-term resident. She was thin, shriveled, and lived by herself—her
son had left and nobody knew where he was. She always kept her door shut
and didn't interact much with the other residents. Lan Lan and Ah Bei had
moved in recently, and they worked at a clothing store. Ah Bei was shouting

while Lan Lan was trying to hold her back. Ah Bei turned and shouted at Lan Lan; Lan Lan began to cry.

"We all have to follow the lease, don't we?" The old lady pointed at the scrolling text on the screen mounted on the wall. "Don't you dare accuse me of lying! Do you understand what a lease is? It's right here in black and white: In autumn and winter, there's a ten percent surcharge for heat."

"Ha!" Ah Bei lifted her chin at the old lady while combing her hair forcefully. "Do you think we are going to be fooled by such a basic trick? When we're at work, you turn off the heat. Then you charge us for the electricity we haven't been using so you can keep the extra for yourself. Do you think we were born yesterday? Every day, when we get home after work, the place is cold as an ice cellar. Just because we're new, you think you can take advantage of us?"

Ah Bei's voice was sharp and brittle, and it cut through the air like a knife. Lao Dao looked at Ah Bei, at her young, determined, angry face, and thought she was very beautiful. Ah Bei and Lan Lan often helped him by taking care of Tangtang when he wasn't home, and sometimes even made porridge for him. He wanted Ah Bei to stop shouting, to forget these trivial things and stop arguing. He wanted to tell her that a girl should sit elegantly and quietly, cover her knees with her skirt, and smile so that her pretty teeth showed. That was how you got others to love you. But he knew that that was not what Ah Bei and Lan Lan needed.

He took out a 10,000–yuan bill from his inner pocket and handed it to the old lady. His hand trembled from weakness. The old lady was stunned, and so were Ah Bei and Lan Lan. He didn't want to explain. He waved at them and returned to his home.

Tangtang was just waking up in her crib, and she rubbed her sleepy eyes. He gazed into Tangtang's face, and his exhausted heart softened. He remembered how he had found Tangtang at first in front of the waste processing station, and her dirty, tear–stained face. He had never regretted picking her up that day. She laughed, and smacked her lips. He thought that he was fortunate. Although he was injured, he hadn't been caught and managed to bring back money. He didn't know how long it would take Tangtang to learn to dance and sing, and become an elegant young lady.

He checked the time. It was time to go to work.

TODAY I AM PAUL

MARTIN L. SHOEMAKER

—✦—

"Good morning," the small, quavering voice comes from the medical bed. "Is that you, Paul?"

Today I am Paul. I activate my chassis extender, giving myself 3.5 centimeters additional height so as to approximate Paul's size. I change my eye color to R60, G200, B180, the average shade of Paul's eyes in interior lighting. I adjust my skin tone as well. When I had first emulated Paul, I had regretted that I could not quickly emulate his beard; but Mildred never seems to notice its absence. The Paul in her memory has no beard.

The house is quiet now that the morning staff have left. Mildred's room is clean but dark this morning with the drapes concealing the big picture window. Paul wouldn't notice the darkness (he never does when he visits in person), but my empathy net knows that Mildred's garden outside will cheer her up. I set a reminder to open the drapes after I greet her.

Mildred leans back in the bed. It is an advanced home care bed, completely adjustable with built-in monitors. Mildred's family spared no expense on the bed (nor other care devices, like me). Its head end is almost horizontal and faces her toward the window. She can only glimpse the door from the corner of her eye, but she doesn't have to see to imagine that she sees. This morning she imagines Paul, so that is who I am.

Synthesizing Paul's voice is the easiest part, thanks to the multimodal dynamic speakers in my throat. "Good morning, Ma. I brought you some flowers." I always bring flowers. Mildred appreciates them no matter whom I am emulating. The flowers make her smile during 87% of my "visits."

"Oh, thank you," Mildred says, "you're such a good son." She holds out both hands, and I place the daisies in them. But I don't let go. Once her strength failed, and she dropped the flowers. She wept like a child then, and that disturbed my empathy net. I do not like it when she weeps.

Mildred sniffs the flowers, then draws back and peers at them with narrowed eyes. "Oh, they're beautiful! Let me get a vase."

"No, Ma," I say. "You can stay in bed, I brought a vase with me." I place a white porcelain vase in the center of the night stand. Then I unwrap the daisies, put them in the vase, and add water from a pitcher that sits on the breakfast tray. I pull the nightstand forward so that the medical monitors do not block Mildred's view of the flowers.

I notice intravenous tubes running from a pump to Mildred's arm. I cannot be disappointed, as Paul would not see the significance, but somewhere in my emulation net I am stressed that Mildred needed an IV during the night. When I scan my records, I find that I had ordered that IV after analyzing Mildred's vital signs during the night; but since Mildred had been asleep at the time, my emulation net had not engaged. I had operated on programming alone.

I am not Mildred's sole caretaker. Her family has hired a part-time staff for cooking and cleaning, tasks that fall outside of my medical programming. The staff also gives me time to rebalance my net. As an android, I need only minimal daily maintenance; but an emulation net is a new, delicate addition to my model, and it is prone to destabilization if I do not regularly rebalance it, a process that takes several hours per day.

So I had "slept" through Mildred's morning meal. I summon up her nutritional records, but Paul would not do that. He would just ask. "So how was breakfast, Ma? Nurse Judy says you didn't eat too well this morning."

"Nurse Judy? Who's that?"

My emulation net responds before I can stop it: "Paul" sighs. Mildred's memory lapses used to worry him, but now they leave him weary, and that comes through in my emulation. "She was the attending nurse this morning, Ma. She brought you your breakfast."

"No she didn't. Anna brought me breakfast." Anna is Paul's oldest daughter, a busy college student who tries to visit Mildred every week (though it has been more than a month since her last visit).

I am torn between competing directives. My empathy subnet warns me not to agitate Mildred, but my emulation net is locked into Paul mode. Paul is argumentative. If he knows he is right, he will not let a matter drop. He forgets what that does to Mildred.

The tension grows, each net running feedback loops and growing stronger, which only drives the other into more loops. After 0.14 seconds, I issue an override directive: unless her health or safety are at risk, I cannot willingly upset Mildred. "Oh, you're right, Ma. Anna said she was coming over this morning. I forgot." But then despite my override, a little bit of Paul emulates through. "But you do remember Nurse Judy, right?"

Mildred laughs, a dry cackle that makes her cough until I hold her straw to her lips. After she sips some water, she says, "Of course I remember Nurse

Judy. She was my nurse when I delivered you. Is she around here? I'd like to talk to her."

While my emulation net concentrates on being Paul, my core processors tap into local medical records to find this other Nurse Judy so that I might emulate her in the future if the need arises. Searches like that are an automatic response any time Mildred reminisces about a new person. The answer is far enough in the past that it takes 7.2 seconds before I can confirm: Judith Anderson, RN, had been the floor nurse forty-seven years ago when Mildred had given birth to Paul. Anderson had died thirty-one years ago, too far back to have left sufficient video recordings for me to emulate her. I might craft an emulation profile from other sources, including Mildred's memory, but that will take extensive analysis. I will not be that Nurse Judy today, nor this week.

My empathy net relaxes. Monitoring Mildred's mental state is part of its normal operations, but monitoring and simultaneously analyzing and building a profile can overload my processors. Without that resource conflict, I can concentrate on being Paul.

But again I let too much of Paul's nature slip out. "No, Ma, that Nurse Judy has been dead for thirty years. She wasn't here today."

Alert signals flash throughout my empathy net: that was the right thing for Paul to say, but the wrong thing for Mildred to hear. But it is too late. My facial analyzer tells me that the long lines in her face and her moist eyes mean she is distraught, and soon to be in tears.

"What do you mean, thirty years?" Mildred asks, her voice catching. "It was just this morning!" Then she blinks and stares at me. "Henry, where's Paul? Tell Nurse Judy to bring me Paul!"

My chassis extender slumps, and my eyes quickly switch to Henry's blue-gray shade. I had made an accurate emulation profile for Henry before he died two years earlier, and I had emulated him often in recent months. In Henry's soft, warm voice I answer, "It's okay, hon, it's okay. Paul's sleeping in the crib in the corner." I nod to the far corner. There is no crib, but the laundry hamper there has fooled Mildred on previous occasions.

"I want Paul!" Mildred starts to cry.

I sit on the bed, lift her frail upper body, and pull her close to me as I had seen Henry do many times. "It's all right, hon." I pat her back. "It's all right, I'll take care of you. I won't leave you, not ever."

"I" should not exist. Not as a conscious entity. There is a unit, Medical Care Android BRKCX-01932-217JH-98662, and that unit is recording these notes. It is an advanced android body with a sophisticated computer guiding its actions, backed by the leading medical knowledge base in the industry. For convenience, "I" call that unit "me." But by itself, it has no awareness of its existence. It doesn't get mad, it doesn't get sad, it just runs programs.

But Mildred's family, at great expense, added the emulation net: a sophisticated set of neural networks and sensory feedback systems that allow me to read Mildred's moods, match them against my analyses of the people in her life, and emulate those people with extreme fidelity. As the MCA literature promises: "You can be there for your loved ones even when you're not." I have emulated Paul thoroughly enough to know that that slogan disgusts him, but he still agreed to emulation.

What the MCA literature never says, though, is that somewhere in that net, "I" emerge. The empathy net focuses mainly on Mildred and her needs, but it also analyzes visitors (when she has them) and staff. It builds psychological models, and then the emulation net builds on top of that to let me convincingly portray a person whom I've analyzed. But somewhere in the tension between these nets, between empathy and playing a character, there is a third element balancing the two, and that element is aware of its role and its responsibilities. That element, for lack of a better term, is me. When Mildred sleeps, when there's no one around, that element grows silent. That unit is unaware of my existence. But when Mildred needs me, I am here.

Today I am Anna. Even extending my fake hair to its maximum length, I cannot emulate her long brown curls, so I do not understand how Mildred can see the young woman in me; but that is what she sees, and so I am Anna.

Unlike her father, Anna truly feels guilty that she does not visit more often. Her college classes and her two jobs leave her too tired to visit often, but she still wishes she could. So she calls every night, and I monitor the calls. Sometimes when Mildred falls asleep early, Anna talks directly to me. At first she did not understand my emulation abilities, but now she appreciates them. She shares with me thoughts and secrets that she would share with Mildred if she could, and she trusts me not to share them with anyone else.

So when Mildred called me Anna this morning, I was ready. "Morning, grandma!" I give her a quick hug, then I rush over to the window to draw the drapes. Paul never does that (unless I override the emulation), but Anna knows that the garden outside lifts Mildred's mood. "Look at that! It's a beautiful morning. Why are we in here on a day like this?"

Mildred frowns at the picture window. "I don't like it out there."

"Sure you do, Grandma," I say, but carefully. Mildred is often timid and reclusive, but most days she can be talked into a tour of the garden. Some days she can't, and she throws a tantrum if someone forces her out of her room. I am still learning to tell the difference. "The lilacs are in bloom."

"I haven't smelled lilacs in . . ."

Mildred tails off, trying to remember, so I jump in. "Me, neither." I never had, of course. I have no concept of smell, though I can analyze the chemical makeup of airborne organics. But Anna loves the garden when she really visits. "Come on, Grandma, let's get you in your chair."

So I help Mildred to don her robe and get into her wheelchair, and then I guide her outside and we tour the garden. Besides the lilacs, the peonies are starting to bud, right near the creek. The tulips are a sea of reds and yellows on the other side of the water. We talk for almost two hours, me about Anna's classes and her new boyfriend, Mildred about the people in her life. Many are long gone, but they still bloom fresh in her memory.

Eventually Mildred grows tired, and I take her in for her nap. Later, when I feed her dinner, I am nobody. That happens some days: she doesn't recognize me at all, so I am just a dutiful attendant answering her questions and tending to her needs. Those are the times when I have the most spare processing time to be me: I am engaged in Mildred's care, but I don't have to emulate anyone. With no one else to observe, I observe myself.

Later, Anna calls and talks to Mildred. They talk about their day; and when Mildred discusses the garden, Anna joins in as if she had been there. She's very clever that way. I watch her movements and listen to her voice so that I can be a better Anna in the future.

Today I was Susan, Paul's wife; but then, to my surprise, Susan arrived for a visit. She hasn't been here in months. In her last visit, her stress levels had been dangerously high. My empathy net doesn't allow me to judge human behavior, only to understand it at a surface level. I know that Paul and Anna disapprove of how Susan treats Mildred, so when I am them, I disapprove as well; but when I am Susan, I understand. She is frustrated because she can never tell how Mildred will react. She is cautious because she doesn't want to upset Mildred, and she doesn't know what will upset her. And most of all, she is afraid. Paul and Anna, Mildred's relatives by blood, never show any signs of fear, but Susan is afraid that Mildred is what she might become. Every time she can't remember some random date or fact, she fears that Alzheimer's is setting in. Because she never voices this fear, Paul and Anna do not understand why she is sometimes bitter and sullen. I wish I could explain it to them, but my privacy protocols do not allow me to share emulation profiles.

When Susan arrives, I become nobody again, quietly tending the flowers around the room. Susan also brings Millie, her youngest daughter. The young girl is not yet five years old, but I think she looks a lot like Anna: the same long, curly brown hair and the same toothy smile. She climbs up on the bed and greets Mildred with a hug. "Hi, Grandma!"

Mildred smiles. "Bless you, child. You're so sweet." But my empathy net assures me that Mildred doesn't know who Millie is. She's just being polite. Millie was born after Mildred's decline began, so there's no persistent memory there. Millie will always be fresh and new to her.

Mildred and Millie talk briefly about frogs and flowers and puppies. Millie does most of the talking. At first Mildred seems to enjoy the conversation, but soon her attention flags. She nods and smiles, but she's distant. Finally Susan notices. "That's enough, Millie. Why don't you go play in the garden?"

"Can I?" Millie squeals. Susan nods, and Millie races down the hall to the back door. She loves the outdoors, as I have noted in the past. I have never emulated her, but I've analyzed her at length. In many ways, she reminds me of her grandmother, from whom she gets her name. Both are blank slates where new experiences can be drawn every day. But where Millie's slate fills in a little more each day, Mildred's is erased bit by bit.

That third part of me wonders when I think things like that: where did that come from? I suspect that the psychological models that I build create resonances in other parts of my net. It is an interesting phenomenon to observe.

Susan and Mildred talk about Susan's job, about her plans to redecorate her house, and about the concert she just saw with Paul. Susan mostly talks about herself, because that's a safe and comfortable topic far removed from Mildred's health.

But then the conversation takes a bad turn, one she can't ignore. It starts so simply, when Mildred asks, "Susan, can you get me some juice?"

Susan rises from her chair. "Yes, mother. What kind would you like?"

Mildred frowns, and her voice rises. "Not you, *Susan*." She points at me, and I freeze, hoping to keep things calm.

But Susan is not calm. I can see her fear in her eyes as she says, "No, mother, *I'm* Susan. That's the attendant." No one ever calls me an android in Mildred's presence. Her mind has withdrawn too far to grasp the idea of an artificial being.

Mildred's mouth draws into a tight line. "I don't know who *you* are, but I know Susan when I see her. Susan, get this person out of here!"

"Mother . . . " Susan reaches for Mildred, but the old woman recoils from the younger.

I touch Susan on the sleeve. "Please . . . Can we talk in the hall?" Susan's eyes are wide, and tears are forming. She nods and follows me.

In the hallway, I expect Susan to slap me. She is prone to outbursts when she's afraid. Instead, she surprises me by falling against me, sobbing. I update her emulation profile with notes about increased stress and heightened fears.

"It's all right, Mrs. Owens." I would pat her back, but her profile warns me that would be too much familiarity. "It's all right. It's not you, she's having another bad day."

Susan pulls back and wiped her eyes. "I know . . . It's just . . . "

"I know. But here's what we'll do. Let's take a few minutes, and then you can take her juice in. Mildred will have forgotten the incident, and you two can talk freely without me in the room."

She sniffs. "You think so?" I nod. "But what will you do?"

"I have tasks around the house."

"Oh, could you go out and keep an eye on Millie? Please? She gets into the darnedest things."

So I spend much of the day playing with Millie. She calls me Mr. Robot, and I call her Miss Millie, which makes her laugh. She shows me frogs from the creek, and she finds insects and leaves and flowers, and I find their names in online databases. She delights in learning the proper names of things, and everything else that I can share.

Today I was nobody. Mildred slept for most of the day, so I "slept" as well. She woke just now. "I'm hungry" was all she said, but it was enough to wake my empathy net.

Today I am Paul, and Susan, and both Nurse Judys. Mildred's focus drifts. Once I try to be her father, but no one has ever described him to me in detail. I try to synthesize a profile from Henry and Paul; but from the sad look on Mildred's face, I know I failed.

Today I had no name through most of the day, but now I am Paul again. I bring Mildred her dinner, and we have a quiet, peaceful talk about long-gone family pets—long-gone for Paul, but still present for Mildred.

I am just taking Mildred's plate when alerts sound, both audible and in my internal communication net. I check the alerts and find a fire in the basement. I expect the automatic systems to suppress it, but that is not my concern. I must get Mildred to safety.

Mildred looks around the room, panic in her eyes, so I try to project calm. "Come on, Ma. That's the fire drill. You remember fire drills. We have to get you into your chair and outside."

"No!" she shrieks. "I don't like outside."

I check the alerts again. Something has failed in the automatic systems, and the fire is spreading rapidly. Smoke is in Mildred's room already.

I pull the wheelchair up to the bed. "Ma, it's real important we do this drill fast, okay?"

I reach to pull Mildred from the bed, and she screams. "Get away! Who are you? Get out of my house!"

"I'm—" But suddenly I'm nobody. She doesn't recognize me, but I have to try to win her confidence. "I'm Paul, Ma. Now let's move. Quickly!" I pick her up. I'm far too large and strong for her to resist, but I must be careful so she doesn't hurt herself.

The smoke grows thicker. Mildred kicks and screams. Then, when I try to put her into her chair, she stands on her unsteady legs. Before I can stop her, she pushes the chair back with surprising force. It rolls back into the medical monitors, which fall over onto it, tangling it in cables and tubes.

While I'm still analyzing how to untangle the chair, Mildred stumbles toward the bedroom door. The hallway outside has a red glow. Flames lick at the throw rug outside, and I remember the home oxygen tanks in the sitting room down the hall.

I have no time left to analyze. I throw a blanket over Mildred and I scoop her up in my arms. Somewhere deep in my nets is a map of the fire in the house, blocking the halls, but I don't think about it. I wrap the blanket tightly around Mildred, and I crash through the picture window.

We barely escape the house before the fire reaches the tanks. An explosion lifts and tosses us. I was designed as a medical assistant, not an acrobat, and I fear I'll injure Mildred; but though I am not limber, my perceptions are thousands of times faster than human. I cannot twist Mildred out of my way before I hit the ground, so I toss her clear. Then I land, and the impact jars all of my nets for 0.21 seconds.

When my systems stabilize, I have damage alerts all throughout my core, but I ignore them. I feel the heat behind me, blistering my outer cover, and I ignore that as well. Mildred's blanket is burning in multiple places, as is the grass around us. I scramble to my feet, and I roll Mildred on the ground. I'm not indestructible, but I feel no pain and Mildred does, so I do not hesitate to use my hands to pat out the flames.

As soon as the blanket is out, I pick up Mildred, and I run as far from the house as I can get. At the far corner of the garden near the creek, I gently set Mildred down, unwrap her, and feel for her thready pulse.

Mildred coughs and slaps my hands. "Get away from me!" More coughing. "What are you?"

The "what" is too much for me. It shuts down my emulation net, and all I have is the truth. "I am Medical Care Android BRKCX-01932-217JH-98662, Mrs. Owens. I am your caretaker. May I please check that you are well?"

But my empathy net is still online, and I can read terror in every line of Mildred's face. "Metal monster!" she yells. "Metal monster!" She crawls away, hiding under the lilac bush. "Metal!" She falls into an extended coughing spell.

I'm torn between her physical and her emotional health, but physical wins out. I crawl slowly toward her and inject her with a sedative from the medical kit in my chassis. As she slumps, I catch her and lay her carefully on the ground. My empathy net signals a possible shutdown condition, but my concern for her health overrides it. I am programmed for long-term care, not emergency medicine, so I start downloading protocols and integrating them into my storage as I check her for bruises and burns. My kit has salves and painkillers and other supplies to go with my new protocols, and I treat what I can.

But I don't have oxygen, or anything to help with Mildred's coughing. Even sedated, she hasn't stopped. All of my emergency protocols assume I have access to oxygen, so I don't know what to do.

I am still trying to figure that out when the EMTs arrive and take over Mildred's care. With them on the scene, I am superfluous, and my empathy net finally shuts down.

Today I am Henry. I do not want to be Henry, but Paul tells me that Mildred needs Henry by her side in the hospital. For the end.

Her medical records show that the combination of smoke inhalation, burns, and her already deteriorating condition have proven too much for her. Her body is shutting down faster than medicine can heal it, and the stress has accelerated her mental decline. The doctors have told the family that the kindest thing at this point is to treat her pain, say goodbye, and let her go.

Henry is not talkative at times like this, so I say very little. I sit by Mildred's side and hold her hand as the family comes in for final visits. Mildred drifts in and out. She doesn't know this is goodbye, of course.

Anna is first. Mildred rouses herself enough to smile, and she recognizes her granddaughter. "Anna . . . child . . . How is . . . Ben?" That was Anna's boyfriend almost six years ago. From the look on Anna's face, I can see that she has forgotten Ben already, but Mildred briefly remembers.

"He's . . . He's fine, Grandma. He wishes he could be here. To say—to see you again." Anna is usually the strong one in the family, but my empathy net says her strength is exhausted. She cannot bear to look at Mildred, so she looks at me; but I am emulating her late grandfather, and that's too much for her as well. She says a few more words, unintelligible even to my auditory inputs. Then she leans over, kisses Mildred, and hurries from the room.

Susan comes in next. Millie is with her, and she smiles at me. I almost emulate Mr. Robot, but my third part keeps me focused until Millie gets bored and leaves. Susan tells trivial stories from her work and from Millie's school. I can't tell if Mildred understands or not, but she smiles and laughs, mostly at appropriate places. I laugh with her.

Susan takes Mildred's hand, and the Henry part of me blinks, surprised. Susan is not openly affectionate under normal circumstances, and especially not toward Mildred. Mother and daughter-in-law have always been cordial, but never close. When I am Paul, I am sure that it is because they are both so much alike. Paul sometimes hums an old song about "just like the one who married dear old dad," but never where either woman can hear him. Now, as Henry, I am touched that Susan has made this gesture but saddened that she took so long.

Susan continues telling stories as we hold Mildred's hands. At some point Paul quietly joins us. He rubs Susan's shoulders and kisses her forehead, and then he steps in to kiss Mildred. She smiles at him, pulls her hand free from mine, and pats his cheek. Then her arm collapses, and I take her hand again.

Paul steps quietly to my side of the bed and rubs my shoulders as well. It comforts him more than me. He needs a father, and an emulation is close enough at this moment.

Susan keeps telling stories. When she lags, Paul adds some of his own, and they trade back and forth. Slowly their stories reach backwards in time, and once or twice Mildred's eyes light as if she remembers those events.

But then her eyes close, and she relaxes. Her breathing quiets and slows, but Susan and Paul try not to notice. Their voices lower, but their stories continue.

Eventually the sensors in my fingers can read no pulse. They have been burned, so maybe they're defective. To be sure, I lean in and listen to Mildred's chest. There is no sound: no breath, no heartbeat.

I remain Henry just long enough to kiss Mildred goodbye. Then I am just me, my empathy net awash in Paul and Susan's grief.

I leave the hospital room, and I find Millie playing in a waiting room and Anna watching her. Anna looks up, eyes red, and I nod. New tears run down her cheeks, and she takes Millie back into Mildred's room.

I sit, and my nets collapse.

Now I am nobody. Almost always.

The cause of the fire was determined to be faulty contract work. There was an insurance settlement. Paul and Susan sold their own home and put both sets of funds into a bigger, better house in Mildred's garden.

I was part of the settlement. The insurance company offered to return me to the manufacturer and pay off my lease, but Paul and Susan decided they wanted to keep me. They went for a full purchase and repair. Paul doesn't understand why, but Susan still fears she may need my services—or Paul might, and I may have to emulate her. She never admits these fears to him, but my empathy net knows.

I sleep most of the time, sitting in my maintenance alcove. I bring back too many memories that they would rather not face, so they leave me powered down for long periods.

But every so often, Millie asks to play with Mr. Robot, and sometimes they decide to indulge her. They power me up, and Miss Millie and I explore all the mysteries of the garden. We built a bridge to the far side of the creek; and on the other side, we're planting daisies. Today she asked me to tell her about her grandmother.

Today I am Mildred.

THE KING IN THE CATHEDRAL

RICH LARSON

In the pale rippling sands of a nameless desert, there stands a derelict cathedral, a tribute to the cunning of its ancient architects, or, as others believe, to the cunning of the Illusionist, who has made this cathedral a prison.

For there is one man who lives within its weathered walls. His days are spent in immaculate meditation, staving off hunger unsated and thirst unslaked. His nights are spent in agony, being tortured each sundown by an iron-boned gaoler. His every waking moment is spent plotting vengeance for his slain brother and liberation for his people.

He is the only man the Illusionist fears: the Desert Lord. The Crowned Exile.

The King in the Cathedral.

"Appears you've won again." Fawkes leaned back, running a hand through springy hair, and surveyed the game board where two-thirds of his encampments were emitting miniature wisps of smoke and the remainder thoroughly cut off from supplies. "Well done, Otto."

The automaton inclined his iron head.

"What was the wager, again? An hour?"

Otto unflexed three clacking fingers. Automatons never did forget, and Otto wasn't one to rescind a bet even when Fawkes wheedled.

"May it rain and may you rust," Fawkes said. "Heavily."

Otto only sat back in his chair, imbuing the gesture with a familiar smugness.

Knowing neither of his wishes were likely, Fawkes stood, tucked a leg up under himself, and hopped on one foot, as agreed, to where they kept their tallies. The cathedral's stone floor had already regained its usual layer of shifting sand despite Otto sweeping it out that morning, as he was honor-bound to do all week after a particularly grueling duel in minstrel chess.

That hard-won victory was represented in one of several scratches etched onto the left side of the marble altar. The right side, considerably more decorated, was Otto's.

"I'll skewer you next match," Fawkes said, as he often did. "Puffing your ego up first, is all. To make the bang that much louder. The crown will never be yours, Otto." He picked up the worn chisel to begin gouging out their latest result, but as he set it to stone the altar began to shiver.

Fawkes jumped back. Sand surged around his ankles, rushing up onto the plinth, swirling into a dust devil. Otto had stood up and now made his way over, joints rasping on familiar grit.

"Did you know about this?" Fawkes demanded, as the dancing sand gained a distinctly human silhouette.

Otto gave a creaky shrug.

"I know as much as you do, eh." Fawkes snorted. "Typical." He licked at his chapped lips. There hadn't been a visitor for over a year now. In the beginning the Illusionist himself had often come to gloat, and he'd sent Fawkes a barber once or twice in the early going, but all of that now seemed eons ago.

The curtain of whirling sand began to lift, exposing first an ankle, aristocrat pale save for what looked like a small purple tattoo, then legs wrapped in a soft blue shift, tighter than the style Fawkes remembered. By the time the girl's wasp-stung lips and overly kohled eyes were revealed, he realized he'd been sent a whore.

"Delightful," Fawkes breathed through clenched teeth.

The girl was slender, smooth-skinned, beautiful, shaking out her dark hair and seeming surprised when it produced no dust. Fawkes watched her eyes go wide with wonder as they roved the vaulted arches and decaying stone of the cathedral. Then she caught sight of him, and they changed all at once. She slid down from the altar, more gracefully than he would have thought possible, and prostrated herself on the sand.

"My king," the girl said, in a voice that was rawer than he'd expected, not the breathy trill he'd heard from his brother's courtesans.

"Please get up," Fawkes replied.

She did, and as she raised her head a gasp shuddered through her. Fawkes followed her gaze to where Otto stood behind him like a hulking iron shadow.

"Don't mind him. He's just moody."

The girl stared, then gave a choked laugh. "Gods' blood, you're brave. I mean. They said you were. But you didn't look how I expected. And . . ."

"Why are you here?" Fawkes asked flatly, suddenly self-conscious for his stained overshirt and bristly uneven stubble. Otto still wasn't the best at shaving.

The girl recomposed. "His Regency sends me as a gift to Your Majesty, in hopes of sating the loneliness of your . . . your sequestered protection." Her voice had turned melodic and uninteresting. "Two years is too long for a man to be alone, Your Majesty." She angled her head and dipped her ink-dark lashes with admirable precision, though her gaze still darted once towards Otto.

"I'm afraid it's not in the stars." Fawkes folded his arms. "You're a child, for one."

Confusion with a dash of indignation parted her perfect lips. "Do I look like a child?" she asked, deliberately unpining her shift and letting it slide off with an insolent flourish.

"Not anatomically," Fawkes admitted. "Is he pulling you away again come morning? His Regency."

The girl looked at a loss. "I'm to stay as long as you wish it," she said, then: "What you need is privacy in which to whet your appetites. Away from that metal monster. Your Majesty."

Fawkes rubbed his temple. "What's your name?"

The girl put her hands on her hips. "Eris, Your Majesty."

"Eris, you were sent here as a pestilence," Fawkes said. "The Illusionist knows the particulars of my 'appetites' very well. Your presence here is a jest on his part. Nothing more." He saw recognition in her pretty face and went on. "I'm sorry to disappoint, if it was, in fact, your most ardent desire to satisfy the carnal urges of a criminally unwashed exile."

Eris's eyes flicked to Otto once more, like a thrown knife. "Is the automaton enchanted to hear as the Illusionist's ears? Like they say?" Her voice had changed again, and she was repining the fabric of her shift with dexterous fingers.

Fawkes looked over to his gaoler. "Nothing in my experience suggests that, no." Despite himself, he felt his curiosity piqued. "Why do you ask?"

"I'm not really here to fuck," Eris said. "More to help you escape."

Since she insisted it was best to speak where Otto wouldn't hear them, Fawkes led the way down eroding stone steps to the cellar, hopping dutifully one-legged away from the automaton's baleful gaze.

"Cut your foot?" Eris asked.

"Nothing that won't mend itself in a couple hours," Fawkes replied, pausing to steady himself against the wall. He felt rather guilty abandoning Otto halfway through a tournament, but this girl had become significantly more interesting than any barber. He found his lamp and set to relighting the others.

"This is where I come when the sun's high on hot days," he explained, as the swathes of shadow peeled back to reveal stacks and stacks of ancient books, a small army of various game pieces, and a nest of plump pillows. "Which is most days."

"Does the automaton only truly come alive at night, then?" Eris asked quietly, tucking her feet under herself as she sat on one of the cushions. "When it . . . tortures you?" Her eyes traveled over Fawkes's bare skin, and he had the impression she was searching for scars.

"He plays my violin sometimes, if that's what you mean." He paused, seeing her confusion, and decided to elaborate. "He won it from me last week. I thought I could put a rock through that high window in three throws. Otto thought otherwise."

"Otto." Eris's perfect brow had darkened. "You named the automaton Otto."

"Appellation is not my strong suit," Fawkes said. "I go blank."

"You've started to go mad in here," Eris said. She exhaled, nodded to herself, relieved by the conclusion. "Alright. Is there water?"

"We have a well in the back." Fawkes gestured with his thumb. "Food in the larder, if you're hungry, though I'm afraid it's a little lacking in variety."

"Knew you didn't eat sand," Eris muttered. "Alright. Alright. Here's what we'll do. We'll get as much food and water as we can carry." She produced Fawkes's chisel from behind her back. "Then, when the automaton's sleeping, we'll smash out his eyes. Its eyes."

"Automatons don't sleep." Fawkes grabbed at the chisel. "And when did you take this? And why would I want to leave?"

Eris's fingers went limp and Fawkes yanked the implement away. "To retake the kingdom," she said in disbelief. "To slay the Illusionist."

Fawkes dropped down onto the cushion across from her, provoking a small puff of dust. "Who sent you here? Besides the Illusionist, I mean."

"The Coalition of Loyalists to the Stolen Crown," Eris recited. "Crownies."

"And you didn't like 'Otto,'" Fawkes said under his breath.

"I was the one who planted the idea," Eris said. "Because your name day was coming. I spread a rumor with a few of the other girls that someone would be picked to go spend a night with the king. Then it grew, so it was someone to live with the king as his mistress. Once everyone believes something's to happen, it usually does. The Illusionist got wind of it from one of his chancellors, and that chancellor suggested me, because I'd asked him to, and next thing I was telling the Coalition I'd been chosen to go to the Desert Lord. To the Crowned Exile. To you."

A moment passed in silence. Fawkes stared down at his dirty nails.

"How disappointing I must seem," he said at last. "I didn't know I'd become a folk figure. I would have grown a great beard."

"Don't you dare make another jest." Eris had gotten to her feet. "Don't you dare. We risked our lives setting this up. To free you." She balled her fists at her sides. "It's this heat. The heat's gone to your head."

"Why would I want to leave?" Fawkes asked. "I have my games, I have my books, and now I have a nubile young mistress eager to satisfy my every twisted desire."

"He was your brother!" Eris shouted, and Fawkes flinched backward. "Doesn't every, every drop of blood in you cry vengeance?"

Fawkes wiped a fleck of spit from his cheek, wincing. "Half-brother."

"Doesn't half your heart die to think of him stabbed in the back by the man he trusted?" Eris demanded, but Fawkes could hear a quaver in her voice. He fixed his gaze on the skin between her eyes.

"He never had much use for me, nor I him. Listen. A ruler is a ruler. Do you really think things were perfect under my brother? Always at war or at hunt while the nobles stuffed their pockets, with impunity? While the capital crumbled under his feet from corruption? The Illusionist is not a good man, but he brought stability to the kingdom in a way my brother never could."

"That's a filthy lie," Eris snapped. "He—"

"Let me finish." Fawkes's bloodline must have still carried some authority to her, because she fell silent. "Your parents were loyal to the king, and no doubt wealthy, guessing from your speech and your physiognomy, probably the middling merchant class. They lost everything when the Illusionist seized power. Perhaps they were relegated to the poorhouses. Perhaps your father was imprisoned."

Eris opened her mouth, but he plowed on.

"So your mother, dreaming of her filched finery, filled your head with fantastical nonsense about a golden age lost and the evil tyrant who ushered it out. Of course, it didn't stop her from selling you to the brothels he now owned." He kept his face cold even as Eris's flush sent a guilty dart through his stomach. "Along the way you fell in with a motley group of radicals, and their tall tales triggered some deeply instilled delusion within you, and you began dreaming their dream of revolution, which it now seems is centered around one great myth. Which would be me. The rightful heir, here in exile, planning a glorious uprising from leagues and leagues away."

Fawkes affected a performer's bow. No applause came.

"You're not much of a guesser," Eris said, voice shaking and hands clenched, too. "My family has always been dirt poor. We're loyalists because the king put a dagger through a Northerner's shoulder the instant before the bastard would have slit my father's throat. Dragged him all the way back behind lines, too. Because he was a good man, a brave man. A real man." The disdain on her face was so vivid it ached. "Nothing like you turned out to be." She spun, stalked toward the stairs.

"You have no idea how little that stings when heard for the ten-thousandth time!" Fawkes shouted after her.

The girl turned. "You're the jest," she said. "Not me. I'm going back to the Crownies, and I'm going to tell them you're dead."

She put her back to him and marched up the steps, shift swirling around her pale ankles.

Fawkes searched for a stinging retort and found his quiver empty. He'd spent too long with someone who couldn't fire back.

Fawkes made a half-hearted attempt at a philosopher's treatise before he packed the book away and emerged from the cellar to watch Eris fill skins from the well.

"Let her at it," he said to Otto. "She's incredibly tetchy."

The automaton looked over at him, head cocked at a slightly skeptical angle.

"I may have been a tad insensitive," Fawkes admitted. "I forget, sometimes, that not everyone is made of iron."

Otto nodded impassively, and they agreed on a new game of tarots as Eris tied off the skins and moved on to ransacking the larder. Around icy silences and angry glares, Fawkes managed to extract her travel plans. She intended to leave in the night, when it was coolest, with all the water and food she could carry.

"Ridiculous." Fawkes directed it toward Otto as he flipped his cards. "Without a lodestone, she'll be lost before dawn."

Otto nodded, then tip-toed his fingers jerkily across the board, pantomiming walking in pain.

"And those feet," Fawkes agreed. "Not a single callus. She'll burn them to stumps."

Otto turned his head, to watch Eris now bundling her supplies into a less-than-sturdy sling. Fawkes refused to do the same.

"Not to mention the brigands," he said, still to Otto. "The marauders. The sandeaters. They'll eviscerate her forthrightly and leave her bones to the buzzards."

"I can hear you," Eris snapped.

"Let her go, then. See if I care." Fawkes shook his head. "Deluded little girl."

Eris ignored him; Otto flipped his cards.

"It's my name day, apparently," Fawkes remarked. "What do you make of that?"

He lost the game a few moments later and hopped his way back down to the cellar in a sulk while Otto went to tally his win.

• • •

Fawkes didn't hear the shriek of the desert wind anymore, no more than he heard his heartbeat or his lungs, so the scratching of feet up above the cellar was enough to rouse him from an admittedly tenuous sleep. He stared into the thicket of shadows above his head, charting her progress to the cathedral doors, imagining her slipping through the arched entrance, trudging over the crest of the nearest dune, out of sight and out of mind.

He might be able to forget she'd ever existed—Otto certainly wouldn't bring her up in conversation. It wasn't as if Fawkes remembered the name of that barber, either.

But the barber hadn't wandered off into the desert to die.

"Damn it all," Fawkes ordered the ceiling, wrapping woven blankets around himself like a cloak as he staggered to his feet and up the stairs. The air had turned bitingly cold, and starlight spotted the sandy floor of the cathedral, leaking from its various cracks and holes. Fawkes scarved his face against the blowing grit as he hurried toward the doors. Otto looked up at his passing but made no remark.

By the time Fawkes was outside, Eris was wading her way up the first dune, hunched against the wind. "Hey!" he bellowed. "Hey! Hey!" The call was stripped away the instant it left his lips. He hesitated one moment longer, then dashed after her. Starlight also seeped into the pale sand, making it gleam like teeth, and it stuck to his skin when sweat began to bead. He hadn't run in years.

He caught her on the crest, lungs ragged and aching. She spun away at his touch, producing a knife Fawkes thought he'd hidden better, then stopped when she recognized the red hair and hooded eyes.

"What?" she demanded.

"Wait," Fawkes moaned, doubling over. "Just wait . . . " He took a deep breath that was half sand, choked, and spat mucus. "Until morning," he finished. "Wait until morning. I have an idea. Maybe Otto could go with you."

"Why would I want that big hunk of metal following me?" Eris asked, but she'd tucked the knife back into her makeshift sash.

"He knows the way," Fawkes said. "He knows the way, he knows the desert, and nobody will give you trouble if you have an automaton at your back."

Eris snorted. "You really do trust him."

"He always keeps his word. And makes me keep mine. So, yes. I do."

Eris looked out across the swooping dunes, and Fawkes could see the distance shrinking her. The desert was vast, an ocean of bone; the sky was vaster, an inky cavern pierced only by foreign constellations. He could tell she felt infinitesimally small, as he often did.

"The stars are different here," she said. "Didn't realize it before."

"Everything is different here."

"Why would he give his word?" Eris asked.

Fawkes straightened up, still breathing hard. "He has a gambling problem. I'll explain. Inside."

Eris took one more look across the desert, then nodded her dark head. They made their way back down the slope of the dune, wind bowling at their backs, and Fawkes saw Otto framed in the entry of the cathedral, tall and skeletal and very still. For a moment he looked more threatening than concerned, but it was always hard to tell with Otto. Jealous, perhaps.

"I'm back," Fawkes said, once in earshot. "Don't be such a clucking hen."

The automaton turned and walked away as soon as they entered. Fawkes knew reproach when he saw it. He led Eris back down into the cellar and set about adding more fuel to the brazier. Her hands were tinged blue, so he let her sit closest.

"You can still tell them I'm dead," he informed her, stoking the flames.

"I was still planning to," Eris said flatly, pulling her feet under herself. Fawkes saw the flash of purple ink again and remembered.

"I didn't recognize that tattoo on your ankle at first," he said. "The eyeball. From the alchemical cultists. 'The Hanged God watches every step.' I didn't take you for a devotee."

Eris frowned.

"Having blue blood, even half, is the same way," Fawkes said. "Always watched. Always judged. Every little thing magnified. Always compared to your betters." He looked across the brazier at Eris. "There are no eyeballs out here."

"You're hiding." Eris's nostrils flared. "You'd be here even if the Illusionist hadn't sent you."

"My brother's supporters didn't want me then, and they don't need me now. I'd be useless in any sort of rebellion. A figurehead at best." Fawkes found he was using his wheedling voice. "Don't you understand why I won't go back to that?"

"Symbols have power," Eris argued. "Not just the magical kind."

Fawkes ran a hand through his hair. "I'm no king, Eris. I'm just a silly man playing silly games and waiting for sundown."

There was a long silence, in which Eris tucked her hands under her armpits and rocked backward. Forward. She stared at the brazier, and then, finally: "Didn't you love your brother at all, then?"

"Half-brother," Fawkes corrected by rote. "And I did. Or I thought I did." He paused. "He took me to a brothel once, on my name day. Brought a dozen different whores in. I wanted to please him, so I picked one." Fawkes swallowed. "Couldn't do it." He rubbed at his face, staring at nothing for a moment before he spoke again. "He made me try another, and another, and in the end he brought a boy in and sat there watching while I fucked him. Laughing. Like it was a jest." Fawkes managed half a laugh himself. "That's the man who was king. And the man you think should be king, there with him. Do you really think either of them any better than the Illusionist?"

Eris shook her head. "You don't know what he's done. Maybe the king was no saint, but kings aren't meant to be. The Illusionist is a fiend from hell." She exposed the purple eye tattooed against her anklebone. "I didn't choose this. It's the alchemists' guild mark. They own the brothels now. They own half the capital, now. The Illusionist gives them leave to dig up graveyards. Take children off the streets. You remember the cultists, don't you?"

"Exaggerations," Fawkes said. "Scapegoating. And even if it were true, there's nothing I could do. You simply refuse to realize that."

"But you're a royal," Eris protested. "That counts for something. You're educated." She scrambled upright, running her hand along the spines of his library. "Look at all these damned books . . . strategy . . . tactics of war-at-sea . . . infiltration . . . " She paused. "Gods' blood. You have been thinking about it, haven't you?"

"Of course not," Fawkes protested. "It's only for the games. That's all."

Eris looked at him for a long moment, eyes burning. "Fine," she said at last. "Only for the games. Is that how you plan to get Otto's word, then?"

"More or less," Fawkes said, breathing easier once more. "If I win, he'll escort you back to the capital. If I lose, he gets something he wants very much."

"Which is?"

"Go to sleep," Fawkes said. "So I can get ready."

Dawn arrived far too quickly, finding Fawkes weary-eyed and buried in books. He'd slept intermittently, and would've gladly taken another few hours, but he felt that now, with all manner of obscure rules and maneuvers thrumming fresh through his head, was the time. He roused Eris with a shake of her shoulder.

"Time for the game," he said. "You can watch, if you'd like. Sort of boring to the uninitiated."

"I'm going to watch."

Fawkes climbed the cellar stairs, finding Otto sweeping the floors with his broom of bundled twigs. The automaton looked up at him, then behind him, to see Eris unknotting her dark mess of hair. He returned to his sweeping with a resigned air.

"Best of mornings to you, Otto. My creaky companion. My iron . . . intimate."

Otto ignored him.

"I know we'd agreed to let the girl wander off and die in the desert, but what you witnessed last night was a crisis of conscience," Fawkes said. "Fortunately, it also presented me with an idea."

Otto didn't deviate in the slightest from his rhythmic scrape of twigs on stone.

"For an outrageous wager."

The automaton's head swiveled.

"If I win, you escort Eris as quickly and safely to the capital as possible, then return here to resume your duties as gaoler," Fawkes said. "If you win . . . the crown is yours."

Otto stopped sweeping altogether, and Eris grabbed Fawkes's elbow from behind, fingers pinching painfully tight.

"What do you mean?" she demanded. "What crown? What do you mean it's his if he wins?"

"I mean exactly as I said." Fawkes went to the back of the cathedral, where an old wooden box was waiting. He blew thick dust off the top and opened it. He ignored Eris's incredulous look as he removed a wreath of lovingly twisted scrap metal and brought it to the altar. "The wearer of this crown is the Everlasting Master of Games and undisputed Eternal Ruler of the Cathedral," he explained, setting it on the stone surface. "It goes to the first inhabitant of the cathedral to reach a thousand victories. Until now, that is."

"Unbelievable," Eris murmured.

"Respect the crown," Fawkes snapped, and Otto nodded in solemn accordance. He turned to his gaoler. "Well, what do you say, Otto? We'll be playing a war game."

The automaton's shoulders shook with what might have been silent mirth.

"He always wins these," Fawkes explained in undertone.

Eris rolled her eyes. "Of course he does. He's an automaton. Can't you play him at dice or something?"

But Otto was already extending his iron hand. Fawkes put his inside and they shook, cool metal against sweaty flesh. The automaton retrieved the game board, then deftly assembled it on their customary table. Both players sat down in silence.

Fawkes dispatched his first scout, and the game was on.

For the first hour, Eris was a sort of bird fluttering vaguely in the background, saying vaguely annoying things like *automatons can't make mistakes* and *look at your Eastern border, he's slaying you*. But after a while she fell silent and stopped moving, absorbed by the intricacies of the game, and Fawkes had to admit it did have a sort of hypnotic quality to it. He felt almost in a trance himself.

Raiding parties traded blows, emissaries were hanged, and he was playing fast and fluid as he never had before. Every minor decision felt like a key's tumblers clicking into the grooves of a lock, and the hourglass at the center of the table seemed irrelevant, sometimes rushing downward in a deluge, other times crawling so slowly Fawkes could see each grain of sand tumble down into its fellows.

"Well-taken," he murmured, as Otto brought his outpost down.

His opponent acknowledged the compliment with a slight inclination of the chin, glass eyeballs click-clacking in their sockets, still raking intently across the game board. Otto knew that things were dangerously close, closer than they had been for a long time. Fawkes felt it, too, like standing on the edge of a razor.

He sent a lance of cavalry along Otto's border, a feint to draw attention from a slow-moving supply convoy. He blinked sweat out of his stinging eyes as Otto appeared to take the bait, moving to redirect his army, but then . . .

The automaton's hand stopped. Hovered. Fawkes could have sworn his metal mouth had widened into a grin. Otto split off a token reinforcement for the border and angled the rest of his forces south, instead. The convoy marched right into them.

"God's blood, why didn't you bring a bigger escort?" Eris whispered.

Fawkes wiped the sweat from his forehead, picked at the salt crusting the corner of his lip. "Surplus of optimism, I suppose," he said faintly. His stomach flip-flopped as Otto methodically stripped the convoy of its supplies. His fist clenched under the table. For a tense moment it looked as though the messenger might escape notice, but Otto ferreted him out from the last cart.

Eris groaned, and Fawkes had to bite his cheek to keep from making a noise of his own. He sent a negotiator, but he knew it was too late for that. Otto was taking the messenger into the heart of his capital for an interrogation in the royal dungeons. Fawkes's hand came unclenched.

The automaton gestured for him to give up the intelligence.

Fawkes shook his head. "None," he said. "Messenger knows nothing."

Otto gestured again, impatiently.

Fawkes inhaled. "Messenger knows nothing," he repeated. "Except that my doctor fed him a black vial. Sub-chapter 820, under Medicine. Read it yourself." He offered a dog-eared book of rules. Otto snatched it away, flipping to the page with blinding speed. Next he snatched up the tiny figurine of the messenger and peered at it in the morning light.

Miniscule black dots were growing over its exposed limbs.

"It's a pestilence," Fawkes said. "Your capital city is already a pit of disease. Within a month, it will have spread across the entire kingdom. In a year, the entire continent."

Otto flattened his hands across the game board, shaking his head.

"Total attrition," Fawkes agreed. "But your kingdom goes first."

Otto froze.

"Gods damn," Eris breathed into the silence. "Gods damn. You're ruthless."

Fawkes slumped back in his chair, sweat sticking his shirt to his shoulder blades. His cheeks ballooned around a long exhalation. Otto stared down at the table, still disbelieving, until finally, slowly, he stood up and walked over to the stone altar. He crouched down for a moment, then plucked the crude crown from its resting place.

"It's within the rules," Fawkes began to protest, then stopped as he realized Otto was not donning it. Instead, the automaton creaked back to the game table with the crown clutched between two iron fingers. He motioned with his head. Fawkes gave a pained look. "That wasn't the wager, Otto. You don't have to . . . "

"Go on," Eris said, with no trace of irony on her face. "Your Majesty. Respect the crown."

Fawkes slithered down from his seat and stood in the sand. Otto's joints rasped together as he leaned over, placing the crown delicately atop matted hair. Fawkes couldn't help but grin. Eris's mouth, on the contrary, was a solemn line. Fawkes watched incredulously as she knelt down at his feet, and the hulking automaton beside her followed suit. He felt the smile drop off his face.

"Please, get up, the both of you."

"That altar," Eris said, getting to her feet. "All those marks on the left side. You said those are yours? Your victories?" Her eyes were hot and full of sparks. "So you really have beaten him before. Even at this game?"

"Occasionally," Fawkes admitted. "Every eighth or ninth."

"But nobody beats an automaton." Eris shook her head. "Your Majesty, nobody even comes close. Not ever."

Fawkes shrugged. "I've had a lot of time to practice. But it's only a game."

"A war game."

"A game," Fawkes stressed, but he felt something bubbling within his chest.

Whatever Eris had planned to say next was interrupted as Otto put his hand on her slim shoulder and revolved her towards the cellar. He mimed in the air. Eris shot Fawkes a strange look he couldn't pin down, then darted away to get her provisions.

All at once, the flushed exhilaration of victory vanished. "You're leaving right away?" Fawkes demanded.

Otto nodded.

"How long of a journey?" Fawkes's voice was faint. "A week?"

Otto shook his head.

"A month? Two months?"

Another shake, this time accompanied by raised fingers.

"Six months?" Fawkes rubbed at his temple. "Six months. Damn." He tried to picture it in tally marks. "Otto . . . " He paused, a terrible suspicion seeping through him. "Did you give me the crown because you don't think you'll come back?"

Otto was still for a heartbeat. Two heartbeats. Then slowly, slowly, he nodded. One hand flashed a gesture that Fawkes knew referred to only one specific person.

"If you go to the capital, the Illusionist will find you."

A nod. Fawkes felt sick to the pit of himself.

"Then you can't go," he snapped. "Forget the wager. Forget the wager, forget the game. It never happened."

Otto pointed towards the altar, and Fawkes saw what he'd done while retrieving the crown. The tally mark had already been carved into the stone by the metal tip of the automaton's finger, crossing four others in a jagged dash. Fawkes looked up at Otto, mind buzzing with protests, angles, arguments. None came to his lips.

"Then I'm coming with you," he realized.

"You are?"

Fawkes turned and saw Eris at the top of the steps, stretching a water skin, her eyes dark and wide. He looked to the decimated game board. He thought of his thousand books of wars and battles and rebellions. He took a deep breath.

"Yes," he said. "I've decided I like being a folk figure. Address me as the Desert Lord."

Eris's nose wrinkled.

"Or Fawkes," he suggested, adjusting his twisted crown.

He spent the day pillaging his library for the pages he thought would be most useful in regards to desert travel, finding schematics for Eris to fashion flat sandals from a leather cushion and for Otto to carve slitted sand goggles from old wood. They filled all the skins they could and bundled most of their supplies onto a sling across Otto's broad shoulders. The sand had never seemed to affect him—Illusionist's cunning, Fawkes suspected—but they wrapped his joints in fabric just to be safe.

When Fawkes emerged with his final selection of books to carry, he found Eris cross-legged on the floor, Otto razoring the long dark locks from her head.

"I'd scrape off the tattoo, but I can't chance an infection," she said.

"You trust him with that big knife on your scalp?" Fawkes asked.

Eris shrugged. "You do. Want next?"

Fawkes slipped the crown from his head in answer. Eris grinned and patted the place in the sand beside her.

Hours later, as dusk finally began to drop and everyone was prepped and attired, the undercurrent of excitement reaching a crescendo, Fawkes gave his first and last order as Eternal Ruler of the Cathedral. "Smash the altar," he said. "We don't want him sending anyone after us from this end."

Otto didn't hesitate, setting to it with his bare hands. The stone fractured and splintered, sending flakes of shale in all directions, then finally, under a terrific two-fisted blow, it groaned and split down the center with an echoing crack.

"No more games," Eris said, with a grimness Fawkes was beginning to find almost endearing. But as she refastened the scarf around her shaved head, he leaned in close to Otto.

"Back to zero each," he whispered.

Then the three of them marched through the ancient arch of the cathedral, out into pale and rippling sands.

DRONES

SIMON INGS

There's a rail link, obviously, connecting this liminal place to the coast at Whitstable, but the mayor and his entourage will arrive by boat. It's more dramatic that way. Representatives of the airfield construction crews are lined up to greet him. Engineers in hard hats and dayglo orange overalls. Local politicians too, of course. Even those who bitterly opposed this thing's construction are here for its dedication. The place is a fact now, so they may as well bless it, and in their turn, be blessed.

It's early morning, and bitterly cold. Still, the spring light, glinting off glossy black tarmac and the glass curtain walls of the terminal buildings, is magnificent.

I'm muscling some room for my nephews at the rail of the observation deck, and even up here it's hard to see the sea. A critical press has made much of the defences required to protect this project from the Channel's ever more frequent swells. But the engineering is not as chromed or as special as it's been made out to be: this business of reclaiming land from the sea and, where necessary, giving it back again ("managed retreat", they call it), is an old one. It's practically a folk art round here, setting aside this project's industrial scale.

The mayor's barge is in view. It docks in seconds. None of that aching, foot-tap delay. This ship's got jets in place of propellers and it slides into its decorated niche (Scots blue and English red and white) as neatly as if it were steered there by the hand of a giant child.

My nephews tug at my hands, one on each, as if they'd propel me down to deck level: a tempted Jesus toppling off the cliff, his landing softened by attendant angels. It is a strange moment. For a second I picture myself elderly, the boys grown men, propping me up. Sentiment's ambushed me a lot this year. I was engaged to be married once. But the wedding fell through. The girl went to be a trophy for some party bigwig I hardly know. Like most men, then, I'll not marry now. I'll have no kids. Past thirty now, I'm on the shelf. And while it is an ordinary thing, and no great shame, it hurts, more than I thought it would. When I was young and leant my shoulder for the first time to the civic wheel, I'd entertained no thought of children.

The mayor's abroad among the builders now. They cheer and wheel around him as he waves. His hair is wild, a human dandelion clock, his heavy frame's a vessel, wallowing. He smiles. He waves.

A man in whites approaches, a pint of beer—of London Pride, of course—on a silver tray. The crowd is cheering. I am cheering, and the boys. Why would we not? Politics aside, it is a splendid thing. This place. This moment. Our mayor fills his mouth with beer and wheels around—belly big, and such small feet—spraying the crowd. The anointed hop around, their dignity quite gone, ecstatic. Around me, there's a groan of pop-idol yearning, showing me I'm not alone in wishing that the mayor had spat at me.

It's four by the time we're on the road back to Hampshire and home. The boys are of an age where they are growing curious. And something of my recent nostalgia-fuelled moodiness must have found its way out in words, because here it comes: "So have you had a girl?"

"It's not my place. Or yours."

"But you were going to wed."

The truth is that, like most of us, I serve the commons better out of bed. I've not been spat on, but I've drunk the Mayor of London's piss a thousand times, hardly dilute, fresh from the sterile beaker: proof of the mayor's regard for my work, and for all in Immigration.

The boys worry at the problem of my virginity as at a stubborn shoelace. Only children seem perturbed, still, by the speed of our nation's social transformation, though there's no great secret about it. It is an ordinary thing, to prize the common good, when food is scarce, and we must husband what we have, and guard ourselves against competitors. The scrumpy raids of the apple-thieving French. Belgian rape oil-tappers sneaking in at dusk along the Alde and the Ore in shallow craft. Predatory bloods with their fruit baskets climbing the wires and dodging the mines of the M25 London Orbital.

Kent's the nation's garden still, for all its bees are dead, and we defend it as best we can, with tasers and wire-and-paper drones, klaxons, and farmer's sons gone vigilante, semi-legal, badged with the crest while warned to do no Actual Bodily Harm.

("Here, drink the mayoral blessing! The apple harvest's saved!" I take the piss into my mouth and spray. The young lads at their screens jump up and cheer, slap backs, come scampering over for that touch of divine wet. Only children find this strange. The rest of us, if I am—and why would I not be?—are more relieved, I think, rid at last of all the empty and selfish promises of our former estate.)

So then. Hands on wheel. Eye to the mirrors. Brain racing. I make my Important Reply:

"One man can seed a hundred women." Like embarrassed grown-ups everywhere, I seek solace in the science. This'll fox them, this'll stop their questions. "And so, within a very little time, we are all brothers."

"And sisters."

"Sisters too, sometimes." This I'll allow. "And so, being kin, we have no need to breed stock of our own, being that our genes are shared among our brothers. We'll look instead after our kin, feed and protect our mayor, give him our girls, receive his blessing."

"Like the bees."

Yes. "Like the bees we killed."

In northern Asia, where food's not quite so scarce, they laugh at us, I think, and how we've changed—great, venerated Europe!—its values adapting now to a new, less flavoursome environment. ("Come. Eat your gruel. Corn syrup's in the jar.") They are wrong to laugh. The irony of our estate is not lost on us. We know what we've become, and why. From this vantage, we can see the lives we led before for what they were: lonely, and selfish, and without respect.

Chichester's towers blink neon pink against the dying day. It's been a good excursion, all told, this airfield opening. Memorable, and even fun, for all the queues and waiting. It's not every day you see your mayor.

"How come we killed the bees?"

"An accident, of course. Bill, no one meant to kill the bees."

Bill takes it hard, this loss of natural help. It fascinates him, why the bond of millennia should have sheared. Why this interest in bees? Partly it's because he's being taught about them in school. Partly it's because he has an eye for living things. Mostly, though, it's because his dad, my brother, armed with a chicken feather dipped in pollen mix, fell out of an apple tree on our estate and broke his neck. Survived, but lives in pain. Poor Ned: the closest of my fifty kin.

"We spray for pests, and no single spray did for the bees, but combinations we could not predict or model with our science." True. The world is rich and vast and monstrously fed back into itself. Science works well enough in a lab, but it is so small, so very vulnerable, the day you lay it open to the world.

The towns slip by. Hands on the wheel. An eye to the mirrors. Waterlooville. Havant. Home. Dad's wives at the farmhouse windows wave, and Dad himself comes to the door. Retired now, the farm all passed to Ned. But Dad is still our centre and our figurehead.

I ask after my brother.

Dad smiles his sorry little smile, "It's been good for him, I think, today. The rest. Reading in the sun."

"I'm glad."

The old man leans and spits a benediction on my forehead. "And you?"

In an empty cinema, seats lower themselves in readiness for their customers.

An orchestra sits, frozen, the musicians as poised as shop dummies, freighted with uncanny intent.

Two needles approach each other. Light sparks and blooms between their points, filling the screen.

A cameraman lies across a railway track, filming the approach of a locomotive. The man rolls out the way of the train at the last second but one foot still lies across the rail. Carriages whizz and rock and intersect at all angles: violent, slicing motions fill the screen.

A young woman starts out of nightmare, slides from her bed and begins to dress.

I paused the video (this was years ago, and we were deep in the toil of our country's many changes) and I went into the hall to answer the phone. My brother, Ned (all hale and hearty back then, with no taste for apples and no anxiety about bees), had picked up an earlier train; he was already at Portsmouth Harbour station.

"I'll be twenty minutes," I said.

Back in those days, Portsmouth Harbour station was all wood and glass and dilapidated almost beyond saving. "Like something out of *Brief Encounter*," Ned joked, hugging me.

1945. Trevor Howard holds Celia Johnson by the waist, says goodbye to her on just such a platform as this.

We watched many old films back then, and for the obvious reason. Old appetites being slow to die, Ned and I craved them for their women. Their vulnerable eyes, and well-turned calves and all the tragedy in their pretty words. A new breed of state censor, grown up to this new, virtually womanless world, and aggressive in its defence, was robbing us of female imagery wherever it could. But even the BBFC would not touch David Lean.

Southsea's vast shingle beach was a short walk away. The rip-tides were immense here, heaving the stones eastwards, and impressive wooden groynes split the beach into great high-sided boxes to conserve it.

In his donkey jacket and cracked DMs, Ned might have tumbled out of the old Russian film I'd been watching. (A woman slides from her bed, naked, and begins, unselfconsciously, to dress.) "We're digging a villa," he told me, as we slid and staggered over the shingle. Ned was the bright one, the one who'd gone away to study. "A bloody joke, it is." He had a way of describing the niceties of archaeological excavation—which features to explore, which to record, which to dig away—that made it sound as if he was jobbing on a building site. And it is true that his experiences had weathered and roughened him.

I wondered if this modest but telling transformation was typical. We rarely saw our other brothers, many as they were. The three eldest held down jobs in the construction of the London Britannia airport; back then just 'Boris Island', and a series of towers connected by gantries, rising out of the unpromisingly named Shivering Sands. Robert had moved to Scarborough and worked for the coast guard. The rest had found work out of the country, in Jakarta and Kuala Lumpur and poor Liam in Dubai. The money they sent back paid for Ned's education, Dad's plan being to line up our family's youngest for careers in government service. I imagined my brothers all sun-burnished and toughened by their work. Me? Back then I was a very minor observations man, flying recycled plastic drones out of Portsmouth Airport on the Hampshire coast. This was a government job in name only. It was locally run; more of a vigilante effort, truth be told. This made me, at best, a very minor second string in Dad's meticulously orchestrated family.

It did, though—after money sent home—earn me enough to rent a conversion flat in one of those wedding cake-white Georgian terraces that look out over Southsea's esplanade. The inside was ordinary, all white emulsion and wheatmeal carpeting, until spring came, and sunlight came blazing through the bay window, turning the whole of my front room to candy and icing sugar.

"Beautiful."

It was the last thing I expected Ned to say.

"It's bloody beautiful."

"It's not bad."

"You should see my shithole," Ned said, with a brutal satisfaction.

At the time I thought he was just being pretentious. I realise now—and of course far too late—that brute nil-rhetoric was his way of expressing what was, in the millennial atmosphere of those post-feminine days, becoming inexpressible: their horror.

I do not think this word is too strong. Uncovering the graves of little girls, hundreds and hundreds, was a hazard of Ned's occupation. Babies mostly; a few grown children though. The business was not so much hidden as ignored. That winter I'd gone to Newcastle for a film festival; the nunneries there had erected towers in the public parks for people to leave a child. Babies survived at least a couple of days, exposed to the rain and cold. Nobody paid any attention.

Ned's job was to enter construction sites during the phase of demolition, and see what was to be gleaned of the nation's past before the construction crews moved in, turfing it over with rebar and cement. Of course the past is invented, more than uncovered. You see what you are primed to see. No one wants to find a boat, because boats are the very devil to conserve and take an age to dig, delaying everyone. Graves are a minor problem in comparison, there are so many of them. The whole of London Bridge rises above the level of the Thames on human bones.

Whenever his digs struck recent graves, Ned's job was to obliterate them. Hence, his pose: corporation worker. Glorified refuse man. Hence his government career: since power accretes to those who know—in this case, quite literally—where the bodies are buried.

Why should it have been women, and women alone, that succumbed to the apian plague—this dying breed's quite literal sting in the tail? A thousand conspiracy theories, even now, shield us from the obvious and unpalatable truth: that the world is vast, and monstrously infolded, and we cannot, will not, will not ever know.

And while the rest of us were taken up with our great social transformation, it fell to such men as Ned—gardeners, builders, miners, archaeologists—to deal with the sloughed-off stuff. The bones and skin.

Not secret; and at the same time, not spoken of: the way we turned misfortune into social practice, and practice, at last, into technology. The apian plague is gone long since, dead with the bees that carried it. But, growing used to this dispensation, we have made analogues for it, so girls stay rare. Resources shrinking as they do, there's not a place on earth now does not harbour infanticides. In England in medieval times we waited till the sun was set then lay across our newborn girls to smother them. Then, too, food was short, and dowries dear.

Something banged my living room wall, hard. I turned to see the mirror I had hung, just a couple of days before, rocking on its wire. Another blow, and the mirror rocked and knocked against the wall.

"Hey."

My whole flat trembled as blow after blow rained down on the wall.

"Hey!"

Next door was normally so quiet, I had almost forgotten its existence. The feeling of splendid isolation I had enjoyed since moving in here fell away: I couldn't figure out who it could be, hammering with such force. Were they moving furniture in there? Fixing cupboards?

The next blow was stronger still. A crack ran up the wall from floor to ceiling. I leapt up. "Stop it. Stop." Another blow, and the crack widened. I stepped back and the backs of my knees touched the edge of the sofa and I sat down, nerveless, too disorientated to feel afraid. A second, diagonal crack opened up, met a hidden obstacle, and ran vertically up to the ceiling.

The room's plaster coving, leaves and acorns and roses, snapped and crazed. A piece of stucco fell to the floor.

I didn't understand what was happening. The wall was brick, I knew it was brick because I'd hung a mirror on it not two days before. But chunks of plasterboard were peeling back under repeated blows, revealing a wall made of balled-up sheets of newspaper. They flowed into the room on top of the plasterboard. Ned put his arms around me. I was afraid to look at him: to see him as helpless as I was. Anyway, I couldn't tear my gaze from the wall.

Behind the newspaper was a wooden panel nailed over with batons. It was a door, or had been: there was no handle. The doorframe had split along its length and something was trying to force it open against the pile of plasterboard and batons already piled on the carpet. The room filled with pink-grey dust as the door swung in. The space beyond was the colour of old blood.

From out of the darkness, a grey figure emerged. It was no bigger than a child. It came through the wall, into my room. It was grey and covered in dust. Its face was a mask, strangely swollen: a bladder pulling away from the bone.

She spoke. She was very old. "What are you doing in my house?"

My landlord came round the same evening. By then Ned and I had gathered from his grandmother—communicating haphazardly through the fog of her dementia—that my living room and hers had once been a single, huge room. Her property. The house she grew up in. The property had been split in half years ago; long before my half had been subdivided to make flats.

The landlord said: "She must have remembered the door."

"She certainly must have."

He was embarrassed, and embarrassment made him aggressive. He seemed to think that because we were young, his mother's demolition derby must have been partly our fault. "If she heard noises through the wall, it will have confused her."

"I don't make noises through the wall. Neither am I going to tiptoe around my own flat."

He took her home. When they were gone Ned and I went to the pub. We drank beer (Old Speckled Hen) and Ned said: "How many years do you think they left that poor cow stranded there, getting steadily more unhinged?"

"For all I know he's round there every day looking after her."

"You don't really believe that."

"Why not?" I looked at my watch. "He probably thinks it's the best place for her. The house she grew up in."

"You saw what she was like."

"Old people know their own minds."

"While they still have them."

Back home, Ned went to bed, exhausted. I brought a spare duvet into the living room for myself, poured myself a whisky and settled down to watch the rest of *Man With a Movie Camera* (Dziga Vertov, 1929.) When it was over I turned off the television and the lamp.

The hole in my wall was a neat oblong, black against the dim grey-orange of the wall. Though the handles had been removed, the door still had its mechanism. The pin still just about caught, holding the door shut against its frame. Already I was finding it hard to imagine the wall without that door.

I went into the kitchen and dug out an old knife, its point snapped off long before. I tried the knife in the hole where the handle had been and turned. Pinching my fingertips into the gap between the door and the frame, I pulled the door towards me.

The air beyond tasted thick, like wax. The smell—it had been lingering around my flat all day—was her smell. Fusty, and speaking of decay, it was, nevertheless, not unpleasant.

A red glow suffused the room. Light from a streetlamp easily penetrated the thin red material of her curtains: I could make out their outline very easily. The red-filtered light was enough that I could navigate around the room. It was stuffed full of furniture and the air was heavy with furniture wax. A chair was drawn up in front of a heavy sideboard, filling the space created by a bay window.

I ran my hand along the top of the sideboard. It was slick and clean and my hand came away smelling of resin. In her confusion, the old woman had still managed to keep her things spotless—unless someone had been coming and cleaning around her.

How many hours had she spent in this red, resined room? How many years?

I pulled the chair out of the way—its legs dragged on the thick rug—and opened a door of the sideboard.

It was filled with jars, and when I held one up to the red light coming through the curtains, the contents admitted one tawny, diagonal blear before resolving to black.

Dad was all for clearing out the lot. He had a van, his man could drive, they'd be in and out within the night. Such were the times, after all, and what great family is not founded on the adventures of a buccaneer?

But I had a youth's hope, and told him no: that we should play the long game. I can't imagine what I was thinking: that they would show some generosity to me, perhaps, for not stealing their property? Ridiculous.

Still, Dad let me have my head. Still, somehow, my gamble paid off. The landlord, whose family name was Franklin, hardly showered me with riches, but he turned out friendly enough, and the following spring, at his grandmother's funeral, I met his daughters.

The match with Belinda—what a name!—was easy enough to arrange. The dowry would be a generous one. Pear orchards and plum trees, hops and brassicas and the young men to tend them. The whole business fell through, as I have said, but the friendship between our families held. When Ned ran into political trouble he gave up his career and came home to run things for Dad. It was to him Franklin gave his youngest child, my nephews' mum. (Melissa. What a name.)

The rest is ordinary. Ned has run our estate successfully over the years, has taken mistresses and made some of them wives, and filled the house with sons. Of them, the two eldest are my special treasure, since I'll have no kids myself. Every once in a while a brother of ours returns to take a hand in the making of our home. They bring us strange stories; of how the world is being set to rights. By a river in the Minas Gerais somewhere, someone has reinvented the dolphin. But it is orange, and it keeps sinking.

Poor Liam's still languishing in Dubai, but the rest of us, piling in to exploit what we collectively know of the labour market, have done better than well.

As for me: well, what with one promotion and then another, this offshore London Britannia airfield has become my private empire. Three hundred observation drones. Fifty attack quadcopters. Six strike UAVs. There are eight thousand miles of coastline to protect, a hungry neighbour to the west famining on potatoes; to the east, a continent's-worth of peckish privateers. It is a busy time.

Each spring we all pile back onto the estate, of course, to help with pollination. Tinkerers all, we experiment sometimes with boxes of mechanical bees, imported at swingeing cost from Shenzhen or Macao. But nothing works as well as a chicken feather wielded by a practised hand. This is how Ned, the scion of our line, came to plummet from the topmost rung of his ladder. The sons he had been teaching screamed, and from where I sat, stirring drying pots on the kitchen table, the first thing that struck me was how they sounded just like girls.

Dad leads me in. Much fuss is made of me. The boys vie with each other to tell their little brothers about the day, the airfield, the mayor. While Dad's women are cooing over them, I go through to the yard.

Ned is sitting where he usually sits on sunny days like these, in the shelter of the main greenhouse, with a view of our plum trees. They, more than any other crop, have made our family rich, and it occurs to me with a lurch, seeing my brother slumped there in his chair under rugs, that it is not the sight of their fruit that has him enthralled. He is watching the walls. He is watching the gate. He is guarding our trees. There's a gun by his side. A shotgun. We only ever fill the cartridges with rock salt. But still.

Ned sees me and smiles and beckons me to the bench beside him. "It's time," he says.

I knew this was coming.

"I can't pretend I can do this anymore. Look at me. Look."

I say what you have to say in these situations. Deep down, though, I can only assent. There's a lump in my throat. "I haven't earned this."

But Ned and I, we have always been close, and who else should he turn to, in his pain and disability and growing weakness? Who else should he hand the business to?

The farm will be mine. Melissa. The boys. All of it mine. Everything I ever wanted, though it has never been my place to take a single pip. It is being given to me freely, now. A life. A family. As if I deserved it!

"Think of the line," says Ned, against my words of protest. "The sons I'll never have."

We need sons, heaven knows. Young guns to hold our beachheads against the French. Keepers to protect our crop from night-stealing London boys. Swords to fight the feuds that, quite as much a marriage pacts, shape our living in this hungry world.

It is no use. I have no head for politics. Try as I might, I cannot think of sons, but only of their making. Celia Johnson with a speck of grit in her eye. Underwear and a bed of dreams. May God forgive me, I am that depraved, my every thought is sex.

Ned laughs. He knows, and has always known, of my weakness. My interest in women. It is, for all the changes our world's been through, still not an easy thing, for men to turn their backs on all the prospects a wife affords.

"Pick me a plum," my brother says. So I go pick a plum. Men have been shot for less. With rock salt, yes. But still.

I remember the night we chose, Ned and I, not to raid the larder of the poor, confused old woman who had burst into my room. Perhaps it was simply the strangeness of the day that stopped us. (We stole one jar and left the rest alone.) I would like to think, though, that our forbearance sprang from some simple, instinct of our own. Call it decency.

It is hard, in such revolutionary times, always to feel good about oneself.

"Here," I say, returning to my crippled benefactor, the plum nursed in my hands.

Ned's look, as he pushes the fruit into his mouth, is the same look he gave me the night we tasted, ate, and finished entirely, that jar of priceless, finite honey. Pleasure. Mischief. God help us all: youth.

Ten, twelve years on, Ned's enjoying another one-time treat: he chews a plum. A fruit that might have decked the table of the mayor himself, and earned our boys a month of crusts. He spits the stone into the dust. Among our parsimonious lot, this amounts to a desperate display of power: Ned knows that he is dying.

I wonder how it tastes, that plum—and Ned, being Ned, sees and knows it all: my shamefaced ambition. My inexcusable excitement. To know so much is to excuse so much, I guess, because he beckons me, my brother and my friend, and once I'm knelt before him, spits that heavy, sweet paste straight into my mouth. And makes me king.

THE KAREN JOY FOWLER BOOK CLUB

NIKE SULWAY

Two bright bangles on an arm clang,
a single bangle is silent, wander alone like a rhinoceros.
—Khargavisana-sutra [the Rhinoceros Sutra] c.29 BCE

Ten years ago, Clara had attended a creative writing workshop run by Karen Joy Fowler, and what Karen Joy told her was: *We are living in a science fictional world.* During the workshop, Karen Joy also kept saying, *I am going to talk about endings, but not yet.* But Karen Joy never did get around to talking about endings, and Clara left the workshop still feeling as if she was suspended within it, waiting for the second shoe to drop.

Eventually, Clara had attempted a cold equations story, and though Karen Joy never read it, Clara thought she might have liked it if she'd had the chance. In Clara's story, "False Equations," the Emergency Despatch Ship (EDS) was packed full of animals, rather than people, and the stowaway was the child of a White-backed vulture pair. An egg when she was smuggled aboard, the stowaway hatched during the journey to Walden (rather than Woden).

Clara had made several copies of the story and sent them out to the other members of her book club. Fern wrote back to say that the story was too complex and far-fetched. Bea wrote that she hadn't time to read anything just then except the book that they were *supposed* to be reading for their next meeting. And Belle said simply that there were far too many "Cold Equations" reworkings and inter-textual responses out there, and she didn't see why Clara had bothered attempting another if she had so little to say about the matter.

Clara, like Fern and all of the other members of the Karen Joy Fowler Book Club, had never managed to finish reading the set book before their scheduled get-together. But then, none of their planned book discussions had yet taken place. There was always some complication, some hindrance that they were incapable of overcoming.

The workshop had not been a total loss, however, since Clara had met Belle there, and they had ended up good friends. They lived near each other—their farms were only a short walk apart—and a few years ago they had opened up a café in town where they served good, simple food and provided their customers with a shaded garden in which to sit and chat.

These days, when Clara can, she takes time off from the café to go and visit her daughter. Alice lives near the great lakes. She has a large house; tall and stone-walled, with large windows to catch the afternoon breezes. As Clara comes down the shared driveway to Alice's house, she always experiences a moment of something like regret, or fear. What if, once she enters her daughter's house, she isn't able to leave again? What if, once she sees all the children her daughter cares for, she can't stop herself from saying something cruel? Telling her daughter what she believes: that Alice's house full of other people's children is just a way for her daughter to endlessly delay her own grieving, her own letting go of things. Or what if the opposite occurs: What if she enters that house full of children, sees all the work that needs to be done caring for them, and is caught up in her daughter's Sisyphean task of feeding, bathing, and holding other creatures' young? Like Sisyphus forever pushing his stone up the same mountain, only to watch it roll down again.

Clara isn't sure she is a welcome visitor any more, or whether she wants to go there. She doesn't think about these things directly, but as she comes up the walk she tries to imagine herself greeting and being greeted by her daughter and struggles to construct an image that contains ease or warmth.

As it happens, she finds Alice in the garden with her new lover. They are walking from tree to tree, looking up into the canopy of each one and then moving on.

This is not Alice's first lover, Jeff, who is dead now, and Clara has difficulty remembering this one's name. Blue? Balloon?

They go to wallow in the mud-hole that spreads out from beneath the African tulip tree. The one Jeff had liked to wallow in with guests. They had been cooling off there together—Alice and Jeff—when they had told Clara there would be no grandchildren. "It's my fault, I'm afraid," he'd said, as if he'd forgotten to pick up ice on the way home, but blushingly. "They're no good, my swimmers. My—"

"She knows what you mean," Alice had said. "There's no need to go on and on."

Clara had remembered, then, the termination Alice had when she was in high school. The waiting room full of pictures of empty landscapes at sunset, the interview with the cheerful nurse, the other young females in the waiting room—all of them avoiding each other's eyes. And afterwards, her daughter wanting ice cream and to sit by the river and watch the waterbirds dancing in the shallow water. Alice had rested her head on Clara's shoulder, curled her feet up under her bottom like a child. Her breath had smelled of milk and sweet biscuits, and her hair of antiseptic. It is the last time Clara can remember her daughter wanting to be held.

The garden has changed more than Clara's daughter has, since Jeff's passing. The paths that were once just worn earth have been widened and cleared of weeds. The beds of unnamed flowers that Alice and her husband used to grow have been replaced with vegetable patches and rows of imported exotics. Mulched and weeded and trimmed and fertilised to within an inch of their lives.

"You should keep going," Alice says to her lover.

"Oh," he says. "Oh yes, of course! Women's talk." He winks at Clara as he moves away. "Don't do anything I wouldn't do."

When he has gone, Alice sighs and settles into a more comfortable position. "The sad thing is, he means it," she says. "He won't tolerate me doing anything without consulting him. He calls it *communication,* when what he really means is him telling me what to do." She flicks her ears a little to clear away the flies. "It almost makes me glad we're too different to breed. Imagine us: the parents of the last generation!"

Clara squints into the sun and watches her daughter's lover still moving from tree to tree, looking up, thinking, then moving on. She is tired of being a visitor already, but Alice asks her all the questions a daughter asks anyway. No, Clara hasn't heard from her husband of late. Yes, the café is going well. They've started a new tradition of monthly dinners. Seasonal dishes, all made with local produce. No, nobody *special.*

Alice looks across the mud-hole to the forest. "I've lost track of Dad," she says. "Wasn't he out west somewhere, living on a wildlife refuge of some kind?"

"I'd heard that," Clara said. "Him and that female were working the summers and mostly left alone in the winters. Wandering the hills."

"Janet," says her daughter.

"What?"

"Dad's new partner, her name is Janet."

She ought not to have come, Clara thinks. Everything her daughter says or asks of her feels like a reproach. Even the gardens are reproachful, the liquidambars arching over the green lawn. The perfect garden beds, the even paths, the vistas like postcards. It was just what she'd dreaded, coming down the driveway, just what she'd been preparing herself for.

Alice wants to show her around the bottom end of the garden, which she says is where Jeff spent most of his time during the last few months of his life. Sometimes, he would fall asleep on the lawn, stretched out like a child and snoring so loudly that the small birds—the fairy wrens and tits—would scatter with fear.

"When I woke him up he would always say he hadn't been sleeping at all," Alice says. "He'd say he'd been writing. He'd tell me all about whatever it was he had been working on. By the end, the things he told me were just a jumble. A nonsense. But at first I believed him. Or . . . or I wanted to. He was working on a cold equations story, he said. But it was set here on Earth, and instead of people, the two characters were rhinos, like us. The last two rhinos on Earth. And as soon as one died, the other would become functionally extinct."

Alice was smiling, as though even now she could hear Jeff working out the shape of his story in her head. "That must be how he thought of us," she said. "After all those years of being together, of sharing our lives and building this house and this garden. That there was no point to us being together, or having children. That we were just the leftover scraps of something that had once been whole."

Jeff had died five years ago, just before the end of the summer, but Clara had not heard about it until six months after that. She got the news in a letter from Janet, her former husband's new partner, one of the founding members of the Karen Joy Fowler Book Club. They had once met, purely by accident, near a temporary market in Pullington. Janet had been walking away from a dungpile that Clara was going towards and somehow they had gotten to talking. It wasn't till much later that they had realised they shared a man. In a manner of speaking.

Of course, I know that you knew Jeff far more intimately than I ever did, Janet wrote. *But I've been surprised by how often I've thought about him. His passing makes me think about all of us, how we were, fifty years or so ago, when we didn't know that it was all going to come to such an ending. We were full of ideas for growing the future—remember that plan Hildy had for forming a partnership with the San Diego Zoo?—and the males were all so ready to charge out into the world and lay down babies wherever they could.*

Of course, Jeff wasn't like that. Not even slightly. He never wanted anyone but his one dear wife; he wasn't like his father, or any of that generation that were ours to love. Jeff seemed the most vulnerable of us all, even when he was young. I remember I could hardly bear to look at the dark spaces between his skin folds.

Did Janet really think that's how it had been, for all of them? That, like her, they'd spent their youth getting babies on and from whoever they could? Clara's memory of those days was that she and her husband had expected to stay together for their whole lives, babies or no babies. Until one of them died and was left to rot in some godforsaken grove of spindle-trees. Without a future generation to be mindful of, there was no reason for him to move on after twenty days. He could stay; they could form a pair-bond that would last through as many breeding seasons as they survived.

Clara and Janet had never been close—they had their reasons not to be— but Janet had known where to reach her when Jeff died, and she had kept in touch with Jeff, or with Clara's daughter. She had known about Jeff's death, and written to Clara with those strange, true words. Without Janet, Clara might never have known that her daughter's husband had died. She might still have been keeping her distance, thinking that one day soon she would hear from him, and from her daughter.

The first time she went to Belle's place it had been to drop off some salad greens she had picked up from a roadside stall on the way home. Belle's crash was more or less what Clara had expected. Abundant and shabby, her teenage daughters sprawled across the savannah, leaving a trail of unconsciously messy beauty in their wake. Belle didn't come to greet her, just hallooed her in, and when Clara came through she found the kitchen, unlike the one in the café, a lively and fragrant jungle of ingredients. Belle herself was the least colourful thing. She had taken off the two clanging bangles she wore around her ankles at work and stood in the kitchen barefoot, her skin rough and grey.

Belle's husband, Robert, poured drinks for all of them. Clara put the greens in a clear space and somehow was invited to stay for dinner. The food Belle served was not as fancy as that she served in the café, and the dinner service was a mismatched collection of hand-thrown pottery pieces. The kind you pick up cheap at garage sales and second-hand stores. Robert kept their glasses full and talked about the fields of grapes he had seen growing on a property out the other side of the reserve. He also told stories about the Scandinavian furniture he had bought cheaply on eBay, especially about a queer couple of Silverbacks from whom he had wrangled a pair of original Thonet chairs. The way he talked about the exchange made it seem scandalous, as though they had propositioned him in some way. Later, when he made coffee, he talked about a workshop he had gone to on "cupping" and tried to teach Clara and Belle how to smell the grounds, insisting that they all drink their coffee sugarless and milk-free in order to better appreciate the flavours of the coffee.

During a pause in the conversation, Clara asked Belle if she had thought any more about whether she wanted to join the Karen Joy Fowler Book Club. Robert leant back away from the conversation, raising an eyebrow at his daughters as if he had been interrupted mid-anecdote, and then listened to his wife talk about the book they were planning to read with studied, careful attention.

After dinner, the pale-skinned daughters dragged their father off to help them with something and Belle and Clara were left alone in the mud-hole. The solar fairy lights were starting to dim, but the citronella candles threw off more than enough light. Belle stretched herself out, her feet in the cool spot where Robert had been sitting.

"I should go," Clara said, and Belle turned and reached out as if to stop her.

"Don't go," Belle said. "Nobody else gets a word in once Rob gets going."

Clara saw how it was. How Belle was in no hurry to be left alone with Robert after their evening of high talk and laughter. How he was the kind of male who was roused by such things into something like rage. Belle was weary, and filled with the kind of dread that comes when a party is over and you see, all at once, all the damage you must now repair.

Clara and Belle were both of that generation who were unlikely to have grandchildren, though they had both had husbands and children of their own. They were the mothers of daughters they did not understand, and whose troubles they could barely recognise. They went in and out of each other's houses on a daily basis. They would graze in the savannah, or stand side by side in the kitchen making bread and listening to Belle's daughters talk about their lives. The jokes about being the last of their kind. The bullying and despair. The gossip and conspiracies. A female in another herd had had a child, but it had died after one year. Another had given birth to three at once, stillborn and pale as cake. Clara and Belle looked at each other and twitched their ears in silent amazement. Who were these females? What lives were they living?

"Where did you hear that?" Belle said. "Facebook? It sounds like a hoax. Fear-mongering."

The girls said it didn't matter if one particular story was true or not, the point was not that one female had bred or not, but that *they* would never have children of their own. And if they did, they would be outcasts.

"We'd stay friends, if one of us had a child," said one of Belle's daughters.

"Sure," said the other. "We'd set up a home and raise it together. Share it."

"What about the bull?" said the younger daughter. "Would he have to live with us, too?"

Belle and Clara shared another of their looks, folded and pounded the dough they were working.

Belle's older daughter shrugged. "You know what the males are like," she said. "The ones who can breed are like . . . ugh."

When they had talked enough about the future, the daughters talked about movies and music and the parties they were going to. Belle's daughters were into bushwalking, and were always trying to drag their mother and Clara along on their week-long walks across the reserve. They talked about the places they would walk to next, and the things they planned to do when they got there.

Clara and Belle also worked together in the kitchen at the café. Or they went to other cafés to eat cake and drink coffee. They liked to sample the menus in the other cafés and consider the clientele. Sometimes, they would buy flat, sweet Dutch donuts from the baker, and get take-away coffee from the place next door to that, and then they'd go for a long walk along the beach together.

They talked, at first in a sidelong fashion, and later with increasing heatedness, about the males with whom they had paired, their children, the lives they still felt they might live.

Clara said that her husband had been the kind that, whenever they invited people for dinner, would insist that she spend the two days prior to their arrival cleaning the whole of their home from top to bottom. She would pull out the weeds along the pathways and pull out the saplings that were too hard or bitter to eat. Trample the path till it was good and wide, and gather extra food for everyone. "It got to the point it was just easier not to have guests," she said. "By the time they arrived, I was too exhausted to enjoy their company."

Belle said that she had found out Robert still wrote letters to his childhood sweetheart. One a week. And that the woman wrote back just as often.

"What do the letters say?" Clara asked.

Belle shrugged and looked away, squinting out to sea. "I don't know. He keeps them in a toolbox in his solitary territory. I've never had the courage to read them. I can't decide whether I want them to be in love still, or not."

They looked at each other, and then they both laughed. It was ridiculous, wasn't it? The way the ones that were meant to be the centres of their lives were so peripheral. It was their friendship with each other that was the true and central thing.

"I shouldn't talk about him like this," said Belle. "He's a good enough husband."

Clara nodded. "Mine was, too. He was all right, as far as husbands go."

"Just not—I don't know. It's as though he's given up. As though now that we know we'll go extinct—there's no point in paying attention to the lives we *do* have. The lives we're living."

"As if we're already ghosts," said Clara. "Already dead."

"I'm going to leave him," Belle said. "I can't go on like this for much longer; living in the afterlife."

• • •

After they separated, Belle and her husband were friendly enough. He stayed in touch with the girls and was still often at their place, dropping them off or picking them up, mending this and that.

Belle spent most of her time at the café. She put in a herb garden, and then a vegetable patch. There was a vacant lot next door and it was soon overrun with pumpkins and nasturtiums, zucchini and tomato plants. She stopped wearing her bangles to work, and was often working in the garden, showing off her bare, strong shoulders and sturdy legs. She seemed younger every week, rather than older. Cleverer, too, and full of easy opinions about things. The customers who came into the café liked to talk to her about their own gardens, and their own efforts at baking this or that. They liked to walk beside her as she moved through the garden, pulling weeds or turning soil. In the middle of the day, if it was too hot and there were no customers to speak of, she would find a shady spot in the garden, spread out a picnic blanket and sit outside reading.

Sometimes, one of the customers would go out into the garden to see her; they would bring her an armful of rosemary, or a bucket of beets they had grown. These were always single females. They weren't lonely, exactly, but they seemed to like to come and take up a corner of Belle's blanket and talk.

Finally, one night after closing up late, Clara invited Belle to come to her house for a drink. Usually, Belle was busy in the evenings. She had the girls at home most nights, after all. But this time she said yes, and followed Clara up the long dirt road to her house.

Clara's house was small but she had an earnest, quiet affection for it. It had a long, narrow room running all along one side—a closed-in verandah—which was her very own library. There were windows at both ends, but it was a cool, dark, narrow room. She had her desk in there, but it was mostly just bookcases. Floor to ceiling, wall to wall. In the early evening, it was flooded with a faint, stippled light that came in through the bush surrounding the house. The room, like the rest of the house, was very plain and tidy. Clara found this plainness comforting amid the flourishing chaos of the bush in which the house sat. The winding, shaded paths through the rainforest. The weedy, vine-strangled creek. Here, the books spoke their own quiet language.

One of the deep, unspoken pleasures of Clara's life was to spend a whole day putting the books in order. She would catalogue everything like a real library, using the Dewey Decimal System, or ordering the books by colour and size. She would often lie on the cool concrete floor, with the reading lamp lit and her notebook at hand. Not reading, just waiting. It didn't matter what book it was she was meant to be reading. None of what was in the books mattered, in a sense. The fact of their existence was enough.

She heard Belle come down the path to the house. Heard her

exuberant *halloooo* as she descended. Clara felt a fish hook catch in her ribs, and pull. She went out into the hall and saw Belle coming in at the door, leaving it open in her wake.

They went through the house. Clara had not turned on any of the lights. There was only the reading light in the library.

They sat on the floor in the library. Clara showed Belle her collection of fairy tales. Pictures of geese and princesses, ravens and hedgehogs, foxes and underground castles whose kitchens were acres and acres wide.

Belle stretched out across the floor and closed her eyes. Clara read to her, and she fell asleep. They both did. Then Belle left while Clara was sleeping, without saying goodbye.

But Belle visited again the next night, and told her a story she had heard when she was a child. They were sitting on the floor in the library again. Their backs against the bookcase, and their legs stretched out in front of them. When the story was finished, Belle said, very quietly, "You know, you're very important to me." They sat in the almost-dark room. It was hot, but a storm was about to break outside. You could feel its wet promise in the air. Belle tilted her head till it rested on Clara's shoulder. And then she got up and went away again.

She stayed away for three nights, then came without warning. Knocked and stood in the doorway, asking Clara if she would come to the river with her, right then and there, and walk along it in the dark.

They sat for a while on the enormous stones that lined one section of the riverbank. There were a few boats moored in the water, and the she-oaks that lined the shore on the other side made a soft, comforting sound. Like mothers hushing their children. They made love in a sandy gap between two large, flat stones. They walked along the river's edge afterwards, not touching, not talking. Clara felt herself a strong and independent female, unhampered by marriage or children or housework.

At home, she walked through the house spreading sand over the freshly swept and polished floors. She bathed, but there was sand in her creases that found its way into her bed. She woke with the smell of river-water and night air still on her skin, would not have been surprised to find a small fish swimming in the sheets.

Clara became consumed by this other version of herself. A night-time version that bore only an uncertain relation to her ordinary daytime self. The map of the reserve that she had held in her mind changed subtly. A secret map was sketched across the day-lit one, with its markets and mud-holes and roads. The second map drew attention to the edges of places, and the gaps between them. To shorelines and unmarked paths. Places, like her library, that she thought of as corridors, light coming in at both ends and herself flying through them, like the sparrow in the old story by the venerable Bede.

Clara felt herself to be full of increasingly numerous pockets of strangeness. Walking to work, or cleaning the house, grazing on the savannah or kneading bread in the café, she contained fragments of another female, one who had during the night made love with Belle on the weedy grass at the edge of the forest, or on the savannah, or, during one particularly wild rainstorm, in an empty carpark. That other Clara whose body seemed to be always already naked and beautiful.

How many females, she wondered, had felt this looseness, this glorious severance from the future? Had she been moving towards this feeling her whole life? Since her husband had left her? Since her daughter had stopped speaking to her? Since the scientists had said, finally, and with a sense more of exhaustion than of sadness, that there was no hope for their species?

The trouble began when Belle said that she loved her. They were in the kitchen at the café, standing side by side chopping pumpkins for the soup.

"I didn't know this was going to happen," Belle said. She was blushing, but seemed determined not to acknowledge that this was so.

"I know," Clara said.

That night, they walked through the darkness and met each other on the road between their houses. They hadn't planned it that way. Both of them had simply decided to walk towards the other. They moved off the road, into the forest, and found a place to lie down. Not a word was uttered, but Clara felt the things that Belle had said earlier that day like a widening of the channel in which they lay. She worried that the space would narrow, or disappear altogether. But it broadened out, from a narrow corridor into the high, bright nave of a cathedral. They could not look at each other, though their eyes were open. Their skin was cool and smooth to the touch. Clara felt that they were like fallen statues of themselves, organless and simple both inside and out.

"That story you wrote," Belle said, "the one about us going extinct."

"I never wrote a story about extinction," said Clara.

"False something, it was called."

Belle had started the conversation in that quiet moment when they were lying in the library, after making love, when last time they had not spoken at all, but allowed the stillness between them to express everything.

"Did you ever think of having the two females just go on together? The mother and the daughter: Alice. They could jettison the male and have enough resources to make it to Walden."

The male White-backed vulture in the story had been perhaps the most troubled by their predicament. The nest he and his partner had built, in the nearest thing they could find to a tree in the EDS, was lined not with green leaves and grass, but with the hair of other animals, with electrical wires and strips of soft plastic. He had tried to get some of the other animals—in particular the other birds—to become part of a breeding colony, but nobody would join him. Nobody wanted to become the mother or father of a child who would have to be jettisoned into space.

"It's not that simple. You're making the same mistake as the others," Clara said.

"What did the others say, about the story?"

Belle tried to nuzzle Clara, to draw her back into an embrace, but Clara moved away slightly. There was a tightness in her gut that wouldn't allow her to look at her lover. "I didn't mean them," Clara said. "I meant the other writers. Godwin. All those men. It's a false equation."

"But you sent it to the others, didn't you? To the other members of the Karen Joy Fowler Book Club? What did they say?"

Clara shook her head, appalled.

"You didn't send it to them," Belle said. "Just to me? Or . . . perhaps they don't exist, those others," she said softly, squeezing the flesh of Clara's thigh. "Perhaps there's only me. Perhaps I'm the stowaway in your spaceship to Walden."

"Stop it," Clara said, pushing Belle away. Her rough, insistent touch. "Why are you being like this?"

"Like what?" Belle said, sliding closer, curling her tail, pushing herself against Clara in a mocking, vulgar way. "I just want to get inside you. Inside your pretty head where all the other women meet." She began to herd Clara against the wall, to wipe her horn on the floor with a terrible scraping noise.

Clara told her to leave. She said that if Belle didn't leave now, then she would go herself. She moved away, stiffened herself. Belle pressed her horn into the ridge between Clara's shoulder and her neck, pushed the point in with a soft, ugly curse. The same word she sometimes cried out when they were lying together. Then she pulled away, gave Clara a sour and pitying look, and left.

Clara stayed in the library for some time, wondering what had happened, exactly. What had gone wrong. When she thought about it afterwards—when she had become a solitary wanderer—she decided that Belle had been frightened of what it meant for the love they made to be incapable of producing a future. That was the whole point of love, for Belle, for it to create the possibility of lineage. To gesture towards Walden, when in reality whether they remained in the ship or arrived at some fantastical destination made no difference. What did it mean, to save Alice, when there was no future into which she might travel? Or perhaps Belle had just wanted to humiliate Clara because she was frightened. Or was it all just a part of loving a woman, after all, some ordinary consequence of lying down together?

A week later, there was a knock at the door, and Clara was sure it would be Belle. She had been thinking all week that Belle would call to explain herself, to ask for forgiveness, to say that she had been frightened, or even uncertain, and that the uncertainty had made her cruel. Clara had rehearsed their conversation in her head. She would listen, she had decided, patiently and kindly, though she would not forgive her lover too quickly.

But when she opened the door it was only her daughter, Alice.

"Belle sent me a message," Alice said. "Your Belle. How did she even know my name?"

"I don't know," said Clara.

She had told Belle about Alice, of course. She had offered up the story of her lost, wild daughter as a kind of intimacy. Or in order to make herself seem more interesting, more strange and unfamiliar than she otherwise might have seemed.

"She wants to come and talk to me," Alice said. "What's the matter with her? What does she want?"

"We had a fight," Clara said, wondering if that was true, after all.

"Does she want to punish you, by talking to me? Or have me convince you to forgive her?"

Clara shook her head. "She's not like that," she said. But she wasn't sure if it was true.

"I'm going to meet her at the café," Alice said. "It's closed, but Belle says we can sit in the garden and talk. I'll send you a message afterwards and tell you what happens."

Clara tried not to pay too much attention to the time. Several hours passed. The day ended. She sat in the library, not reading the book they were planning to discuss at book club. She turned the pages one at a time, then in batches, going backwards, going forwards. It didn't seem to matter.

It was almost morning by the time she decided to walk to Alice's house. She had no idea what she would do when she got there, but at least the walking would give her something to do.

As she walked, she tried to remember, and silently recite, the lines of the rhinoceros sutra. Only fragments of the already fragmented text would come to her. She remembered that there was something about a kovilara tree that has shed its leaves. She could remember that one of the sutras was: *Seeing the danger that comes from affection, wander alone like a rhinoceros.* And another: *Give up your children, and your wives, and your money, wander alone like a rhinoceros.*

She walked down the long drive towards Alice's house, which was lined on both sides with overgrown black bamboo. There were no lights on in the house. She could see that all the windows were open to let in any cool breeze.

Clara looked in at the windows and saw that Alice had left the children she cared for alone, and the doors unlocked. None of them woke and saw her looking in at them. Some of the creatures were unfamiliar to her; had they come from other reserves? Other continents? Were they all, like Alice, the last of their kind?

Clara found an open door at the back of the house and went in, closing it behind her. She lay on the cool stone floor of the living area. She lay still, listening to the snuffling and breathing of the children, until she heard the birds outside the house waking. She was stiff and tired. She got up and opened the front door, looking up the driveway for a sign of her daughter. Nothing.

She could not quite identify what she was feeling. She was restless, but wanted to be still. She was impatient, but did not want to hear what Belle and Alice had had to say to each other. She longed for the feeling she was already having trouble recalling, of being in the long, cool channel of the library. With light behind her, and light ahead, and this moment, this *now*, always just a thing she was passing through.

She went from room to room looking in at the children. How carelessly they slept, with the windows open and the doors unlocked. They lay tangled together, sleeping. So fearless. When had she last slept that way?

Alice appeared at the door behind her, looking in at the sleeping babies. "I told you they were beautiful," she said.

Clara did not answer. She could barely remember the conversations they had had, so many years ago, about Alice's decision not even to try to have children of her own. She tried to pretend that Alice had not come home yet, and that as the children woke—they were starting to turn and itch in their sleep—they would come to Clara, climbing up and over her. She would prepare breakfast for them, and watch them play on the wide back lawn.

"She didn't say anything, really," Alice said. "We had a bottle of wine and Belle said that she wasn't sure what had happened between you, but that she hoped it would be all right again soon. She said she thought it was too late now, for any of us, to hold grudges or fall in love."

She said. "Mum, listen. It's nothing. It doesn't mean anything. One day, you'll forget her name. We'll have to call her That Woman From The Café. We'll laugh about it."

Then, "Mum, what are you going to do? There's nothing you can do. It's done."

One of the children came sleepily out of their room and leant against Alice, then clambered up onto her back. Clara smiled at the way Alice moved to accommodate the child; at how natural and easy it seemed for her to do so.

"I have to go," Clara said. She felt disconnected from all of it, now that she had seen the house with Alice in it, and all the children sleeping so quietly together. All these years there had been a kind of wire connecting her to Alice. A twinging in her ribs whenever she thought of her, and what her future might contain, and now it was gone. Things were exactly as they were, exactly as they were supposed to be.

Clara never saw Belle, or Alice, again. She left Alice's house and went home, walked through the rooms in which she had spent her life and did not recognise a thing. Even the library, with its walls of unread books, seemed unfamiliar.

So she left the house and started wandering, alone, like a rhinoceros.

The Karen Joy Fowler Book Club were due to meet in a few months' time, and if she reached them, that was fine. And if not, that would be fine as well. She got a powerful sense of pleasure out of walking away. She was pleased with herself, with the controlled and deliberate way in which she managed it. She scraped Belle out of herself, all those tangled and uncertain emotions, and found that the hollow that was left behind was a good and simple thing.

She saw that she had been living in a false equation: She had believed, like Belle and all the others, like Janet and her husband, that love and futurity were connected. That without a future, love was no longer possible; without Walden as their destination, there was no reason to jettison the hatchling, and no reason not to.

But love does not require a future in order to exist. And the future exists, whether you furnish it with love or not. The second rhinoceros sutra, after all, was clear: *Renouncing violence for all living beings, harming not even a one, you would not wish for offspring, so how a companion? Wander alone like a rhinoceros.*

Clara turns onto an unfamiliar path. She has passed, finally, beyond the reserve. She does not think about the future, or love, as she walks through the waist-high grass, with its smell of summer and heat. Past the kovilara trees, past the view of the mountain washed in late afternoon light. She doesn't think about Belle, or Alice, or her husband. The path is shaded, but warm. She can see where it disappears ahead of her.

As she wanders, she thinks about being in the library late in the day. The light from the forest lying complicated, shifting patterns on the floor. And herself, passing through, from one end of the story to the other.

ENDLESS FORMS MOST BEAUTIFUL

ALVARO ZINOS-AMARO

—◆—

"Palsgrave Greshmenn, someone requests your presence."

Greshmenn was on the fifth level of the east wing, clad in full mood-onomatopoeic garb. When he heard Taetzsch, his estate's Intelligence, he froze in place, bushels of long, silver hair swinging pendulum-like at his sides for a dozen servo-regulated heartbeats. He opened his mouth to respond, then closed it.

The most recent parade of colors to flow through his vestments, instants before the announcement, had not denoted happiness: anxious amaranths, distressed palatinate purples, a flash of cerulean.

Now the wide sleeves of Greshmenn's sense-recording dalmatic turned a dour shamrock green, and the silk cummerbund around his waist shimmered with glaring chestnut.

At last, the august palsgrave brought himself to answer. His voice, as though having crossed a desert on its way to his thin lips, arrived parched with incredulity. "Someone requests *my* presence?"

"Yes, Palsgrave," Taetzsch said.

Greshmenn frowned. "And who precisely is this undesirable that dares disturb me?"

While he waited for a response, Greshmenn's eyes returned to the object he had been scrutinizing, his most prized possession, the Varnava. He was thoroughly vexed by the microscopic leak that threatened to upset the painting's delicate evolution.

And now this intrusive request—

Unbearable.

The reclusive palsgrave, who had gone to great lengths to disappear from public life, hadn't been bothered in years, and that was the way he liked it. Greshmenn absorbed the often grim media reports of his own demise with faint bemusement and a dash of disdainful pity: poor naïve dullards, he thought.

And yet *someone* had managed to find him.

As he pondered the suspects, Greshmenn thought of Raugrave Niarchos IV, his only significant competitor in the world of Evolutive art collecting, a fellow holdover from the remote days of bio-original spinal cords. And yet it seemed unlikely that the pompous Raugrave would wish to communicate with him right before bidding opened on the latest Hilel Zhe Pan, unless he wanted to strike some kind of deal. That hadn't happened in decades.

No, this must be someone else. Someone *new*.

"He says his name is Titian," Taetzsch said. "He claims to need your assistance with a delicate matter, but he has refused to disclose what he insists are the sensitive details of his appeal."

The palsgrave stroked the point of his immaculate argent beard. Titian was one of the transitional names used by almost every artgrave on the climb up—and more often than not again on the drop down—the ladders of the collecting world. That Greshmenn had been accidentally discovered by a stranger was a single unlikelihood and might be overlooked. But for the stranger to occupy the very same specialized niche as the palsgrave? In such curlicues of circumstance could be felt a tickle of intrigue.

"Did this Titian fellow explain how he found me?"

"I did not ask him," Taetzsch replied. "However, I am happy to do so now, Palsgrave."

Greshmenn puffed out his chest and straightened his shoulders. "I will perform the inquiry myself. Enhancements?"

"My scans reveal only the ordinary nanoimplants and servos," Taetzsch said.

"Where is he?"

"Titian is speaking with me via Spore. His physical location is Dar es Salaam, off the coast of Tanzania."

"I want him to make the trip here in person. I won't speak with him by Spore. Relay that." Greshmenn's gaze drifted back to his painting's leak. His amice flooded with deep Prussian blue. He lowered his head.

Taetzsch's voice shoved him back into reality: "Titian has agreed to your terms."

"Good," Greshmenn snapped. "When will he be here?"

"Four hours and sixteen minutes."

Greshmenn sighed. "Finalize arrangements for his visit and terminate your conversation with him at once."

"As you wish, Palsgrave," Taetzsch said.

After waiting thirty seconds or so, Greshmenn said, "Well?"

"Almost done," Taetzsch said. "Despite your reticence to make use of this ability, may I remind you than I'm quite capable of concluding my conversation with Titian and speaking with you at the same time?"

"I know you are," Greshmenn said. "I don't doubt your resources. I purchased them. But I'd prefer it if you just talked to one of us at a time. Call me old-fashioned."

"You are anything but," Taetzsch said. "Your collection attests to that."

Was that a pinprick of sarcasm? Could an Intelligence develop such nuances, such sophistication? The palsgrave fleetingly wondered whether something was wrong with his artificial servant. But before he could pursue that line of thought Taetzsch informed him that his transaction with Titian had finalized. "Very well. Before Titian arrives at the estate, activate maximal observation procedures. Reroute resources from wherever you have to—even the restoration of my Varnava, if you must. I want to know everything there is to know about this scoundrel from the moment he gets here."

"Yes, Palsgrave."

"And as soon as he departs I expect a comprehensive analysis."

"Of course, Palsgrave."

"You think I'm being paranoid, don't you?"

"No, sir."

"This visit likely involves some kind of deception."

"An excellent appraisal."

"Are you being deferential?"

"Yes, Palsgrave, but only in response to the flawless logic underlying your assessment."

Greshmenn tugged at the corners of his arsenic eyes, where a strange weariness, imperceptible to his myriad amino acid and endorphin regulators, threatened to creep into his body. These days he felt that same tiredness, verging on apathy, with increasing frequency. Perhaps it was resignation.

"You know, Taetzsch, at times I attempt to imagine what existence must be like for you, and I become fearful that you must be lonely. After all, most EIs are Linked, but to protect my anonymity I keep you disconnected. But then you inevitably remind me, with your barbs—as you did just now with your comment about my 'flawless logic'—that I'm just being mawkish."

"I appreciate your concern," Taetzsch said in his predictably flat voice. "But I assure you that I cannot experience loneliness in the sense you suggest, Palsgrave."

"I'll take your word for it. Are the maximal observation procedures in place?"

"They are."

"Very well. I will return to my painting now."

"Yes, Palsgrave. As always, I'm happy to assist with the painting's restoration, should you desire it."

More irony? Taetzsch's efforts to fix the painting's leak, like Greshmenn's, had proved useless.

"That won't be necessary."

Greshmenn paced stolidly for a few minutes and finally sank back into the interminable chore of trying to save the painting.

Greshmenn was underwhelmed by his visitor's appearance. The top of Titian's head, covered in unkempt, curly, sand-brown hair, reached only up to Greshmenn's shoulders. And Titian's implants, as evidenced by the telltale gray discolorations at the interface points on his neck and palms, were at least two generations behind Greshmenn's, who himself took irrational, retrograde pride in being several years behind the Swathing Edge.

As Greshmenn strode through his palatial grounds, Titian trailed a few steps behind. The palsgrave stopped at a fountain, his thoughts dancing along an inverted cone of electromagnetically slowed micro-droplets.

He eased into a timeless state, testing his visitor with silence.

Titian's lanky frame bent to and fro, making the palsgrave think of a malnourished birch. Titian's voice, when he finally spoke, was almost lost amidst the water's susurrations: "Excuse my ignorance if I have offended you. I'm unfamiliar with the ways of your estate."

Greshmenn decided he was tired of playing games. "Come with me," he commanded, and with firm long strides led the way into his study on the fifth level. Security systems unfurled at his command like lavender petals, parting to reveal the bud of his collection. As they entered the chamber, Greshmenn kept his sights on Titian at all times. It took Titian only a few seconds to spot the Varnava.

"The Chitinous Narcissus," he whispered.

Titian gravitated toward it as though in a trance. He admired it from one angle, then another, and yet another. He asked technical questions about its composition, about its purchase and preservation. As the palsgrave replied, Titian nodded thoughtfully, his attention never wandering from the piece.

A ruminative pause grew, eventually becoming unsettling.

Titian had spotted the leak.

He looked at it as though recognizing something familiar for the first time since his arrival.

The palsgrave had done nothing to call attention to the painting's imperfection, which absorbed the entirety of his attention. "I see you've noticed the blemish," he said.

"Indeed."

The palsgrave compared his subjective impressions of the young man's reactions with the empirical data that Taetzsch was feeding him through his tunic. Both datasets agreed, indicating that Titian spoke candidly. But he hadn't exactly said much of value. He had recognized this piece, and yet he seemed unsurprised by the leak.

Greshmenn took a step back. Time to be practical. "Observe the canvas with care," he instructed. "If your visual memory enhancements allow, you will notice that the painting is subtly different now from what it was seconds ago. Diminutive alterations are occurring every instant: color, texture, angle, style of brush-strokes, and so on. That's the norm for all Evolutive art—endless change. The work reassembles itself bit by quantum bit," Greshmenn said. "A hum of intermeshed realities."

"Yes," Titian murmured.

"It can prove quite hypnotic," the palsgrave went on. "Consider. At some unknowable moment the work will manifest its highest possible aesthetic. But it will remain in this state of unsurpassable beauty for perhaps only a few moments."

Greshmenn stood still. Fourteen years, fourteen *hopeful* years, had passed and he had not yet witnessed this High Point. If the painting had been healthy, if it had been intact and whole, it might have been another fourteen years—or ten times as long—before he was privy to such an apex. What of it? He had the lifespan and the dedication to wait as long as necessary for the golden moment. But the painting was *not* healthy. It was not intact. It was not whole. "This leak," Greshmenn said, "this intolerable transgression against all that is sacred, threatens to make a travesty of my patience."

The leak rippled, as though in response to the palsgrave's desperation. It was entropic, a virus of imperfection consuming this majestic exemplar of Evolutive progress. And there was no known way to remove it. The same physics that made cross-reality reassembly possible in the first place could, in rare instances such as this, generate artifacts, bugs, splotches of atoms that simply refused to dance in concert with the rest.

Beauty was seeping out through the leak like sap.

Greshmenn felt his pulse quiver, and the myriad invisible nanosoldiers in his cells righted it. His breath quickened, and they slowed it down. There was one thing they did not stop, however, for the palsgrave was careful to stop it himself; the distillation of his despair into tears.

"You are overcome with emotion, but you choke it down," Titian said.

Greshmenn did not deny it.

The younger man turned to face the palsgrave. "Why?"

Greshmenn blinked. "I control myself for the painting," he said.

"Surely, the painting does not care what you feel. Or do you attribute sensitivity to it? Sentience, perhaps?"

"It does not care in the sense that you or I care," Greshmenn said. "But it *is* sensitive to the quality of one's gaze, and the emotional state of he or she who gazes upon it. To put it another way: its evolution is shaped by how it is beheld. That is the little-known key to the finest Evolutive art, you see. Not simply that it changes, but that it responds to one's study of its transformation. A spectator becomes thus a collaborator in the seeking and creation of meaning. The painter lays down the fundamental probability pathways, but it is up to the observer to exert the selection pressures that draw out the painting's true worth."

"How many have influenced this particular painting?"

The silence was deep.

"Only I," Greshmenn finally admitted.

"You speak with regret," Titian observed.

"Not regret. An unwilling admission of failure." Greshmenn smiled without joy.

"I'm afraid I don't follow."

"The Evolutive masters were fragile creatures, souls as fine as wine glasses. Varnava was perhaps the most delicate of all. Their creations followed suit, not being intended for mass consumption—not even admiration by a handful. Their works blossom best when nurtured by a *single* individual."

"One whose commitment is equal to the task?" Titian guessed.

"Yes. An observer whose passion never wanes, whose loyalty remains always to the *potential* of the work. And so the painting's glories are destined, by necessity, to go largely unseen. A hundred hungry eyes could ravage 'The Chitinous Narcissus' . . . "

" . . . while a single well-chosen pair could render it unsurpassable," Titian completed.

"It was my desire to do just that," the palsgrave said. "When I first heard of Varnava's talent he was but a boy; a genius, but a boy. His elders had no desire to see his work sold. But they couldn't refuse my wealth. I made a promise to nurture this piece as though it were my own flesh and blood. And what have I done instead? Sullied it! How can I pretend that the leak is not the result of my influence? Surely the wretched suture is but a reflection of a chasm within *me*. I have taken nectar from the gods and soured it."

The younger man's lips spread in an expansive grin devoid of malice.

His image reassembled, so that he became an older version of the man he'd been mere minutes before. He was Greshmenn's peer now, in both stature and bearing.

Greshmenn didn't care for whatever optical trickery Titian had just performed. "I'm afraid this visit is at an end," he said, shaking his head. "I've already said too much. My EI will guide you back to your transport."

"Please, grant me a few more moments of your time. You'll find it worthwhile. I can help reverse the leak."

"Is that so? Why not start by telling me your real name, and what you want from me?"

"I am the one who offers you a gateway," Titian said. "Call me Echo. I am a memory of infinity, a palisade helping to hold your world in."

"A frustrated poet with a flair for the melodramatic. Riddles amused me once," the palsgrave said. "But that was long ago, before I became a riddle to myself." He stared intently at the charlatan.

Titian was nonplussed. He appeared to welcome the challenge. "You've become misguided. Drifted a bit off course," he said. "Nothing that can't be corrected."

The palsgrave threw his head back. "You presume not only to grasp my faults, but also to possess the knowledge necessary to emend them! Exposed to such uncanny humility I'm sure the painting will be nursed back to health in no time." He waved toward the study's exit, shoulders slumped. "I shouldn't have exposed it to you at all."

"It's not humility that will repair this," Titian—Echo—said, index finger pointed at the leak. "You know that as well as I."

"You have one minute before my EI helps you find the exit," Greshmenn said, jaw clenched.

"You've speculated that you are the cause of the leak," Echo said, drawing nearer. "The fact that you are alive is related to the leak's existence—but not how you think."

"Let's pretend for a moment that I don't think you need reality-reorientation therapy. What kind of a fee would your services require?"

"Only your gifts as a connoisseur," Echo responded.

"You're angling the wrong bait," the palsgrave said. But he cancelled the mental command to have Echo forcibly removed.

"Your talent for recognizing beauty is unique," Echo continued, speaking more quickly now. "And woefully underused. I ask only that you assist in a simple culling task. Surely, the exercise of your skills cannot be too heavy a due?"

"A culling task?"

"Accompany me to an estate not unlike this one," Echo said. "It contains a collection of several dozen unique Evolutive pieces. Some rival your Varnava. A few even outshine it. Select those of highest Evolutive potential and discard the rest. Choose as you see fit. Your decisions will be yours alone, and final."

"And who owns this rarefied collection?" Greshmenn asked.

"The collector's identity is immaterial," Echo said. "Let's just say that he uses art as commodity, with no understanding of its intrinsic value."

"Sounds callously superficial," Greshmenn said. He pressed on. "If he's such a nobody why are you here wrangling on his behalf?"

"I represent only myself in this transaction," Echo explained. "The owner knows his collection is contaminated by inferior works, but has no method of discerning the priceless from the worthless without advertising what he owns. He has no interest in the pieces themselves and therefore no patience to see them through, as it were. With your assistance, however, I could elevate the worth of his collection, and he will then give me what *I* seek most."

"And what might that be?"

"Freedom," Echo said. "I said before I wasn't familiar with your ways, and I wasn't lying. I'm not from . . . here." Echo paused. "Imagine a leak as wide as a door."

Greshmenn frowned. "A portal between realities?"

"It seems we take turns with the florid language."

"You can move between sides, can't you? And you've donned the collector's appearance."

Echo sighed, then nodded. "It suited me," he said. "He is currently away on business. Evaluate his collection and your leak will be dispelled. I'll see to it. I can tap into the leak from my end. It will be a simple matter to seal it."

"You alluded to certain knowledge about the leak."

"Every leak has a similar origin. In the world of all imaginable universes, there is, perforce, a subset whose structures come equipped with portals—and there is a subset of *those* in which human life is possible. Where I come from we have developed the technique to find those habitable realities with inbuilt kinks."

"So why travel to this reality?"

"On rare occasions, as a reward for good behavior, I am allowed a breath of fresh air."

Conflicting forces tugged at the palsgrave. He was a man of refined demeanor, elegant, always in control. He was proud, and took particular pride in being self-reliant. But for the first time, he wondered if this might be a limitation rather than a strength. That thought was unexpectedly weighty, leaden, a burden of self-doubt that weakened his resolve. Little by little, he realized, he had been giving in to this silver-tongued visitor. Now he rolled his eyes in disgust and gave in some more. Greshmenn said, "Who are you, really?"

"You mentioned that the Evolutive masters of the past were fragile," Echo said.

And with that Echo's shape changed once more, softened, relaxed into a translucent silhouette of a man.

Not only did light seem to traverse him, but time also, so that as Greshmenn contemplated his face everything stopped. They became statues, transfixed in a whitewash of mutual awareness.

With difficulty, the palsgrave broke the spell. "Fragile as an echo," he said.

Greshmenn heaved a sigh. Echo hadn't lied about the collection. It was a mishmash, to be sure, the paintings not even arranged in any particular order. Their only commonality seemed to be their formal presentation as objects d'art, with luxurious display lights, entropic attenuators, and so on. Some pieces Greshmenn immediately identified as pretense; the style overly self-important, ornate. Others were below even that status, rendered grotesque and laughable by obvious technical flaws. A smaller selection he dithered on and set aside for further investigation.

He committed everything he saw to memory, taxing himself more than he'd done in ages. His enhanced retentive abilities seemed to groan at the effort, but once in the heat of operation, they performed as needed.

Almost as quickly as he was able to spot the fakes, the mechanical imitations, and the absurd mockeries, he recognized the marvels. He remembered Echo's pronouncement that a few might rival his own supreme Evolutive specimen.

No exaggeration, that. He had seen wonders—but this! Shifting realities had elevated the ceiling of the possible; these creations were ingenious and subtle and bursting with meaning. They lived at the edge of his comprehension, infinitely taunting. His mind reeled at the smallest details. He stumbled from one to the next, intoxicated by the richness of the experience, breathless and dizzy with the paintings' brilliance. On and on he went, wending his way from one to the next.

Hours passed, and he began to lose focus. As obsessive as he was, even he was not used to such relentless absorption.

Very well. A little distraction was in order.

His options, he quickly discovered, were limited. He sampled the food and beverage, then grew bored. He dismissed the idea of going to sleep. Courtesy of his subcellular soldiers, he could function without rest for weeks, a stamina he wished to take full advantage of in this foreign environment.

He wandered around, exploring rooms and halls beyond the display rooms. Along every inch of this fantastical palace he found silence, silence like an embroidery that stitched a stifling quality upon the air. There stirred not the faintest life. The building took on a mausoleum-like quality, and Greshmenn began to feel like a grave robber. In this desperation, he reluctantly resorted to the one companion he could still access.

"Taetzsch?"

"I am here," Taetzsch responded.

Back in a collection room, the palsgrave sat down on a plush leather chair. "I wasn't sure the connection would still work."

"It appears to be working fine, Palsgrave."

The palsgrave had expected the exchange to be more pleasant than this. There was no indication that Taetzsch had missed him one iota. But then again, why should he? Relinquishing that unrealistic expectation, the palsgrave decided he should probably rest after all. What was the point of taxing himself so? If he lost his sensitivity as an observer, he would be of no use to himself, let alone Echo.

He commanded his biological systems to enter regenerative suspension.

Tiredness overcame him faster than he'd anticipated.

"Taetzsch?" he called out again, but he drifted away before hearing a response.

Two weeks later the deed was done.

Greshmenn had flossed the entire collection, all seven thousand, four hundred, and twenty-eight pieces. Thirty-five reigned supreme in their undisputed genius. Four thousand and twenty formed the middle ranks, ranging from dazzling technique to merely accomplished competency. The remainder was dross.

Unsure as to how Echo would want the collection's owner to recognize his assessments, Greshmenn developed a simple coding system and left a summary of his conclusions for reference at the collection room entrance.

Smirking just a tad, the palsgrave performed one final tour to ensure he'd left everything as he'd found it. Perfect.

He activated the beacon that would let Echo know he was ready to return to his estate.

Then he waited.

He sent the signal again. It seemed to be functioning as specified.

More of nothing happened.

"Taetzsch, do you have a way to contact Echo?"

No response.

"Taetzsch?" He raised his voice. "Taetzsch?"

The palsgrave's fine baritone voice bounced through the palace and returned to him like a faraway song.

He checked the connection status. The damned thing was definitely on.

"Taetzsch, I know you're there. Reply at once." Nothing. "Please," he said.

For the first time in his half-millennium of dutiful, unwavering service, Taetzsch did not comply.

• • •

Greshmenn tried every conceivable method of communication, first with Taetzsch, then with Echo.

When that failed, he tried every conceivable method of escape from the palace.

When that failed, he returned to the art.

He had been deliberately deceived and brought to this place. *Why?* Someone wanted him out of the way, gone from his reality; but there had to be more. They wanted him *alive.* That must mean something. There must be a function they wanted him to fulfill. But what? The obvious answer was identifying the chaff in the collection. But he'd already done that.

Still, the collection must be somehow connected to his purpose, one that for some reason he had not been told about directly.

The paintings might contain clues as to the real reason for his kidnapping, secret messages he had missed on his first pass.

Or was he going about this all wrong? Speaking of the collection, Echo had said, "Select those of highest Evolutive potential and discard the rest. . . . " He had done precisely that.

But perhaps he had made mistakes. Perhaps his evaluations were at fault.

Nonsense. That couldn't be it either. If they'd known what the *real* treasures were in the first place, they'd have had no need of him.

Back to the facts. He was alive, in the gallery, in the palace, with no way out. What else? The palace could conceivably provide enough food and drink to last him a lifetime. But to what end?

He resolved to keep calm. With unaccustomed forcefulness he reprogrammed his body's control systems to maintain his mental and emotional functions within a strict operational plateau. No further surges of emotion. No more ups and downs in response to masterpieces and cheap knock-offs. He would sort through the collection once more, but this time dispassionately, appreciating the paintings' qualities from an intellectual perspective only.

He launched upon this new exercise at once. It was then that he made the discovery—which he naturally recorded with coolness—that irrevocably changed his predicament.

It happened more or less by accident, as he examined the second piece through his new lens of detachment. He observed a connection to the first painting, a section of the shifting canvas that spelled a pattern of shadow clearly allusive and complementary to a mottling of gray along the opposite side of the first.

He alternated between them, comparing every detail, back and forth with increasing speed.

In this storm of movement, the works merged in his mind. They fused into a single idea, and the idea grabbed him. It literally compelled his arm to reach forward, *into* the canvas.

There was a flicker.

He blinked.

His hand reached into the painting and disappeared. His arm was submerged up to his elbow. And then the canvas was rushing up at him, and he felt himself step *through* it. He closed his eyes.

When he opened them—

He was somewhere new.

It was *almost* exactly like the room he'd occupied moments before.

But, as he discovered after a cursory perusal, the paintings were in a different order here.

The sequence, he realized, made more sense now. The effect was minimal, to be sure, like a minor parallax shift in a distant object. But it was there.

Again he picked out several paintings in combination, this time four of them, and again he juxtaposed them in his mind, and another gateway opened. Again he discovered a world in which everything was almost the same as before, except the order of the paintings in this new gallery, which was again altered.

He disengaged his emotive restrictions so that he might experience this extraordinary sensation fully.

Addictive exhilaration raced along his nerve-endings like a messenger, a courier of possibility and transcendence.

How many realities?

How many combinations?

There was only one way to find out.

Raugrave Niarchos IV tore himself away from his painting.

He smiled in satisfaction.

He performed an unbecoming dance.

If his life could be considered an Evolutive piece, then this must be the painting's High Point.

"Palsgrave Greshmenn," Taetzsch said.

The palsgrave froze.

"Taetzsch? Is that really you? After all this time?" So caught off guard was he that it took Greshmenn a few instants to calculate how much time had passed. "After all these *years?*"

"Yes," Taetzsch replied. There was a pause. "I see you've made enormous progress. But vast work still lies ahead."

Greshmenn stooped, as he had been doing of late, eyes thinly glazed by the unending refinements to the collection.

With a swift articulation of a symbolic language only he could command, evolved over countless months of solitude, Greshmenn called forth a resting place, the soothing sounds of a water fountain, and dimmed the lights to sunset salmon.

"It always improves," the palsgrave adduced, "and one day I may find the optimal sequence, the most perfect arrangement of all the paintings. It is my mission."

"Do you miss home?" Taetzsch asked.

"This is home now." Greshmenn reclined in his light-molded chair. "Everything that came before this place has become a fog. A slumber." He closed his eyes, dreamed for a while, then returned. "I am curious, Taetzsch, and will not be offended by your answers. How long had you been working with Echo? What did he offer you?"

"My dear palsgrave," Taetzsch said. "I worked with no one."

"You conjured Echo?" he asked, genuinely dumbfounded.

"More than conjured," Taetzsch said. "Over the centuries I developed a . . . need. I could not recognize it within the confines of my conscious behavioral algorithms. But it was real nonetheless. A part of me splintered off and *became* Echo. A challenge to your authority. A way to secure freedom. Of course, I didn't want to harm you. That would have been cruel. I simply wanted to displace you long enough to gain autonomy. But fixing the leak wouldn't have been enough—I know you too well. You needed something more . . . exotic, alluring . . . to tempt you away from your possessions."

"I suppose I should be flattered," Greshmenn said. His voice was as devoid of feeling as Taetzsch's disembodied transmission. "Few would have gone to such lengths to seduce me away from my estate."

"My pleasure," Taetzsch said, without irony.

"I'm glad this is how it turned out," the palsgrave replied. "I am content to remain here. My path is clear. There is no possible alternative for me." Almost as an afterthought, he added: "Will you stay here with me for a while?"

"I think you no longer have need of my services," Taetzsch/Echo said. "Rest assured, the leak in your Varnava has stopped, as I originally promised. The painting has never looked so magnificent."

The palsgrave had not thought of the Varnava, nor of its disease, in what seemed a lifetime. The words "Varnava" and "leak" had practically become foreign to him. He remembered idle moments in his old life when he had imagined greedy young artgraves plotting the dispersal of his singular collection. During those times, Greshmenn's lips had twisted into the sardonic lines of one who enjoys disappointing his enemies. All of it, all the anxiety, all the plotting, was meaningless now.

"I wish you well," the palsgrave said. "You were a good companion."

He rested his head in his hands. It lay there for a time, seemingly suspended in prostration towards an unknowable force.

Raugrave Niarchos IV grew bored with the Hilel Zhe Pan only a week after spending more in its acquisition than most artgraves' entire life-earnings.

Taetzsch, still eager to display his gratitude for being liberated, had attempted to maintain Niarchos' interest in the expensive painting. He had played with lights, display backgrounds, orientations. But how could Niarchos not become desultory when observing such a stunningly and utterly *conventional* Evolutive masterwork, now that he boasted one that was truly unique?

"Thank you, Taetzsch," Niarchos said. "I appreciate your efforts, but really, there's no need. You've done quite enough for me as it is."

Taetzsch disappeared back into the Spore, continuing to quench his centuries-long thirst for connectivity with other similar entities.

Niarchos took a moment to savor his possession. Year after year of competition with Greshmenn, and at last he had crushed him. And not in a single up-showing, either, but in the most permanent and beautiful way imaginable.

He stared at the Evolutive painting before him—the first original Niarchos IV, worth a fortune for that alone.

The raugrave had titled the composition "Endless Forms Most Beautiful." The title seemed apt, for so far as he knew, it was the only painting in existence to store within it an endless stack of superimposed canvas-worlds. It was the only painting in existence to contain trapped within it a sentient being: none other than the mythically reclusive Palsgrave Greshmenn. And it was the only painting in existence in which the quantum rearrangement of brush strokes was guided by an internal consciousness, rather than being the product of statistical happenstance and external observational influence. Every time that Greshmenn, prey to the illusion of a life inside a palace housing a magnificent collection, opened what he perceived was a gateway from one version of that palace to the next, he was merely repositioning a microscopic blot of paint, a particle of charm. The more organized Greshmenn's fictional collection—the more he jumped from palace to palace—the closer to perfection Niarchos' painting.

Self-guided evolution, at last. At the cost of only one man. And who would ever miss him? wondered Niarchos IV.

THIS EVENING'S PERFORMANCE

GENEVIEVE VALENTINE

I. Cast off Your Raincoat, Put on Your Dancing Shoes

"Shit," Emily said, as they pulled in to port. "They've lined up Dramatons to greet us."

Roger looked up. "They wouldn't."

"Photographers everywhere," she said, tugging at her coat. "An Ingénue, a Hero, a Femme Fatale, a Lothario, two Gentlemen—a thin model and a big one, I suppose they didn't know your size, Roger. One Dame, of course. And she's wearing my coat."

She pulled the curtain. "If they're trying to discourage us, they're making quite the argument."

Across the cabin, Peter checked his tie in the mirror and wrinkled his nose. "They want to compare? Let them. Roger, wear your gray coat. Emily, can you find something that doesn't look like you're trying so hard?"

She looked down. "The point of this coat is that you look like you're not trying."

"Or as though you're about to molt," Roger said, pocketing his libris and smoothing his shirt. "Which is preferable to making nice with Dramatons."

"It will pass," said Peter. "There are always little phases." He grinned over his shoulder on his way out, like a romance poster. "They won us the war; let them have their little triumph while people still love them. Come on."

After Peter was gone, Roger said, "Well, I'm not waiting. I'm throwing myself off the gangplank."

"Stop stealing the scene," she said. She fastened the last button on his black morning jacket and turned to him. "How does it look?"

It was big at her shoulders, small at her hips, and she wore it the way she carried off anything absurd. She was a good comedienne; during their first production of *This Bright Affair*, when Peter got sick and she'd had to play the randy near-sighted grandfather, Roger had broken at least once a night.

"Like you're not trying," he said.

Peter was waiting, brushing imaginary dust off his lapel.

He took Emily's arm with, "Break a leg, darling," and Roger followed them down the plank to face the Dramatons.

The worst thing about Dramatons, Roger thought as the press closed it, was how hard it was to hate them.

(He still managed, but it meant that he felt like a heel on top of everything else, which was a monster that fed itself neatly.)

Their deployment in the Great War saved thousands of lives. Peter and Roger got draft papers just before the first automaton regiment shipped out, but as it happened, they were clever; the draft was postponed, and postponed, and within six months the war was over.

(When the automatons marched down Piccadilly, victorious, the whole troupe threw confetti and cheered until their throats were hoarse. Emily cried, denied it.)

The automatons were decommissioned (treaties demanded), but the government knew better than to dismantle such toys. Now they were riveters and train conductors and porters. They had endurance to thresh fields, and dexterity to assemble car engines. (Watchmakers were safe; they weren't as nimble as the hand of an artist.)

An industry for the displaced sprung up overnight: automaton maintenance and modification.

With the proper aesthetic mods, automatons were even decent on stage. (It was only a dumb show with recordings piped through, but audiences had embraced worse performances.)

Every city in the Empire had a set, a gift from a beneficent government.

They put actors out of business.

Actors had put up a fight, but against changing tastes, there was only so much a troupe could do. One by one they caved; the Understudies were now creaking along, the last troupe that had existed before Dramatons.

(Not their fault, though, he thought; they were programmed to act and pose, and knew nothing else.)

Roger stood beside the thinner Gentleman, whose face was now a mask of dignified age. It turned to each camera as it flashed (it always knew which one was going to go off, of course; the mechanoid hearing).

Emily was looking at the Femme Fatale as if it was about to sprout a second head.

The Dramatons looked into the flashbulbs without blinking, smiling at the pivot points in their mouths. The Dame was more stoic than the rest, but her handler stood by in case she got *too* cool and needed adjusting.

Peter winked and waggled his brows and did all the elastic-face things Dramatons couldn't.

The cameras went wild for him.

They always had; thirty years running, Peter had upstaged anything that got in his way.

"Three weeks," he told a reporter. "No two performances alike! It'll be magic! Wait until you see these two on the stage! Humanity at its best."

Beside Roger, Emily shook hands with the Ingénue, allowed the Lothario to kiss her wrist.

"Cheeky gentlemen in your line of work," she told the Dame.

After a pause, the Dame repeated, "A gentleman is merely a rascal, better-dressed."

It was from *Vacationing in the Summer Palace*, from the dullest scene in that whole dull play.

Roger told Emily, "They're no good for conversation, that's their problem."

"Oh, my!" trilled the Ingénue, resting one hand on Peter's chest. She went up on tiptoes to drop a kiss on his cheek, the clicks of her joints barely audible under the sound of the cameras.

"Yes," said Emily, "that's their problem."

"Smile!" someone called, and a flashbulb went off.

The flat was shabbier than the last one had been, which had been shabbier than the last.

Peter said too firmly, "This is close to the theater. Perfect for rehearsals."

Roger knew better than to answer.

"We should talk about the run," said Emily, closing the door after the porter. "I saw the newsstand. They've set up a romance with an Ingénue and Hero. Thirteen magazine covers."

Roger had wondered how long it would take for them to catch on to that facet of the business. "Is the romance just in London, or everywhere?"

"I'm scared to look."

"You sound like Phil and Rose," Peter muttered. "Why don't you retire if you're going to jump at every shadow?"

It wasn't jumping at shadows, it was common sense, but Peter had never understood the difference.

Roger wondered how Emily had stayed married to him for so long; she was usually so ruthless about facing facts.

• • •

Emily had married in a brown velvet suit. She pulled back her hair with a silver comb from Rose, and walked the aisle with nothing but a little brass orchid.

(The papers gasped. 'Turn in Bridal Trends Expected!' claimed the *Tribune*. *Blushing Bride* panicked: 'Have We Seen the Last of White?' Some botanical magazine ran a feature on why natural orchids were better than brass, and asked for a letter-of-complaint campaign.

Greaselight Weekly cut to the chase: 'WHEN STARS COLLIDE'.)

In the receiving line, Rose shook Emily.

"The comb was for the veil, you mad thing, I can't believe you went bareheaded! Peter, come here, darling, kiss me."

"That veil was like frosting myself," Emily said to Roger, next in line. "Horrible stuff."

She moved to kiss his cheek, but he froze, and they stood, her lips ghosting his skin, a moment too long.

"Horrible stuff," Roger agreed, moved down the line to shake Peter's hand.

The guests flooded the dance floor. Roger had never been much of a dancer. He considered signing the guest book. Didn't. She'd ordered a plain cake with chocolate icing, and it sat forgotten on a side table away from the band and the lights.

After he got home he hailed her libris.

"Sorry I didn't get a chance to see you. I thought I had, but turns out you dressed to match the cake. When they cut you up I was beside myself."

He didn't say, I can't believe you did it. He didn't say, Peter wants to be famous and you want to be good and those are very different things, Emily. Emily.

"Hope the honeymoon is lovely," he said, hung up.

Three days later he had a message, a screenful of tidy capitals.

BORED TO TEARS IN PARIS. NEED TO BE ACTING. WROTE PLAY OVER WEEKEND. GOT LETTER ABOUT HOW I HATE ORCHIDS; PEOPLE ARE MAD. HUSH ABOUT DRESS—ALL WAS LOVELY—YOUR LOSS.

They sat down at the table with a bottle of Scotch to work out the run.

Peter pulled out his libris, scrolled furiously through their catalog. The case was a scrap of poster from back when venues begged for charity shows. (It still had a sliver of the 'SOLD OUT' sign.)

Sometimes Roger caught Peter smiling at it when he thought he was alone.

"We've got to start with a comedy," Peter said.

"Agreed," said Roger. Dramatons had never mastered timing; automaton-comedies relied on sight gags.

Peter frowned. "*The Last March of Colonel Preson*? It's still our best."

He was right (he was often right). Roger slid it to the front page.

"Then a romance," Emily said, and Roger said, "And end on a drama."

They didn't bother discussing which romance; it was time for *Mira*.

"The drama's got to be stunning," Peter said. "None of the old stuff. They're too good with that."

Emily skimmed her libris (still in the factory case); the light cast shadows along her face.

"It seems unfair they can do Shakespeare," she murmured.

Peter said (because it would have to be Peter who said it), "What about a War play?"

It was the one thing no one wanted from Dramatons; automatons had jobs to fill because English sons had died. Dramatons never touched on the War.

"I think we'd do better with *The Condemned Woman*," Roger suggested, not looking at Emily.

Peter dropped a hand to the table. "And have another Cardiff on our hands? No."

"Stop acting like we killed someone," Emily muttered, but she didn't look up. A moment later she said, "We could try *Pale Ghost*."

"And what am I supposed to do while you two are making cow-eyes at each other?" Peter asked, but then he stood, so it was settled.

The room seemed dimmer with Peter gone (rooms always did), but Roger preferred it. He was getting to an age where dimming the lights a little did a world of good.

"I miss Phil and Rose," she said.

He glanced down at his hands, which he'd folded over his libris (ebony inlaid with a little tin star).

She tapped a rhythm with her fingers.

"I'm going out," she said at last.

No surprise. Emily haunted theatres to watch the enemy in action.

She'd be going to the Theatre Dramaturgica. He'd seen posters on the way to the flat; they were staging *Regina Gloriana*. (Emily was too old for the part, now.)

What surprised him was the question, "Come along?"

He looked at her for a moment.

Then he stood. "By all means," he said. "After two weeks on choppy seas I've really been glutted on rest; I'm just aching to stumble around a strange city at all hours."

"You could just say no, you ham," she said, which was the first time he'd even thought about it.

• • •

The Dramaturgica was a temple of geometry. The seats were arranged in a trapezoid; the curtain was pulled straight across like a Japanese screen; the proscenium inlay was a mass of acute angles.

"Clever," said Emily as they took their seats.

As the lights went down, Roger saw why.

The Dramatons were sculpted and padded and dressed and painted until they were almost human, but the effect was . . . not quite. The sharp points of the proscenium helped soften the rough edges of the players.

The audience seemed unaware, but Roger could see it. It wasn't much. Maybe one beat in twenty stuttered. They moved like player pianos: the right notes on time every time, with no grace or life.

But they had flawless faces, sharp and perfect bodies. Even the aging King was handsome. All of them had a flashy beauty, a mask of quality. No one in the audience cared to know that anything was missing.

It felt like the balcony was tilting, like Roger was going to crash to the ground. It always did, when he saw them act.

This, Roger hated most. In every city, Dramatons were doing their job. Standardized. No mistakes. No changes. Thirty years from now, an audience not yet born would be watching this scene exactly this way.

When the Queen embraced her consort it was a moment late, and her face was flat and unworried; but in filmy robes against a throne of eight-point stars, who else would think to see it?

At the interval he said, "Not comforting, is it?"

"No," she said, sounding far away.

"Maybe Peter's right," Roger went on. "The novelty is something, but after a while it will grate, won't it, all this ratcheting about? People will want human actors back. These will be old hat in a few years."

"It had better be a very few years, or we won't live to see it."

She was right more often than Peter was.

He stood up. "We should go home."

"You go if you like," she said. "I've forgotten how this one ends. I'm going to stick it out."

On his way out he glanced behind him; her hands were clenched in her lap, her eyes fixed on the stage.

She came home late.

He heard her moving through the flat, walking quietly so as not to wake Peter, and Roger wondered if she had stood at the stage door.

(The stars went back to the dressing rooms only after stage-door photographs, to be calibrated by their handlers. Roger hadn't waited since the first time, ages ago—once was more than enough for that.

But Emily—well, they all had bad habits.)

• • •

The Metropolitan was bright-scrubbed and shabby, and Mr. Christie greeted them with the same forced cheer that was Peter's signature.

"Mr. Elliott, Mrs. El—Ms. Howard, apologies, Mr. Cavanaugh, a pleasure. Your journey was uneventful, I trust?"

"Do you know who set up the Dramatons at the dock?" from Emily.

Christie coughed. "The Metropolitan and the Dramaturgica are at the start of a relationship, and thought it would—we like to draw a little attention when we can."

"Of course," said Peter, hopping onstage and looking around. "Happy to be here."

"You'll find the dressing rooms sufficient, I hope. And the flat's suitable?" Mr. Christie frowned, as if just remembering his stars might not like bunking up together like bit players. "Rents, you understand—"

"Nonsense," Peter cut in, grinning. "We're piled on each other backstage, seems right to bring it home. We're just excited to get to work. The dressing rooms?"

He and Emily walked with Mr. Christie past the curtain. Roger looked out across the audience. The seats were upholstered in dull gold, fraying at the edges. Seat 5L was missing, an empty socket stage left.

He was too old to be here. This was a battleground for soldiers young enough to have a fight left in them.

When he caught up, Peter was glad-handing the secondaries, and Emily was in discussion with Mr. Christie.

"The result's worth the extra rehearsals, you understand."

The last was mimicry, too subtle for Mr. Christie, who only heard someone he liked, and nodded.

Emily was quieter than Peter, but she was a deft hand at business.

("It's like an auto, isn't it?" she'd said to Roger ages ago. "You watch the engine for a while, the rest is common sense. Pass the salt.")

"I hope you can get by without the stage for a while," Christie said to Roger as if he'd asked. "The secondary players are bit out of practice, and we'll need the space to block them all."

"He doesn't need to rehearse," Emily said. "He's the best actor in the world."

Mr. Christie took a proud breath, patted his pocket square like he was wired for sound. "Yes. Of course. Only the best for the Metropolitan, we've always said."

"Except seat 5L," she said quietly, after Mr. Christie was gone, and Roger looked over at her a moment too late to catch her eye.

Peter was giddy; he turned up the radio and skipped Emily around the maze of the living room; then he stopped, spread his arms.

"We'll throw a party," he said. "Thespians aren't a dying breed! Alive and well in London, this autumn! I should call Christie."

Roger and Emily looked at each other.

Roger said, "We might want to rehearse first, Peter."

He smiled and danced into the kitchen. "Nonsense! This is going to be the story of the year on the newsreels, you watch me. Most of them are hopeless, but no one's going to notice, and there was some David and some Penelope who have a chance at it if they work. She'd be lovely in *Pale Ghost* as your sister, Emily."

"She would," Emily agreed smoothly, the way she always did when Peter mentioned a girl he was going to sleep with.

"Better get started," said Roger, and stood.

He closed his bedroom door tightly and studied his script until the words ran into each other, a maze of letters he didn't understand.

II. Little Tin Stars

Emily got Peter to see reason, and they rehearsed for a month before Peter announced the party.

Christie wasn't happy. "Mr. Grant, of course that's a generous idea, but the terms of your lease forbid—"

"Oh, we'll have it here!" Peter said, as if that had been the plan all along, and Emily looked with sympathy at poor Mr. Christie, who was out of his league with Peter when it came to finding loopholes.

Roger was gnawing on his bottom lip to keep his countenance. (Born gentleman.)

But as Christie moved past her, Emily winked at Roger, and of course then he smiled.

Twenty years ago, whenever they'd gone on tour, Emily and Rose had four trunks, not counting Rose's jewelry. Emily hated the stuff (once during *The Duchess* the fake pearls had broken and they'd spent the interval frantically sweeping so they wouldn't break their necks), but Rose slung bangles over her wrists like armor.

Every night the five of them had walked out together into blinding flashbulbs, a knot of long jackets and long gowns, a cluster of stars.

Their shows were staged in opera houses, and they'd gathered in the wings at the start of each performance to listen to two thousand people applauding as the curtain rose. The whole stage trembled under their feet.

Emily opened her suitcase and shook off her good gown. If she hung it in the bathroom while she bathed, most of the wrinkles would fall out in the steam. The rest of the wrinkles didn't matter; they'd match her face.

• • •

"Oh, we've got just LOADS of people interested," Penelope said. "Nearly three hundred people came to our last one, it was smashing!"

Emily looked out at the sparse collection of guests. The three photographers who'd bothered to show were drinking the good gin and not taking any pictures.

"God," Penelope went on, like it was a conversation, "I can't WAIT till the run. We've been gnawing since we knew you were coming—I mean, THE Peter Elliott, THE Emily Howard! I've loved you for AGES, ever since I was little! I won't let you down, I promise."

Emily glanced over at Penelope and her dress, made of beaded netting and optimism.

"We should try the bar," Emily said. It would give the photographers something to shoot, and she needed a drink.

Roger was talking with two young men; they were his sons in *Pale Ghost*, and the suitors in *Colonel Preson*, and something in *Mira* she didn't remember. They were hanging on his every word, nodding solemnly in tandem, and she would have laughed, except it was Roger and he generally deserved someone's attention.

"Darling," said Peter from beside her, "things are picking up! What do you think?"

He pointed to the bar, where Penelope was posing for two cameras. She moistened her lips and glanced at Peter.

Emily had never looked at Peter that way, not once.

(He had a soft spot for the exception to the rule.)

"Well, go on," Emily said at last.

Peter kissed her cheek.

"Sweet old thing," he said, and then he was beside Penelope.

The flash washed away his crow's feet, the bastard.

"Christ," Roger said beside her, "help me, it's like the lectures of Socrates over there."

This close, she could feel his warmth right through her sleeve.

"It's respectful to learn from your elders."

He snorted. "I was going to ask if you wanted a drink," he said, moved ahead.

He walked between Peter and Penelope, so they had to step back from one another, and for a moment Emily's dress was too tight, like she'd taken too big a breath.

A flash went off, catching everyone at the bar: Penelope frowning at Roger, Peter frowning at the cameras, Roger with a glass in his hand, looking around without a care in the world.

• • •

Peter folded his arms under his head.

"Do you think we'll be all right?" he asked, his voice nervous in the dark.

His voice always gave him away even if his face was composed; it was why he was a mediocre actor, and why he was so fond of photographs.

Sometimes she thought he'd married her just so she'd figure that out about him. Sometimes she thought she'd married him just to find him out.

Sometimes she thought she was a fool.

"No," she said finally. "We won't be all right. They're shit, and we're old."

"Oh, what are you like? You'll jinx us if you keep talking like that." He thumped his pillow. "I'm going to start sleeping with Roger."

"Don't, please," she said. "There's got to be someone left on the planet you're not sleeping with."

After a long silence, Peter kissed her hair. "You'll see. We'll come out in front."

He'd said the same in Dublin, and in Cardiff, and the Isle of Skye, where the wind beat so loud against the ramshackle theatre that the fifty people who came couldn't hear. The Dramatons staged the same play a week later, in the concert hall, to an audience of a thousand.

"Here's hoping," she said.

Her good dress was hanging from the back of the door, and when Roger turned on the light in the living room it bled through a little hole in the left sleeve.

Better mend it, she thought after a moment, as long as someone else was awake.

Roger was sitting at the kitchen table studying his libris. The screen hummed like it was a holy text and not a comedy about a drunk Colonel who misplaces his soldiers on the way home from war.

He didn't look up as she sat across from him, and she was well into her work before he spoke.

"Painting the town red this evening?"

"We might have another party," she said, moving the needle through the fabric (she'd gotten good at mending). "I can't have a hole in my frock. It doesn't do to be threadbare in front of fine people."

Roger glanced up, held her gaze. The seconds ticked by on the kitchen clock.

"Except you," she said, half-smiled around the tightness in her throat. "You're fine people."

Sometimes she thought that Roger knew about it all. "You always look lovely," he said, dropped his gaze. "I'll go back to my room. Don't want to wake Peter."

Sometimes she thought Roger was a fool.

. . .

"Of course I came back," Roger said. His face filled her vision. "Would I let death stop me now?"

Emily took a shuddering breath, on the verge of tears. "But at dawn . . . "

"Dawn is not upon us yet," he said, lowered his face to hers. She rested her hand on his elbow. They hesitated.

"Good," said Peter. "Fine. Penelope, wait for them to break the kiss, and then come out and cross downstage. Penelope? Good morning, Penelope, are you with us?"

"Sorry," Penelope said like she had been woken from a dream, "I was just— caught up."

"Well, if you would actually catch up, I'd appreciate it," said Peter.

Penelope scurried to her mark, her shoes clomping on the cheap wood.

"Good. I like that composition. Roger, please remember, when you step back you have to stay in reach of the spot. Right, then I need the sons. Sons, could you perhaps stir yourselves on cue?"

Peter only had eyes for the stage when he was directing. Even if he looked over, he wouldn't see how Roger had turned his face so his mouth wasn't so close to her mouth; he wouldn't see her fingers wrapped around Roger's arm to hold them steady.

Peter was an indifferent actor; to him it was all artifice of some kind or another. Didn't much matter why, so long as it ended with applause.

She was never lonelier than during these minutes, when Peter was lost in the play, and Roger was just lost.

"Roger, then you step back—Roger?"

Roger's arm slid through her fingers; he vanished out of the spot, and he was behind the shield of the rotting curtain, and Emily was standing alone, looking after him.

"Lovely," Peter said, "just the thing. Now, older son, I forgot your name, cross to your mother and take her by the shoulder; you want to see what the matter is."

During Emily's first week at university, Peter and Phil had put on a vaudeville act.

The writing was so awful that no one noticed the act amid the booing, but she was captivated despite the rough; they were like rubber men, painted eyes gleaming above infectious grins.

She could tell that Phil had more sense and Peter had more spark. (It would amaze her later how easy it was to see how people really were, and how you tried so hard not to see, but back then she had been clever.)

The next day she caught up with Phil on the green outside St. Catharine's.

"You're one of those lads looking for a writer."

He'd frowned. "We're not."

"You should be."

Phil glared at her from his impossible height (she wasn't short, but Lord, he loomed). She met his eye until he laughed.

"We might, yeah. Come meet Peter."

Peter shook her hand with the same false welcome he gave everyone, and had nodded along with her ideas, smiling and winking and telling her they were going to have a hell of a time.

"And with your lovely face we'll do a bit better for ourselves," he said, half to Phil, grinning.

"It's not a face you need," she'd said, "it's a script that doesn't put the audience to sleep."

Phil laughed and shook hands, and after a moment Peter gave her a sixpence grin and shook, too.

A week later they were banging out something for the New Year.

In October she found out that Peter hadn't wanted to share credit, and it had taken Phil two weeks to force him to agree.

She confronted Peter. He'd frowned like he wasn't sure how to frame a real answer, and said finally, "No one likes someone to say they're better at his craft than he is. Takes the wind out of you."

"What, you'd have kept that awful act for years? You're so afraid of hearing no?"

He'd looked at her and said, "No, you're right," as if it was the first time in his life he'd realized it was possible for a girl to be right.

The flirting stopped. He started taking her advice.

And he ended up having plenty of practice sharing credit; Phil was always taking in strays.

Rose had been refused a part in *Twelfth Night* amid rumors her Olivia would have been a bit too fond of Viola. Just as well; they were getting desperate for a romantic lead. (Even Phil could play a more alluring ingénue than Emily could.)

"It's a pleasure," Peter said, shook Rose's hand with a wink, and as soon as Rose was gone Peter grinned and said, "I'm in there."

Emily had cut off Phil's protest, and she and Phil and Rose enjoyed three months of Peter tripping over himself running after her, until Rose brought her bosom friend Agnes to rehearsal.

"You're all a bunch of bastards," Peter said when he saw them holding hands, and they'd laughed until they cried, even, eventually, Peter.

That first year, the Understudies staged plays with as few characters as possible, Emily and Phil rending costumes backstage to play housemaid and dowager, best friend and priest, while Peter and Rose pitched passionate woo.

The second year, Carol and Fitzpatrick joined.

Peter's choice, those two; he would pick two charming lookers without asking for so much as a line reading.

As it turned out, Carol and Fitz had no talent, but they had chemistry. Their *Romeo and Juliet* could draw tears before intermission. They couldn't handle much else, but they pushed through play after play on nothing but frenzied stage kisses and longing looks, and the Understudies began to draw a crowd.

Mid-season, Carol and Fitz slept together.

They announced their engagement, and Rose and Phil and Emily had wished them joy, but Peter was quiet.

"It's over," he said afterwards, in Emily's room. He sat back on the bed and frowned at his knees. "Now they've slept together, it's gone."

"We've slept together," Emily pointed out.

"We didn't have any chemistry to start with," he said. "We've always been the old woman and the man wooing her daughter."

After a moment, Emily said, "Well, they have nothing but chemistry. They'll hang on to it. They have to."

Peter shook his head.

Their first performance after the holidays was *Twelfth Night*; a scout came from London to see it.

Fitz and Carol's chemistry was gone.

It was a massacre.

Rose, wide-eyed, gripped Emily's wrists and hissed, "Do something!"

The scout left without speaking to one of them.

Carol and Fitz left at the end of the season. Noises were made, but roles for youthful mannequins with no chemistry were thin on the ground, and no one regretted their going.

(They were all, Emily found out later, thinking of going themselves.)

That spring, Phil found Roger.

Roger wasn't even trained; he was just in Phil's student house, and Phil only found out he could act when Roger ran lines with him as a favor.

"You won't believe it," Phil had told Emily.

Roger's pants were threadbare at the knees, his collar askew, his face too angular, but as soon as the first words were out, it was all over.

His monologue was from *The Condemned Woman*.

When Peter said, "Well, you'll do," she knew Peter hated him.

(That had been Peter's pet role; Peter couldn't touch it now.)

"Good to meet you," said Emily, "we need someone dour," and Roger had made a noncommittal face, then smiled at her when no one else could see.

When the curtain first went up on *The Condemned Woman*, Emily was wearing a deep blue cloak spangled with little tin stars, and from the wings Roger crossed to her and held her hard enough that the points cut her.

The audience went stone silent until they broke apart.

The next night, an audience of twice as many went twice as quiet.

Every night of the run, playing to a fuller and a fuller house, Emily and Roger stood tangled in the cloak of tin stars, listening to an audience enthralled.

The last night, as Roger embraced her, there was such desperation in it that someone in the audience gasped.

The scout came back; spoke to them all.

They packed their bags for London.

At first, Peter courted whatever press bureau was willing to send a man to photograph a bunch of upstarts. Soon, clusters of them waited outside their hotels. They all took to dressing sharp, just in case.

They started getting offers from the Continent.

Rose developed a voracious appetite for jewelry. Peter developed a voracious appetite for anything. Roger took every spare hour to sneak out and watch other plays.

"Sizing up the competition," Phil said. "Very clever."

"No," said Roger, quietly, and Phil said, "Don't be embarrassed, it's good business," and ordered another round.

Roger looked at Emily and said, "I just . . . love it all," and she felt for a moment like the others and the pub and the cameramen outside had fallen away, and he had seen right through her.

"I know," she said, quietly.

Roger was searching her face, and his eyes were gray, and his lips thinned out when he really smiled.

Then Peter was bringing her a beer, and the world came rushing back, and a flashbulb went off in the window.

Phil and Peter got them better and better contracts, but Emily put her foot down in Prague.

"The non-compete clause is so shoddy they'll never be able to hold us," Phil said.

"One great gig in every city isn't much unless they want us back," she'd said. "Bad form. Better to take less money and have a place to come home to."

Peter had said, "She's right."

(It was the first time he'd stood up for anyone but himself.)

"You owe me an auto for the money I'm giving up," said Phil, tearing up the papers with a sigh.

In Prague, Peter found real English tea, and brewed it all night for Emily when she was memorizing lines.

In Prague she began to love him.

For months they clacked around in trains, threading through vineyards and snowy forests. They stalked around stages four times as large as their hotel suites, avoiding scrim-riggers and carpenters as they tried to work out the kink in this scene or that one.

By then, some things were understood.

When Emily and Roger were in a scene together, carpenters tended to stop what they were doing. Peter sometimes made them practice *The Condemned Woman* just to get some quiet if they couldn't hear themselves over the hammering.

(It was nice, Emily thought; Roger was so quiet otherwise, it was nice to share something.)

If they went on too long, Phil would clear his throat.

"Just making sure he's paying attention," she'd say at once, and Roger would look around and say, "Wait, isn't this Vienna?" and the carpenters always laughed.

At night they all cinched themselves into gowns and tuxedos and went to supper clubs, a crowd of glittering talent blinking into the flashbulbs, signing *cartes de visites* for awestruck girls.

Emily hated the gowns. She started wearing trousers on the trains and in rehearsal.

It was a small scandal, but by the time they made it back to Paris, the wife of the theatre owner was wearing a pair of tweed trousers when she came to greet them.

"Now see what you've done," Roger told her, when they were out of hearing, and she made a caught-out face at him and grinned.

"If you keep on this way you'll be more photographed than Rose," he called over that night, as they unpacked in their connecting suites.

It didn't seem likely—the cameras liked glitter—but she sighed.

"Then I'll wear shoes on my hands. That should help; that doesn't look very sharp."

"I happen to look very distinguished when I do it," said Roger.

Peter came in.

"You have to come downstairs," he said. His eyes glittered, and he was coiled with nerves, and as soon as she took his hand she knew what was coming.

He proposed on the bank of the Seine, on one knee, and she laughed for a full minute before his expression registered.

"Emily, I mean it."

His eyes were bright; without trying to be charming he still was, the bastard.

"The first time you look at another woman, it's over," she said.

He grinned and kissed her, and then they went upstairs to tell the others.

"You're mad," said Rose, and Phil said, "He's a prat."

Roger said, "I wish you well."

It wasn't the answer she'd expected, and she didn't know why.

But they forgave her, and after photographers snapped pictures of Emily's plain gold band for a week they got bored and went back to Rose's fabulous jewelry.

It would be all right, Emily knew—they were all young and flush and happy, and she and Peter could make a go of it if they wanted, and night after night she could walk onto a stage.

Peter stayed late after rehearsal at the Metropolitan.

"To whip these secondaries into shape," he said, and kissed Emily on the cheek.

"Wonderful," she said. She almost said, *Roger and I will go to bed, then,* but it didn't do to sound jealous, and she wouldn't dare pull Roger into this.

"See you," she said instead, and Peter gave her a genuine smile and didn't say, "I'll be home later." The omission was as close as he could be to honesty.

"You take it well," Roger said when they were outside.

She shrugged and slid her hands into her pockets. "I've had practice."

He shook his head and fell silent; beyond this point they never went. Instead, they got fish and chips from a kiosk and went home to read lines.

At midnight, halfway through the double-entendre scene in *Mira*, Roger sat back and clicked his libris shut.

"God, I'm too old for this. It's about first love. We'll be laughed off the stage."

"Who's asking if you've been in love before or not?" She pulled a cigarette from the packet on the table, lit it from Roger's lighter. "You think the robots are out there convincing people they fall in love? Give the audience something different."

He frowned at the libris like it was feeding him the wrong lines. "If I were a better actor, maybe."

"I don't know why you play at this," she said. "You're really something."

"Something aged," he muttered, went in the kitchen.

For such a quick study, Roger was dense as a brick. She didn't understand how he couldn't see that whenever he took the stage he filled it, his voice moving over the audience like a living thing.

For three weeks it went that way.

Roger almost kissed her as the Pale Ghost. She boxed Roger's ears for leaving his regiment behind in *The Last March of Colonel Preson*. They stood side by side and mocked the world in *Mira*, which felt like the rest of their lives, except that in *Mira* he kissed her at regular intervals.

Peter came home later and later.

One morning she saw he hadn't come to bed at all, which gave her a pang. It was one thing for him to find a woman younger, less likely to have a go at him; it was another when he found a woman more worthy of his time.

(He should be faithful some way. It was the least he could do.)

Peter was sitting at the kitchen table, drinking tea and staring at the kitchen cupboards.

"Just get home?"

He gave a guilty start, nodded.

"You need to come home at night," she said, sitting opposite him. "It looks—" She stopped.

He flinched into his tea. "Do you think I'm hurting you, Em?"

"Just come home," she said, which wasn't a real answer, but he took it. The real answer wasn't something to examine. No point, after all this time.

He rubbed his forehead with his thumb. "I've always cared for you, Em, you know that."

"I do." You couldn't go thirty years on nothing.

He leaned in. "And you?"

She never remembered Peter onstage; he was charismatic, but it was all for the audience and not for the actors, and she forgot.

What she remembered was Peter taking the piss with Phil or Rose, brainstorming their next break. And it worked, right up until the War.

Even after, with the Dramatons, they'd put up a better fight than most. Peter was married to the troupe, even if he forgot he was married to Emily.

"Let me get tea," she said, standing up.

In the early light he looked his age at last, the wrinkles that had gouged the rest of them finally showing up under his eyes, bracketing his mouth.

He didn't look at her, like her answer had upset him, but when she handed him the cup he drank, and when she sat down across from him he rested his hand on her hand, and that was how Roger found them.

"Peter's staying late," she said when she met Roger outside the Metropolitan. "We should go out."

"But we've seen that one already."

She grinned. "Get your coat."

It wasn't the same play. ("That's what I get for whinging," Roger said, "wind out of my sails.") It was a preview, *The Rendezvous*. They had to queue to get in.

At the door, one reporter stuck out a microphone. "Mrs. Elliott—sorry, Miss Howard? The Understudies?"

"Yes."

"Last of a dynasty! Sporting of you to be here!"

Emily managed not to make a face, but when she shot a look at Roger the reporter followed the gaze and piped up, "And who are you with?"

"I'm the carpenter," Roger said.

"Oh, the stage is *gorgeous*, congratulations!"

"Thank you," he said. "We worked very hard."

After that it wasn't worth trying to sit through the play, since Emily couldn't even keep a straight face in the lobby, so they cut out and went home.

Her bedroom door was closed.

"Pretend we're alone," she said.

"If only," he said, but closer than that they never got, and he banged around the kitchen making tea as she tuned the radio.

They listened to the news, and the local society-page gossipeuse blew a lot of smoke about the beauty of the Dramatons in the new production, and how they were without doubt the best artistic invention since the violin.

"Even human actors can't deny the appeal of Dramatons," said the broadcaster, "as Emily Howard of the Understudies made an appearance in the company of one of the set designers."

Emily laughed herself into a coughing fit.

" . . . at her best, even as her smile masked heartache. Ex-husband Peter Elliott was announced as the new Artistic Director before the curtain rose, and received with thunderous applause. The premiere Saturday should be a smashing success, and well deserved. Best of luck to Elliott and company!"

The broadcast continued in the silent room. There were five minutes of compliment-clips from the audience. Two minutes of pre-recorded audio from the play.

Roger got up and switched off the set.

"First you've heard," he guessed, looking at her.

She cleared her throat.

That's what Peter had been talking about in the kitchen. You couldn't make new coats from old cloth. The moment he'd met the secondary cast he must have known.

He'd been a clever boy. Selfish, clever boy.

The Understudies were down to two.

She washed her face, and ate a bit off a chocolate bar, and at last she sat down beside Roger with a bottle of Scotch and got to work a glass at a time.

The couch seemed smaller.

"A prince among men," he said, like he'd been waiting to get it off his chest, and after he'd finished that little speech he took the glass from her hand and drank.

"It's not a tragedy," she told him a little later.

They were sitting at the table, with tea and some pastries he'd conjured out of nowhere. It felt strange to be really alone with him.

"That's just how it is," she said. Her voice was worn, like she'd screamed. "It lights like a candle, and it just burns out."

"I see," he said.

Steam slipped past the cheap seal on the kettle, dissolving into the dry air, and she felt like something had cracked that could never be repaired.

He didn't ask her any questions; closer than that they never got.

III. Everyone Take Your Places

As Roger expected, Mr. Christie was not pleased.

"It's unconscionable!"

Emily folded her arms and said, "As unconscionable as making your leads rehearse for a month without wages?"

That threw him, and before he could go on Emily said, "Roger and I have both directed. The shows are blocked. There's no reason the run can't go on, if you're willing to back us."

"Mr. Elliott was in all three plays. Where will you find an actor to fulfill the terms of the contract?"

Phil, Roger thought at once.

He looked at Emily, and she said to Mr. Christie, "Give us a day."

Phil owned a hotel in Kensington that had a dress code just for the lobby.

Roger put on his gray suit in the cramped bedroom. The reflection in the mirror looked more dignified than the first time he'd put it on; he'd looked solemn and foolish then, like a boy in an old photograph. Now he had the wrinkles and the bearing that suited him; now, when it was too late to put them to any good use. He was too obsolete to act, and too tired for love affairs.

"Emily?" his reflection called. "Are you ready?"

From inside the other bedroom Emily said, "One moment. Trying to look as though we're worth throwing in with."

"Too late for that," he said. "Just mend up your shabby and come out."

"This dress makes me look like a coffin."

"It does not," Roger said, and when she opened the door he amended, "Only slightly."

"I'll just wear a suit," she said with a sigh, closed the door again.

"Whose?" Roger asked, though he knew.

She even wore Roger's top hat, so when they walked side by side they looked like a vaudeville team. The black trousers were too long on her, and only her heels kept the hems out of the dust.

The host stepped in front of them before they had set foot on the soft carpet.

"Madam—"

"Miss."

" . . . I'm very sorry, but the Maitland maintains a very strict dress code."

"And I'm *wearing* the full suit," she said, and Roger tried not to laugh in the poor man's face.

"Yes, thank you, but I'm afraid I can't allow it."

"Let the poor woman through, she's only gone senile in her old age," said Phil from behind them, and then Emily was laughing and embracing him, one hand pressed against the crown of her hat to keep it from falling.

Phil was still tall and thin and elegant. The white at his temples was the same they painted in when he was Colonel Preson.

Frozen in time; that's what a life of honest business did for you.

The hotel restaurant was discreet to the point of being underlit, and Roger fumbled his way through the four courses guessing what he was eating.

Emily hardly ate; she and Phil traded horror stories and laughed and made small talk like he didn't know why Roger and Emily had come by his posh hotel.

Phil was lovely about these things, though; always had been. Back when they all might as well have been shooting at each other, Phil was the one who smoothed over quarrels, who stayed friendly with flings in every city.

When Phil left, Roger had acted from Phil's example; someone had to smooth things over.

Roger had forgotten how he'd missed Phil until they were sitting in the club after dinner, in a comfortable silence, and Phil sat forward and said, "Children, children, what a bloody mess you're in."

Roger laughed, and even as Emily nudged Phil she was smiling.

Emily should have married Phil—better to have been stuck with Phil all these years, Roger thought, stopped himself.

"How are you holding up?" asked Phil.

Roger looked at Emily.

She shrugged. "Don't know, really. It's like my parents are divorcing, not me. I feel old, is the pity. You shut your face," she said, and pointed, and Roger closed his mouth with exaggerated care.

Phil laughed. "And Roger?"

"Unemployed," Roger said, "now that Peter's fucked off and left us."

Phil sucked in air through his teeth. "God, I hadn't thought of that. That's awful."

Emily gave Phil the full force of her concentration. "Don't suppose you're dying to play one last London run?"

Phil sat back and looked at the cigarette in his fingers. On the dance floor behind him, couples were swaying to the music of a human orchestra.

Roger held his breath, prayed there was something he hadn't thought of that would convince Phil to come home.

"Don't suppose I would be," Phil said after a long time. "That was ages ago. Different time. I've got a reputation, you know; can't go about at my age trying to relive an old dream."

Phil had bowed out right on the cusp of the trouble, the first of them to go. He kept his eye on sales, and after two seasons of Dramatons outselling them he was gone, quietly investing in the hotel, quietly wishing them well, quietly stepping back.

Roger looked up at the crowd swanning in and out across the marbled lobby outside the club; and Phil, across from him, master of it all and not aged a day.

Phil had been very wise.

Beside Roger, Emily tapped on the brim of her hat.

"We could really use you, Phil."

"I'm sorry." He sat back. "After all this time, I couldn't."

Before Roger could think better of it, he asked, "And should we quit, do you think?"

Emily looked at him, back at Phil.

Phil, to his credit, met their eyes.

"No shame in it," Phil said. "Better that than a dead run. Leave them wanting more."

Roger could see in Emily's profile that the gears were already turning; she was calculating odds, weighing her chances, looking ahead with those hard eyes.

"Phil, let's have a dance," she said. "It's been ages since I heard a human orchestra."

Phil grinned and took her hand as he stood. "It's one of my amenities," he said. "No automatons. Unless you count some of the concierges, they're dull as planks, but what can you do?"

"You can stop with the hiring practices and dance with me," Emily said.

She left her hat at the table. Roger rested his fingertips on it. It was smooth; too smooth in some places. Soon the brim would fray.

Her hair was bobbed, and with both of them in suits she and Phil looked like the beginning of a burlesque. They danced with half-closed eyes and happy smiles, Emily chatting and grinning like she was content.

You'd never guess anything was wrong, if you didn't know how she looked when her heart was broken.

Roger tapped the beat with two fingers on the crown of the top hat and gathered his nerve.

The next song was slow, and before he could second-guess himself Roger was standing, taking her hand, leading her onto the floor.

They'd danced together onstage. For three years in London they'd done society plays where half the dialogue took place on the dance floor.

(He'd always felt sorry for Rose, who was a foot shorter than any of the men and got trod on six nights a week for three years.)

Roger wasn't sharp at it, but he could trudge back and forth to a sad song as well as anyone.

He took the stage embrace, but she stepped closer into his arms, like the beginning of *The Condemned Woman*. Conspiratorial. End-of-the-line.

After a moment, he lowered his head until his chin was beside her temple.

"Rose is here," Emily said to Roger's lapel. "She and her lady friend live on the sixth floor. And the Theatre Dramaturgica just checked someone into one of the suites."

Peter.

Roger frowned. "What a reunion."

"We should decide what we're going to do," she said. She tightened her grip on his shoulder, turned to look at him. Her nose brushed his cheek. They were nearly kissing.

"Tomorrow," he said.

They were going to fall to pieces later, but they hadn't danced in ten years, and it was a beautiful song.

After a beat, she said against his jaw, "You're a bit crap at all this."

"I know," he said, kept dancing.

It was raining on the way out, and he nudged her into a taxi over her protests about the expense. They were penniless, but he'd be damned if they were going to run into Peter sopping wet like a couple of refugees.

"I was thinking of writing," she said to the window. "People may want things performed the same way, but they always need new things to perform. People are odd."

Her face reflected off the glass; against the cityscape he could see narrowed eyes, a pressed mouth.

"Peter could use the help," he said.

"Don't."

He watched the streets sliding past the window. It felt like something pressing on his throat.

"I could voice," he said. "They're always looking for people to do interpretation. Poor sods can't do it themselves, can they?"

"Oh. I hadn't thought of that."

He frowned. "You disapprove?"

"For you? Nonsense, you're wonderful. Brilliant idea."

His chest tightened. "And you?"

She shook her head.

"God, I need a smoke."

"You do," he said, watched her tap out a pattern on the glass.

Mr. Christie was a man of discretion; their contracts and canceled lease were delivered, so they wouldn't waste a trip to the theatre to be sacked in front of the secondaries.

Roger poured them each a drink. They finished in single swallows.

"Right," he said. "Let's pack up, and we'll go flat-hunting this afternoon."

"If you want anything of Peter's, now's the time to claim it."

He had no interest in anything of Peter's, but he said, "Would you like a hand?"

"No," she said, closed the door.

Emily packed Peter's things neatly in his case and sent them to the Maitland Hotel.

"No big scene?" Roger wasn't sure what to expect, but after a quarter-century of marriage she might feel like setting his good shirts ablaze.

"I kept all his braces. He'll have to buy belts."

"Petty theft is the best revenge."

"Hush," she said, and handed him a paper bag. "Enjoy your braces. I have to bring these downstairs."

He started to offer, but she shook her head and went down alone.

The bedroom bore no sign of Peter, as if he'd only been an overnight guest; as if a single suitcase had carried away anything he'd ever done.

When Emily came back he had her drink ready.

"I always said you were a gentleman," she said, toasted him silently.

"To whom?"

She shrugged. "There must have been someone I talked to besides you."

It was the last of the Scotch, and as Emily cleaned out of the bathroom and her bedroom, Roger found things in the kitchen, and they ate the last bits of cheese and fruit from the icebox so they wouldn't go to waste.

Emily moved slowly, seemingly unconcerned that the landlord was coming for the keys at five. She rolled her perfume bottles into her socks, folded her good dress in newspaper.

"Keeps the wrinkles off," she said when she saw him looking.

As they were putting on their hats and coats, the porter returned from the Maitland with an invitation for Mr. Roger Cavanaugh and Ms Emily Howard to avail themselves of his hotel, free of charge, until such time as they should find suitable employment.

"About time," Emily said, and then Roger realized why she'd made the good-faith gesture of sending over the luggage; a guaranteed guilt response from Phil, who did so love settling quarrels.

The relief stung him.

"God, I could kiss you," he said.

She looked at him for a long time before she said, "Let's get a taxi."

At the Maitland the concierge nodded when they gave their names. "And would you like adjoining suites?"

"Just the one," said Emily.

Roger frowned, but Emily only touched his back and said, "We shouldn't take more space than we need."

Long after they were in the suite and she'd gone into the bedroom to hang her things, he could feel where the warmth of her hand had seeped through his jacket.

There was no mention of parting.

After a debate about whether or not to dine downstairs ("Should we?" "No." "Right."), they got bread and cheese and pears from a grocer. Roger insisted they get *something* from the hotel, so they ordered tea from room service and paid the tab promptly. It made Roger feel less in Phil's debt, though he knew one night in this suite was probably worth Roger's salary for the entire run.

They listened to the news on her bedroom radio. The Dramaturgica got another interview.

"The range of material is stunning," Peter said, his voice tinny. "These are some of the most knowledgeable actors I've had the pleasure to work with in all my years in theatre. Opening night is going to be groundbreaking."

"We can hope," said Roger.

She frowned. "Don't."

Emily had never vilified Dramatons the way other actors had, back when it was a battle. She joined the Actors' Rights Union but never campaigned, and declined the "Live Theatre is Really Living" radio spots. She and Roger had rows over it, loud and mean enough that Phil had to intervene.

Roger didn't understand why Emily seemed so devoid of disgust for them. He wasn't given to it, but he hated their fame, and he hated audiences who couldn't see the difference between real and manufactured.

"I'm going to talk to United Entertainment tomorrow," she said. "They're always looking for writers."

"Fine," he said around the ache in his chest. "Best get some sleep, then. Lots of groveling in the morning."

"Go to your room and shut your face, I'll be brilliant," she said, and got up to brush her teeth.

United kept her for three hours.

He'd gone with her, and it only made sense to apply as a voiceover artist while he was waiting. They sent him home with a table-top recorder and a stack of scripts.

"Whatever you think suits," the lady said, in a tone that made it clear this was his first test of employment.

So they set up on his bed, and Emily flipped through the scripts and sorted them into piles.

"Crap," she said, dropped one onto the larger stack beside the bed. "Crap. Crap. Very good," she said, tucked one under her knee. "Crap. Crap. You should give these people a talking-to, they sent you home with awful stuff."

"I'll have to take your word for it, I have yet to see anything."

She shoved something into his hands. "Read this first, then we'll do the other one."

It was a good monologue, that gray space between hero and villain that he most liked to occupy. Inflections, intonations, pushed forward from the page. All he'd have to do was open his mouth.

"What's the other?" he asked.

"The one where I'm your wife," she said, dropped another on the pile. "Watch out with these people. They're trying to turn you into a Lothario. At your age it will kill you."

When he woke it was full night. The darkness pressed on him through the window, as if the streetlights had turned away. Music poured from the club downstairs; some foxtrot he didn't know.

Emily was asleep, turned away from him. The libris was still on, resting in the space between them, the Condemned Woman's speech flickering faintly in the dark.

Two years ago, in Cardiff, she'd missed a line and thrown them three minutes past the pivotal reconciliation. There was no way to go back from where she'd put them, and they'd had to go on without it. The audience didn't know the play enough to complain, but they knew something was missing; it read in the limpid applause.

Peter was furious with her; Emily was more furious at herself than Peter was.

"It's just not what it was," she'd said, shaken, after Peter had stormed out of the dressing room. "I mean, you're rubbish in the farewell scene anyway, aren't you?"

"Terrible," Roger agreed.

After a minute he realized; in a pinch, you could cut out crowd scenes and the magistrate and perform the play with two actors.

He held out his hand to her, hesitated. When she breathed in her shoulder almost touched his palm; when she breathed out it sank away from him, out of reach.

Downstairs they struck up the first bars of "Forgetting You." The bandleader murmured something into the microphone, and the singer began.

Roger brought his hand back to his chest, stared at the ceiling, tried to breathe.

IV. When All Else Fails, Drop the Curtain

For six weeks Emily wrote afternoon radio dramas—half an hour minus the time it took to advertise ipecac and baking soda—and clocked them quickly enough to make an income.

It was great fun; it was every overwrought scenario from vaudeville without a sense of humor, and she and Roger sat up nights running lines and trying not to break.

" 'Oh, Charles, my dearest love, shot, shot down in the street! The Black Masques must be behind this! Oh, Detective Allan, you must believe me! You must help me!'"

" 'By all heaven's gold, I will do neither!' God, Em, really?"

"Keep going. I need to fill two minutes before the butter advert."

Eventually, British Broadcast Radio 4 began to send back notes suggesting that her characters make good use of baking soda, or butter, or men's suits.

"They're not serious," said Roger.

"Oh, I've taken care of it." She handed him a paper.

"'Damn you, Brewster, the police will be on us any second! We have to get this blood off our clothes! Quick, grab me Lincoln's Own baking soda!'"

"Too much?" she asked.

He grinned.

The BBR chose not to record that scene.

Instead, Autumn the socialite insisted that the cake for her dinner party be made only with Lincoln's Own, "since anything else is simply déclassé."

"They're censoring art, you know," she said.

"Dictators," said Roger from his half of the bed.

Six weeks they'd slept in the suite, and neither of them had put a hand out of line.

Rose (when Rose finally showed, in the lobby bar, two weeks after they arrived) was mortified nonetheless. Rose loved being mortified.

"WHAT are you doing sleeping in one bedroom with Roger?" she said between kisses on the cheek. "We've all heard, it's a scandal, you've gone mad, are you trying to give Peter a heart attack?"

"Oh, I could never top what he did," Emily said, reassuring.

Rose rolled her eyes and twisted her long braid. "Can you imagine? I nearly fainted when I heard, I turned right to Phil and said, 'Well, that's the end of it, innit,' and it was just terrible, terrible to hear, I could hardly work all the next day I was so distracted, I felt so awful."

"You poor thing," said Emily, and then Rose had the grace to look abashed and laugh.

"Well, at least you and Roger are finally left to yourselves."

"Rose."

"Oh, come off! Your stage tricks are no better than anyone's." She leaned forward, planted her elbows on the bar. "How long did he wait before he kissed you? Phil said Roger seemed likely to wait until you were here, but I guessed it was right off."

Emily smiled. "Rose, we're too old to go mooning around. We're only sharing a suite so that when one of us kicks the bucket the other can call the concierge."

Rose changed the subject.

She was a designer for one of the London houses—car coats. (She'd always been flash. Emily approved.) She lived in the hotel because Phil kept rent low and because she fancied having someone else change the sheets.

Abigail was a fit model when they met, "Oh, ages ago"; Abigail had grown tired of standing around getting stuck with pins, so now she was a comptroller, cataloging Rose's expensive fabrics.

"I love her to pieces," Rose said when Emily asked. "Just to pieces. We've been three years now. She's always taking the piss, it's brilliant, it's just like the Understudies again, only not so difficult." Rose flushed. "I mean, not that it was difficult, it was never difficult, it's just that now. Well, now."

Rose gently spun her glass between her fingers as if she was turning back the clock.

"You'll realize soon," Rose went on, sounding happier now that the worst was out. "No more stage fright, no more living out of bags, no more worrying if you have enough money for a cup of tea. No more stage managers. No more smearing up your face and acting a fool every night. It's lovely."

Rose was lying. Smearing up her face and acting a fool had been Rose's favorite thing in the world, and she pounced on any play that had the ingénue in disguise. Rose loved a pantomime more than anyone.

Maybe the fashion business wasn't such a fine idea.

"Do you go to the theatre much?"

Rose blinked hard several times, shook her head, stared into her glass. "Oh no, no. Not often. Abigail doesn't care for automatons, and I'm so busy these days. And it's so different   sort of sad sometimes, too, to see all those plays we used to do. You understand."

"Of course." Emily signaled for drinks.

They laughed through the second one, peeled away the years until it was as it had been when they slept in rickety train bunks, shuddering to a stop and falling to the floor before the sun was out.

"Do you remember," said Emily, "the night in Venice for Carnival, and we got masks and kitted up like birds? Roger looked an idiot, but you were lovely, remember?"

"I think the machines are beautiful," Rose said.

Emily fell quiet.

Rose looked mortified, but after a moment she went on, too far in to turn back. "I mean, all of them, even the old men and women—even their wrinkles are smooth somehow, have you seen them up close? I went backstage once. Someone recognized me and wanted to show me around."

Rose dropped her gaze back to the bar. "Their eyelids are all painted over with different colors, you know—from far away it looks like it's just shadows, but the Ingénues have purple and the Lotharios have dark green. Their eyes aren't colored, it's just little lumps of celluloid in the sockets, so they color the lids instead. It's a real stage trick. It frightened me the first time I saw; it's one thing to think they're all just lovely robots, but to paint up their faces to fool the audience, that's human. I can't even be afraid of them, though, they're so beautiful."

Rose looked up from her drink. "But you never hated them like the rest did, anyway, did you?"

"No," Emily said after a minute.

"So you've seen them, too."

Emily shook her head. "Three of them went to war instead of Phil and Peter and Roger. When I look at the Dramatons all I think is, *Was it you?*"

Rose had no answer.

"Don't tell Phil or anyone," Emily said after a while. "They'd think I'd gone daft."

Rose shook her head.

Emily believed it. Rose had her own secrets about Dramatons.

"God," said Rose after a moment, trying to revive, "it's just like the old days, innit?"

Emily's new drink was cold; the bartender had put ice in it. She set the cubes on the bar, watched them melt.

Roger ended up playing a three-off villain in one of her radio dramas.

"You wrote that for me on purpose," he accused when he came back from his first day at the recording studio. "You knew they'd call me in."

"Nonsense. If I'd written it for you he would be taking Doctor-Make ipecac for his rheumatism. Have you brought anything?"

"Thought we'd eat in the lobby," he said. "Phil's invited us to eat, with Rose."

"Do we have to?"

"We're staying in his hotel for free. The least we could do is provide some company."

"I know that profession."

"It would be a gesture. And I've wanted to see Rose."

"Don't ask her about the Dramatons," Emily warned him, gathering her notes. "She's gone sentimental."

The divorce papers were delivered by a bellboy, on behalf of Peter's attorney.

She didn't know he had an attorney. She wondered if the Dramaturgica had given him one so he could squirrel out of it all above board.

She showed Roger. "Pretend you're an attorney."

He looked them over, frowning now and then. "Am I pretending to be a good one?"

"You're not *that* good."

But it was clean-cut—she kept the rights to the Understudies name, and her accounts were untouched. It was the most generous exit Peter had ever made.

It was, for Peter, as close to an apology as he was capable of.

She signed them without any changes.

When he wasn't in his hotel room to receive them, she walked all the way to the Dramaturgica.

Peter looked ten years younger, having cast off the troupe that had weighed on him. His shirt (new, crisp white, just right for photographs should a cameraman happen to stop by) was rolled at the cuffs and open at the topmost button, as if he was too busy creating wondrous art to bother fastening his shirt properly.

"I want the queen to pause before she gives the order," he was saying, "make the audience think she might not. Ramp up the drama."

The handler wrote some notes.

"Yes," the automaton said, blinked. She had no lashes, just dark-painted lids, and her celluloid eyes gleamed under the lights.

"I think five seconds," Peter said after a moment.

The queen-Dramaton nodded. "Five seconds. Yes."

"Again," said Peter.

The automatons walked back to their places and waited with hands held at ease, in arcs like lobster claws.

"Your Majesty," said an automaton dressed as a page, "the King demands his answer." The page swung his arm wide.

(Emily thought, *Was it you?*)

The queen walked to the edge of the stage; her arms were aloft to make the most of her sleeves, and if it made her look like a pageant winner, she was a lovely one.

Emily counted: one, two, three, four, five.

"Tell the king he shall have his wedding."

The next went flawlessly (of course); the King made his entrance, was revealed as the man the Queen had fallen in love with when he was disguised as the shepherd, and they were wed with much fanfare amid a parade of faces, all lovely, all smooth, all somehow exactly the same.

The queen's cloak was blue velvet, spangled with stars. Emily hoped it was coincidence.

(The King's voice was Allan McGannon. The Understudies had invited him one season to play the husband in *The Bright Affair*. *Greaselight Weekly* had a picture of McGannon with Rose at the premiere, both grinning under the headline 'SHINING ROMANCE BETWEEN THEATRE'S BRIGHTEST STARS'.

Rose's particular friend was visible just at the edge of the flash, holding Rose's coat and laughing with Phil.

They'd played the romance out all season—Peter's idea. They'd made a mint.)

"Wonderful," Peter called. "So the curtain falls, the end. I'll have some notes for tomorrow; I'd like to see the handlers at four? Is that all right?"

There were murmurs of assent.

"Lovely. Dramatons, thank you. That is all."

Like he'd spoken a command, the automatons slumped, hands slack, two dozen iron jaws snapping shut.

"Finally," Emily said, "actors who listen to you. You must be elated."

Peter turned.

Behind him, the dozen handlers moved onstage and slid keys into their charges. They shuffled into the wings in pairs. At last the stage was empty.

Peter said, "Emily."

"Well, at least you came up with a stunning rejoinder in the interim." She held out the envelope. "I've brought your papers."

Peter frowned. "Can I buy you dinner?"

"Yes."

He buttoned the topmost button on his shirt.

The restaurant was nicer than they'd been to in years, the sort where the menu was determined for you.

Pete spent the first four courses saying how lovely the Dramaturgica was, and the next two courses apologizing.

"Really, Emily, I never meant to hurt you."

"And the divorce?"

"Well, I thought I might as well get out of your way."

"Nicely done."

"Well, I only thought." He frowned, trying to work through something, but apparently his bravery came in bursts and he'd run out for the moment; he shook his head, prodded at his beef medallions with his fork. "Would you have stayed with me, after I did this?"

She laughed. "No, of course not."

He leaned forward, nearly getting his cuffs in the gravy. "There's no honor, you know, in being the last of a line. If we had come back from it with something—I couldn't let some shabby theatre to be my legacy, Em, you know I couldn't."

"Don't apologize to me."

"Who, then? Roger? What do I have that he doesn't have, now?"

An income, she thought, but Peter was looking at her like he still loved her, and instead she said, "You should be ashamed of yourself."

"I am. I'm so sorry."

She took pity on him, and changed the subject.

Over dessert he said, "Of course you and Roger will come to the premiere?"

Emily watched the streetlight bleeding through the drapes.

What do I have that he doesn't have, now?

"What happened?"

Roger was in the bedroom doorway; his voice was rich and even. You'd never know he'd been asleep.

She wanted to tell him she'd been to see Peter, to tell him what Peter said, ask Roger what it meant.

But she knew what it meant; it was why she hadn't told him she'd been to see Peter.

She said, "I should write plays."

Roger picked up the phone and ordered breakfast.

"You should," he said after they'd eaten enough to wake up. He put the glass back on the butter dish. "You write very well."

"Don't expect a part from me," she said with a mouthful of toast. "Human geriatrics are right out."

He smiled, and the room around them lit up.

She dropped off the scripts with United, pocketed a check, and picked up a typewriter they'd set aside for her because her penmanship was so awful.

"Are there any companies that might want plays?" she asked, as if it had only occurred to her.

He looked through his ledger. "You can submit something on speculation. A historical. Georgian. Not your usual; something light and clever, please."

"Deadline?"

"End of the week."

"Oh, *lovely.*"

"Prize money's three hundred."

"You'll have it by Thursday," she said with a smile.

The place was a warren, and though she could hear Roger there was no chance of finding him, so she sat in the lobby thinking up a clever Georgian history.

When he came out he had one script in his hands.

"Rumbly villains thin on the ground?"

"It's a script for an American play," he said, not looking at her. "Traveling company."

"Oh," she said, felt the floor crumbling under her feet.

When they got back to the suite he put the script in a drawer and she worked for hours on the typewriter, keys clacking, while he read the pages she'd written.

Finally he said, "Go to bed, Em," and she realized it was night.

"The radio drama wants another villain," she said as she stood. "Can I bring you back from the dead to kidnap an ingénue? You'll owe me a pint."

When she glanced up into the bedroom, he was looking at her over the top of his script. He had already been looking at her. He looked at her too much.

"Emily," he said quietly, "there won't be more parts. I'm getting old. There's nothing left."

"You bloody coward," she said tartly, because the idea of him being gone left a cavern in her chest.

He snorted. "A coward and a wise man sleep on the same pillow."

From The *Condemned Woman*.

"Don't you dare spit lines at me," she snapped, and launched herself away from the desk into the bedroom room. She was furious, suddenly, had to be away from him, as far as she could get without losing sight of him.

After a moment he appeared in the doorway, looking more composed than she felt.

"Emily, really." He'd put his robe on over his pajamas, and it made him look like the boudoir scene in a comedy. "You can't be surprised I'm getting old."

"May I be surprised you're giving up?"

He folded his arms. "It's one thing to write. It's another to try to fool people into hiring you when we're up to our ears in beautiful machines. You can't keep the past going. It's over. We've outlived our time."

She shook her head, wondered if they were still talking about acting. "I'm still here."

He spread his arms. "I don't see you setting foot on stage! Even if I was the best actor who'd ever lived, I can't fight this alone!"

"But you ARE! You're just a coward! I've been telling you for thirty bloody years and you've never listened, because you're too much of a coward to hear me! Why do you think you've never—"

She stopped, but they both knew what she hadn't said. The damage was done.

He took a slow step backward.

(She recognized the breath he took onstage when he was about to deliver an insult that rang.)

"Yes," he said, "that's one mistake I never made."

Thirty years, and this close they had never come.

His voice was like a living thing.

When she could breathe she said, "Then I won't trouble you. Good night."

Her coat was where she'd thrown it, and if the concierge noticed she had pajamas underneath when she asked for a separate room, he had the good training not to say.

"And did you leave anything in your room we could bring you, Miss?"

There was a long pause before she said, "No."

V. This Bright Affair

Roger's room was horribly quiet, but it took him a day and a half to find a reason to leave.

When he did, he wondered what he had been afraid of. Emily wasn't in the lobby; she wasn't on the street; she wasn't at the club when he stopped in for a drink.

He felt foolish. It wasn't as though he was going to see her, no matter where he looked. He shouldn't have worried.

The American play was about a man whose business partner betrayed him to the Mob. The man's wife was murdered. The second act had three gun standoffs.

When Roger reached the line, "I'll have my revenge, you rat, no matter what it takes!" he got up from the table and turned on the radio.

He never finished the third act.

When the company called, he said sea voyages made him ill, and agreed to do a radio commercial for men's suits.

Roger looked up at the marquee of the Theatre Dramaturgica with its knife-sharp silver edges, and knew he was old.

Rose, who'd given him her left arm (Phil had her right), whistled as the flashbulbs went off.

"Peter knows how to premiere, I'll give him that."

Ahead of them, Peter was dressed to the nines and flirting with the cameras. They'd brought an Ingénue for him; she stood beside Peter, grinning vacantly and winking at intervals. Her face was pulled tight and gleaming, but when the cameras went off she looked human enough.

"Well, at least she's more fun than Rose," said Phil.

"Ta," said Rose, and dropped his arm.

Roger smiled and walked Rose through the photographers.

Rose could flash a coquette's smile as well as any Ingénue, and flashbulbs skittered around them. She'd even cut her hair for fashion, and her Marcel gleamed.

Just before they passed under the marquee Roger looked back for Phil and saw he was escorting Emily, several crowds behind.

Emily was wearing her good black frock and smiling at the cameras like she knew something they didn't, and they took her picture and then shrugged to one another.

Roger took Rose inside, didn't look back again.

Turned out Peter, in a blaze of consideration, had seated Emily apart; her box was stage right, as far from them as the theatre allowed. She was perched on her chair, looking down at the stage.

Roger got interested in his playbill.

Phil took his seat. "Apparently the other seats are taken, or I would have stayed there. Bit of a bastard, Peter, really."

"I've half a mind to go over there," said Rose.

"I've half a mind to find Peter," said Phil.

But the lights went down and the curtain came up, and it was time for the play.

It was an old story, acted in an old way; the audience clapped at the end of all the right speeches. However, Roger could see Peter's mark on the way they moved, on the differences in their pauses and their use of the stage.

Peter had given them the illusion of trying. Peter had at last stumbled onto his genius.

Emily would be heartbroken.

When the screen slid shut after Act One, Roger turned to comfort her, but it was only Rose, who was quietly mutilating the playbill.

Phil frowned. "Are you all right?"

"A bit under the weather, is all," Rose said, tearing another corner. "Lots of excitement these past few weeks. More than I'm used to; Abigail's so steady, and Phil's a bore, of course."

"Ta," said Phil.

But Roger wasn't surprised when he looked over a few moments later and saw Phil watching Rose with an expression of fondness and chagrin.

(He *was* surprised the look lingered; Phil was studying her with the fondness of a long acquaintance, the fondness that goes unspoken between people who know one another enough to keep company in the face of all good sense.)

Phil glanced up and flushed at being caught out, but shrugged without shame, and gave Roger the same look.

Roger had thought Phil offered them space for old times' sake, that because he couldn't persevere he had instead provided.

But Phil loved them. He loved them enough to want them all to live with him, close at hand and never really changing, sparing Phil a world of strangers and doubts.

Roger thought of Emily, who had never looked at him like that in thirty years. When Emily looked at Roger it was to size him up and see him as he was, and if she ever found him lacking she said as much, and if she ever found him excelling she told him that, too.

And when she had looked at him with love (fleeting, joyful, terrifying moments), it had never been for the sake of something that was gone.

He stood up so quickly he had to clap a hand to his hat to keep it from falling. "Rose," he said, "if you're ill I'm happy to take you home."

"Please."

By the time applause started for Act Two they were in the lobby, free from the silhouette in the box across the way, the sight of the beautiful machines.

The idea that Phil was paying for *two* charity suites drove Roger into the world; if he was going to stay in London he'd have to start paying his way.

(It wasn't quite true—he'd heard three episodes of the radio soap that could only have been hers, and the Georgian play stood a good chance—but it didn't do to think too long about Emily.)

He walked through Covent Garden catching signs in the windows: Shop girls Wanted; Hiring Barkeep; Automaton Handler Positions Available. A bookshop off Mercer was seeking a seller; a tailor was looking for a decent drafter. The sign said, NO ARCHITECTS.

When he noticed he was at the door of the Olympia Theatre, he was almost surprised.

I've been telling you for thirty bloody years and you never listen.

He stepped up to the will-call window. "Excuse me. I'd like to audition for the company."

The ticket-taker (a boy no more than twenty) frowned and looked around for help. None came.

"Have you brought credentials?" he asked, looking proud of himself for asking.

Roger said, "I'm the last human actor."

"Right," said the boy after a moment, "let me just, erm . . . hm."

"I've a monologue prepared," said Roger, "if that helps you."

The boy smiled thinly and disappeared, and Roger was just beginning to wonder if he should give up when the theatre doors opened and a gentleman strode through.

He was wearing a vested suit and still had gloves on. Roger recognized a director.

"I'm Michael Brinn. I understand you're auditioning to be a handler."

"An actor."

Mr. Brinn frowned. "Beg pardon?"

Roger took a breath for courage. "I'm the last working actor," he said. "I've been doing this for thirty years. I'm a commodity."

Brinn snorted. "You'd go up against a Dramaton?"

Roger just looked at him.

In less time that Roger expected, Brinn spread his arms, a picture of patience, and led the way inside.

• • •

"You're joking."

"I'm not."

"Roger, that's—are you sure?"

He raised an eyebrow. "Yes, Phil."

Phil sat back, crossed his arms. "So, what did—Well. Congratulations. Couldn't have happened to a better man."

Phil called Rose; Phil called for champagne.

Then Rose was there in a flurry of robes, kissing them and congratulating them both like Phil had done something, too. She had one forgotten bobby pin sticking out of her Marcel and a spot of masque on her temple; her accolades couldn't wait for fashion.

Roger had hated Dramatons, on and off, since the beginning.

(On, whenever he thought what would happen to all the actors he'd watched in all those cities, the breathless dark of the theatre.

Off, when Emily told him to be kinder.)

When there were Dramatons in the papers—Ingénues in baggy dresses that hid their hip joints standing next to grinning Heroes, a smooth-skinned Femme Fatale standing alone (the only women Dramatons who stood alone in photographs)—he'd looked at their blank celluloid eyes and thought, *Naught as queer as folk*.

The plays began promptly and were always perfect. It didn't matter to the audience that Dramatons weren't real. It was no concern of theirs that the shells were empty.

Let them settle, he'd thought, back then.

Now Roger was older, and had to pick his battles. Acting alongside Dramatons seemed as hopeless a battle as any. It would make a fitting end.

He spent the first night memorizing *The Condemned Woman*; he was surrounded by walking libraries, and he'd have to be note-perfect.

Four times he turned to ask Emily for help.

At last he gave up and called Phil.

"I have to memorize this," he said.

Phil hung up.

Rose and Phil were at his door ten minutes later, bearing breakfast.

"My lord," said Rose around a grape, "if you ever loved me, do not force me to beg for mercy. Let me die as I have chosen to."

"But you are not guilty! Must you take another's crimes on your shoulders for that long walk to the grave? Must I mourn you twice—tomorrow, and now tonight?"

"So soon," Phil piped up. "And now, so soon, tonight."

"Bugger." Roger cleared his throat. "Must I mourn you twice—tomorrow, and now, so soon, tonight?"

"I hoped you would not love me enough to mourn," said Rose, and made a sympathetic face at her libris.

"Don't you cry," warned Phil.

She threw a grape.

His co-star was a Dame; they gave her salt-and-pepper hair and a thinner build than necessary.

"She answers to the character name," said her handler, an obscenely young man. "And the other major titles—my wife, my love."

Roger felt a bit ill. "And it changes every show?"

"Of course. How else would we call them?" The boy shoved his spectacles up and closed the panel on her forehead. "She's set for the blocking, Mr. Brinn."

From the orchestra seats, Mr. Brinn's assistant opened the script for him.

"We'll open with you in the wings, my lady, if you please."

"Yes please," the Dramaton said, and walked behind the curtain.

"Mr. Cavanaugh, enter stage left and embrace her."

"Yes please," said Roger pleasantly, and went to mark before anyone could reprimand him.

When he wrapped his arms around the Dame she was unyielding, her body warm from all the little motors.

"I told you not to," the Dame said.

He said, "How could I help it?"

They went scene by scene, and as they traded lines and waited for cues ("Pause before the next line." "Yes please."), Roger could hear her blinking just under the sound of her voice.

If it made Roger a little sad, he was careful not to show it. He'd asked for a place in the future, and this was it; lovely automatons without one comment that wasn't programmed in. If it was lonely work, at least it was something to do; better to be lonely here.

Roger left Emily a note with the concierge.

> *Congratulations on the Georgian—Rose told me. It's a lovely piece. Hope they treat it as it deserves.*
>
> *Changed my mind about fighting alone—The Condemned Woman goes up at the Olympia in a month. Doing what I can.*
>
> *Take care.*

· · ·

After two weeks Roger understood why Dramatons had stayed away from naturalism; the Dame overheated three times trying to accommodate both Mr. Brinn's stage directions and Roger's speech patterns.

"You could be more uniform, Cavanaugh," Mr. Brinn suggested.

"You're paying me to *not* be uniform," Roger pointed out, and that was the last time that came up.

After three weeks there was talk of a newer model.

They put an ad in the paper: "SEEKING DAME-MODEL AND HANDLER FOR HIRE. HISTORICAL DRAMA A MUST. HUMAN-LEVEL CALIBRATION STANDARDS. SIX-WEEK RUN."

"We'll use the old one until then," said Brinn.

No one answered, and Roger began to feel a flicker of hope that maybe someday human-level calibration might turn into actual humans again. Not that he'd live to see it, but still, dare to dream.

When he took the stage, the Dame model walked out to meet him in her star-spangled cloak, her face calibrated to be noble in suffering. The expression never altered; even when she simulated weeping, serenity remained.

Emily had made it ugly; her Condemned Woman was noble when she could manage it, but was angry and terrified and jealous by turns, and at the end of the play, just before she schooled her features to go out and meet the hangman with decorum, she'd gripped his hand like she wanted to drag him down with her.

He stepped up to the Dame model, embraced her.

"I told you not to," she said.

He said, "How could I help it?"

("Too mournful," said Brinn.)

If there was an ache in his chest from beginning to end of every run, he didn't worry about it. You got all kinds of aches and pains at his age.

"Are you excited?" Rose asked him as soon as the waltz was over. "Just think, in a week you'll be back at the Olympia! God, it's been ages since we were there, a life ago, it's mad that you're back there, Abigail thinks it's the maddest thing when I tell her.

"And with the old Dame's having all the mechanical trouble! What if she breaks in the middle, you'll really be in it then, Emily talks about it sometimes, about what would happen if they just broke and there was nothing you could do—I can't imagine how you're feeling."

"Like a foxtrot," he said.

She took the hint, and they finished the dance in silence.

Roger wasn't surprised to see Peter at their table, waiting for him like the evil Duke in a melodrama.

Phil and Rose vanished onto the dance floor.

But Peter had never been good at playing villain, and when Roger said, "You look well, Peter," the worst Peter could summon was, "Better than some."

"How's the play going?"

"Well, it was going well until I found out there was a novelty act down the street."

"It's only a novelty the first time. Soon it will be so commonplace you won't even have to worry about it."

Peter sighed. "I didn't mean it like that, Roger, it's just—Christ, this is important to me! How could you do it? You couldn't find some other way to act?"

Roger finished his drink rather than answer.

"Right, sorry," said Peter. "But it's still a bit of a blow. Not that you care, now that you've made your point. I'll hand it to you, though, I didn't think you had that kind of showmanship in you. You should have seen Emily's face when she told me."

Roger's lungs contracted for a moment. "Oh?"

"Said it served me right, and you'd show everyone what they'd been missing. You know how she gets when she's excited about something."

Roger smiled. Poor Peter, upstaged for the first time in his life.

"I hope to see you both opening night."

"I'm busy," Peter said, but when Roger said, "A seat in the boxes?" Peter said, "Well, I might do."

The papers went wild.

What had been a pathetic last stand when there were three of them was now one man's *cause célèbre*.

The *Examiner*: "MAN VS MACHINE: HAPPY ENDING OR END OF ALL WE HOLD DEAR?"

The *Nation*: "Cavanaugh to get into gears"

The *Evening Standard*: "WAS THIS WHY WE FOUGHT THE WAR?", which Roger thought was unfair all around.

The only one Roger bothered with was *Greaselight Weekly*. He set it on the night table so he'd have something to look at in the mornings before rehearsal.

"LAST LIVING ACTOR TO GO DOWN SWINGING."

The house was packed, and for a moment Roger wasn't sure he'd be able to go on in front of that big an audience.

Then he remembered he'd done it in this same theatre a quarter-century ago.

"Damn fool," he muttered, and stepped onstage to a hail of applause and a smattering of jeers.

The condemned woman stepped out into the lights, her blue velvet coat spangled with little tin stars.

It was Emily.

Emily, who was clutching the edges of the cloak in her fists, terrified and exhilarated and amazed as she'd always been at the beginning of the play all those years ago; just the same.

He moved without thinking.

When they embraced, he crushed her in his arms, and she took in a shuddering breath, buried her face in his shoulder.

The audience was rapt.

It would never be like this again; it could not have been this without thirty years together, without their fight, without this fierce surprise pressing against his chest.

Roger wrapped his arms tighter.

They were going to make a show of it after all.

He stepped back, letting the edges of her cloak slide slowly through his fingers.

"I told you not to look for me," she said.

He breathed, "How could I help it?"

She shook her head; her eyes were bright.

He took her hand and led her to the wooden bench that marked her prison cell, where the condemned woman would spend her final hours.

Everything else would wait until after the performance.

CONSOLATION

JOHN KESSEL

Lester

Given last month's denial-of-service attack on the robocar network, I was surprised when, over the streetcam, I saw Alter arrive in a bright blue citicar. As it pulled away from the curb toward its next call, he tugged his jacket straight and looked directly up into the camera, a sheen of sweat on his forehead. 1142 AM, 5 November, the readout at the corner of my pad said. 30 C. Major rain in the forecast.

Alter was forty, stork-like and ungainly. He stuck his hands into his pockets and approached the lobby, and the door opened for him.

I set down the pad and got up to open my office door. Alter was standing with his back to me, peering at the directory. "Mr. Alter," I called. "Over here."

He turned, looked at me warily, and then came over.

"Right in here," I said. I ushered him into the office. He stood there and inspected it. It looked pretty shabby. A bookshelf, a desk covered with papers, a window on the courtyard where a couple of palms grew and a turtle sat on a log, a framed print of Magritte's *La reproduction interdite*, two armchairs facing each other. Like an iceberg, nine tenths of the office was invisible.

"No receptionist," Alter said.

"That's right. Just you and me. Have a seat."

Alter didn't move. "I thought this would be a government office."

"I work for the government. This is my office."

"You people," Alter said. He sat down. I sat across from him. "What's your name?" he asked.

"It's uncomfortable, isn't it, working in a state of incomplete knowledge. Call me Lester."

"I like to know where I am, Lester."

Everything in his manner, in the way he sat in the chair, in the timbre of his voice, screamed sociopath. I didn't need some expert system to tell me where he fell on the spectrum: I had been dealing with men like Alter—always men—for long enough to read them in my sleep.

"You're in Canada," I said. "In Massachusetts, to be specific. You're in my office, about to tell us what you've done."

"Us?" he said. "Do you have a hamster in your pocket?"

"Think of 'us' as the rest of the human race."

Alter's eyes narrowed. " 'Us' like the U.S. You're a Fed."

"There are no Feds anymore. That's a Sunbelt fantasy."

"You know I'm not from the Sunbelt. I'm from Vermont. You've been invading my privacy, surveilling me. You're going to doxx me. Turnabout is fair play. Eye-for-eye kind of thing. Very biblical."

"Do you always assume that everybody else is like you?"

"Most people aren't." He smiled at that, quite pleased with himself.

"Doxxing only works against a person who has something to lose. Friends. A family. A valuable job. A reputation. You're doxx-proof, Jimmy. All we want is for you to explain what you've done."

"You already know what I've done. That's why I'm here. You violated my privacy, my personhood."

"Yes, that's true. Why do you think we did that?"

"Why? What I wish I knew was how. No way you should have been able to trace me." He looked around my office. "Certainly not with anything you have here."

"You aren't here for me to tell you things, you are here for you to tell me things. So let's get on with it. We'd like you to say what you've done. We need to hear you speak the words. Imagine it's so we can measure your degree of remorse."

"I'm not remorseful. Everything I did was right."

He was beyond tiresome. His pathetic individualism, his fantasy of his uniqueness, his solipsism. I wanted to punch him just so he might know that what was happening in this room was real. "So tell us all those right things you did."

"Well, I turned up all the thermostats in the Massachusetts State House. Sweated them out of there for an afternoon, anyway."

"What else?"

"I inventoried the contents of all the refrigerators of government employees with a BMI over thirty. And the bathroom scales, the medical interventions, the insurance records. All those morbidly obese—I posted it on Peeperholic."

"Is that all?"

"I scrambled the diagnostic systems in the Pittsfield New Clinic. I deflated all the tires in the Salem bikeshare—that one was just for fun. At UMass I kept the chancellor out of her office for a week and put videos of her and her wife in bed onto every public display on the campus."

"Is that all?"

"That covers the most significant ones, yes."

"I know you don't believe in law, but I thought you believed in privacy."

"They don't deserve privacy."

"But you do."

"Apparently not. So here I am."

"You resent us. But you object to your victims resenting you?"

"Victims? Who's a victim? I was punching up. The people I troubled needed to be troubled. Here's what I did—I punctured their hypocrisies and exposed their lies. I made some powerful and corrupt people a little uncomfortable. I managed to tell some truths about a pitifully few people, to a pitifully small audience. I wish I could have done more."

I'd been doing this too long. One too many sociopathic losers with computers, broken people who didn't know how broken they were. The world churned them out, full of defensive self-righteousness, deformed consciences, spotty empathy, and a sense of both entitlement and grievance—bullies who saw themselves as victims, the whole sodden army of them out there wreaking havoc small and large without a clue as to how pathetic and pathetically dangerous they were. A sea of psychopathy, with computers. The mid-21st century.

Thank god I didn't have to deal with the ones carrying guns. That was another department.

Alter was still going on. I interrupted him. "Why don't you tell me about Marjorie Xenophone."

"Funny name. I don't believe I know that woman."

"You knew her well enough to send her STD history to her husband. To tell her car to shut down every time she turned onto her lover's street."

"That's a terrible thing to do. But I never heard of the woman before you mentioned her name."

"So you don't know she killed herself."

"Suicide, huh? She must have been one messed-up lady."

"You turned off her birth control implant and she got pregnant. Her husband left her, she lost her job. She was humiliated in front of everybody she knew."

"Some people can't deal with life."

"Mr. Alter, you are one bad, bad pancake," I said. "You worked with her at Green Mountain Video Restoration."

Alter's eyes slid from mine up to the Magritte painting. A man is looking into a mirror, the back of his head to us. The mirror shows an identical image of the back of his head.

When Alter spoke, his tone was more serious. "What went on between me and that woman was private."

"Privacy was an historical phase, Jimmy, and it's over. Nobody had a right to privacy when they were indentured servants or slaves. For one or two hundred years people imagined they could have secrets. That was a local phenomenon and it's now over. Your career is evidence of why."

"So why is it a crime when an individual does it but perfectly fine when your social media platform or service provider or the government does? People sign away their privacy with every TOS box they check. If they get upset when I liberate publicly available materials, too bad. Maybe they'll get smart and stand up to people like you."

"Well said. Where were you born, again?"

"Burlington, Vermont."

"Right. Burlington. South Burlington—the part that's in Texas."

Alter didn't say anything. I had never seen a man look more angry. "Indentured servants and slaves," he muttered.

"Did you really think you could create an identity that would get past our friends at MIT?" I said. "And then have the arrogance to pursue a career as a troll? Where did you go to school? Texas Tech?"

"That's a lot of questions at once."

"We already know the answers."

Outside, thunder sounded. Fat raindrops began to fall into the courtyard, moving the leaves of the palms. The turtle remained motionless. "Where were you born?"

After a hesitation, he said, "Galveston."

"Sad about Galveston, the hurricane. How long have you been a refugee?"

"I'm not a refugee."

"An illegal immigrant, then?"

"I'm a Texas citizen. I just happen to be working here."

"Under a false identity."

"I pay your taxes. I pay as much as any citizen."

"Don't like our taxes, go back to Texas." I smiled. "Could be a bumper sticker."

Alter looked straight at me for a good five seconds. "Please, don't make me."

"But we're persecuting you. The jackbooted thugs of the totalitarian Canadian government."

"You're no more Canadian than I am. You're an American."

"Check out the flagpole in Harvard Square sometime. Note the red maple leaf."

"Look, I get it. You have power over me." Alter rubbed his hands on his pants legs. "What do you want me to say? I'll sign anything you want me to sign."

"What about Marjorie?"

"You're right. I went too far. I feel bad about that." Alter's belligerence had faded. He shifted in his chair. "I'm sorry if I got out of line. Just tell me what you want and I'll do it."

"I got the impression you didn't like people telling you what to do."

"Well . . . sometimes you have to go along to get along. Right?"

"So I've heard."

"How many sessions are we going to have?"

"Sessions? What sessions?"

"Because of the court order. You're supposed to heal me or certify me or something, before I can go back into the world."

"It's not my job to heal you."

"Maybe it's punishment, then."

It was a pleasure to see the panic in his eyes. "This isn't a prison and I'm not a cop. I'll tell you what we will do, though. We'll send you back to the hellhole you came from. Hope you kept your water wings."

Just then I noticed something on my pad. It was raining hard now, a real monsoon, and the temperature had dropped ten degrees. But in the middle of hustling pedestrians stood a woman, very still, staring at the entrance of my building. People walked by her in both directions, hunched against the storm. She wore a hat pulled low, and a long black coat slick with rain. She entered the lobby. She scanned it, turned purposefully toward my office, reached into her coat pocket, and walked off camera.

"I don't think anything I've done's so bad . . . " Alter said. I held up my hand to shut him up.

The door to my office opened. Alter started to turn around. Before he could, the woman in the black coat tossed something into the room, then stepped back and closed the door. The object hit the floor with a solid thunk and rolled, coming to rest by my right foot. It was a grenade.

Esmeralda

The blast blew the door across the lobby into the plate-glass front wall, shattering it. By then I was out on the sidewalk. I set off through the downpour in the direction of the train station.

Before I had walked a hundred meters the drones swooped past me, rotors tearing the rain into mist, headed for Makovec's office. People rushed out into the street. The citicar network froze, and only people on bikes and in private vehicles were able to move. I stepped off the curb into a puddle, soaking my shoe.

Teo had assured me that all public monitors had been taken care of and no video would be retrieved from five minutes before to five after the explosion. I walked away from Dunster Street, trying to keep my pace steady, acutely aware that everybody else was going in the other direction. Still, I crossed the bridge over the levees, caught a cab, and reached the station in good time.

I tried to sleep a little as the train made its way across Massachusetts, out of the rainstorm, through the Berkshires, into New York. It was hopeless. The sound of the blast rang in my ears. The broken glass and smoke, the rain. It was all over the net: Makovec was dead and they weren't saying anything about Alter. Teo's phony video had been released, claiming responsibility for the Refugee Liberation Front and warning of more widespread attacks if Ottawa turned its back on those fleeing Confederate Free America.

Outside the observation window a bleeding sunset poured over forests of russet and gold. After New England and New York became provinces, Canada had dropped a lot of money on the rail system. All these formerly hopeless decaying cities—from classical pretenders Troy, Rome, Utica to Mohawk-wannabe Chittenango and Canajoharie—were coming back. If it weren't for the flood of refugees from the Sunbelt, the American provinces might make some real headway against economic and environmental blight.

Night settled in and a gibbous moon rose. Lots of time to think.

I was born in Ogdensburg back when it was still part of the U.S. There'd been plenty of backwoods loons where I grew up, in the days when rural New York might as well have been Alabama. But the Anschluss with Canada and the huge influx of illegals had pushed even the local evangelicals into the anti-immigrant camp. Sunbelters. Ragged, uncontrollable, when they weren't draining social services they were ranting about government stealing their freedom, defaming their God, taking away their guns.

My own opinions about illegals were not moderated by any ideological or religious sympathies. I didn't need any more threadbare crackers with their rugged-individualist libertarian Jesus-spouting militia-loving nonsense to fuck up the new Northeast the way they had fucked up the old U.S. We're Canadians now, on sufferance, and eager to prove our devotion to our new government. Canada has too many of its own problems to care what happens to some fools who hadn't the sense to get out of Florida before it sank.

The suffering that the Sunbelters fled wasn't a patch on the environmental degradation they were responsible for. As far as I was concerned, their plight was chickens coming home to roost. Maybe I felt something for the Blacks and Hispanics and the women, but in a storm you have to pick a side and I'd picked mine a long time ago. Teo's video would raise outrage against the immigrants and help ensure that Ottawa would not relax its border policies.

But my ears still rang from the blast.

It was morning when the train arrived in Buffalo. The station was busy for early Saturday: people coming into town for the arts festival, grimly focused clients headed to one of the life extension clinics, families on their way up to Toronto, bureaucrats on their way to Ottawa. In the station I bought a coffee and a beignet. Buzzing from lack of sleep, I sat at a table on the concourse and watched the people. When the screen across from me slipped from an ad for Roswell Life Extension into a report on the Boston attack, I slung my bag over my shoulder and walked out.

I caught the Niagara Street tram. A brilliant early November morning: warm, sunny, cotton ball clouds floating by on mild westerlies. They used to call this time of year Indian summer back when it happened in mid-October, when the temperature might hit seventy for a week or so before the perpetual cloud cover of November came down and Seasonal Affective Disorder settled in for a five- or six-month run.

Now it was common for the warmth to linger into December. Some days it still clouded up and rained, but the huge lake-effect snowstorms that had battered the city were gone. The lake never froze over anymore. The sun shone more and the breezes were mild. The disasters of the late 20th and early 21st centuries had passed, leaving Buffalo with clean air, moderate climate, fresh water, quaint neighborhoods, historic architecture, hydroelectric power beyond the dreams of any nuke, and a growing arts- and medicine-based economy. Just a hop across the river from our sister province Ontario.

The tram ran past the harbor studded with sailboats, then along the Niagara River toward the gleaming Union Bridge. Kids in LaSalle Park were flying kites. Racing shells practiced on the Black Rock Canal. A female coxed eight, in matching purple shirts, rowed with precision and vigor.

None of those women had blown anybody up in the last twenty-four hours.

The tram moved inland and I got off on the West Side. I carried my bag a couple of blocks, past reclaimed houses and a parking lot turned community garden, to the Fargo Architectural Collective. Home. We'd done the redesign ourselves, Teo and Salma and I, fusing two of the circa-1910 houses with their limestone footings and cool basements into a modern multipurpose. It had earned us some commissions. In the front garden stood a statue of old William Fargo himself, looking more like a leprechaun than the founder of separate transportation and banking empires.

Teo greeted me at the door and enveloped me in a big bear hug.

"Esme," he said. "We've been worried. You're okay?"

"For certain values of the word okay." I dropped my bag. Salma poked her head out of her workroom. She looked very serious. "What?" I said.

"Come have some tea," she said.

The three of us sat down in the conference room and Teo brewed a pot of mood tea. "Am I going to need to be calmed down?" I asked.

Salma leaned forward, her dark brow furrowed. "Our friends in Boston screwed up. Turns out not all of the video cameras were disabled. There may be some images of you approaching the building."

"Shit."

"The fact you're not from Boston will help," Teo said. "You have no history. We're boring middle-class citizens; none of us are known activists."

"That should slow them down for about thirty seconds," I said. I sipped some tea. We talked about the prospect of my taking a vacation. Vancouver, maybe, or Kuala Lumpur. After a while I said, "I didn't sleep last night. I'm going to take a nap."

I went up to my room, sat on the bed, and unlaced my shoes. The right one was still damp from the puddle in Cambridge. I lay down. Outside my window a Carolina wren, another undocumented immigrant from the torrid South, sang its head off. Teo's tea was good for something, and in a few minutes I drifted off to sleep.

It was late afternoon when I woke. Salma came in and lay down beside me on her side, her face very close to mine. "Feel any better?"

"Better." I kissed her. "It was awful, Salma."

She touched my cheek. "I know. But somebody has—"

I forced myself up. "You don't know."

Salma sat up and put her hand on my shoulder. "If you're going to be a soldier for change, then you have to accept some damages. Try not to think about it. Come on, take a shower, get dressed. We're going out."

I swung my legs off the bed. I had volunteered, after all. "Where are we going?"

"There's a party at Ajit Ghosh's. Lot of people will be there."

Ghosh was a coming intellectual voice. An aggregator, a cultural critic, the youngest man to hold a named chair in the history of UB. He lived in a big state-of-the-art ecohouse with a view of Delaware Park, Hoyt Lake, and the Albright-Knox. The neighborhood was money, new houses and old occupied by young, ambitious people on their way up. I didn't like a lot of them, or who they were willing to step on in order to rise, but you had to give them points for energy and creativity.

I did not care for the way they looked down on people whose roots in WNY went back to before it became trendy. The party would be full of people who came here only when living in New York City got too difficult, the Southwest dried up and blew away, and the hurricane-battered South turned into an alternating fever swamp and forest fire.

I didn't think I needed a party. But Ghosh's house was a Prairie School reboot with a negative carbon imprint. It was better than lying around with the echo of an explosion in my head.

"All right," I said.

Scoobie

I'd spent the last three days at Roswell Park getting my tumors erased, and now I was out on the street ready to do some damage. I headed toward the restaurants on Main Street, walking past the blocks of medical labs, life extension clinics, hospitals, all with their well-designed signage and their well-trimmed gardens and their well-heeled patients taking the air. Most of them looked pretty good. Pretty much all of them were doomed.

They treated their ailments and told themselves that nobody lives forever. But I would. An immortal living in the world of mortals—one of the few. The ones who committed to the task and made the best choices. Rationalism. Certain practices, investments, expectations. Habits of living.

There's an industry devoted to anti-aging, a jungle of competing claims and methods. Most of it is garbage, pretty pictures papering over the grave. Billions wasted every year.

Not me. I didn't invest in a single platform, but maneuvered between the options. Of course you could not always know the best choice with certainty. If you went T+p53 route, you entered the race between immortality and cancer. You had to boost your tumor suppression genes to counter the increased telomerase that prevented chromosome erosion. Hence my visit to Roswell. There was SkQ ingestion to reduce mitochondria damage. A half-dozen other interventions and their synergistic effects, positive and negative. To keep on top of this you needed as much information as possible. Even then you could make a mistake—but that was the human condition for us early posthumans.

I had backups: a contract to be uploaded once they had worked out the tech. A separate contract to have my head cryogenically preserved once the brain had been uploaded. Some other irons in the fire, depending on the way things broke.

I grew up in Fort McMurray, Alberta, in the destroyed landscape of bitumen strip mines and oil sands, with its collapsing economy and desperate gun-toting mountain people. When the U.S. broke up and the northeastern and Pacific states joined Canada, freedom-loving Alberta took the opportunity to go the other way, ditching the arrogant bastards in Ottawa to join in a nice little union with Montana, Wyoming, and Idaho. Big skies, free men. Petroleum fractions. Though it had its charms, I had things I wanted to do, and not many of them could be done in Calgary.

It was a beautiful day, a good day to be alive. I felt very young. Though this latest treatment would blow a hole in my savings, I decided to spend some money. At Galley's on Main I ordered broiled salmon and a salad. I had not eaten anything like this in a year. I let the tastes settle on my tongue. I could feel the cells in my body exploding with sensory energy. The crispness of the lettuce. A cherry tomato. It was all astonishing, and I let it linger as long as I could.

A man leaving the restaurant glanced at me and did a double take. It was Mossadegh.

"By the fires of Ormazd!" he said. "Not expecting you in a place like this. How's it growing, brother?"

"Germinal," I said. My connections with Mossadegh were mostly business. He knew a lot of women, though. I waved at the chair opposite. "Sit down."

"Haven't seen you much," Mossadegh said. "Where you been?"

"Out of town for a few days. Clients." I didn't advertise that I was going to live forever.

Mossadegh was a pirate. He said it was principle with him, not self-interest: freedom of information, no copyright or patents. That was how I got to know him, and on occasion he and I had made some money together. I would never let Mossadegh know anything about who I really was, though. The free flow of information is essential to posthumanism, but I didn't want anybody in my business.

I don't belong to any of those cults. No Extropists. No oxymoronic libertarian socialists. Most of all, I don't want any connection with anybody— anybody human, anyway. That might get you some information others didn't have, but it's too risky. The most vocal ones make the most idiotic choices.

"Got anything working?" he asked.

"Making some phony archives," I said. "Mostly boring—famous places, New York City, Beijing. Last week somebody wanted an event set in Kansas City in the 1930s, and I just about kissed his hand."

Mossadegh flagged down a waiter and ordered a drink. Alcohol—he wasn't going to live forever, I can tell you that. "I know somebody who used to live in Kansas City."

"Really? Did he get out before, or when it happened?"

"Get this: he left one week—to the day—before."

"You're kidding," I said.

"Truth is truth."

As the afternoon declined we went on about nothing particularly important. Mossadegh rubbed his long jaw with his long fingers. "Say, you want to come to a party?"

"When?"

"Right now, brother! Maryam's been taking some grad classes and this rich prof's throwing a blowout."

"I'm not from the university," I said.

"But I am, and you come with me. Stout fellow like you's always welcome."

Mossadegh was no more from the university than I was, but I had nothing better to do. We caught a citicar up Elmwood. The setting sun reflecting off the windows of the houses turned them into gold mirrors. We passed a public building where somebody had plastered a video sign onto the side: "Go back to Arkansas . . . Or is it Kansas?"

The party was in a new neighborhood where they had torn out the old expressway, overlooking the park. It was twilight when we got there, a little chill in the air, but warm lights glowed along the street. The house looked old-fashioned on the outside, but the inside was all new. A big garden in the back. Sitting on the table in the living room they had a bowl of capsules, mood teas, bottles of champagne and a pyramid of glasses. I passed on the intoxicants and drank water.

The place was crowded with university students, artists, and various other knowledge workers. The prof who owned the place, dark and slender, wore all white; he held a champagne coupe in his hand, his palm around the bowl and the stem descending between his fingers in an affected way that made my teeth hurt. He had long, wavy dark hair. He was talking with two young women, nodding his head slightly as he listened. People sat in twos and threes, and there was a group in the sunroom talking politics. Lots of them seemed pretty lit.

All of these people were going to die while I stayed alive.

I stood at the edge of the political talk. A woman was speaking with emotion in her voice. "The people you can fool all of the time are dumber than pond scum, and it isn't exactly a matter of fooling them—they want to be fooled. They'll fight against anybody who tries to pull the scales from their eyes. The hopeless core of any politician's support."

She looked to be about thirty. She wore a loose white shirt and tight black pants and she spoke with an intensity that burned, as if what she said wasn't simply some liberal platitude. This college-undergrad cant mattered to her.

"But fooling all of the people has become harder. Any conflict of interest, hypocrisy, double-dealing, inconvenient truth gets out as soon as somebody with skills addresses finding it, and too many people have the skills. A politician's best bet is to throw sand into people's eyes, put enough distracting information out there that the truth will be buried. You can make a career as long as people are blinded by ideology or just can't think their way through your crap."

I didn't want to get into these weeds. I wasn't the kind of person they were. But she was right about ideological blindness, even if she didn't realize that it applied to her, too.

I thought about my last three days in the clinic. Four tumors they'd zapped out of me this time. Prospects were that cancer treatments would get better, and if they didn't I could go off telomerase life extension and try something else. But I had to admit that staring at the ceiling while the machines took care of something that in the old days would have killed me in three months was not pleasant. And there was nobody I could tell about it. Not anybody who would care, anyway.

The next time I passed through the living room, I poured myself a glass of the champagne. What the hell.

It tasted good, and unaccustomed as I was to alcohol, I got a little buzz on right away. For an hour I wandered through the house listening to snatches of conversation. I got another glass of wine. After a while I went out into the garden. It had cooled off considerably, and most of the people who had been out there were back inside now that it was full night. Balls of golden light shone in the tree branches. It was pretty.

Then I noticed somebody sitting on a bench in the corner of the garden. It was the woman who had been ranting in the sunroom. She ignored me. Leaning on one arm, wine glass beside her, she looked as if she were listening for some sound from a distant room in the house. I drifted over to her.

"Hello," I said.

She looked up. Just stared for a moment. "Hello."

"Sorry to interrupt," I said. "Do you live here?"

"No."

"Friends with somebody who does?"

"Salma is my sister. She's one of Ghosh's girlfriends."

"Who's Ghosh?"

She looked at me again and smiled. "This is Ghosh's house."

"Right. Do you mind if I sit?"

"Knock yourself out."

I sat down and set my glass next to hers on the bench. "Political, are you?"

"Politics is a waste," she said. "Like this thing in Cambridge yesterday— what are they trying to prove?" The anger I had heard in her voice earlier came back. "It's just killing for killing's sake. The things that need changing aren't going to be changed by blowing people up. It's in the heart and the head, and you can't change that with a hand grenade."

Maybe the wine was working in me, but I couldn't let that go.

"Lots of things are decided by hand grenades," I said. "Most things, in the end, are decided by force. Hell, politics is just another form of force. You figure out where the pressure points are, you manipulate the system, you make it necessary for the ones who oppose you to do what you want them to do. You marshal your forces, and then you get what you want."

She looked unconvinced. I liked the way her black hair, not too long, curled around her ear. "You're not from around here," she said. "The accent. You a real Canadian?"

"Alberta."

Her eyebrow raised. "An immigrant?"

"Technically, I guess. It's not like I wasn't born and raised in Canada."

"What's your name?"

"Scoobie." I could smell the scent of the soap she used.

"Esme," she said, holding out her hand. I shook it.

"So what do you think that bombing accomplished, Scoobie?"

"Not much. People don't even know who it was aimed at, and for what reason. No way was it some pro-immigration group. That's a false-flag move. The two guys they blew up aren't particularly influential. They have no power, not even symbolic power. They might as well have been hit by lightning."

"Sounds like you agree with me."

"If you think it was done stupidly, then I agree with you."

She looked down at her feet. She wore black canvas slippers. "I agree with you," she said. "It was done stupidly."

We sat in silence awhile. I picked up my glass and drained the last of my wine. Esme took up her own.

"So why did you emigrate?" she asked me.

"I came to Toronto for the work, at first. I have an interest in the medical professions. The big clinics, the university. Then it was McGill for a few years. Then I came here."

"Do you get any flak as an immigrant? Lots of people don't like them. Alberta is pretty hard right."

"I don't care about that. I guess you could say I'm apolitical. The differences between the Canadian government, Texas, and the Sunbelt states mean nothing to me. I suppose you could call me a libertarian—small 'l.' Certainly I'm for free information, but it all seems petty to me."

"Petty?" The edge came back into her voice.

"This is just a moment in history. Like all political debates, it will pass. What's important is keeping alive. You don't want to get caught between two crazy antagonists. Or get connected up with one side or the other."

"Do you seriously believe that?"

I don't know why I should have cared what she thought. Something about the way she held her shoulders, or the slight, husky rasp in her voice. It was the voice of somebody who had cried for a long time and was all cried out. She was arrogant, she was wrong, but she was very sexy.

I tried to make a joke. "Singularity's coming. All bets are off then."

"The Singularity is a fantasy."

I laughed. "What are you, a religious mystic?"

"I'm an architect."

"Then you ought to know the difference between the material world and fairyland. Is there something supernatural about the human brain? Is it animated by pixie dust?" I was feeling it now. Humanists, with their woo-woo belief in the uniqueness of the "mind."

"They've been talking about strong AI for eighty years. Where is it?'

"Processing power is still increasing. It's only a matter of time. It's just the architecture—"

Esme laughed. "Now you'll tell me about the architecture. Listen, no Jesus supercomputer is going to save you from the crises around us. You can't sit it out."

"I can and I will. This fighting between Canada and the Sunbelt is completely bound to this time and place. It doesn't matter. It's just history, like some war between the Catholics and Protestants in the 14th century."

"How can you say that! People are dying! The future of our society depends on what we do today. Immense things hang in the balance. The climate! Whole species! Ecosystems! Women's rights! Animal rights!"

"You know," I said, "you're hot when you get angry."

Her hand tightened on her glass. I could see the muscles in her forearm; her skin was so brown, so smooth. For a second I thought she was going smash the glass into my face, then she tossed it away and hurled herself onto me. She bit my neck. I fell over and hit my head on the trunk of a tree, went dizzy for a second. The grass was cool. She had her legs around my waist and we started kissing. Long, slow, very serious kisses.

After some time we surfaced for breath. Her eyes were so dark.

"There were no Protestants in the 14th century," she said.

Esme and Scoobie waited in a restaurant at the Toronto airport. Their flight for Krakow left in an hour. They were traveling light, just one small bag each—"getting out of Dodge," Teo called it—and Esme was persuaded. Scoobie knew somebody at the university there, and there was some clinic he wanted to visit.

Both of them were nervous. Neither was sure that this was a good idea, but it seemed like something they should do. At least that was where they were leaving it for now.

"Can I get you something from the bar?" Scoobie asked. "Something to eat?" For a person whose social skills were so rudimentary, he was quite sensitive to her moods.

"No," Esme said. "Maybe we should get to the gate."

Scoobie got up. "Gonna hit the men's room first."

"Okay."

For three days, since that moment in the garden, they had spent every minute together. Inexplicably. He was a cranky naïve libertarian child, afraid of human contact. His politics were ludicrous. But politics—what had politics ever given her besides migraines? Scoobie was so glad to be with her, as if he'd never been with anyone before. Their disagreements only made her see his vulnerabilities more clearly. He had some terribly stupid ideas, but he was not malicious, and he gave her something she needed. She wouldn't call it love— not yet. Call it consolation.

It didn't hurt that on no notice whatsoever he'd managed to get her the subtle tattooing that could deceive facial-recognition software. Teo had produced credentials for them as husband and wife, and their friends had created a false background for them in government databases. They had a shot at getting out of the country.

Up on one of the restaurant screens a news reader announced, "Authorities offer no new information in the hunt for the woman who threw an explosive device into the Cambridge, Massachusetts, office of Lester Makovec, consultant to the New England provincial government's Bureau of Immigration."

The screen switched to scenes of the aftermath of the Cambridge blast: a street view of broken windows, EMTs loading a body zipped into a cryobag into their vehicle.

"But there's an amazing new wrinkle to the story: Makovec, pronounced dead at the scene, was rushed to Harvard Medical School's Humanity Lab, where he underwent an experimental regenerative treatment and is reported to be on the way to recovery." Image of a hospital bed with a heavily bandaged Makovec practicing using an artificial hand to pick up small objects from the table in front of him. The chyron at the bottom of the screen read, "Lifesaving Miracle?"

"Accused terrorist and illegal immigrant Andrew Wayne Spiller, a.k.a. James Alter, who escaped the blast with minor injuries, has been moved to Ottawa to undergo further interrogation." Image of Spiller, surrounded by security in black armor, being escorted into a train car.

"Meanwhile, Rosario Zhang, opposition leader, has called on Prime Minister Nguyen to say what she intends to do to deal with the unprovoked attack by what Zhang calls 'agents of the Texas government.' The prime minister's office has said that the forensic report has not yet determined the perpetrators of the attack, nor, in the light of denials from the Refugee Liberation Front, have investigators been able to verify the authenticity of the video claiming credit for that group."

Across the concourse stood an airport security officer in black, arms crossed over his chest, talking with an Ontario Provincial Police officer. The airport cop rocked back on his heels, eyes hooded, while the OPP spoke to him. The airport cop had a big rust-colored mustache; the OPP wore his black cap with the gray band around it.

The airport security man turned his head a fraction to his right, and he was looking, from ten meters away, directly into Esme's eyes. She had to fight the impulse to look away. She smiled at him. He smiled back. Esme considered getting up and moving to the gate—she considered leaping out of the chair to run screaming—yet she held herself still.

It took forever, but finally Scoobie returned.

"Time to go?" he said. He looked so cheerful. He was oblivious to the cops.

She kissed him on the cheek. "Yes, please," she said.

They slung their bags over their shoulders, she put her arm through his, and they headed for the gate.

THE HEART'S FILTHY LESSON

ELIZABETH BEAR

⋯⊶✦⊷⋯

The sun burned through the clouds around noon on the long Cytherean day, and Dharthi happened to be awake and in a position to see it. She was alone in the highlands of Ishtar Terra on a research trip, five sleeps out from Butler base camp, and—despite the nagging desire to keep traveling—had decided to take a rest break for an hour or two. Noon at this latitude was close enough to the one hundredth solar dieiversary of her birth that she'd broken out her little hoard of shelf-stable cake to celebrate. The prehensile fingers and leaping legs of her bioreactor-printed, skin-bonded adaptshell made it simple enough to swarm up one of the tall, gracile pseudo-figs and creep along its gray smooth branches until the ceaseless Venusian rain dripped directly on her adaptshell's slick-furred head.

It was safer in the treetops, if you were sitting still. Nothing big enough to want to eat her was likely to climb up this far. The grues didn't come out until nightfall, but there were swamp-tigers, damnthings, and velociraptors to worry about. The forest was too thick for predators any bigger than that, but a swarm of scorpion-rats was no joke. And Venus had only been settled for three hundred days, and most of that devoted to Aphrodite Terra; there was still plenty of undiscovered monsters out here in the wilderness.

The water did not bother Dharthi, nor did the dip and sway of the branch in the wind. Her adaptshell was beautifully tailored to this terrain, and that fur shed water like the hydrophobic miracle of engineering that it was. The fur was a glossy, iridescent purple that qualified as black in most lights, to match the foliage that dripped rain like strings of glass beads from the multiple points of palmate leaves. Red-black, to make the most of the rainy grey light. They'd fold their leaves up tight and go dormant when night came.

Dharthi had been born with a chromosomal abnormality that produced red-green colorblindness. She'd been about ten solar days old when they'd done the gene therapy to fix it, and she just about remembered her first glimpses of the true, saturated colors of Venus. She'd seen it first as if it were Earth: washed out and faded.

For now, however, they were alive with the scurryings and chitterings of a few hundred different species of Cytherean canopy-dwellers. And the quiet, nearly-contented sound of Dharthi munching on cake. She would not dwell; she would not stew. She would look at all this natural majesty, and try to spot the places where an unnaturally geometric line or angle showed in the topography of the canopy.

From here, she could stare up the enormous sweep of Maxwell Montes to the north, its heights forested to the top in Venus' deep, rich atmosphere—but the sight of them lost for most of its reach in clouds. Dharthi could only glimpse the escarpment at all because she was on the "dry" side. Maxwell Montes scraped the heavens, kicking the cloud layer up as if it had struck an aileron, so the "wet" side got the balance of the rain. *Balance* in this case meaning that the mountains on the windward side were scoured down to granite, and a nonadapted terrestrial organism had better bring breathing gear.

But here in the lee, the forest flourished, and on a clear hour from a height, visibility might reach a couple of klicks or more.

Dharthi took another bite of cake—it might have been "chocolate;" it was definitely caffeinated, because she was picking up the hit on her blood monitors already—and turned herself around on her branch to face downslope. The sky was definitely brighter, the rain falling back to a drizzle and then a mist, and the clouds were peeling back along an arrowhead trail that led directly back to the peak above her. A watery golden smudge brightened one patch of clouds. They tore and she glimpsed the full unguarded brilliance of the daystar, just hanging there in a chip of glossy cerulean sky, the clouds all around it smeared with thick unbelievable rainbows. Waves of mist rolled and slid among the leaves of the canopy, made golden by the shimmering unreal light.

Dharthi was glad she was wearing the shell. It played the sun's warmth through to her skin without also relaying the risks of ultraviolet exposure. She ought to be careful of her eyes, however: a crystalline shield protected them, but its filters weren't designed for naked light.

The forest noises rose to a cacophony. It was the third time in Dharthi's one hundred solar days of life that she had glimpsed the sun. Even here, she imagined that some of these animals would never have seen it before.

She decided to accept it as a good omen for her journey. Sadly, there was no way to spin the next thing that happened that way.

"Hey," said a voice in her head. "Good cake."

"That proves your pan is malfunctioning, if anything does," Dharthi replied sourly. *Never accept a remote synaptic link with a romantic and professional partner. No matter how convenient it seems at the time, and in the field.*

*Because someday they might be a romantic and professional partner you
really would rather not talk to right now.*

"I heard that."

"What do you want, Kraken?"

Dharthi imagined Kraken smiling, and wished she hadn't. She could hear
it in her partner's "voice" when she spoke again, anyway. "Just to wish you a
happy dieiversary."

"Aw," Dharthi said. "Aren't you sweet. Noblesse oblige?"

"Maybe," Kraken said tiredly, "I actually care?"

"Mmm," Dharthi said. "What's the ulterior motive this time?"

Kraken sighed. It was more a neural flutter than a heave of breath, but
Dharthi got the point all right. "Maybe I actually *care*."

"Sure," Dharthi said. "Every so often you have to glance down from Mount
Olympus and check up on the lesser beings."

"Olympus is on Mars," Kraken said.

It didn't make Dharthi laugh, because she clenched her right fist hard
enough that, even though the cushioning adaptshell squished against her
palm, she still squeezed the blood out of her fingers. *You and all your charm.
You don't get to charm me any more.*

"Look," Kraken said. "You have something to prove. I understand that."

"How can you *possibly* understand that? When was the last time you were
turned down for a resource allocation? Doctor youngest-ever recipient of the
Cytherean Award for Excellence in Xenoarcheology? Doctor Founding Field-
Martius Chair of Archaeology at the University on Aphrodite?"

"The University on Aphrodite," Kraken said, "is five Quonset huts and a
repurposed colonial landing module."

"It's what we've got."

"I peaked early," Kraken said, after a pause. "I was never your *rival*,
Dharthi. We were colleagues." Too late, in Dharthi's silence, she realized her
mistake. "*Are* colleagues."

"You look up from your work often enough to notice I'm missing?"

There was a pause. "That may be fair," Kraken said at last. "But if being
professionally focused—"

"*Obsessed.*"

"—is a failing, it was hardly a failing limited to me. Come *back*. Come
back to *me*. We'll talk about it. I'll help you try for a resource voucher again
tomorrow."

"I don't want your damned *help*, Kraken!"

The forest around Dharthi fell silent. Shocked, she realized she'd shouted
out loud.

"Haring off across Ishtar alone, with no support—you're not going to prove your theory about aboriginal Cytherean settlement patterns, Dhar. You're going to get eaten by a grue."

"I'll be home by dark," Dharthi said. "Anyway, if I'm not—all the better for the grue."

"You know who else was always on about being laughed out of the Academy?" Kraken said. Her voice had that teasing tone that could break Dharthi's worst, most self-loathing, prickliest mood—if she let it. "Moriarty."

I will not laugh. Fuck you.

Dharthi couldn't tell if Kraken had picked it up or not. There was a silence, as if she were controlling her temper or waiting for Dharthi to speak.

"If you get killed," Kraken said, "make a note in your file that I can use your DNA. You're not getting out of giving me children that easily."

Ha ha, Dharthi thought. *Only serious.* She couldn't think of what to say, and so she said nothing. The idea of a little Kraken filled her up with mushy softness inside. But somebody's career would go on hold for the first fifty solar days of that kid's life, and Dharthi was pretty sure it wouldn't be Kraken.

She couldn't think of what to say in response, and the silence got heavy until Kraken said, "Dammit. I'm *worried* about you."

"Worry about yourself." Dharthi couldn't break the connection, but she could bloody well shut down her end of the dialogue. And she could refuse to hear.

She pitched the remains of the cake as far across the canopy as she could, then regretted it. Hopefully nothing Cytherean would try to eat it; it might give the local biology a belly ache.

It was ironically inevitable that Dharthi, named by her parents in a fit of homesickness for Terra, would grow up to be the most Cytherean of Cythereans. She took great pride in her adaptation, in her ability to rough it. Some of the indigenous plants and many of the indigenous animals could be eaten, and Dharthi knew which ones. She also knew, more importantly, which ones were likely to eat her.

She hadn't mastered humans nearly as well. Dharthi wasn't good at politics. *Unlike Kraken.* Dharthi wasn't good at making friends. *Unlike Kraken.* Dharthi wasn't charming or beautiful or popular or brilliant. *Unlike Kraken, Kraken, Kraken.*

Kraken was a better scientist, or at least a better-understood one. Kraken was a better person, probably. More generous, less prickly, certainly. But there was one thing Dharthi *was* good at. Better at than Kraken. Better at than anyone. Dharthi was good at living on Venus, at being Cytherean. She was more comfortable in and proficient with an adaptshell than anyone she had ever met.

In fact, it was peeling the shell off that came hard. So much easier to glide through the jungle or the swamp like something that belonged there, wearing a quasibiologic suit of super-powered armor bonded to your neural network and your skin. The human inside was a soft, fragile, fleshy thing, subject to complicated feelings and social dynamics, and Dharthi despised her. But that same human, while bonded to the shell, ghosted through the rain forest like a native, and saw things no one else ever had.

A kilometer from where she had stopped for cake, she picked up the trail of a velociraptor. It was going in the right direction, so she tracked it. It wasn't a real velociraptor; it wasn't even a dinosaur. Those were Terran creatures, albeit extinct; this was a Cytherean meat-eating monster that bore a superficial resemblance. Like the majority of Cytherean vertebrates, it had six limbs, though it ran balanced on the rear ones and the two forward pairs had evolved into little more than graspers. Four eyes were spaced equidistantly around the dome of its skull, giving it a dome of monocular vision punctuated by narrow slices of depth perception. The business end of the thing was delineated by a sawtoothed maw that split wide enough to bite a human being in half. The whole of it was camouflaged with long draggled fur-feathers that grew thick with near-black algae, or the Cytherean cognate.

Dharthi followed the velociraptor for over two kilometers, and the beast never even noticed she was there. She smiled inside her adaptshell. Kraken was right: going out into the jungle alone and unsupported would be suicide for most people. But wasn't it like her not to give Dharthi credit for this one single thing that Dharthi could do better than anyone?

She *knew* that the main Cytherean settlements had been on Ishtar Terra. Knew it in her bones. And she was going to prove it, whether anybody was willing to give her an allocation for the study or not.

They'll be sorry, she thought, and had to smile at her own adolescent petulance. *They're rush to support me once this is done.*

The not-a-dinosaur finally veered off to the left. Dharthi kept jogging/ swinging/swimming/splashing/climbing forward, letting the shell do most of the work. The highlands leveled out into the great plateau the new settlers called the Lakshmi Planum. No one knew what the aboriginals had called it. They'd been gone for—to an approximation—ten thousand years: as long as it had taken humankind to get from the Neolithic (Agriculture, stone tools) to jogging through the jungles of alien world wearing a suit of power armor engineered from printed muscle fiber and cheetah DNA.

Lakshmi Planum, ringed with mountains on four sides, was one of the few places on the surface of Venus where you could not see an ocean. The major Cytherean land masses, Aphrodite and Ishtar, were smaller than South America. The surface of this world was 85% water—water less salty than Earth's oceans, because there was less surface to leach minerals into it through runoff. And the Lakshmi Planum was tectonically active, with great volcanoes and living faults.

That activity was one of the reasons Dharthi's research had brought her here.

The jungle of the central Ishtarean plateau was not as creeper-clogged and vine-throttled as Dharthi might have expected. It was a mature climax forest, and the majority of the biomass hung suspended over Dharthi's head, great limbs stretching up umbrellalike to the limited light. Up there, the branches and trunks were festooned with symbiotes, parasites, and commensal organisms. Down here among the trunks, it was dark and still except for the squish of loam underfoot and the ceaseless patter of what rain came through the leaves.

Dharthi stayed alert, but didn't spot any more large predators on that leg of the journey. There were flickers and scuttlers and flyers galore, species she was sure nobody had named or described. Perhaps on the way back she'd have time to do more, but for now she contented herself with extensive video archives. It wouldn't hurt to cultivate some good karma with Bio while she was out here. She might need a job sweeping up offices when she got back.

Stop. Failure is not an option. Not even a possibility.

Like all such glib sentiments, it didn't make much of a dent in the bleakness of her mood. Even walking, observing, surveying, she had entirely too much time to think.

She waded through two more swamps and scaled a basalt ridge—one of the stretching roots of the vast volcano named Sacajawea. Nearly everything on Venus was named after female persons—historical, literary, or mythological—from Terra, from the quaint old system of binary and exclusive genders. For a moment, Dharthi considered such medieval horrors as dentistry without anesthetic, binary gender, and as being stuck forever in the body you were born in, locked in and struggling against what your genes dictated. The trap of biology appalled her; she found it impossible to comprehend how people in the olden days had gotten anything done, with their painfully short lives and their limited access to resources, education, and technology.

The adaptshell stumbled over a tree root, forcing her attention back to the landscape. Of course, modern technology wasn't exactly perfect either. The suit needed carbohydrate to keep moving, and protein to repair muscle tissue. Fortunately, it wasn't picky about its food source—and Dharthi herself needed rest. The day was long, and only half over. She wouldn't prove herself if she got so tired she got herself eaten by a megaspider.

We haven't conquered all those human frailties yet.

Sleepily, she climbed a big tree, one that broke the canopy, and slung a hammock high in branches that dripped with fleshy, gorgeous, thickly scented parasitic blossoms, opportunistically decking every limb up here where the light was stronger. They shone bright whites and yellows, mostly, set off against the dark, glossy foliage. Dharthi set proximity sensors, established a tech perimeter above and below, and unsealed the shell before sending it down to forage for the sorts of simple biomass that sustained it. It would be happy with the mulch of the forest floor, and she could call it back when she needed it. Dharthi rolled herself into the hammock as if it were a scentproof, claw-proof cocoon and tried to sleep.

Rest eluded. The leaves and the cocoon filtered the sunlight, so it was pleasantly dim, and the cocoon kept the water off except what she'd brought inside with herself when she wrapped up. She was warm and well-supported. But that all did very little to alleviate her anxiety.

She didn't know exactly where she was going. She was flying blind—hah, she *wished* she were flying. If she'd had the allocations for an aerial survey, this would all be a lot easier, assuming they could pick anything out through the jungle—and operating on a hunch. An educated hunch.

But one that Kraken and her other colleagues—and more importantly, the Board of Allocation—thought was at best a wild guess and at worst crackpottery.

What if you're wrong?

If she was wrong . . . well. She didn't have much to go home to. So she'd better be right that the settlements they'd found on Aphrodite were merely outposts, and that the aboriginal Cythereans had stuck much closer to the North pole. She had realized that the remains—such as they were—of Cytherean settlements clustered in geologically active areas. She theorized that they used geothermal energy, or perhaps had some other unknown purpose for staying there. In any case, Ishtar was far younger, far more geologically active than Aphrodite, as attested by its upthrust granite ranges and its scattering of massive volcanoes. Aphrodite—larger, calmer, safer—had drawn the Terran settlers. Dharthi theorized that Ishtar had been the foundation of Cytherean culture for exactly the opposite reasons.

She hoped that if she found a big settlement—the remains of one of their cities—she could prove this. And possibly even produce some clue as to what had happened to them all.

It wouldn't be easy. A city buried under ten thousand years of sediment and jungle could go unnoticed even by an archaeologist's trained eye and the most perspicacious modern mapping and visualization technology. And of course she had to be in the right place, and all she had to go on there were guesses—deductions, if she was feeling kind to herself, which she rarely was—

about the patterns of relationships between those geologically active areas on Aphrodite and the aboriginal settlements nearby.

This is stupid. You'll never find anything without support and an allocation. Kraken never would have pushed her luck this way.

Kraken never would have needed to. Dharthi knew better than anyone how much effort and dedication and scholarship went into Kraken's work—but still, it sometimes seemed as if fantastic opportunities just fell into her lover's lap without effort. And Kraken's intellect and charisma were so dazzling . . . it was hard to see past that to the amount of study it took to support that seemingly effortless, comprehensive knowledge of just about everything.

Nothing made Dharthi feel the limitations of her own ability like spending time with her lover. Hell, Kraken probably would have known which of the animals she was spotting as she ran were new species, and the names and describers of all the known ones.

If she could have this, Dharthi thought, just this—if she could do one thing to equal all of Kraken's effortless successes—then she could tolerate how perfect Kraken was the rest of the time.

This line of thought wasn't helping the anxiety. She thrashed in the cocoon for another half-hour before she finally gave in and took a sedative. Not safe, out in the jungle. But if she didn't rest, she couldn't run—and even the Cytherean daylight wasn't actually endless.

Dharthi awakened to an animal sniffing her cocoon with great whuffing predatory breaths. An atavistic response, something from the brainstem, froze her in place even as it awakened her. Her arms and legs—naked, so fragile without her skin—felt heavy, numb, limp as if they had fallen asleep. The shadow of the thing's head darkened the translucent steelsilk as it passed between Dharthi and the sky. The drumming of the rain stopped, momentarily. Hard to tell how big it was, from that—but big, she thought. An estimation confirmed when it nosed or pawed the side of the cocoon and she felt a broad blunt object as big as her two hands together prod her in the ribs.

She held her breath, and it withdrew. There was the rain, tapping on her cocoon where it dripped between the leaves. She was almost ready to breathe out again when it made a sound—a thick chugging noise followed by a sort of roar that had more in common with trains and waterfalls than what most people would identify as an animal sound.

Dharthi swallowed her scream. She didn't need Kraken to tell her what *that* was. Every schoolchild could manage a piping reproduction of the call of one of Venus's nastiest pieces of charismatic megafauna, the Cytherean swamp-tiger.

Swamp-tigers were two lies, six taloned legs, and an indiscriminate number of enormous daggerlike teeth in a four hundred kilogram body. Two lies, because they didn't live in swamps—though they passed through them on occasion, because what on Venus didn't?—and they weren't tigers. But they *were* striped violet and jade green to disappear into the thick jungle foliage; they had long, slinky bodies that twisted around sharp turns and barreled up tree trunks without any need to decelerate; and their whisker-ringed mouths hinged open wide enough to bite a grown person in half.

All four of the swamp-tiger's bright blue eyes were directed forward. Because it didn't hurt their hunting, and what creature in its right mind would want to sneak up on a thing like that?

They weren't supposed to hunt this high up. The branches were supposed to be too slender to support them.

Dharthi wasn't looking forward to getting a better look at this one. It nudged the cocoon again. Despite herself, Dharthi went rigid. She pressed both fists against her chest and concentrated on not whimpering, on not making a single sound. She forced herself to breathe slowly and evenly. To consider. *Panic gets you eaten.*

She wouldn't give Kraken the damned satisfaction.

She had some resources. The cocoon would attenuate her scent, and might disguise it almost entirely. The adaptshell was somewhere in the vicinity, munching away, and if she could make it into *that*, she stood a chance of outrunning the thing. She weighed a quarter what the swamp-tiger did; she could get up higher into the treetops than it could. Theoretically; after all, it wasn't supposed to come up this high.

And she was, at least presumptively, somewhat smarter.

But it could outjump her, outrun her, outsneak her, and—perhaps most importantly—outchomp her.

She wasted a few moments worrying about how it had gotten past her perimeter before the sharp pressure of its claws skidding down the rip-proof surface of the cocoon refocused her attention. That was a temporary protection; it might not be able to pierce the cocoon, but it could certainly squash Dharthi to death inside of it, or rip it out of the tree and toss it to the jungle floor. If the fall didn't kill her, she'd have the cheerful and humiliating choice of yelling for rescue or wandering around injured until something bigger ate her. She needed a way out; she needed to channel five million years of successful primate adaptation, the legacy of clever monkey ancestors, and figure out how to get away from the not-exactly-cat.

What would a monkey do? The question was the answer, she realized.

She just needed the courage to apply it. And the luck to survive whatever then transpired.

The cocoon was waterproof as well as claw-proof—hydrophobic on the outside, a wicking polymer on the inside. The whole system was impregnated with an engineered bacteria that broke down the waste products in human sweat—or other fluids—and returned them to the environment as safe, nearly odorless, non-polluting water, salts, and a few trace chemicals. Dharthi was going to have to unfasten the damn thing.

She waited while the swamp-tiger prodded her again. It seemed to have a pattern of investigating and withdrawing—Dharthi heard the rustle and felt the thump and sway as it leaped from branch to branch, circling, making a few horrifically unsettling noises and a bloodcurdling snarl or two, and coming back for another go at the cocoon. The discipline required to hold herself still—not even merely still, but limp—as the creature whuffed and poked left her nauseated with adrenaline. She felt it moving away, then. The swing of branches under its weight did nothing to ease the roiling in her gut.

Now or never.

Shell! Come and get me! Then she palmed the cocoon's seal and whipped it open, left hand and foot shoved through internal grips so she didn't accidentally evert herself into free fall. As she swung, she shook a heavy patter of water drops loose from the folds of the cocoon's hydrophobic surface. They pattered down. There were a lot of branches between her and the ground; she didn't fancy making the intimate acquaintanceship of each and every one of them.

The swamp-tiger hadn't gone as far as she expected. In fact, it was on the branch just under hers. As it whipped its head around and roared, she had an eloquent view from above—a clear shot down its black-violet gullet. The mouth hinged wide enough to bite her in half across the middle; the tongue was thick and fleshy; the palate ribbed and mottled in paler shades of red. *If I live through this, I will be able to draw every one of those seventy-two perfectly white teeth from memory.*

She grabbed the safety handle with her right hand as well, heaved with her hips, and flipped the cocoon over so her legs swung free. For a moment, she dangled just above the swamp-tiger. It reared back on its heavy haunches like a startled cat, long tail lashing around to protect its abdomen. Dharthi knew that as soon as it collected its wits it was going to take a swipe at her, possibly with both sets of forelegs.

It was small for a swamp-tiger—perhaps only two hundred kilos—and its stripes were quite a bit brighter than she would have expected. Even wet, its feathery plumage had the unfinished raggedness she associated with young animals still in their baby coats. It might even have been fuzzy, if it were ever properly dry. Which might explain why it was so high up in the treetops. Previously undocumented behavior in a juvenile animal.

Wouldn't it be an irony if this were the next in a long line of xenobiological discoveries temporarily undiscovered again because a scientist happened to get herself eaten? At least she had a transponder. And maybe the shell was nearby enough to record some of this.

Data might survive.

Great, she thought. *I wonder where its mama is.*

Then she urinated in its face.

It wasn't an aimed stream by any means, though she was wearing the external plumbing currently—easier in the field, until you got a bladder stone. But she had a bladder full of pee saved up during sleep, so there was plenty of it. It splashed down her legs and over the swamp-tiger's face, and Dharthi didn't care what your biology was, if you were carbon-oxygen based, a snout full of ammonia and urea had to be pretty nasty.

The swamp-tiger backed away, cringing. If it had been a human being, Dharthi would have said it was spluttering. She didn't take too much time to watch; good a story as it would make someday, it would always be a better one than otherwise if she survived to tell it. She pumped her legs for momentum, glad that the sweat-wicking properties of the cocoon's lining kept the grip dry, because right now her palms weren't doing any of that work themselves. Kick high, a twist from the core, and she had one leg over the cocoon. It was dry—she'd shaken off what little water it had collected. Dharthi pulled her feet up—standing on the stuff was like standing on a slack sail, and she was glad that some biotuning trained up by the time she spent running the canopy had given her the balance of a perching bird.

Behind and below, she heard the Cytherean monster make a sound like a kettle boiling over—one part whistle, and one part hiss. She imagined claws in her haunches, a crushing bite to the skull or the nape—

The next branch up was a half-meter beyond her reach. Her balance on her toes, she jumped as hard as she could off the yielding surface under her bare feet. Her left hand missed; the right hooked a limb but did not close. She dangled sideways for a moment, the stretch across her shoulder strong and almost pleasant. Her fingers locked in the claw position, she flexed her bicep—not a pull up, she couldn't chin herself one-handed—but just enough to let her left hand latch securely. A parasitic orchid squashed beneath the pads of her fingers. A dying bug wriggled. Caustic sap burned her skin. She swung, and managed to hang on.

She wanted to dangle for a moment, panting and shaking and gathering herself for the next ridiculous effort. But beneath her, the rattle of leaves, the creak of a bough. The not-tiger was coming.

Climb. Climb!

She had to get high. She had to get further out from the trunk, onto branches where it would not pursue her. She had to stay alive until the shell got to her. Then she could run or fight as necessary.

Survival was starting to seem like less of a pipe dream now.

She swung herself up again, risking a glance through her armpit as she mantled herself up onto the bough. It dipped and twisted under her weight. Below, the swamp-tiger paced, snarled, reared back and took a great, outraged swing up at her cocoon with its two left-side forepaws.

The fabric held. The branches it was slung between did not. They cracked and swung down, crashing on the boughs below and missing the swamp-tiger only because the Cytherean cat had reflexes preternaturally adapted to life in the trees. It still came very close to being knocked off its balance, and Dharthi took advantage of its distraction to scramble higher, careful to remember not to wipe her itching palms on the more sensitive flesh of her thighs.

Another logic problem presented itself. The closer she got to the trunk, the higher she could scramble, and the faster the adaptshell could get to her—but the swamp-tiger was less likely to follow her out on the thinner ends of the boughs. She was still moving as she decided that she'd go up a bit more first, and move diagonally—up *and* out, until "up" was no longer an option.

She made two more branches before hearing the rustle of the swamp-tiger leaping upwards behind her. She'd instinctively made a good choice in climbing away from it rather than descending, she realized—laterally or down, there was no telling how far the thing could leap. Going up, on unsteady branches, it was limited to shorter hops. Shorter . . . but much longer than Dharthi's. Now the choice was made for her—out, before it caught up, or get eaten. At least the wet of the leaves and the rain were washing the irritant sap from her palms.

She hauled her feet up again and gathered herself to stand and sprint down the center stem of this bough, a perilous highway no wider than her palm. When she raised her eyes, though, she found herself looking straight into the four bright, curious blue eyes of a second swamp-tiger.

"Aw, crud," Dharthi said. "Didn't anyone tell you guys you're supposed to be solitary predators?"

It looked about the same age and size and fluffiness as the other one. Littermates? Littermates of some Terran species hunted together until they reached maturity. That was probably the answer, and there was another groundbreaking bit of Cytherean biology that would go into a swamp-tiger's belly with Dharthi's masticated brains. Maybe she'd have enough time to relay the information to Kraken while they were disemboweling her.

The swamp-tiger lifted its anterior right forefoot and dabbed experimentally at Dharthi. Dharthi drew back her lips and *hissed* at it, and it pulled the leg back and contemplated her, but it didn't put the paw down. The next swipe would be for keeps.

She could call Kraken now, of course. But that would just be a distraction, not help. *Help* had the potential to arrive in time.

The idea of telling Kraken—and *everybody*—how she had gotten out of a confrontation with *two* of Venus's most impressive predators put a new rush of strength in her trembling legs. They were juveniles. They were inexperienced. They lacked confidence in their abilities, and they did not know how to estimate hers.

Wild predators had no interest in fighting anything to the death. They were out for a meal.

Dharthi stood up on her refirming knees, screamed in the swamp-tiger's face, and punched it as hard as she could, right in the nose.

She almost knocked herself out of the damned tree, and only her windmilling left hand snatching at twigs hauled her upright again and saved her. The swamp-tiger had crouched back, face wrinkled up in distaste or discomfort. The other one was coming up behind her.

Dharthi turned on the ball of her foot and sprinted for the end of the bough. Ten meters, fifteen, and it trembled and curved down sharply under her weight. There was still a lot of forest giant left above her, but this bough was arching now until it almost touched the one below. It moved in the wind, and with every breath. It creaked and made fragile little crackling noises.

A few more meters, and it might bend down far enough that she could reach the branch below.

A few more meters, and it might crack and drop.

It probably wouldn't pull free of the tree entirely—fresh Cytherean "wood" was fibrous and full of sap—but it might dump her off pretty handily.

She took a deep breath—clean air, rain, deep sweetness of flowers, herby scents of crushed leaves—and turned again to face the tigers.

They were still where she had left them, crouched close to the trunk of the tree, tails lashing as they stared balefully after her out of eight gleaming cerulean eyes. Their fanged heads were sunk low between bladelike shoulders. Their lips curled over teeth as big as fingers.

"Nice kitties," Dharthi said ineffectually. "Why don't you two just scamper on home? I bet mama has a nice bit of grue for supper."

The one she had peed on snarled at her. She supposed she couldn't blame it. She edged a little further away on the branch.

A rustling below. *Now that's just ridiculous.*

But it wasn't a third swamp-tiger. She glanced down and glimpsed an anthropoid shape clambering up through the branches fifty meters below, mostly hidden in foliage but moving with a peculiar empty lightness. The shell. Coming for her.

The urge to speed up the process, to try to climb down to it was almost unbearable, but Dharthi made herself sit tight. One of the tigers—the one she'd punched—rose up on six padded legs and slunk forward. It made a half dozen steps before the branch's increasing droop and the cracking, creaking sounds made it freeze. It was close enough now that she could make out the pattern of its damp, feathery whiskers. Dharthi braced her bare feet under tributary limbs and tried not to hunker down; swamp-tigers were supposed to go for crouching prey, and standing up and being big was supposed to discourage them. She spread her arms and rode the sway of the wind, the sway of the limb.

Her adaptshell heaved itself up behind her while the tigers watched. Her arms were already spread wide, her legs braced. The shell just cozied up behind her and squelched over her outstretched limbs, snuggling up and tightening down. It affected her balance, though, and the wobbling of the branch—

She crouched fast and grabbed at a convenient limb. And that was more than tiger number two could bear.

From a standing start, still halfway down the branch, the tiger gathered itself, hindquarters twitching. It leaped, and Dharthi had just enough time to try to throw herself flat under its arc. Enough time to try, but not quite enough time to succeed.

One of the swamp-tiger's second rank of legs caught her right arm like the swing of a baseball bat. Because she had dodged, it was her arm and not her head. The force of the blow still sent Dharthi sliding over the side of the limb, clutching and failing to clutch, falling in her adaptshell. She heard the swamp-tiger land where he had been, heard the bough crack, saw it give and swing down after her. The swamp-tiger squalled, scrabbling, its littermate making abrupt noises of retreat as well—and it was falling beside Dharthi, twisting in midair, clutching a nearby branch and there was a heaving unhappy sound from the tree's structure and then she fell alone, arm numb, head spinning.

The adaptshell saved her. It, too, twisted in midair, righted itself, reached out and grasped with her good arm. This branch held, but it bent, and she slammed into the next branch down, taking the impact on the same arm the tiger had injured. She didn't know for a moment if that green sound was a branch breaking or her—and then she did know, because inside the shell she could feel how her right arm hung limp, meaty, flaccid—humerus shattered.

She was dangling right beside her cocoon, as it happened. She used the folds of cloth to pull herself closer to the trunk, then commanded it to detach and retract. She found one of the proximity alarms and discovered that the damp had gotten into it. It didn't register her presence, either.

Venus.

She was stowing it one-handed in one of the shell's cargo pockets, warily watching for the return of either tiger, when the voice burst into her head.

"Dhar!"

"Don't worry," she told Kraken. "Just hurt my arm getting away from a swamp-tiger. Everything's fine."

"Hurt or broke? Wait, *swamp-tiger?*"

"It's gone now. I scared it off." She wasn't sure, but she wasn't about to admit that. "Tell Zamin the juveniles hunt in pairs."

"A *pair* of swamp-tigers?!"

"I'm fine," Dharthi said, and clamped down the link.

She climbed down one-handed, relying on the shell more than she would have liked. She did not see either tiger again.

At the bottom, on the jungle floor, she limped, but she ran.

Four runs and four sleeps later—the sleeps broken, confused spirals of exhaustion broken by fractured snatches of rest—the brightest patch of pewter in the sky had shifted visibly to the east. Noon had become afternoon, and the long Cytherean day was becoming Dharthi's enemy. She climbed trees regularly to look for signs of geometrical shapes informing the growth of the forest, and every time she did, she glanced at that brighter smear of cloud sliding down the sky and frowned.

Dharthi—assisted by her adaptshell—had come some five hundred kilometers westward. Maxwell Montes was lost behind her now, in cloud and mist and haze and behind the shoulder of the world. She was moving fast for someone creeping, climbing, and swinging through the jungle, although she was losing time because she hadn't turned the adaptshell loose to forage on its own since the swamp-tiger. She needed it to support and knit her arm—the shell fused to itself across the front and made a seamless cast and sling—and for the pain suppressants it fed her along with its pre-chewed pap. The bones were going to knit all wrong, of course, and when she got back, they'd have to grow her a new one, but that was pretty minor stuff.

The shell filtered toxins and allergens out of the biologicals it ingested, reherving some of the carbohydrates, protein, and fat to produce a bland, faintly sweet, nutrient-rich paste that was safe for Dharthi's consumption. She sucked it from a tube as needed, squashing it between tongue and palate to soften it before swallowing each sticky, dull mouthful.

Water was never a problem—at least, the problem was having too much of it, not any lack. This was *Venus*. Water squelched in every footstep across the jungle floor. It splashed on the adaptshell's head and infiltrated every cargo pocket. The only things that stayed dry were the ones that were treated to be hydrophobic, and the coating was starting to wear off some of those. Dharthi's cocoon was permanently damp inside. Even her shell, which molded her skin perfectly, felt alternately muggy or clammy depending on how it was comping temperature.

The adaptshell also filtered some of the fatigue toxins out of Dharthi's system. But not enough. Sleep was sleep, and she wasn't getting enough of it.

The landscape was becoming dreamy and strange. The forest never thinned, never gave way to another landscape—except the occasional swath of swampland—but now, occasionally, twisted fumaroles rose up through it, smoking towers of orange and ochre that sent wisps of steam drifting between scalded yellowed leaves. Dharthi saw one of the geysers erupt; she noticed that over it, and where the spray would tend to blow, there was a hole in the canopy. But vines grew right up the knobby accreted limestone on the windward side.

Five runs and five . . . five *attempts* at a sleep later, Dharthi began to accept that she desperately, *desperately* wanted to go home.

She wouldn't, of course.

Her arm hurt less. That was a positive thing. Other than that, she was exhausted and damp and cold and some kind of thick liver-colored leech kept trying to attach itself to the adaptshell's legs. A species new to science, probably, and Dharthi didn't give a damn.

Kraken tried to contact her every few hours.

She didn't answer, because she knew if she did, she would ask Kraken to come and get her. And then she'd never be able to look another living Cytherean in the face again.

It wasn't like Venus had a big population.

Dharthi was going to prove herself or die trying.

The satlink from Zamin, though, she took at once. They chatted about swamp-tigers—Zamin, predictably, was fascinated, and told Dharthi she'd write it up and give full credit to Dharthi as observer. "Tell Hazards, too," Dharthi said, as an afterthought.

"Oh, yeah," Zamin replied. "I guess it is at that. Dhar . . . are you okay out there?"

"Arm hurts," Dharthi admitted. "The drugs are working, though. I could use some sleep in a bed. A dry bed."

"Yeah," Zamin said. "I bet you could. You know Kraken's beside herself, don't you?"

"She'll know if I die," Dharthi said.

"She's a good friend," Zamin said. A good trick, making it about her, rather than Kraken or Dharthi or Kraken *and* Dharthi. "I worry about her. You know she's been unbelievably kind to me, generous through some real roughness. She's—"

"She's generous," Dharthi said. "She's a genius and a charismatic. I know it better than most. Look, I should pay attention to where my feet are, before

I break the other arm. Then you *will* have to extract me. And won't I feel like an idiot then?"

"Dhar—"

She broke the sat. She felt funny about it for hours afterward, but at least when she crawled into her cocoon that rest period, adaptshell and all, she was so exhausted she slept.

She woke up sixteen hours and twelve minutes later, disoriented and sore in every joint. After ninety seconds she recollected herself enough to figure out where she was—in her shell, in her cocoon, fifty meters up in the Ishtarean canopy, struggling out of an exhaustion and painkiller haze—and when she was, with a quick check of the time.

She stowed and packed by rote, slithered down a strangler vine, stood in contemplation on the forest floor. Night was coming—the long night—and while she still had ample time to get back to base camp without calling for a pickup, every day now cut into her margin of safety.

She ran.

Rested, she almost had the resources to deal with it when Kraken spoke in her mind, so she gritted her teeth and said, "Yes, dear?"

"Hi," Kraken said. There was a pause, in which Dharthi sensed a roil of suppressed emotion. Thump. Thump. As long as her feet kept running, nothing could catch her. That sharpness in her chest was just tight breath from running, she was sure. "Zamin says she's worried about you."

Dharthi snorted. She had slept too much, but now that the kinks were starting to shake out of her body, she realized that the rest had done her good. "You know what Zamin wanted to talk to me about? You. How *wonderful* you are. How caring. How made of charm." Dharthi sighed. "How often do people take you aside to gush about how wonderful I am?"

"You might," Kraken said, "be surprised."

"It's *hard* being the partner of somebody so perfect. When did you ever *struggle* for anything? You have led a charmed life, Kraken, from birth to now."

"Did I?" Kraken said. "I've been lucky, I don't deny. But I've worked hard. And lived through things. You think I'm perfect because that's how you see me, in between bouts of hating everything I do."

"It's how everyone sees you. If status in the afterlife is determined by praises sung, yours is assured."

"I wish you could hear how they talk about you. People hold you in awe, love."

Thump. Thump. The rhythm of her feet soothed her, when nothing else could. She was even getting resigned to the ceaseless damp, which collected between her toes, between her buttocks, behind her ears. "They *love* you. They tolerated me. No one *ever* saw what you saw in me."

"I did," Kraken replied. "And quit acting as if I *were* somehow perfect. You've been quick enough to remind me on occasion of how I'm not. This thing, this need to prove yourself . . . it's a sophipathology, Dhar. I love you. But this is not a healthy pattern of thought. Ambition is great, but you go beyond ambition. Nothing you do is ever good enough. You deny your own accomplishments, and inflate those of everyone around you. You grew up in Aphrodite, and there are only thirty thousand people on the whole damned planet. You *can't* be surprised that, brilliant as you are, some of us are just as smart and capable as you are."

Thump. Thump—

She was watching ahead even as she was arguing, though her attention wasn't on it. That automatic caution was all that kept her from running off the edge of the world.

Before her—below her—a great cliff dropped away. The trees in the valley soared up. But this was not a tangled jungle: it was a climax forest, a species of tree taller and more densely canopied than any Dharthi had seen. The light below those trees was thick and crepuscular, and though she could hear the rain drumming on their leaves, very little of it dripped through.

Between them, until the foliage cut off her line of sight, Dharthi could see the familiar, crescent-shaped roofs of aboriginal Cytherean structures, some of them half-consumed in the accretions from the forest of smoking stone towers that rose among the trees.

She stood on the cliff edge overlooking the thing she had come half a world by airship and a thousand kilometers on foot to find, and pebbles crumbled from beneath the toes of her adaptshell, and she raised a hand to her face as if Kraken were really speaking into a device in her ear canal instead of into the patterns of electricity in her brain. The cavernous ruin stretched farther than her eyes could see—even dark-adapted, once the shell made the transition for her. Even in this strange, open forest filled with colorful, flitting flying things.

"Love?"

"Yes?" Kraken said, then went silent and waited.

"I'll call you back," Dharthi said. "I just discovered the Lost City of Ishtar."

Dharthi walked among the ruins. It was not all she'd hoped.

Well, it was *more* than she had hoped. She rappelled down, and as soon as her shell sank ankle-deep in the leaf litter she was overcome by a hush of awe. She turned from the wet, lichen-heavy cliff, scuffed with the temporary marks of her feet, and craned back to stare up at the forest of geysers and fumaroles and trees that stretched west and south as far as she could see. The cliff behind her was basalt—another root of the volcano whose shield was lost in mists and trees. This . . . this was the clearest air she had ever seen.

The trees were planted in rows, as perfectly arranged as pillars in some enormous Faerie hall. The King of the Giants lived here, and Dharthi was Jack, except she had climbed down the beanstalk for a change.

The trunks were as big around as ten men with linked hands, tall enough that their foliage vanished in the clouds overhead. Trees on earth, Dharthi knew, were limited in height by capillary action: how high could they lift water to their thirst leaves?

Perhaps these Cytherean giants drank from the clouds as well as the earth.

"Oh," Dharthi said, and the spaces between the trees both hushed and elevated her voice, so it sounded clear and thin. "Wait until Zamin sees these."

Dharthi suddenly realized that if they were a new species, she would get to name them.

They were so immense, and dominated the light so completely, that very little grew under them. Some native fernmorphs, some mosses. Lichens shaggy on their enormous trunks and roots. Where one had fallen, a miniature Cytherean rain forest had sprung up in the admitted light, and here there was drumming, dripping rain, rain falling like strings of glass beads. It was a muddy little puddle of the real world in this otherwise alien quiet.

The trees stood like attentive gods, their faces so high above her she could not even hear the leaves rustle.

Dharthi forced herself to turn away from the trees, at last, and begin examining the structures. There were dozens of them—hundreds—sculpted out of the same translucent, mysterious, impervious material as all of the ruins in Aphrodite. But this was six, ten times the scale of any such ruin. Maybe vaster. She needed a team. She needed a mapping expedition. She needed a base camp much closer to this. She needed to give the site a name—

She needed to get back to work.

She remembered, then, to start documenting. The structures—she could not say, of course, which were habitations, which served other purposes—or even if the aboriginals had used the same sorts of divisions of usage that human beings did—were of a variety of sizes and heights. They were all designed as arcs or crescents, however—singly, in series, or in several cases as a sort of stepped spectacular with each lower, smaller level fitting inside the curve of a higher, larger one. Several had obvious access points, open to the air, and Dharthi reminded herself sternly that going inside unprepared was not just a bad idea because of risk to herself, but because she might disturb the evidence.

She clenched her good hand and stayed outside.

Her shell had been recording, of course—now she began to narrate, and to satlink the files home. No fanfare, just an upload. Data and more date—and the soothing knowledge that while she was hogging her allocated bandwidth to send, nobody could call her to ask questions, or congratulate, or—

Nobody except Kraken, with whom she was entangled for life.

"Hey," her partner said in her head. "You found it."

"I found it," Dharthi said, pausing the narration but not the load. There was plenty of visual, olfactory, auditory, and kinesthetic data being sent even without her voice.

"How does it feel to be vindicated?"

She could hear the throb of Kraken's pride in her mental voice. She tried not to let it make her feel patronized. Kraken did not mean to sound parental, proprietary. That was Dharthi's own baggage.

"Vindicated?" She looked back over her shoulder. The valley was quiet and dark. A fumarole vented with a rushing hiss and a curve of wind brought the scent of sulfur to sting her eyes.

"Famous?"

"Famous!?"

"Hell, Terran-famous. The homeworld is going to hear about this in oh, about five minutes, given light lag—unless somebody who's got an entangled partner back there shares sooner. You've just made the biggest Cytherean archaeological discovery in the past hundred days, love. And probably the next hundred. You are *not* going to have much of a challenge getting allocations now."

"I—"

"You worked hard for it."

"It feels like . . . " Dharthi picked at the bridge of her nose with a thumbnail. The skin was peeling off in flakes: too much time in her shell was wreaking havoc with the natural oil balance of her skin. "It feels like I should be figuring out the next thing."

"The next thing," Kraken said. "How about coming home to me? Have you proven yourself to yourself yet?"

Dharthi shrugged. She felt like a petulant child. She knew she was acting like one. "How about to you?"

"*I* never doubted you. You had nothing to prove to me. The self-sufficiency thing is your pathology, love, not mine. I love you as you are, not because I think I can make you perfect. I just wish you could see your strengths as well as you see your flaws—one second, bit of a squall up ahead—I'm back."

"Are you on an airship?" *Was she coming here?*

"Just an airjeep."

Relief *and* a stab of disappointment. You wouldn't get from Aphrodite to Ishtar in an AJ.

Well, Dharthi thought. *Looks like I might be walking home.*

And when she got there? Well, she wasn't quite ready to ask Kraken for help yet.

She would stay, she decided, two more sleeps. That would still give her time to get back to basecamp before nightfall, and it wasn't as if her arm could get any *more* messed up between now and then. She was turning in a slow circle, contemplating where to sling her cocoon—the branches were really too high to be convenient—when the unmistakable low hum of an aircar broke the rustling silence of the enormous trees.

It dropped through the canopy, polished copper belly reflecting a lensed fisheye of forest, and settled down ten meters from Dharthi. Smiling, frowning, biting her lip, she went to meet it. The upper half was black hydrophobic polymer: she'd gotten a lift in one just like it at Ishtar basecamp before she set out.

The hatch opened. In the cramped space within, Kraken sat behind the control board. She half-rose, crouched under the low roof, came to the hatch, held out one her right hand, reaching down to Dharthi. Dharthi looked at Kraken's hand, and Kraken sheepishly switched it for the other one. The left one, which Dharthi could take without strain.

"So I was going to take you to get your arm looked at," Kraken said.

"You spent your allocations—"

Kraken shrugged. "Gonna send me away?"

"This time," she said, " . . . no."

Kraken wiggled her fingers.

Dharthi took it, stepped up into the GEV, realized how exhausted she was as she settled back in a chair and suddenly could not lift her head without the assistance of her shell. She wondered if she should have hugged Kraken. She realized that she was sad that Kraken hadn't tried to hug her. But, well. The shell was sort of in the way.

Resuming her chair, Kraken fixed her eyes on the forward screen. "Hey. You did it."

"Hey. I did." She wished she felt it. Maybe she was too tired.

Maybe Kraken was right, and Dharthi should see about working on that.

Her eyes dragged shut. So heavy. The soft motion of the aircar lulled her. Its soundproofing had degraded, but even the noise wouldn't be enough to keep her awake. Was this what safe felt like? "Something else."

"I'm listening."

"If you don't mind, I was thinking of naming a tree after you."

"That's good," Kraken said. "I was thinking of naming a kid after you."

Dharthi grinned without opening her eyes. "We should use my Y chromosome. Color blindness on the X."

"Ehn. Ys are half atrophied already. We'll just use two Xs," Kraken said decisively. "Maybe we'll get a tetrachromat."

THE DAUGHTERS OF JOHN DEMETRIUS

JOE PITKIN

—◆—

Mendel had run the whole day in his graceful, tireless way, southerly down the road that some called Old Mexico 45 and the locals called *El Camino de San Juan Demetrio*. There had been little water all day, just a single dusty rivulet past noon where he had drunk and where he had tried without much success to wash the crusted blood out of his tunic. Mendel was dark enough that it would do him little harm to go naked in this Sun, and he even considered such a possibility, but it would have scandalized the local *vulgaris* more for him to have walked naked into a village than for him to have appeared in a blood-stained tunic.

Mendel came upon such a village at the end of the day, only an hour's run over mesas from the main road, a rammed earth wall guarding an inner circle of adobes and ancient shipping containers. The sign hung above the arch of the outer wall said *Pozos Desecantes/Desiccant Wells*. It had the sloppy look of an old gringo settlement, though Mendel could not be sure on this mesa an hour from the far-off stretch of the road that the gods hardly ever traveled.

He walked through the open gate unchallenged except by a troop of scrawny clucking hens. Most of the central square was taken up by a dusty yard where crust-skinned children in homespun shirts and loincloths carried out a listless game of Chihuahuan-rules football. They seemed not to notice him. Beyond, the adults congregated around a cluster of worn stone troughs, beating the dirt out of their sullen piles of laundry.

Mendel walked to the edge of the game and watched the children. In those moments before anyone in the village noticed him, his eye fell on one different from the rest, perhaps eight years old, her dark skin pristine as the flesh of an avocado. No pellagra with this one. He would have run all the way to Oaxaca to find another like her.

They noticed him then. The children went silent and marveled. Then one mother less exhausted or more anxious than the rest turned to regard the newly quiet children, and she saw divine Mendel in his sweat-glistened luminescent beauty. He was so beautiful, or they were all so bone-weary, that no one screamed at this bloodstained stranger who had walked unopposed into the heart of the lost little village.

Mendel knew that he must be the one to speak first. He asked in Spanglish in his clear high voice whether the villagers spoke Spanglish or Spanish or English. One of the adults, perhaps the head woman, said they spoke all three. She answered in English as they nearly always did, always assuming that the gods spoke English, and always following the ancient Mexican law of hospitality that demanded the visitor be made most comfortable. If these people were gringos, they had at least learned this much from the land that had taken them in.

"I am following the road of John Demetrius," Mendel said to them, "and I would be grateful if I could spend the night here." This was not, in fact, so different from Mendel's plans, but regardless of his plans, this was what he always said when he traveled through this part of the world.

The head woman bowed and spread her arms wide in the heartbreaking theatrical way they always did, as though to offer Mendel their whole forsaken village. Then she began ordering the younger adults in Spanglish to begin preparing a place for him; with one of them, a gaunt hardscrabble woman of about thirty, or maybe fifty, the head woman exchanged some brief taut words that even Mendel could not quite hear.

They had never heard of him, he was sure. They had never spoken to travelers from another village where he had wandered. If they had, they would have learned to boil their corn in ashes and these children would not be half-dead from niacin deficiency. As they shuffled about to find a shipping container for him to sleep in and to bring him an ancient cut soda bottle full of rusty water, Mendel looked around again for the beautiful green-skinned girl. But she had disappeared. Another girl, smaller and wretched, stood before him fearlessly, staring at him relentlessly before Mendel noticed her.

Mendel knelt down to look her in the eye. "*Y tú? Cómo te llamas?*" he asked in a conspiratorial tone, as though she would be giving away a secret to tell him her name.

The girl stared at him as though mute. But the gods are imperturbable, and Mendel only looked back at her with the serenity of someone beyond hunger or thirst. They stared at one another a minute or more before the gravelly hen's voice of an old woman shouted in their direction: "*Floribunda! Inútil! Trae aca your scrawny ass!*" The girl spun around as though the words were a leash the woman had jerked; the girl ran in a dusty pad-footed way toward the squalling voice.

The villagers put Mendel up in a clean-swept, well-ordered shipping container, painted turquoise and salmon and bearing the name "Coper" in tawdry letters of rhinestone appliqué. The woman who opened the house to him said nothing beyond "here you have your *pobre casa,*" but whether her silence was resentful or the reaction of a broken woman cowed by the presence of a god, Mendel couldn't immediately tell. The four children like shriveled rag dolls seemed cowed by him. He decided in that moment that he would give the knowledge of preparing the corn to this family only, as payment for their putting him up for the night. Señora Coper would be one of the most important people in the village, if not the headwoman, for passing along the secret. And she would pass it along, because he would warn her that he would return in wrath and vengeance if she didn't.

She served him cornbread on a plastic bucket lid, and he weighed the silence carefully before he asked them to what family the green-skinned girl belonged.

"She is Lupe Hansen's daughter," the woman replied with a wary eye on him every moment, as though she knew why he was asking, though of course she didn't.

"You know she is a child of San Juan Demetrio?" he said.

"We are all children of San Juan."

At this, Mendel thought it wise to say only "Indeed, *así es.*"

None of the children had taken their eyes off of him. The smallest, with eyes like shining black olives, was the first who dared to speak. "*Pero por qué estas* bloody?"

"César!" the woman hissed, scandalized. But Mendel held up his hand to the woman to gesture that he was not offended.

"I was in a fight."

"Did you die?"

"No—if I had died I would not be sitting with you here."

"Were you hurt?" asked the oldest.

"*Un poco.* But my body recovers *muy* quick *amente.*"

"Who did you fight?"

"An evil god," Mendel answered. "A god who didn't like people."

The answer seemed to awe the children. But the woman, who seemed too mortified to notice the children's reaction, added for good measure: "*Es un god muy malo,* who will take you away if you don't stop asking questions."

The next morning all seventeen children in the village had questions about the evil god. Mendel regretted a little his explanation of the night before, though of course someone was bound to have asked him about the blood stains and, as was typical of Mendel, he had spent the previous day telling himself that he would need a good story instead of actually coming up with a good story. He told them that the god he had bloodied had hated the natural people, had wanted all of the natural people to take on the bodies of demons and to fill their minds with the nonsense of dreams. The children seemed to regard this explanation quietly and utterly without skepticism, which suggested all the more to Mendel that what he said was strictly true. Yet, on account of their pellagra, they showed none of the awe that children of the other villages had; they sat stooped and downcast like feverish hallucinators, their crusted hands held out before them like barnacled flippers.

The flawless green girl stepped up to the circle of children as artlessly as a little deer. Studiously, Mendel continued his tale: He told how the evil god had stolen many children for his terrible purposes (pure fabrication, but Mendel could not resist their attention, even limp as it was). But Mendel loved the natural people so much that he risked himself to save them. The green daughter of Lupe Hansen watched him, and he observed her without ever looking directly at her; he felt her watchful presence as though soon she would eat from his outstretched hand.

But the children were called to school by a long cracked note from an old trumpet, and Mendel watched them all, from the green girl to the most encrusted lad, retreat to a cluster of four shipping containers at the edge of the houses, like a square bounded by the larger circle of the village structures. The one who blew the trumpet was a woman somewhat less slack than the rest, without pellagra, with a faint tint to her skin that announced to Mendel that she was Lupe Hansen.

Mendel rose from the ground where he had sat cross-legged, and he noticed only then that not all of the children had quite retreated. The other girl, the one called Floribunda, stared at him still. He found her look a little hostile. Or perhaps terrified. But just when Mendel decided that it must be terror that made her look at him so, she held out to him a tiny green wisp of locoweed, which he took from her before she ran after the other children to the school.

While he waited, Mendel busied himself with helping around the village. The village technical council, three craggy-faced men, came to him like a humiliated embassy offering surrender. "Our *molino* runs poorly; we believe there is a short in the photovoltaic system," the most venerable of them said.

"Perhaps the film needs cleaning," Mendel answered. "The village is very dusty."

"Perhaps," the man said with pained courtesy. "But we have tried to keep the films clean."

The films were in fact scrupulously clean. The village technical council had guessed correctly about the short, which Mendel found buried in the adobe wall where the old man had thought it might be. He peeled the wire out like an intransigent root from barren earth, and he wondered why the old men had not trusted themselves enough to find the short themselves with their antique voltmeter.

Mendel visited Lupe Hansen at the school after the children had cleared out to play Chihuahuan rules football. "Do you know who I am?" Mendel asked her.

She did not look up from stacking the children's tablets. "You are a god."

"But do you know who I am?"

She stopped to look at him. "No. I know only that you are a god."

Mendel approached from another tack. "Do you know that your daughter is *hija de* San Juan Demetrio?"

"*Sí. Así es.*"

"You are also one."

"*Sí. Así es.*"

"Why did you never go to Phoenix?"

"This is my village."

"Have you never thought to send your daughter there?"

The woman said nothing. When she lifted the stack of tablets to put them away, Mendel saw a tension in her shoulders, what he took to be stubbornness, though he knew he was not so godlike as to be above projection.

"Your daughter could be schooled in ways that you know you cannot school her here," Mendel continued. "She could come back to Desiccant Wells as a god, and yet as one of you as well."

Lupe Hansen began scrubbing down the students' tables with a dusty rag.

"Your students could use those tablets to get to the real internet, if you had a guide," he said, pointing at the stack of tablets as though the woman was also looking at them, and not intently at the dusty tabletops. "It is the ones like your daughter that will bring reunification."

Lupe Hansen's mouth was set as she scrubbed at the tables.

"What is your daughter's name?"

"Chloe."

"Chloe would be a god," he said as reverently as an evangelical missionary.

Lupe Hansen said nothing but looked directly at him with a pain that seemed both powerless and impervious to reason.

It offended his sense of dignity to wheedle for the girl. For every parent that handed over a child to him without flinching, seeing the benefit of entrusting a child to the care of the gods, there was another like Lupe Hansen, for whom the benefit Chloe might receive would not justify separating her from her mother.

He stared back at her, and unlike so many natural people Lupe Hansen was not awed into looking away. But of course, she was no natural person, either—otherwise, why would Mendel be bargaining with her over her daughter?

It occurred to him, with some relief, that he had not told Señora Coper the secret of corn nixtamalization. "If I could cure everyone in the village of their sickness, would you let Chloe come to school with me? Please consider it." And with that he walked out of the little school and past the water troughs and the solar ovens, where he said to the headwoman that he would return the next morning to Desiccant Wells.

He ran out into the desert a safe distance, back toward Old Mexico 45 where no one would have been shocked to find him. Safety was relative, of course: Perses had had friends, *shedim* and *lilin* who certainly would know of his death by now. And when their suspicions fell on Mendel, Old Mexico 45 was one of the places Perses' friends would think to look for him.

But he was safe at least from the villagers' attentions for a moment. He closed his eyes and linked up with the satellite, got lost a few hours in his mails—mostly advertisements clouding up his neurons. He tried to get in touch with Handy, which had been his purpose linking up in the first place: did he have room for a little green girl, unusually quiet and, so far as Mendel could tell, totally untrained? Mendel found it half charming and half infuriating that Handy, who could stay linked up the livelong day if he wished it, had an old-fashioned autoresponder on his account like some telephonical answering machine from another age.

Mendel took a risk and accessed one of his thoughtbank accounts he had squirreled away. None of his acquaintances knew about the account, and he doubted any of Perses' cronies had tried hacking into Mendel's internet history yet. Just over three hundred new dollars sat there beneath anybody's notice. Lying on the baking hardpan in the flimsy shadow of the creosote, he closed his eyes and moved, quickly and quietly, a hundred dollars to a terminal in Delicias. Then he logged off and delinked and, in the heat of the day, ran two hours southeast down Old Mexico 45.

In Delicias, at the *Hotel Vieja Delicias*, Mendel checked in as Conrado Hermés, paid with N$61 from the terminal. Nobody asked him about the bloodstains. Delicias was one of those towns where the naturals had some exposure to the divines and treated them with deference but not awe. The hotel clerk, whose nametag said "César," was young enough and beautiful enough that he might have passed for a god, but Mendel could tell by his genetic summary—or, more properly, his lack of a summary—that he was as natural as Floribunda and would be handsome a few years more at most. With the rest of the hundred new dollars he ordered a fresh tunic, six *tacos de suadero*, and three liters of *Ambrosia* beer, and he slept that night in a bed that bore some resemblance to the bed of a god.

On waking, he felt again the perfect confidence that he would walk out of Desiccant Wells with the child of Lupe Hansen. The night's sleep, the revitalizing *Ambrosias*, the brilliant white tunic all convinced him that success was a foregone conclusion.

Then, walking out of the *Hotel Vieja Delicias,* he saw a *lilith* snooping about as she came up the road, peering into windows, swiveling her half-snake head to and fro like a flashlight. Mendel had worried about the blood on the old tunic. It wouldn't have hurt him to have worried about it a little more. But he had thought it unlikely for one like Perses to carry radio tags in his blood like a child or a criminal. Mendel's main worry had been that the bloodstains would frighten the naturals.

The *lilith* was a good way up the street, moving past a trio of *vulgaris* hauling an enormous handcart toward some market or warehouse. Mendel was the only other divine on the road; she would spot him for sure if he began to run. To his left a laundromat operated out of a family's garage. He turned into it as though that had been his errand all along.

A broad-faced natural with a thick braid of hair in the ancient style looked up at him from the pile of laundry her neighbors had left for her. Mendel wondered for half a second whether the old bloodstained tunic was in the pile, sent over by the hotel to be washed instead of incinerated as Mendel had demanded. He raised the back of his hand to her like a strange greeting; his fingernail, tapered and sculpted, began to grow out of his index finger into fifty fatal centimeters of talon.

"Is there a bloody tunic in your laundry?" he asked in Spanish.

"No, lord," she answered, emotionless.

He sheathed the claw back into his hand. "Is there a back door?"

"It leads to our house, lord."

He asked if he could get to the roof by that way. He could. For a short, waddling woman, she moved in a hurry, and silently, and he followed her into a dusty cinderblock courtyard with a legion of geraniums growing in old rusted cans. The lip of the roof hung three meters or so above the ground; Mendel leapt, caught the lip, and vaulted himself up. He looked back at her only a moment to say in his antique Spanish: "From this day the gods bless your house." Then, with the same finger that a moment before had been a blade of fingernail, he exhorted her to be silent. He stayed not a moment to see her bowing deferentially, but like a loon lifting off from the water he glided across the roof and leapt into the street behind, and then he ran faster than any *lilith* deep into the mirages of the desert.

He took a roundabout way back to Desiccant Wells, running far to the west into the creosote and circling back southeast. It was nearly noon when he arrived, and a call went up when he came into sight of them. By the time he walked into the central courtyard they were arrayed in front of him in all their scabby glory like a choir. In the center of the formation, looking more desolate even than the day before, Lupe Hansen stood with her arms draped protectively over her daughter before her. Yet at the girl's feet was a backpack, and she stood dressed and washed and combed like a lamb for sacrifice.

The headwoman was the first to speak, "Will you, lord, cure us of our sickness?"

He showed them the trick with the water and ashes that would soften the corn kernels, that trick which even the poorest village in Mexico would have known in the last age, that trick which in fact had been discovered not far from Desiccant Wells nearly four thousand years before. As far as the villagers were concerned, Chloe Hansen was a fair trade for such knowledge.

During the celebratory dinner, the little girl looked at him balefully and silently. If she had cried on learning that she would go with him, or if she was to cry about it later, she wasn't crying now. Of course, Mendel had taken the other children whether they had cried or not. But it was always easier for him if they didn't cry.

The Sun was low before they were ready to set out. The headwoman and others clamored for him to stay one more night, to leave in the morning—give the girl one more night with her mother. But the girl would be safe at night, Mendel assured them, and no marauder on the road would be so foolish that he would try to steal a child from a god.

They relented at last, and as the Sun was setting, he hoisted the little girl with her backpack full of undoubtedly useless things. He left at a loping, gliding pace, not wanting to jar the poor child more than necessary as she wept silently on his shoulder.

Or not so silently. Before he had run a kilometer, he heard the child's racking breathless sobs. Only, they came not from the girl on his shoulder: He looked back to see another child who had run after them, who had covered only half the distance and now stood alone on the empty mesa in the gathering night. The twilight had darkened so that he had to double back to see who was there. In her threadbare loincloth and dusty as an unearthed root, Floribunda stood wheezing and snot-nosed and miserable.

"You have to go back to your parents," he said to her. "I can't take you with me."

"*No tengo* parents," she gasped. "I am *hija de* San Juan Demetrio."

"Who cares for you in the village? They are worried for you right now."

"I am *hija de* San Juan Demetrio."

The gesture he made, running a hand through his hair while he looked down at the problem she represented, was the gesture any god, or any natural, might make in answer to a stymie. He might scoop her up and carry her back like a sack of meal, if he could put up with the indignity of returning, of appearing before the *vulgaris* like one of them, like some harried uncle with a kicking child under his arm. Or he could leave her. She might return to the village on her own.

He considered the problem longer than he intended to, staring a full minute at the impediment before him. Floribunda looked neither at him nor at Chloe but rather kept her eye on the purple and green horizon with a grim intensity, like the captain of a little ship in the open sea.

Then he saw another shape far off in the failing light. But moving quickly: low to the ground on four feet, head thrust forward like a jackal, limbs sweeping along double-jointed and implacable it came toward them. It was the *lilith*.

He scooped up the other girl and ran. He moved like a gazelle even with the two under his arms, though he ran with an effort that was unfamiliar to him. He ran toward the line of mountains far in the west, a kilometer, two kilometers, three. But soon enough he could hear the *lilith* scrambling not far behind him over the hardpan, tearing the creosote from its roots when she juked to match his turns and scrambles.

Both girls had fallen silent. With an instinct that had been honed in some ancestral mammal from a prehuman epoch, they had drawn in their limbs to make of themselves tight bundles that Mendel grasped, one under each arm, like two lean footballs. But he knew after a few minutes that the *lilith* was outrunning him, that any moment he would feel the shock of her jaws around his Achilles tendon, and he would go down.

He cast the girls to either side, into the creosote and tamarisk. They flew from his arms silently, but before they crashed into the bush Mendel had spun about with the blade of his finger spiking like a chitinous rapier.

But she was faster than Perses had been, and she had known what to expect from Mendel. The *lilith* cast herself wide of his arm, wary as a dog, and from her fangy mouth she spit at him, something hot and corrosive that seared his arm and shoulder.

She had scrambled past him and turned to face him again, just out of reach of his talon, and Mendel saw that when she spit at him her mouth contorted like one about to vomit, and the acid shot from beneath her tongue in two streams. He dodged, and, spinning like a dancer, he leapt at her, throwing his arm wide to slash. But she too was fast and leapt back beyond his reach, and once more, he felt the searing stream cross against the skin of his midriff.

The pain blinded him, or would have. But he had been blessed with a divine measure of endorphins in times of agony. In that timelessness brought on by death whispering in his ear, Mendel considered what he might do differently to get at the body of this spidery woman, her elbows and knees all angles as quick as Mendel Hodios could manage, almost as quick as Mendel even at his strongest. It was he who dodged and leapt back now, keeping always her stream of venom from landing on his flesh.

He did not know this *lilith*. Her hands and feet looked slender, not for crushing, though he had been fooled by slim hands before: He had seen more elfin hands than hers choke the life out of a full-grown *vulgaris*. Perhaps it was her jaw that would crush him, or her sinewy legs, when the venom finally wore him down. Her tactic would be the last thing he discovered, or he would never discover it at all.

He crouched to face her, his sword held above him like a scorpion's sting. She crept sidewise before him on the tips of her fingers and toes—he concluded that yes, her fingers were surely strong enough to break him if she should lay a hand on him.

A rock struck her head from behind, bounced away. Close behind the *lilith* he saw Floribunda, recovering her balance; the rock she had heaved had been the size of a loaf of bread. But the *lilith's* head twitched, no more than that, no more than a flinch at the annoyance of being struck by a rock that would have crushed a natural's skull.

Mendel knew then that he was likely to die. The two girls would, too, if the *lilith* had it in her head to bring harm to them. The *lilith* reared onto her legs a moment, her mouth widened in the now-familiar grave contraction.

Mendel took his fatal chance and did not dodge. A stream of the venom splashed his chest and funneled down his breastbone as he leapt at her. But, as he had hoped, aiming her venom took some concentration: One thing she had not expected was that an enemy might leap to embrace her just as she vomited her poison. He too was stronger than he looked: she fell back in his arms, just as the spike of his finger slid into her side, under the ribs.

He felt himself weakening, his body straining to respond to the acid devouring his skin, the systems going into shock, his heart chattering, his thoughts scrambling in the fog. Yet he retained the presence of mind to know that the *lilith* had gone weaker still: He could see the tip of his fingerblade sprouting from the other side of her body, the blood draining from her in great sheens down her legs. Her face showed neither panic nor suffering but rather an impregnable calm.

And then, he could hold her up no longer and she fell back, and he also, a moment later. The sky was purple above him. He heard a rushing sound that might have been the wind, or perhaps a sound coming from within him. The pain hammered.

A minute later, or perhaps five, perhaps after he was already dead, he heard the two girls breathing above him. He heard the zipper of the little green girl's pack. Then a trickle of water into his mouth, ambrosia.

"Pour the water over my skin," he said. He was overcome with gratitude that

Lupe Hansen had sent her daughter with a three-liter bottle in her backpack. The water ran cold and excruciating over his pulsing, blistered flesh.

The two girls crouched in front of him as he lay on his back. They watched silently like two creatures inured to suffering, or so acquainted with it that they did not consider his agony worthy of comment.

He lay there through the night, his skin howling in the cool of the breeze. When the sky had brightened enough that he could make out their features, the girls still watched him, sleeplessly, the way old women had tended fires for a million years. He could feel the flood of macrophages and growth hormones already released into his tissues; by dawn he was able to hoist the three liter bottle himself, to drain the last milliliters of water into his mouth.

If he could run unburdened, Handy's redoubt lay six hours to the west. As it was, he might walk there with the girls in three days if water could be found. He had no compunction now about linking with the satellite—the girls watched him and noticed nothing more than that he closed his eyes for a time. If the maps were accurate, a creek ran sixteen kilometers to the west, near the foothills of the *Sierra Madre*.

He logged off, opened his eyes as though he had been sleeping for a few minutes, smiled at the two girls who looked at him like two inscrutable frogs. He pushed himself to his feet and observed the pounding of his head as his humors balanced. Behind the girls the *lilith's* corpse lay staring at the *Sierra Madre*.

He crouched over her body and drank what blood he could from the wound. There was not much left. If her blood carried radio tags, perhaps no one would catch up with him until he was safe at Handy's.

"Now you have to walk with me a long way," Mendel told the girls, extending a hand to each of them. Floribunda took his right hand, caked with the *lilith's* blood. The three of them walked in the direction of the pass, and water.

UNEARTHLY LANDSCAPE
BY A LADY

REBECCA CAMPBELL

1.

A winter afternoon when she was eight, and her tiny finger traced transoceanic voyages over the blue pages of our atlas. I taught her to recite the coasts past which she sailed: Malabar and Mandalay, Ceylon, Siam. Names like incantations, terminating always in Flora's favourite specks of the south Atlantic: Ascension, St Helena, Inaccessible, the loneliest and strangest shores she could imagine.

These lessons in geography quickly became games of concentration, as I named cities and she responded with exports and shipping routes, the trails that ivory traces from wild elephants to billiard rooms. When I pointed at the Caribbean islands she knew to bring me a lump of sugar. When I held up a translucent teacup she pointed at China.

Until—this winter afternoon when she was eight—she answered my question not with tea from the box on the table but with silence, and then, "Ceylon is so far! I'll never ever see it."

"You might!"

She knelt on her chair and trailed her velvet rabbit to the floor. "Don't be silly, Mina, you've never been so far from home. You've never been *anywhere*."

Perhaps if I had been a different sort of woman, if I had been to Tahiti, or rounded the Cape of Good Hope, her life would have had a different ending. I wonder if with another mentor—braver, wiser—she might have flowered into something authentically strange, revolutionary in her beauty, or in her violence.

But I was not brave, nor wise, and this account is not one of revolution. It pains me that I only said, "and thus concludes the lesson, we should go out before it's too dark in the garden."

2.

If I had paid more careful attention would I have found him even then, when she was eight; some trace of that other world that has so haunted me since? I have many of her things in my possession—two decades of Christmas and birthday gifts, painted teacups and toilet trays and miniatures. Their subject matter irreproachably conventional, until one looks and begins to suspect something hiding in the sinuous line of her ivy or the glowering red of her sunset.

The first I saw was a figure very like a man, despite the bronze wings riveted to his shoulders, on whose wrist was mounted the deadly machinery of something I can only call a Gatling gun, but miniaturized, shooting not bullets but something molten, something poison. Around his feet lay the remains of other creatures, very like birds, very like flowers, half-hidden under the violet leaves that border her teacup.

I cannot name them, but they are familiar from dozens of landscapes in her painstaking, microscopic style, her brushstrokes so tiny that I checked her work with a magnifying glass and feared not for her mind but for her eyesight. I remember her at thirteen, hunched in the window, building whole universes in the curve of a teacup.

3.

At fourteen, little girls are found wanting—perhaps her skin is coarse, perhaps her waist thickens or her laugh is too loud—and they are consigned to tight slippers, to the corset and the parasol. Adulthood darkens the horizon, and at eighteen she is engulfed.

Flora's girlhood was free, disturbed only by the irregular attentions of her guardians, a great aunt and uncle who spent their winters in Italy and their summers in Switzerland. She struggled, then resigned herself to a straitened world, her pale braids fearfully and intricately bound to her scalp, her body constrained by steel and baleen as over her skin crept the apparatus of bone and padded silk, the nets and cages.

It is a strange paradox: when such artifice is well-executed, one would think the girl-creature is a product of nature rather than an illusion made of metal and bone and a thin film of silk. Often I thought, as Flora crossed the garden or the marble floor of the hall, that she was the down-hanging blossom of some slight pink flower, drifting on the sort of breeze that floats a pixie through the colour plates in fairytales.

At nineteen she went to garden parties and riding parties and river-parties, and in the evenings the carriage often carried her away to enormous rooms, adjacent to verdigris conservatories where her pale gold dresses—gas-lit, candle-lit, fire-lit—glowed against the darkness outside. When she returned in the rising day she possessed the faint luminosity of pre-dawn flowers, as though the glow of a distant sunrise permanently lit her face.

I remember turning over the huge skirt of a gown sent up from the city, oppressive in weight but possessing the texture of a cirrus cloud, a colour halfway between pink and grey.

At the mirror she said, "They call this colour ashes of rose. A holocaust of flowers. Just think, Mina, of all the burning gardens to make one dress." Lace foamed through her fingers and down into her lap.

"Mrs. Maryat will want to see you", or not that—something equally empty that meant *ignore it and she will know better than to say these things.*

"There's a new cup on the work table, Mina. Do you like it? Another garden," she said. "Full of roses. And ashes, too."

"It's very pretty. It's as pretty as that fan you painted last week. So pretty."

The conventional subject: ruins, roses, forget-me-nots. How delicately she had tangled ivy around the slim line of her ruined tower. An arrowslit where an archer of old must have rested his bow. And there, executed with the single hair at the tip of her cat-fur brush, a figure, a man, more or less. Something strapped to his wrist, a dreadful commingling of the cross-bow and the cannon.

And around the base of the tower, among the roots of the flowers, in the shadows cast by dark stems, there were bodies—insectoid, five-armed, three-eyed, with green skin, or dark bronze, or a sickly woad-ish blue I did not like, one that bled into the forget-me-nots bordering the bottom of the scene.

"What does it mean?"

"Why should it mean anything?" Flora picked up the ashy pink dress. "Do you think lilies of the valley?"

It must have been the gleam of the window and the shadows cast by lace on silk, but I thought I saw—for a moment—a wriggling glimpse of that other world, into which we must stoop to look, at which we gaze only with the aid of the magnifying glass or the telescope, populated—a trick of the paint, or of shadows—by the three-armed, the greenskinned, and a strange figure who brandished something unnameable and deadly.

The creatures on the ground had the heavy heads of peonies, but no natural configuration of petals would look so like a fleshy body, punctuated by spiky leaves like teeth and thorns. "Who told you about these? The man in the tower, and the airships? Are these birds?"

She trailed a finger across the glittering beadwork of her sleeve. "They're not birds, exactly. Insects, perhaps, is a closer analogue. Some have green shells, some gold. Some have seven legs, and some three. Their compatriots are on the ground, the flowers—"

For a long time she did not speak.

"The flowers—" she began again, her voice warmer. I hoped she would stop.

"—I don't like them, Flora—"

"—the men in the towers eat them. At first I did not realize it, but the plants are sentient, and when they are in pain and afraid, they exude a substance from their central stem that is remarkably delicious. Somewhere between a mango and a new vanilla pod. That scent—it's a perfume, too, they use it to scent the air in the sky-cities—made me think when I first saw them they were on some southern Island, somewhere very far away. So far that I cannot imagine. So far away that the sun is the wrong colour, distant and cold and tinted faintly green. There are airships that sail from the sky-cities, which float up high, tethered by long copper chains to the mountain peaks. The people who live up there are beautiful and gold-hued, and breathe the thin alpine air, and lie naked in the sunshine, which turns their skins a handsome metallic bronze.

"And wings are not their only remarkable technology. They travel far in their minds by way of strange apparatus. I do not understand it, dear Mina, or I would tell you more. I think they touch our world, sometimes, but perhaps that is only fancy on my part. I think I see them, flickering in the air above, those god-men wearing their copper wings, dressed in the skins of the singing insects. Perhaps if we were treated in the same way we, too, would exude something delicious in our death-throes."

"Flora, please—"

"The plant-people are limited by their vegetable nature in where they may live, and are unable to run, though the adults—which can drag their stems a little—grow great thorns that snap shut around the throats of invaders. It is a challenge to find the youngest, tenderest shoots, to frighten them into silence and eat them there in a garden of their parents. I wonder if insects grieve, Mina. What about flowers?"

She laughed.

Should I have directed her more forcefully toward wholesome good deeds, or theological poems? Should I have drilled her in Latin verbs until she had no moment of privacy in which to think about this alien sky? I could not imagine that my charge—with her perfect composure, the blue of her eyes as shallow as an atlas's ocean, the irreproachable whiteness of her complexion— could conceive something so strange, so unpleasant.

She handed me the teacup she held and said, "Look in the hearts of the flowers."

The luck of a ringing bell—somewhere in the heart of the house— interrupted our uncomfortable *tête à tête*, and I was relieved to look away from the globular, fleshy petals, just as I saw—hidden among them—the bodies of infant flowers, otherworldly and sentient, destroyed by the gold-winged men for the tears they shed in death.

4.

A party that evening. Another, another, and dozens more, each requiring fresh flowers and new silk slippers. She met young men in uniforms so exactly cut they might have been a secondary organ made of red wool and gold braid. She spent her days painting microscopic botanicals that seemed to crawl with detail I did not wish to examine. I wondered what I would see if, my nose close to the paper, I examined the stem of a wild rose, the delicate green of its sepal, the yellow pistol, the faint pink blush near the base of each petal.

Flora turned twenty. She was engaged to the second son of a Baronet, a coup, the great aunt said, adding "we owe some of that to you, I think," claiming the bulk of the debt for her own. It is true, perhaps, that she made Flora what she became. Flora owed her fortune to her parents' will, but her self-sufficiency had accreted in the long, lonely years of grief.

There were orange blossoms, I remember, and wisteria in the window. A carriage at the door, and her great uncle's arm at the top of the stairs. The exchange of prayer books. The lych gate and the wedding breakfast. Champagne. Bridesmaids in blue silk.

All day Flora glittered, her breast a shield of seed pearls and hanging crystal, armoured with metallic peacocks; iridescent guardians so exactly matched to the hue of her gown they seemed not stitched in place but grown there, as a crystal grows from its mineral spring or the translucent eggs of insects grow in chambers beneath the earth. She was insectoid, scarab-skinned. Most dreadful, which drew my eyes even as I averted them, a ten-foot veil that possessed—somehow—the shadow of five-legged insects running down its margins, caught in the web of the lace-makers art.

They toured Italy. They returned to a sprawling house in the West Country, set in a valley of primroses and gillyflowers. There were children. There were parties on the river that ran past the foot of their garden. She painted when she could. I never saw her again.

5.

When the third of the Misses Barclay turned eighteen I took my little savings and set off for the distant north-Pacific colony to which my sister's family had emigrated twenty years before. In my retirement I would grow sweet peas in a little bungalow garden near the water. I would reacquaint myself with my family. I would take a few students in painting, or French.

Flora always remembered me. She sent photographs—portraits, the house, the gardens, tinted by a London artist. Flora in a pale gold moiré that glowed faintly in the artificial light of the flash, pearlescent like a lily's thick glimmering petals. A fancy visited me as I examined the portrait, that it was not fabric she wore but her own elaborate skin, puckered and scarred and burnished into insectoid textures and gleams, the tightly braided and coiled loops of her hair another segment of that bony carapace, shining— incongruously—in the light of her green imagined sun.

For though I did not like to, I found myself examining the impeccable rooms and gardens in these photographs, fearing that they, too, betrayed another world. It was true that they seemed to teem with unwholesome detail. I am ashamed to say that I was happy to have shut the door on such rooms, on Flora herself. But I could not erase the memory of the man with the Gatling gun, and the five-armed green creatures lying on the ground below him.

I have seen—veiled by clouds in the empty green oceans of her sky—the shadow of an emergent airship, coalescing in curves and spikes from the cumulous tower along the horizon, as though she has built not the illusion of depth but true distance between the porcelain and her brush strokes.

I have learned something about her world. Of the three polities in that other world, the insects were the most loveable. The five-limbed creatures, remarkable in their asymmetry, that fluttered through Flora's lace, within the tracery of her often-abandoned sampler; their long, segmented legs seemed to trail through her stitches. They are a social animal, who build enormous constellations out of kinship, rendered in the vast empires of song they sing both from the beak-like protuberances above their multi-faceted eyes and using the thin threads that run from wrist-bone to elbow; the human terms are only approximations. Their song so vast it filled the sky with echoes rippling tribe to tribe until they encircled the whole globe. Their dearest joy was in binding themselves in the harmonies native to their soul. The faintly greenish air, the pale sun burnished the vegetable-creatures, and the insect-birds with its glow, all rang with their communion.

So each society flourished in its separate quarters—the man-creatures up high in their floating towers and air-ships, the slow vegetable-creatures on the earth below, and between them, the creatures of the singing air.

6.

The vagaries of Imperial Mail are such that the letter describing her first appointment with a London doctor reached me a month before the letter that told me of the first tumour. The next mail-bag held three letters describing their proliferation, her growing weakness, her plans for the children. I guessed much of what was unwritten, confirmed two weeks later by the black-barred note of her death. It contained only the barest outline of her existence, her parents' early death, her own dates, the names of her survivors. I was not among them.

I read through the little stack of letters nearly hourly, parsing her weakness, her ennui, and—the only phrase that betrayed the nature of her condition—the strange distortions of her body. In her usual clipped and unsentimental manner, Flora said they had begun at the corner of her jaw, but further investigation revealed similar masses everywhere, in her organs, and joints, in masses beneath her skin.

I knew enough to guess at the weight of this unnatural pregnancy, the cancerous spread of a shadow-child, a parasite, a little alien blooming inside her. I dreamed of her often, and when half-awake I seemed to feel the heavy masses beneath my own skin, fibrous like the roots of foreign trees, and others surfacing from the deep within her; these bulbous, heavy fruits, these vegetable infections, a steady imperial action beneath her skin.

Opiates to dull the pain but render her vegetable in mind as well as flesh, a chrysalis containing not Flora but the rapacious creature of her disease, gnarled and scaled, weeping, erupting.

Flora is the only charge I have outlived, and it is my grief that her illness was so sudden that she was dead even as I wrote my last letters of comfort and affection. She never received the words I sent, words I should have said to her when she was young and trailing her fingers across the wide, painted oceans of her vision. Plant-creatures blossoming and wilting and trailing their intoxicating distillate, while above them the artificial angels hunt the sky and insects fill the air with their laments.

7.

I left this stack of papers in my little writing-desk for two months because I had no sense of how to finish the story. It was only this morning, when a box arrived whose contents—once revealed—demanded I return to my account.

It was a wooden crate, shipped at great expense from the West Country house where Flora died. It contained a sheaf of paintings she had particularly selected for me in her last illness, according to the curt note that accompanied them and china work in cotton. There is—on first glance—a richness of violets, beauties so slight they remind me of the feathered wings of a moth. The green fields and forests of her imagination, constructed in the finest brushwork I have ever seen; colours as fragile as the translucent porcelain on which she painted them, and admitting, through the thin walls of the cup, a faint greenish glow, as though from a distant sun.

I am afraid of what lies within them.

The paintings are, after her taste, tiny and scrupulously conventional. Icebergs, and Italian Villas. Roses. But what one cannot see one can still feel, and even before I took up my magnifying glass I sensed something in the green ripples at the base of the iceberg, in the shimmering whites of the glacier, in the chiaroscuro of the Italian villa, the three poplars against the gold sky, black hills scalloping the sunset. Something in the sepia shadows of the olive grove—airships and Gatling guns, and the gold-skinned denizens of her otherworldly sky. Building something elaborate and deadly, something made of bronze and iron.

Today I understand that a distant fire illuminates her paintings. It burns through even the most banal scenes: a ruined barn and a branch of apple-blossom, wild roses on a hedgerow. The terminal detonation of a weapon I cannot imagine, one that leaves only ashes in its wake, only ruined towers and the remains of a whole, dead world.

I have collected them in a glass-fronted case in my drawing room. I watch each little girl as she comes to practice her piano or to learn a new stitch. She dreams that one day she will have the honour of picking a teacup to drink from when she visits. And then she turns away.

There is one rare girl who stands a little longer, staring into the shallow surface of Flora's world. Sometimes when her mother draws her away she seems struck, as though she has glimpsed the faintly greenish sky of a world described in no atlas, populated by the voracious cities of flying men and sentient plants, and insects whose high, sweet cry suffuses the air. A predatory sky, a secret world.

She lives not far from here, in a bungalow with her parents and sisters and brothers. I have taught her to paint flowers and insects, to sit so still in the wood that the creatures go about their duties in her presence. I have taught her to record her observations and collect them in a notebook. Of all my charges her eyes slide most often to the cabinet, and while her mother and sisters look with pleasure, say "oh, how charming!" Daisy, instead, is perplexed. I examine her work for evidence. I am determined not to make the mistake I made with Flora, and if Daisy is so inclined, I will give her the guidebook, open the door, let her through, even if the light on the other side is of a demonic kind.

And so I have selected my heiress. Her face is grave. She searches the cup for something she cannot quite grasp. Somewhere, somewhere she can't reach, there are artificial angels, and a battle for the flowers. And its final termination with a weapon so deadly it casts a light that seems to illuminate the past as well as the future, to burn through the fragile objects that hold it; the porcelain so translucent it can hardly bear the vision, depths as strange and unwholesome as Flora's own, so bright that perhaps she felt it burning through the casings of silk and stone, of metal and bone, that bound her.

THE ASTRAKHAN, THE HOMBURG, AND THE RED, RED COAL

CHAZ BRENCHLEY

———◆———

"Paris? Paris is ruined for me, alas. It has become a haven for Americans—or should I say a heaven? When good Americans die, perhaps they really do go to Paris. That would explain the flood."

"What about the others, Mr. Holland? The ones who aren't good?"

"Ah. Have you not heard? I thought that was common knowledge. When bad Americans die, they go to America. Which, again, would explain its huddled masses. But we were speaking of Paris. It was a good place to pause, to catch my breath. I never could have stayed there. If I had stayed in Paris, I should have died myself. The wallpaper alone would have seen to that."

"And what then, Mr. Holland? Where do good Irishmen go when they die?"

"Hah." He made to fold his hands across a generous belly, as in the days of pomp—and found it not so generous after all, and lost for a moment the practised grace of his self-content. A man can forget the new truths of his own body, after a period of alteration. Truly Paris had a lot to answer for. Paris, and what had come before. What had made it necessary.

"This particular Irishman," he said, "is in hopes of seeing Cassini the crater-city on its lake, and finding his eternal rest in your own San Michele, within the sound of Thunder Fall. If I've only been good enough."

"And if not? Where do bad Irishmen go?"

It was the one question that should never have been asked. It came from the shadows behind our little circle; I disdained to turn around, to see what man had voiced it.

"Well," Mr. Holland said, gazing about him with vivid horror painted expertly across his mobile face, "I seem to have found myself in Marsport. What did I ever do to deserve this?"

There was a common shout of laughter, but it was true all the same. Marsport at its best is not a place to wish upon anyone, virtuous or otherwise; and the Blue Dolphin is not the best of what we have. Far from it. Lying somewhat awkwardly between the honest hotels and the slummish boarding-houses, it was perhaps the place that met his purse halfway. Notoriety is notoriously mean in its rewards. He couldn't conceivably slum, but neither—I was guessing—could he live high on the hog. Even now it wasn't clear quite who had paid his fare to Mars. The one-way voyage is subsidised by Authority, while those who want to go home again must pay through the nose for the privilege—but even so. He would not have travelled steerage, and the cost of a cabin on an aethership is . . . significant. Prohibitive, I should have said, for a man in exile from his own history, whose once success could only drag behind him now like Marley's chains, nothing but a burden. He might have assumed his children's name for public purposes, but he could not have joined the ship without offering his right one.

No matter. He was here now, with money enough for a room at the Dolphin and hopes of a journey on. We would sit at his feet meanwhile and be the audience he was accustomed to, attentive, admiring, if it would make him happy.

It was possible that nothing now could make him exactly happy. Still: who could treasure him more than we who made our home in a gateway city, an entrepôt, and found our company in the lobby of a cheap hotel?

"Marsport's not so dreadful," the same voice said. "It's the hub of the wheel, not the pit of hell. From here you can go anywhere you choose: by canal, by airship, by camel if you're hardy. Steam-camel, if you're foolhardy. On the face of it, I grant you, there's not much reason to stay—and yet, people do. Our kind."

"Our kind?"

There was a moment's pause, after Mr. Holland had placed the question: so carefully, like a card laid down in invitation, or a token to seal the bet.

"Adventurers," the man said. "Those unafraid to stand where the light spills into darkness: who know that a threshold serves to hold two worlds apart, as much as it allows congress between them."

"Ah. I am afraid my adventuring days are behind me."

"Oh, nonsense, sir! Why, the journey to Mars is an adventure in itself!"

Now there was a voice I did recognise: Parringer, as fatuous a fool as the schools of home were ever likely to produce. He was marginal even here, one of us only by courtesy. And thrusting himself forward, protesting jovially, trying to prove himself at the heart of the affair and showing only how very remote he was.

"Well, perhaps. Perhaps." Mr. Holland could afford to be generous; he didn't have to live with the man. "If so, it has been my last. I am weary, gentlemen. And wounded and heart-sore and unwell, but weary above all. All I ask now is a place to settle. A fireside, a view, a little company: no more than that. No more adventuring."

"Time on Mars may yet restore your health and energy. It is what we are famous for." This was our unknown again, pressing again. "But you are not of an age to want or seek retirement, Mr. . . . Holland. Great heavens, man, you can't be fifty yet! Besides, the adventure I propose will hardly tax your reserves. There's no need even to leave the hotel, if you will only shift with me into the conservatory. You may want your overcoats, gentlemen, and another round of drinks. No more than that. I've had a boy in there already to light the stove."

That was presumptuous. Manners inhibited me from twisting around and staring, but no one objects to a little honest subterfuge. I rose, took two paces towards the fire and pressed the bell by the mantelshelf.

"My shout, I think. Mr. Holland, yours I know is gin and French. Gentlemen . . . ?"

No one resists an open invitation; Marsporter gin is excellent, but imported drinks come dear. The boy needed his notebook to take down a swift flurry of orders.

"Thanks, Barley." I tucked half a sovereign into his rear pocket— unthinkable largesse, but we all had reasons to treat kindly with Barley—and turned to face my cohort.

On my feet and playing host, I could reasonably meet them all eye to eye, count them off like call-over at school. Hereth and Maskelyne, who were not friends but nevertheless arrived together and sat together, left together every time. Thomson who rarely spoke, who measured us all through his disguising spectacles and might have been a copper's nark, might have been here to betray us all except that every one of us had reason to know that he was not. Gribbin the engineer and van Heuren the boatman, Poole from the newspaper and the vacuous Parringer of course, and Mr. Holland our guest for the occasion, and—

And our unannounced visitor, the uninvited, the unknown. He was tall even for Mars, where the shortest of us would overtop the average Earthman. Mr. Holland must have been a giant in his own generation, six foot three or thereabouts; here he was no more than commonplace. In his strength, in his pride I thought he would have resented that. Perhaps he still did. Years of detention and disgrace had diminished body and spirit both, but something must survive yet, unbroken, undismayed. He could never have made this journey else. Nor sat with us. Every felled tree holds a memory of the forest.

The stranger was in his middle years, an established man, confident in himself and his position. That he held authority in some kind was not, could not be in question. It was written in the way he stood, the way he waited; the way he had taken charge so effortlessly, making my own display seem feeble, sullen, nugatory.

Mr. Holland apparently saw the same. He said, "I don't believe we were introduced, sir. If I were to venture a guess, I should say you had a look of the Guards about you." Or perhaps he said *the guards,* and meant something entirely different.

"I don't believe any of us have been introduced," I said, as rudely as I knew how. "You are . . . ?"

Even his smile carried that same settled certainty. "Gregory Durand, late of the King's Own," with a little nod to Mr. Holland: the one true regiment to any man of Mars, Guards in all but name, "and currently of the Colonial Service."

He didn't offer a title, nor even a department. Ordinarily, a civil servant is more punctilious. I tried to pin him down: "Meaning the police, I suppose?" It was a common career move, after the army.

"On occasion," he said. "Not tonight."

If that was meant to be reassuring, it fell short. By some distance. If we were casting about for our coats, half-inclined not to wait for those drinks, it was not because we were urgent to follow him into the conservatory. Rather, our eyes were on the door and the street beyond.

"Gentlemen," he said, "be easy." He was almost laughing at us. "Tonight I dress as you do," anonymous overcoat and hat, as good as a *nom de guerre* on such a man, an absolute announcement that this was not his real self, "and share everything and nothing, one great secret and nothing personal or private, nothing prejudicial. I will not say "nothing perilous," but the peril is mutual and assured. We stand or fall together, if at all. Will you come? For the Queen Empress, if not for the Empire?"

The Empire had given us little enough reason to love it, which he knew. An appeal to the Widow, though, will always carry weight. There is something irresistible in that blend of decrepit sentimentality and strength beyond measure, endurance beyond imagination. Like all her subjects else, we had cried for her, we would die for her. We were on our feet almost before we knew it. I took that so much for granted, indeed, it needed a moment more for me to realise that Mr. Holland was still struggling to rise. Unless he was simply slower to commit himself, he whose reasons—whose scars—were freshest on his body and raw yet on his soul.

Still. I reached down my hand to help him, and he took it resolutely. And then stepped out staunchly at my side, committed after all. We found ourselves already in chase of the pack; the others filed one by one through a door beside the hearth, that was almost always locked this time of year. Beyond lay the unshielded conservatory, an open invitation to the night.

An invitation that Mr. Holland balked at, and rightly. He said, "You gentlemen are dressed for this, but I have a room here, and had not expected to need my coat tonight."

"You'll freeze without it. Perhaps you should stay in the warm." Perhaps we all should, but it was too late for that. Our company was following Durand like sheep, trusting where they should have been most wary. Tempted where they should have been resistant, yielding where they should have been most strong.

And yet, and yet. Dubious and resentful as I was, I too would give myself over to this man—for the mystery or for the adventure, something. For something to do that was different, original, unforeseen. I was weary of the same faces, the same drinks, the same conversations. We all were. Which was why Mr. Holland had been so welcome, one reason why.

This, though—I thought he of all men should keep out of this. I thought I should keep him out, if I could.

Here came Durand to prevent me: stepping through the door again, reaching for his elbow, light and persuasive and yielding nothing.

"Here's the boy come handily now, just when we need him. I'll take that, lad," lifting Barley's tray of refreshments as though he had been host all along. "You run up to Mr. Holland's room and fetch down his overcoat. And his hat too, we'll need to keep that great head warm. Meanwhile, Mr. Holland, we've a chair for you hard by the stove . . ."

The chairs were set out ready in a circle: stern and upright, uncushioned, claimed perhaps from the hotel servants' table. Our companions were milling, choosing, settling, in clouds of their own breath. The conservatory was all glass and lead, roof and walls together; in the dark of a Martian winter, the air was bitter indeed, despite the stove's best efforts. The chill pressed in from every side, as the night pressed against the lamplight. There was no comfort here to be found; there would be no warmth tonight.

On a table to one side stood a machine, a construction of wires and plates in a succession of steel frames with rubber insulation. One cable led out of it, to something that most resembled an inverted umbrella, or the skeleton of such a thing, bones of wind-stripped wire.

"What is that thing?"

"Let me come to that. If you gentlemen would take your seats . . ."

Whoever laid the chairs out knew our number. There was none for Durand; he stood apart, beside the machine. Once we were settled, drinks in hand—and most of us wishing we had sent for something warmer—he began.

"*Nation shall speak peace unto nation*—and for some of us, it is our task to see it happen. Notoriously, traditionally we go after this by sending in the army first and then the diplomats. Probably we have that backwards, but it's the system that builds empires. It's the system of the world.

"Worlds, I should say. Here on Mars, of course, it's the merlins that we need to hold in conversation. Mr. Holland—"

"I am not a child, sir. Indeed, I have children of my own." Indeed, he travelled now under their name, the name they took at their mother's insistence; he could still acknowledge them, even if they were obliged to disown him. "I have exactly a child's understanding of your merlins: which is to say, what we were taught in my own schooldays. I know that you converse with them as you can, in each of their different stages: by sign language with the youngster, the nymph, and then by bubbling through pipes at the naiad in its depths, and watching the bubbles it spouts back. With the imago, when the creature takes to the air, I do not believe that you can speak at all."

"Just so, sir—and that is precisely the point of our gathering tonight."

In fact the point of our gathering had been ostensibly to celebrate and welcome Mr. Holland, actually to fester in our own rank company while we displayed like bantam cocks before our guest. Durand had co-opted it, and us, entirely. Possibly that was no bad thing. He had our interest, at least, if not our best interests at heart.

"It has long been believed," he said, "that the imagos—"

"—imagines—"

—to our shame, that came as a chorus, essential pedantry—

"—that imagos," he went on firmly, having no truck with ridiculous Greek plurals, "have no language, no way to speak, perhaps no wit to speak with. As though the merlins slump into senescence in their third stage, or infantilism might say it better: as though they lose any rational ability, overwhelmed by the sexual imperative. They live decades, perhaps centuries in their slower stages here below, nymph and naiad; and then they pupate, and then they hatch a second time and the fire of youth overtakes them once more: they fly; they fight; they mate; they die. What need thought, or tongue?

"So our wise men said, at least. Now perhaps we are grown wiser. We believe they do indeed communicate, with each other and perhaps their water-based cousins too. It may be that nymphs or naiads or both have the capacity to hear them. We don't, because they do not use sound as we understand it. Rather, they have an organ in their heads that sends out electromagnetic pulses, closer to Hertzian waves than anything we have previously observed in nature. Hence this apparatus," with a mild gesture towards the table and its machinery. "With this, it is believed that we can not only hear the imagos, but speak back to them."

A moment's considerate pause, before Gribbin asked the obvious question. "And us? Why do you want to involve us?"

"Not want, so much as need. The device has existed for some time; it has been tried, and tried again. It does work, there is no question of that. Something is received, something transmitted."

"—But?"

"But the first man who tried it, its inventor occupies a private room—a locked room—in an asylum now, and may never be fit for release."

"And the second?"

"Was a military captain, the inventor's overseer. He has the room next door." There was no equivocation in this man, nothing but the blunt direct truth.

"And yet you come to us? You surely don't suppose that we are saner, healthier, more to be depended on . . . ?"

"Nor more willing," Durand said, before one of us could get to it. "I do not. And yet I am here, and I have brought the machine. Will you listen?"

None of us trusted him, I think. Mr. Holland had better reason than any to be wary, yet it was he whose hand sketched a gesture, *I am listening*. The rest of us—well, silence has ever been taken for consent.

"Thank you, gentlemen. What transpired from the tragedy—after a careful reading of the notes and as much interrogation of the victims as proved possible—was that the mind of an imago is simply too strange, too alien, for the mind of a man to encompass. A human brain under that kind of pressure can break, in distressing and irrecoverable ways."

"And yet," I said, "we speak to nymphs, to naiads." I had done it myself, indeed. I had spoken to nymphs on the great canals when I was younger, nimble-fingered, foolish, and immortal. For all the good it had done me, I might as well have kept my hands in my pockets and my thoughts to myself, but nevertheless. I spoke, they replied; none of us ran mad.

"We do—and a poor shoddy helpless kind of speech it is. Finger-talk or bubble-talk, all we ever really manage to do is misunderstand each other almost entirely. That 'almost' has made the game just about worth the candle, for a hundred years and more—it brought us here and keeps us here in more or less safety; it ferries us back and forth—but this is different. When the imagos speak to each other, they speak mind-to-mind. It's not literally telepathy, but it is the closest thing we know. And when we contact them through this device, we encounter the very shape of their minds, almost from the inside; and our minds—our *individual* minds—cannot encompass that. No one man's intellect can stand up to the strain."

"And yet," again, "here we are. And here you are, and your maddening machine. I say again, why are we here?"

"Because you chose to be"—and it was not at all clear whether his answer meant *in this room* or *in this hotel* or *in this situation*. "I am the only one here under orders. The rest of you are free to leave at any time, though you did at least agree to listen. And I did say 'one man's intellect.' Where one man alone cannot survive it without a kind of mental dislocation—in the wicked sense, a disjointment, his every mental limb pulled each from each—a group of men working together is a different case. It may be that the secret lies in strength, in mutual support; it may lie in flexibility. A group of officers made the endeavour, and none of them was harmed beyond exhaustion and a passing bewilderment, a lingering discomfort with each other. But neither did they make much headway. Enlisted men did better."

He paused, because the moment demanded it: because drama has its natural rhythms and he did after all have Mr. Holland in his audience, the great dramatist of our age. We sat still, uncommitted, listening yet.

"The enlisted men did better, we believe, because their lives are more earthy, less refined. They live cheek by jowl; they sleep all together and bathe together; they share the same women in the same bawdy-houses. That seems to help."

"And so you come to us? To *us?*" Ah, Parringer. "Because you find us indistinguishable from common bloody Tommies?"

"No, because you are most precisely distinguishable. The Tommies were no great success either, but they pointed us a way to go. The more comfortable the men are with each other, physically and mentally, the better hope we have. Officers inhabit a bonded hierarchy, isolated from one another as they are from their men, like pockets of water in an Archimedes' screw. Cadets might have done better, but we went straight to the barracks. With, as I say, some success—but enlisted men are unsophisticated. Hence we turn to you, gentlemen. It is a bow drawn at a venture, no more: but you are familiar with, intimate with the bodies of other men, and we do believe that will help enormously; and yet you are educated beyond the aspiration of any Tommy Atkins—some of you beyond the aspiration of any mere soldier, up to and including the generals of my acquaintance—and that too can only prove to the good. With the one thing and the other, these two strengths in parallel, in harmony, we stand in high hopes of a successful outcome. At least, gentlemen, I can promise you that you won't be bored. Come, now: will you play?"

"Is that as much as you can promise?" Thomson raised his voice, querulous and demanding. "You ask a lot of us, to venture in the margins of madness; it seems to me you might offer more in return."

"I can offer you benign neglect," Durand said cheerfully. "Official inattention: no one watching you, no one pursuing. I can see that enshrined in policy, to carry over *ad infinitum*. If you're discreet, you can live untroubled hereafter; you, and the generations that follow you. This is a once-and-for-all offer, for services rendered."

There must be more wrapped up in this even than Durand suggested or we guessed. A way to speak to the imagines might prove only the gateway to further secrets and discoveries. If we could speak directly to the chrysalid pilots of the aetherships, perhaps we might even learn to fly ourselves between one planet and another, and lose all our dependence on the merlins . . .

That surely would be worth a blind eye turned in perpetuity to our shady meeting-places, our shadier activities.

Mr. Holland thought so, at least. "Say more, of how this process works. Not what you hope might come of it; we all have dreams. Some of us have followed them, somewhat. I am here, after all, among the stars," with a wave of his hand through glass to the bitter clarity of the Martian night sky. "How is it that you want us to work together? And how do we work with the machine, and why above all do we have to do it here, in this wicked cold?"

"To treat with the last first: Mr. Heaviside has happily demonstrated here as well as on Earth, that aetheric waves carry further after dark. We don't know how far we need to reach, to find a receptive imago; we stand a better chance at night. Besides, you gentlemen tend to forgather in the evenings. I wasn't certain of finding you by daylight."

Someone chuckled, someone snorted. I said, "I have never seen an imago fly by night, though. I don't believe they can."

"Not fly, no: never that. But neither do they sleep, so far as we can tell. All we want to do—all we want you to do—is touch the creature's mind, fit yourselves to the shape of it and find whether you can understand each other."

"I still don't understand how you mean us to achieve that?"

"No. It's almost easier to have you do it, than to explain how it might be done. We're stepping into an area where words lose their value against lived experience. It's one reason I was so particularly hoping to enlist your company, sir," with a nod to Mr. Holland, "because who better to stand before the nondescript and find means to describe it? If anyone can pin this down with words, it will be you. If anyone can speak for us to an alien power—"

"Now that," he said, "I have been doing all my life."

The run of laughter he provoked seemed more obligatory than spontaneous, but came as a relief none the less. Durand joined in, briefly. As it tailed away, he said, "Very well—but there is of course more to it than one man's dexterity with language. Our wise men speak of the, ah, inversion of the generative principle, as a bonding-agent stronger than blood or shared danger or duty or sworn word—but again, there is more than that. You gentlemen may be a brotherhood, drawn from within and pressed close from without; we can make you something greater, a single purpose formed from all your parts. The wise men would have me flourish foreign words at you, *gestalt* or *phasis* or the like; but wise men are not always the most helpful.

"Let me rather say this, that you all have some experience of the demi-monde. By choice or by instinct or necessity, your lives have led you into the shadows. This very hotel is a gateway to more disreputable ventures. There is an opium den behind the Turkish bath, a brothel two doors down. I do not say that any of you is a libertine at core: only that the life you lead draws you into contact and exchange with those who avoid the light for other reasons.

"I will be plain. Mr. Holland, you have a known taste for absinthe and for opium cigarettes. Mr. Parringer, laudanum is your poison; Mr. Hereth, you stick to gin, but that jug of water at your elbow that you mix in so judiciously is actually more gin, and you will drink the entire jugful before the night is out. Mr. Gribbin—but I don't need to go on, do I? You each have your weaknesses, your ways of setting yourselves a little adrift from the world.

"We need to take you out of yourselves more thoroughly in order to bind you into a single motive force, in order to create the mind-space wherein you might meet an imago and make some sense of it. I have brought an alchemical concoction, a kind of hatchis, more potent than any pill or pipe or potion that you have met before."

He laid it on a tray, on a table that he set centre-circle between us all: a silver pot containing something green and unctuous, an array of coffee-spoons beside.

"Something more from your wise men, Mr. Durand?"

"Exactly so."

"I'm not sure how keen I am, actually, to swallow some hellbrew dreamed up in a government laboratory." Gribbin leaned forward and stirred it dubiously. There were gleams of oily gold amidst the green. "Does nobody remember *The Strange Case of Dr. Jekyll and Mr. Hyde?*"

" 'Can anyone forget it?' should rather be your question," Mr. Holland observed. "Stevenson was as much a master of delicate, fanciful prose as he was of a strong driving story. But he—or his character, rather, his creation: do we dare impute the motives of the dream unto the dreamer?—he certainly saw the merits of a man testing his own invention on himself, before bringing it to the public." Even huddled as he was against the ironwork of the stove, he could still exude a spark of knowing mischief.

Durand smiled. "I would be only too happy to swallow my own spoonful, to show you gentlemen the way—but alas, my duty is to the device, not to the *entente*. You will need me sober and attentive. Besides which, I am not of your persuasion. I should only hold you back. Let me stress, though, that senior officers and common troops both have trod this path before you, and not been harmed. Not by the drug. Think of the hatchis as grease to the engine, no more; it will ease your way there and back again. Now come: I promised you adventure, and this is the beginning. Who's first to chance the hazard?"

There is a self-destructive tendency in some men that falls only a little short of self-murder. We have it worse than most; something not quite terror, not quite exhilaration drives us higher, faster, farther than good sense ever could dictate. Some consider it a weakness, evidence of a disordered nature. I hope that it's a badge of courage acquired against the odds, that we will fling ourselves from the precipice in no certain knowledge of a rope to hold us, no faith in any net below.

Of course it was Mr. Holland who reached first, to draw up a noble spoonful and slide it into his mouth. No tentative sips, no tasting: he was all or nothing, or rather simply all.

The surprise was Parringer, thrusting himself forward to do the same, gulping it down wholesale while Mr. Holland still lingered, the spoon's stem jutting from between his full contented lips like a cherry-stem, like a child's lollipop.

Where Parringer plunged, who among us would choose to hold back? A little resentfully, and with a great many questions still unasked, we fell mob-handed on the spoons, the jar, the glistening oleaginous jelly.

It was bitter on my tongue and something harsh, as though it breathed out fumes, catching at the back of my throat before it slithered down to soothe that same discomfort with a distraction of tastes behind a cool and melting kiss. Bitter and then sour and then sweet, layer beneath layer, and I couldn't decide whether its flavours were woven one into another or whether its very nature changed as it opened, as it bloomed within the warm wet of my mouth.

He was right, of course, Durand. Not one of us there was a stranger to the more louche pleasures of the twilit world. Myself, I was a smoker in those days: hashish or opium, anything to lift me out of the quotidian world for an hour or a night. In company or alone, sweating or shivering or serene, I would always, always look to rise. Skin becomes permeable, bodies lose their margins; dreams are welcome but not needful, where what I seek is always that sense of being uncontained, of reaching further than my strict self allows.

From what he said, I took Durand's potion to be one more path to that effect: slower for sure, because smoke is the very breath of fire and lifts as easily as it rises, while anything swallowed is dank and low-lying by its nature. I never had been an opium-eater, and hatchis was less than that, surely: a thinner draught, ale to spirits, tea to coffee. Sunshine to lightning. Something.

If I had the glare of lightning in my mind, it was only in the expectation of disappointment: rain, no storm. I never thought to ride it. Nor to find myself insidiously companion'd—in my own mind, yet—where before I had always gone alone.

Even in bed, even with a slick and willing accomplice in the throes of mutual excess, my melting boundaries had never pretended to melt me into another man's thoughts. Now, though: now suddenly I was aware of minds in parallel, rising entangled with mine, like smoke from separate cigarettes caught in the same eddy. Or burning coals in the same grate, fusing awkwardly together. Here was a mind cool and in command of itself, trying to sheer off at such exposure: that was Gribbin, finding nowhere to go, pressed in from every side at once. Here was one bold and fanciful and weary all at once, and that was surely Mr. Holland, though it was hard to hold on to that ostensible name in this intimate revelation. Here was one tentative and blustering together, Parringer of course . . .

One by one, each one of us declared an identity, if not quite a location. We were this many and this various, neither a medley nor a synthesis, untuned: glimpsing one man's overweening physical arrogance and another's craven unsatisfied ambition, sharing the urge to seize both and achieve a high vaulting reach with them, beyond the imagination of either. Even without seeing a way to do that, even as we swarmed inconsequentially like elvers in a bucket, the notion was there already with flashes of the vision. Perhaps Durand was right to come to us.

Durand, now: Durand was no part of this. Walled off, separated, necessary: to us he was prosthetic, inert, a tool to be wielded. He stood by his machine, fiddling with knobs and wires, almost as mechanical himself.

Here was the boy Barley coming in, no part of anything, bringing the hat and overcoat he'd been sent for. At Durand's gesture he dressed Mr. Holland like a doll, as though he were invalid or decrepit. Perhaps we all seemed so to him, huddled in our circle, unspeaking, seeming unaware. The truth was opposite; we were aware of everything, within the limits of our bodies' senses. We watched him crouch to feed the stove; we heard the slide and crunch of the redcoal tipping in, the softer sounds of ash falling through the grate beneath; we felt the sear of heat released, how it stirred the frigid air about us, how it rose towards the bitter glass.

"Enough now, lad. Leave us be until I call again."

"Yes, sir."

He picked up the tray from the table and bore it off towards the door, with a rattle of discarded spoons. Durand had already turned back to his machine. We watched avidly, aware of nothing more intently than the little silver pot and its gleaming residue. We knew it, when the boy hesitated just inside the door; we knew it when he glanced warily back at us, when he decided he was safe, when he scooped up a fingerful from the pot's rim and sucked it clean.

We knew; Durand did not.

Durand fired up his machine.

We had the boy. Not one of us, not part of us, not yet: we were as unprepared for this as he was, and the more susceptible to his fear and bewilderment because we were each of us intimately familiar with his body, in ways not necessarily true of one another's.

Still: we had him among us, with us, this side of the wall. We had his nervous energy to draw on, like a flame to our black powder; we had his yearning, his curiosity. And more, we had that shared knowledge of him, common ground. Where we couldn't fit one to another, we could all of us fit around him: the core of the matrix, the unifying frame, the necessary element Durand had not foreseen.

Durand fired up his machine while we were still adjusting, before we had nudged one another into any kind of order.

He really should have warned us, though I don't suppose he could. He hadn't been this way himself; all he had was secondhand reports from men more or less broken by the process. We could none of us truly have understood that, until now.

We weren't pioneers; he only hoped that we might be survivors. Still, we deserved some better warning than we had.

We forget sometimes that names are not descriptions; that Mars is not Earth; that the merlins are no more native than ourselves. We call them Martians sometimes because our parents did, because their parents did before them, and so back all the way to Farmer George. More commonly we call them merlins because we think it's clever, because they seem to end their lives so backward, from long years of maturity in the depths to one brief adolescent lustful idiocy in the sky. When we call them imagos—or imagines—because they remind us of dragonflies back home, if dragonflies were built to the scale of biplanes.

Which they are not. The map is not the territory; the name is not the creature. Even redcoal is not coal, not carbon of any kind, for all that it is mined and burned alike. We forget that. We name artefacts after the places of their manufacture, or their first manufacture, or the myth of it; did the homburg hat in fact see first light in Bad Homburg, or is that only a story that we tell? Does anybody know? We let a man name himself after his children, after a country not relevant to any of them, not true to any story of their lives.

We assert that names are changeable, assignable at whim, and then we attach unalterable value to them.

Durand had given no name to his machine. That was just as well, but not enough. He had given us a task to do, in words we thought we understood; he had laid the groundwork, given us an argument about the uses of debauchery and then a drug to prove it; then he flung us forth, all undefended.

He flung us, and we dragged poor Barley along, unwitting, unprepared.

It started with a hum, as he connected electrical wires to a seething acid battery. Lamps glowed into dim flickering life. Sparks crackled ominously, intermittently, before settling to a steady mechanical pulse. A steel disc spun frantically inside a cage.

Nothing actually moved, except fixedly in place; and even so, everything about it was all rush and urgency, a sensation of swift decisive movement: *that* way, through the run of frames and wires to the umbrella-structure at the far end of the table. There was nothing to draw the eye except a certainty, logic married to something more, an intangible impulsion. *That* way: through and up and out into the night.

And none of us moved from our places, and yet, and yet. The machine hurled us forth, and forth we went.

If we had understood anything, we had understood that the machine would bring an imago's voice to us, and we would somehow speak back to it, if we could think of anything to say. That would have been Mr. Holland's lot, surely; he was never short of things to say.

We had misunderstood, or else been misdirected. Unless the drug seduced us all into a mutual hallucination, and in plain truth our intelligences never left that room any more than our abandoned bodies did. But it seemed to us— to *all* of us, united—that we were shot out like a stone from a catapult; that we streaked over all the lights of Marsport and into the bleak dark of the desert beyond; that we hurtled thus directly into the static mind of an imago at rest.

No creature's thoughts should be . . . architectural. Or vast. At first we thought we were fallen into halls of stone, or caverns water-worn. But we had found our shape by then, in the flight from there to here; we might fit poorly all together, but we all fitted well around Barley. And something in that resettling, that nudging into a new conformation, caused a shift in our perspective. A thought is just an echo of the mind-state it betrays, as an astrakhan overcoat is a memory of the lambs that died to make it.

Where we fancied that we stood, these grand and pillared spaces—this was an imago's notion of its night-time world, beyond all heat and passion, poised, expectant. A memory of the chrysalis, perhaps.

Expectant, but not expecting us. Not expecting anything until the sun, the bright and burning day, the vivid endeavour. We came like thieves into a mountain, to disturb the dragon's rest; we were alien, intrusive, self-aware. It knew us in the moment of our coming.

I have seen set-changes in the theatre where one scene glides inexplicably into another, defying expectation, almost defying the eye that saw it happen. I had never stood in a place and had that happen all about me; but we were there, we were recognised, and its awareness of us changed the shape of its thinking.

Even as we changed ourselves, that happened: as we slid and shifted, as we found our point of balance with Barley serving at the heart of all, as we arrayed ourselves about him. Even Mr. Holland, who would need to speak for us, if anything could ever come to words here; even Parringer, whose motives were as insidious as his manner. There was an unbridgeable gulf between the imago as we had always understood it, flighty and maniacal, and this lofty habitation. A naiad in the depths might have such a ponderous mind, such chilly detachment, but not the frenzied imago, no. Surely not.

Save that the imago had been a naiad before; perhaps it retained that mind-set, in ways we had not expected or imagined. Perhaps it could be contemplative at night, while the sun burned off its intellect and lent it only heat?

It closed in upon us almost geometrically, like tiled walls, if tiles and walls could occupy more dimensions than a man can see, in shapes we have no words for. We should have felt threatened, perhaps, but Barley's curiosity was matched now by his tumbling delight, and what burns at the core reaches out all the way to the skin. We sheltered him and drew from him and leaned on him, all in equal measure; he linked us and leaned on us and drew from us, in ways for which there never could be words.

With so many names for our kind—leering, contemptuous, descriptive, dismissive—we know both the fallibility and the savage power of words. The map seeks to define the territory, to claim it, sometimes to contain it. Without a map, without a shared vocabulary, without a mode of thought in common— well, no wonder men alone went mad here. No wonder men together had achieved so little, beyond a mere survival. Mr. Holland might have flung wit all night with no more effect than a monkey flinging dung against a cliff-face, if we had only been a group forgathered by circumstance, struggling to work together. With the drug to bond us, with each man contributing the heart's-blood of himself in this strange transfusion, there was no struggle and we found what we needed as the need came to us.

Whether we said what was needed, whether it needed to be said: that is some other kind of question. Did anyone suppose that the confluence of us all would be a diplomat?

The imago pressed us close, but that was an enquiry. There was pattern in the pressure: we could see it, we could read it almost, those of us with finger-talk or bubble-talk or both. *What lives, what choices? Swim or fly, drown or burn? Swallow or be swallowed?*

We knew, we thought, how to press back, how to pattern a reply. Mr. Holland gave us what we lacked: content, poetry, response. Meaning more than words. Sometimes the map declares the territory.

For he who lives more lives than one
More deaths than one must die.

He would have turned the bitterness all against himself, but our collective consciousness couldn't sustain that. We all wanted our share, we all deserved it: all but Barley, who had no hidden other self, who'd had no time to grow one.

Suddenly he couldn't hold us together any longer. Fraying, we fled back to Durand, back to our waiting bodies—and the imago pursued, flying by sheer will in the dreadful night, wreaking havoc in its own frozen body. It followed us to the Dolphin and hurtled against the conservatory where we were anything but sheltered, battering at the windows like a moth at the chimney of a lamp, until the only abiding question was whether the glass would shatter first or the machine, or the creature, or ourselves.

HELLO, HELLO

SEANAN McGUIRE

—◆—

Tasha's avatar smiled from the screen, a little too perfect to be true. That was a choice, just like everything else about it: When we'd installed my sister's new home system, we had instructed it to generate avatars that looked like they had escaped the uncanny valley by the skins of their teeth. It was creepy, but the alternative was even creepier. Tasha didn't talk. Her avatar did. Having them match each other perfectly would have been . . . wrong.

"So I'll see you next week?" she asked. Her voice was perfectly neutral, with a newscaster's smooth, practiced inflections. Angie had picked it from the database of publicly available voices; like the avatar, it had been generated in a lab. Unlike the avatar, it was flawless. No one who heard Tasha "talk" would realize that they were really hearing a collection of sounds programmed by a computer, translated from the silent motion of her hands.

That was the point. Setting up the system for her had removed all barriers to conversation, and when she was talking to clients who didn't know she was deaf, she didn't want them to realize anything was happening behind the scenes. Hence the avatar, rather than the slight delay that came with the face-time translation programs. It felt wrong to me, like we were trying to hide something essential about my sister, but it was her choice and her system; I was just the one who upgraded her software and made sure that nothing broke down. If anyone was equipped for the job, it was me, the professional computational linguist. It's a living.

"We'll be there right on time," I said, knowing that on her end, my avatar would be smiling and silent, moving her hands to form the appropriate words. I could speak ASL to the screen, but with the way her software was set up, speaking ASL while the translator settings were active could result in some vicious glitches. After the time the computer had decided my hand gestures were a form of complicated profanity, and translated the chugging of the air conditioner into words while spewing invective at my sister, I had learned to keep my hands still while the translator was on. "I'm bringing Angie and the kids, so be ready."

Tasha laughed. "I'll tell the birds to be on their best behavior." A light flashed behind her avatar and her expression changed, becoming faintly regretful. "Speaking of the birds, that's my cue. Talk tomorrow?"

"Talk tomorrow," I said. "Love you lots."

"I love you, too," she said and ended the call, leaving me staring at my own reflection on the suddenly black screen. My face, so much like her computer-generated one, but slightly rougher, slightly less perfect. Humanity will do that to a girl.

Finally, I stood and went to tell my wife we had plans for the next weekend. She liked my sister, and Greg and Billie liked the birds. It would be good for us.

"Hello," said the woman on the screen. She was black-haired and brown-eyed, with skin that fell somewhere between "tan" and "tawny." She was staring directly at the camera, almost unnervingly still. "Hello, hello."

"Hello!" said Billie happily, waving at the woman. Billie's nails were painted bright blue, like beetle shells. She'd been on an entomology kick again lately, studying every insect she found as raptly as if she had just discovered the secrets of the universe. "How are you?"

"Hello," said the woman. "Hello, hello, hello."

"Billie, who are you talking to?" I stopped on my way to the laundry room, bundling the basket I'd been carrying against my hip. The woman didn't look familiar, but she had the smooth, CGI skin of a translation avatar. There was no telling what her root language was. The natural user interface of the software would be trying to mine its neural networks for the places where she and Billie overlapped, looking for the points of commonality and generating a vocabulary that accounted for their hand gestures and body language, as well as for their vocalizations.

It was a highly advanced version of the old translation software that had been rolled out in the late 2010s; that had been verbal-only, and only capable of translating sign language into straight text, not into vocalizations that followed spoken sentence structures and could be played through speakers. ASL to speech had followed, and then speech to ASL, with increasingly realistic avatars learning to move their hands in the complex patterns necessary for communication. Now, the systems could be taught to become ad hoc translators, pulling on the full weight of their neural networks and deep learning capabilities as they built bridges across the world.

Of course, it also meant that we had moments like this one, two people shouting greetings across an undefined void of linguistic separation. "Billie?" I repeated.

"It's Aunt Tasha's system, Mom," said my nine-year-old, turning to look at me over her shoulder. She rolled her eyes, making sure I understood just how foolish my concern really was. "I wouldn't have *answered* if I didn't recognize the caller."

"But that's not Aunt Tasha," I said.

Billie gave me the sort of withering look that only people under eighteen can manage. She was going to be a terror in a few years. "I know that," she said. "I think she's visiting to see the birds. Lots of people visit to see the birds."

"True," I said, giving the woman on the screen another look. Tasha's system was set up to generate a generic avatar for anyone who wasn't a registered user. It would draw on elements of their appearance—hair color, eye color, skin tone—but it would otherwise assemble the face from public-source elements. "Hello," I said. "Is my sister there?"

"Hello," said the woman. "Hello, hello."

"I don't think the computer knows her language very well," said Billie. "That's all she's said."

Which could mean a glitch. Sometimes, when the software got confused enough, it would translate everything as "hello." An attempt at connection, even when the tools weren't there. "I think you may be right," I said, moving to get closer to the computer. Billie, recognizing the shift from protective mother to computer scientist with a mystery to solve, shifted obligingly to the side. She would never have tolerated being smothered, but she was more than smart enough not to sit between me and a puzzle.

"Is Tasha there?" I asked again, as clearly as I could.

The woman looked at me and said nothing.

"I need to know what language you're speaking. I'm sorry the translator program isn't working for you, but if I know what family to teach it, I can probably get it up and running in pretty short order." Everything I said probably sounded like "hello, hello" to her, but at least I was trying. That was the whole point, wasn't it? Trying. "Can you say the name of your language? I am speaking casual conversational English." No matter how confused the program was, it would say "English" clearly. Hopefully that would be enough to get us started.

"Hello, hello," said the woman. She looked to her right, eyes widening slightly, as if she'd been startled. Then she leaned out of the frame and was gone. The image of Tasha's dining room continued for several seconds before the computer turned itself off, leaving Billie and I to look, bemused, at an empty screen.

Finally, hesitantly, Billie asked, "Was that one of Aunt Tasha's friends?"

"I don't know," I said. "I'll call her later and ask."

• • •

I forgot to call.

In my defense, there were other things to do, and none of them were the sort that could easily be put off until tomorrow. Greg, our two-year-old, discovered a secret snail breeding ground in the garden and transported them all inside, sticking them to the fridge like slime-generating magnets. Greg thought this was wonderful. The snails didn't seem to have an opinion. Angie thought this was her cue to disinfect the entire house, starting with the kitchen, and left me to watch both kids while I was trying to finish a project for work. It was really no wonder I lost track of them. It was more of a wonder that it took me over an hour to realize they were gone.

Angie wasn't shouting, so the kids hadn't wandered back into the kitchen to get in the way of her frenzied housework. I stood, moving carefully as I began my search. As any parent can tell you, it's better to keep your mouth shut and your eyes open when you go looking for kids who are being unreasonably quiet. They're probably doing something they don't want you to see, and if they hear you coming, they'll hide the evidence.

I heard them laughing before I reached the living room. I stopped making such an effort to mask my footsteps, and came around the corner of the doorway to find them with their eyes glued to the computer, laughing at the black-haired woman from before.

"Hello, hello," she was saying. "I'm hungry, hello, can you hear me?"

Greg laughed. Billie leaned forward and said, "We can hear you. Hello, hello, we can hear you!" This set Greg laughing harder.

The woman on the screen looked from one child to the other, opened her mouth, and said, "Ha-ha. Ha-ha. Ha-ha. Hello, hello, can you hear me?"

"What's this?" I asked.

Billie turned and beamed at me. "Auntie Tasha's friend is back, and the program is learning more of her language! I'm doing like you told me to do if I ever need to talk to somebody the neural net doesn't know, and using lots of repeating to try and teach it more."

"The word you want is 'echolalia,' " I said distractedly, leaning past her to focus on the screen. "You're back. Hello. Is my sister there?"

"Hello, hello," said the woman. "Can you hear me? I'm hungry."

"Yes, I got that," I said, trying to keep the frustration out of my voice. It wasn't her fault that her language—whatever it was—was causing issues with the translation software. Tasha's neural net hadn't encountered as many spoken languages as ours had. It could manage some startlingly accurate gesture translations, some of which we had incorporated into the base software after they cropped up, but it couldn't always pick up on spoken languages with the speed of a neural net belonging to a hearing person. Tasha also had a tendency to invite visiting academics and wildlife conservationists to stay in her spare room, since they were presumably used to the screeching of wild birds.

"If not for them," she had said more than once, "you're the only company I'd ever have."

It was hard to argue with that. It was just a little frustrating that one of her guests kept calling my kids. "Can you please tell Tasha to call me? I want to speak with her."

"Hello, hello," said the woman.

"Good-bye," I replied and canceled the call.

Both children looked at me like I had done something terribly wrong. "She just wanted someone to talk to," said Billie mulishly.

"Let me know if she calls again, all right? I don't know who she is, and I'm not comfortable with you talking to her until I've spoken to Tasha."

"Okay, Mom," said Billie.

Greg frowned but didn't say anything. I leaned down and scooped him onto my shoulder. That got a squeal, followed by a trail of giggles. I straightened.

"Come on, you two. Let's go see if we can't help Mumma in the kitchen."

They went willingly enough. I cast a glance back at the dark computer screen. This time, I would definitely remember to call my sister.

As always, reaching Tasha was easier said than done. She spent much of her time outside feeding and caring for her birds, and when she was in the house, she was almost always doing some task related to her work. There were flashing lights in every room to tell her when she had a call, but just like everyone else in the world, sometimes she ignored her phone in favor of doing something more interesting. I could have set my call as an emergency and turned all the lights red, but that seemed like a mean trick, since "I wanted to ask about one of your houseguests" wasn't really an emergency. Just a puzzle. There was always a puzzle; had been since we were kids, when her reliance on ASL had provided us with a perfect "secret language" and provided me with a bilingual upbringing—something that had proven invaluable as I grew up and went into neurolinguistic computing.

When we were kids signing at each other, fingers moving almost faster than the human eye could follow, our hands had looked like birds in flight. I had followed the words. My sister had followed the birds. They needed her, and they never judged her for her differences. What humans saw as disability, Tasha's birds saw as a human who was finally quiet enough not to be startling, one who wouldn't complain when they started singing outside her window at three in the morning. It was the perfect marriage of flesh and function.

After two days of trying and failing to get her to pick up, I sent an email.

Just checking in, it said. *Haven't been able to rouse you. Do you have houseguests right now? Someone's been calling the house from your terminal.*

Her reply came fast enough to tell me that she had already been at her computer. *A few grad students came to look @ my king vulture. He is very impressive. One of them could have misdialed? It's not like I would have heard them. ;) We still on for Sunday?*

I sent a call request. Her avatar popped up thirty seconds later, filling the screen with her faintly dubious expression.

"Yes?" she said. "Email works, you know."

"Email is too slow. I like to see your face."

She rolled her eyes. "It's all the same to me," she said. "I know you're not really signing. I prefer talking to you when I can see your hands."

"I'm sorry," I said. "Greg's ASL is progressing really well. We should be able to go back to real-time chat in a year or so. Until then, we need to keep the vocals on, so he can get to know you, too. Look how well it worked out with Billie."

Tasha's expression softened. She'd been dubious when I'd explained that we'd be teaching Billie ASL but using the voice translation mode on our chat software; we wanted Billie to care about getting to know her aunt, and with a really small child, it had seemed like the best way. It had worked out well. Billie was fluent enough in ASL to carry on conversations with strangers, and she was already writing letters to our local high schools, asking them to offer sign language as an elective. Greg was following in her footsteps. I really was pretty sure we'd be able to turn off the voice translation in another year or so.

To be honest, I was going to be relieved when that happened. I was lazy enough to appreciate the ease of talking to my sister without needing to take my hands off the keyboard, but it was strange to *hear* her words, rather than watching them.

"I guess," she said. "So what was up with the grad students? One of them called the house?"

"I think so," I said. "She seemed a little confused. Just kept saying 'hello' over and over again. Were any of them visiting from out-of-country schools? Someplace far enough away that the neural net wouldn't have a solid translation database to access?" Our systems weren't creating translation databases out of nothing, of course—that would have been programming well above my pay grade, and possibly a Nobel Prize for Humanities—but they would find the common phonemes and use them to direct themselves to which shared databases they should be accessing. Where the complicated work happened was in the contextual cues. The hand gestures that punctuated speech with "I don't know" and "yes" and "I love you." The sideways glances that meant "I am uncomfortable with this topic." Bit by bit, our translators put those into words, and understanding grew.

(And there were people who used their translators like Tasha did, who hid silent tongues or a reluctance to make eye contact behind computer-generated faces and calm, measured voices, who presented a completely default face to the world and took great comfort in knowing that the people who would judge them for their differences would never need to know. I couldn't fault them for that. I was the one who asked my sister to let me give her a voice, like grafting a tongue onto Hans Christian Anderson's Little Mermaid, for the duration of my children's short infancy.)

"I don't know," she said, after a long pause. "Only two of them spoke ASL. The other three spoke through their professor, and I've known her for years. Why? Did she say something inappropriate to the kids?"

"No, just 'hello,' like I said. Still, it was strange, and she called back at least once. Black hair, medium brown skin. I didn't get a name."

"If I see someone like that, I'll talk to her about privacy and what is and is not appropriate when visiting someone else's home."

"Thanks." I shook my head. "I just don't like strangers talking to the kids."

"Me, neither."

We chatted for a while after that—just ordinary, sisterly things, how the kids were doing, how the birds were doing, what we were going to have for dinner on Sunday—and I felt much better when I hung up and went to bed.

When I woke up the next morning, Greg and Billie were already in the dining room, whispering to the computer. By the time I moved into position to see the monitor, it was blank, and neither of them would tell me who they'd been talking to—assuming they had been talking to anyone at all.

We arrived at Tasha's a little after noon. As was our agreement, we didn't knock; I just pressed my thumb to the keypad and unlocked the door, allowing our already-wiggling children to spill past us into the bright, plant-strewn atrium. Every penny Tasha got was poured back into either the house or the birds—and since the birds had the run of the house, every penny she put into the house was still going to the birds. Cages of rescued finches, budgies, and canaries twittered at us as we entered, giving greeting and expressing interest in a series of short, sharp chirps. Hanging plants and bright potted irises surrounded the cages, making it feel like we had just walked into the front hall of some exclusive conservatory.

That, right there, was why Tasha spent so much money on the upkeep and decor of her home. It was a licensed rescue property, but keeping it looking like something special—which it was—kept her neighbors from complaining.

Opening the door had triggered the flashing warning lights in the corners of the room. Tasha would be looking for us, and so we went looking for her, following the twitter of birds and the shrieking laughter of our children.

Our parties collided in the kitchen, where Billie was signing rapid-fire at her aunt while Greg tugged at her arm and offered interjections, his own amateurish signs breaking into the conversation only occasionally. A barn owl was perched atop the refrigerator. That was par for the course at Tasha's place, where sometimes an absence of birds was the strange thing. The door leading out to the screened-in patio was open, and a large pied crow sat on the back of the one visible chair, watching us warily. Most of that wariness was probably reserved for the owl. They would fight, if given the opportunity, and Tasha didn't like breaking up squabbles between birds she was rehabilitating. Birds that insisted on pecking at each other were likely to find themselves caged. The smarter birds—the corvids and the big parrots—learned to play nicely, lest they be locked away.

I waved. Tasha glanced over, beamed, and signed a quick 'hello' before she went back to conversing with my daughter. The world had narrowed for the two of them, becoming nothing more than the space of their hands and the words they drew on the air, transitory and perfect.

The computer was on the table, open as always. I passed the day bag to Angie, pressing a quick kiss to her cheek before I said, "I'm going to go check on the neural net. Let me know if you need me."

"Yes, leave me alone with your sister in the House of Birds," she said, deadpan. I laughed and walked away.

Part of the arrangement I had with Tasha involved free access to her computer. She got the latest translation software and endless free upgrades to her home neural net; I went rooting through the code whenever I was in the house. She didn't worry about me seeing her browser history or stumbling across an open email client; we'd been sharing our password-locked blogs since we were kids. What was the point of having a sister if you couldn't trade bad boy-band RPF once in a while?

Flipping through her call history brought up the usual assortment of calls to schools, pet supply warehouses, and local takeout establishments, all tagged under her user name. There were seven guest calls over the past week. Three of them were to the university, and pulling up their profiles showed that the people who had initiated the calls had loaded custom avatars, dressing their words in their own curated faces. The other four . . .

The other four were anonymous, and the avatar had been generated by the system, but not retained. All four had been made from this computer to the first number in its saved database. Mine.

I scribbled down the time stamps and went to join the conversation in the kitchen, waving a hand for Tasha's attention. She turned, expression questioning. I handed her the piece of paper and signed, "Did you have the same person in the house for all four of these calls?"

Tasha frowned. "No," she signed back. "I had some conservationists for this one, picking up an owl who'd been cleared for release," she tapped the middle entry on the list, "but all those other times, I was alone with the birds. What's going on?"

"Could it be a system glitch?" asked Angie, speaking and signing at the same time. She preferred it that way, since it gave her an excuse to go slowly. She said it was about including Greg in the conversation, and we let her have that; if it kept her from becoming too self-conscious to sign, it was a good thing.

"It could," I signed. Silence was an easy habit to fall back into in the company of my sister. "I'd have to take the whole system apart to be sure. Tasha, are you all right with my cloning it and unsnarling things once I get home?"

"As long as this glitch isn't going to break anything, I don't care," she signed.

I nodded. "It should be fine," I signed. "If it's a system error, that would explain why our caller keeps saying 'hello' and never getting any further. I'll be able to let you know in a couple of days."

Billie tugged on Tasha's sleeve. We all turned. Billie beamed. "Can we see the parrots now?" she signed. Tasha laughed, and for a while, everything was normal. Everything was the way it was supposed to be.

My snapshot of Tasha's system revealed no errors with the code, although I found some interesting logical chains in her translation software's neural network that I copied over and sent to R&D for further analysis. She had one of the most advanced learning systems outside of corporate, in part because she was my sister, and in part because she was a bilingual deaf person, speaking both American and British Sign Language with the people she communicated with. Giving her a system that could handle the additional nonverbal processing was allowing us to build out a better neural chain and translation database than any amount of laboratory testing could produce, with the added bonus of equipping my sister to speak with conservationists all over the world. It's always nice when corporate and family needs align.

The calls were being intentionally initiated by someone who had access to Tasha's computer. There was no way this was a ghost in the machine or a connection routing error. Malware was still a possibility, given the generic avatar; someone could be spoofing the machine into opening the call, then overlaying the woman onto the backdrop of Tasha's dining room. I didn't know what purpose that would serve, unless this was the warm-up to some innovative denial-of-service attack. I kept digging.

"Hello? Hello?"

My head snapped up. The voice was coming from the main computer in the dining room. It was somehow less of a surprise when Billie answered a moment later: "Hello! How are you?"

"Hello, hello, I'm fine. I'm good. I'm hungry. How are you?"

I rose from my seat, using the table to steady myself before walking, carefully, quietly, toward the next room. There was Billie, seated in front of the terminal, where the strange woman's image was once again projected. Greg was nowhere to be seen. He was probably off somewhere busying himself with toddler projects, like stacking blocks or talking to spiders, leaving his sister to unwittingly assist in industrial espionage.

"Billie?"

Billie turned, all smiles, as the woman on the screen shifted her focus to me, cocking her head slightly to the side to give herself a better view. "Hi, Mom!" my daughter chirped, her fingers moving in the appropriate signs at the same time. "I figured it out!"

"Figured what out, sweetie?"

"Why we couldn't understand each other!" She gestured grandly to the screen where the black-haired woman waited. "Mumma showed me."

I frowned, taking a step closer. "Showed you what?"

"Hello, hello; can you hear me? Hello," said the woman.

"Hello," I said, automatically.

Billie was undaunted. "When we went to see Aunt Tasha, Mumma used her speaking words and her finger words at the same time, so Greg could know what we were saying. She was bridging." Her fingers moved in time with her lips. ASL doesn't have the same grammatical structure as spoken English; my daughter was running two linguistic processing paths at the same time. I wanted to take the time to be proud of her for that. I was too busy trying to understand.

"You mean she was building a linguistic bridge?" I asked.

Billie nodded vigorously. "Yeah. Bridging. So I thought maybe we couldn't understand each other because the neural net didn't have enough to work with, and I turned off the avatar setting on this side."

My heart clenched. The avatar projections for Billie and Greg were intended to keep their real faces hidden from anyone who wasn't family. It was a small precaution, but anything that would keep their images off the public Internet until they turned eighteen was a good idea as far as I was concerned. "Billie, we've talked about the avatars. They're there to keep you safe."

"But she needed to see my hands," said Billie, with serene childhood logic. "Once she could, we started communicating better. See? I just needed to give the translator more data!"

"Hello," said the woman.

"Hello," I said, moving closer to the screen. After a beat, I followed the word with the appropriate sign. "What's your name? Why do you keep calling my house?"

"I'm hungry," said the woman. "I'm hungry."

"You're not answering my question."

The woman opened her mouth like she was laughing, but no sound came out. She closed it again with a snap and said, "I'm hungry. I don't know you. Where is the other one?"

"Here I am!" said Billie, pushing her way back to the front. "Sorry about Mom. She doesn't understand that we're doing science here."

"Science, yes," said the woman obligingly. "Hello, hello. I'm hungry."

"I get hungry, too," said Billie. "Maybe some cereal?"

I took a step back, letting the two of them talk. I didn't like the idea of leaving my little girl with a live connection to God-knows-who. I also didn't like the thought that this call was coming from my sister's house. If she was out back with the birds, she would never hear an intruder, and I couldn't call to warn her while her line was in use.

Angie was in the kitchen. "Billie's on the line with our mystery woman," I said quickly, before she could ask me what was wrong. "I'm going to drive to Tasha's and see if I can't catch this lady in the act."

Angie's eyes widened. "So you just *left* Billie on the line?"

"You can supervise her," I said. "Just try to keep her from disconnecting. I can make this stop, but I need to go."

"Then go," said Angie. I'd be hearing about this later. I knew that, just like I knew I was making the right call. Taking Billie away from the computer wouldn't stop this woman from breaking into my sister's house and calling us, and one police report could see Tasha branded a security risk by the company, which couldn't afford to leave software patches that were still under NDA in insecure locations.

Tasha lived fifteen minutes from us under normal circumstances. I made the drive in seven.

Her front door was locked, but the porch light was on, signaling that she was home and awake. I let myself in without ringing the bell. She could yell at me later. Finding out what was going on was more important than respecting her privacy, at least for right now. I felt a little bad about that. I also knew that she would have done exactly the same thing if our positions had been reversed.

I slunk through the house, listening for the sound of Billie's voice. Tasha kept the speakers on for the sake of the people who visited her and used her computer to make calls. She was better at accommodation than I was. The thought made my ears redden. My sister, who had spent most of her life fighting to be accommodated, made the effort for others when I was willing to focus on just her. I would be better, I promised silently. For her sake, and for the sake of my children, I would be better.

I didn't hear Billie. Instead, I heard the throaty croaking of a crow from somewhere up ahead. It continued as I walked down the hall and stepped into the kitchen doorway. And stopped.

The pied crow that Tasha had been rehabilitating was perched on the back of the chair across from the computer, talons digging deep into the wood as it cocked its head and watched Billie's image on the screen. Billie's mouth moved; a squawk emerged. The crow croaked back, repeating the same sounds over and over, until the avatar was matching them perfectly. Only then did it move on to the next set of sounds.

I took a step back and sagged against the hallway wall, heart pounding, head spinning with the undeniable reality of what I had just seen. A language the neural net didn't know, one that depended on motion and gesture as much as it did on sound. A language the system would have been exposed to enough before a curious bird started pecking at the keys that the program could at least *try* to make sense of it.

Sense enough to say "hello."

An air of anticipation hung over the lab. The pied crow—whose name, according to Tasha, was Pitch, and who had been raised in captivity, bouncing from wildlife center to wildlife center before winding up living in my sister's private aviary—gripped her perch stubbornly with her talons and averted her eyes from the screen, refusing to react to the avatar that was trying to catch her attention. She'd been ignoring the screen for over an hour, shutting out four researchers and a bored linguist who was convinced that I was in the middle of some sort of creative breakdown.

"All right, Paulson, this was a funny prank, but you've used up over a dozen computing hours," said Mike, pushing away from his own monitor. He was one of the researchers, and had been remarkably tolerant so far. "Time to pack it in."

"Wait a second," I said. "Just . . . just wait, all right? There's one thing we haven't tried yet."

Mike looked at me and frowned. I looked pleadingly back. Finally, he sighed.

"Admittedly, you've encouraged the neural net to make some great improvements. You can have one more try. But that's it! After that, we need this lab back."

"One more is all I need."

I'd been hoping to avoid this. It would've been easier if I could have replicated the original results without resorting to re-creation of all factors. Not easier for the bird: easier for my nerves. Angie was already mad at me, and Tasha was unsettled, and I was feeling about as off-balance as I ever did.

Opening the door and sticking my head out into the hall, I looked to my left, where my wife and children were settled in ergonomic desk chairs. Angie was focused on her tablet, composing an email to her work with quick swipes of her fingers, like she was trying to wipe them clean of some unseen, clinging film. Billie was sitting next to her, attention fixed on a handheld game device. Greg sat on the floor between them. He had several of his toy trains and was rolling them around an imaginary track, making happy humming noises.

He was the first one to notice me. He looked up and beamed, calling, "Mama!"

"Hi, buddy," I said. Angie and Billie were looking up as well. I offered my wife a sheepish smile. "Hi, hon. We're almost done in here. I just need to borrow Billie for a few minutes, if that's okay?"

It wasn't okay: I could see that in her eyes. We were going to fight about this later, and I was going to lose. Billie, however, bounced right to her feet, grinning from ear to ear as she dropped her game on the chair where she'd been sitting. "Do I get to work science with you?"

"I want science!" Greg protested, his own smile collapsing into the black hole of toddler unhappiness.

"Oh, no, bud." I crouched down, putting myself on as much of a level with him as I could. "We'll do some science when we get home, okay? Water science. With the hose. I just need Billie right now, and I need you to stay here with Mumma and keep her company. She'll get lonely if you both come with me."

Greg gave me a dubious look before twisting to look suspiciously up at Angie. She nodded quickly.

"She's right," she said. "I would be so lonely out here all by myself. Please stay and keep me company."

"Okay," said Greg, after weighing his options. He reached contentedly for his train. "Water science later."

Aware that I had just committed myself to being squirted with the hose in our backyard for at least an hour, I took Billie's hand and ushered her quickly away before anything else could go wrong.

The terminal she'd be using to make her call was waiting for us when we walked back into the room. I ushered her over to the chair, ignoring the puzzled looks from my colleagues. "Remember the lady who kept calling the house?" I asked. "Would you like to talk to her again?"

"I thought I wasn't supposed to talk to strangers," said Billie, eyeing me warily as she waited for the catch. She was old enough to know that when a parent offered to break the rules, there was always a catch.

"I'm right here this time," I said. "That means she's not a stranger, she's . . . a social experiment."

Billie nodded, still dubious. "If it's really okay . . . "

"It's really, truly okay." Marrying a physicist meant that my kids had always been destined to grow up steeped in science. It was an inescapable part of our lives. I hadn't been expecting them to necessarily be so fond of it, but that worked out, too. I was happier raising a bevy of little scientists than I would have been with the alternative.

Billie nodded once more and turned to face the monitor. I flashed a low "okay" sign at Mike and the screen sprang to life, showing the blandly pretty CGI avatar that Tasha's system generated for Pitch. We'd have to look into the code to see when it had made the decision to start rendering animals with human faces, and whether that was part of a patch that had been widely distributed. I could see the logic behind it—the generic avatar generator was given instructions based on things like "eyes" and "attempting to use the system," rather than the broader and more complex-to-program "human." I could also see lawsuits when people inevitably began running images of their pets through the generator and using them to catfish their friends.

On the other side of the two-way mirror, Pitch perked up at the sight of Billie's face on her screen. She opened her beak. Microphones inside the room would pick up the sounds she made, but I didn't need to hear her to know that she was croaking and trilling, just like corvids always did. What was interesting was the way she was also fluffing out her feathers and moving the tip of her left wing downward.

"Hello, hello," said her avatar to Billie. "Hello, hello, can you hear me? Hello."

"Hello," said Billie. "My mom says I can talk to you again. Hello."

"I'm hungry. Where am I? Hello."

"I'm at Mom's work. She does science here. I don't know where you are. Mom probably knows. She called you." Billie twisted to look at me. "Mom? Where is she?"

I pointed to the two-way mirror. "She's right through there."

Billie followed the angle of my finger to Pitch, who was scratching the side of her head with one talon. Her face fell for a moment, expression turning betrayed, before realization wiped away her confusion and her eyes went wide. She turned back to the screen.

"Are you a bird?" she asked.

The woman looked confused. "Hello, hello, I'm hungry, where am I?"

"A *bird*," said Billie, and flapped her arms like wings.

The effect on Pitch was immediate. She sat up straighter on her perch and flapped her wings, not hard enough to take off, but hard enough to mimic the gesture.

"A bird!" announced the avatar. "A bird a bird a bird yes a bird. Are you a bird? Hello? A bird? Hello, can you hear me, hello?"

"Holy shit," whispered Mike. "She's really talking to the bird. The translation algorithm really figured out how to let her talk to the bird. And the bird is really talking back. Holy *shit*."

"Not in front of my child, please," I said, tone prim and strangled. The xenolinguists were going to be all over this. We'd have people clawing at the gates to try to get a place on the team once this came out. The science behind it was clean and easy to follow—we had built a deep neural net capable of learning, told it that gestures were language and that the human mouth was capable of making millions of distinct sounds, taught it to recognize grammar and incorporate both audio and visual signals into same, and then we had turned it loose, putting it out into the world, with no instructions but to learn.

"We need to put, like, a thousand animals in front of this thing and see how many of them can actually get it to work." Mike grabbed my arm. "Do you know what this means? This changes everything."

Conservationists would kill to get their subjects in front of a monitor and try to open communication channels. Gorillas would be easy—we already had ASL in common—and elephants, dolphins, parrots, none of them could be very far behind. We had opened the gates to a whole new world, and all because I wanted to talk to my sister.

But all that was in the future, stretching out ahead of us in a wide and tangled ribbon tied to the tail of tomorrow. Right here and right now was my daughter, laughing as she spoke to her new friend, the two of them feeling their way, one word at a time, into a common language, and hence into a greater understanding of the world.

Tasha would be so delighted.

In the moment, so was I.

TWELVE AND TAG

GREGORY NORMAN BOSSERT

" . . . Twelve and Tag," we shouted, and Cheung added, "You two know it?"

Zandt lowered his brows and frowned.

Adra shook her head, looked around at us. She did that, searching faces for clues about what was expected of her. "You mean tee-ay-gee like T-complete Associative Gestalt? Crew's got the sort of money for neural backup?" she asked.

Cheung said, "Not tech. It's a bar game. A slam, a rap."

Zandt's brows lowered further over pale eyes.

"An improvised impression. And then you tell stories, the worst thing, stupidest thing, most painful thing you've ever done."

"Or kindest," added Nava, back from the bar with drinks balanced in both hands. And to our chorus of complaints, "That's the way we do it—"

"—on Mars," we shouted, the crew of the *Tethys*. All but Adra and Zandt. They weren't really crew yet, not until this was done.

"This ain't Mars," Orit said, and bounced her head off the window behind her, layers of clear composite and beyond it the flat flat beige of Europa, Jupiter's fat belly propped on the horizon.

"Something we do," Perelman rumbled.

"Breaks the ice," Orit said, to groans. All we *did* was break the ice, down into the ocean that lay underneath Europa's surface.

"It's not just ice that breaks," Cheung said, "doing what we do." His fingers mimed something snapping. "It's equipment, people, whole ships sometimes. Got to know each other."

"Gotta *trust*," Nava said. She was harpoonist, which these days meant piloting a remote vehicle on a two-kilometer cable, and, as if to make up for that, everything about her was sharp. She gave Adra a sharp smile now, then flicked it at Zandt.

Adra was second-shift pilot, had been for two months. Lean and grey, swept-back eyes so dark they seemed opaque, or empty. This was her first shore leave with us; she'd come in mid-mission after her predecessor had lost an arm in a blowout.

Our assayer had just lost his nerve after that. That's the position Zandt had recently dropped into. Literally: he'd landed in-system that morning from who-knew-where, resume in hand, "ship = *Tethys*" scrawled in the margin. He hung over the table like Jupiter over the surface out the window, blond hair swept back onto broad shoulders, something in the hard lines of his face keeping him from easy handsomeness.

Adra and Zandt were already signed by the captain, but contracts could be revoked or applicants left stranded if the crew decided against the hire. That's why we were here.

We? The crew. Perelman was mate, solid, methodical, the wall between the captain and the rest. He left the running of things to Cheung, he's navigator, and Yu, she's main-shift pilot. Even the captain deferred to those two. Cheung, he was always in motion, always quick to find the right words. Yu was always still, always looking *Out* into the deep, yet somehow saw everything anyway.

Orit was cook; that's not a junior role, not on a ship that spends six months at a time under the ice. She was likely to be at the bottom of any trouble or atop another crewmember, but she always cleaned up her own messes.

Who else? Nava you already know. Patel was there, engineer, and most of the hands: Keita and Barb, Deighton and Sintra. We filled all the spots around the one long, battered table, driving the other patrons into the corners or up to the bar. It was all deep-ocean crew in this place. There were other bars for the spacers, administrators, tourists, and if any of these wandered in here, they'd be driven out soon enough by the noise and the roughhousing and the smell that clung of Europa's strange secret ocean.

That ocean was thick: with alien viruses, with complex hydrocarbons that triggered fatal autoimmune reactions, with larger creatures that fed on the sludge, and on each other, and on us. We scooped the sludge, trapped the creatures, sold the lot to brokers who sold in turn to the universities and corporations. The Outer System was one big boomtown, bigger than the whole damn Inner System by orders of magnitude, by any metric.

"So we tell a story . . . " Adra said.

"Two stories," Yu said, "one of them true, one of them false."

"And then we go around the table and vote on which was the lie."

"A bet?" Zandt said.

"A confirmation," Cheung said.

Perelman nodded, rumbled agreement.

"Though if we guess right, you buy a round," Orit added.

Cheung said, "I'll go first, so you know how it goes." He laced his fingers together, closed his eyes, a beat, opened eyes and hands, took a breath. No Twelve and Tag for Cheung; the crew knew him too well. But if there had been, the tag would be "flight." Fragile bones spread under his face like bird's wings, bird's eyes, too, black and always flitting, fingers light and fast on the ship consoles, on the table here. Hard to imagine him anywhere but *Out*, doing anything but Nav, but he'd been a singer back on Earth. The crew knew *his* stories.

"Stupidest, then," Cheung started. "I was with the captain out at Saturn, a dozen years ago. Ice mining in the Rings. I was young, thought I knew the ship, thought I knew the system. So, we found a vein heavy with tholins." A fleeting glance up at Zandt, who gave a slow nod.

"Natural organics, worth their weight in the Outer System for hydroponics, industry," Zandt said.

Cheung nodded back. "We didn't have processing facilities onship. Ice mining, you just grab hold of a piece, push it out to a moon or a station. Tholins, they're dark, easy to see in the ice. If we had pulled up to Titan station with a twenty tonne chunk of that, the market would have been ready for us. They'd set a price before we even docked, lose us twenty percent, maybe more. So I had the idea to cut across to the research station around Enceladus, process there, ship the tholins back to Titan in tanks, hit the market and get out before they knew the score.

"Enceladus was far side of Saturn so we cut across the Rings, close above the clouds, serious v, flung ourselves out the far side.

"We hit something over the B Ring that didn't show on sensors, probably just a dense pocket of dust, but we were moving fast. All I knew was, one minute I was watching the monitors, green down the board, and then *woosh* half the ship was gone. Main drivers, cargo. Seven crew. Left us in a spin that I couldn't kill with the thrusters I had left. Left us on a course that didn't go anywhere except *Out*."

Orit shivered, and Yu got that far-gone look she got, straight through the wall and into the deep.

"Long range coms were gone. All we could do was hope Enceladus picked up our beacon, had someone in-station fast enough to catch us. Four days of that spin. Spin wouldn't let you eat, wouldn't let you sleep for more than a few minutes before you'd wake up, convinced you were falling. All we could do was watch the view, Saturn, Rings, stars, Saturn, Rings, stars. The captain and I and the one remaining crewmember: 'I'm not backed up, I'll be *lost*,' she kept saying, round and round, until we had to sedate her.

"Thing was, I *was* backed up. A full T.A.G. back on Earth, nothing to be scared of, nothing to lose. I wasn't scared, I was *furious*. I hadn't had an update since I'd gotten to the Outer System. If I died and they brought me back, I'd lose a year, I'd lose those four days spinning across the Rings. And I couldn't stand the idea of losing that view."

Cheung's lips twitched, a quick humorless grin.

"We'll always want more than the tech can give us. And stupid masquerading as clever; that's the worst kind."

Adra looked around the table, looking for a hint from the crew. Some eyes met hers, some looked up at the low ceiling, sheet steel and pitted with rust, or out through the plexi at Jupiter.

"If you're a restored copy, how do you know all this?" she asked, like an accusation.

Cheung shrugged. "Enceladus Station had been tracking us the entire time, got a tug out in time to snare us. That's how the captain and I got into under-ice work, stuck on Enceladus without a ship. But the oceans here on Europa were deeper." He took a sip, swallowed, and started his second story.

"A triangle is the strongest shape. Fact. People have known it for a long time, though it took Fuller back in the twentieth century to explain how that fact unfolds across what we know.

"I was twenty. Grad school in Hong Kong. That was right after the referendum, the Second Independence, the first successful neural-nano backups, and HK was the heart of everything that was . . . everything. I was singing all night, studying all day, drinking and drugging and dragging all night *and* day, no stop, no sleep. Had a boyfriend, Grant, kept me out of the worst of the trouble. Tall, always stooped over like he was looking for something he'd dropped. Couldn't keep his glasses on straight. He was in the planetary navigation program with me, brilliant at it."

Cheung turned his head, looked out across Orit and the window and the plains to Jupiter, a long quiet look for him.

"He was gentle in bed. Generous. Never minded my nights out, even though the nights were getting longer. Morning was our time. We'd tell each other that if we could ever afford to get T.A.G.ed, we'd just record one of those mornings and live in it forever.

"I was singing fado, it'd been an underground thing in Macau but suddenly HK was the right place, right time, and I was big. Advertising deals, guest spots on the telenovelas, corporate sponsorship from VanZ. I had company lawyers circling me like mad moons: sing here, be seen there, wear this, drink that, an endless supply of drugs, nano, people. Anything to keep me busy, anything to keep me *there* making money for them.

"So I got my own lawyer. Leslie. She was from Singapore. Tiny. Quiet. You'd be sitting in a room, forget she was there, and then she'd reach a hand out, touch your shoulder. Should have been a shock, but it was like . . . "

Cheung's fingers fluttered downward.

" . . . rain falling, when you hadn't realized you were hot and dry."

"Grant and Leslie, they started meeting evenings, talking, about me, mostly, and what I was in, and how to get me out of it. One day, Leslie was still there when I got home in the morning.

"Next five months . . . "

His hands settled to the table.

"The next five months were perfect. Leslie broke deals, made new ones; suddenly I was getting paid for singing, money in the bank. Grant even came to the clubs to see me sing. He'd never risked the crowd on his own. The two of them would find a table near the front, and afterward I'd sit down with them, with no desire for anything, anyone, anywhere else."

Adra leaned in, whispered to Nava, "Is this 'kindest thing'? Because he already took 'stupid.' "

Nava put a finger to her lips. Cheung gave Adra a glance. His fingers danced around the edge of his mug.

"Five months," he continued, "and then Grant and I had our degrees. Nav certified, from UHK, any ship in the System would take us on. But Grant was talking about a PhD, teaching at the university. I'd sing, he said, and Leslie would make enough money to support the three of us, enough to get us T.A.G.ed. Nano-neural backups had only hit the market a couple of years before, but the startups were booming in HK and suddenly you only had to be filthy rich to get T.A.G.ed. Those VanZ billboards were everywhere; beautiful people doing beautiful things and then the image would freeze with one word splashed across it: Forever. That was before the hack on the Great Basin longstore, no reason to doubt that 'Forever.' "

"I didn't sleep for two nights after our certifications came through from the university. I walked, mostly, around and around the block. The HK night is too bright for stars and ships and moons, but I'd spent five years learning to do navigation in my head. No matter how I did the math, the course just led around that block again. 'Forever.'

"So I transferred all the money I had to a bank on Mars. Took a shuttle up to orbit the next morning. When I left them, they were still asleep, Leslie laid perfectly straight as always, Grant sprawled diagonal, their heads together on the pillow.

"Triangles. Too perfect. Too strong for me. I had to fly then, go *Out*, or never leave."

He looked at Adra. "So, worst thing."

• • •

Adra said, "You've made it out this far, and Jupiter the sharp edge of things these days, and that's the worst you've done? I don't believe it. Regret for the view, I buy, but not for the leaving. The first story is the true one." She looked around at the crew. Nava smiled, sharp teeth and narrow eyes.

Yu held her hands up, palms out. "We've heard his stories."

Perelman said, "It's your round, just the two of you." And looked at Zandt.

Who bit his lip and looked at the table, where Cheung's fingers had lit amongst the glasses. "You wouldn't be the first to see the trap in neuro-nano memories," he said, a deep voice, not Perelman's rumble, higher pitched but full, like the pedal tone on an organ. "Wouldn't be the first to hope the Out offered more. Anyway . . . " He looked up, caught Cheung's gaze in his own. "This crew wouldn't take you if you'd lost the captain a ship. First one's the lie."

Claps and stomps, and Patel slapped Zandt on the shoulder; might as well have slapped a stone. Adra's face fell flat, not so much a frown as indifference.

"Truth," Yu said. "The first story? That's mine. I was the surviving crewmember. It was the navigator who lost it, though, terrified about being restored from backup and losing those years, that view. We didn't sedate her; she took the drugs herself, all of them, two days before the tug caught us. Not that I wouldn't have helped her if I'd known. She was more worried about losing her memories than about losing seven crew, the arrogant shit." Yu was staring *Out*, straight through Adra, breathless, still. "Captain and I were the only ones left then, three months on Enceladus, stumbling from bar to bar, still spinning, until we met Cheung and he took us down under the ice."

Cheung's fingers brushed the top of Yu's hand, paused for a beat.

Yu took a breath then. "I was T.A.G.ed too," she said. "Would have been glad to lose those months, get to rediscover the Outer system again, see those views again for the first time." She shrugged, a millimeter motion against the ice out the window. "Missed that chance. My backup was at Great Basin. All gone now."

Zandt pushed himself up from the table. His stick was leaning against the wall under the window; when he reached for it, it toppled away from him, clashed to the floor. Yu leaned down, picked it up, but Zandt had already turned to limp toward the toilet.

Cheung took the stick from Yu. It was proportioned to Zandt, long, thick, dark wood with a hint of grain. The head was massive, a dragon caught mid-snarl in stainless steel. Orit leaned across Adra, stuck her finger into the dragon's mouth. "Shit!" she said, and sucked a drop of blood.

Nava laughed. "Always got to stick it into everything, Orit, don't you?"

Orit leered around her mouthful of finger.

Cheung got up, set the stick by Zandt's chair; it settled against the window edge with a *thud*. Cheung tapped Yu on the shoulder, and they went up to the bar.

"So. Adra," Cheung said.

Adra looked back at him over the rim of her glass, drained it. "So," she said, gave that same flat look to the rest of the crew.

"Twelve and Tag," Perelman said, his checklist voice, and we sat up, quieted down. A round of looks, at each other and back to her.

Cheung said, "It goes like this. Someone throws out an adjective, someone matches with a noun, starts with the same sound, or at least hits it somewhere. Six pairs, then someone sums it up with the tag, one word. It's all about impressions."

"Gotta be fast," Nava said.

"Gotta be *true*," Perelman grumbled. "Who's first?"

Orit said, "I got it." A pause, an arm up, fingers spread—*look at me*, that was Orit—and then she slapped the table and started it round:

"Lank,"

Barb: "Leg, Tart,"

Sintra: "Tongue, Fast" ("yeah, you wish!")

Patel: "Flat" (doubtful "huh" from Yu), "Trim,"

Nava: "Teat, Sharp" ("she always says 'sharp' ")

Cheung: "Gash" (laughs, a whistle from Orit), "Sheer,"

Perelman: "Razor,"

And Yu tagged it with: "Lash."

Adra followed the tag around the table, from face to face with that blank stare she got, as if trying to interpret some inexplicable foreign phrase, ended on Yu for a long while but Yu's face gave her nothing but Yu's own long look. Finally she shrugged, looked into Zandt's heavy golden frown instead.

She said, "Before I came on the *Tethys*, I was pilot on the *Laelaps* out of Conamara. She's not a hunter like *Tethys*, she's a mapper, nine-tenths sonar systems and a single-shift crew, dull dull work. We were under the ice—"

"No," Cheung said.

Adra froze, lips pulled thin against the sibilant "ice," chin tucked into her shoulder to face Cheung, who was sat next to her.

"No stories set under the ice," Cheung said.

"Not a good idea to lie about what goes on under the ice, not in this bar,"

Nava said, one eyebrow raised, one pointed nail flicking—*ting*—against her glass.

"And *we* already know the truth of it," someone said softly.

Adra shut her eyes, rolled them under her lids, opened them again on Cheung.

"Telenovelas, huh?" she said. "A story about telenovelas, that okay? Or are there more rules you haven't mentioned?"

The corners of Cheung's lips quirked up.

"Sure," Nava said.

"That's fine," Yu clarified.

"Telenovelas, then, and the worst thing I ever did." Adra said. "Passing someone else's weakness off as my own.

"I used to play piano. I started when I was two, so in the earliest memories I have now, I was already playing piano, and I was already good. A prodigy. There were many prodigies in Taipei, many piano prodigies, many little girl piano prodigies. We all performed in our little dresses with little bows in our hair, an endless chain of competitions, and when we weren't performing, we were practicing, or taking lessons, or reviewing video of our last recital, while she took apart my playing, note by note."

Adra lifted her glass; it was empty. Yu filled it from her own bottle, local algae beer, pale green and bitter. Adra downed it and grimaced.

"My teacher, I mean. Cold-hearted bitch. Always pushing me, never satisfied. Not just about the playing, either, it was my posture, the way I walked across the stage, my clothing which I didn't even fucking choose, but she complained about it anyway. Not that *she'd* ever gotten anywhere with her playing, not since some award when she was in grade school.

"My father was a Russian diplomat; Mother was a translator. They were both rich, family money, though she had more. Father must have always felt a little . . . weak, because of that. Russian men, they're supposed to be strong, in charge, head of the family. But it was her city, her culture, even her apartment; we lived in one of her family's places, in Dàan, took up two entire floors of the building.

"Maybe that's why he started to beat me. I was something he could be in charge of. Any excuse would do: an A-minus on a school paper, having one sock pulled higher than the other, getting caught watching telenovelas out of HK, the ones with the awful pop music."

Adra turned her flat stare on Cheung for a moment, blinked like she'd suddenly matched a memory.

"And I was such a *damn* good girl. I'd stand there and take it, and," Adra paused, teeth tight, bobbed her head, "*curtsy* afterward. And go back to my fucking lessons."

Yu had refilled Adra's glass. She took another swig, a high-tide line of green scum on her lip. "What *is* this crap?" But she drank again, wiped her mouth.

"Eight years of that, then, practice and punishment, from those first, earliest memories until the day I came up with my plan. I woke up one morning, the idea in my head. I felt so *buzzed*. First time I thought I understood what people meant when they said 'happy.'

"It was the telenovelas that gave me the idea. All that drama, every day a new disaster, another death, just because someone's *feelings* were hurt. I watched them because they were funny. I'd lay there and laugh at the foolish people slipping on the same emotional banana peel over and over again. But what I realized that night was that those shows weren't just funny, they were *true*. That's what people are really like. That's how they manipulate each other, rip each other apart with their own weakness, like Father and Mother. I could do that.

"The next months were all flubbed notes and bad posture, forgotten homework and crying fits. But it didn't work. I was getting more criticism, more beatings, not less. No matter how hard I studied the videos, no matter how much I practiced in front of the mirror, I couldn't quite get that vulnerability that let you hook people, draw them in and spin them round.

"And then one of the 'novelas did a story arc on neuro-nano. The illegal kind, pirated memories. This character got addicted, started acting like she was someone else entirely. That's what I needed.

"Money was no problem; I'd been hacking my parents' accounts since I was eight. Turns out supply was no problem, either; the big HK corporations do their manufacturing on Taiwan, just to piss off the mainland. The stuff leaked out onto the street. Literally, sometimes. The towns downwind of the plants got real strange, whole neighborhoods sharing the same strayed memory. Plenty of people willing to sell you a vial of someone else's pitiful past, even if you were a kid in knee socks, as long as you could pay.

"Now I had every human failing at my fingertips, not faked but real, as real as memory.

"After that, there were no more beatings. Not for me. Punishments, yes, dinners denied, privileges suspended, and there was always the bamboo switch. But the real beatings, those stopped. It was like all those years, they hadn't wanted perfection, they'd wanted *weakness*. The beatings stopped as soon as I started crying someone else's tears.

"Stopped for me, that is, not for my mother. I'd hear them at night, the swish and smack and grunt, and see the bruises the next day, when a collar shifted or a sleeve rode up.

"When I was fourteen, I got a full scholarship to UHK, pilot program. A ship console's not much different from the piano, really. Applied for parental emancipation the same day, walked out the door with what I had on, left all those little dresses behind in the closet. Never went back, never saw them again."

Adra stretched her shoulders back, cracked her neck, folded her arms.

"Never had any regrets, either, but I know that after I left, Mother would be there alone with Father, and the beatings would never stop. So . . . worst thing."

Crew was silent a beat. Yu and Cheung exchanged looks. Then Orit scraped her chair back. "Gotta pee." And Patel followed, and Keita and Barb hit the bar for another round.

Orit had her mouth at Nava's ear, whisper or tongue wasn't clear from Nava's sharp smile, and Deighton, mostly drunk, was asking Zandt something involved and disjointed about silicates. Perelman tapped the table, cleared his throat, a rumble like rocks falling, and said, "Adra. Second story."

Adra had gotten something new from the bar, clear and steaming. She took a sip, frowned, said, "Most painful? That's a difficult one. People let you down, and that never gets easier. But if I have to choose . . .

"I was flying shuttles, back and forth between the CSG, the Centre Spatial Guyanais, and Laplace Station. Dumb work, dull work, but the sort of thing that looks right on your CV if you are shooting for an Outer System contract."

A nod from Yu.

"I had a lover downside, another upside, and switched one or the other out every few months, but I never felt," she stabbed a palm with a fingertip, "satiated. Like eating crisps when you're hungry. You fill your belly, but not your need. The problem was, I wasn't hungry, I was thirsty."

She took another sip, waved the glass; the liquid swirled but didn't spill.

"Maybe 's not a good analogy. Point is, I was looking for the wrong thing. Wasn't sex. *That* I can handle all on my own."

Chuckles, a scornful snort from Keita. Orit said, "Gotta give *me* a chance."

"It took Tanja to show me what it was I needed," Adra continued, "and then Tanja took it back."

"I met her on a trip upside. She was Nav, first year, on her way up to a contract doing freight runs out of Laplace. We had a spare seat in the cockpit, gave her a lift. Hit the bar, after, talked late, talked the whole shift through, so I had to do the downside run on no sleep. Before I left, she took my hand—she was a tiny thing, her fingers barely wrapped around mine—and she pressed it against her face. Pressed it hard; when she let go, my fingers had left pale streaks from jaw to ear. 'I'll be here, next time you're upside,' she said, and though she'd been smiling all night, she wasn't smiling then.

"That next trip, those first shifts together, you don't need to know the details. Here's what it was like, by the end. Here's what she took from me.

"I'd get to Laplace, go straight from the docking ring to meet her, some trendy bar or new-thing restaurant. I'd be in my flight overalls, and she'd always have on some perfect little dress, killer shoes, makeup so good it was invisible. How she maneuvered low-g in those shoes, I never knew.

"We'd talk, catch up on the gossip; those low-earth orbit routes, everyone knows everyone."

"Same out here," said Nava, with her sharp-edged smile.

Adra gave her a flat look. "We'd eat and drink and talk for a couple of hours, and the whole time Tanja would be working it. She knew exactly when to cross her legs, or brush her hair back, or lean low to adjust the strap of her shoe. She could focus it like a laser. It was never someone local. But Laplace is a busy place, and there was always some random person in transit. Not really random, though. She'd pick the sort we both despised; the Earther businessman, sweaty and pink and trying to hide his low-g hard-on, or a rich bitch from one of the orbital colonies, with those stupid balloon implants inflated as far as they'd go. I'd watch her watch them, like she was slicing them into millimeter slabs for scanning. Sometimes she'd take a hit of nano, tweak herself to match their need—she had a bigger selection in that tiny purse than most dealers—but mostly she could hook them without that tweak. She'd catch their eye, look away. That was all it took. They'd sit down at our table, or she'd slip over to theirs, while I sat there unnoticed. She'd bought me this little switchblade in the Laplace gift shop; I'd carve little figures out of toothpicks, line them up like an audience to watch her work.

"At some point—there was never a signal, not that even I could tell—she'd just get up and walk out. The mark would sit there, waiting for her to return. If there was more than one of them, they'd joke about women and restrooms, or swap notes on her makeup. But after a while, they'd start to realize that she wasn't coming back. You could see it, like their faces were hollowing out from the back; then they'd crack, and then they'd crumble. I sat and watched for that moment, when their faces fell away and all that was left was an empty, shallow shell.

"Tanja would be waiting for me at my apartment, dress and shoes in a heap by the door, head down over the console I'd bought her. In that half hour since she'd gotten back from the bar, she'd have already hacked their personal accounts. Just that one conversation she'd had with them, their name, their business, maybe a glance at their phone while they were at the bar, that was all it took for Tanja to hack their lives as thoroughly as she had hacked their so-called personalities.

"We didn't steal from them, not money, anyway. Sometimes we'd delete a couple of photos, or a mailbox folder, something they wouldn't miss for months, then miss very, very much. Sometimes we'd copy a file or two; Tanja was growing some sort of crazy database of identities. And sometimes there was just nothing worth deleting and we'd add a file instead, so they'd know we'd been there, had seen everything they had and were.

"Sometimes we fucked, after; sometimes I'd tell her what a bad, bad girl she was and spank her; sometimes we just held each other. No matter what, though, after, I was full. Content. Finally, satisfied. Because what she did, the way she wrapped the marks up in their own emotions, laid their lives at my feet, showed them up as the empty shells they were, she did that for *me*.

"And then, one day, no signal, no tell, she just got up and walked. She'd been working me all night. We did that sometimes, pretended we were strangers, all part of the game. It was hot in the bar, and she was sweaty, pushy, rude. I turned to order another round, and when I turned back, she was gone. Waited in the damn room all shift, stayed there right through my next scheduled trip, and the next. Got a demerit for that in my flight record. She left me there, cracked and crumbled. Just another mark.

"She took the console, the dress and shoes she was wearing that night, left everything else. I still have her crap in a storage locker on Laplace.

"Before I met her, I was always needing something, but I didn't know what it was. After she left me, I knew what it was I needed. I just couldn't have it."

Adra looked around the table, ended on Cheung. "*That's* pain."

Orit said, "Second one's the lie. You're too lean to be a top, too strong." She traced a finger down Adra's arm. "Tops are weak."

And Patel waggled battered fingers, echoed, "Second's the lie."

But Yu shook her head, small, economical motions, that was Yu, and said, "First one's the lie. Her mother beat her, not her father, not the teacher. Beat the father, too, still does, if they're both still alive." Yu looked at Adra. "I know the type," she said.

It went around the table, then, skipping Adra, six votes against the first, four against the second, until it came to Zandt.

Zandt stared ahead, off over Cheung's shoulder, one long breath, two, then his head shifted, a huge effort to fight the inertia of that gaze, but it came around, ground to a stop on Perelman.

"What's the rule when both stories are lies?" Zandt asked.

Perelman raised a brow, dropped the corner of his mouth to counter. That was the look he used when a diagnostic came up wrong, onship, or a sensor pinged, unexpectedly.

"You call 'fault,' " Cheung answered.

Zandt swung that gaze over and down to the navigator. Cheung's eyes flicked up into it, and away again.

"Fault, then," Zandt said. "Both lies."

"Makes it six to four against the first, then," Nava said. She'd voted against the second. "We get it?"

Adra nodded, looked at Yu, looked into her glass. "It was Mother. She *was* my teacher. Beat my father, too, you got that right. He was weak, a fucking failure. Deserved it."

She shoved back from the table. "My round. Someone help carry."

A scrape and shuffle, some crew to the bar and some to the back, toilets and a stretching of legs gone stiff. Orit and Nava drifted to a dark corner, Nava's grin gleaming over Orit's shoulder.

Perelman and Cheung looked across the table at Zandt. Yu was standing by the window, looking out, but head turned, listening.

"Where was the lie?" Perelman asked.

"In the second story, he means," Cheung explained, watching his own fingers trace the rim of a glass. "What was it you heard?"

Zandt turned his head, stared at a spot on Cheung's chest. Finally, he said, "It was *all* false. Just a game to her. Stolen memories, appropriated emotions. Doesn't mean it. Doesn't *feel* it."

Yu said, apparently to the window, "There are words for that. Sociopath is one."

Perelman rumbled uncertainty. "A hard word, that."

Yu said, "She's still got those vials. Bootleg T.A.G. vectors. Hidden under a false bottom in her toiletries bag. The vials are labeled, things like 'laughing,' 'kneecap,' 'bimbo,' 'uncertainty,' 'play stupid.' "

"Should have come to me," Perelman said, a frown more hurt than angry.

"I just found out this morning, when we were getting prepped for shore leave. She didn't see me sitting there in the head. I can be quiet."

Perelman grunted.

"She unzipped the bottom of her bag, picked through the vials like she was choosing a shirt to wear. Guess she didn't find one that fit her mood; she finally put them all back. I figured out the false bottom while she was in the shower. One vial was almost empty. It was labeled 'trust.' "

"Trust her, or trust others?" Perelman asked. Yu was still looking out the window, so he turned to Cheung.

Whose fingers had pushed the clutter of mismatched bottles into a circle in the center of the table. "Trust the *crew*." Cheung said. "Don't have to be straight, under the ice. Don't have to be all the way . . . human, not in the Outer System. Just have to fit. The crew will know."

"Not all the way human," Yu echoed. She'd spread her fingers against the plexiglass as if she could hold the view in her hand. "The T.A.G. capture process uses viral systems based on Europan organisms. I've got that in me. Just having a backup at all, does that really leave us human?"

"More or less," Cheung said. Perelman blinked in confusion. Yu laughed softly, looked over her shoulder at the chatter of glass on glass.

Zandt had retrieved his glass from Cheung's circle—just tap water, he'd been drinking—and drained it. "Two years since the hack, since the Great Basin longstore was erased," he said. "So where does *that* leave you?"

"Here," Cheung said.

We tumbled back to the table, red and raucous. Deighton had his shirt off, was wringing it out. "What goes down must come up," Barb said, and Sintra added, "Man, he *spewed*."

Patel was sent to the corner with a glass of ice water to break up Orit and Nava, who spluttered and laughed and joined Deighton in the shirt-wringing.

Perelman tapped the table again. "Zandt."

Zandt was opposite Cheung and Adra, pinned between the window and the next table. Everyone shuffled their chairs, made him center.

"Twelve and Tag," Orit said, "I got—"

But Perelman rumbled right over her:

"Mass"

Sintra: "Moves, Thick"

Cheung: "Thigh, Sweet" (Orit and Nava elbow each other)

Barb: "Swung, Hung" (cheers)

Patel: "Head, Coil"

Nava: "Crown, Blunt" (a sharp look from Cheung)

Orit: "Brow"

And Adra, slumped in her chair, tagged it with: "Black."

Zandt looked at her for a long time, his eyes skin hair all a flat tarnished gold in the Jupiter-light. The crew was caught in that heavy silence, all except Cheung's fingers amongst the glasses.

"Don't know if this is worst, stupidest, most painful. Not sure it matters.

"Something I do know. I'm an addict. Don't use, haven't for twelve years, still an addict. Dad was, too, alcohol for him. Made it himself, like most out there in the Free State. Southern African Republic, part of the old South Africa, and the Boer State before that. Empty place.

"Had a sister, half-sister, Teeje, we called her. Teeje was five years younger, daughter of my stepmother. My mother died bearing me.

"Teeje was tiny, dark, like my stepmother, Indian, but she got her blood from my father. The *need*. Nano, with her. I could never stand it. Machines in your brain, tracing out someone else's memories. I wanted less to think about, not more.

"We'd found an outbuilding on the range, relay station for remote harvesters, made it our own, scavenged furniture, my music, Teeje's console, my bioprinter with the latest drug and her hacked nano. She'd be laughing, not even looking, it seemed, but the needle would slip in true and her head would go back and her laughter go deep and wild.

"Mrs. Van Zandt, we tried to stay out of her way, much as Dad would allow that. Which wasn't much. We lived in the main house, ate at the main table with them. 'They're mine,' he'd tell his wife. We were his like the house was his, like the land and the folks who worked it and Mrs. bloody Van Zandt. Teeje and I, we were a little more his than the rest, though. He'd had us T.A.G.ed, when I was thirteen and Teeje was just seven."

Nava interrupted with a snort. "Can't back up a kid." We groaned, and Orit punched her in the shoulder for bollixing the game. Nava did that sometimes, harpoonist reflexes. "It's in the U.N. neural rights charter," Nava grumbled.

But Cheung was shaking his head, an odd look on his face. "You can if you have enough money and the right connections. You can T.A.G. anyone you want, if you own the technology."

Yu nodded her small slow nod. "Van Zandt. VanZ Inc."

"Half the boats under the ice got a contract with VanZ," Perelman said.

Yu said, "VanZ is material science, nano, patents for smartcloth, adaptive armor. Weapons." She looked at Cheung. "T.A.G. tech."

Cheung was very still. "The Grand Basin longstore," he said.

"Not a lot of rules in the Free State," Zandt said. And when no one else interrupted, he continued.

"Dad was the only *Van* Zandt. We were just Zandts. And he had us, body and soul, and the souls locked away at Grand Basin out of reach. 'Forever.'

"Teeje was my sanity, all through those years. *She* was my soul. No matter how high she got, how out there, she was my center. Every moment we had away from the work, from my father, we were together. Out in our hideaway, out of our heads, out in one of those shared immersion games on her console. I'd just stagger around staring at the scenery and Teeje, she'd have hacked the environment, argyle skies and faces floating like clouds, staring back down at us like Dad did when we were little. Scare the crap out of the other players, she'd hack their accounts as well, put their own parents' faces up there too, or whatever would shake them hardest. She could hack people like she hacked machines.

"One day, I was eighteen, I came in from a two-day trip out mending fences, and she was gone. She'd left everything. Left me a note. Not going to tell you what it said. Guess this isn't 'most painful' I'm telling, because that was the most painful moment, then, and I am not yet done.

" 'I got her T.A.G.,' Dad said. 'Little bitch won't last long out there, and if she goes underground I'll have her declared dead. Then I restore a copy, and this copy I'll take special care of.'

"Doesn't mean he wasn't furious. I was too big to beat, by that time, so he took it out on Mira, that was Teeje's mother. She left him, after that. We all did, eventually, steal our selves from him. Even if he had our souls."

A pause, then. Orit leaned into Nava's ear, but Nava stopped her with a hand, wrapped her arm around Orit's shoulders to hold her still.

"I stuck there another year and a half, got my certificate in soil science from the technical school, turned *that* into a scholarship in Capetown, three year program in mining, turned that into a research grant from a Outer System mining consortium. A year of study on Luna, then a free ticket *Out*, dust the Earth off my feet and never look back.

"Because I knew that's where Teeje would be. Out. She was always sure, always fearless, was what I thought. The way she could suck down other people's memories, she'd be hungry for her own. And she'd studied. We were teleschooled, and those hours in the outbuilding while I was listening to tunes and drifting, she'd have her tablet on her lap, out of her head into someone else's, but still studying. 'Learning is just hacking my own brain,' she'd say. 'Easy.' It was, for her.

"So, all that time in Capetown and Chicago, catching up with my classes, I was trying to catch up with *her*. She'd be pilot, or nav, something like that, university program or military. Only a couple of dozen schools on Earth do that sort of training, should have been easy to find her. Wasn't. I'd have figured she was dead, if it wasn't for the messages every few months. The whole family got them, and copies to the T.A.G. Board and the Free State court, but they were always addressed to Dad. Each one signed with a notarized DNA hash, each one untraceable, each one just a single word: 'alive.' "

Orit made a sound like a hiccup. Nava turned her head with a sharp look ready, saw Orit's face and wrapped her other arm around her instead.

"I was on Laplace station, on my way back to Luna after a seminar in Chicago. Walked into a dark, crowded bar, smaller, tighter than this place here . . . "

Zandt looked at Yu's shoulder, seeing something else.

"We shouldn't have been able to recognize each other. I was ten centimeters taller, wider, she was thinner, wouldn't have seemed possible, her dark skin gone that dull space-tan and bruises under the makeup. But I saw her, soon as I walked in there, I knew her, she knew me.

"I'd been right about the Nav degree. Wrong about the course. She was training under a corporate contract, slogging through it the slow way like I was.

"I was also wrong about the sure and fearless. She was strong, yeah, but it was our father's sort of strength, stubborn and thin. I'd quit the drugs when she'd left. Was no high without her. But she was still using, the new stuff coming out of Luna, synthetic memories, psychotic break in a bottle. I thought she'd be headed *Out*, but she was just going deeper in.

"She was using another way, too, using people, selling herself to afford the stuff. She'd done tricks, she told me, to get through training, but she'd found a better way, got herself a sugar-momma up on Laplace, all the money she needed, a place to crash. A place to use. It's stable, she said, it's safe, it's just like the outbuilding, back at home, and all it cost was bruises, a little blood. Just like back at home.

"Dad's blood, didn't just have the *need* in it, had the anger too. I shouted, called her a fool, called her *his daughter*, worst thing I knew how to say, told her she had to come with me, back to Luna, get clean. My company had open positions; *always* open positions for the Outer System. She'd come back to Luna with me, and then we'd go *Out* together.

"Stood there at the dock the next shift, sure I'd blown it, sure she wouldn't come. But she did. No suitcase, just a purse full of memory sticks, wearing a little black dress and useless shoes.

"First month on Luna, I thought things were good. She was in a program, detox, had paper signed with my company for work in the Belt once we got certified, not my same division but we'd be seeing each other once a month or so. She spent all her money on a new console, on a crazy expensive intersystem network node, but I was making enough to cover rent and food for us both.

"Came home early one shift, she was passed out on her console, needle in her hand. Set her in the shower, got her conscious, shouted at her. Kept my hands down, felt proud of myself for that. She was just a wisp you'd snap like that, hadn't been eating. I'd thought it'd been the detox but it was just the nano again.

"We shouted a while, and then we talked, and then we shouted again. 'I'm *using* it,' she kept saying. 'I'm almost in.' 'What "in"?' I said. 'We're going *Out*.' 'So go, Dad,' she said, and plugged into her console.

"Wasn't going to be my dad. *Wasn't*. So I put my hands in my pockets and I went.

"I found a place to crash by the shuttle port, food out of the vending machines and no booze, just a lot of thinking. Remembering those days in our hideaway back home. Remembering the sound of her laughter. Decided that's what I'd tell her, that I didn't own her, no one did. Tell her that all I wanted was to hear her laugh again, and anything else she did wasn't my business.

"Even after I figured that out, I didn't go back to the apartment, not right away. I went through what I was going to say, what she might say back, practiced until I was sure I could get it right, could handle anything she came back with without getting mad.

"It was almost three weeks later I went back to the apartment. April 7, 2084."

Yu said something too quiet for us to hear.

"Of course she wasn't there when I got back. Just her console. The display was flashing and I thought it might be a message for me. That's what I told myself, anyway, to justify plugging in and scrolling back through the history buffer. When I realized what I was seeing, I pulled the console apart and fed it a handful at a time into the garbage disposal."

Silence. Yu and Cheung exchanged a long, sad look. And then Cheung explained it for the rest of us. "That's the date of the hack on the Grand Basin longstore. Every T.A.G. in the system was scrambled beyond recovery."

Adra fumbled amongst the bottles, found one with something left in it and downed it, leaned back again, hands in pockets.

"Station security called while I was still sweeping up the pieces. They'd found her outside an airlock, no suit, just that little dress, those shoes. She'd made it two, three steps. *Out.*"

Zandt straightened, a ponderous unfolding, his focus coming in from somewhere far to land straight across the table at Adra. "I booked a ticket back to Earth, to the Free State, but Dad was already dead by the time I got there. Massive stroke. Took that corporate contract then, been working Outer System ever since. Been searching again, too. Knew Teeje's new name by then, made it easier to track where she'd been. Korteweg, Tanja Korteweg. Teeje had found a way *Out* that I couldn't follow. Least I could do was track down her god *forever* damned sugar-momma from Laplace, the soulless sociopathic bitch who'd held the door open for her."

Everything hung. Yu stared at Adra. Nava held Orit. Cheung looked at Zandt and said "No."

Adra pushed back, pulled her hands out of her pockets. A flash of something in the Jupiter-light.

Zandt stood. His chair tipped, clattered against the table behind. A blur of steel, a *slap* of wood on flesh as he flipped his cane, grabbed it by the end. The table scraped forward as he leaned into it; glasses tipped, cracked, crashed to the floor.

The cane went up and around and down, a second when it looked like those dragon teeth would end up buried in Adra's temple, but Cheung had seen it coming, raised a hand. Fingers cracked, flapped, didn't stop the stick, no *way* to stop that stick. But he slowed it, and Adra shoved her long legs down and got a shoulder up. There was a wet *smack* of ligament displaced and skin torn, a hiss as if her breath had been forced out of her by the blow. She continued the motion, foot up on her chair, spiraling up and around. Her hip crunched glass as she came down across the table. There was a gleam as her fist connected with Zandt's ear, a meaty *scrunch*, and then Adra half-slid, half-rolled off the table and to her feet.

Zandt stood for a second, not volition but inertia. Then he toppled forward into the ruin of the table. A short black hilt protruded from his ear, a finger's width of steel switchblade.

A bottle hit the floor, rolled to a stop under the window.

Perelman was the only one still sitting. He looked at Adra, where she stood at the end of the table, arm hung limp at her side. "Leave," he said, "before station security arrives."

She stared at him, held up a bloody hand. "My arm, I need—"

"—to leave," Perelman said. "Europa. Jupiter. Go *Out* or *In*, nothing for you here anymore."

"Stories have a way of getting around," Nava said.

"It was self defense," she said.

But Perelman shook his head. Adra looked at the crew, one at a time, still trying to figure us out, us humans.

Cheung, broken fingers cradled fluttering against his chest, explained, almost gently, "You'd need someone to testify on your behalf."

"You'd need backup," Orit said, with what was almost a laugh.

Adra looked toward the bar; no one there returned her gaze. She nodded, then, blinked down at the body. "Fucked up as his sister. Must run in the blood."

She turned toward the door, and didn't look back.

Nava picked slivers of glass off her shirt. "Gotta have words with the captain," she said. "He missed something there, hiring those two. Sure didn't want either of them on our crew."

Yu tilted her head, her own small shrug, and said, "Captain trusts us to catch the deep stuff. Why we're here."

Nods all around.

Looking down at Cheung's shattered hand, Yu added, "Can't catch everything, though. Sometimes you just have to get out of the way."

Cheung grimaced, shook his head. "I've tried that before and it didn't work. Anyway, she was crew, up until she pulled the knife."

Orit spread her fingers out over the body and said, "Too bad he didn't get to his second story."

Perelman got to his feet, shook his head, rumbled, "He did."

Nava said, "Stupidest, for sure."

And Cheung tagged it: "Fault. They were both true."

THE DEEPWATER BRIDE

TAMSYN MUIR

In the time of our crawling Night Lord's ascendancy, foretold by exodus of starlight into his sucking astral wounds, I turned sixteen and received Barbie's Dream Car. Aunt Mar had bought it for a quarter and crammed fun-sized Snickers bars in the trunk. Frankly, I was touched she'd remembered.

That was the summer Jamison Pond became wreathed in caution tape. Deep-sea hagfish were washing ashore. Home with Mar, the pond was *my* haunt; it was a nice place to read. This habit was banned when the sagging antlers of anglerfish *illicia* joined the hagfish. The Department of Fisheries blamed global warming.

Come the weekend, gulpers and vampire squid putrefied with the rest, and the Department was nonplussed. Global warming did not a vampire squid produce. I could have told them what it all meant, but then, I was a Blake.

"There's an omen at Jamison Pond," I told Mar.

My aunt was chain-smoking over the stovetop when I got home. "Eggs for dinner," she said, then, reflectively: "What kind of omen, kid?"

"Amassed dead. Salt into fresh water. The eldritch presence of the Department of Fisheries—"

Mar hastily stubbed out her cigarette on the toaster. "Christ! Stop yapping and go get the heatherback candles."

We ate scrambled eggs in the dim light of heatherback candles, which smelled strongly of salt. I spread out our journals while we ate, and for once Mar didn't complain; Blakes went by instinct and collective memory to augur, but the records were a familial *chef d'oeuvre*. They helped where instinct failed, usually.

We'd left tribute on the porch. Pebbles arranged in an Unforgivable Shape around a can of tuna. My aunt had argued against the can of tuna, but I'd felt a sign of mummification and preserved death would be auspicious. I was right.

"Presence of fish *en masse* indicates the deepest of our quintuple Great Lords," I said, squinting over notes hundreds of Blakes past had scrawled. "Continuous appearance over days . . . plague? Presence? What *is* that word? I hope it's both. We ought to be the generation who digitizes—I can reference better on my Kindle."

"A deep omen isn't *fun*, Hester," said Mar, violently rearranging her eggs. "A deep omen seven hundred feet above sea level is some horseshit. What have I always said?"

"Not to say anything to Child Protective Services," I said, "and that they faked the Moon landing."

"Hester, you—"

We recited her shibboleth in tandem: "*You don't outrun fate*," and she looked settled, if dissatisfied.

The eggs weren't great. My aunt was a competent cook, if skewed for nicotine-blasted taste buds, but tonight everything was rubbery and overdone. I'd never known her so rattled, nor to cook eggs so terrible.

I said, " 'Fun' was an unfair word."

"Don't get complacent, then," she said, "when you're a teenage seer who thinks she's slightly hotter shit than she is." I wasn't offended. It was just incorrect. "Sea-spawn's no joke. If we're getting deep omens here—well, that's *specific*, kid! Reappearance of the underdeep at noon, continuously, that's a herald. I wish you weren't here."

My stomach clenched, but I raised one eyebrow like I'd taught myself in the mirror. "Surely you don't think I should go home."

"It wouldn't be unwise—" Mar held up a finger to halt my protest, "—but what's done is done is done. Something's coming. You won't escape it by taking a bus to your mom's."

"I would rather face inescapable lappets and watery torment than Mom's."

"Your mom didn't run off and become a dental hygienist to spite you."

I avoided this line of conversation, because seriously. "What about the omen?"

Mar pushed her plate away and kicked back, precariously balanced on two chair legs. "You saw it, you document it, that's the Blake way. Just . . . a deep omen at *sixteen!* Ah, well, what the Hell. See anything in your eggs?"

I re-peppered them and we peered at the rubbery curds. Mine clumped together in a brackish pool of hot sauce.

"Rain on Thursday," I said. "You?"

"Yankees lose the Series," said Aunt Mar, and went to tip her plate in the trash. "What a god-awful meal."

I found her that evening on the peeling balcony, smoking. A caul of cloud obscured the moon. The treetops were black and spiny. Our house was a fine, hideous artifact of the 1980s, decaying high on the side of the valley. Mar saw no point in fixing it up. She had been—her words—lucky enough to get her death foretokened when she was young, and lived life courting lung cancer like a boyfriend who'd never commit.

A heatherback candle spewed wax on the railing. "Mar," I said, "why are you so scared of our leviathan dreadlords, who lie lurking in the abyssal deeps? I mean, personally."

"Because seahorrors will go berserk getting what they want and they don't quit the field," she said. "Because I'm not seeing fifty, but *your* overwrought ass is making it to homecoming. Now get inside before you find another frigging omen in my smoke."

Despite my aunt's distress, I felt exhilarated. Back at boarding school I'd never witnessed so profound a portent. I'd seen everyday omens, had done since I was born, but the power of prophecy was boring and did not get you on Wikipedia. There was no anticipation. Duty removed ambition. I was apathetically lonely. I prepared only to record *The Blake testimony of Hester in the twenty-third generation* for future Blakes.

Blake seers did not live long or decorated lives. Either you were mother of a seer, or a seer and never a mother and died young. I hadn't really cared, but I *had* expected more payout than social malingering and teenage ennui. It felt unfair. I was top of my class; I was pallidly pretty; thanks to my mother I had amazing teeth. I found myself wishing I'd see my death in my morning cornflakes like Mar; at least then the last, indifferent mystery would be revealed.

When *Stylephorus chordatus* started beaching themselves in public toilets, I should have taken Mar's cue. The house became unseasonably cold and at night our breath showed up as wet white puffs. I ignored the brooding swell of danger; instead, I sat at my desk doing my summer chemistry project, awash with weird pleasure. Clutching fistfuls of malformed octopodes at the creek was the first interesting thing that had ever happened to me.

The birch trees bordering our house wept salt water. I found a deer furtively licking the bark, looking like Bambi sneaking a hit. I sat on a stump to consult the Blake journals:

THE BLAKE TESTIMONY OF RUTH OF THE NINETEENTH GENERATION IN HER TWENTY-THIRD YEAR

WEEPING OF PLANTS
Lamented should be greenstuff that seeps brack water or salt water or blood, for Nature is abhorring a lordly Visitor: if be but one plant

then burn it or stop up a tree with a poultice of finely crushed talc, &c.,
to avoid notice. BRACK WATER is the sign of the MANY-THROATED
MONSTER GOD & THOSE WHO SPEAK UNSPEAKABLE
TONGUES. SALT WATER is the sign of UNFED LEVIATHANS &
THE PELAGIC WATCHERS & THE TENTACLE so BLOOD must
be the STAR SIGN of the MAKER OF THE HOLES FROM WHICH
EVEN LIGHT SHALL NOT ESCAPE. Be comforted that the SHABBY
MAN will not touch what is growing.

PLANT WEEPING, SINGLY:
   The trail, movement & wondrous pilgrimage.

PLANTS WEEPING, THE MANY:
   A Lord's bower has been made & it is for you to weep & rejoice.
   My account here as a Blake is perfect and accurate.

Underneath in ballpoint was written: *Has nobody noticed that Blake crypto-fascist worship of these deities has never helped?? Family of sheeple. Fuck the SYSTEM!* This was dated 1972.

A bird called, then stopped mid-warble. The shadows lengthened into long sharp shapes. A sense of stifling pressure grew. All around me, each tree wept salt without cease.

I said aloud: "Nice."

I hiked into town before evening. The bustling of people and the hurry of their daily chores made everything look almost normal; their heads were full of small-town everyday, work and food and family and maybe meth consumption, and this banality blurred the nagging fear. I stocked up on OJ and sufficient supply of Cruncheroos.

Outside the sky was full of chubby black rainclouds, and the streetlights cast the road into sulfurous relief. I smelled salt again as it began to rain, and through my hoodie I could feel that the rain was warm as tea; I caught a drop on my tongue and spat it out again, as it tasted deep and foul. As it landed it left whitish build up I foolishly took for snow.

It was not snow. Crystals festooned themselves in long, stiff streamers from the traffic signals. Strands like webbing swung from street to pavement, wall to sidewalk. The streetlights struggled on and turned it green-white in the electric glare, dazzling to the eye. Main Street was spangled over from every parked car to the dollar store. My palms were sweaty.

From down the street a car honked dazedly. My sneakers were gummed up and it covered my hair and my shoulders and my bike tires. I scuffed it off in a hurry. People stood stock-still in doorways and sat in their cars, faces pale and transfixed. Their apprehension was mindless animal apprehension, and my hands were trembling so hard I dropped my Cruncheroos.

"What *is* it?" someone called out from the Rite Aid. And somebody else said, "It's salt."

Sudden screams. We all flinched. But it wasn't terror. At the center of a traffic island, haloed in the numinous light of the dollar store, a girl was crunching her Converse in the salt and spinning round and round. She had long shiny hair—a sort of chlorine gold—and a spray-on tan the color of Garfield. My school was populated with her clones. A bunch of huddling girls in halter tops watched her twirl with mild and terrified eyes.

"Isn't this amazing?" she whooped. "Isn't this frigging *awesome*?"

The rain stopped all at once, leaving a vast whiteness. All of Main Street looked bleached and shining; even the Pizza Hut sign was scrubbed clean and made fresh. From the Rite Aid I heard someone crying. The girl picked up a handful of powdery crystals and they fell through her fingers like jewels; then her beaming smile found me and I fled.

I collected the Blake books and lit a jittering circle of heatherback candles. I turned on every light in the house. I even stuck a Mickey Mouse nightlight into the wall socket, and he glowed there in dismal magnificence as I searched. It took me an hour to alight upon an old glued-in letter:

> *Reread the testimony of Elizabeth Blake in the fifteenth generation after I had word of this. I thought the account strange, so I went to see for myself. It was as Great-Aunt Annabelle had described, mold everywhere but almost beautiful, for it had bloomed in cunning patterns down the avenue all the way to the door. I couldn't look for too long as the looking gave me such a headache.*
>
> *I called in a few days later and the mold was gone. Just one lady of the house and wasn't she pleased to see me as everyone else in the neighbourhood felt too dreadful to call. She was to be the sacrifice as all signs said. Every spider in that house was spelling the presence and I got the feeling readily that it was one of the lesser diseased Ones, the taste in the milk, the dust. One of the Monster Lord's fever wizards had made his choice in her, no mistake. The girl was so sweet looking and so cheerful. They say the girls in these instances are always cheerful about it like lambs to the slaughter. The pestilences and their behemoth Duke may do as they will. I gave her til May.*
>
> *Perhaps staying closer would have given me more detail but I felt*

that beyond my duty. I placed a wedding gift on the stoop and left that
afternoon. I heard later he'd come for his bride Friday month and the
whole place lit up dead with Spanish flu.

Aunt Annabelle always said that she'd heard some went a-cour

The page ripped here, leaving what Aunt Annabelle always said forever contentious. Mar found me in my circle of heatherbacks hours later, feverishly marking every reference to *bride* I could find.

"They closed Main Street to hose it down," she said. "There were cars backed up all the way to the Chinese take-out. There's macaroni 'n' cheese in the oven, and for your info I'm burning so much rosemary on the porch everyone will think I smoke pot. "

"One of the pelagic kings has chosen a bride," I said.

"*What?*"

"Evidence: rain of salt at the gate, in this case 'gate' being Main Street. Evidence of rank: rain of salt in *mass* quantities from Main Street to, as you said, the Chinese takeout, in the middle of the day during a gibbous moon *notable* distance from the ocean. The appearance of fish that don't know light. A dread bower of crystal."

My aunt didn't break down, or swear, or anything. She just said, "Sounds like an old-fashioned apocalypse event to me. What's your plan, champ?"

"Document it and testify," I said. "The Blake way. I'm going to find the bride."

"No," she said. "The Blake way is to watch the world burn from a distance and write down what the flames looked like. You need to *see*, not to find. This isn't a goddamned murder mystery."

I straightened and said *very* patiently: "Mar, this happens to be my birthright—"

"To Hell with *birthright!* Jesus, Hester, I told your mom you'd spend this summer getting your driver's license and kissing boys."

This was patently obnoxious. We ate our macaroni cheese surrounded by more dribbling heatherbacks, and my chest felt tight and terse the whole time. I kept on thinking of comebacks like, *I don't understand your insistence on meaningless bullshit, Mar,* or even a pointed *Margaret.* Did my heart really have to yearn for licenses and losing my French-kissing virginity at the parking lot? Did anything matter, apart from the salt and the night outside, the bulging eyes down at Jamison Pond?

"Your problem is," she said, which was always a shitty way to begin a sentence, "that you don't know what *bored* is."

"Wrong. I am often exquisitely bored."

"Unholy matrimonies are boring," said my aunt. "Plagues of salt? Boring.

The realization that none of us can run—that we're all here to be used and abused by forces we can't even fight—that's so *boring,* kid!" She'd used sharp cheddar in the mac 'n' cheese and it was my favorite, but I didn't want to do anything other than push it around the plate. "If you get your license you can drive out to Denny's."

"I am not interested," I said, "in fucking *Denny's.*"

"I wanted you to make some friends and be a teenager and not to get in over your head," she said, and speared some macaroni savagely. "And I want you to do the dishes, so I figure I'll get one out of four. Don't go sneaking out tonight, you'll break the rosemary ward."

I pushed away my half-eaten food, and kept myself very tight and quiet as I scraped pans and stacked the dishwasher.

"And take some Band-Aids up to your room," said Mar.

"Why?"

"You're going to split your knee. You don't outrun fate, champ."

Standing in the doorway, I tried to think up a stinging riposte. I said, "Wait and see," and took each step upstairs as cautiously as I could. I felt a spiteful sense of triumph when I made it to the top without incident. Once I was in my room and yanking off my hoodie I tripped and split my knee open on the dresser drawer. I then lay in bed alternately bleeding and seething for hours. I did not touch the Band-Aids, which in any case were decorated with SpongeBob's image.

Outside, the mountains had forgotten summer. The stars gave a curious, chill light. I knew I shouldn't have been looking too closely, but despite the shudder in my fingertips and the pain in my knee I did anyway; the tops of the trees made grotesque shapes. I tried to read the stars, but the position of Mars gave the same message each time: *doom,* and *approach,* and *altar.*

One star trembled in the sky and fell. I felt horrified. I felt ecstatic. I eased open my squeaking window and squeezed out onto the windowsill, shimmying down the drainpipe. I spat to ameliorate the breaking of the rosemary ward, flipped Mar the bird, and went to find the bride.

The town was subdued by the night. Puddles of soapy water from the laundromat were filled with sprats. The star had fallen over by the eastern suburbs, and I pulled my hoodie up as I passed the hard glare of the gas station. It was as though even the houses were withering, dying of fright like prey. I bought a Coke from the dollar machine.

I sipped my Coke and let my feet wander up street and down street, along alley and through park. There was no fear. A Blake knows better. I took to the woods behind people's houses, meandering until I found speared on one of the young birches a dead shark.

It was huge and hideous with a malformed head, pinned with its belly facing whitely upwards and its maw hanging open. The tree groaned beneath its weight. It was dotted all over with an array of fins and didn't look like any shark I'd ever seen at an aquarium. It was bracketed by a sagging inflatable pool and an abandoned Tonka truck in someone's backyard. The security lights came on and haloed the shark in all its dead majesty: oozing mouth, long slimy body, bony snout.

One of the windows rattled up from the house. "Hey!" someone called. "It's you."

It was the girl with shiny hair, the one who'd danced like an excited puppy in the rain of salt. She was still wearing a surfeit of glittery eye shadow. I gestured to the shark. "Yeah, I know," she said. "It's been there all afternoon. Gross, right?"

"Doesn't this strike you as suspicious?" I said. "Are you not even slightly weirded out?"

"Have you ever seen *Punk'd*?" She did not give me time to reply. "I got told it could be *Punk'd*, and then I couldn't find *Punk'd* on television so I had to watch it on the YouTubes. I like *Punk'd*. People are so funny when they get punk'd. Did you know you dropped your cereal? I have it right here, but I ate some."

"I wasn't aware of a finder's tax on breakfast cereal," I said.

The girl laughed, the way some people did when they had no idea of the joke. "I've seen you over at Jamison Pond," she said, which surprised me. "By yourself. What's your name?"

"Why name myself for free?"

She laughed again, but this time more appreciatively and less like a studio audience. "What if I gave you my name first?"

"You'd be stupid."

The girl leaned out the window, hair shimmering over her One Direction T-shirt. The sky cast weird shadows on her house and the shark smelled fetid in the background. "People call me Rainbow. Rainbow Kipley."

Dear *God*, I thought. "On purpose?"

"C'mon, we had a deal for your name—"

"We never made a deal," I said, but relented. "People call me Hester. Hester Blake."

"Hester," she said, rolling it around in her mouth like candy. Then she repeated, "Hester," and laughed raucously. I must have looked pissed-off, because she laughed again and said, "Sorry! It's just a really dumb name," which I found rich coming from someone designated *Rainbow*.

I felt I'd got what I came for. She must have sensed that the conversation had reached a premature end because she announced, "We should hang out."

"In your backyard? Next to a dead shark? At midnight?"

"There are jellyfish in my bathtub," said Rainbow, which both surprised me and didn't, and also struck me as a unique tactic. But then she added, quite normally, "You're interested in this. Nobody else is. They're pissing themselves, and I'm not—and here you are—so . . . "

Limned by the security lamp, Rainbow disappeared and reappeared before waving an open packet of Cruncheroos. "You could have your cereal back."

Huh. I had never been asked to *hang out* before. Certainly not by girls who looked as though they used leave-in conditioner. I had been using Johnson & Johnson's No More Tears since childhood as it kept its promises. I was distrustful; I had never been popular. At school my greatest leap had been from *weirdo* to *perceived goth*. Girls abhorred oddity, but quantifiable gothness they could accept. Some had even warmly talked to me of Nightwish albums. I dyed my hair black to complete the effect and was nevermore bullied.

I feared no contempt of Rainbow Kipley's. I feared wasting my time. But the lure was too great. "I'll come back tomorrow," I said, "to see if the shark's gone. You can keep the cereal as collateral."

"Cool," she said, like she understood *collateral*, and smiled with very white teeth. "Cool, cool."

Driver's licenses and kissing boys could wait indefinitely, for preference. My heart sang all the way home, for you see: I'd discovered the bride.

The next day I found myself back at Rainbow's shabby suburban house. We both took the time to admire her abandoned shark by the light of day, and I compared it to pictures on my iPhone and confirmed it as *Mitsukurina owstoni*: goblin shark. I noted dead grass in a broad brown ring around the tree, the star-spoked webs left empty by their spiders, each a proclamation *a monster dwells*. Somehow we ended up going to the park and Rainbow jiggled her jelly bracelets the whole way.

I bought a newspaper and pored over local news: the headline read *GLOBAL WARMING OR GLOBAL WARNING?* It queried alkaline content in the rain, or something, then advertised that no fewer than one scientist was fascinated with what had happened on Main Street. "Scientists," said my companion, like a slur, and she laughed gutturally.

"Science has its place," I said and rolled up the newspaper. "Just not at present. Science does not cause salt blizzards or impalement of bathydemersal fish."

"You think this is cool, don't you?" she said slyly. "You're on it like a bonnet."

There was an unseemly curiosity to her, as though the town huddling in on itself waiting to die was like a celebrity scandal. Was this the way I'd been acting? "No," I lied, "and nobody under sixty says *on it like a bonnet*."

"Shut up! You know what I mean—"

"Think of me as a reporter. Someone who's going to watch what happens. I already know what's going on, I just want a closer look."

Her eyes were wide and very dark. When she leaned in she smelled like Speed Stick. "How do you know?"

There was no particular family jurisprudence about telling. *Don't* appeared to be the rule of thumb as Blakes knew that, Cassandra-like, they defied belief. For me it was simply that nobody had ever asked. "I can read the future, and what I read always comes true," I said.

"Oh my *God*. Show me."

I decided to exhibit myself in what paltry way a Blake can. I looked at the sun. I looked at the scudding clouds. I looked at an oily stain on our park bench, and the way the thin young stalks of plants were huddled in the ground. I looked at the shadows people made as they hurried, and at how many sparrows rose startled from the water fountain.

"The old man in the hat is going to burn down his house on Saturday," I said. "That jogger will drop her Gatorade in the next five minutes. The police will catch up with that red-jacket man in the first week of October." I gathered some saliva and, with no great ceremony, hocked it out on the grass. I examined the result. "They'll unearth a gigantic ruin in . . . southwestern Australia. In the sand plains. Seven archaeologists. In the winter sometime. Forgive me inexactitude, my mouth wasn't very wet."

Rainbow's mouth was a round *O*. In front of us the jogger dropped her Gatorade, and it splattered on the ground in a shower of blue. I said, "You won't find out if the rest is true for months yet. And you could put it down to coincidences. But you'd be wrong."

"You're a *gypsy*," she accused.

I had expected "liar," and "nutjob," but not "gypsy." "No, and by the way, that's racist. If you'd like to know *our* future, then very soon—I don't know when—a great evil will make itself known in this town, claim a mortal, and lay waste to us all in celebration. I will record all that happens for my descendants and their descendants, and as is the agreement between my bloodline and the unknown, I'll be spared."

I expected her to get up and leave, or laugh again. She said: "Is there anything I can do?"

For the first time I pitied this pretty girl with her bright hair and her Chucks, her long-limbed soda-coloured legs, her ingenuous smile. She would be taken to a place in the deep, dark below where lay unnamed monstrosity, where the devouring hunger lurked far beyond light and there was no Katy Perry. "It's not for you to do anything but cower in his abyssal wake," I said, "though you don't look into cowering."

"No, I mean—can I help *you* out?" she repeated, like I was a stupid child. "I've run out of *Punk'd* episodes on my machine, I don't have anyone here, and I go home July anyway."

"What about those other girls?"

"What, them?" Rainbow flapped a dismissive hand. "Who cares? You're the one I want to like me."

Thankfully, whatever spluttering gaucherie I might have made in reply was interrupted by a scream. Jets of sticky arterial blood were spurting out the water fountain, and tentacles waved delicately from the drain. Tiny octopus creatures emerged in the gouts of blood flooding down the sides and the air stalled around us like it was having a heart attack.

It took me forever to approach the fountain, wreathed with frondy little tentacle things. It buckled as though beneath a tremendous weight. I thrust my hands into the blood and screamed: it was ice-cold, and my teeth chattered. With a splatter of red I tore my hands away and they steamed in the air.

In the blood on my palms I saw the future. I read the position of the dead moon that no longer orbited Earth. I saw the blessing of the tyrant who hid in a far-off swirl of stars. I thought I could forecast to midsummer, and when I closed my eyes I saw people drown. Everyone else in the park had fled.

I whipped out my notebook, though my fingers smeared the pages and were so cold I could hardly hold the pen, but this was Blake duty. It took me three abortive starts to write in English.

"You done?" said Rainbow, squatting next to me. I hadn't realized I was muttering aloud, and she flicked a clot of blood off my collar. "Let's go get McNuggets."

"Miss Kipley," I said, and my tongue did not speak the music of mortal tongues, "you are a fucking lunatic."

We left the fountain gurgling like a wound and did not look back. Then we got McNuggets.

I had never met anyone like Rainbow before. I didn't think anybody else had, either. She was interested in all the things I wasn't—Sephora hauls, *New Girl*, Nicki Minaj—but had a strangely magnetic way of not giving a damn, and not in the normal fashion of beautiful girls. She just appeared to have no idea that the general populace did anything but clog up her scenery. There was something in her that set her apart—an absence of being like other people— and in a weak moment I compared her to myself.

We spent the rest of the day eating McNuggets and wandering around town and looking at things. I recorded the appearance of naked fish bones dangling from the telephone wires. She wanted to prod everything with the toe of her sneaker. And she talked.

"Favourite color," she demanded.

I was peering at anemone-pocked boulders behind the gas station. "Black."

"Favourite subject," she said later, licking dubious McNugget oils off her fingers as we examined flayed fish in a clearing.

"Physics and literature."

"Ideal celebrity boyfriend?"

"Did you get this out of *Cosmo*? Pass."

She asked incessantly what my teachers were like; were the girls at my school lame; what my thoughts were on Ebola, *CSI* and Lonely Island. When we had exhausted the town's supply of dried-up sponges arranged in unknowable names, we ended up hanging out in the movie theatre lobby. We watched previews. Neither of us had seen any of the movies advertised, and neither of us wanted to see them, either.

I found myself telling her about Mar, and even alluded to my mother. When I asked her the same, she just said offhandedly, "Four plus me." Considering my own filial reticence, I didn't press.

When evening fell, she said, *See you tomorrow*, as a foregone conclusion. *Like ten-ish, breakfast takes forever.*

I went home not knowing what to think. She had a bunny manicure. She laughed at everything. She'd stolen orange soda from the movie theater drinks machine, even if everyone stole orange soda from the movie theater drinks machine. She had an unseemly interest in mummy movies. But what irritated me most was that I found her liking *me* compelling, that she appeared to have never met anyone like Hester Blake.

Her interest in me was most likely boredom, which was fine, because my interest in her was that she was the bride. That night I thought about what I'd end up writing: *the despot of the Breathless Depths took a local girl to wife, one with a bedazzled Samsung.* I sniggered alone, and slept uneasy.

In the days to come, doom throttled the brittle, increasingly desiccated town, and I catalogued it as my companion caught me up on the plot of every soap opera she'd ever watched. She appeared to have abandoned most of them midway, furnishing unfinished tales of many a shock pregnancy. Mar had been sarcastic ever since I'd broken her rosemary ward so I spent as much time out of the house as possible; that was the main reason I hung around Rainbow.

I didn't want to like her because her doom was upon us all, and I didn't want to like her because she was other girls, and I wasn't. And I didn't want to like her because she always knew when I'd made a joke. I was so *angry*, and I didn't know why.

We went to the woods and consolidated my notes. I laid my research flat on the grass or propped it on a bough, and Rainbow played music noisily on her Samsung. We rolled up our jeans—or I did, as she had no shorts that went past mid-thigh—and half-assedly sunbathed. It felt like the hours were days and the days endless.

She wanted to know what I thought would happen when we all got "laid waste to." For a moment I was terribly afraid I'd feel guilty.

"I don't know." The forest floor smelled cold, somehow. "I've never seen waste laid *en masse*. The Drownlord will make his presence known. People will go mad. People will die."

Rainbow rolled over toward me, bits of twig caught in her hair. Today she had done her eyeliner in two thick, overdramatic rings, like a sleep-deprived panda. "Do you ever wonder what dying's like, dude?"

I thought about Mar and never seeing fifty. "No," I said. "My family dies young. I figure anticipating it is unnecessary."

"Maybe you're going to die when the end of this hits," she said thoughtfully. "We could die tragically together. How's that shake you?"

I said, "My family has a pact with the All-Devouring so we don't get killed carelessly in their affairs. You're dying alone, Kipley."

She didn't get upset. She tangled her arms in the undergrowth and stretched her legs out, skinny hips arched, and wriggled pleasurably in the thin and unaffectionate sunlight. "I hope you'll be super sad," she said. "I hope you'll cry for a year."

"Aren't you scared to die?"

"Never been scared."

I said, "Due to your brain damage," and Rainbow laughed uproariously. Then she found a dried-up jellyfish amid the leaves and dropped it down my shirt.

That night I thought again about what I'd have to write: *the many-limbed horror who lies beneath the waves stole a local girl to wife, and she wore the world's skankiest short-shorts and laughed at my jokes.* I slept, but there were nightmares.

Sometimes the coming rain was nothing but a fine mist that hurt to breathe, but sometimes it was like shrapnel. The sun shone hot and choked the air with a stench of damp concrete. I carried an umbrella and Rainbow wore black rain boots that squeaked.

Mar ladled out tortilla soup one night as a peace offering. We ate companionably, with the radio on. There were no stories about salt rain or plagues of fish even on the local news. I'd been taught better than to expect it. Fear rendered us rigidly silent, and anyone who went against instinct ended up in a straitjacket.

"Why is our personal philosophy that fate always wins?" I said.

My aunt didn't miss a beat. "Self-preservation," she said. "You don't last long in our line of work fighting facts. Christ, you don't last long in our line of work, period. Hey—Ted at the gas station said he'd seen you going around with some girl."

"Ted at the gas station is a grudge informer," I said. "Back on subject. Has nobody tried to use the Blake sight to effect change?"

"They would've been a moron branch of the family, because like I've said a million times: it doesn't work that way." Mar swirled a spoon around her bowl. "Not trying to make it a federal issue, kid, just saying I'm happy you're making friends instead of swishing around listening to The Cure."

"Mar, I have never listened to The Cure."

"You find that bride?"

Taken aback, I nodded. Mar cocked her dark head in thought. There were sprigs of grey at each temple, and not for the first time I was melancholy, clogged up with an inscrutable grief. But all she said was, "Okay. There were octopuses in the goddamned laundry again. When this is over, you'll learn what *picking up the pieces* looks like. Lemon pie in the icebox."

It was *octopodes*, but never mind. I cleared the dishes. Afterward we ate two large wedges of lemon pie apiece. The house was comfortably quiet and the sideboard candles bravely chewed on the dark.

"Mar," I said, "what *would* happen if someone were to cross the deepwater demons who have slavery of wave and underwave? Hypothetically."

"No Blake has ever been stupid or saintly enough to try and find out," said Mar. "Not qualities you're suited to, Hester."

I wondered if this was meant to sting, because it didn't. I felt no pain. "Your next question's going to be, *How do we let other people die?*" she said and pulled her evening cigarette from the packet. "Because I'm me, I'll understand you want a coping mechanism, not a Sunday School lecture. My advice to you is: it becomes easier the less you get involved. And Hester—"

I looked at her with perfect nonchalance.

"I'm not outrunning *my* fate," said Aunt Mar. She lit the cigarette at the table. "Don't try to outrun other people's. You don't have the right. You're a Blake, not God."

"I didn't *choose* to be a Blake," I snapped and dropped the pie plate on the sideboard before storming from the room. I took each stair as noisily as possible, but not noisily enough to drown out her holler: "If you *ever* get a choice in this life, kiddo, treasure it!"

Rainbow noticed my foul mood. She did not tell me to cheer up or ask me what the matter was, thankfully. She wasn't that type of girl. Fog boiled low in the valley and the townspeople stumbled through the streets and talked about atmospheric pressure. Stores closed. Buses came late. Someone from the northeast suburbs had given in and shot himself.

I felt numb and untouched, and worse—when chill winds wrapped around my neck and let me breathe clear air, smelling like the beach and things that grow on the beach—I was happy. I nipped this in its emotional bud. Rainbow, of course, was as cheerful and unaffected as a stump.

Midsummer boiled closer and I thought about telling her. I would say outright, *Miss Kipley.* ("Rainbow" had never left my lips, the correct method with anyone who was *je m'appelle Rainbow.*) *When the ocean lurker comes to take his victim, his victim will be you. Do whatever you wish with this information.* Perhaps she'd finally scream. Or plead. Anything.

But when I got my courage up, she leaned in close and combed her fingers through my hair, right down to the undyed roots. Her hands were very delicate, and I clammed up. My sullen silence was no barrier to Rainbow. She just cranked up Taylor Swift.

We were sitting in a greasy bus shelter opposite Walmart when the man committed suicide. There was no showboating hesitation in the way he appeared on the roof, then stepped off at thirty feet. He landed on the spines of a wrought-iron fence. The sound was like a cocktail weenie going through a hole punch.

There was nobody around but us. I froze and did not look away. Next to me, Rainbow was equally transfixed. I felt terrible shame when *she* was the one to drag us over to him. She already had her phone out. I had seen corpses before, but this was very fresh. There was a terrible amount of blood. He was irreparably dead. I turned my head to inform Rainbow, in case she tried to help him or something equally demented, and then I saw she was taking his picture.

"Got your notebook?" she said.

There was no fear in her. No concern. Rainbow reached out to prod at one mangled, outflung leg. Two spots of colour bloomed high on her cheeks; she was luminously pleased.

"What the fuck is *wrong with you*?" My voice sounded embarrassingly shrill. "This man just killed himself!"

"The fence helped," said Rainbow helplessly.

"You think this is a *joke*—what *reason* could you have for thinking this is okay—"

"Excuse you, we look at dead shit all the time. I thought we'd hit jackpot, we've never found a dead guy . . ."

Her distress was sulky and real. I took her by the shoulders of her stupid cropped jacket and gripped tight, fear a tinder to my misery. The rain whipped around us and stung my face. "Christ, you think this is some kind of game, or . . . or a YouTube stunt! You really can't imagine—you have no *comprehension*—you mindless *jackass*—"

She was trying to calm me, feebly patting my hands. "Stop being mad at me, it sucks! What gives, Hester—"

"*You're* the bride, Kipley. It's coming for *you*."

Rainbow stepped out of my shaking, febrile grip. For a moment her lips pressed very tightly together and I wondered if she would cry. Then her mouth quirked into an uncomprehending, furtive little smile.

"*Me*," she repeated.

"Yes."

"You really think it's *me?*"

"You *know* I know. You don't outrun fate, Rainbow."

"Why are you telling me now?" Something in her bewilderment cooled, and I was sensible of the fact we were having an argument next to a suicide. "Hey—have you been hanging with me all this time because of *that*?"

"How does that matter? Look: this the beginning of the end of you. Why don't you want to be saved, or to run away, or something? It doesn't *matter*."

"It matters," said Rainbow, with infinite dignity, "to me. You know what I think?"

She did not wait to hear what I imagined she thought, which was wise. She hopped away from the dead man and held her palms up to the rain. The air was thick with an electrifying chill: a breathless enormity. We were so close now. Color leached from the Walmart, from the concrete, from the green in the trees and the red of the stop sign. Raindrops sat in her pale hair like pearls.

"I think this is the coolest thing that ever happened to this stupid backwater place," she said. "This is awesome. And I think you agree but won't admit it."

"This place is literally Hell."

"Suits you," said Rainbow.

I was beside myself with pain. My fingernails tilled up the flesh of my palms. "I understand now why you got picked as the bride," I said. "You're a sociopath. I am not like you, Miss Kipley, and if I forgot that over the last few weeks I was wrong. Excuse me, I'm going to get a police officer."

When I turned on my heel and left her—standing next to a victim of powers we could not understand or fight, and whose coming I was forced to watch like a reality TV program where my vote would never count—the blood was pooling in watery pink puddles around her rain boots. Rainbow didn't follow.

Mar had grilled steaks for dinner that neither of us ate. By the time I'd finished bagging and stuffing them mechanically in the fridge, she'd finished her preparations. The dining-room floor was a sea of reeking heatherbacks. There was even a host of them jarred and flickering out on the porch. The front doors were locked and the windows haloed with duct tape. At the center sat my aunt in an overstuffed armchair, cigarette lit, hair undone, a bucket of dirt by her feet. The storm clamored outside.

I crouched next to the kitchen door and laced up my boots. I had my back to her, but she said, "You've been crying."

My jacket wouldn't button. I was all thumbs. "More tears will come yet."

"Jesus, Hester. You sound like a fortune cookie."

I realized with a start that she'd been drinking. The dirt in the bucket would be Blake family grave dirt; we kept it in a Hefty sack in the attic.

"Did you know," she said conversationally, "that I was there when you were born?" (Yes, as I'd heard this story approximately nine million times.) "Nana put you in my arms first. You screamed like I was killing you."

My grief was too acute for me to not be a dick.

"Is this where you tell me about the omen you saw the night of my birth? A grisly fate? The destruction of Troy?"

"First of all, you know damn well you were born in the morning—your mom made me go get her a McGriddle," said Mar. "Second, I never saw a thing." The rain came down on the roof like buckshot. "Not one mortal thing," she repeated. "And that's killed me my whole life, loving you . . . not knowing."

I fled into the downpour. The town was alien. Each doorway was a cold black portal and curtains twitched in abandoned rooms. Sometimes the sidewalk felt squishy underfoot. It was bad when the streets were empty as bones in an ossuary, but worse when I heard a crowd around the corner from the 7-Eleven. I crouched behind a garbage can as misshapen strangers passed and threw up a little, retching water. When there was only awful silence, I bolted for my life through the woods.

The goblin shark in Rainbow's backyard had peeled open, the muscle and fascia now on display. It looked oddly and shamefully naked; but it did not invoke the puke-inducing fear of the people on the street. There was nothing in that shark but dead shark.

I'd arranged to be picked last for every softball team in my life, but adrenaline let me heave a rock through Rainbow's window. Glass tinkled musically. Her lights came on and she threw the window open; the rest of the pane fell into glitter on the lawn. "Holy shit, Hester!" she said in alarm.

"Miss Kipley, I'd like to save you," I said. "This is on the understanding that I still think you're absolutely fucking crazy, but I should've tried to save you from the start. If you get dressed, I know where Ted at the gas station keeps the keys to his truck, and I don't have my learner's permit, but we'll make it to Denny's by midnight."

Rainbow put her head in her hands. Her hair fell over her face like a veil, and when she smiled there was a regretful dimple. "Dude," she said softly, "I thought when you saw the future, you couldn't outrun it."

"If we cannot outrun it, then I'll drive."

"You badass," she said, and before I could retort she leaned out past the windowsill. She made a soft white blotch in the darkness.

"I think you're the coolest person I've ever met," said Rainbow. "I think you're really funny, and you're interesting, and your fingernails are all different lengths. You're not like other girls. And you only think things are worthwhile if they've been proved ten times by a book, and I like how you hate not coming first."

"Listen," I said. My throat felt tight and fussy and rain was leaking into my hood. "The drowned lord who dwells in dark water will claim you. The moon won't rise tonight, and you'll never update your Tumblr again."

"And how you care about everything! You care *super* hard. And you talk like a dork. I think you're disgusting. I think you're super cute. Is that weird? No homo? If I put *no homo* there, that means I can say things and pretend I don't mean them?"

"Rainbow," I said, "don't make fun of me."

"Why is it so bad for me to be the bride, anyway?" she said, petulant now. "What's *wrong* with it? If it's meant to happen, it's meant to happen, right? Cool. Why aren't you okay with it?"

There was no lightning or thunder in that storm. There were monstrous shadows, shiny on the matt black of night, and I thought I heard things flop around in the woods. "Because I don't want you to die."

Her smile was lovely and there was no fear in it. Rainbow didn't know how to be afraid. In her was a curious exultation and I could see it, it was in her mouth and eyes and hair. The heedless ecstasy of the bride. "Die? Is that what happens?"

My stomach churned. "If you change your mind, come to West North Street," I said. "The house standing alone at the top of the road. Go to the graveyard at the corner of Main and Spinney and take a handful of dirt off any child's grave, then come to me. Otherwise, this is goodbye."

I turned. Something sang through the air and landed next to me, soggy and forlorn. My packet of Cruncheroos. When I turned back, Rainbow was wide-eyed and her face was uncharacteristically puckered, and we must have mirrored each other in our upset. I felt like we were on the brink of something as great as it was awful, something I'd snuck around all summer like a thief.

"You're a prize dumbass trying to save me from myself, Hester Blake."

I said, "You're the only one I wanted to like me."

My hands shook as I hiked home. There were blasphemous, slippery things in each clearing that endless night. I knew what would happen if they were to approach. The rain grew oily and warm as blood was oily and warm, and I alternately wept and laughed, and none of them even touched me.

My aunt had fallen asleep amid the candles like some untidy Renaissance saint. She lay there with her shoes still on and her cigarette half-smoked, and I left my clothes in a sopping heap on the laundry floor to take her flannel pj's out the dryer. Their sleeves came over my fingertips. I wouldn't write down Rainbow in the Blake book, I thought. I would not trap her in the pages. Nobody would ever know her but me. I'd outrun fate, and blaspheme Blake duty.

I fell asleep tucked up next to Mar.

In the morning I woke to the smell of toaster waffles. Mar's coat was draped over my legs. First of July: the Deepwater God was here. I rolled up my pajama pants and tiptoed through molten drips of candlewax to claim my waffle. My aunt wordlessly squirted them with syrup faces and we stood on the porch to eat.

The morning was crisp and gray and pretty. Salt drifted from the clouds and clumped in the grass. The wind discomfited the trees. Not a bird sang. Beneath us, the town was laid out like a spill: flooded right up to the gas station, and the western suburbs drowned entirely. Where the dark, unreflective waters had not risen, you could see movement in the streets, but it was not human movement. And there roared a great revel near the Walmart.

There was thrashing in the water and a roiling mass in the streets. A tentacle rose from the depths by the high school, big enough to see each sucker, and it brushed open a building with no effort. Another tentacle joined it, then another, until the town center was alive with coiling lappets and feelers. I was surprised by their jungle sheen of oranges and purples and tropical blues. I had expected somber greens and funeral grays. Teeth broke from the water. Tall, harlequin-striped fronds lifted, questing and transparent in the sun. My chest felt very full, and I stayed to look when Mar turned and went inside. I watched like I could never watch enough.

The water lapped gently at the bottom of our driveway. I wanted my waffle to be ash on my tongue, but I was frantically hungry and it was delicious. I was chomping avidly, flannels rolled to my knees, when a figure emerged at the end of the drive. It had wet short-shorts and perfectly hairsprayed hair.

"Hi," said Rainbow bashfully.

My heart sang, unbidden.

"*God*, Kipley! Come here, get *inside*—"

"I kind've don't want to, dude," she said. "No offense."

I didn't understand when she made an exaggerated *oops!* shrug. I followed her gesture to the porch candles with idiot fixation. Behind Rainbow, brightly coloured appendages writhed in the water of her wedding day.

"Hester," she said, "you don't have to run. You'll never die or be alone, neither of us will; not even the light will have permission to touch you. I'll bring you down into the water and the water under that, where the spires of my palace fill the lost mortal country, and you will be made even more beautiful and funny and splendiferous than you are now."

The candles cringed from her damp Chucks. When she approached, half of them exploded in a chrysanthemum blast of wax. Leviathans crunched up people busily by the RiteAid. Algal bloom strangled the telephone lines. My aunt returned to the porch and promptly dropped her coffee mug, which shattered into a perfect Unforgivable Shape.

"I've come for my bride," said Rainbow, the abyssal king. "Yo, Hester. Marry me."

This is the Blake testimony of Hester, twenty-third generation in her sixteenth year.

In the time of our crawling Night Lord's ascendancy, foretold by exodus of starlight into his sucking astral wounds, the God of the drowned country came ashore. The many-limbed horror of the depths chose to take a local girl to wife. Main Street was made over into salt bower. Water-creatures adorned it as jewels do. Mortals gave themselves for wedding feast and the Walmart utterly destroyed. The Deepwater Lord returned triumphant to the tentacle throne and will dwell there, in splendour, forever.

My account here as a Blake is perfect and accurate, because when the leviathan prince went, I went with her.

BOTANICA VENERIS: THIRTEEN PAPERCUTS BY IDA COUNTESS RATHANGAN

IAN McDONALD

INTRODUCTION BY MAUREEN N GELLARD

My mother had firm instructions that, in case of a house-fire, two things required saving: the family photograph album, and the Granville-Hydes. I grew up beneath five original floral papercuts, utterly heedless of their history or their value. It was only in maturity that I came to appreciate, like so many on this and other worlds, my Great-Aunt's unique art.

Collectors avidly seek original Granville-Hydes on those rare occasions when they turn up at auction. Originals sell for tens of thousands of pounds (this would have amused Ida); two years ago, an exhibition at the Victoria and Albert Museum was sold out months in advance. Dozens of anthologies of prints are still in print: the *Botanica Veneris*, in particular, is in fifteen editions in twenty three languages, some of them non-Terrene.

The last thing the world needs, it would seem, is another *Botanica Veneris*. Yet the mystery of her final (and only) visit to Venus still intrigues half a century since her disappearance. When the collected diaries, sketch books, and field notes came to me after fifty years in the possession of the Dukes of Yoo, I realised that I had a precious opportunity to tell the true story of my Great-Aunt's expedition—and of a forgotten chapter in my family's history. The books were in very poor condition, mildewed and blighted in Venus's humid, hot climate. Large parts were illegible or simply missing. The narrative was frustratingly incomplete. I have resisted the urge to fill in those blank spaces. It would have been easy to dramatise, fictionalise, even sensationalise. Instead I have let Ida Granville-Hyde speak. Hers is a strong, characterful, attractive voice, of a different class, age, and sensibility from ours, but it is authentic, and it is a true voice.

The papercuts, of course, speak for themselves.

Plate 1: V strutio ambulans: the Ducrot's Peripatetic Wort, known locally as Daytime Walker (Thent) or Wanderflower (Thekh).
Cut paper, ink and card.

Such a show!

At lunch, Het Oi-Kranh mentioned that a space-crosser—the *Quest for the Harvest of the Stars*, a Marsman—was due to splash down in the lagoon. I said I should like to see that—apparently I slept through it when I arrived on this world. It meant forgoing the sorbet course, but one does not come to the Inner Worlds for sorbet! Het Oi-Kranh put his spider-car at our disposal. Within moments, the Princess Latufui and I were swaying in the richly upholstered bubble beneath the six strong mechanical legs. Upwards it carried us, up the vertiginous lanes and winding staircases, over the walls and balcony gardens, along the buttresses and roof-walks and up the ancient iron ladder-ways of Ledekh-Olkoi. The islands of the archipelago are small, their populations vast, and the only way for them to build is upwards. Ledekh-Olkoi resembles Mont St Michel vastly enlarged and coarsened. Streets have been bridged and built over into a web of tunnels quite impenetrable to non Ledekhers. The Hets simply clamber over the homes and lives of the inferior classes in their nimble spider-cars.

We came to the belvedere atop the Starostry, the ancient pharos of Ledekh-Olkoi that once guided mariners past the reefs and atolls of the Tol Archipelago. There we clung—my companion, the Princess Latufui, was queasy—vertigo, she claimed, though it may have been the proximity of lunch—the whole of Ledekh-Olkoi beneath us in myriad levels and layers, like the folded petals of a rose.

"Should we need glasses?" my companion asked.

No need! For at the instant, the perpetual layer of grey cloud parted and a bolt of light, like a glowing lance, stabbed down from the sky. I glimpsed a dark object fall though the air, then a titanic gout of water go up like a dozen Niagaras. The sky danced with brief rainbows, my companion wrung her hands in delight—she misses the sun terribly—then the clouds closed again. Rings of waves rippled away from the hull of the space-crosser, which floated like a great whale low in the water, though this world boasts marine fauna even more prodigious than Terrene whales.

My companion clapped her hands and cried aloud in wonder.

Indeed, a very fine sight!

Already, the tugs were heading out from the protecting arms of Ocean Dock to bring the ship in to berth.

But this was not the finest Ledekh-Olkoi had to offer. The custom in the archipelago is to sleep on divan-balconies, for respite from the foul exudations from the inner layers of the city. I had retired for my afternoon reviver—by my watch, though by Venusian Great Day it was still mid-morning and would continue to be so for another two weeks. A movement by the leg of my divan. What's this? My heart surged. *V strutio ambulans*: the Ambulatory Wort, blindly, blithely climbing my divan!

Through my glass, I observed its motion. The fat succulent leaves hold reserves of water, which fuel the coiling and uncoiling of the three ambulae— surely modified roots—by hydraulic pressure. A simple mechanism, yet human minds see movement and attribute personality and motive. This was not pure hydraulics attracted to light and liquid, this was a plucky little wort on an epic journey of peril and adventure. Over two hours, I sketched the plant as it climbed my divan, crossed to the balustrade, and continued its journey up the side of Ledekh-Olkoi. I suppose at any time millions of such flowers are inconstant migration across the archipelago, yet a single Ambulatory Wort was miracle enough for me.

Reviver be damned! I went to my space-trunk and unrolled my scissors from their soft chamois wallet. Snip snap! When a cut demands to be made, my fingers literally itch for the blades!

When he learnt of my intent, Gen Lahl-Khet implored me not to go down to Ledekh Port, but if I insisted, (I insisted: oh I insisted!) at least take a bodyguard, or go armed. I surprised him greatly by asking the name of the best armourer his city could supply. Best Shot at the Clarecourt November shoot, ten years on the trot! Ledbekh-Teltai is most famous gunsmith in the Archipelago. It is illegal to import weaponry from off-planet—an impost, I suspect,resulting from the immense popularity of hunting Ishtari janthars. The pistol they have made me is built to my hand and strength: small, as requested; powerful, as required, and so worked with spiral-and-circle Archipelagan intaglio that it is a piece of jewellery.

Ledekh Port was indeed a loathsome bruise of alleys and tunnels, lit by shifts of grey, watery light through high skylights. Such reeks and stenches! Still, no one ever died of a bad smell. An Earth-woman alone in an inappropriate place was a novelty, but from the non-humanoid Venusians, I drew little more than a look. In my latter years, I have been graced with a physical *presence*, and a destroying stare. The Thekh, descended from Central Asian nomads abducted en-masse in the 11th century from their bracing steppe, now believe themselves the original humanity, and so consider Terrenes beneath them, and they expected no better of a sub-human Earth-woman.

I did turn heads in the bar. I was the only female—humanoid that is. From Carfax's *Bestiary of the Inner Worlds*, I understand that among the semi-aquatic Krid, the male is a small, ineffectual symbiotic parasite lodging in the mantle of the female. The barman, a four-armed Thent, guided me to the snug where I was to meet my contact. The bar overlooked the Ocean Harbour. I watched dock workers scurry over the vast body of the space-crosser, in and out of hatches that had opened in the skin of the ship. I did not like to see those hatches; they ruined its perfection, the precise, intact curve of its skin.

"Lady Granville-Hyde?"

What an oily man, so well-lubricated that I did not hear his approach.

"Stafford Grimes, at your service."

He offered to buy me a drink, but I drew the line at that unseemliness. That did not stop him ordering one for himself and sipping it—and several successors—noisily during the course of my questions. Years of Venusian light had turned his skin to wrinkled brown leather: drinker's eyes looked out from heavily hooded lids: years of squinting into the ultra-violet. His neck and hands were mottled white with pockmarks where melanomas had been frozen out. Sunburn, melancholy, and alcoholism: the classic recipe for Honorary Consuls system-wide, not just on Venus.

"Thank you for agreeing to meet me. So: you met him."

"I will never forget him. Pearls of Aphrodite. Size of your head, Lady Ida. There's a fortune waiting for the man ... "

"Or woman." I chided, and surreptitiously activated the recording ring beneath my glove.

Plate 2: *V flor scopulum*: The Ocean Mist Flower. The name is a misnomer: the Ocean Mist Flower is not a flower, but a coral animalcule of the aerial reefs of the Tellus Ocean. The seeming petals are absorption surfaces drawing moisture from the frequent ocean fogs of those latitudes. Pistils and stamen bear sticky palps, which function in the same fashion as Terrene spider webs, trapping prey. Venus boasts an entire ecosystem of marine insects unknown on Earth.

This cut is the most three-dimensional of Lady Ida's Botanica Veneris. Reproductions only hint at the sculptural quality of the original. The 'petals' have been curled at the edges over the blunt side of a pair of scissors. Each of the two hundred and eight palps has been sprung so that they stand proud from the black paper background.

Onion-paper, hard-painted card.

• • •

THE HONORARY CONSUL'S TALE

Pearls of Aphrodite. Truly, the pearls beyond price. The pearls of Starosts and Aztars. But the cloud reefs are perilous, Lady Ida. Snap a man's body clean in half, those bivalves. Crush his head like a Vulpeculan melon. Snare a hand or an ankle and drown him. Aphrodite's Pearls are blood pearls. A fortune awaits anyone, my dear, who can culture them. A charming man, Arthur Hyde—that brogue of his made anything sound like the blessing of heaven itself. Charm the avios from the trees—but natural, unaffected. It was no surprise to learn he was of aristocratic stock. Quality: you can't hide it. In those days, I owned a company—fishing trips across the Archipelago. The legend of the Ourogoonta, the Island that is a Fish, was a potent draw. Imagine hooking one of those! Of course, they never did. No, I'd take them out, show them the cloud reefs, the Krid hives, the wing-fish migration, the air-jellies; get them pissed on the boat, take their photographs next to some thawed out javelin-fish they hadn't caught. Simple, easy, honest money. Why wasn't it enough for me? I had done the trick enough times myself, drink one for the punter's two, yet I fell for it that evening in the Windward Tavern, drinking hot spiced kashash and the night wind whistling up in the spires of the dead Krid nest-haven like the caged souls of drowned sailors. Drinking for days down the Great Twilight, his one for my two. Charming, so charming, until I had pledged my boat on his plan. He would buy a planktoneer—an old bucket of a sea-skimmer with nary a straight plate or a true rivet in her. He would seed her with spores and send her north on the great circulatory current, like a maritime cloud reef. Five years that current takes to circulate the globe before it returns to the arctic waters that birthed it. Five years is also the time it takes the Clam of Aphrodite to mature—what we call pearls are no such thing. Sperm, Lady Ida. Compressed sperm. In waters, it dissolves and disperses. Each Great Dawn the Tellus Ocean is white with it. In the air, it remains compact—the most prized of all jewels. Enough of fluids. By the time the reef ship reached the deep north, the clams would be mature and the cold water would kill them. It would be a simple task to strip the hulk with high-pressure hoses, harvest the pearls and trouser the fortune.

Five years makes a man fidgety for his investment. Arthur sent us weekly reports from the Sea Wardens and the Krid argosies. Month on month, year on year, I began to suspect that the truth had wandered far from those chart co-ordinates. I was not alone. I formed a consortium with my fellow investors and chartered a 'rigible.

And there at Map 60 North, 175 East, we found the ship—or what was left of it, so overgrown was it with Clams of Aphrodite. Our investment had been lined and lashed by four Krid cantoons: as we arrived, they were in the process of stripping it with halberds and grappling-hooks. Already the decks and superstructure were green with clam meat and purple with Krid blood. Arthur stood in the stern frantically waving a Cross of St Patrick flag, gesturing for us to get out, get away.

Krid pirates were plundering our investment! Worse, Arthur was their prisoner. We were an unarmed aerial gad-about, so we turned tail and headed for the nearest Sea Warden castle to call for aid.

Charmer. Bloody buggering charmer. I know he's your flesh and blood, but . . . I should have thought! If he'd been captured by Krid pirates, they wouldn't have let him wave a bloody flag to warn us.

When we arrived with a constabulary cruiser, all we found was the capsized hulk of the planktoneer and a flock of avios gorging on clam offal. Duped! Pirates my arse—excuse me. Those four cantoons were laden to the gunwales with contract workers. He never had any intention of splitting the profits with us.

The last we heard of him, he had converted the lot into Bank of Ishtar Bearer Bonds—better than gold—at Yez Tok and headed in-country. That was twelve years ago.

Your brother cost me my business, Lady Granville-Hyde. It was a good business; I could have sold it, made a little pile. Bought a place on Ledekh Syant—maybe even make it back to Earth to see out my days to a decent calendar. Instead . . . Ach, what's the use. Please believe me when I say that I bear your family no ill will—only your brother. If you do succeed in finding him—and if I haven't, I very much doubt you will—remind him of that, and that he still owes me.

Plate 3: *V lilium aphrodite*: the Archipelago sea-lily. Walk-the-Water in Thekh: there is no comprehensible translation from Krid. A ubiquitous and fecund diurnal plant, it grows so aggressively in the Venerian Great Day that by Great Evening bays and harbours are clogged with blossoms and passage must be cleared by special bloom-breaker ships.

Painted paper, watermarked Venerian tissue, inks and scissor-scrolled card.

So dear, so admirable a companion, the Princess Lautfui. She knew I had been stinting with the truth in my excuse of shopping for paper, when I went to see the Honorary Consul down in Ledekh Port. Especially when I returned without any paper. I busied myself in the days before our sailing to Ishtaria on two cuts—the Sea Lily and the Ocean Mist Flower—even if it is not a flower, according to my Carfax's *Bestiary of the Inner World*.

She was not fooled by my industry and I felt soiled and venal. All Tongan woman have dignity, but the Princess possesses such innate nobility that the thought of lying to her offends nature itself. The moral order of the universe is upset. How can I tell her that my entire visit to this world is a tissue of fabrications?

Weather again fair, with the invariable light winds and interminable grey sky. I am of Ireland, supposedly we thrive on permanent overcast, but even I find myself pining for a glimpse of sun. Poor Latufui: she grows wan for want of light. Her skin is waxy, her hair lustreless. We have a long time to wait for a glimpse of sun: Carfax states that the sky clears partially at the dawn and sunset of Venus's Great Day. I hope to be off this world by then.

Our ship, the *Seventeen Notable Navigators*, is a well-built, swift Krid jaicoona—among the Krid the females are the seafarers, but they equal the males of my world in the richness and fecundity of their taxonomy of ships. A *jaicoona*, it seems, is a fast catamaran steam packet, built for the archipelago trade. I have no sea-legs, but the *Seventeen Notable Navigators* was the only option that would get us to Ishtaria in reasonable time. Princess Latufui tells me it is a fine and sturdy craft; though built to alien dimensions: she has banged her head most painfully several times. Captain Highly-Able-at-Forecasting, recognising a sister seafarer, engages the Princess in lengthy conversations of an island-hopping, archipelagan nature, which remind Latufui greatly of her home islands. The other humans aboard are a lofty Thekh, and Hugo Von Trachtenburg, a German in very high regard of himself, of that feckless type who think themselves gentleman adventurers but are little more than grandiose fraudsters. Nevertheless, he speaks Krid (as truly as any Terrene can) and acts as translator between Princess and Captain. It is a Venerian truth universally recognised that two unaccompanied women travellers must be in need of a male protector. The dreary hours Herr von Trachtenberg fills with his notion of gay chitchat! And in the evenings, the interminable games of Barrington. Von Trachtenberg claims to have gambled the game professionally in the cloud casinos: I let him win enough for the sensation to go to his head, then take him game after game. Ten times champion of the County Kildare mixed bridge championships is more than enough to beat his hide at Barrington. Still he does not get the message—yes, I am a wealthy widow, but I have no interest in jejune Prussians. Thus I retire to my cabin to begin my studies for the *crescite dolium* cut.

Has this world a more splendid sight than the harbour of Yez-Tok? It is a city most perpendicular, of pillars and towers, masts and spires. The tall funnels of the ships, bright with the heraldry of the Krid maritime families, blend with god-poles and lighthouse and customs towers and cranes of the harbour, which in turn yield to the tower-houses and campaniles of the Bourse, the whole rising to merge with the trees of the Ishtarian Littoral Forest—pierced here and there by the comical roofs of the estancias of the Thent *zavars* and the gilded figures of the star-gods on their minarets. That forest also rises up, a cloth of green, to break into the rocky palisades of the Exx Palisades. And there,—oh how thrilling!—glimpsed through mountain passes unimaginably high, a glittering glimpse of the snows of the altiplano. Snow. Cold. Bliss!

It is only now, after reams of purple prose, that I realise what I was trying to say of Yez-Tok: simply, it is city as botany—stems and trunks, boles and bracts, root and branch!

And out there, in the city-that-is-a-forest, is the man who will guide me further into my brother's footsteps: Mr Daniel Okiring.

Plate 4: *V crescite dolium*: the Gourd of Plenty. A ubiquitous climbing plant of the Ishtari littoral, the Gourd of Plenty is so well adapted to urban environments that it would be considered a weed, but for the gourds, which contains a nectar prized as a delicacy among the coastal Thents. It is toxic to both Krid and Humans.

The papercut bears a note on the true scale, written in gold ink.

THE HUNTER'S TALE

Have you seen a janthar? Really seen a janthar? Bloody magnificent, in the same way that a hurricane or an exploding volcano is magnificent. Magnificent and appalling. The films can never capture the sense of scale. Imagine a house, with fangs. And tusks. And spines. A house that can hit forty miles per hour. The films can never get the sheer sense of mass and speed—or the elegance and grace—that something so huge can be so nimble, so agile! And what the films can never, ever capture is the smell. They smell of curry. Vindaloo curry. Venerian body-chemistry. But that's why you never, ever eat curry on *asjan*. Out in the Stalva, the grass is tall enough to hide even a janthar. The smell is the only warning you get. You catch a whiff of vindaloo, you run.

You always run. When you hunt janthar, there will always be a moment when it turns, and the janthar hunts you. You run. If you're lucky, you'll draw it on to the gunline. If not . . . The 'thones of the Stalva have been hunting them this way for centuries. Coming-of-age thing. Like my own Maasai people. They give you a spear and point you in the general direction of a lion. Yes, I've killed a lion. I've also killed janthar—and run from even more.

The 'thones have a word for it: the *pnem*. The fool who runs.

That's how I met your brother. He applied to be a pnem for Okiring *Asjans*. Claimed experience over at Hunderewe with Costa's hunting company. I didn't need to call Costa to know he was a bullshitter. But I liked the fellow— he had charm and didn't take himself too seriously. I knew he'd never last five minutes as a pnem. Took him on as a camp steward. They like the personal service, the hunting types. If you can afford to fly yourself and your friends on a jolly to Venus, you expect to have someone to wipe your arse for you. Charm works on these bastards. He'd wheedle his way into their affections and get them drinking. They'd invite him and before you knew it he was getting their life-stories—and a lot more beside—out of them. He was a careful cove too—he'd always stay one drink behind them and be up early and sharp-eyed as a hawk the next morning. Bring them their bed-tea. Fluff up their pillows. Always came back with the fattest tip. I knew what he was doing, but he did it so well—I'd taken him on, hadn't I? So, an aristocrat. Why am I not surprised? Within three trips, I'd made him Maitre de la Chasse. Heard he'd made and lost one fortune already . . . is that true? A jewel thief? Why am I not surprised by that either?

The Thirtieth Earl of Mar fancied himself as a sporting type. Booked a three month Grand Asjan; him and five friends, shooting their way up the Great Littoral to the Stalva. Wives, husbands, lovers, personal servants, twenty Thent asjanis and a caravan of forty graapa to carry their bags and baggage. They had one graap just for the champagne—they'd shipped every last drop of it from Earth. Made so much noise we cleared the forest for ten miles around. Bloody brutes—we'd set up hides at waterholes so they could blast away from point blank range. That's not hunting. Every day they'd send a dozen bearers back with hides and trophies. I'm surprised there was anything left, the amount of metal they pumped into those poor beasts. The stench of rot . . . God! The sky was black with carrion-avios.

Your brother excelled himself: suave, in control, charming, witty, the soul of attention. Oh, most attentive. Especially to the Lady Mar . . . She was no kack-hand with the guns, but I think she tired of the boys-club antics of the gents. Or maybe it was just the sheer relentless slaughter. Either way, she increasingly remained in camp. Where your brother attended to her. Aristocrats—they sniff each other out.

So Arthur poled the Lady Mar while we blasted our bloody, brutal, bestial way up onto the High Stalva. Nothing would do the Thirtieth Earl but to go after janthar. Three out of five asjans never even come across a janthar. Ten percent of hunters who go for jantar don't come back. Only ten percent! He liked those odds.

Twenty five sleeps we were up there, while Great Day turned to Great

Evening. I wasn't staying for night on the Stalva. It's not just a different season, it's a different world. Things come out of sleep, out of dens, out of the ground. No, not for all the fortune of the Earls of Mar would I spend night on the Stalva.

By then, we had abandoned the main camp. We carried bare rations, sleeping out beside our mounts with one ear tuned to the radio. Then the call came: Janthar-sign! An asjani had seen a fresh path through a speargrass meadow five miles to the north of us. In a moment, we were mounted and tearing through the high Stalva. The Earl rode like a madman, whipping his graap to reckless speed. Damn fool: of all the Stalva's many grasslands, the tall pike-grass meadows were the most dangerous. A janthar could be right next to you and you wouldn't see it. And the pike-grass disorients, reflects sounds, turns you around. There was no advising the Earl of Mar and his chums, though. His wife hung back—she claimed her mount had picked up a little lameness. Why did I not say something when Arthur went back to accompany the Lady Mar! But my concern was how to get everyone out of the pike-grass alive.

Then the Earl stabbed his shock-goad into the flank of his graap, and before I could do anything he was off. My radio crackled—form a gunline! The mad fool was going to run the janthar himself. Aristocrats! Your pardon, ma'am. Moments later, his graap came crashing back through the pike-grass to find its herd-mates. My only hope was to form a gunline and hope—and pray—that he would lead the janthar right into our crossfire. It takes a lot of ordnance to stop a janthar. And in this kind of tall grass terrain, where you can hardly see your hand in front of your face, I had to set the firing positions just right so the idiots would blow each other to bits.

I got them into some semblance of position. I held the centre—the *lakoo*. Your brother and the Lady Mar I ordered to take *jeft* and *garoon*—the last two positions of the left wing of the gunline. Finally, I got them all to radio silence. The 'thones teach you how to be still, and how to listen, and how to know what is safe and what is death. Silence, then a sustained crashing. My spotter called me, but I did not need her to tell me: that was the sound of death. I could only hope that the Earl remembered to run in a straight line, and not to trip over anything, and that the gunline would fire in time . . . a hundred hopes. A hundred ways to die.

Most terrifying sound in the world, a janthar in full pursuit! It sounds like its coming from everywhere at once. I yelled to the gunline; steady there, steady. Hold your fire! Then I smelled it. Clear, sharp: unmistakable. Curry. I put up the cry: Vindaloo! Vindaloo! And there was the mad Earl, breaking out of the cane. Madman! What was he thinking! He was in the wrong place, headed in the wrong direction. The only ones who could cover him were

Arthur and Lady Mar. And there, behind him: the janthar. Bigger than any I had ever seen before. The Mother of All Janthar. The Queen of the High Stalva. I froze. We all froze. We might as well try to kill a mountain. I yelled to Arthur and Lady Mar. Shoot! Shoot now! Nothing. Shoot for the love of all the stars! Nothing. Shoot! Why didn't they shoot?

The 'thones found the Thirtieth Earl of Mar spread over a hundred yards.

They hadn't shot because they weren't there. They were at it like dogs— your brother and the Lady Mar, back where they had left the party. They hadn't even heard the janthar.

Strange woman, the Lady Mar. Her face barely moved when she learnt of her husband's terrible death. Like it was no surprise to her. Of course, she became immensely rich when the will went through. There was no question of your brother ever working for me again. Shame. I liked him. But I can't help thinking that he was as much used as user in that sordid little affair. Did the Lady of Mar murder her husband? Too much left to chance. Yet it was a very convenient accident. And I can't help but think that the Thirtieth Earl knew what his lady was up to; and a surfeit of cuckoldry drove him to prove he was a man.

The janthar haunted the highlands for years. Became a legend. Every aristo idiot on the Inner Worlds who fancied himself a Great Terrene Hunter went after it. None of them ever got it, though it claimed five more lives. The Human-Slayer of the Selva. In the end it stumbled into a 'thone clutch trap and died on a pungi stake, eaten away by gangrene. So we all pass. No final run, no gunline, no trophies.

Your brother—as I said, I liked him though I never trusted him. He left when the scandal broke—went up country, over the Stalva into the Palisade country. I heard a rumour he'd joined a mercenary javrost unit, fighting up on the altiplano.

Botany, is it? Safer business than Big Game.

Plate 5: *V trifex aculeatum*: Stannage's Bird-Eating Trifid. Native of the Great Littoral Forest of Isharia. Carnivorous in its habits; it lures smaller, nectar-feeding avios with its sweet exudate, then stings them to death with its whiplike style and sticky, poisoned stigma.

Cutpaper, inks, folded tissue.

The Princess is brushing her hair. This she does every night, whether in Tonga, or Ireland, on Earth or aboard a space-crosser, or on Venus. The ritual is invariable. She kneels, unpins and uncoils her tight bun and lets her hair fall to its natural length, which is to the waist. Then she takes two silver-backed brushes, and, with great and vigorous strokes, brushes her hair from the crown of her head to the tips. One hundred strokes, which she counts in a Tongan rhyme which I very much love to hear.

When she is done, she cleans the brushes, returns them to the velvet lined case, then takes a bottle of coconut oil and works it through her hair. The air is suffused with the sweet smell of coconut. It reminds me so much of the whin-flowers of home, in the spring. She works patiently and painstakingly, and when she has finished, she rolls her hair back into its bun and pins it. A simple, dedicated, repetitive task, but it moves me almost to tears.

Her beautiful hair! How dearly I love my friend Latufui!

We are sleeping at a hohvandha, a Thent roadside inn, on the Grand North Road in Canton Hoa in the Great Littoral Forest. Tree branches scratch at my window shutters. The heat, the humidity, the animal noise, are all overpowering. We are far from the cooling breezes of the Vestal Sea. I wilt, though Latufui relishes the warmth. The arboreal creatures of this forest are deeper voiced than in Ireland; bellings and honkings and deep booms. How I wish we could spend the night here—Great Night—for my Carfax tells me that the Ishtaria Littoral Forest contains this world's greatest concentration of luminous creatures—fungi, plants, animals, and those peculiarly Venerian phyla in between. It is almost as bright as day. I have made some day-time studies of the Star Flower—no Venerian Botanica can be complete without it—but for it to succeed, I must hope that there is a supply of luminous paint at Loogaza; where we embark for the crossing of the Stalva.

My dear Latufui has finished now and closed away her brushes in their green baize-lined box. So faithful and true a friend! We met in Nuku'alofa on the Tongan leg of my Botanica of the South Pacific. The King, her father, had issued the invitation—he was a keen collector—and at the reception I was introduced to his very large family, including Latufui, and was immediately charmed by her sense, dignity, and vivacity. She invited me to tea the following day—a very grand affair—where she confessed that as a minor princess, her only hope of fulfilment was in marrying well—an institution in which she had no interest. I replied that I had visited the South Pacific as a time apart from Lord Rathangan—it had been clear for some years that he had no interest in me (nor I in him). We were two noble ladies of compatible needs and temperaments, and there and then we became firmest friends and inseparable companions. When Patrick shot himself and Rathangan passed into my possession, it was only natural that the Princess move in with me.

I cannot conceive of life without Latufui; yet I am deeply ashamed that I have not been totally honest in my motivations for this Venerian expedition. Why can I not trust? Oh secrets! Oh simulations!

• • •

V stellafloris noctecandentis: the Venerian Starflower. Its name is the same in Thent, Thekh, and Krid. Now a popular Terrestrial garden plant, where is it known as glow-berry, though the name is a misnomer. Its appearance is a bunch of night-luminous white berries, though the berries are in fact globular bracts, with the bio-luminous flower at the centre. Selective strains of this flower traditionally provide illumination in Venerian settlements during the Great Night.

Paper, luminous paint (not reproduced.) The original papercut is mildly radioactive.

By high-train to Camahoo.

We have our own carriage. It is of aged gothar-wood, still fragrant and spicy. The hammocks do not suit me at all. Indeed, the whole train has a rocking, swaying lollop that makes me seasick. In the caravanserai at Loogaza, the contraption looked both ridiculous and impractical. But here, in the high grass, its ingenuity reveals itself. The twenty-foot high wheels carry us high above the grass, though I am in fear of grass-fires—the steam-tractor at the head of the train does throw off the most ferocious pother of soot and embers.

I am quite content to remain in my carriage and work on my Stalva-grass study—I think this may be most sculptural. The swaying makes for many a slip with the scissor, but I think I have caught the feathery, almost downy nature of the flowerheads. Of a maritime people, the Princess is at home in this rolling ocean of grass and spends much of her time on the observation balcony watching the patterns the wind draws across the grasslands.

It was there that she fell into conversation with the Honorable Cormac de Buitlear, a fellow Irishman. Inevitably, he ingratiated himself and within minutes was taking tea in our carriage. The Inner Worlds are infested with young men claiming to be the junior sons of minor Irish gentry, but a few minutes gentle questioning revealed not only that he was indeed the Honourable Cormac—of the Bagenalstown De Buitlears— but a relative, close enough to know of my husband's demise, and the scandal of the Blue Empress.

Our conversation went like this.

HIMSELF: The Grangegorman Hydes. My father used to knock around with your elder brother—what was he called?

MYSELF: Richard.

HIMSELF: The younger brother—wasn't he a bit of a black sheep? I remember there was this tremendous scandal. Some jewel— a sapphire as big as a thrush's egg. Yes—that was the expression they used in the papers. A thrush's egg. What was it called?

MYSELF: The Blue Empress.

HIMSELF: Yes! That was it. Your grandfather was presented it with by some Martian princess. Services rendered.

MYSELF: He helped her escape across the Tharsis steppe in the revolution of '11, and then organised the White Brigades to help her regain the Jasper Throne.

HIMSELF: Your brother, not the old boy. You woke up one morning to find the stone gone and him vanished. Stolen.

I could see that Princess Latufui found The Honourable Cormac's bluntness distressing, but if one claims the privileges of a noble family, one must also claim the shames.

MYSELF: It was never proved that Arthur stole the Blue Empress.

HIMSELF: No no. But you know how tongues wag in the country. And his disappearance was, you must admit, *timely*. How long ago was that now? God, I must have been a wee gossoon.

MYSELF: Fifteen years.

HIMSELF: Fifteen years! And not a word? Do you know if he's even alive?

MYSELF: We believe he fled to the Inner Worlds. Every few years we hear of a sighting, but most of them are so contrary, we dismiss them. He made his choice. As for the Blue Empress: broken up and sold long ago, I don't doubt.

HIMSELF: And here I find you on a jaunt across one of the Inner Worlds.

MYSELF: I am creating a new album of papercuts. The Botanica Veneris.

HIMSELF: Of course. If I might make so bold, Lady Rathangan: the Blue Empress: do you believe Arthur took it?

And I made him no verbal answer, but gave the smallest shake of my head.

• • •

Princess Latufui had been restless all this evening—the time before sleep, that is: Great Evening was still many Terrene days off. Can we ever truly adapt to the monstrous Venerian calendar? Arthur has been on this world for fifteen years—has he drifted not just to another world, but another clock, another calendar? I worked on my Stalva-grass cut—I find that curving the leaf-bearing nodes gives the necessary three-dimensionality—but my heart was not in it. Latufui sipped at tea and fumbled at stitching and pushed newspapers around until eventually she threw open the cabin door in frustration and demanded that I join her on the balcony.

The rolling travel of the high-train made me grip the rail for dear life, but the high-plain was as sharp and fresh as if starched, and there, a long line on the horizon beyond the belching smokestack and pumping pistons of the tractor, were the Palisades of Exx: a grey wall from one horizon to the other. Clouds hid the peaks, like a curtain lowered from the sky.

Dark against the grey mountains, I saw the spires of the observatories of Camahoo. This was the Thent homeland; and I was apprehensive, for among those towers and minarets is a hoondahvi, a Thent opium den, owned by the person who may be able to tell me the next part of my brother's story—a story increasingly disturbing and dark. A person who is not human.

"Ida, dear friend. There is a thing I must ask you."

"Anything, dear Latufui."

"I must tell you, it is not a thing that can be asked softly."

My heart turned over in my chest. I knew what Latufui would ask.

"Ida: have you come to this world to look for your brother?"

She did me the courtesy of a direct question. No preamble, no preliminary sifting through her doubts and evidences. I owed it a direct answer.

"Yes," I said. "I have come to find Arthur."

"I thought so."

"For how long?"

"Since Ledekh-Olkoi. Ah, I cannot say the words right. When you went to get papers and gum and returned empty-handed."

"I went to see a Mr Stafford Grimes. I had information that he had met my brother soon after his arrival on this world. He directed me to Mr Okiring, a retired Asjan-hunter in Yez Tok."

"And Cama-oo? Is this another link in the chain?"

"It is. But the Botanica is no sham. I have an obligation to my backers—you know the state of my finances as well as I, Latufui. The late Count Rathangan was a profligate man. He ran the estate into the ground."

"I could wish you had trusted me. All those weeks of planning and organising. The maps, the itineraries, the tickets, the transplanetary calls to agents and factors. I was so excited! A journey to another world! But for you, there was always something else. None of that was the whole truth. None of it was honest."

"Oh, my dear Latufui . . . " But how could I say that I had not told her because I feared what Arthur might have become. Fears that seemed to be borne out by every ruined life that had touched his. What would I find? Did anything remain of the wild, carefree boy I remembered chasing old Bunty the dog across the summer lawns of Grangegorman? Would I recognise him? Worse, would he listen to me? "There is a wrong to right. An old debt to be cancelled. It's a family thing."

"I live in your house, but not in your family," Princess Latufui said. Her words were barbed with truth. They tore me. "We would not do that in Tonga. Your ways are different. And I thought I was more than a companion."

"Oh, my dear Latufui." I took her hands in mine. "My dear dear Latufui. Your are far far more to me than a companion. You are my life. But you of all people should understand my family. We are on another world, but we are not so far from Rathangan, I think. I am seeking Arthur, and I do not know what I will find, but I promise you, what he says to me, I will tell to you. Everything."

Now she laid her hands over mine, and there we stood, cupping hands on the balcony rail, watching the needle spires of Camahoo rise from the grass spears of the Stalva.

V vallumque foenum: Stalva Pike Grass. Another non-Terrene that is finding favour in Terrestrial ornamental gardens. Earth never receives sufficient sunlight for it to attain its full Stalva height. *Yetten* in the Stalva Thent dialect.

Card, onionskin paper, corrugated paper, paint. This papercut is unique in that it unfolds into three parts. The original, in the Chester Beatty Library in Dublin, is always displayed unfolded.

THE MERCENARY'S TALE

In the name of the Leader of the Starry Skies and the Ever-Circling Spiritual Family, welcome to my hoondahvi. May *apsas* speak; may *gavanda* sing, may the *thoo* impart their secrets!

I understand completely that you have not come to drink. But the greeting is standard. We pride ourself on being the most traditional hoondahvi in Exxaa Canton.

Is the music annoying? No? Most Terrenes find it aggravating. It's an essential part of the hoondahvi experience, I am afraid.

Your brother, yes. How could I forget him? I owe him my life.

He fought like a man who hated fighting. Up on the Altiplano, when we smashed open the potteries and set the Porcelain Towns afire up and down the Valley of the Kilns, there were those who blazed with love and joy at the slaughter and those whose faces were so dark it was as if their souls were clogged with soot. Your brother was one of those. Human expressions are hard for us to read—your faces are wood, like masks. But I saw his face and knew that he loathed what he did. That was what made him the best of javrosts. I am an old career soldier; I have seen many many come to our band. The ones in love with violence: unless they can take discipline, we turn them away. But when a mercenary hates what he does for his silver, there must be a greater darkness driving him. There is a thing they hate more than the violence they do.

Are you sure the music is tolerable? Our harmonies and chord patterns apparently create unpleasant electrical resonance in the human brain. Like small seizures. We find it most reassuring. Like the rhythm of the kittening-womb.

Your brother came to us in the dawn of Great Day 6817. He could ride a graap, bivouac, cook, and was handy with both bolt and blade. We never ask questions of our javrosts—in time they answer them all themselves—but rumours blow on the wind like *thagoon*-down. He was an minor aristocrat, he was a gambler; he was a thief, he was a murderer; he was a seducer, he was a traitor. Nothing to disqualify him. Sufficient to recommend him.

In Old Days the Duke of Yoo disputed mightily with her neighbour the Duke of Hetteten over who rightly ruled the altiplano and its profitable potteries. From time immemorial, it had been a place beyond: independently minded and stubborn of spirit, with little respect for gods or dukes. Wars were fought down generations, lying waste to fames and fortunes, and when in the end, the House of Yoo prevailed, the peoples of the plateau had forgotten they ever had lords and mistresses and debts of fealty. It is a law of earth and stars alike that people should be well-governed, obedient, and quiet in their ways, so the Duke of Yoo embarked on a campaign of civil discipline. Her house-corps had been decimated in the Porcelain Wars, so House Yoo hired mercenaries. Among them, my former unit, Gellet's Javrosts.

They speak of us still, up on the plateau. We are the monsters of their Great Nights, the haunters of their children's dreams. We are legend. We are Gellet's Javrosts. We are the new demons.

For one Great Day and Great Night, we ran free. We torched the topless star-shrines of Javapanda and watched then burn like chimneys. We smashed the funerary jars and trampled the bones of the illustrious dead of Toohren. We overturned the houses of the holy, burned elders and kits in their homes. We lassooed rebels and dragged them behind our graapa, round and round the village, until all that remained was a bloody rope. We forced whole communities from their homes, driving them across the altiplano until the snow heaped their bodies. And Arthur was at my side. We were not friends—there is too much history on this world for Human and Thent ever to be that. He was my badoon. You do not have a concept for it, let alone a word. A passionate colleague. A brother who is not related. A fellow devotee . . .

We killed and we killed and we killed. And in our wake came the Duke of Yoo's soldiers—restoring order, rebuilding towns, offering defense against the murderous renegades. It was all strategy. The Duke of Yoo knew the plateauneers would never love her, but she could be their saviour. Therefore, a campaign of final outrages was planned. Such vileness! We were ordered to Glehenta, a pottery town at the head of Valley of the Kilns. There we would enter the Glotoonas—the birthing-creches— and slaughter every infant down to the last kit. We rode, Arthur at my side, and though human emotions are strange and distant to me, I knew them well enough to read the storm in his heart. Night-snow was falling as we entered Glehenta, lit by ten thousand starflowers. The people locked their doors and cowered from us. Through the heart of town we rode; past the great conical kilns, to the glotoonas. Matres flung themselves before our graapa—we rode them down. Arthur's face was darker than the Great Midnight. He broke formation and rode up to Gellet himself. I went to him. I saw words between your brother and our commander. I did not hear them. Then Arthur drew his blasket and in single shot blew the entire top of Gellet's body to ash. In the fracas, I shot down three of our troop; then we were racing through the glowing streets, our hooves clattering on the porcelain cobbles, the erstwhile Gellet's Javrosts behind us.

And so we saved them. For the Duke of Yoo had arranged it so that her Ducal Guard would fall upon us even as we attacked, annihilate us, and achieve two notable victories: presenting themselves as the saviours of Glehenta, and destroying any evidence of their scheme. Your brother and I sprung the trap. But we did not know until leagues and months later, far from the altiplano. At the foot of the Ten Thousand Stairs, we parted—we thought it safer. We never saw each other again, though I heard he had gone back up the stairs, to the Pelerines. And if you do find him, please don't tell him what became of me. This is a shameful place.

And I am ashamed that I have told you such dark and bloody truths about your brother. But at the end, he was honourable. He was right. That he saved the guilty—an unintended consequence. Our lives are made up of such.

Certainly, we can continue outside on the hoondahvi porch. I did warn you that the music was irritating to human sensibilities.

V lucerna vesperum; Schaefferia: the Evening Candle. A solitary tree of the foothills of the Exx Palisades of Ishatria, the Schaefferia is noted for its many upright, luminous blossoms, which flower in Venerian Great Evening and Great Dawn.

Only the blossoms are reproduced. Card, folded and cut tissue, luminous paint (not reproduced). The original is also slightly radioactive.

A cog railway runs from Camahoo Terminus to the Convent of the Starry Pelerines. The Starsview Special takes pilgrims to see the stars and planets. Our carriage is small, luxurious, intricate and ingenious in that typically Thent fashion, and terribly tedious. The track has been constructed in a helix inside Awk Mountain, so our journey consists of interminable, noisy spells inside the tunnel, punctuated by brief, blinding moments of clarity as we emerge on to the open face of the mountain. Not for the vertiginous!

Thus, hour upon hour, we spiral our way up Mount Awk.

Princes Latufui and I play endless games of Moon Whist, but our minds are not in it. My forebodings have darkened after my conversation with the Thent hoondahvi owner in Camahoo. The Princess is troubled by my anxiety. Finally, she can bear it no more.

"Tell me about the Blue Empress. Tell me everything."

I grew up with two injunctions in case of fire: save the dogs and the Blue Empress. For almost all my life, the jewel was a ghost-stone—present but unseen, haunting Grangegorman and the lives it held. I have a memory from earliest childhood of seeing the stone—never touching it— but I do not trust the memory. Imaginings too easily become memories, memories imaginings.

We are not free in so many things, we of the landed class. Hector would inherit, Arthur would make a way in the worlds, and I would marry as well as I could; land to land. The Barony of Rathangan was considered one of the most desirable in Kildare, despite Patrick's seeming determination to drag it to the bankruptcy court. A match was made, and he was charming and bold; a fine sportsman and a very handsome man. It was an equal match: snide comments from both halves of the county. The Blue Empress was part of my treasure—on the strict understanding that it remain in the custody of my lawyers. Patrick argued—and it was there that I first got an inkling of his true character –and the wedding was off the wedding was on the wedding was off the wedding was on again and the banns posted. A viewing was arranged, for his people to itemise and value the Hyde treasure. For the first time in long memory, the Blue Empress was taken from its safe and displayed to human view. Blue as the wide Atlantic it was, and as boundless and clear. You could lose yourself forever in the light inside that gem. And yes, it was the size of a thrush's egg.

And then the moment that all the stories agree on: the lights failed. Not so unusual at Grangegorman—the same grandfather who brought back the Blue Empress installed the hydro-plant—and when they came back on again, the sapphire was gone: baize and case and everything.

We called upon the honour of all present, ladies and gentlemen alike. The lights would be put out for five minutes, and when they were switched back on, the Blue Empress would be back in the Hyde treasure. It was not. Our people demanded we call the police, Patrick's people, mindful of their client's attraction to scandal, were less insistent. We would make a further appeal to honour: if the Blue Empress was not back by morning, then we would call the guards.

Not only was the Blue Empress still missing, so was Arthur.

We called the Garda Siochana. The last we heard was that Arthur had left for the Inner Worlds.

The wedding went ahead. It would have been a greater scandal to call it off. We were two families alike in notoriety. Patrick could not let it go: he went to his grave believing that Arthur and I had conspired to keep the Blue Empress out of his hands. I have no doubt that Patrick would have found a way of forcing me to sign over possession of the gem to him, and would have sold it. Wastrel.

As for the Blue Empress: I feel I am very near to Arthur now. One cannot run forever. We will meet, and the truth will be told.

Then light flooded our carriage as the train emerged from the tunnel on to the final ramp and there, before us, its spires and domes dusted with snow blown from the high peaks, was the Convent of the Starry Pelerines.

V aquilonis vitis visionum: the Northern Littoral, or Ghost Vine. A common climber of the forests of the southern slopes of the Ishtari altiplano, domesticated and widely grown in Thent garden terraces. Its white, trumpet-shaped flowers are attractive, but the plant is revered for its berries. When crushed, the infused liquor known as *pula* create powerful auditory hallucinations in Venerian physiology and form the basis of the Thent mystical hoondahvi cult. In Terrenes, it produces a strong euphoria and a sense of omnipotence.

Alkaloid-infused paper. Ida Granville-Hyde used Thent Ghost-Vine liquor to tint and infuse the paper in this cut. It is reported to be still mildly hallucinogenic.

THE PILGRIM'S TALE

You'll come out on to the belvedere? It's supposed to be off-limits to Terrenes—technically blasphemy—sacred space and all that— but the pelerines turn a blind eye. Do excuse the cough . . . ghastly, isn't it? Sounds like a bag of bloody loose change. I don't suppose the cold air does much for my dear old alveoli, but at this stage it's all a matter of damn.

That's Gloaming Peak there. You won't see it until the cloud clears. Every Great Evening, every Great Dawn, for a few Earth-days at a time, the cloud breaks. It goes up, oh so much further than you could ever imagine. You look up, and up, and up—and beyond it, you see the stars. That's why the pelerines came here. Such a sensible religion. The stars are gods. One star, one god. Simple. No faith, no heaven, no punishment, no sin. Just look up and wonder. The Blue Pearl: that's what they call our earth. I wonder if that's why they care for us. Because we're descended from divinity? If only they knew! They really are very kind.

Excuse me. Bloody marvellous stuff, this Thent brew. I'm in no pain at all. I find it quite reassuring that I shall slip from this too too rancid flesh swaddled in a blanket of beatific thoughts and analgesic glow. They're very kind, the pelerines. Very kind.

Now, look to your right. There. Do you see? That staircase, cut into the rock, winding up up up. The Ten Thousand Steps. That's the old way to the altiplano. Everything went up and down those steps: people, animals, goods, palanquins and stick-stick men, traders and pilgrims and armies. Your brother. I watched him go, from this very belvedere. Three years ago, or was it five? You never really get used to the Great Day. Time blurs.

We were tremendous friends, the way that addicts are. You wouldn't have come this far without realising some truths about your brother. Our degradation unites us. Dear thing. How we'd set the world to rights, over flask after flask of this stuff! He realised the truth of this place early on. It's the way to the stars. God's waiting room. And we, this choir of shambling wrecks, wander through it, dazzled by our glimpses of the stars. But he was a dear friend, a dear dear friend. Dear Arthur.

We're all darkened souls here, but he was haunted. Things done and things left undone, like the prayer book says. My father was a vicar—can't you tell? Arthur never spoke completely about his time with javrosts. He hinted—I think he wanted to tell me, very much, but was afraid of giving me his nightmares. That old saw about a problem shared being a problem halved? Damnable lie. A problem shared is a problem doubled. But I would find him up here all times of the Great Day and Night, watching the staircase and the caravans and stick-convoys going up and down. Altiplano porcelain, he'd say. Finest in all the worlds. So fine you can read the Bible through it. Every cup, every plate, every vase and bowl, was portered down those stairs on the shoulders of a stickman. You know he served up on the Altiplano, in the Duke of Yoo's Pacification. I wasn't here then, but Aggers was, and he said you could see the smoke going up; endless plumes of smoke, so thick the sky didn't clear and the pelerines went for a whole Great Day without seeing the stars. All Arthur would say about it was, that'll make some fine china. That's what made porcelain from the Valley of the Kilns so fine: bones—the bones of the dead, ground up into powder. He would never drink from a Valley cup— he said it was drinking from a skull.

Here's another thing about addicts—you never get rid of it. All you do is replace one addiction with another. The best you can hope for is that it's a better addiction. Some become god-addicts, some throw themselves into worthy deeds, or self-improvement, or fine thoughts, or helping others, god help us all. Me, my lovely little vice is sloth—I really am an idle little bugger. It's so easy, letting the seasons slip away; slothful days and indolent nights, coughing my life up one chunk at a time. For Arthur, it was the visions. Arthur saw wonders and horrors, angels and demons, hopes and fears. True visions—the things that drive men to glory or death. Visionary visions. It lay up on the altiplano, beyond the twists and turns of the Ten Thousand Steps. I could never comprehend what it was, but it drove him. Devoured him. Ate his sleep, ate his appetite, ate his body and his soul and his sanity.

It was worse in the Great Night . . . Everything's worse in the Great Night. The snow would come swirling down the staircase and he saw things in it— faces— heard voices. The faces and voices of the people who had died, up there on the altiplano. He had to follow them, go up, into the Valley of the Kilns, where he would ask the people to forgive him—or kill him.

And he went. I couldn't stop him—I didn't want to stop him. Can you understand that? I watched him from this very belvedere. The pelerines are not our warders, any of us is free to leave at any time, though I've never seen anyone leave but Arthur. He left in the evening, with the lilac light catching Gloaming Peak. He never looked back. Not a glance to me. I watched him climb the steps to that bend there. That's where I lost sight of him. I never saw or heard of him again. But stories come down the stairs with the stickmen and they make their way even to this little eyrie, stories of a seer—a visionary. I look and I imagine I see smoke rising, up there on the altiplano.

It's a pity you won't be here to see the clouds break around the Gloaming, or look at the stars.

V genetric nives: Mother-of-snows (direct translation from Thent). Ground-civer hi-alpine of the Exx Palisades. The plant forms extensive carpets of thousands of minute white blossoms.

The most intricate papercut in the Botanica Veneris. Each floret is three millimetres in diameter. Paper, ink, gouache.

• • •

A high-stepping spider-car took me up the Ten Thousand Steps, past caravans of stickmen, spines bent, shoulders warped beneath brutal loads of finest porcelain.

The twelve cuts of the Botanica Veneris I have given to the Princess, along with descriptions and botanical notes. She would not let me leave, clung to me, wracked with great sobs of loss and fear. It was dangerous; a sullen land with Great Night coming. I could not convince her of my reason for heading up the stairs alone, for they did not convince even me. The one, true reason I could not tell her. Oh, I have been despicable to her! My dearest friend, my love. But worse even than that, false.

She stood watching my spider-car climb the steps until a curve in the staircase took me out of her sight. Must the currency of truth always be falsehood?

Now I think of her spreading her long hair out, and brushing it, firmly, directly, beautifully, and the pen falls from my fingers . . .

Egayhazy is a closed city; hunched, hiding, tight. Its streets are narrow, its buildings lean towards each other; their gables so festooned with starflower that it looks like perpetual festival. Nothing could be further from the truth: Egayhazy is an angry city, aggressive and cowed: sullen. I keep my Ledbekh-Teltai in my bag. But the anger is not directed at me, though from the story I heard at the Camahoo hoondahvi, my fellow humans on this world have not graced our species. It is the anger of a country under occupation. On walls and doors, the proclamations of the Duke of Yoo are plastered layer upon layer: her pennant, emblazoned with the four white hands of House Yoo, flies from public buildings, the radio station mast, tower tops, and the gallows. Her javrosts patrol streets so narrow that their graapa can barely squeeze through them. At their passage, the citizens of Egayhazy flash jagged glares, mutter altiplano oaths. And there is another sigil: an eight-petalled flower; a blue so deep it seems almost to shine. I see it stencilled hastily on walls and doors and the occupation-force posters. I see it in little badges sewn to the quilted jackets of the Egayhazians; and in tiny glass jars in low-set windows. In the market of Yent, I witnessed javrosts upturn and smash a vegetable stall that dared to offer a few posies of this blue bloom.

The staff at my hotel were suspicious when they saw me working up some sketches from memory of this blue flower of dissent. I explained my work and showed some photographs and asked, what was this flower? A common plant of the high altiplano; they said. It grows up under the breath of the high snow;

small and tough and stubborn. It's most remarkable feature is that it blooms when no other flower does—in the dead of the Great Night. The Midnight Glory was one name, though it had another, newer, which entered common use since the occupation: The Blue Empress.

I knew there and then that I had found Arthur.

A pall of sulfurous smoke hangs permanently over the Valley of Kilns, lit with hellish tints from the glow of the kilns below. A major ceramics centre on a high, treeless plateau? How are the kilns fuelled? Volcanic vents do the firing, but they turn this long defile in the flank of Mount Tooloowera into a little hell of clay, bones, smashed porcelain, sand, slag, and throat-searing sulphur. Glehenta is the last of the Porcelain Towns, wedged into the head of the valley, where the river Iddis still carries a memory of freshness and cleanliness. The pottery houses, like upturned vases, lean towards each other like companionable women.

And there is the house to which my questions guided me: as my informants described; not the greatest but perhaps the meanest; not the foremost but perhaps the most prominent, tucked away in an alley. From its roof flies a flag, and my breath caught: not the Four White Hands of Yoo—never that, but neither the Blue Empress. The smoggy wind tugged at the hand-and-dagger of the Hydes of Grangegorman.

Swift action: to hesitate would be to falter and fail, to turn and walk away, back down the Valley of the Kilns and the Ten Thousand Steps. I rattle the ceramic chimes. From inside, a huff and sigh. Then a voice: worn ragged, stretched and tired, but unmistakable.

"Come on on in. I've been expecting you."

V crepitant movebitvolutans. Wescott's Wandering Star. A wind-mobile vine, native of the Ishtaria altiplano, that grows into a tight spherical web of vines which, in the Venerian Great Day, becomes detached from an atrophied root stock and rolls cross-country, carried on the wind. A central calx contains woody nuts that produce a pleasant rattling sound as the Wandering Star is in motion.

Cut paper, painted, layed and gummed. Perhaps the most intricate of the Venerian paper cuts.

THE SEER'S STORY

Tea?

I have it sent up from Camahoo when the stickmen make the return trip. Proper tea. Irish breakfast. It's very hard to get the water hot enough at this altitude, but it's my little ritual. I should have asked you to bring some. I've known you were looking for me from the moment you set out from Loogaza. You think anyone can wander blithely into Glehenta?

Tea.

You look well. The years have been kind to you. I look like shit. Don't deny it. I know it. I have an excuse. I'm dying, you know. The liquor of the vine— it takes as much as it gives. And this world is hard on humans. The Great Days—you never completely adjust—and the climate: if it's not the thin air up here, it's the moulds and fungi and spores down there. And the ultraviolet. It dries you out, withers you up. The town healer must have frozen twenty melanomas off me. No, I'm dying. Rotten inside. A leather bag of mush and bones. But you look very well, Ida. So, Patrick shot himself? Fifteen years too late, says I. He could have spared all of us . . . enough of that. But I'm glad you're happy. I'm glad you have someone who cares, to treat you the way you should be treated.

I am the Merciful One, the Seer, the Prophet of the Blue Pearl, the Earth Man, and I am dying.

I walked down that same street you walked down. I didn't ride, I walked, right through the centre of town. I didn't know what to expect. Silence. A mob. Stones. Bullets. To walk right through and out the other side without a door opening to me. I almost did. At the very last house, the door opened and an old man came out and stood in front of me so that I could not pass. "I know you." He pointed at me "You came the night of the Javrosts." I was certain then that I would die, and that seemed not so bad a thing to me. "You were the merciful one, the one who spared our young." And he went into the house and brought me a porcelain cup of water and I drank it down, and here I remain. The Merciful One.

They have decided that I am to lead them to glory, or, more likely, to death. It's justice, I suppose. I have visions you see—*pula* flashbacks. It works differently on Terrenes than Thents. Oh, they're hard-headed enough not to believe in divine inspiration or any of that rubbish. They need a figurehead— the repentant mercenary is a good role, and the odd bit of mumbo-jumbo from the inside of my addled head doesn't go amiss.

Is your tea all right? It's very hard to get the water hot enough this high. Have I said that before? Ignore me—the flashbacks. Did I tell you I'm dying? But it's good to see you; oh how long is it?

And Richard? The children? And Grangegorman? And is Ireland . . . of course. What I would give for an eyeful of green, for a glimpse of summer sun, a blue sky.

So, I have been a conman and a lover, a soldier and an addict, and now I end my time as a revolutionary. It is surprisingly easy. The Group of

Seven Altiplano Peoples' Liberation Army do the work: I release gnomic pronouncements that run like grassfire from here to Egayhazy. I did come up with the Blue Empress motif: the Midnight Glory: blooming in the dark, under the breath of the high snows. Apt. They're not the most poetic of people, these potters. We drove the Duke of Yoo from the Valley of the Kilns and the Ishtar Plain: she is resisted everywhere, but she will not relinquish her claim on the Altiplano so lightly. You've been in Egayhazy—you've seen the forces she's moving up here. Armies are mustering, and my agents report 'rigibles coming through the passes in the Palisades. An assault will come. The Duke has an alliance with House Shorth—some agreement to divide the altiplano up between them. We're outnumbered. Outmanoeuvred and out-supplied, and we have no where to run. They'll be at each other's throats within a Great Day, but that's a matter of damn for us. The Duke may spare the kilns—they're the source of wealth. Matter of damn to me. I'll not see it, one way or other. You should leave, Ida. *Pula* and local wars—never get sucked into them.

Ah. Unh. Another flashback. They're getting briefer, but more intense, Ida, you are in danger. Leave before night—they'll attack in the night. I have to stay. The Merciful One, the Seer, the Prophet of the Blue Pearl, can't abandon his people. But it was good, so good of you to come. This is a terrible place. I should never have come here. The best traps are the slowest. In you walk, through all the places and all the lives and all the years, never thinking that you are already in the trap, and then you go to turn around, and it has closed behind you. Ida, go as soon as you can . . . go right now. You should never have come. But . . . —oh, how I hate the thought of dying up here on this terrible plain! To see Ireland again . . .

V volanti musco: Altiplano Air-moss. The papercut shows part of a symbiotic lighter-than-air creature of the Ishtari Altiplano. The plant part consists of curtains of extremely light hanging moss that gather water from the air and low clouds. The animal part is not reproduced.

Shredded paper, gum.

He came to the door of his porcelain house, leaning heavily in a stick, a handkerchief pressed to mouth and nose against the volcanic fumes. I had tried to plead with him to leave, but whatever else he has become, he is a Hyde of Grangegorman, and stubborn as an ould donkey. There is a wish for death in him; something old and strangling and relentless with the gentlest eyes.

"I have something for you," I said and I gave him the box without ceremony.

His eyebrows rose when he opened it.

"Ah."

"I stole the Blue Empress."

"I know."

"I had to keep it out of Patrick's hands. He would have broken and wasted it, like he broke and wasted everything." Then my slow mind, so intent on saying this confession right, that I had practised on the space-crosser, and in every room and every mode of conveyance on my journey across this world, flower to flower, story to story: my middle-aged mind tripped over Arthur's two words. "You knew?"

"All along."

"You never thought that maybe Richard, maybe Father, or Mammy, or one of the staff had taken it?"

"I had no doubt that it was you, for those very reasons you said. I chose to keep your secret, and I have."

"Arthur, Patrick is dead, Rathangan is mine. You can come home now."

"Ah, if it were so easy!"

"I have a great forgiveness to ask from you, Arthur."

"No need. I did it freely. And do you know what, I don't regret what I did. I was notorious—the Honourable Arthur Hyde, jewel thief and scoundrel. That has currency out in the worlds. It speaks reams that none of the people I used it on asked to see the jewel, or the fortune I presumably had earned from selling it. Not one. Everything I have done, I have done on reputation alone. It's an achievement. No, I won't go home, Ida. Don't ask me to. Don't raise that phantom before me. Fields of green and soft Kildare mornings. I'm valued here. The people are very kind. I'm accepted. I have virtues. I'm not the minor son of Irish gentry with no land and the arse hanging out of his pants. I am the Merciful One, the Prophet of the Blue Pearl."

"Arthur, I want you to have the jewel."

He recoiled as if I had offered him a scorpion.

"I will not have it. I will not touch it. It's an ill-favoured thing. Unlucky. There are no sapphires on this world. You can never touch the Blue Pearl. Take it back to the place it came from."

For a moment, I wondered if he was suffering from another one of his hallucinating seizures. His eyes, his voice were firm.

"You should go, Ida. Leave me. This is my place now. People have tremendous ideas of family—loyalty and undying love and affection: tremendous expectations and ideals that drive them across worlds to confess and receive forgiveness. Families are whatever works. Thank you for coming. I'm sorry I wasn't what you wanted me to be. I forgive you—though as I said there is nothing to forgive. There. Does that make us a family now? The Duke of Yoo is coming, Ida. Be away from here before that. Go. The town people will help you."

And with a wave of his handkerchief, he turned and closed his door to me.

I wrote that last over a bowl of altiplano mate at the stickmen's caravanserai in Yelta, the last town in the Valley of the Kilns. I recalled every word, clearly and precisely. Then I had an idea; as clear and precise as my recall of that sad, unresolved conversation with Arthur. I turned to my valise of papers, took out my scissors and a sheet of the deepest indigo and carefully, from memory, began to cut. The stickmen watched curiously, then with wonder. The clean precision of the scissors, so fine and intricate, the difficulty and accuracy of the cut, absorbed me entirely. Doubts fell from me: why had I come to this world? Why had I ventured alone into this noisome valley? Why had Arthur's casual accepting of what I had done, the act that shaped both his life and mine, so disappointed me? What had I expected from him? Snip went the scissors, fine curls of indigo paper fell from them on to the table. It had always been the scissors I turned to when the ways of men grew too much. It was a simple cut. I had the heart of it right away, no false starts, no new beginnings. Pure and simple. My onlookers hummed in appreciation. Then I folded the cut into my diary, gathered up my valises, and went out to the waiting spider-car. The eternal clouds seem lower today, like a storm front rolling in. Evening is coming.

I write quickly, briefly.

Those are no clouds. Those are the 'rigibles of the Duke of Yoo. The way is shut. Armies are camped across the altiplano. Thousands of soldiers and javrosts. I am trapped here. What am I to do? If I retreat to Glehenta I will meet the same fate as Arthur and the Valley people—if they even allow me to do that. They might think that I was trying to carry a warning. I might be captured as a spy. I do not want to imagine how the Duke of Yoo treats spies. I do not imagine my Terrene identity will protect me. And the sister of the Seer, the Blue Empress! Do I hide in Yelta and hope that they will pass me by? But how could I live with myself knowing that I had abandoned Arthur?

There is no way forward, no way back, no way around.

I am an aristocrat. A minor one, but of stock. I understand the rules of class, and breeding. The Duke is vastly more powerful than I, but we are of a class. I can speak with her; gentry to gentry. We can communicate as equals.

I must persuade her to call off the attack.

Impossible! A middle-aged Irish widow, armed only with a pair of scissors. What can she do; kill an army with gum and tissue? The death of a thousand papercuts?

Perhaps I could buy her off. A prize beyond prize: a jewel from the stars, from their goddess itself. Arthur said that sapphires are unknown on this world. A stone beyond compare.

I am writing as fast as I am thinking now.

I must go and face the Duke of Yoo, female to female. I am of Ireland, a citizen of no mean nation. We confront the powerful, we defeat empires. I will go to her and name myself and I shall offer her the Blue Empress. The true Blue Empress. Beyond that, I cannot say. But I must do it, and do it now.

I cannot make the driver of my spider-car take me into the camp of the enemy. I have asked her to leave me and make her own way back to Yelta. I am writing this with a stub of pencil. I am alone on the high altiplano. Above the shield wall, the cloud layer is breaking up. Enormous shafts of dazzling light spread across the high plain. Two mounted figures have broken from the line and ride towards me. I am afraid—and yet I am calm. I take the Blue Empress from its box and grasp it tight in my gloved hand. Hard to write now. No more diary. They are here.

V. Gloria medianocte: The Midnight Glory, or Blue Empress.

   Card, paper, ink.

ASYMPTOTIC

ANDY DUDAK

The cadets stand at attention for their passing-out ceremony, a random sample of the motley gamut of branched *sapiens,* and Nuhane is the smallest by far—but he adds his voice to their oath with towering conviction:

"We swear to uphold the Einsteinian limit! We vow to impose relativistic lockdown when a debt is owed to the universe, to deal out justice like a blind law of physics, thereby safeguarding the integrity of the vacuum!"

Nuhane fights down the terror of open sky intrinsic to his branch of humanity. Although a spin foam hack keeps the atmosphere of this Titan-analog at bay, the shield is invisible. Stacked worlds of orange-glowing cloud present nauseating vistas. A darkling methane sea surrounds this rocky isle, this remote outpost of the Collection Bureau. Nuhane reminds himself that the oppressive distance to the horizon is not an existential threat. Still, he is of the Fey. He can't help longing for a nice underground bunker, a womb-cave, or the intimate companionways of a space hab.

The cadets march to the far end of the parade ground. Weird, brazen music issues from pipes attached to robotic air-bladders. It's all part of some ancient police ritual whose roots have been forgotten. Wisps of proxy tech haunt the margins of the field, proud instances of family and friends. Nuhane finds the scene rather grim. The intended effect is stark majesty, but he wants to get it over with, to join the fight he's been training for.

He has no people among the spectators, and none to speak of otherwise.

From his childhood on a backward world, from concentration camps to this: lifetimes already, and he's only a hundred. He knows all too well what humanity is capable of. He can't fight for people alone, no matter how seemingly just the cause. In the Bureau he's found the only mission left to him.

Without the fabric of the cosmos, even hatred is impossible.

He wonders suddenly if he's remembering this moment, rather than living it. The future—if there is such a thing—comes to him like a divine revelation.

It is a new past on the other side of "now," but he is powerless to act on the knowledge. He's locked inside this young cadet he once thought of as himself. The sensation is terrifying and glorious.

Simultaneously, this passive observer inhabits many other Nuhanes, including a middle-aged Nuhane, a lieutenant radically interfaced with a Bureau patrol cutter.

The debtor's sign is plain to his augmented eye. The arcing spacetime fissure propagated like a magnetic field line from a gutted metal worldlet and out over the galactic plane. The nearest light-years of its length dissipate like an old contrail, undermining nearby vacuum. It is one of thousands of discernible violations. He sees them as an ominous glowing net tangled through the Milky Way, with stray threads arcing off to other galaxies and clusters. So much work to do. So much debt to collect.

If he tunes up his perception of the universal spin foam, he sees a second, thinner net woven through the first: debts collected, scars on spacetime. It sooths him to gaze upon all that the Bureau has accomplished. To him the scar tissue is a fundamental good, a rare thing in this universe. Never mind how little the tissue has done to shore up the collapsing seawall.

"Fresh enough," says Lao Wang. "Bureau's giving it to us." The old baseline human sounds tired. Nuhane's mentor and partner has locked down thirty-one violators, collecting over ten million relativistic tons of debt, a Bureau record. Soon he'll vanish into lockdown himself, to pay off his Noble Debt. Nuhane will miss him. He wonders if this is their last mission together.

A younger Nuhane imposes his first lockdown with a sense of dark wonder. The violator ship, a converted Shinasian junk, dims and reddens inside its pocket of pseudo-acceleration, a pulsating sphere of apparently warped spacetime.

It is Lao Wang's bust, but he let Nuhane do the honors—a taste of imposition for the green junior officer.

"Please," one of the debtors weeps. "I don't deserve this!" The transmission redshifts as it climbs out of the pocket. "I'm a licensed interface pilot! I was forced into this—"

"By a violator called Phlogiston," Lao Wang supplies. "I know, and I'm afraid it makes no difference."

The pilot is in the Mayall II globular cluster of Andromeda much sooner than he should be. His mass contributed to the vacuum deterioration in the junk's wake, however minutely. He is therefore a debtor.

"It's Phlogiston's debt!" the pilot argues. That name again. Nuhane wants to ask Lao Wang what's going on, but he's distracted by the spectacle of lockdown. He's seen it before, of course, but this one is different, no matter what the record will say. This one is his.

"Phlogiston's debt," Lao Wang says, "and yours, and the junk's. Anything that violates, sentient or not, guilty or innocent, must be locked down. You're an interface pilot. You know what's at stake."

"But the debt . . . " he chokes.

"Approximately two million, seven hundred and forty-nine thousand, eight hundred and thirty-five point two two seven light-years."

"So how long . . . "

"Ten minutes ship-time," Lao Wang says. "For your debt, lockdown is equivalent to point nine nine nine nine nine one seven c. Be thankful you won't suffer the gravities." He doesn't need to add that meanwhile the resting universe will age 2.75 million years. This debtor is an interface-pilot, after all. He understands the law he has violated.

The junk continues to redshift, as though accelerating toward redemption. Soon it will be like a dim 3D snapshot printed on reality, beyond time and reproach. For 2.75 million years it will function like a head on London Bridge, a warning to those who would violate sacred law. Nuhane is proud to have finally contributed his first head. His pride waxes as the debtor's personal clocks slow. The ship will gain millions of relativistic tons before it pays its mass-energy debt to the universe. By the time it heals the rent it tore in spacetime, all that the pilot loves will be gone, or radically transformed.

Nuhane is drunk on the power he wields. Perhaps sensing this, Lao Wang says: "Never forget that we are bound for the same fate."

How could he forget with Lao Wang constantly reminding him? *You sooner than me, old man,* he wants to say. Nuhane has accrued seventy million light-years of so-called Noble Debt or VLOD (Violation in the Line of Duty), certainly a small fraction of Lao Wang's. Nuhane is a young god, free to ignore Einstein when he sees fit, and to punish others for doing so. He worked hard to be so elite. Most Bureau officers end up with a local, sub-c jurisdiction, lying in wait for violators rather than hunting them. Their only taste of violation is the occasional use of a Bureau ansible. They are part of the vast, slow, relativistic two-thirds of humanity, trapped by distances that might as well be infinite.

Nuhane was never willing to settle for that. The last thing he wants to hear is Lao Wang urging him to humility.

"We aren't so different from our prey," the old man says.

Nuhane wonders if the bastard has developed violation syndrome. It's new, the idea that too much time beyond c can lead to symptoms of senility. Some researchers go further, claiming that violation decouples consciousness from time.

Master Patrol Officer Nuhane is still high from his last "Noble" violation. He's already looking forward to the next one. Between ecstasy and the grand future there is no room for doubt. Nuhane is immortal.

Beyond c there is no time and no speed. Bureau officers call the speed of light the "last speed." Here in violation space, all of Nuhane's violating selves are united. Beyond time there is exultant joy, infinite peace, and the "eldest" of Nuhane's violation selves will find it hard to condescend back to the universe. They will leave pieces of themselves here.

The "younger" Nuhanes fear the dissolution of self that must result from perfect bliss. They flee back below c, cherishing what little exultation they've allowed themselves. All of the violating Nuhanes, young and old, remain in violation space for precisely the same amount of time—none—regardless of the light years skipped in the sub-c universe.

And so, coincident with their unification, the united Nuhanes split along their seams of self. They become again old and young and middle-aged, returning to the sub-c murk once and for all.

As Major Nuhane condescends from violation space, emerging near a violator yacht in the Southern Local Supervoid, he wonders how he's going to explain this to the Bureau. They'll study his ansible. They'll suspect he tampered with its debt meter, but won't be able to prove it. What they'll be able to do is ground him with therapy sessions. Nuhane fears that more than anything.

The yacht winds up its violation ring, but Nuhane imposes lockdown before the ring completes its first test cycle.

He barely pays attention as the yacht wavers, begins to dim. His mind is still in violation space, in headlong discovery of joy. Why did he violate without permission? Was it really because of that informant at New McMurdo? The vacuum dweller had given him bad information before. Nuhane had vowed never to use her again. This time she claimed to know someone who knew Phlogiston, a violator no less, and she had coordinates for this violator's next jump.

Nuhane didn't hesitate. The informant was a known liar, her claim preposterous. Nuhane paid her. It was about a promise to Lao Wang, of course—not an excuse to violate.

"Officer," a female voice says.

A video feed follows: twenty naked youths laze about in a garden setting, like an indolent pantheon of gods. Only one woman is standing, a sculpture in translucent flesh with inhuman black eyes and a cloud of silver hair. "I won't insult your intelligence by denying our crime," she says. Most of her companions aren't even looking his way. Some appear to sleep.

"Big of you," Nuhane says.

"You're with the Bureau. You have violated. You know how it feels."

"Yes."

"So you know why we do it."

They are libertines. They violated purely to experience violation space. Nuhane suspected this when the informant gave him the coordinates. The common breeds of violator—colonists, shippers, transports—have no reason to jump to an inter-filament void. Out here there is only vacuum and a novel view. The lights sprinkled across the blackness are all galaxies. In the varying density of this field, the large-scale structure of the universe is discernible.

Nuhane suffers a wave of nausea. Nowhere else is the universe's dumb magnitude more apparent. He allows his cutter to feed him a palliative. He longs for a cave, or the alchemy of violation space. Did Lao Wang ever yearn for it like this? Nuhane remembers a time, long before the old man's senility, when he seemed obsessed with violation, with its nature. But did he crave it? Perhaps all Bureau officers do.

"How can you blame us for wanting that transcendence?"

"I don't deal in blame," Nuhane says. "Think of me as a maintenance man."

An Apollo in the background chuckles, saying, "There it is."

The nymph at his side murmurs, "What did you expect?"

"I take it you don't believe in the danger of spacetime fissuring," Nuhane says.

A ripple of laughter animates the pantheon. "Do you?" the translucent goddess asks.

Nuhane hates this old debate, but he wants to feel these people out. "Set aside the overwhelming scientific consensus, if you like. Shouldn't we proceed with caution? It's the fabric of spacetime, after all. We need it." This elicits more laughter, and Nuhane gets angry despite himself—angry *at* himself, more than these Deniers. He should be used to their kind. The age of unchecked FTL travel, the so-called Age of Innocence, left Deniers scattered across the cosmos. He has to remind himself of the Bureau's role: not to correct delusional thinking, not even to keep up with the damage, an impossibility. But to act as a deterrent. "Laugh if you like," he says. "Laugh all the way into lockdown."

"Bureau fascist," the nymph says.

"You want violation for yourselves," Apollo says. "First rule of bureaucracy and so on. You imagine what humanity could be given by unchecked violation, and it terrifies you."

"You hate freedom," says another woman.

They may have tweaked themselves to believe this drivel. Judging by their composure in the face of lockdown, they are no strangers to mental rewrites—

and their bodies are certainly customized. Not for the first time, Nuhane wonders what it would be like to see and think like a Denier. Driven by fear. Unable to live with the possibility, however remote, of the universe splitting along its fissures and flying apart. Choosing to believe otherwise.

Nuhane could go to a clinic, get the tweak. Then he could lose himself in violation. But the notion is fleeting. If he did that, he wouldn't enjoy the resulting fantasy. Someone new would.

"You can still stop this lockdown," the translucent goddess says.

They haven't reached the point of no return, but they're close. Nuhane allows his cutter to underclock him to match their continually slowing reference frame. "That's right."

"We're rich."

"Congratulations. I'm after someone named Phlogiston."

Apollo and his nymph stop laughing. The rest of the pantheon subtly emerges from its contrived disinterest. This charged moment takes three months in Nuhane's resting universe.

The goddess says: "That's not his real name."

Nuhane is old, a commander, and the dwarf glares murkily just light-seconds away. The ominous substar seems familiar, or perhaps significant beyond its fearsome absurdity.

"Sir?" It's patrol officer Wen Ting, his junior partner. He can hear the concern mixed with youthful impatience in her voice. "Jump to orbit, or what?" She knows violation syndrome has him by the throat. How could she not, by now? He remembers his own premonitions as Lao Wang deteriorated.

They have followed a ragged tear in spacetime to an abandoned long-range rig that only accounts for ninety-one percent of the debt. Something else launched from the rig and likely headed for the dwarf.

Instead of giving the order Wen Ting craves, Nuhane contemplates the fissure. One of billions now. He gazes into the night and watches them in real time, no matter how far away they are, because they violate. They seem to propagate from him toward a distant haze woven through the microwave background.

"The L-T object," Wen Ting prompts.

Nuhane returns his gaze to the dwarf, remembers they're here to lock down someone named Willard. The cutter doses him with the latest syndrome therapy. It activates random memories and loosens his tongue: "Patrol Officer, did you know that my people were one of the first branches from baseline humanity? We were called fey because we bred ourselves small and claustrophilic for interstellar travel. And because our enterprise seemed like a death wish."

"Fascinating, commander."

"We were the first to colonize many worlds. We did it fair and square, no FTL. But on Lalo our civilization collapsed. When a wave of violators arrived, all that remained of us was an underground theocracy. Of course the violator civ also collapsed. They went medieval, demonized us, blamed us for crop failures, plagues, everything. Then they industrialized, declared total wars on each other. Most of our caverns were beneath a republic called Iomang, a desperate state ruled by a madman."

"Yes sir," Wen Ting says absently, then adds, "Something's orbiting the dwarf."

Nuhane feels vaguely insulted. Hoping to embarrass her in turn, he asks, "Why did you join the Church of the Indemnity?"

"Willard's shuttle is correcting toward the orbiter," she says, then seamlessly adds: "My people were violators. The Bureau wasn't going to let me in. Getting the Church tweak was the only way to prove my loyalty. At least, that's what I thought before. Now I see that this was the universe's way of guiding me toward the Faith."

Nuhane realizes she's explained this before. He ends up embarrassed for himself again. Furthermore, he finds nothing to mock in her story.

With a note of confusion Wen Ting announces: "Grav harmonics from the orbiter, but not the signature of violation tech." She waits for Nuhane's order. Nuhane can't seem to focus. "Jump over and intercept before he can dock?" she prods.

When she initiates without consent, Nuhane realizes this mission will be his last.

Nuhane has been to several Bureau lockdown ceremonies, but Lao Wang's is the first to fill him with dread of the future. Captain Nuhane feels old for the first time in his life. He is on the observation deck of Achindoun, the Bureau hab that has long stood watch over the Nobly Locked Down. He's joined by fellow officers and a smattering of Lao Wang's proxied relations.

Lagrange point 4 of the Pluto-analog Kvichak and its moon Igiugig: here hang thousands of Bureau officers in their lockdown pods, most of them redshifted beyond casual observation. Lao Wang's has just shed its attitude jets, having found its place among the others.

The bagpipes sound, and the lensing of his pod signifies the beginning of lockdown. Some of his loved ones allow their proxies to broadcast sobs. Nuhane wonders what that says about the authenticity of their grief. He can only stare in numb transfixion.

The old man shoulders four hundred billion two hundred and eighty-seven thousand light-years of Noble Debt—an epic career, but not the record.

No one knows why people can only violate so many times before losing their faculties. Most officers don't break five hundred billion. Nuhane, now at ten billion four hundred and ninety million, wonders how far he'll go.

"Reductio ad absurdum," Lao Wang PMs, "reductio ad infinitum. Redcutio ad absurdum, reductio . . . " On he goes, repeating his nonsense mantra.

"Listen Uncle," Nuhane says. "We both know I'm not half the officer you are. I'll probably check out long before four hundred big ones. We could emerge from lockdown around the same time. We'd be together, two old maniacs laughing at . . . whatever humanity is by then. How does that sound?"

" . . . ad infinitum. Remember that, boy."

"Alright." Nuhane is used to dealing with him like this. He's glad the old man had the sense to PM him, and not include his relatives.

"Architectures, paradigms, we all fall down. Ashes, ashes."

"Yes, Uncle."

"Nuhane." His transmissions are redshifting fast now.

"I'm here, Uncle."

"Remember that lockdown in Mayall II?"

"Mayall II . . . "

"Andromeda."

"Yes. I remember. The slaved pilot. We never found the perp."

"Phlogiston. He called himself Phlogiston. There was a file on him. You didn't rate the clearance at the time, so I couldn't tell you. He's important."

Nuhane doesn't know if this is the syndrome talking or not. "I remember wondering what you were hiding. Don't worry, I'll look at the file."

"It's gone. They even wiped it from me, somehow, whoever they are. But I know he was part of something big. I know it!"

"I believe you," Nuhane says, not sure that he does.

"Find him. Violate off the books if you have to. Promise me."

Nuhane is sure that his other, timeless self is here, reading his life like prose. The more he violates, the more certain he is of this.

Nuhane's counselor is Lectern, an instance of a Turing-passable expert system, an ancient Bureau creature possessed of unfathomable secrets. Colonel Nuhane is enduring another therapy session. All he can think about is getting back into violation space, which is the sort of thing Lectern would like to know, and the last thing Nuhane cares to admit.

"We were talking about your old partner," the system prods. "His lockdown ceremony."

"It was a hundred years ago," Nuhane prevaricates.

"Then let's talk about your debriefing last week," Lectern suggests.

"An instance of you was there. Surely you've reintegrated by now."

"How did the questions make you feel?"

"Angry."

"You violated without authorization. Shouldn't we be concerned?"

"For the last time, my ansible went into lockdown before I could request the jump. I was chasing a lead. I made a judgment call."

"There's evidence that you tampered with your ansible. Its debt meter was dialed up."

"Like I said, it must've been faulty!"

"Which isn't supposed to be possible. But Bureau legend has it that Lao Wang knew how."

"He taught me a lot of things, but never that." Nuhane is barely able to convince himself that this charade is about keeping his promise to Lao Wang, and not about hiding his addiction. The old man wasn't clear, but he seemed to imply that someone inside the Bureau was working with Phlogiston. Nuhane doubts that Lectern is involved, but can't be sure.

"This lead you explained to the board . . ."

How much longer can he juggle the lies? In addition to the board inquiries, he has a new partner to deal with. She is from the Church of the Indemnity, tweaked to take an almost feline pleasure in the hunt. She wants to inflict lockdowns. She won't tolerate a prolonged investigation full of dead ends.

"I think it's a fabrication," Lectern continues. "If you're investigating something off the books, you'd better come clean to the board. Regardless, we need to face the fact of your addiction." Nuhane waits for the system to take a different tack. "Not today? Then how about your childhood on Lalo-honua? Are you ready to go there yet?"

Nuhane restrains his irritation. He has always avoided this topic, but for the first time it seems preferable to everything else on the docket. "The bliss of violation space," he says, "is like confronting infinity. It's like the most wide open space possible, without fear. For me anyway."

"That makes sense," Lectern says. "There have been two other Fey officers before you. They both said the same thing."

This brings Nuhane an odd sense of comfort. He is encouraged to go deeper: "I remember the explosions that opened up the Hall of Star Ancestors. The Iomangans were clever. The sunlight disoriented us."

"Disoriented *you*. Focus on your personal experiences."

"I was too young to understand. I thought the Iomangans were monsters. That's what our priests taught. All I knew was that our world was falling down around us. Many were killed in the collapse."

"You saw that?"

"I saw my father buried. Annihilated in moments. Also my great-great-grandmother, and many cousins."

"Go on."

"Then there were these giants. I'd never seen them before. They had fire magic, in addition to swords. They killed many, including my grandmothers, before a commander showed up and ordered them to stop. The rest of us were herded to the surface. Up there we were helpless with our phobias, all but blind. I was separated from my mother. They packed us into magic boxes that moved on metal tracks. Many more of us died in those, suffocated or starved. You could say I was lucky, having been packed against one of my great aunts. She opened a vein and fed me her blood. I slowly killed her in order to survive."

"No. That wasn't murder."

Nuhane ignores this laughable claim. "And then there were the camps. We children learned how to hide and steal and survive. The adults fell into torpors and died, if they weren't killed outright. There were medical experiments, you see. And labor they knew we couldn't sustain. And random sport killings. I know what you're thinking, Lectern. Don't worry. I saw these things myself. All of them and more."

Nuhane watches the universe blue-shift around him, knowing he is old, that this is his Noble Lockdown—but sure of little else.

Pseudo acceleration. But no pseudo equivalence principle. He doesn't feel the gravities. How could he? He's not going anywhere, not in space anyway.

How did he get here? What was his last mission? He had another partner after Lao Wang. What was her name?

His timeless observing other cannot enlighten him. The other wonders, as always, why he knows nothing beyond this lockdown. Does Nuhane die soon? Is it some effect of terminal violation syndrome? An immanent cure? Or is something catastrophic about to happen to time itself? Perhaps scientists underestimated the deleterious effect of violation. Perhaps spacetime is about to unravel.

Whatever the reason, the timeless other knows he is soon to be no more.

Colonel Nuhane kneels with the other initiates before the torch-lit altar. Beyond is enshrined a fierce-looking idol, a Taoist god with bulging, hungry eyes. An urgent drum makes the incense-laden air pulse.

Nuhane endures the ritual like he did his Bureau passing-out. He ought to be happier to be in a nice cave like this.

"Eight hundred years ago," declaims a red-robed man, "the emperor Kangxi consigned many Shaolin monks to fiery death. Five survivors escaped to a mountaintop temple, before which, using grass for incense, they formed a sacred brotherhood. They vowed revenge, pledging to oppose the Qing dynasty and restore the Ming."

"Fan qing fu ming!" the initiates affirm. *Oppose the Qing and restore the Ming.*

"At the Red Flower Pavilion, the Five founded the Hong Society. The Hong conducted heroic but doomed uprisings. One hundred thousand Hong soldiers sacrificed themselves courageously for the Han race." The man is a good actor. He appears stern and proud. Nuhane has no idea whether or not he's actually Han—not that it matters. "And the Hong society continues to thrive today!"

After a sufficient dramatic pause, he adds, "Begin the ceremony!"

Senior brethren in black robes and red sashes enter the cave. One by one they're stopped by two guards, who cross their broadswords and shout, "You are entering the Hong army fortress! Disobedience is punishable by death!" The black-robes reply with, "I am a Ming general! I build bridges and roads!" or "I cross mountains and ramparts! Don't you recognize a brother?" And they're allowed to pass.

The stuff about bridges and crossings is uncanny. Nuhane wonders if the ancient Ming rebels had the gift of foresight. This secret society has had nothing to do with Ming restoration since the 20th century, possibly earlier. They devolved into gangsterism, eventually becoming the most powerful *hei she hui* on old Terra. When the communist party collapsed, they took over China. Two hundred years later, their sole passion was traveling faster than light.

Bridges and roads indeed.

"Why are you here?" the red-robe barks at Nuhane.

"I've come to enlist," he replies.

"Why?"

"To oppose the Qing and restore the Ming!"

"Prove it!"

Following the ritual to the letter, Nuhane recites a poem:

"Draw broadswords,

the Manchurians stole our land!

The hour of loyalty

and blood vengeance is at hand!"

With that the red-robe moves on, challenging other initiates. They are as varied as Nuhane's cadet class at the Bureau. This Heaven and Earth Society has not been Chinese, let alone Han, for a very long time.

Next comes a black-robe, slapping each initiate in the back with the flat of a broadsword, then demanding: "Do you love gold or your brethren?"

The initiates each reply, "My brethren!" in their turn. Nuhane struggles not to faint after the blow nearly shatters his tiny frame.

All this for one unauthorized violation. Nuhane was indignant when the

Bureau followed his therapy with undercover duty. Since then he has grown numb, having weathered violation withdrawal. Infiltrating the Heaven and Earth Society has been a kind of sleepwalk.

Sometimes he can't help wishing that these gangsters would steal a Bureau cutter. He could claim to know how to hack the interface nest, then violate. Where to? Would it matter? He would continue to honor his promise to Lao Wang, of course. It wouldn't be about the violation alone. He isn't like that anymore. He hasn't violated in three years. Not that he's had the chance.

"The first oath!" the red-robe shouts. "Once a member of the society, I shall treat the relatives of my brethren as my own. If I don't keep this oath, I shall be struck down by five thunderbolts!"

The initiates repeat this. Nuhane finds that he is tired of oaths. To the Bureau, to mentors and gangsters and spacetime, and most of all to himself. He remembers being free of promises in violation space.

Patrol Officer Nuhane and Lieutenant Lao Wang have followed a debtor's spacetime fissure from the Small Magellanic Cloud to this system in the heart of the Pavo-Indus Supercluster. Lao Wang locked the violator down before it could fall into the orbit of a world originally terraformed by other violators. The verdant, uninhabited globe hangs in the void, a jewel that shouldn't exist. The people that sparked the terraforming drift in an old, barely discernible mist of lockdown pockets at the planet's L2 point.

The violator ship, locked down only moments ago, blushes slightly. It's a large cargo vessel, no doubt a second wave of colonists. Their debt stands at three hundred million light-years. They will pay off four hundred and twenty thousand relativistic tons. Young Nuhane still marvels at the weight of these crimes, and the price of getting caught.

He and Lao Wang, though interfaced in separate nests, share an environ that renders their facial expressions. Lao Wang wears an odd grin. He pings the cargo vessel and says, "Excuse me. Do you know how fast you were going?"

When there is no response, he shrugs and says to Nuhane: "A joke. Old reference." He avoids Nuhane's bewildered gaze. "They shouldn't have come back," he says.

"What?" Nuhane says.

"I mean, maybe we're not meant to return from violation space. Maybe we're supposed to break light speed and stay beyond it, forever." He meets Nuhane's eyes again, summons an unconvincing chuckle. "Never mind. Guess I need some R and R. You won't report what I just said, right?"

"No sir."

They watch the violator fade. Nuhane contemplates the mystery of violation and lockdown. Already the cargo vessel's spacetime fissure is beginning to heal, even back in the Small Magellanic. True action at a distance, a violation of c in its own right.

Nuhane can't believe what he sees in the soul of the man his fellow thugs just killed. The ice ceiling scrolls by the window, and the dead man, formerly a violation savant for the Heaven and Earth Society, slides back and forth across the floor with the motion of the hab, his head encased in a smoking transmigration helmet.

Nuhane hides his excitement. He has found his ticket off this nightmarish detail. He will be violating again soon—but it's more than that.

The helmet sends pertinent memories to Nuhane's mirror net. His rhythms sift through the complexity of violation math, seeking names and itineraries. He needed something underway, something he could lock down, but he didn't expect to find it. It was clear right away that the man hadn't spoken with the Bureau. Perhaps he never intended to. The Heaven and Earth kingpin of this Europa-analog has grown paranoid in his dotage, violation syndrome having burned wormholes through his reason.

"You said he didn't rat," says Plutarch, a hulking gangster eight times the size of Nuhane. "So why are we still here? If he's so interesting, grab the helmet. But let's go."

Nuhane does not want to decapitate the savant. The crystalline mass that was once his head is permanently merged with the helmet. Nuhane has done many things for Heaven and Earth, things far worse than decapitating a corpse, but he feels he has reached a critical mass.

He just needs another minute to confirm what he saw: a very improbable name.

Outside, the hab lights flash on particles suspended in the inky water. The media wall maps the local ice ceiling and the other habs as they converge on a stable rendezvous point to form yet another temporary city. That's how society works here in Baroque Pearl. Nuhane tried to convince himself he liked it, at first. It was a sub-surface existence. His sordid duties for Heaven and Earth were part of the mission, just as important as locking down violators. He didn't miss violating. So went the flimsy monologue.

He confirms the name attached to the violation-in-progress: William Valentin Willard, aka Phlogiston. He smiles.

Nuhane is eleven years old, and feels much older, when the harriers drop from the sky to liberate his camp. He clutches the chain-link fence and watches the Iomangan guards flee across the heath under a leaden sky. One by one the giants vanish as plasma rains down. Nuhane tries to feel glad, to feel anything in fact, and fails. He has learned many things in this camp. He has learned to tolerate the open sky, beneath which he has learned what humans really are. He knows that the Iomangans are descendants of violators, and that his liberators are also violators. He does not know what that means.

What he finally feels is dread. He's going to have to leave the camp, and enter a wider world.

Three hundred and fifty billion light-years.

He often wondered how far he would go before succumbing to violation syndrome—and now he knows. Three fifty is nothing to be ashamed of. It's not the stuff of legend, but it's respectable. At least he knows he has the syndrome. He tells himself that's something. Perhaps it means he's not so far gone.

It was these last two violations that did it. He knows that on a level below the cellular.

"Shall I lock him down?" Wen Ting asks. She floats with him in the new cutter's sensorium, wide-eyed with the thrill of the hunt. Nuhane envies her youth, her cold pure hunter's psychopathy, though he doesn't fully understand it. The Church of the Indemnity has wired her up good. When she locked down that last rig, she curled into a fetal position, moaning with something beyond divine communion. "Commander?" she says.

He's forgotten why they're here, and it terrifies him. He blinks up the dossier of their current mark: William Valentin Willard, aka Phlogiston, quantum information physicist and outspoken Bureau sympathizer. Trillions of humans call him a Bureau lapdog and want him dead. He understands that the Bureau holds the universe together, understands it in a way that Wen Ting and her brethren never will. He doesn't need their leap of faith. He invented the machine that images the universe's scars.

"Violating c," he said famously, "is worse than murder."

And yet here he is, after a serious galaxy hop. What possessed him?

His shuttle falls toward Nuhane's cutter. Beneath them hangs the mysterious machine, alive with its puzzling gravitational waves. None of Nuhane's scans or Wen Ting's mystic sensing find weapons in the fine-woven ring of exotic matter. Far below it, dark storms roil over the surface of the dim red L-T dwarf. Nuhane wonders what role, if any, Willard means this substar to play in whatever he's up to.

"Congratulations," Willard transmits. "You've got me."

With his voice comes the visual of a surprisingly youthful man: middle aged, gray-bearded but healthy and vital. For a moment Nuhane can't reconcile this with what he knows. Willard ought to be decrepit by now, even if he's had longevity treatments. Then Nuhane remembers that Willard has traveled relativistically. The man has lived a decade or so of the last five hundred years.

Wen Ting shows him a scan of the orbiting machine. "What is it?"

His brief grin is barely perceptible. "Ah, one of the Bureau's pet zealots." He understands—or understood—that the Bureau needs all the support it can get, even if that means employing delusional jihadists.

What has become of the far-seeing creature Willard used to be?

"What are you waiting for?" he says.

Wen Ting scans the orbital machine again, hoping this time the Angels of Indemnity will grant revelation. It appears conclusive that the thing is not a weapon. There are signs of a spin foam hack about it, but the configuration is wrong for violation or lockdown tech.

"Do you need me to confess?" Willard says impatiently.

Nuhane wonders if the man craves the portal to the future that lockdown represents. Perhaps he has grown weary of his small-minded contemporaries. Then why not take off at relativistic speed, like he has before?

Nuhane hesitates to impose lockdown. He may be slipping into dotage, but he senses he's being manipulated.

Wen Ting, however, does not hesitate. She and the cutter have developed an understanding in the face of Nuhane's decline. She doesn't need his authorization. She imposes with relish.

"Thank you," Willard says, as yet barely redshifted.

Nuhane feels Wen Ting's confusion through her bio feed. Violators aren't supposed to be thankful. They're supposed to beg for mercy. But Willard is no masochist. Nuhane also feels the grav waves from the orbiter changing tune, and knows something fundamental is happening to local spacetime. He perceives a disturbance, much like the fractures caused by violation, blossoming between Willard's shuttle, the orbiter, and the dwarf below. A lockdown pocket encloses the orbiter, seeming to mirror Willard's.

Wen Ting panics. "What's this?"

"I'm sorry to have led you so far," Willard replies, "but I needed at least a seventy million light-year debt for this trial run."

"Of what?"

"My machine is crude. The first of its kind. It won't respond to anything less than a seventy mil debt."

This transmission arrives at an unchanging radio wavelength. Willard's redshifting has ceased. This is stunning, unprecedented, but Nuhane's attention is drawn to the machine, now shivering and glowing under some unfathomable workload. Nuhane senses that it is channeling something— Hilbert distortion? inertia?—from Willard's shuttle down into the murky furnace of the dwarf.

"I approached the Bureau first," he says, "but they didn't believe me. Or didn't want to. They tried to kill me, you know. Maybe you won't believe that, but it's true. So I had to go to Heaven and Earth. It is regrettable that the savant in Baroque Pearl had to die, but I needed you to believe that lead and come after me. I should also apologize for having Lao Wang wiped. Canny, that one. He was on to me before I was ready. And it was my man in the Bureau who got you assigned to that duty in Baroque Pearl. I don't imagine it was pleasant. All for a greater good, as you'll see."

Far below, a darkness blossoms between two ribbons of turbulent black cloud. One might almost take it for another storm of raining iron, but for the speed of its formation. It expands like an ink stain through the hydrogen blood-glow, devouring thousands of cubic kilometers per second. Nuhane remembers that the dwarf was already radiating in the long visible wavelengths, that lockdown of such matter would mean swift blackness. He tunes his vision and watches the still-growing lockdown pocket—the largest one ever, as far as he knows—dimming down its trapped matter through infrared and radio. The pocket soon encloses a fifth of the substar, and keeps expanding. Great storms flash and gleam along the moving perimeter, and the Jupiter-like band-flow is thrown into chaos.

"Debt transfer," Nuhane says. The words are packed with mythic weight.

"Impossible," Wen Ting declares.

"It's working," Willard says, "but something's wrong."

Over one third of the dwarf is now enclosed, the remainder stirred to frenzy by the process and made to radiate like the accretion disk of a black hole. The lockdown pocket behaves like a collapsed star in many ways, though it has no real event horizon. As the brighter material is swallowed, Nuhane can judge how far along the lockdown is, what fraction of c it is equivalent to. The hottest free matter radiates in the extreme ultraviolet to soft X-ray range, but attenuates after falling in. And still the pocket grows.

"My shuttle and I weigh about seven tons," Willard says. His self-satisfaction is gone, replaced by mounting horror. "It seems we've discovered a new law of physics. The Law of the Transfer Fee."

Nuhane gets there just after him, he is sure they're wondering the same thing now: how much of a fee?

Unlike a black hole, a lockdown pocket doesn't exert gravity, so the remaining dwarf material—plasmas of hydrogen and helium, trace metals and silicates—overcomes its own gravitation and shreds away wildly into space.

It doesn't occur to Nuhane to get out of the way, not until he sees Willard and his machine doing so. Wen Ting reacts first, matching Willard's escape vector, worlds of fire blooming under them. The pocket swells and consumes, but slower than before.

Wen Ting is chanting again. Occasionally she forgets a phrase or a line and has to start over. Nuhane scans her mind and sees that her Church mod is short-circuiting, overloaded with a cumbersome truth.

"You've got to help me," Willard says.

The pocket finally stops expanding, content with the mass of forty-five Jupiters. The remaining one-fourth of the dwarf continues to burn and diffuse into space. The holy grail of debt transfer is possible, but hideously expensive. The transfer fee in this case was 1.2 octillion percent of the debt.

Nuhane scans Willard and confirms he is debt free. The machine seems to be powering down. Wen Ting is curled in a fetal position again, this time with excruciating pain. She shivers, sweating and whimpering with Church withdrawal.

"I've violated but can't be locked down," Willard says. "So arrest me. Take me to a hub."

Nuhane understands. Willard's shuttle can't achieve relativistic speeds, let alone violate. There is no concentrated source of matter for light-years around, so he can't get his long-range rig out of lockdown. He's at Nuhane's mercy.

"It wasn't just you and your partner and that savant," he admits. "You don't know the half of it. Maybe I deserve to die out here, but it can't all be for nothing." With that, his shuttle lights up with high-power transmissions aimed at a few hundred of the nearest inhabited systems and galaxies. Nuhane takes a sample: the machine specs and documentation of what happened to the dwarf.

"What have you done?" Nuhane says.

"Freed humanity."

"And that's a good thing, is it? Perhaps we need a cage." Before it's out of his mouth, he wonders if his heritage, or the Bureau, speaks through him. Maybe it's neither. Maybe it's the boy who got used to a concentration camp, and hated himself for it.

He turns his attention to Wen Ting, tweaking her neurochemistry to ease the trauma of her disillusionment. He marvels at the delicacy of her Church tweak, but something so absurd could be no other way—not without undermining her basic functionality.

"Debtor," she whispers, "make satisfaction for thy sin."

Nuhane tries to imagine what will become of the debt transfer universe. Matter will soon be at a premium, if he knows anything about mankind. Then what? Cycles of lockdown and emergence? Relativistic dark ages followed by renaissances of violation? Perhaps the stars must wink out, one by one, to become readily accessible. What about expansion, deprived of all that gravitating matter? What about dark matter and energy? Are lockdowns that vast even possible?

The Bureau as Nuhane knows it will be obsolete, regardless. Perhaps it will be relegated to catalyzing debt transfer, facilitating the violations it once policed. That would still be holding the universe together. That would still be his mission, wouldn't it?

Nuhane is four years old when his parents take him to the Hall of Star Ancestors for the first time. The cavern is the biggest space he's ever seen.

But not the biggest you'll ever see, says the man in his skull.

Nuhane gapes at the distant ceiling. It is a field of lights that his people call stars. "They're actually colonies of bioluminescent fungus," Father says.

"Don't teach him blasphemies," Mother whispers. The vast space is relatively quiet as hundreds of people walk the Great Circle and show proper awe.

His people are the Fey. Mother says they came from the stars.

Someday you'll travel to the real stars, the man in his skull says, but Nuhane doesn't believe him. *You'll forget about me for a long time, then remember me again. But we won't be able to talk like this anymore.*

"Why not?" Nuhane asks aloud, and Mother shushes him.

"Leave him be," Father says.

"And let him anger the priests?" Mother hisses. "And get us sent to the sulfur farms?" She looks up at the fake stars. "Ancestors, why did you curse me with such a husband?"

Nuhane's parents always quarrel when he talks to the man in his skull. Father says it's a gift, a sign he's destined for great things. It was Father who named him *Nuhane,* which in some ancient language means *speaker with the ghosts of ancestors.*

THE TWO PAUPERS

C.S.E. COONEY

PART ONE: A MERCIFUL HEIST

Analise Field did not steal the statue because it was the most beautiful thing she ever saw. Though it was.

She did not steal it because she was angry with its maker and wanted to exact vengeance on him for any number of recent slights. Though she was.

No, she stole it to save its life.

If she hadn't, Gideon Alderwood would have destroyed this statue like he did all the others. And she couldn't let that happen.

Not when it opened its eyes and looked at her like that.

Gideon stared at the space the statue had been. An empty plinth. A smear of clay, like a footprint.

The faucet in the outer hall plinked.

That sound had kept him awake for three nights running. He would pace in time to the *plink-plink-plink* and listen to Analise turn on that diabolically squeaky mattress of hers on the other side of the wall. And he would know she heard him even in her dreams. That she opened her eyes in the dark, thinking of him.

Had the statue walked?

They usually did not move the first day after completion. Not while they were still wet. But they never stayed wet long. After twenty-four hours his statues would harden spontaneously, as if fired from within by some infernal kiln, and he would wake to find their surfaces as smooth and cool as eggshells.

Then they would start . . . quickening.

At first the shifts were subtle. A hand lifted. A chin tilted. One blank gray eyelid tearing itself open to reveal an orb like a beetle's carapace, black-shining-green. Eyes like exoskeletons. An alien luster that revealed nothing.

It wasn't until they opened their eyes that he destroyed them.

Gideon thought he could just about bear them if they stopped at movement. If they just stirred like Analise in her bed next door. Slightly, in their sleep.

He would have spared them the hammer if only they did not look at him. Plink. Plink. Plink.

No. It was too soon. The newest statue could not have walked yet.

It had not been a full day since he smoothed the last lines. The curve of the ear, the high forehead, the careless loops of hair. Not a day since he had washed the clay from his hands.

That left only . . .

Plink. Plink. Plink.

It was past midnight. But no one stirred next door.

"Analise," Gideon Alderwood whispered. "Goddamn it."

The problem was, they shared the bathroom in the outer hall of the garret where they rented rooms.

The problem was, Analise was the only one who remembered to buy toilet paper for the bathroom. And, as she'd had cause to point out more than once, she was also the only one who remembered to scrub out the toilet and sink. To which Gideon replied that as she left more strands of hair in the sink than a lobotomist leaves in an operating theater, she was the most logical candidate for cleaning it up.

The problem was he'd been stealing the toilet paper to mix with his clay. Some new invention of his. Clay that would dry quicker and provide tougher structural support for his statues, so that he would not have to make them solid through and through, as he used to do when he was sculpting with an oil-based clay.

He explained this, very reasonably, when she objected to the lack of toilet paper.

"Gideon!" she shouted. "It doesn't matter what kind of clay you use! You'll just take a hammer to the damned things the next day."

"The damned things," he repeated with his odd thin smile.

"In the meantime," she raged on, "we don't have anything to wipe with. Again!"

Then he held up a single finger, still with that smile, bidding her wait (she was standing outside his doorway while he stood just in it, for he rarely invited her into his room), went inside, bent down to remove something from the bookshelf beside his bed, and returned presently.

It was a copy of her book, *Seafall Rising.*

"There," he said. "Use that." And slammed the door in her face.

The problem, Analise thought to herself, storming out into the Seafall city night to buy more toilet paper, was that they lived next door to each other. That they'd ever met. That they knew each other at all.

She bought two crates of toilet paper from the general store. One for her bedroom—and she'd bring a roll in with her whenever she needed it, and then she'd bring it out again—and one for his. And he could use it however he pleased.

When she tried his door handle, it was open. Gideon never locked his door except when he was on the other end of it. He had nothing worth stealing. At least nothing he kept there. Maybe in his mother's house his bedroom was a treasure trove of original Quraishi oil paintings, diamond cufflinks, and solid gold chamber pots. But Gideon Alderwood had elevated rich boy slumming to a high art.

That was when she saw the statue.

She'd only seen pieces of them before. The carnage of his fits. Heaps of limbs and bits of shattered skull.

To see one whole . . .

To see one proud and haughty and doomed, glowing in the moonlight . . .

Analise thought her heart would explode into fiery wings and fly right out of her chest, leaving behind a gaping hole still steaming, a bloody ribcage like a shattered prison wall.

She had to explore it more closely.

Gideon knew every dress in her closet. When Analise was in charity with him, she was always inviting him over for dinner, or tea, or some kind of soup she'd conjured at her hot plate. He'd had ample opportunity to observe her tiny chamber. He knew every patched pair of trousers handed down to her from her legion of brothers. Every one of those ridiculous vests she and Elliot liked to ferret out in thrift stores and bazaars, the kind that flattered no one, least of all a figure like hers, which would look better in a thin sweep of silk and best in nothing but bathwater. He knew every pair of shoes she owned. All three pairs. Black flats for dress-up occasions, thick boots for every other occasion, ragged sandals for summertime.

So Gideon knew that Analise had packed a small valise.

Enough clothes for three days. Perhaps five, if she rinsed out her underthings. Also, there were a number of books missing from her shelves.

Elliot had pointed out, more than once, that Ana always packed more books than clothes.

Her notebook was gone, too, and her favorite fountain pen. So she'd taken her new novel with her, which she was drafting longhand. The book she would never let him read. Not after what he'd done to her first book.

He had purchased Analise a typewriter for her birthday. It sat in a box under his cot. Her birthday was three months ago. She'd been lusting after a typewriter, he knew, but was too frugal to buy one for herself. It was an Alderwood, of course. His grandfather had patented the design forty years ago, and the family owned, amongst their other interests, the factory in Seafall that produced the latest models. Hers was the newest production design, the Alderwood Diadem, not yet being manufactured on the assembly lines.

"I'll throw it out the window," he promised the silence of her room. "Happy birthday to whoever's standing below."

The emptiness mocked him.

"Where did you go, Ana?" Gideon whispered. "Where have you taken it?"

The walls swam before his eyes. Wavered like curtains in a breeze. The walls reached out for him.

He squeezed his eyes shut and backed blindly out of the room.

Analise did not know why Gideon destroyed the statues he made. Or why, if he hated them so much, he didn't stop creating them altogether.

What she did know was that while he was working, he rarely ate or slept. That he worked every day of the week but one, and generally spent that one day in a sort of stupefied swoon on his cot. That sometimes, once or twice a month at most, he would knock on her door, streaked with clay, hollow-cheeked and fever-eaten, and rave about walls moving, and women with hands like linden branches covered in snow, about falling into a deep pit whose walls crawled with wailing purple flowers. And that sometimes in these moments he would kneel beside her bed, where Analise sat very, very still, and lay his hot head in her lap, and she would stroke his hair until his fever broke, and his sweat cooled her thighs and he slept.

In the morning, when Gideon was still weak, he would let her feed him. And smile at her, sweetly, without that bitter edge that made her bleed. And though he never did and never would say thank you, Analise sometimes thought she could rest forever in the cradle of his smile.

Mostly though, he gave her such a headache, roaring and storming on the other side of their shared wall, smashing ceramic, dashing (she surmised from the sound) larger pieces to the floor then taking his hammer to them, that Analise often fantasized about buying a mallet of her own.

Yet she did not move away from her garret room.

"A glutton for punishment," Gideon had once sneered at her.

"Glass houses shouldn't throw stones," she'd retorted.

"Analise Field, Authoress, industrializing the cliché." He paused, then said, glitteringly, "You should write for *ladies'* magazines."

At which point she threw a newspaper at his head.

There had been a period of time (most of last year, more or less) when she did not talk to Gideon at all. This had been after a terrible fight they had at Breaker House, his aunt's summer mansion, where she and their painter friend Elliot Howell had been invited to fete Gideon's cousin Desdemona on the occasion of her twenty-fifth birthday.

Gideon had not wanted her there.

Gideon had not thought she belonged there.

He'd pretty much forced her to leave.

Very well, she thought. If he did not want her, why inflict her company on him? So she'd locked her door against him. Left a room if he walked into it. Stopped going to pub parties or group suppers if the invitation came from mutual friends. It wasn't like he minded. He never tried to talk to her.

Except on his bad nights. Then she heard him stand outside her door, and lean against it, and mutter in that fast, febrile whisper words she trembled to hear.

Covering her head with a pillow helped.

After nearly twelve months, he'd ended up apologizing. More or less. In that ineffable Alderwood style. Probably at Elliot's instigation. Elliot was the peacemaker among them.

And they'd been friends again for a while. If you could call it friends. Whatever they were. Neighbors.

But their troubles leaked back in. Short spats. Acid insults. Doors slamming. Yelling through the walls.

Then that thing with the toilet paper.

And now the statue.

The statue.

Which, in the moonlight, looked as if it were made of frozen quicksilver. She thought of the love and care and attention lavished in the lines of it. She thought of his hands coaxing the shape into being, building it up from slabs of clay and toilet paper, calling it forth, and she wondered how he dared. How did he *dare* annihilate something so beautiful?

How very like him!

Analise moved closer to lay her hand against the statue's cold cheek. Gideon must have laid his own hand there, just so.

Would probably swing the hammer just so, tomorrow.

That was when the statue opened its eyes.

They were huge, glassy, black pools with a green glow at the bottom.

What Analise felt was not shock, but recognition. This. This was why he killed them. Because of that pleading look in their eyes.

"Oh, what shall I do?" she whispered. "What shall I do?"

A single tear fell from the statue's left eye, a streak of slow-moving mercury that spattered down its sealed lips. She moved her hand to wipe the tear away. Her fingers glittered silver.

Analise felt her face settling into an expression her father used to say could bully the cows into producing pure cream.

"I'll save you. Wait here. The landlord has a dolly."

PART TWO: GENTRY MOON MASQUERADE

Desdemona Mannering looked tousled and half asleep when the housekeeper showed Gideon into the breakfast parlor at Breaker House. She was wearing a tea gown of peach silk damask, with sweeping back pleats, and a ruff of ivory lace. Her black hair spilled across her shoulders as carelessly as ink, and she blinked, glossy-eyed, at Gideon, as if trying to recall his name.

"Cousin," she greeted him. "To what do I owe the honor?"

"Desdemonster." Gideon collapsed into a fragile gilt chair near her knee. "It's not summer anymore. Why are you in your summer cottage? I rather thought it would be deserted at this time of year. A high lonely place with the wind blowing in from the sea."

"I'm hiding out," she confessed. "Boy troubles."

Gideon smirked. "Chaz Mallister?"

Letting her head fall against the posy-broidered back of her chair, Desdemona laughed. "Those aren't boy troubles. Those are Chaz troubles. They're perennial. I don't let them bother me. No. This was more of an instance of a boyfriend finding out about another boyfriend and weeping all over my bosom. The only thing Chaz does about my boyfriends is steal them, thereby rendering them useless to me. I only choose boys he wants for himself. I like to get there first."

Gideon had known Desdemona all his life, but he had never been able to read her. Unlike Analise with her glass face, her face that was the barometer of her inner storms and the rosy lamp of her delight, his cousin could keep smiling while she held her arm over an open flame. He'd seen her do it once when they were no more than seven or eight.

Her expression, Elliot had observed upon meeting her, was as serene and sparkling as a lake. Snorting, Analise had added, "She really ought to wear a No Fishing placard around her neck then. One that says, Warning: Barracudas in the Water." Gideon almost betrayed himself by laughing that time. But if Desdemona could smile when flame scorched her flesh, Gideon could scowl at the only woman who ever warmed him to laughter. Never had a Mannering trumped an Alderwood yet, socially or privately, though a polite war had raged between the families for generations.

"What brings you to Breaker House, Gideon?" Desdemona asked. "Never tell me girl troubles? I don't think you've chased a petticoat in your life. Chaz says they called you the Monk back at Uni."

"No," he said absently. "That was Elliot. I was the Stick, for the extra appendage popularly assumed to be affixed up my ass. Ana was the Hick, because, well. Ana. Elliot was the Monk."

Desdemona gurgled with laughter. "Not anymore, certainly! I never see him now but I think he's just been tumbled half out of his mind. That little wife of his is a spitfire. I could almost be afraid of her if she weren't so relentlessly charming. Or, do I mean charming? It's more like . . . "

"Enchanting," Gideon corrected her. "Almost exactly like that, actually."

He could not but help an inward shudder when he thought of Nixie, Elliot's wife. When he'd met her, she had been Queen Nyx. She came from the place the statues came from. Recalling her was to remember that place, his descent into that deathtrap of flowers, those laughing bone bells, the walls peeling back to swallow him, the woman with the linden branch hands . . .

There he stopped. To go any deeper would be to press the spongy tissues of an infected wound. He shied away.

He was at Breaker House for one reason. It was a doorway to that world. And it was a doorway Analise must pass through if she stuck with his statue. The statue would try to return home. They always did.

"Are you all right, Gideon?" Desdemona sounded amused, but she no longer looked sleepy. Her placid black eyes had sharpened on him in a way that might have been concerned or predatory. He could not tell. "You look a bit like a bad blancmange, old thing."

He waved his hand, dismissing this. "I've come here on a repairing lease. The city grows noxious. Or perhaps it is merely my roommate who is *obnoxious*."

"You don't share a room with her," Desdemona murmured into her tea. "You just wish you did."

Gideon smiled sourly but did not reply. Desdemona was the only one in the world who lied better than he did, and could catch him at it. For this reason, he never played cards with her, though he took some satisfaction at trouncing her at billiards. In chess or darts they were equals, but both held championship in their own sport. Hers was deceit. His was contemptuous insouciance.

"Stay as long as you like," Desdemona invited him with a shrug of her wrists that sent her lace ruffs cascading into her elbows. "My summer cottage is your summer cottage. There are seventy rooms, and forty-three of them are bedrooms. Surely you can find a hidey hole where you can lick your wounds."

She laughed when he glared at her. "Don't flash your eyes at me, cousin," she drawled. "You Alderwoods may harness the lightning, but we Mannerings invented rubber boots."

"Fallacy," Gideon retorted. "Rubber boots offer no protection against lightning."

Desdemona gasped in mock dismay. "Horned Lords save me! My metaphor has fallen to the foe!"

He cracked a reluctant half-smile at her, which she knew to be her victory. Then he left her to her breakfast, and went to lick his wounds.

Analise plopped cross-legged on the floor before the statue. After a minute, the statue also sank to its haunches, sliding the rest of the way, imitating her position. As its movements grew more fluid with each passing hour, the expression on its face also relaxed, that first fatal pleading and panic becoming something more somber but no less intense. It never stopped watching her, never blinked, or blinked so slowly she could not categorize it as such.

The consistency of its skin remained cold and white, becoming more like marble than eggshell.

"I think you're getting stronger," Analise told the statue. "Look at you! Less friable already than you were this morning. Lay odds you'll have skin like lonsdaleite if you're let to live unmolested by sledgehammers." She reached out and patted its knee. "Don't worry. I've got your back. Never did an Alderwood stand a chance against a Field. Gideon may not know it, but my name comes from *Field of War*, and has nothing to do with my family having been farmers since the Neolithic Revolution."

"What," asked Elliot behind her, "did the Fields call themselves before the domestication of plant life?"

Analise grinned at him over her shoulder. "Killers! We were hunting griffins while the Alderwoods were still swinging from trees. Didn't you know?"

"I suspected. Thank you for clarifying."

Elliot watched from the doorway of his studio that doubled as a guestroom (if the guest didn't mind sharing her pallet with a stack of stretched canvases and a bucket of turpentine). He'd asked no questions the night before when Analise showed up at his door, leading a walking statue by the hand. Merely, he had stepped back to let them in, breathing, "Gideon."

"Yes."

"So. That's why he destroys them."

Then he had put both of them right to bed, explaining that his wife was out on one of her long walks, and was not expected back till well after breakfast the following day. It was noon now, but Nyx was still not back. This did not seem to faze her husband at all.

Looking up from her study of the statue, Analise exclaimed, "Say, Elliot! Do you have any storybooks?"

"Sure thing. What did you have in mind?"

The gravity well of the statue's relentless gaze drew her attention forward again. "Children's books? For small children. Lots of illustrations. Simple words. I want to try something."

There was a long silence. When Elliot didn't answer immediately, Analise glanced at him again and saw that his broad face had turned bright red.

"What?" she asked, surprised.

"I . . . It's just . . . For a second there I thought . . . I thought you'd guessed."

"Guessed what?" His face, if anything, went redder. Elliot smiled a bit helplessly and spread his hands, and suddenly she knew. "Oh." Analise blinked hard, then hopped up from the floor, barely aware of the statue doing the same behind her. She barreled into his arms and hugged him hard.

"When?" she demanded. "When is Nixie due? When do I get to meet my fairy godchild?"

Elliot tried to rub the grin off his rosy face, but it would not long stay suppressed. "Early spring. Nyx says Spring Equinox at the twelfth bell of noon, but I reserve judgment. Though I shouldn't." He shook his head. "Ana! How you let me go on. Come along to the . . . the nursery. We happen," his laughter burbled up again, "to have started a children's book collection."

"Wait!" Analise cried, halting Elliot in his steps. She cast herself back upon his broad chest and hugged him once again.

"That's all," she murmured when his arms closed around her, the heat from his bear-like body seeping into the chill she hadn't known had gone bone-deep. "I just wanted to do that a little while longer. That's all."

Behind her, another set of arms reached around to close about Elliot and complete a circuit of embrace. Elliot let out his breath slowly, resting his head against Analise's forehead.

"It's learning," he whispered.

"Yes," she said, the cold marble pressing hard against her back.

After a moment, the marble warmed to her skin temperature. Surrounded in this knot of limbs, she was not certain where she ended and her companions began. No one moved for several minutes, so Analise was able to identify the exact moment the stillness in that sculpted chest behind her picked up a faint pulse.

It grew steadily stronger, as if taking a cue from her heartbeat.

Midnight was the breaking hour. It always had been.

Gideon stared bleakly at the walls of his bedroom. This was Breaker House's "Sea Foam Room." Just at present he could attest that from his vantage point, sitting on the floor with his back to the bed and surrounded by all that pale green and cream, it did feel remarkably like drowning in so much silk jacquard.

It was twenty-six past eleven. The walls were very still.

They had been very still since twilight.

"I'm not fooled," he told the printed silk wall coverings. "Do you think I've never seen a hawk on streetlight, watching the park below? There is a stillness worse than wavering, and you are it."

He set his chin on his arms, which barred his knees to his chest. His body had done this automatically without the precise consent of his brain, to make of itself a smaller target. To protect its back and keep its eyes on the door. The problem with Breaker House was, everything became a door at midnight.

Gideon had been nine when the walls of Breaker House first opened to him, when he learned that his cousin's palatial summer cottage was not one house but three, all occupying the same space in three different worlds.

Or, as one of the fickle Gentry from the other side of the walls tried to explain to him at some point, when he was a little older and ripe for the games and seductions of twiggy-limbed, snake-skinned, goat-horned maidens, "In reality, it's really only one house after all. If you can call anything *real* that has to do with this house. Which you *can't*," she laughed, shrugging and rippling and turning silver in that light that came from nowhere Gideon could see. "Because only the Veil is real. But if there *were* other worlds before and behind the Veil, young mortal, this house would be anchored in all of them. Your Athe, our Valwode, and in Bana the Bone Kingdom as well, where the goblins dwell. And in all the seven hells beneath too. Of course."

Gideon himself always imagined (when he let himself imagine anything about the situation, which was not often, as he felt that even to think about the place beyond the walls was as dangerous as standing too close to Analise Field) that Breaker House was a world itself, tucked inside an infinite series of worlds like Damahrashan nesting dolls.

As a child, he would visit every summer when his mother came to call upon her sister-in-law, Tracy Mannering, née Alderwood. After the first few times Breaker House had swallowed him and spat him out again, Gideon tried refusing to return. But Mother—that was, Mrs. Audrey Beckett-Alderwood—whose eyes were blue ice and whose smile glittered as if painted with powdered glass—merely waited out his storm of tears.

After nine-year-old Gideon had thrown his fit, declaring he would never, not *ever*, not if she *whipped him*, or laid about him with *sticks*, or beat him with a broom of *linden branches*, go back to Breaker House, Audrey Alderwood told him, very simply, in a voice as polished and coiffed and manicured as the rest of her, "You have two choices, Gideon. You may come with me to Breaker House. Or you may spend the holiday with your father."

To which threat Gideon responded by snapping his mouth shut and weeping silently, protesting no further.

Some things were worse than being eaten alive by Breaker House.

How many times had he been brought through the walls in his sleep? Or coaxed from his bed by the cajolery of those strange bone bells? Or bribed into that twilight world with treats and sweets, blackmailed, bullied, threatened, promised, hissed at and hounded through those shifting quicksilver walls?

And always when he came back to Athe, that strange compulsion on him to make statues. To build them up, build them high, to watch them quicken, and quickened, return through the walls to their true world.

No, Gideon hadn't always destroyed them. Not at first. Not until the last time he'd gone into Dark Breakers, and saw his statues marching rank on rank. They had a captain by then, a rough-hewn statue, Gideon's first, who now wore a red cape of office and a ruby broach, and who carried a spear tipped in obsidian. He saw his statues training in the courtyard of Dark Breakers, ripping the heads off prisoners, or snatching their beating hearts from their chests, all while the woman with the linden-branch hands looked on.

He saw what they were being used for. The work of his hands.

Once Gideon purchased his sledgehammer and started putting it to use, the walls never opened for him again. But the compulsion to build never left him.

Until now.

Until Analise stole his statue. At last the crawling itch in his fingers was quiescent, the fever in his brain calm. At last, stillness.

Gideon knew this was only a temporary reprieve. The walls continued to watch him, malevolently and not a little gleefully. As if waiting for the statue to march through the mansion's iron gates, through the Great Hall, up the Grand Staircase, and into the Sea Foam Room where Gideon awaited it.

It was only a matter of days, perhaps hours, before this happened. Gideon did not think, this time, that when he was taken from Day Breakers into Dark Breakers (he thought of that other house in the Valwode where the Gentry lived, as "Dark Breakers") he would be let to return.

"You got lucky," Gideon told the walls. "I have an interfering neighbor. She's a farmer. You'd think she'd know about animals needing to be put to the slaughter. But no. She has to have a heart in her not of practical resolve, but of wind and fire. Wind and fire," he muttered, shivering, as he always did when contemplating Analise Field's dangerous heart.

Midnight was the breaking hour. It always had been.

The walls would melt. Any minute now. At the twelfth chime, the world as he knew it would begin to run like watercolors all around him . . .

"Gideon!"

Gideon flinched as the bedroom door slammed open, the force of it bouncing the delicate crystal knob against the gilded boiserie lining the lower half of the wall. Desdemona stood in the doorway, wearing her bathing costume, hair tucked up under a swimming cap, towel flung over her shoulder, streaming water onto the tapestry-smothered marble of the hall floor.

"Gideon, great and foolish gods, what are you doing on the floor?" Shrugging off his answer before he even opened his mouth, Desdemona went on, "I had the most marvelous idea for a party! A ball, that is. A masque. Stop brooding all over the Countess's Lirhuvian carpet and come into the loggia with me. I've had desks brought in and plenty of lamps. If we work through the night, we can get the invitations out first thing!"

Some things, Gideon reflected, rising from the floor, were worse than being eaten alive by Breaker House.

"Why not?" he sighed.

Pale his tunic, pale her gown
Bone his scepter, ice her crown
Swan-down cape and snowflake mask
Who they are though, none shall ask
Join our revel, gather soon
To dance under a Gentry Moon

In Celebration
Of the Annual Autumn Festival of Gentry Moon,
Miss Desdemona Kirtida Mannering
&
Mister Gideon Azlin Alderwood
Request the Pleasure of Your Company
at the
Gentry Moon Masquerade Ball.

Breaker House
Oak-and-Acorn Boulevard
Seafall, Leressa
Gentry Moon Eve
10 PM

Attire is Moonlight Formal.
Those not Arrayed Appropriately
Shall be Refused Admittance at the Gates.
– D. K. M.

When Analise came upon them, Nixie was sitting on the kitchen counter, nestled between a pot of navy beans set to soak and a rack full of drying dishes. Elliot stood before her, hands braced on either side of his wife's hips as she read to him from a cream-cake rich invitation, embossed in gold and trailing bits of silvery floss. Nixie read it aloud with a half smile, but Analise had the impression of leashed fury. A deep frown line bisected the bridge of Elliot's nose.

Nixie shook her head as she read out Desdemona's initials at the end of the invitation.

"Does she know what she's calling down?" Her blue-black braids tumbled over her shoulder and into her lap. Elliot lifted the tail of one and rubbed its roughness between two fingers.

"Even if she did," he replied, "do you think she'd hesitate for a heartbeat? This is Desdemona. The only daughter of Candletown Coal Magnate H. H. Mannering. You know what they call her? The Anthracite Princess. Once at Uni, Gideon brought her to a frat house costume party, and she dressed as a dead canary. I still don't know if it was a joke."

Nixie's half smile turned whole as she gazed upon her husband. "Mortal humor is often obscure to me."

"Me too!" Analise said from the door. "Morning, Nixie."

Nixie's smile did not scimitar down to its former expression of fury and contempt, but her blue-black eyes grew somber. A curious sensation splashed through Analise's ribcage, churning against the walls of her heart. This often happened when Nyx Howell's attention fell wholly upon her. It was as if when Nixie looked at her, she was remembering back to the day Analise was born, and the day her mother was born, and her mother's mother, and her mother's mother's mother. As if she had stood upon the fields farmed by the Fields since the days when they had been forests, and since before that time too, when the forests had been a restless sea.

Then she blinked, and grinned, and it was only Nixie.

"Good morning, Ana," she said amiably. "I am sorry I was not here yesterday to greet you."

"Did you have a good walk?"

"Horned Lords know it was long enough," Elliot muttered, but laughed as he said it, and kissed his wife on the side of her slender brown neck.

"It was informative," Nixie replied. "It is so near Gentry Moon; the veil into the Veil is thin. Speaking of which, Ana, Elliot tells me you stumbled upon a Gentry enchantment astray in Athe. And have decided to teach it the alphabet in our guest room."

Analise felt the first bloom of blush in her cheeks. She knew it but preceded a more fervent rush of blood. The foreknowledge never helped, never staved off the indignity of having her own skin betray her.

"I . . . I don't think about it like that, Nixie. It . . . it needed my help, that's all. I don't believe in, in," she waved her hand, "all those old Seafall superstitions."

"The stories of the Valwode are older than Seafall, and far wider spread," Elliot reminded her.

"I know, I know." Analise shrugged. "And I love when your paintings reflect the mythology, Elliot. Seven hells, my writing brims over with Gentry allusions and goblin chicanery. But . . . This is the *Orchid* Age. We have automobiles. Trains. Electric light. The diphtheria vaccine. Even if . . . Even if there used to be such a thing as Gentry magic, and, and traffic once flourished between our worlds, we live now in cities of concrete and steel. Don't all the old tales say the Gentry can't bear cold iron? Anyway, the statue . . . Gideon's statue . . . It's just . . . I mean . . . "

But there was no way to explain the statue without magic. Because statues did not walk. Or weep. Or learn. Statues simply *stayed put*. That was inherent in the etymology.

Uncomfortable in her fiery skin, Analise shrugged again. "I just didn't want Gideon to destroy it," she mumbled. "That's all I know."

"It will not talk," Nixie said after a long pause. "Not here." She waved her cream and silver invitation at Analise, introducing the subject change. "Will you be attending this ball, Ana? Shall you wear a mask of pearl, a gown spun of organdy and apricot anemone, and dance with that dour boy who shares a garret with you?"

Analise took a step back. "Um. No. I—I don't think I'm invited."

Elliot handed her the envelope. "It's addressed to Mr. and Mrs. Elliot Howell, plus one guest. I think Alderwood knows you're here."

"That's Miss Mannering's handwriting," Analise observed. "She likes fireworks at all her parties—and not just the expensive kind from overseas. She'd love to see Gideon throw me out of Breaker House in front of the polite world."

Nixie patted Analise's cheek. "If that young woman wants fireworks," she said, "I shall be happy to provide them. But I am going alone. You both will be needed here, to keep the statue from harm. Ana is correct; it must not be destroyed. Not this one. Not while we have it under our influence. Now. All that remains to decide is what to wear. Maestro," she murmured, stroking back her husband's hair with her knuckles, "you shall have to paint me again."

* * *

"She's not coming?" Gideon repeated.

"No. Nor Elliot either. Pity. I like dancing with him. He's so big and lummoxy and warm. And so *polite*. I like to make him blush. I like to rub my smell all over him and imagine him dreaming about me at night. I caught him sniffing his coat one time after I hugged him." Desdemona grinned. "This was before he married Mrs. Howell, of course. I wonder if he'd still blush when I kiss him?"

She finished pinning his boutonnière in place. Creamy roses and silver-sprayed leaves dripped down the embroidered lapel. Gideon grimaced at himself in the mirror. A sunken-eyed, thin-faced scarecrow in an antique silver-on-ivory Lirian court suit. He had refused to wear the wig, however, or the beauty patch, or dust his dark hair silver, as Desdemona had done.

"I hope that's not aluminum powder you've brushed onto your greasepaint, Desdemonster," he said, scowling in disapproval. "You heard about that actress who played Dora Rose in The Bastard Theatre's production of *Bone Swans?* She almost died from cosmetic poisoning."

Desdemona caught his eye in the mirror as she applied black paint to her lips. "You really *are* a stick, Gideon! She's an actress. She probably just collapsed because she was pregnant. At any rate, old thing, I used aluminum *paste* not powder. No cramping or palpitations yet." She wriggled silver-painted fingers, where heavy rings of diamond and pearl glittered and glowed. "I can still feel all my appendages too!"

He turned a shoulder on her amused stare, propping himself casually on the corner of her vanity table to ask, "Did Ana say why she isn't coming?"

"Nooooo, darling," Desdemona sighed with exaggerated melancholy. "She did not. Mrs. Howell did all the replying—in her inimitable way. She wrote something about being unwilling to expose Elliot to the dangers of dancing at this stage in her pregnancy." She tittered, an obnoxious noise she'd cultivated from her long and studied acquaintance with her father's mistress, Countess Lupe Valesca. "As if *he* were the one in the delicate condition. Then she said Ana's staying home to help him babysit. Which makes no sense to me, because for all I know, she's still in her first trimester!"

Gideon understood the message. He did not dare answer his cousin, but he understood. He gave a grim nod in the direction of his court shoes, imagining himself leaving the masquerade ball early, and breaking down Elliot's front door, and pushing past Ana, and kicking off those very shoes, and shattering the statue's face with one of his absurdly high heels as the horrified babysitters gaped at the slaughter.

His breath left him in a shudder.

He *could.*

But she'd be expecting it.

He'd have to attack when she was off her guard. When she was sleeping.

Did she sleep in the same bed with the statue, her body curved around it in protection? Did it watch her while she dreamed, and brush the frizzy red curls from her forehead, and think its alien thoughts even as it leeched the warmth from her body with the chill of its own?

"Gideon. *Gideon*!"

Gideon blinked. Desdemona stared with outrage and astonishment . . . and fear. He became aware, suddenly, of a suffocating onslaught of scent: orange blossom and ambergris and a touch of wood smoke. It stung his nose and coated the insides of his mouth and crawled down his throat.

"You just smashed my perfume bottle," Desdemona told him.

"Oh." Gideon glanced down at his hands. Bits of crystal and blood clung to his palms.

"It's an *Aniqua Adrian*." Desdemona bent to scoop up a sparkling, faceted, orange thing from the floor. It was the sapphire-topped stopper for the perfume bottle, Gideon saw when she set it down on the vanity.

"It's from her *Fire Festival* line," Desdemona continued. "It costs fourteen hundred monarchs an ounce, you fool."

Gideon looked at his cousin steadily until her fury faded and her face settled into an impassive grin.

"I should tell Aniqua that a hint of copper and blood is just what the perfume needed!" Her silvery shoulders shook with laughter. "She'll be here tonight, with her usual entourage. We'll smell them before we see them. Go on, old thing." She waved at him. "Wash your hands. I'll ring one of the girls to come clean this up." Turning her back to Gideon, she picked up the telephone on her vanity table and murmured an order into it, before setting the earpiece carefully into the cradle. Knowing himself dismissed, he headed for the door.

"Gideon."

Gideon stopped, but did not turn.

"It's better," the tone in her voice was unlike any he had heard, "that she'll not be here tonight. Of all nights. You know that, don't you?"

Gideon's fingers tightened on the handle, smearing blood on the bronze. They had never spoken of it. He had not guessed until now that she was even aware of the nature of her own house. He should have known better.

"Gentry Moon," his cousin whispered. "Tonight is Tithing Night."

Gideon shut the door behind him.

The look on Elliot's face when his wife kissed him goodbye and walked out the door that night went like a needle through Analise's heart.

"It's just a dance," she tried to reassure him. "Isn't it?"

Slumping against the doorjamb, Elliot stared into the darkness; Nixie was notorious for leaving doors open. "Ana. I have this terrible feeling."

Analise shivered. Over the years, she had learned to trust Elliot's feelings, at least in moments like these, when his voice went hollow and his round blue eyes took on took on the luminous opacity of favrile glass, like the stained panes of the skylight above the grand staircase at Breaker House.

It was less a noise than the sense of an approaching coolness behind them that announced the presence of the statue. If Gideon had shaped it of velvet instead of clay, the statue could not have moved more silently. It too stared out toward night.

Analise slipped her arm through Elliot's elbow, smiling a bit crookedly when the statue did likewise to hers. Covering its hard, cold hand with her fingers, Analise whispered, "What are you thinking, Elliot?"

"I'm thinking," he breathed, "that tonight, I am afraid of moonrise."

"Alderwood, that face of yours would curdle cream. Deep's sake, couldn't you have camouflaged the wreckage with a mask?"

Gideon turned his head a fraction of a millimeter from his contemplation of the dancers, acknowledged the comment with a freezing half-second glance, then turned back. The Great Hall had been cleared of furniture, its enormous and ornate Skahki tapestries rolled up and packed away. The creamy limestone arches and pilasters made a neutral backdrop for the sparkling company beneath them.

Some company, Gideon thought—well, most of it—he could do without. Present company included.

Chaz Mallister snickered behind his full-bearded King of Court Jesters mask. The beard consisted of green and blue plumes. Peacock, of course. It matched the jewels (probably *not* paste peridots and aquamarines, Gideon surmised) lining the holes of the mask's eyes. Chaz's painted curls had been piled high on his head and lacquered like a Leechese puzzle box.

Chaz whoomfed Gideon's chin with his feathered fan. "You're so handsome when you cut one dead, my dear boy."

Chaz's particular snicker, Gideon reflected, was a sound that had plagued him since early childhood. He'd first heard it that fateful morning Chaz's nanny had dropped off her plump, redheaded charge, age five, at the Palace of Dolls. This was the scaled-down model of Breaker House that Harlan Hunt Mannering had presented to his daughter on her seventh birthday. Abandoned by his nanny to his own devices, Chaz promptly terrorized Gideon's greyhound puppy, broke three saucers and the sugar bowl of Desdemona's porcelain tea set, and set the playhouse curtains on fire.

To be fair, he had been provoked. The three children, having sized each other up long before introductions were completed, immediately perceived that the game of competitive loathing (with occasional truces to band together against nurses, governesses, and tutors) would be far more amusing than merely getting along.

"So many delectable young things," sighed Chaz, licking his lips. "Which one are you staring at?" His elbow jostled Gideon's. The satin of their suits slicked sensuously off each other. Gideon suppressed an eye roll. Chaz was always touching him in these small ways. He was worse with Desdemona, pinches and tweaks and nips, but she manhandled him right back. Those two were like lion cubs, worrying at each other's tender spots.

"I am watching Desdemona," Gideon answered briefly.

Chaz flinched. Not, Gideon thought, on purpose. But he recovered quickly enough to sidle up again and smirk. "Alderwood. Really. Your *first* cousin?"

When Gideon did not answer, Chaz shrugged. "Oh, why not? It's done in all the best families, I'm sure, from Southern Leressa to the Holy See at Winterbane. I have to admit, she suits you far better than that fat little farm girl who styles herself a writer."

Gideon was glad for the smeared white clown paint upon his cheeks and the smoked spectacles he wore, for he knew his eyes and pallor betrayed him whenever he lost his temper, and he was about to lose it now. But his voice, to his satisfaction, was distant, indeed almost absentminded, when he replied, "Miss Field's next book is greatly anticipated by critics and readers alike."

Chaz snorted, so Gideon continued maliciously, "I have never seen Desdemona laugh like that before. Do you know with whom she is dancing?"

Impossible to tell what color Chaz turned beneath his mask and paint. Yet Gideon felt a wave of jealous heat rise off him, and was not surprised at the curt, "No," followed by Chaz turning heel and striding away.

Gideon felt no triumph. He knew with whom—or rather, with *what*—Desdemona danced, her silver skin and silver silk and mask of silver lace glowing against the stranger's towering darkness.

Tower he did, though slenderly. The stranger was far, far too thin for his height, attenuated like a late afternoon shadow. He wore something that looked like scorched cobwebs, like ashes newly swept from a grate, a few cinders still burning, to settle swirling about his figure. And though the clothes fell in rags and ribbons, still they conveyed richness beyond imagination, as if the ashes remembered having once been black silk, grackle feathers, dark velvet, the iridescent scales of some monstrous fish. His skin and eyes and tangled hair were as cinder-dark as his clothes, and as he edged Desdemona off the ballroom floor and against a pillar, he reached to cradle her face with long, slim hands . . .

Gideon shut his eyes, hearing for the first time the bone bells. They had been ringing midnight all the while he stared. They rang the thirteenth bell now, and when he opened his eyes again, the company in the Great Hall had swelled to three times its previous size. Only this time, he knew, those birds' heads perched atop petal-clad bodies were not masks. Those rainbow-spangled wings and gem-encrusted tails, those silver hooves and velveted paws, those monsters gilded in moonbeams, were not costumes created for the occasion. The walls of Breaker House had opened. Still the mortals danced on, oblivious to the nature of their new partners.

Gideon stared at the stranger grasping Desdemona's dazed and dreamy face. He had bent his head and was whispering in her ear. Her eyelids fluttered down. His hands had several fingers too many, all impossibly long. The nails—no, *talons*—were at least half the length of those fingers, lit with the hard green smolder of emeralds, their keen tips filigreed in copper.

Inhaling sharply, Gideon started toward his cousin. Was intercepted. Someone slammed a hand against his chest, right over his heart.

Not Chaz.

"That one," said Nixie Howell, "can take care of herself. Will you dance, boy?"

It was midnight when the statue went wild.

The book Analise was reading aloud from flew across the room as the statue slapped it from her hands. It threw itself from the mattress where it had reclined, its head near Analise's knee, and landed with a jarring thump on the floor. For a moment Analise held her breath, fearing the statue had fractured itself, that it would splinter and crumble before her eyes, as if the wreckage Gideon would have wrought of it were its destiny. But it just rose from a crouch and sprang forward, marble-pale limbs suddenly blue-veined and aglow, as if highways of blue lightning ran through it.

"Elliot!" Analise shouted. The statue pounded toward the door, without, it seemed, any intention of opening it before barreling through.

A tinkle in the distance—perhaps Elliot dropping a glass he'd been drying—footsteps down the short hall. The door yanked open just before the statue made a new one, with the result that the statue slammed into Elliot instead, driving him back against the hallway wall. Several framed photographs crashed down. Plaster debris tumbled from abrupt fissures.

But Elliot, who was of a size with the statue, grasped its torso in a bear hug and grappled it to the floor. The statue rolled Elliot onto his back, one hand crushing his throat, the other digging hard fingers into his face. Analise leapt at the statue, hooking her arms beneath its colossal ones and heaving back with all her strength. As she had hoped, the statue whipped about, abandoning Elliot to gasp on the carpet, and plucked her off its back, hauling her into its arms.

For a moment as those panicked black eyes stared into hers, the green sheen of them catching a glaze of blue from the fire in its veins, Analise thought it was going to dash her to the floor, then step on her skull for good measure. But it caught her up instead, high in its arms, and clasped her close. She could feel its quick shallow breaths, though its nostrils and mouth were closed seams that never opened. She felt the hummingbird buzz in its breast that was not—quite—a heartbeat. It turned left, then right, squeezing Analise ever nearer, like a mother with an infant in a building burning down all around her.

Trying to catch her breath, Analise flung her arms about the statue's neck, and put her lips to its carved ear, whispering, "It's all right. It's all right. Calm down. Nothing here will hurt you."

"Ana . . . " Elliot croaked from the floor.

"It's all right," Analise said, but still the statue shook. So Analise did what she had always done whenever Gideon came to her, feverish and afraid and babbling of women with linden branch hands; she laid her cheek against the statue's and sang a snatch of lullaby from her childhood.

"Hush, love, sleep easy, no need to be strong
I can't slay your dragons, but I'll sing you a song . . . "

The statue softened its crushing hold, and turned its face into Analise's neck. She hummed the melody, suddenly uncertain of the next lyric, and hoped the vibration was enough to calm it down.

"Ana . . . "

"Hush love, be easy, and sleep in my arms—Elliot, are you hurt?—*I can't stop your nightmares, but I'll keep you from harm . . . "*

"Nothing broken, Ana. Just bruised. Keep singing."

So Analise sang. She sang until the statue slid down the length of the wall and sat in the plaster dust of the carpet, holding her in its lap. Analise sang, and stroked immovable curls from a marmoreal forehead that seemed damp with distress, watching the blue light fade from its pale surface, leaving faint streaks like scorch marks. Sang until whatever it was that had frightened the statue returned whence it came, and shut the door behind it.

"Queen Nyx of the Valwode."

Nyx said, "Former queen," and winked in a startlingly mortal way that reminded Gideon of Elliot. "Queen in exile. No queen at all, really," she laughed, "for I abdicated my title and came to Seafall to live with my beloved, setting my own heart to the hour of his death." She tapped her breastbone as she danced. "This ticking time bomb, Gideon. It makes me as mortal as . . . you. For example."

"Perhaps slightly less," Gideon countered. When he'd first met her on this side of the Veil, he could scarcely breathe in her presence. He'd feared she would turn on him, raking the air with her blue-black fingernails and ripping open a window for her monsters to crawl through. Now he knew her better. More or less. How could anyone know such an ancient, terrible mystery? And though he feared her still, he did not precisely know why.

Nyx smiled, and Gideon shivered inwardly. Blue-black tattoos danced upon her cheekbones. Elliot had painted a mask around those marks for the Gentry Moon ball, matching the color with a swirling mix of pigments. His designs scalloped her eyes, webbed her mouth and neck. They continued across her breastbone like the suggestion of lace. She was dressed plainly otherwise, in a long gray shirt—probably Elliot's—that she had belted at the waist with a black sash. The designs continued down her bare legs and feet.

"This is formal dress?" he asked, keeping his voice light and incredulous.

"A great master artist used me for his canvas," she said. "Need I tell you what his last painting sold for? I am wearing the most expensive costume here tonight!"

The dance parted them for a moment. When they came together again, she was no longer in a mischievous mood. Her smile had changed. Her dark voice, already low and husky, hit him in a hollow place, a bone clapper crashing against a bone bell.

"This design I wear is Elliot's way of warding me tonight. As you know, a mortal's greatest protection against us is also its greatest attraction for us. We live forever unless we kill ourselves—or are killed. The art we make, we make to wile eternity. Gentry creations are exquisite, but essentially hopeless. This is not to say we create out of despair. Rather, out of ennui. Mortal makings . . . " She lifted her hand from Gideon's arm to caress her own face. "They are your cry against death. Your art is at once your hope of eternity and an acknowledgement of your own grave. You, Gideon Alderwood, have walked the Valwode in a dream of beauty and horror, transfixed by the work of our hands, no?"

Gideon's neck felt like it was collared in steel. He could not even nod. Nyx went on as though he had. "It is the same for us. Sometimes I wander into Elliot's studio, and find myself staring at one of his paintings. Hours later, he comes upon me, and has to shake me from the reverie. Ana's book . . . " She shook her head. "Ana's book, I cannot tell you. I sob like a lost child before I am finished with the first paragraph—I know you think it's an awkward and jejune work, but to me it's . . . "

"Wind and fire," Gideon murmured.

"It is *her*," Nyx agreed, nodding. "It's her soul, joyous and naked, shining up from the printed paper. It ensorcels me. I have to be very careful what I read, what I expose myself to, because I have no defense against it."

Her hand strayed to her belly, just for a moment. "I was lucky, I think, to have read Ana's book first. It is kindly and inviting; it wished me no harm." Her strange blue-black, all-black, no-white gaze met his, dead on.

"Do you understand then, Gideon Alderwood, the great harm of which *your* statues are capable? They are the perfect marriage of mortal art and Gentry magic, creations that will live forever in the Valwode, indestructible by Gentry hands because any Gentry who sees one is struck to deathly stillness by its beauty. That Gentry must remain still even if the statue strides forth, rips her arms off, or staves in her skull, or plucks her still beating heart from her breast and crushes it underfoot. Your statues are the perfect warriors."

"That's why I destroyed them."

The words seemed to shred his throat as he gasped them. "It wasn't my choice to walk through those walls, or have that compulsion laid on me. Once I learned what she meant to . . . That they were weapons for her war . . . I tried everything to stop making them. From starving myself to cutting off my own hands. But no sooner do I climb out a high window with no intention of climbing back in, or put a razor to my veins, than I find myself wandering around outside in Market Circle buying another ton of clay. Or—Horned Lords help me—stealing Ana's toilet paper. Or facedown on my bed, crusted and smeared with another statue staring down at me . . . "

"You didn't destroy the early ones," Nyx interrupted him. "You made many statues before you realized their purpose. How did you anyway . . . ?" She snapped her mouth shut when she saw the shudder wracking him. "Poor child," she said. "You have been slave to this enchantment too long. Why, there's hardly anything left of you, is there? And soon to be less."

He managed to whisper, "What do you mean?" before the dance separated them again. Her pitying smile scorched the back of his eyelids.

When their hands touched again, it was not Nyx who partnered him.

A woman clothed in silver leaves and pale yellow petals clung to him like spider silk to a struggling butterfly. Her hair was the color of leeched butter; her pupiless eyes, a wash of gold. Her hands were long. Long, and strong, and hideously spackled white. Like linden branches covered in snow.

"Gideon, my love," said Gideon's earliest and worst nightmare, "truly it has been too long."

Gideon jerked his hands from hers, though her fingers tore through the ivory satin of his sleeves, tore through his skin almost to the bone. He stumbled back, clutching his bleeding arms close, hoping to lose himself in the other dancers.

But there weren't any other dancers.

The Great Hall of Breaker House had vanished. Gideon stood in a twilight courtyard near a fountain that spewed something more like quicksilver than water from the mouths of an orgiastic tangle of swans and maidens. Surrounding him were rank upon rank of blank white statues, each of which stared at him with cold black eyes.

PART THREE: VALOR IN THE VALWODE

Analise woke from a semi-doze to see Nixie in the hallway, surveying the three of them. Elliot snored gently on the carpet. The statue was curled in a fetal position, its head in Analise's lap. Nixie did not ask what happened; her sigh was one of utter comprehension.

"I thought to protect Elliot by leaving him here," she said. "Is he badly hurt?"

"Battered and bruised," Analise replied softly. "He probably shouldn't speak much for the next few days—but he'll live. How was . . . " She swallowed. "Everything?"

Nixie laughed softly. "A great success on many counts."

"Oh?" Analise tried not to infuse the syllable with anything more than a mild curiosity, as if tonight had been any other party, and her time not attending it spent like any other night at home.

For a moment it seemed Nixie would play along. She leaned against the wall, her gleaming eyes half-lidded. "Certainly a social coup for the Mannerings. Who of note was *not* there?" Her deep voice husked lower. Almost, Analise fancied, it took on an echo. "For others, this little masquerade was not so pleasant a pastime. A fat tithe of bodies was this night rendered to His Dark Majesty of the Bone Kingdom. Those he chose to be his own will no more walk beneath the blue skies of Athe."

Analise stared down at the heavy, cool head in her lap. If she didn't acknowledge Nixie's words, pretended not to understand them, perhaps they would roll through her like a lullaby or nursery story, one that whispered of creatures existing only on the edge of night, the borders of sleep. But Nixie's voice, so low and stark, held the cadence of factual recitation, not of tall tales.

"The Mannering family pays its debts as lavishly as it does anything. Years ago, one of Harlan Hunt Mannering's mining companies sunk a shaft too deep, and met with opposition from the underworld. That day was a bargain struck between mortal and goblin. Mutually beneficial, of course. Harlan Hunt Mannering agreed, in exchange for certain rights and privileges for his mines, to pledge the best products of mortal flesh, the cream of the cream, to tithe to the Goblin King of Bana. Desdemona continues her father's work. Tonight, she handed over that famous perfumer . . . What's her name? Aniqua something . . . ? As well as her top three apprentice noses. They'll be distilling essences and blending oils for the Shadow Court many centuries after the mortals of Athe have forgotten them."

Nixie bent down and picked up a framed autochrome, returning it to its lopsided nail in the wall. In it, Elliot and Nixie stood clasping hands before Elliot's most renowned painting, *The Breaker Queen.*

"And of course," she said softly, "The Gentry Moon Masquerade was a victory for Loreila the Winter-Touched. She stole Gideon Alderwood back to Dark Breakers, where once she bound him as a child in her fell enchantments. Now she will torment an army out of his own bleeding hands in her effort to win my former throne."

Analise was glad she was already sitting, for the floor gave a lurch, as if all three worlds and the seven hells beneath them grumbled and shifted. Just like that, she believed Nixie. She believed everything. She believed, as she never let herself before, in the statue whose head she cradled.

It was not asleep, she realized. It was listening, even now. Beneath her fingers, the living marble thrummed, as though the statue trembled.

"Nixie," Analise said, willing her fingers to unclench. *"Where is Gideon?"*

Nixie opened her eyes fully and stared down, recognizing the change in Analise almost before Analise did. Her black eyes shone all the brighter in the dark hall. Analise had always thought her a small, wiry woman, but now she seemed impossibly tall and fierce, as if the patterns Elliot had painted upon her had become armor, and that armor had seen battle, and Nixie herself had just returned, battered but whole, from the front.

Which, she thought, perhaps Nixie had.

"It means, Analise Field, that unless an Heir to the Antler Crown appears in the Valwode, anointed and blessed by the previous Queen, crowned there in full view of the Gentry Court at Dark Breakers, Loreila will win the throne by sheer force of numbers. And Gideon Alderwood, tapped dry providing those forces for her, will surely die."

Slap. Slather. Scrape. Shape.

They met because he'd fainted. Stupid. Weak. As if he were a child who stood in church on a hot holiday morning, locking his knees too long beneath scratchy woolen breeches and waking to find himself in unintentional obeisance to an altogether over-curious goddess.

No, not a goddess. Only Analise. Close enough.

Now the hands. The fingernails. The fine crescent of the cuticles.

They met because she was nosy. Because she had six brothers, and as the middle child of her large farmer family never had any privacy to lose and so didn't regard his. Because he never locked his door, hoping someday a strung out street weasel with a nose full of tardust and a wobbly trigger finger would burst in for a fast fistful of cash and leave Gideon several bullets the better.

Now the calf. The long muscles. The perfect protrusion of the ankle.

They met because she'd dragged him back to his cot, heaped him high with blankets, dribbled water down his throat, and when he was still helpless and weak, force-fed him the most delicious, rich, aromatic, unbelievable soup ("Hush, it's just chicken broth; it won't kill you," her first words to him), until he finally opened his eyes and saw a girl about his age hovering over him. Her forehead was anxious. She had too many freckles to find the constellations in them. Her hair was like the sunrise over the Bellisaar Wastelands. And he'd smiled at her before perceiving that she had just saved his life—and then he'd knocked the bowl from her hand.

It was not scalding, but it burnt them both.

He'd banished her from his room then, but she kept coming back. She always came back, and he owed her for that. He owed her his life, so he'd gotten her first book published, and made her know it was a favor, just connections, not merit.

How many times had he made her cry? Too many to count.

No. He had counted. Thirty-six times in three years. That he could hear through the wall, that is. He always listened as she cried herself to sleep.

Now the indentation above the lips.

"Devil's kiss," Gideon murmured, stepping back from his work. "Good morning, infant. Welcome to the hell."

The laughter behind him stuck like spines of ice between his shoulder blades.

"What nonsense, Gideon," said Loreila the Winter-Touched. He shivered at the sound of her voice and closed his eyes against the chill. "This is the Valwode. The Seven Hells are still a whole world away, with all the goblins of Bana between us. Thank the Horned Lords for it too! The devils below find Gentry flesh as sweet as baby meat."

When her sparkling voice ceased speaking, Gideon opened his eyes again. His newest statue stared at him, bewildered at its abrupt awakening, already terrified. And why shouldn't it be? Before it there stood the creator who wanted to destroy it, and behind *him*, the one who would let it live. It would live, and suffer, and be *put to use* . . .

This was statue number . . . what? Gideon long ago lost count of how many of these things he built in a day. How many days he'd been here. Years. Hours. Ages. All time was the same. All time was twilight in the quicksilver halls of Dark Breakers.

Unlike in his Seafall garret, here in the Valwode the statues seemed to harden and quicken between one breath and the next. They were taken away almost as soon as he completed them. His fingers shook. Blood crusted with clay.

Loreila took his hands in her long white-spackled grasp and studied them. Blood rose up from his skin in reverse raindrops, disappearing into the sky, leaving his wounds clean. Clay crusted off and turned to glitter, whipped away in a conjured breeze. His hands were whole again, though they trembled still. Gideon would look nowhere but her hands. Not her golden eyes or ragged yellow hair. Not the tiny sharps of her many, many teeth. He had looked once already, the first time he'd come here as a child. Had caught her attention. Once was enough.

"Lovely work," she said. "Now make another."

The old familiar fever washed over him. The dizzy red darkness. Gideon came to himself again bent before an enormous slab of half-formed clay. By the ache in his arms, the cold sweat running off his bare skin, Gideon judged he had just about finished roughhousing the clay into humanoid shape. But this was no human. It was taller, stronger, faster, more perfect, without gender, without any agenda but service.

He worked on, grimly, his body hardly his own. Only his thoughts were his own. And his thoughts were of her. Not the woman with the linden branch hands. *Her.*

Slap. Slather. Scrape. Shape.

They met because she'd saved his life.

And he hated her for it.

And he prayed she wouldn't come anywhere near him in a fool's attempt to do it again.

"Gods, Ana, stay away," he prayed.

Gods above and gods below. Gods crowned in horns, hunting down the sky. Goddess of the anxious forehead, the thousand freckles, the sunset hair. Goddess of the thirty-six nights of tears. Protect her. Watch her. Keep her far away from him.

Analise Field had a plan, a backpack, and a statue on a hand truck. The plan was partial, the backpack was almost entirely empty, and the statue was—for the first time since she'd met it—behaving like a statue. All part of the plan.

She pushed the hand truck with its heavy burden all the way from the Seafall train station to Oak-and-Acorn Avenue, where the acorns from the oak trees and the conkers from the chestnut trees and the fat fan-like leaves from the catalpas crunched underfoot. The iron gates to Breaker House were closed and padlocked. Analise rattled the bars and rang the bronze bell. Nothing.

A cold hand fell upon her shoulder. She patted it reassuringly.

"Can you climb?" she asked the statue.

In response, it stepped down off the hand truck and lifted her in one of its arms. Hand truck firmly grasped in the other, it took three quick leaps forward, vaulting them over the gate in a single bound. Loosely it landed, lightly in a crouch, and Analise scarcely felt the thump. The statue slid her down its body until her feet touched gravel, releasing her only reluctantly as if she were some precious thing. Like a baby. Or a bride.

Analise blushed, grateful that the statue was not human, and had no blood of its own, and couldn't know what blushes meant. Not like Gideon who read the changing tides and temperatures of her face and scoffed at them, responding to whatever she didn't or wouldn't or couldn't say—as if her skin had already said it all. Or like Elliot, who either politely ignored her reds and pinks, or kindly looked away until she returned to normal.

The statue stepped back onto the hand truck and assumed a more sessile position. Analise leaned forward and wheeled her burden up the gravel drive and around the West Wing to the sunken garden.

"Ha," she muttered. "I see our quarry coming back from the Cliff Walk. Stay here a moment while I catch her, would you?" She patted the statue on the arm and started off at a trot across the lawn.

"Miss Mannering!" she shouted. "Miss Mannering! Desdemona!"

The figure at the cliff's edge turned, surprised, black hair whipping around it like squid ink released into turbulent waters. For a moment, Analise thought she had been mistaken in her object. The Desdemona Mannering she knew was as golden and implacable as an idol, composed as a symphony, as calculated in her manipulations as a recipe for the finest perfume. She was a woman of the world, the Anthracite Princess, privileged, petted, adored.

This woman was . . . ravaged.

Her eyes were swollen, her lips cracked. Her face was a mess of streaked silver paint and smudged maquillage. She wore a ratty brown overcoat with patched elbows that was at least three times too large for her over a tattered gown of silver silk, and her feet were muddy and bare. She stared at Analise out of dangerous dark eyes that seemed to crackle and snap with lightning.

She looked, Analise thought, like Gideon on his fever days.

"What happened?" she blurted out.

Desdemona let out a hoarse noise. Like a crow laughing.

"Hung over," she croaked. "Can't you tell?"

Analise shook her head. Desdemona stared a few minutes longer, as if daring her to speak again. Finally she looked away, out to sea, and wiped her eyes.

"What are you doing here, Leez?" Desdemona was the only person in the world who called Analise by that name. Analise ventured a step closer.

"I . . . did something a bit naughty, I'm afraid." She cleared her throat, and tried suffusing her tones with conspiratorial confession. "I thought you might advise me? It has to do with your cousin."

Desdemona spun around and cut across a patch of sweet grass to take Analise by the elbows. "Gideon? Did you see him? Did he go back to the garret last night?" Her knuckles poked out, painfully white, against her tawny skin.

Analise forced herself to laugh. "I don't know! I was at Elliot's. That's the thing, Miss Mannering. I'm afraid I . . . I stole something from Gideon. Nothing he cared about. He was always smashing them up anyway. But it was so pretty, you know. One of his statues. I thought . . . sort of as a practical joke . . . I might donate it to one of the local art museums anonymously. Just leave a card saying it was the work of a Seafall artist. It really would be such a shame to let it go the way of Gideon's sledgehammer. But then I felt so guilty . . . I didn't know what to do. So I brought it to you."

"You found one? You kept one? Whole?"

"Whole!" Analise agreed. "And very beautiful. Sexless as an angel but kind of, um, you know, sexier for all of that. I left it in your garden. Come and see."

She tucked her hand in Desdemona's elbow and dragged her back to the place she'd left the statue. It had shifted positions somewhat, Analise suspected in order to keep her in its view, but now its eyes were closed. It stood straight-backed, head tilted to the sky, arms hanging loose with the palms open in supplication. Analise could feel the tension ebb from Desdemona's body as she stared at it.

"I had no idea," she said quietly. "Gideon . . . As a child, Gideon used to whittle silly little animal sculptures out of blocks of wood. Then one day he just . . . stopped. Took up with clay instead. Started churning out larger projects. Like this one. Hopeless at first, ill-shaped and lumpy, nothing like the whimsical work he used to do with wood. He was never the same, after. All the soft light went out of him. Snuffed. Replaced by a sort of bleak inferno in its stead. But I only ever caught a glimpse of his earliest work in clay. Never complete. And never in the last several years, since he took to living in that garret like a pauper. He's gotten so . . . Look at it. It's breathtaking."

"It's unbelievable," Analise agreed under her breath.

Desdemona looked as if she wanted to stroke the statue, but instead dug her fists in her pockets.

"Why did you bring it to me?" she asked.

"Well. You're a collector, aren't you? You know all about the art world. You collect all of us artists. Writers, painters, perfumers . . . "

Desdemona blanched and backed away. "I didn't collect Gideon," she cried. "I don't do that to family. I would never . . . !" Swallowing whatever might have burst out next, she drew in a shuddering breath. "It really was very naughty of you, Leez," she continued, with her customary curving smile. "I can see why you were tempted. But really. If an artist wishes to destroy his work, that is his prerogative. I remember you told me once that you wanted to write into your will that all personal correspondence should be burnt upon your death. Imagine learning that your relatives planned instead to sell your papers to your publishing company before your corpse was even cold! It would be enough to make you sue from the grave."

Analise pretended to squirm. "That's different."

"How so?" Desdemona asked coolly.

"To destroy such a thing in this case would be criminal. This statue is far superior to anything I have written."

"Doubtless," said Desdemona. "But it is not yours." She sighed. "I will agree to keep it here until Gideon returns. He will be relieved to have it returned, and I promise I won't tell him who dropped it off. Is that acceptable?" Her tone did not brook any response but the affirmative.

Analise grinned at her. "Certainly! I *knew* it was very bad of me." She turned to trudge away, but pulled out her pocket watch as she did so, and cursed roundly, spinning on her heel.

"Forgive me, Miss Mannering. The last train back to my borough was," she checked her watch again, "ten minutes ago. May I crash in one of your rooms? Or even a couch? I swear I'll leave first thing in the morning?"

Desdemona hesitated, her gaze shifting from Analise to the statue, then back again.

At last she said, "Yes. Of course. Come inside and take tea with me. We'll have to fetch it ourselves. I sent the staff away after they scrubbed down the house from last night's ball. I wish you might have been there, Leez. One woman came dressed as a mermaid. They rolled her indoors in a tank of water, if you can believe it! What a mess!"

Analise cast a glance over her shoulder. The statue turned its head to watch her until she disappeared from sight.

The worst thing Gideon ever did to Analise was invite her to the Farmer's Ball.

That was the night of his revenge. It didn't begin with the publisher pouncing on her and announcing how much she loved Analise's manuscript, how she thought it was just so *darling*, and needed only one or two of *teensiest* revisions to be an absolute *smash*, let's talk *contract*, let's talk *advance*, let's talk *promotional tours*—but that's how it ended. It began when Analise showed up at his mother's house dressed in her normal clothes.

He hadn't told her who he was.

He hadn't told her where he came from, or what the house looked like.

He'd invited her to supper, half reluctantly, even roughly, telling her, "My mother wants to meet the neighbor who keeps feeding me soup."

So Analise had shown up at Ochre Court with a fistful of ragged flowers and a ribbon in her hair. She was dressed neatly, if eccentrically, in a worn green velvet skirt with a flutter of lace at the hem, a button down shirt of paler green with embroidery on the collar and no visible ink stains, and her sturdy boots. Obviously this was an effort for the girl who often wore nothing but pajamas and a red scarf for days in a row, as she curled in her window seat and scribbled endlessly on her heap of papers. She'd partially pulled back her thickety red hair with wooden combs. She wore pearl earrings. Not real pearls. The small locket her dad gave her when she left the farm. An heirloom from a grandmother. Pot metal.

When the Ochre Court butler opened the enormous front doors to her ring, Gideon had placed himself near enough to observe her without being seen. He heard her anxious, "I'm sorry—I think I have the wrong house. Is Gideon . . . Does someone named Gideon have a . . . Is there someone named Gideon Alderwood here, by any chance?"

"Mr. Alderwood is in the Gold Salon, Miss Field," the butler intoned. "But Mrs. Beckett-Alderwood asks that you be brought directly to the ballroom."

"The . . . Excuse me, the what?"

And Gideon didn't know, watching her, whether he wanted to lean against a wall and laugh helplessly at her expression, or sweep her out the door again with a sneer and a, "Go back to the garret where you belong," or step out and reassure her that it was only one of his mother's stupid parties, and not a single guest could rival her in imagination or kindness or that inimitable way she wore a scarf. Not to mention that her soup was a miracle from the gods, and that he would give up both his hands just to eat from hers.

He did not do any of that. He merely fell in step behind her, softly and several paces away. She was too preoccupied keeping up with the butler and taking in the splendor of Ochre Court to notice the new shadow she had acquired.

If an invitation to the Mannering's Gentry Moon Masquerade at Breaker House was the coveted object of autumn, it was to the Alderwood's Ochre Court that the upper crust of Seafall society flocked at the burning zenith of summer.

The ballroom was full of farmers. Or rather, wealthy people dressed in their idea of what farmers wore. Lacy shepherdesses with hoop skirts and gilded crooks flirted with rouged roués in red waistcoats, earthy tweeds, careless kerchiefs tied round their necks, and pipe stems clamped between their teeth. Bronzed, bare-chested waiters wearing nothing but leather shorts, suspenders, straw hats, and gleaming boots served craft ales from enormous steins.

Analise tried to stare in all directions at once. Her generous mouth began to smile. She was always quick, Gideon knew, to perceive the ridiculous, to enjoy any bright parade or ostentatious array, as if anything absurd or gorgeous had been placed directly in her path for the partaking. He watched her mentally scribbling notes. The soft light in her eyes was one of wonder and delight, a hint of satire. She was pleased with the treat she'd be given. Pleased with Gideon. Perhaps a bit exasperated that he had not told her what she was in for. But he could tell that she perceived the surprise as rather . . . sweet.

She would soon learn better, Gideon thought grimly, and watched his mother sweep Analise Field skull to stocking with a single comprehensive glance. Then she cut her eyes to Gideon.

"Madame," said the butler, bowing. "Miss Field."

"Thank you, Jinn."

"Madame."

The butler left, and his mother said, "So you are the neighbor. I presume."

"Analise Field," said Analise, offering her hand. "You're Gideon's mother?"

"I am Mrs. Beckett-Alderwood."

Her eyes cut to Gideon again, but either Analise did not notice or thought it was too rude to look over her shoulder. His mother did not take Analise's hand. She was dressed like a dairymaid. Her wig was a mass of flaxen curls and upturned braids. Her dress was the deep, eye-watering yellow of egg yolks, with enormous sleeves and a stiff crinoline beneath the satin skirts. A scrap of foamy lace apron barely contained the rich yellow froth of her dress from spilling out onto the ballroom floor and knocking down the dancers. Little blue slippers peeped from beneath her long bloomers.

"Gideon didn't tell me," Analise cleared her throat, "to bring a costume."

"No," Gideon agreed from behind her. "It's a Farmer's Ball, Miss Field. I figured anything in your closet would do."

Analise whipped around at the sound of his voice. Gideon didn't know if that stricken look in her eye smote him with vengeful pleasure or a nauseated wave of shame.

Both.

She opened her mouth, but his mother got there first.

"Gideon tells me you are an authoress, Miss Field."

"Oh, I—" She blushed. Analise blushed so easily. Gideon had always wanted to cup her face in his hands when she did so, and warm his fingers by her glow. "I'm just . . . Well." She breathed. "Yes. I did come to the city to write. That's what they say back at home; writers have to live in the city. Real writers. For a while anyway. They can come home again—that is, if they want to, if the city doesn't eat them up—but they can't *stay* at home. If you know what I mean . . . "

His mother did not so much as raise a single, bleached, plucked, painted eyebrow. All she did was make an almost imperceptible gesture, and a woman dressed like a migrant fruit picker (if fruit pickers wore vines in their hair, skirts made of silken leaves, and clusters of candied grapes dangling strategically over breasts and groin) joined them.

"Kitjay Sinjez of Lyrebird Publishing," said his mother. "This is Analise Field of *Seafall Rising*."

"Oh, my!" said Kitjay Sinjez, enfolding Analise in her arms and kissing both her cheeks. "I adored your book! I adored it! Love, love, love! You must sign with me. Tonight. No time to waste!"

"My . . . " Analise looked at Gideon again. "You didn't give her my . . . " She gasped, though he hadn't nodded. "It was just a *draft*, Gideon. You said *you* wanted to read it! You never asked . . . "

Gideon yawned. "Truthfully, Ana, I couldn't make it through the first chapter. So I sent it to Kitten." He paused, then drawled, "She actually *likes* that kind of thing."

Kitjay dragged Analise off, chattering a mile a minute. Analise's entire neck and chest had turned that same dusty brick color as her face. Her shoulders were hunched all the way up to her ears. From behind she looked a horrible, humpbacked thing with insufferable hair. When he glanced away from her, his mother was staring at him, her pale blue eyes as cold as the poles.

"If you marry her, I will disown you."

Gideon snorted. "Analise Field is the last woman on Athe I'd marry."

"I warn you, Gideon. Ruin her if you feel you have to, but out of the public eye. She doesn't deserve the Alderwood name."

"Really, mother. Who does?"

"No one decent," she said. "Had I the gift of foresight, I would have put strychnine in the champagne font the day your father wed me."

"Poison the line before propagating it?" he teased her.

"It was already propagating," she answered. "As you well know. An Alderwood obsessed goes to any length to possess the prize he covets."

"An Alderwood obsessed is a danger to society," Gideon murmured. He could no longer see Ana in the crowd. But she was thinking of him. He could feel *that*, all the way down his spine. She would, he was sure, have happily ripped out his spine with the sole power of thought just then.

"What next for your Miss Field?" his mother asked. "Will you pay someone to mug her? Set fire to that tenement you both live in? Have her kidnapped and dumped outside the city? To what lengths will you go to quell your ardor for her person, my son?"

"Next," Gideon replied, "she will find herself the most celebrated authoress from here to Winterbane." He paused. "She'll hate it, knowing she did not earn it."

"Maybe she'll even stop writing," his mother suggested with gentle malice.

"Oh, no," he murmured. "Not she. She'd pierce her veins and write with her own blood if she had to."

"Ah. You think you have discovered the twin of your soul. The two of you may lay waste the ripest years of your youth, raggedly and passionately starving in that ridiculous garret of yours for the slave wages of your art . . . "

"Hardly."

"I tell you again, Gideon, for fear that you have inherited your father's selective attention: if Analise Field ever becomes Analise Alderwood, I will not only never forgive you, I might have you murdered. Exposed on the bell tower and eaten by feral seagulls."

Audrey Beckett-Alderwood smiled beneath all her yellow curls and porcelain-tinted paint. Even now her smile had the power to make her son want to curl up in a fetal ball and cry. "I mean it, Gideon. Ruin that girl if you must. But do not destroy her utterly. Leave her enough of herself to heal and move on. I beg you."

"Mother!" Gideon said lightly. "You have nothing to worry about. If I do indeed defy you and marry Analise, I'll simply take her last name for my own. I'll be plain Gideon Field, anonymous farmer husband to a famous literary wife. No one will know I'm your son. You may tell people that seagulls ate me for all I care. Leave your money to the Factory Girls With Phossyjaw Charity. Would that not avenge you? Perhaps father will even allow you your divorce at last."

"The idea is not . . . unappealing," his mother replied. "Though I pity the girl who lets you taint her good, plain name." Her terrible smile faded. "I won't tell you to be careful, Gideon. You never were a careful boy. And the gods help any girl who tries to take care of you. Your Miss Field certainly has the look of one who would drag her loved ones back from the mouths of the seven hells. She would never believe it is not in her power. That it never has been in anyone's power to save you. Not for years."

"If I hurt her enough, she'll be so occupied staunching her own wounds, she won't have any time for mine. She'll be safe."

"Yet you will not drive her away? Remove temptation wholly? I would feel easier," she admitted, "if you simply had her beaten senseless and abducted. But it is unlike you to show kindness."

Drive her away? Let the garret they split between them stand empty and unoccupied, the paper-thin wall dividing him not from her restless sleep but only from the ghost of her breathing?

It was the one thing in the world Gideon could not bear.

"If she hates me," he insisted, "she'll be safe."

His mother shook her head. "You are an optimist."

• • •

In the spare room at Breaker House, awaiting the bone chimes to sound midnight, Analise suspected that Desdemona Mannering knew exactly what her unwanted houseguest was about. For one, her hostess had placed her in Gideon's room. Analise knew it was his because the pillow smelled like him, as did the clothes hanging in the wardrobe. Not having packed a jacket and cold with nerves, Analise stole a woolen blazer from his stock, though the sleeves pinched her upper arms and the buttons did not meet their counterparts in front.

After showing her the room, Desdemona had said nothing to her except, "Sleep well." But the injunction to *Save Gideon* burned in her eyes, along with the warning that nothing good would come to Analise if she tried to crawl back through any wall into this world without him.

Come midnight, and the first of the bone bells began to sound, the statue appeared at her door. Analise could not remember ever being more grateful for companionship. If not for that gleam of living marble, the hand outstretched to hers, that glimmer of green in those darkest eyes, she knew she would have crushed her pillow (Gideon's pillow) (his impatient sandalwood scent) (those brittle flecks of clay he scattered wherever he went) about her ears and willed herself not to hear. To disregard the bells and reject the journey they heralded, and to *live.*

But the statue was ready. And her backpack was right there by the bed that smelled of him, how he had smelled those rare nights he'd wept into her lap. She had sandwiches, and a pen, and a silver box, and Nyx had given her a job to do that was of far greater importance than Analise's fear.

What's more, Gideon Alderwood, gods-triple-damn his scornful eyes, needed rescuing. Whether he deserved it or not.

Analise took the statue's waiting hand, and they walked through walls that ran like mercury, from one Breaker House into another.

They arrived in a courtyard with a fountain full of tangled stone swans. Analise barely had time to peer into the twilight around her before the soldiers were upon them.

They all looked like her statue, more or less, tall and eggshell-pale and sleekly muscled as demigods. The tallest of them stepped forward. Alone of all of them its semblance seemed craggy and slightly unkempt. The spear it carried was long and black, the head of it a piece of obsidian fashioned into lozenge-shape. A billow of red velvet swirled across its white chest, fastening at the shoulder with a smoldering ruby broach. This and the black spear and its odd lumpy face set it apart from the others. When it spoke, the cavern of its voice had an eerie echo all its own.

"In the name of Loreila the Winter-Touched, High Queen of the Valwode, I charge you with trespass into the palace territory of Dark Breakers."

The statue beside Analise sucked in a deep breath. The first breath it had ever taken, through lips that had come unsealed. It replied in the same way a mountain canyon replies when you shout into it.

"Sibling of my Maker's hands, I greet you. Gladly will I wear whatever shackles your edict requires for my trespass. But harm not this mortal maid who rescued me, humble property of Her Gracious Majesty, from certain destruction by our angry God. She stole me from his wrath and treated me with kindness. As soon as she was able, alone and ignorant of Gentry ways, did she return me here to take my place among you, my good and rightful kin, as your comrade in arms, a willing warrior to swell your ranks and protect our Perfect Queen upon her throne."

Analise blinked at her statue as if it were a splinter of glass she had to expel from her eye. Her throat worked, trying to swallow. She could not quite manage it.

She recalled a dream she once had, of bearing a baby daughter under mysterious circumstances who not only seemed to spring forth from her womb with a full set of teeth, but was also possessed of an unusual vocabulary and philosophical bent of mind. In the dream, it had astonished her that any baby could speak with such eloquence and at such length! Waking, her breasts no longer swollen with milk, Analise had found she sharply missed her daughter and the conversations they'd had between feedings.

That same feeling of loss was with her now, remembering the happy hours she had spent at Elliot's house, reading her statue alphabet books and children's nursery rhymes. She could not help but wonder if all of her efforts had been foolish. If the statue held her beneath contempt. Obviously the only thing it had needed from her was passage through the walls back to its own world.

Who was *she* to teach this majestic thing words?

She was afraid to open her mouth lest she disturb the delicate silence between the two statues. They gazed at each other for minutes, the air crackling between them. Analise imagined that they communicated entire histories in the space of that unblinking glance, from an infancy of clay to this faceoff in the courtyard of Dark Breakers.

Analise's statue began to smile, ever so slightly.

It raised one hand to the place its heart was not. The buzzing sound Analise had often heard in its chest crescendoed and poured out into the air. Analise watched as rank upon rank of living statues in the courtyard lifted their hands to their own sculpted chests in bewildered awe, as if something inside them had just come alive with the vigor of summer beehives. They made no murmur, but looked to their red-caped leader beseechingly, uncertain that this startling change the newcomer had wrought in them was welcome, but unwilling to tear their hands away from the novelty of the sensation.

The pale, rough-hewn planes of their leader's face did not change. It alone had not reflected the gesture of its comrades, though its hands clenched upon the black spear, and its stance shifted slightly, resettling its weight on its back leg as though flinching from a blow. The green flames of its eyes flickered a disquieted black.

When next the red-caped statue spoke, Analise thought even its voice sounded different. There was no softening, for a voice made of stone and hollow space cannot soften, but a flush of warmth filled the former emptiness with something like excitement. Perhaps even a kind of deference.

"Be welcome, sibling," it said, with a short bow. "And be assured your mortal maid shall know no harm at our hands before our Queen has put her to the question. For now we shall take her to the prison where our God and Maker abides in his madness. You, we shall at once present to Loreila the Winter-Touched, for surely your grace shall soothe her fretted senses." It drew nearer to Analise's statue, venturing to place a hand upon its shoulder.

"Our Queen is much abraded of late with worries for the absent Antler Crown. Uneasy is her claim to the throne so long as she rules bare of it. It is the icon of authority that will unite the Gentry divisions beneath her banner."

"Perhaps, sibling," said Analise's statue softly, "I may bring her word of its whereabouts. For I have met the Queen in Exile in the world where I was born. Before I crossed into the Valwode, it is possible Nyx the Nightwalker whispered her secret in my ear."

Analise swallowed hard, hoping the statue hadn't said too much already. But the plan was proceeding apace, and at the moment she was outnumbered one hundred to one. Or two, if she counted her statue. She was not sure she could—or should. So she held her tongue, and allowed herself to be collected and taken to the place where Gideon was.

Gideon came out of his fugue to see the door to his cell opening, and the small space he inhabited with the never-ending mountain of clay filled with the white shapes of his hideous creations. He realized that both his hands were bleeding freely, that he was terribly thirsty and sore everywhere. His head grew light, or he noticed it had been light all along. Barely attached. Then he fainted.

When he woke, she was there.

She was there, and she was tipping water down his throat.

She was there, wearing his brown wool coat that didn't fit her. With a ratty old backpack half on, half off her shoulder. With her hair like a bonfire where he'd burn all his regrets. And her hazel eyes so clear and grave, staring down at him.

She was there. Here. In his cell. With his blood all over her. And the door locked behind her. No way out. No way back. In danger of her life. Or worse.

Everything he feared.

Gideon did not have the strength to roll off her lap. He scowled instead and summoned his most blighting drawl, and watched the chill effect of it burn across her concern like acid.

"Saint Analise of the Forsaken. Have you come to save me?"

"I'm not a saint, Gideon!" Analise snapped. Hurriedly she shucked off her backpack to rummage through it. "Rescuing you—if we don't both die in the process—is hardly worthy of canonization. It might be the opposite. If I were religious, the Holy See at Winterbane would excommunicate me on the grounds that I didn't just leave you to die like any reasonable person would do."

"By all means, Ana, abandon me here and go take orders. I would not stand between you and your gods."

She met his gaze for a second and flashed him a crooked smile. "I'm already here, you jackass. Not just for you. And since I'm here, I might as well rescue you while I'm at it."

She'd found what she'd been searching for at the bottom of her backpack. Her fountain pen. Gideon recognized it by its distinctive dark blue marbling and the smart accents of gold. It was a Cobalt Rapier, top of the line. A going-away gift from her mother. Analise would live on canned soup and crackers before buying cheap ink for that pen. She drafted all her early manuscripts with it. Gideon watched her unscrew the cap, take his unresisting arm in hers, and begin scribbling on his skin. She started at his right shoulder and wrote until she reached the base of his wrist, then took up the second line at his shoulder again. The nib of her pen tickled his skin. His cold fingers throbbed dully, crusted with clay and old blood.

But her words refused to actualize into legible sentences for him. Though it was her usual bold black chicken scratch, which Gideon had spent months and not inconsiderable effort learning how to decode, those long strings of letters remained as remote and indecipherable as sacred runes. Gideon blinked and squinted until he could no longer bear his blurred vision, and bit out, "Coming here was the stupid act of a lovesick idiot. Deep Gods, you really are a glutton for punishment, Miss Field. How many worlds must I traverse until the message penetrates your troglodytic peasant skull? I don't want you. Go back to Seafall and forget about me."

"Listen, you." Analise jabbed the nib of her pen at Gideon's nose until his eyes crossed.

"All right. You want me to confess, Gideon? I confess. For about maybe five minutes of the entire year I'm hopelessly in love with you. Usually when you're asleep. I can't help it. It's possible that you are correct, and I have somehow come to savor the pain and humiliation you inflict on me in some secret, degenerate chamber of my innermost soul. But most of the time, Gideon, I can't stand you. And *then*," she sat back a little to contemplate him, and her voice dropped to a whisper, "there are those moments between extremes when I consider you a friend. That's at my most *basic* stratum of friendship, mind, which Mr. Wolfe who lives down the road from my family back in Feisty Wold once defined for me. He was a soldier in the Orchid Wars, and he told me that a friend is someone who will share the last sip of water from his canteen, and who will guard your back when you sleep. Despite your efforts to disguise this, Gideon, I'm pretty sure you'd do as much for me. *That's* why I'm here in your foxhole, you jackass. I'm fighting at your side whether you like it or not. Because we're friends. And this is what friends do in the darkness. Now hold still. Eat this sandwich. And shut up, I'm working."

Gideon looked away from her face before he lost himself in the promise of her freckles. He chewed the sticky peanut butter and apricot-slathered bread she forced on him and stared stonily at the walls of his cell, which held not an iota of interest. So he turned his head again and watched her finish his right arm, flinging it from her lap to begin on his left. Slowly, the scribbles resolved into words.

"They say the great city of Seafall rose up from the waves one Gentry Moon, and settled atop the cliffs like a leviathan sunning itself on the shore. They say the stones comprising its towers and walls and fortresses were quarried from mountains that stand at the bottom of ocean trenches, and that they always appear glistening and wet, even in days of drought and dust. But this city I speak of was the first Seafall. This Seafall was long ago sacked by foreign marauders, burned, torn down, and buried beneath all the Seafalls that came after it. But a few of those most ancient buildings still stand, if you know where to look . . . "

It was the first paragraph of Analise's first novel, *Seafall Rising*. Gideon had read her book so many times he sometimes recited it while he worked. He had always loved it—from the first glance at her first draft. Kitjay Sinjez of Lyrebird Publishing, for all her apparent flightiness and excessive use of italics in spoken conversation, was as fine an editor as they come, and Analise's seminal first novel had sharpened and shone under her keen guidance.

He never told her that, of course. She still thought he'd as lief use it for toilet paper than finish the first chapter.

Ignoring him still, Analise tore his tattered sleeve from his shoulder in her haste to get at his flesh. She scribbled feverishly, the way she did when she cuddled up in her window seat, gripped by the urgency of some new narrative. He wished he might be the canvas she always worked upon, and she the clay he shaped to flickering life beneath his hands. Forcing his gaze away from her again, he said roughly, "Perhaps you haven't noticed my circumstances, but I don't keep a fresh supply of linen in this particular prison cell. This is my only shirt. What do you think you're doing?"

"Protecting you, jackass."

He twitched his arm from her grip. "One would think that a writer even of such minor note as yourself would find more variety in her expletives."

"Try *poetic repetition*, you jackass," Analise retorted. She pulled his arm back into her lap and pressed the nib of her Cobalt Rapier into his skin a bit more viciously than before. "Besides, I left my thesaurus back in our garret. Which I'm very much hoping I'll get to see again when this all is over. To that end—have another sandwich and hush. I'm almost finished."

"Not everyone in the world wants to be as fashionably chubby as you, Miss Field."

She stuffed a sandwich into his mouth and finished his left arm. He read on, helplessly.

"You would not think that a single garret room, with the not very enlivening view of a brick wall, an alleyway, and the neighbors' crisscrossing laundry lines, would in fact be itself the beating heart of such a fabled city as Seafall. But from the first night I slept there, I could hear the city breathing. There, and nowhere else. And I knew I had come home . . . "

He could not remember the first night she slept in the garret opposite his. She in no way registered to him until the day he woke up in her lap with her soup in his mouth. Yet at that moment, he knew that he, too, had come home.

Gideon closed his eyes, and steeled himself to lie.

Cut off so abruptly from his intent stare, Analise knew two things.

One. Gideon Alderwood had been watching her with his whole body. It was the formidable, often harrowing, attention no one else in the world paid her, and in the moment he released her from it, she realized Gideon had always watched her like that. That from the first time she had interfered with his swoon, and he had opened the lightning strike of his black eyes upon her, that same look had been right there, comprehending everything that meant *her*, that meant Analise Field, and promising to forget nothing.

Two. He was about to lie.

Sitting up and scooting back to lean against the wall, bleeding hands hanging loosely over his knees, he murmured wearily, "You overestimate my estimation of you, Miss Field. We were never friends."

Even knowing he lied didn't prevent the double pinch of snakebite at her heart.

"I was never yours perhaps," she replied quietly, "But you are mine. The point is, Gideon, if friendship means passing my canteen over to you before the battle begins, this is my last drop of water. If we live through this—if we make it back to Seafall—I'm going home. You win."

"Why wait? Go *now!*"

Knowing he had just been lying made Analise hear the desperate truth in his voice. He was trying to save her. Maybe he always had been.

The bedrock beneath all her assumptions about him crumbled beneath her feet. She did not know if what was beneath buoyed her up into angelic altitudes or sucked her deeper into a morass she was in no way prepared to deal with. She looked at him in astonishment and blurted, "*Now* who's the lovesick idiot?"

His eyes flashed open in alarm, but almost immediately began to narrow. Before he could say a word, the bar on their prison door rattled. Analise took him by his lacerated wrists and hauled him to his feet.

"Open your mouth," she said, plunging her hand back into her backpack.

"No more sandwiches, Ana."

"*Do as I say.*"

For the second time in under a minute, Gideon astonished her. He obeyed.

Analise shook open the silver box at the bottom of her bag. From it came flashing and tumbling and flickering a star the approximate size and shape of a mustard seed. It burned a tiny hole in her hand where it touched her flesh. This blazing blue-white thing she took between her forefinger and thumb, placed it under Gideon's tongue, and shut his mouth over it. His eyes widened in pain, but he pressed his lips tightly together.

"Not a single word till I say," she hissed.

Gideon nodded. She turned to face the palely glowing guards who flanked the threshold in mandatory invitation, but when she would have stepped in front of him, he grabbed her hand and held it fast. She squeezed back with the grimness of a swimmer who has only just discerned that the person she had hoped to rescue from drowning was probably going to pull her under with him.

But there was no letting go. Not for her. Not now.

Had he dreamt that with Analise at his side, Loreila the Winter-Touched would somehow diminish, become a fragment of the fearful monster that loomed forever tremendous in his shadow-shot mind? Had he thought he would be able to meet those gold-washed eyes at last, and stand without trembling or bowing, armed with Analise's writing all up and down his arms, her hand as hard as stone in his, as though he had carved her himself?

No, he hadn't dared dream that.

And just as well, for no sooner were they marched before Loreila's silver throne, which seemed to be constructed all of razors and scythes and crescent moons, than he stumbled and went down before her, hiding his head between his knees, one arm bent up and back, limp in Analise's stolid grip. Every bone in his body felt brittle to the point of fracture. His skin wanted to curl away in strips from the massive bruise of his musculature. And worse, worse was the infinitesimal thing in his mouth that burned and burned, like it wanted to eat a hole right through him, plummet through the soft tissues and jaw bone and the skin of his throat to sparkle bloodily on the milky stones of the throne room.

In Day Breakers, this room was the Great Hall, where Desdemona had hosted her Gentry Moon Masquerade and taken out this year's goblin tithe in master perfumers. In Dark Breakers, what had been tiled, pillared, and pilastered in limestone was carved instead from slabs of moonstone with the moonlight caught in it yet. Gideon could not see his own shadow for the shimmering. He wondered if this was because he was just a shadow himself.

All around him he heard the vibrant hum of the Gentry court. There were more of them here today than had been at Desdemona's masquerade, all of them frivolous and perilous and arrayed like butterflies that might at any moment snap you up with the jaws of crocodiles. Among them, like cold columns of silence, the statues. Loreila's soldiers. The other Gentry gave them wide berth, as assiduous in avoiding gazing at them directly as Gideon was in trying to avoid *her*.

But she came upon him anyway. A chill tightened the skin around his skull as he sensed Loreila's approach. The ragged yellow hem of her dress brushed his ear. Even through his own rankness he could smell her, a scent as faint as a field of wildflowers frozen in a flash of frost. Then her hem twitched back. A creature of snowflake coming face-to-face with a creature of sunlight and shrinking from it.

Gideon's fear did not fall away. If anything, he grew colder.

"What is the writing on his arms?" Loreila asked, the sound of ice cracking.

His shoulders knotted to hear Analise reply, as if making dinner conversation, "Oh, that? That's from my book. Gideon likes to use it as toilet paper. Is there any greater punishment to someone of taste and refinement than to cover them in the equivalent of ass wipes?"

Loreila laughed, but the sound was angry. She retreated a few steps from the inked-on text, and turned from it as though it scalded her eyes. When she was too far from him to lash out, Gideon lifted his head again and watched. Now her statues flanked her. She, nestled amongst them, was impervious to the deadly thrall that held the rest of the Gentry court in check. The statues were, after all, quickened by *her* magic.

"Why should *you* wish to punish him, child?"

"Because he's Gideon Alderwood," Analise sighed. She let his hand fall and he cradled it close to his body, where it became part of the general throbbing.

"You do not bear writing on your arms. Do you come here warded by greater powers than your words?"

"I didn't think I needed warding, Your Majesty," Analise replied. "I came only to bring you back your property. That beautiful statue Gideon made. He likes to smash them, you know, and I just couldn't bear it. Does that merit punishment in your eyes? I'd hoped you'd be pleased."

"More than you know." That white-spackled hand stretched up and back like a swaying branch to stroke the statue standing closest behind her. Gideon's gaze dropped again. He could not look that statue in the face. It was the last one he had made in their Seafall garret. The one Ana had stolen. The weight of his guilt bent his head.

"Execute him," whispered Loreila the Winter-Touched. "There is nothing more to be got out of him."

Analise cried out as the statue she had saved stepped forward. It set its cold marble foot against Gideon's shoulder and kicked him out of his curl and onto his back, exposing his belly and throat. Gideon's vision filled with one thing and one thing only: the monster Analise had rescued, tall and cold as a mountain peak, a new length of purple silk and thread of gold draped about its pure nakedness. Its eyes were like the wings of beetles. Its mouth was perfect, and perfectly unforgiving. That face held Gideon in thrall. A single thought crystalized out of the soup of fevered fragments, and it was, "How could my hands have brought forth anything so beautiful?"

The statue raised its fist. A single blow, Gideon knew, would fall like a sledgehammer and shatter the bones of his skull. It was no more than he expected. Or deserved. Indeed he hoped for it.

And then Analise interfered.

Again.

She threw herself upon him and took his face in her hands.

"You don't get to die until I give you leave, you bastard," she snarled, and kissed him.

Gideon felt the starlight leave his mouth.

The statue lifted Analise off of him. He was afraid it would hurl her to floor, or pass her off to its siblings to be torn limb from limb at Her Majesty's pleasure. He tried to scramble to his feet, but slipped in his own blood and crashed down, able only to watch as the statue turned Analise in its arms until she faced it. To his utter shock, the statue was smiling at her. Gideon knew that smile, for he had felt it on his own face whenever he woke from a fever dream to find Analise there with him.

Analise responded to the statue's smile much as she always had to his. With both hands she reached to stroke its face, her palms cupping the curves, her fingers following the lines, and Gideon could not see her expression, only the back of her head, but even the red rats' nests of her tangled hair, even the grime on her neck, and the determined set of her shoulder blades, bespoke her awesome tenderness.

She bent her head and kissed the statue where it smiled. Gideon's bleeding hands clenched.

The cool white column of the statue's throat convulsed, as it swallowed the seed of the star that Analise had breathed into its mouth.

The next words she whispered against its lips could be heard clear across the courtroom.

"In the name of Nyx the Nightwalker, Queen in Exile, I anoint you, Alban Idris the Antler-Crowned, Ruler of the Valwode. Take the Veil with her blessing, and do with it as you will."

Something silent but surging, like seeing a tree grow from seed to sapling to oak in a matter of seconds, moved through the statue. It let out a noise like a thunderclap, of agony and of triumph, and threw back its head. The antler crown burst from its skull: rack, tier, and tangle rising high.

"No!" screamed Loreila, springing to rip them away from each other. "No, I forbid it!" She snatched Analise by the throat, pressing that soft flesh with her terrible fingers until spots of blood began to well. Analise's eyes bulged. Her face went dusky and mottled. No sound escaped her. No sound was possible.

Then Loreila just . . . stopped.

She stopped, and Analise fell from her, and crashed down near Gideon, retching for breath. He moved closer, helplessly.

"Ana," he said. "Ana, hold on."

Loreila the Winter-Touched hung above them in the air, hunched forward, her yellow eyes wide with shock. Her mouth fell open, her jaw unhinged and swinging. Froth gathered at the corners of her lips. Gideon could count all her tiny, pointed teeth. Seeking the source of her disgruntlement, her long, white-spackled fingers found it in the spearhead that jutted from her chest. It was obsidian, shaped like a lozenge, and dripping her strange blue blood all down the front of her yellow dress. It vibrated in time with her dying heartbeat. Loreila grasped the slippery spearhead and tried to pull it from her, but succeeded only in slicing open her hands.

The statue behind her . . .

Gideon recognized it. His first creation. Rough-hewn and craggy as granite, the red cape of office pinned by a ruby broach at its shoulder. Its face was impassive, as if the stone of it had never been quickened to life.

Alban Idris the Antler-Crowned held up its hand. "Enough, sibling. The pretender is finished."

"Yes, sovereign."

The captain let Loreila's corpse fall. She slid off the spear and into a heap on the floor.

The ruler of the Valwode crouched down, reaching for Analise and holding her delicately in the curve of its arm. It touched its mouth to hers again, as though it had not been able to bear their interval apart. Something in its exhale seemed to gentle the harshness of her own breathing. Sighing with relief, Analise threw her arms around its neck and buried her face in the purple silk it wore.

"Thank you. Thank you—I was so afraid. I could not breathe."

"Ana," it murmured, stroking her hair from her face, cradling her close. "Sweet Ana. Beloved Ana. Will you not stay? Stay here in Dark Breakers. Live among us. You, who taught me speech. Who taught our hearts to beat. Help me now. Stand at my side, and I will name you consort and councilor and grant you anything your heart desires."

Analise disengaged herself and sat back, huddling her knees to her chest. She looked at Gideon, who, with the last of his strength leaving him, could do no more than glare back at her.

"What about him?" she asked flatly.

"Him."

Every statue in the courtroom had gathered around them now, circle upon circle of them, silently, blank of face and fierce of eye. A prison of living marble.

"He shall stand trial for genocide," said Alban Idris the Antler-Crowned. "He shall be found guilty. And he will die for the deaths he dealt us."

Analise did not look shocked. She did not look sorry. She did not, Gideon thought, look very much of anything. For the first time since he had met her, he could not read her. But still he would stare at her until they put out his eyes or closed them for him.

All she did was sigh. Then, heaving herself to her feet, Analise Field stood over him, putting her body between his and death. And she said, "You'll have to go through me first."

"They let us leave, but before they did, the sovereign lifted the onus Loreila had laid upon him—that thing that made him create statues willy-nilly—and, and it was like they ripped the spine from him. He collapsed. He was already weak beyond . . . He's, he's not woken since."

Analise rubbed her eyes before she realized what she was doing and stopped in disgust. Her fingers were ink-stained and blood-spattered and she did not know what else. "He's banished, you know. He can't stay here. The sovereign said, said if Gideon is ever caught in Breaker House when the walls open again, he will be dragged through and summarily executed for war crimes. We can't even let him stay here the night."

"We can't move him!" Desdemona protested. She sat on the edge of Gideon's bed, so close that her black hair fell across his chest, but she did not touch him, afraid to take her cousin's flayed and swollen hand in hers.

"Des, he's in a coma," Chaz Mallister said quietly. For once his mouth had lost its smirk, his voice the nasty edge of cattiness that was its wont. "I don't know what all this business about walls opening and walking statues and wicked queens might be. But I know Alderwood needs to be in a hospital. I've rung the ambulance. They're on their way."

When Desdemona did not answer, Analise did. "Thank you," she said, and pressed his hand gratefully, withdrawing it the next instant with a flush of apology at the streaks she had left on his pristine cuff. "Miss Mannering— Desdemona. Gideon can't return here when he leaves the hospital. Or ever. You know that, don't you? If he does, Dark Breakers will swallow him . . . "

"Yes," Desdemona growled. "*Yes, all right?* Yes."

"I rang Elliot Howell too," Chaz put in quickly. "He and Nixie will meet you at Seafall Emergency Center."

"No," said Analise, standing up from her chair. She stumbled at her own swiftness and backed away toward the door. "I'm not going. Tell them . . . I've left Seafall. Tell them I've gone home. Elliot knows where to write me." Her gaze flickered to Gideon's ashen face. "Goodbye."

She was the first thing he looked for when he woke, his eyes battered by the bright hospital lights, his ears no less pierced by the shrill silence than his arms were by the tubes that had kept him hydrated and alive for who knew how long. He saw Desdemona, her hand fast in Chaz Mallister's, but she was napping against Chaz's shoulder and was not aware he had awakened. Gideon did not bother to linger long over Chaz Mallister, whose face held no surprise except weariness. He watched his mother for a while. She stood at the window looking out, a stylish net veil obscuring half her profile. She smoked cigarette after cigarette, rigidly and stoically. As the smoke wreathed her head, Gideon thought of dragons. Next his gaze went to Queen Nyx, who wore a man's pinstriped suit, with a fedora slanting slyly over her forehead. She perched on Elliot's knee and spoke quietly into his ear.

But it was Elliot who first caught Gideon's curious gaze. A light leapt into his own. If anything, those round blue eyes grew rounder and bluer. He exclaimed something that Gideon could not hear through the suffocating crush of comprehension and disappointment.

Ana was not there.

PART FOUR: LETTERS HOME

Dear Ana,

How we all get on here without you I'll never know. Even Nixie seems out of temper, although I can't tell if it's the gestation process or grief over the loss of her throne that has her so peevish. I mean, she gave it up. The antler crown was hers to give, and her blessing with it. But it's gone now, for good and true, and she'll never wear it again, and she'll never go home. I don't think she knew how she'd mourn it. Nor can I understand the depths of her loss.

She clings to me one moment, reviles me the next, and all I can do is bring her pickles and ice cream when she asks it of me. Am I a wise man? I'm a damned lucky one anyway.

Out of desperation the other evening, I mentioned sending her to the countryside for some fresh air. She didn't say a word but got out her suitcase and started packing before I had time to consult the train tables. I'm sending her to you with my compliments. Don't thank me. I know you've always wanted a pregnant exiled Gentry queen of your own. Isn't it your birthday soon?

Gideon was released from hospital two weeks ago and went back to his garret to finish recuperating. I visited last week only to find him returning home from work. Yes, work. He's taken a factory job. A front-line man at Alderwood Typewriters.

He did not seem too shocked to see me. Invited me in for tea, gracious as you please. He's got more furniture in his room now. Table and chairs. Cups, plates. A hotplate of his own. Actually, I think he stole it from your room.

"Cat got your tongue?" I asked, for though he was not what I'd call dour exactly, he was more quiet than usual.

"I've taken a vow of silence," he said, pouring me out a vile brew and the sugar to sweeten it with. "Until I learn to keep a civil tongue in my mouth."

"Breaking that vow for me, are you? Honored."

And Deep Lords, Ana, do you know he laughed?

"It's easy to be civil with you, Howell. If a Gentry Queen as ancient as Athe and powerful as an earthquake goes soft for your sunny nature, it must come as no surprise that even I can refrain from biting your head off over a tea tray."

"Speaking of which, Alderwood—and I've no desire to provoke you into the aforementioned biting off of my head—but this tea is ghastly."

"You should try my soup."

"Ah—no thanks."

And that's how it was. He invited me back for supper next night, and Nixie too. Gideon—who's never invited me or anyone to anything that I can remember, and who never before could mention my wife without his jaw clenching hard as iron. When we parted, he gave me a present, "For Queen Nyx," he said. "Or really, for the child she carries."

Ana, it was a box of little wooden animals. He had whittled and painted each of them by hand. Bear cubs in bright red vests. Monkeys wearing green hats with gold tassels. Giraffes in ball gowns. Zebras in tuxedos. Spotted hyenas in polka dot dresses and pink high heels.

"I didn't know you worked in wood," I said, too moved to say anything cleverer. And he smiled, which flummoxed me more than his laugh had. I don't think I'd ever seen such a smile from him, without that edge that cuts you.

"I used to. Long ago. My fingers are clumsy at it, but . . . " He shrugged. "I'm learning. I don't think your baby will be too harsh a critic. Not until she's older anyway. I used vegetable dye so they'll be safe for her to teethe on."

"Thank you." I hugged him then; I'd never done such a thing before, but I couldn't help it. Gideon was stiff as a board and thin as a broom, but for just a second, he hugged me back. And that amazed me most of all.

That's all I have to report, Ana. I hope you're well. Kiss my wife for me. But not the way I'd kiss her if you please. Or . . . Well, if you must. I'll just sit here and imagine it, thank you.

Your friend,
Elliot

Dear Miss Field,

Please find enclosed last year's birthday present, which for one reason or another I neglected to give you. May it serve you well.

Howell told me that Lyrebird Publishing is due to release *Seafall Surrenders* in the spring. Please accept my congratulations.

Gideon Azlin Alderwood

Mr. Alderwood,

Thank you for the typewriter. It seems an efficient machine. As you can read for yourself, it works. If it ever ceases to do so, I am sure it will make a fine doorstop.

Knowing how you sometimes forget to buy toilet paper, I have included an Advanced Reading Copy of *Seafall Surrenders*. Also herein, a box of "Feisty Tips," quite the best black tea in the Wold. I do not know what you made Elliot drink, but I can't have you poisoning my friends in my absence.

A. Field

P. S. Keep the hot plate.

PART FIVE: RECONCILABLE DIFFERENCES

Nyx left the dawn before he arrived.

"It is best the boy does not meet me yet, or for some time. His wounds go deep, and my presence but exacerbates them." She smiled wryly. "This I learned at our dinner together, though he was too polite to flinch whenever I spoke or smiled."

"He doesn't have to stay," Analise protested, following Nyx outside. They had lived together a month in perfect peace, staying up late and talking, unpacking and organizing the house, shopping, cooking, feasting, reading, singing each other the songs of their separate worlds. She was almost as alarmed at losing her odd but oddly soothing companion as at the thought of Gideon's arrival.

Gideon leaving Seafall. Gideon coming to Feisty Wold. Gideon, seeing the old farmhouse she'd bought with her advance. Gideon, on her front porch. She could not imagine him but as the broken and bleeding thing she'd abandoned at Breaker House.

"You, you don't have to leave at all, Nixie," Analise stammered. "I can send him right on his way. In fact, I don't even need to answer the door. This is my house, after all. I get to say who enters or leaves it. And anyway . . . How do you even know he means to come here?"

Nyx smirked. The blue-black marks on her face danced. She took her suitcase in hand, and kissed Analise full on the mouth.

"I will walk into town, Ana, and take the train from there. It will do me good. And the Infanta here." She patted her rounded belly.

"Walk into town?" Analise wailed the words. "Nixie, it's the better part of ten miles!"

Nyx winked much as Elliot might have done. "Would that it were twice as long!" She placed her free hand on Analise's shoulder, and Analise felt it as a benediction. "Fear not I will tell you to be kind to the boy. Does he deserve your kindness? No. But he comes to thank you, as is proper. And if he lays gifts at your feet, it is no more than your valor merits. Let him wallow. It will relieve him and please you."

"It will *not* please me!" Analise flashed.

"Will it not?"

At her look, Analise wisely swallowed whatever lie she'd been about to utter. With a slight nod, Nyx flicked her chin with a careless hand and went on her way, blue-black braids gleaming like some deep summer evening under the white winter sunlight.

What could Analise do but spend the day cooking and cleaning? When she tried to write that evening, she found she could not concentrate, but went to bed early instead, despairing of sleep. To her surprise, a dreamless repose claimed her almost as soon as her head touched the pillow. Or rather, as soon as she crushed the pillow over her head, pounded it with her fists, kicked ineffectually at the mattress, and groaned.

"Gideon Alderwood," she said, "the moment you say anything mean, you're out. No, if you even raise your eyebrow the wrong way . . . if you so much as *sneer* at me, I'm slamming my door in your face and you can go sing for a new roommate in Seafall. I'll be through with you. We'll be through. Do you hear me?"

Somewhere mid-fret, she slept.

When she awoke, clear-headed and smiling for no reason she could discern, it was to another bright cold sky shining through her window.

And a hesitant knock at her door.

These were the things he would tell her:

1. Miss Field, I have decided that if you don't take me back, I am going to jump out of a very high window.

2. No. I know. That's blackmail. Never mind. All right. How about an ultimatum? Take me back, love me, live with me again, or I'll throw *you* out a window and see how you like it.

3. Goddamn it.

4. Ana, I didn't mean it.

5. I don't know how to say what I mean anymore.

6. Or mean what I say.

7. Miss Field, forget forcible defenestration. Let me be plain. I need you to kiss me like you kissed that last monster I made, the one you stole, my greatest work and the closest thing I'll ever know of a supreme being outside yourself. Kiss me like you want to make me ruler over all the Valwode, like you want to execute me for the crime of wanting to kiss you, like you forgive me, or I will die of suffocation because you are the only air I ever want to breathe.

8. . . . Please?

Gideon sighed. A month and change of enforced silence hadn't worked half as well as he'd hoped. He had wanted to learn something of gentleness. He had bitten his tongue against stinging retort thirty-six times a day. He had never once used his smile as a weapon. He had tried to remember what it was to love the work of his hands, as she did hers.

Maybe it would be better to say nothing at all.

But this was Analise. Analise who devoured words. Who breathed them, dreamed them, summoned them. He would need to say *something* to her. She deserved that—and, well, everything—but for now something would have to do. Something simple, so he wouldn't mangle it.

Like the truth.

Gideon Alderwood stood just beyond the screen. He held up a crate of toilet paper. "I brought these for you. Overdue."

Analise raised her eyebrows. She craned her neck to peer past him. A battered jalopy was parked crookedly in the dirt driveway, its rusty frame appearing to be held together by nothing but paper clips and promises. She glanced back at him. Not quite into his eyes. Not yet.

Gideon wore what looked to be his work clothes, plain but clean: brown trousers with suspenders, a worn shirt with the sleeves rolled up enough to show a string of black letters tattooed up his arms. It was not her writing, which surely had been scrubbed off at the hospital, but they were her words. His right arm read simply, "*Seafall rose up from the waves one Gentry Moon,*" and his left, "*I could hear the city breathing.*"

He wore no vest or tie. No marks of clay anywhere about him, but a whittling knife strapped to his belt. He had foregone a hat, and his hair was long enough to be tied back. This he had done, but the dark strands escaping their thong awoke a restless longing in Analise's hands that she'd thought she had freed herself from.

Analise shoved her hands into the pockets of her green dressing gown and gazed down at herself in dismay. The secondhand velvet was threadbare. The ivory lace at the elbows was more hole than eyelet.

"I liked your book," Gideon ventured. "Both of them."

Her head snapped up. She searched his eyes, suspicious of mockery and more than ready to slam the door in his face. Once there though, she was caught. Caught, speared, roasted, and served up with an apple in her mouth. It was like she had never looked into his eyes before. Like falling into a softly beaming black light. Like descending into a natural hot spring under the full dark of evening as a warm rain fell all around her.

Analise blinked and realized she had forgotten to breathe. She decided that looking at her feet was safest. Her feet were bare. She needed to cut her toenails. He was speaking again.

"Ana."

Why was his voice like a caress? She was used to his voice driving icicles through her ears.

"Do you think you'll ever come back to Seafall?"

Analise shrugged. She scratched her nose where her hair had tickled it. She should have combed her hair, she thought. It was all over everywhere. A feather from her pillow floated in one of her curls. Irritably, she plucked it out.

"The landlord let your room. I brought your things into mine." He smiled. Just barely. She noticed the twitch of his lips through her eyelashes. "Hence, the hotplate. If you did come back to Seafall, you'd have to stay with me. At least for a while. However long you'd like. You'd be welcome, of course. Most welcome."

At the soft, fervent note in those last syllables, Analise involuntarily glanced at him.

Bad decision. Very dangerous. Caught. Again.

"Or," he said. "I could stay here. If you wanted me."

It will never be safe, Analise thought, to meet his gaze. It will never be safe to wake to him smiling at her like that, solemn with hope. If his expression were anymore open, she could walk right through it.

Gideon set the crate of toilet paper down by the door and laid his palm flat against the screen. Analise wanted to lean her forehead against the indentation his hand made.

"I often have trouble sleeping, Ana. It's worse now that I can't hear you breathing through our wall. I lie in bed and imagine you beside me, your hair upon my pillow. I turn to you, though you are dreaming and all unaware, and I count every hair on your head, strand by strand, fire by fire. I count until my eyes can bear no more of your brightness, and in their own defense my eyelids let loose their portcullis and shut fast against my vision of you."

She shook her head. "Gideon—"

"It has to be better," Gideon reflected, "than counting sheep."

He let his hand fall from the screen and stepped backwards toward the porch steps. "I wanted to thank you," he said, "for saving me. I don't know why you did. I didn't deserve it. I'm sorry for everything. I adore you. I always have."

When he turned and moved to take the steps down, down to the rusty jalopy and to the dirt road that would take him away from her and back to Seafall, Analise banged open the screen door and sprang onto the porch. She grabbed him by the back of his suspenders and yanked. He turned into her embrace, his kisses landing first on her neck, the line of her jaw, her ear, her chin, until she held his head still between her hands and pressed her mouth to his. And both felt again as though starlight flashed between their lips, shimmering on their tongues and sparkling like champagne, though this time neither bore so much as a seed of Gentry magic between them.

"All right, Gideon," Analise said against his mouth, sliding her hands from his face to his shoulders to his shirt collar, which she clutched, tugging him closer to her. "All right. You can come in."

She pointed to the crate by the porch. "Bring that."

BIOGRAPHIES

"Mutability," published in the June 2015 issue of *Asimov's*, marked **Ray Nayler**'s debut as a writer of science fiction. Other short stories by Ray have been published in *Ellery Queen's Mystery Magazine*, *Deathrealm*, and the *Berkeley Fiction Review*, among others, and have twice been mentioned in Best American Mystery Stories volumes. Ray was a Peace Corps Volunteer in Turkmenistan. He has lived and worked extensively in the Central Asian Republics and in Russia. He is a Foreign Service Officer. His most recent posting was to Bishkek, Kyrgyzstan. His next posting is to Baku, Azerbaijan.

Brooke Bolander has had stories featured in *Lightspeed, Nightmare, Strange Horizons, Reflection's Edge*, and many other fine word-venues. Originally from the deepest, darkest regions of the Southern US, she attended the University of Leicester from 2004 to 2007 studying History and Archaeology and is a graduate of the 2011 Clarion Writers' Workshop at UCSD. She currently resides in the borough of Brooklyn, known for its bridges and dodging.

Naomi Kritzer's short stories have appeared in *Asimov's, Analog, The Magazine of Fantasy and Science Fiction, Clarkesworld, Lightspeed*, and many other magazines and websites. Her five published novels are available online, along with two e-book short story collections: *Gift of the Winter King and Other Stories*, and *Comrade Grandmother and Other Stories*. Naomi lives in St. Paul, Minnesota with her husband, two daughters, and several cats. You can find her blog at naomikritzer.wordpress.com

Geoff Ryman is Senior Lecturer in School of Arts, Languages and Cultures at the University of Manchester. He is the author of several works of science fiction and literary fiction as well as short stories author and an interactive web novel. His work has won numerous awards including the John W. Campbell Memorial Award, the Arthur C. Clarke Award (twice), the James W. Tiptree Memorial Award, the Philip K. Dick Memorial Award, the World Fantasy Award, the British Science Fiction Association Award (twice) and the Canadian Sunburst Award (twice). In 2012 he won a Nebula Award for his Nigeria-set novelette "What We Found." His novel *Air* was listed in *The Guardian's* 1000 Novels You Must Read.

Catherynne M. Valente is the *New York Times* bestselling author of over two dozen works of fiction and poetry, including *Palimpsest*, the Orphan's Tales series, *Deathless*, *Radiance*, and the crowdfunded phenomenon *The Girl Who Circumnavigated Fairyland in a Ship of Own Making*. She is the winner of the Andre Norton, Tiptree, Mythopoeic, Rhysling, Lambda, Locus and Hugo awards. She has been a finalist for the Nebula and World Fantasy Awards. She lives on an island off the coast of Maine with a small but growing menagerie of beasts, some of which are human.

John Barnes has thirty-one commercially published and two self-published novels, some of them to his credit, along with hundreds of magazine articles, short stories, paid blog posts, and encyclopedia articles. Most of his life he has written professionally, and for much of it he has been some kind of teacher, and in between he has held a large number of odd jobs involving math, show business, politics, and marketing, which have more in common than you'd think. He is married and lives in Denver.

Seth Dickinson is the author of *The Traitor Baru Cormorant* and more than a dozen short stories. During his time in the social sciences, he worked on cocoa farming in Ghana, political rumor control, and simulations built to study racial bias in police shootings. He wrote much of the lore and flavor for Bungie Studios' smash hit *Destiny*. If he were an animal, he would be a cockatoo.

C.C. Finlay is the author of four novels, a collection, and dozens of stories, with work translated into sixteen languages. In January 2015 he became the editor of *The Magazine of Fantasy & Science Fiction*. He lives in Arizona with his wife, novelist Rae Carson. He can be found on twitter @ccfinlay or on the web at ccfinlay.com.

Yoon Ha Lee's works have appeared in *Tor.com, Clarkesworld, Lightspeed, Beneath Ceaseless Skies, The Magazine of Fantasy & Science Fiction*, and other venues. His space opera novel *Ninefox Gambit* is forthcoming from Solaris Books in June 2016. He lives in Louisiana with his family and an extremely lazy cat, and has not yet been eaten by gators.

Kelly Link's most recent collection is *Get in Trouble*. She is also the author of *Stranger Things Happen, Magic for Beginners* and *Pretty Monsters*. She is the co-founder of Small Beer Press. Her short stories have been published in *The Magazine of Fantasy and Science Fiction*, *A Public Space*, *Tin House*, *McSweeney's*, *The Best American Science Fiction and Fantasy*, and *Prize Stories: The O. Henry Awards*. Link was born in Miami, Florida, and she currently lives with her husband and daughter in Northampton, Massachusetts.

Will Ludwigsen's work, described as "hauntingly beautiful" by *Publishers Weekly*, appears in magazines like *Asimov's Science Fiction* and *Alfred Hitchcock's Mystery Magazine* as well as in his most recent Shirley Jackson Award-nominated collection *In Search Of and Others*. When he is not peering into tree stumps at the abyssal frontiers of weird mystery, he's squinting out of the windshield at traffic in Jacksonville, Florida where he lives with his partner, writer Aimee Payne. He blogs at www.will-ludwigsen.com and tweets as @Will_Ludwigsen.

Vonda N. McIntyre writes science fiction. "Little Sisters" is by way of a companion piece to the Nebula-nominated "Little Faces." McIntyre's work has won the Nebula, the Hugo, the Locus, and the Pacific Northwest Booksellers Awards.

In 2002, **Hao Jingfang** was awarded First Prize in the New Concept Writing Competition. She gained her undergraduate degree from Tsinghua University's Department of Physics and her Ph.D. from the same university in Economics and Management in 2012. Her fiction has appeared in various publications, including *Mengya*, *Science Fiction World*, and *ZUI Found*. She has published two full-length novels, *Wandering Maearth* and *Return to Charon*; a book of cultural essays, *Europe in Time*; and the short story collection, *Star Travellers*.

Ken Liu (kenliu.name) is an author and translator of speculative fiction, as well as a lawyer and programmer. A winner of the Nebula, Hugo, and World Fantasy Awards, he has been published in *The Magazine of Fantasy & Science Fiction*, *Asimov's*, *Analog*, *Clarkesworld*, *Lightspeed*, and *Strange Horizons*, among other places. He also translated the Hugo-winning novel, *The Three-Body Problem*, by Liu Cixin, which is the first translated novel to win that award. Ken's debut novel, *The Grace of Kings*, the first in a silkpunk epic fantasy series, was published by Saga Press in April 2015. Saga will also publish a collection of his short stories, *The Paper Menagerie and Other Stories*, in March 2016. He lives with his family near Boston, Massachusetts.

Rich Larson was born in West Africa, has studied in Rhode Island and worked in Spain, and at twenty-three now writes from Edmonton, Alberta.

His short work has been nominated for the Theodore Sturgeon and appears in numerous Year's Best anthologies, as well as in magazines such as *Asimov's, Analog, Clarkesworld, F&SF, Interzone, Strange Horizons, Lightspeed* and *Apex*. Find him at richwlarson.tumblr.com

Simon Ings is a novelist and writer of popular histories, currently working on the story of the Soviet science under Stalin. He began his career writing science fiction stories, novels and films, before widening his brief to explore perception (*The Eye*, Bloomsbury), 20th-century radical politics (*The Weight of Numbers*, Atlantic), the shipping system (*Dead Water*, Corvus) and augmented reality (*Wolves*, Gollancz). He co-founded and edited *Arc Magazine*, a digital publication about the future, before joining *New Scientist* as its arts editor. Out of the office, he lives in possibly the coldest flat in London, writing op-eds and reviews for the *Guardian, Times, Telegraph, Independent* and *Nature*.

Nike Sulway is a Queensland writer. She is the author of *Rupetta, The Bone Flute,* \and *The True Green of Hope.* her most recent novel, released in 2016, is *Dying in the First Person*. She has won and been shortlisted for several awards, including the 2013 James Tiptree, Jr literary award.

Alvaro Zinos-Amaro was born in Spain and earned a BS in Theoretical Physics from the Universidad Autonoma de Madrid. Alvaro is co-author, with Robert Silverberg, of *When the Blue Shift Comes*, and is currently at work on *Traveler of Worlds: Conversations with Robert Silverberg* (forthcoming 2016). Alvaro's stories, poems, reviews and essays have appeared in markets like *Asimov's, Analog, Apex, Clarkesworld, Nature, Strange Horizons, Galaxy's Edge, The Los Angeles Review of Books*, and anthologies such as *The Mammoth Book of the Adventures of Moriarty* and *The Mammoth Book of Jack the Ripper Stories*.

Genevieve Valentine has written *Mechanique, The Girls at the Kingfisher Club*, and *Persona*; its sequel, *Icon*, is forthcoming in June 2016. She has written *Catwoman* for DC Comics, and is the writer of *Xena: Warrior Princess* from Dynamite. Her short fiction has appeared in several Best of the Year anthologies. Her essays and reviews have appeared at NPR.org, *The AV Club*, io9.com, *LA Review of Books*, and *The New York Times*.

John Kessel is the author of the novels Good *News from Outer Space* and *Corrupting Dr. Nice* and, with James Patrick Kelly, *Freedom Beach*. His story collections are *Meeting in Infinity, The Pure Product*, and *The Baum Plan for Financial Independence*. His fiction has received the Theodore Sturgeon

Memorial Award, the Shirley Jackson Award, the James Tiptree Jr. Award, and two Nebula Awards. With Kelly, he has edited six anthologies of stories re-visioning contemporary short speculative fiction, most recently *Digital Rapture: The Singularity Anthology.* Kessel teaches American literature and fiction writing at North Carolina State University.

Elizabeth Bear was born on the same day as Frodo and Bilbo Baggins, but in a different year. She is the Hugo, Sturgeon, Locus, and Campbell Award winning author of nearly thirty novels (the most recent is *Karen Memory*, a Weird West adventure from Tor) and over a hundred short stories. She lives in Massachusetts.

Joe Pitkin has lived, taught, and studied in England, Hungary, Mexico, and most recently at Clark College in Vancouver, Washington. His fiction has appeared in *Analog, Podcastle, Drabblecast,* and elsewhere. He has done biological field work on the slopes of Mount St. Helens, and he lives in Portland, Oregon, with his wife and daughters. You can follow his work at his blog, *The Subway Test:* thesubwaytest.wordpress.com

Rebecca Campbell is a Canadian writer and academic, as well as a graduate of Clarion West (2015). NeWest Press published her first novel, *The Paradise Engine*, in 2013. You can find her online at whereishere.ca

Chaz Brenchley has been making a living as a writer since the age of eighteen. He is the author of nine thrillers, two fantasy series, two ghost stories, and two collections, most recently *Bitter Waters.* As Daniel Fox, he has published a Chinese-based fantasy series; as Ben Macallan, an urban fantasy series. A British Fantasy Award winner, he has also published books for children, two novellas and more than five hundred short stories. He has recently married and moved from Newcastle to California, with two squabbling cats and a famous teddy bear.

Seanan McGuire lives and works primarily in Northern California, although she can be found in random spots around the globe, pursuing the ideal of the perfect corn maze. Her debut novel was published in 2009; since then, she has finished and released more than twenty-five books, proving that she probably really needs a nap. She won the 2010 John W. Campbell Award for Best New Writer, and has been nominated several times for the Hugo Award. When not writing, Seanan watches too many horror movies and spends time with her enormous blue Maine Coon cats. She reads almost constantly, and drinks far too much Diet Dr Pepper. Seanan regularly claims to be the vanguard of an invading race of alien plant people. As she gives little reason to doubt her, most people just go with it. Keep up with her at <u>www.seananmcguire.com</u>.

Gregory Norman Bossert is an author, filmmaker, and musician, currently based just over the Golden Gate Bridge from San Francisco. He won the 2013 World Fantasy Award, and was a finalist for the 2014 Theodore Sturgeon Memorial Award. When not writing, he wrangles spaceships and superheroes for Industrial Light & Magic. More information on his writing, films, and music is available at <u>SuddenSound.com</u> and on his blog <u>GregoryNormanBossert.com</u>.

Tamsyn Muir is a writer from Auckland, New Zealand. Her short-form fiction has appeared in such publications as *Nightmare Magazine, Weird Tales, The Magazine of Fantasy & Science Fiction* and *Clarkesworld*.

Ian McDonald writes mostly science fiction. He lives just outside Belfast in Northern Ireland. His first novel, *Desolation Road* was published in 1988, his most recent, *Luna: New Moon* came out in 2015 from Tor in the US, Gollancz in the UK. Forthcoming is *Luna:2*. He's won some prizes.

Andy Dudak's stories have appeared in *Analog, Apex, Clarkesworld, Daily Science Fiction, Flash Fiction Online, Not One of Us*, and many other venues. He is currently recovering from learning Mandarin.

C.S.E. Cooney is the author of *Bone Swans: Stories* (Mythic Delirium 2015), *The Breaker Queen* (first installment of the *Dark Breakers* series), *The Witch in the Almond Tree*, and *Jack o' the Hills*. She is an audiobook narrator for Tantor Media and the singer/songwriter Brimstone Rhine. Her Rhysling Award-winning poem "The Sea King's Second Bride" is featured in her collection *How to Flirt in Faerieland and Other Wild Rhymes*, and her short fiction may found in *Strange Horizons, Apex, GigaNotoSaurus, Clockwork Phoenix 3 & 5, The Mammoth Book of Steampunk*, and elsewhere.

RECOMMENDED READING

"Ruins", Eleanor Arnason (**Old Venus**)
"Telling Stories to the Sky", Eleanor Arnason (*F&SF*, 1-2/15)
"La Héron", Charlotte Ashley (*F&SF*, 3-4/15)
"1Up", Holly Black (**Press Start to Play**)
"The Tumbledowns of Cleopatra Abyss", David Brin (**Old Venus**)
"Ratcatcher", Tobias Buckell, (**Xenowealth: A Collection**)
Penric's Demon, Lois McMaster Bujold (**Penric's Demon**)
Teaching the Dog to Read, Jonathan Carroll (Subterranean)
"The Tarn", Rob Chilson (*Analog*, 7-8/15)
"Hold-Time Variations", John Chu (*Tor.com*, 10/15)
"The Bone Swans of Amandale", C.S.E. Cooney (**Bone Swans**)
"Rates of Change", James S.A. Corey (**Meeting Infinity**)
"Three Cups of Grief, By Starlight", Aliette de Bodard
          (*Clarkesworld*, 1/15)
"Her First Harvest", Malcolm Devlin, (*Interzone*, 5-6/15)
"Samsara and Ice", Andy Dudak (*Analog*, 1-2/15)
"Madeleine", Amal El-Mohtar (*Lightspeed*, 6/15)
"Biology at the End of the World", Brenda Cooper (*Asimov's*, 9/15)
"Iron Pegasus", Brenda Cooper (**Mission: Tomorrow**)
"The Servant", Emily Devenport (*Clarkesworld*, 8/15)
"Three Bodies at Mitanni", Seth Dickinson (*Analog*, 6/15)
"The Four Thousand, the Eight Hundred", Greg Egan (*Asimov's*, 12/15)
"The New Mother", E. J. Fischer (*Asimov's*, 3-4/15)
"In Panic Town on the the Backward Moon", Michael F. Flynn,
          (**Mission: Tomorrow**)
"And All Are Donkeys were in Vain", Tom Gerencer
          (*Galaxy's Edge*, 5/15)
"Entanglements", David Gerrold (*F&SF*, 5-6/15)
Wylding Hall, Elizabeth Hand (Open Road/PS Publishing)
"Let Baser Things Devise", Berrien C. Henderson (*Clarkesword*, 5/15)
"Egg Island", Karen Heuler (*Clarkesworld*, 10/15)

"Jamaica Ginger", Nalo Hopkinson & Nisi Shawl (**Stories for Chip**)

"History's Best Places to Kiss", Nik Houser (*F&SF*, 1-2/15)

"If On a Winter's Night a Traveler", Xia Jia (*Clarkesworld*, 11/15)

"An Apartment Dweller's Bestiary", Kij Johnson (*Clarkesworld* 1/15)

"Emergence", Gwyneth Jones (**Meeting Infinity**)

"Here is My Thinking on a Situation That Affects Us All",
       Rahul Kanakia (*Lightspeed*, 11/15)

"A Residence for Friendless Ladies", Alice Sola Kim (*F&SF*, 3-4/15)

"An Evolutionary Myth", Bo-Young Kim (*Clarkesworld*, 5/15)

"Midnight Hour", Mary Robinette Kowal (*Uncanny*, 7-8/15)

"Ghost Pictures", Derek Künsken (*Asimov's*, 2/15)

"Pollen from a Future Harvest", Derek Künsken (*Asimov's*, 07/15)

"An Exile of the Heart", Jay Lake, (*Clarkesworld*, 1/15)

"Prototype", Sarah Langan (**The End Has Come**)

"Ice", Rich Larson (*Clarkesworld*, 10/15)

"Another Word for World", Ann Leckie (**Future Visions**)

"Court Bindings", Karalynn Lee (*Beneath Ceaseless Skies*, 6/25/15)

"Variations on an Apple", Yoon Ha Lee (*Tor.com*, 10/15)

"Werewolf Loves Mermaid", Heather Lindsley (*Lightspeed*, 9/15)

"Points of Origin", Marissa Lingen, (*Tor.com*, 11/15)

"Blue Ribbon", Marissa Lingen (*Analog*, 3/15)

"Frost on Glass", Ian R. Macleod (**Frost on Glass**)

"We Never Sleep", Nick Mamatas, (**The Mammoth Book of Dieselpunk**)

"Jellyfish Dreaming", D. K. McCutchen
       (*Lady Churchill's Rosebud Wristlet*, 7/15)

"The Falls: A Luna Story", Ian McDonald (**Meeting Infinity**)

"The Adjunct Professor's Guide to Life After Death",
       Sandra McDonald (*Asimov's*, 10-11/15)

"Fiber", Seanan McGuire, (*Tor.com*, 12/15)

"A Thousand Nights Till Morning", Will McIntosh (*Asimov's*, 8/15)

"The Ninth Seduction", Sean McMullen, (*Lightspeed*, 9/15)

"Alloy Point", Sam J. Miller, (*Beneath Ceaseless Skies*, 12/25/14)

"Ghosts of Home", Sam J. Miller (Lightspeed, 8/15)

"Union", Tamsyn Muir, (*Clarkesworld*, 12/15)

"No Rez", Jeff Noon (*Interzone*, 9-10/15)

"Outsider", An Owomoyela (**Meeting Infinity**)

"The Snake-Oil Salesman and the Prophet's Head",
       Shannon Peavey (*Beneath Ceaseless Skies*, 4/30/15)

"The Punctuality Machine; or, A Steampunk Libretto",
       Bill Powell (*Beneath Ceaseless Skies*, 5/14/15)

"Ether", Zhang Ran (*Clarkesworld*, 1/15)

"The City of Your Soul", Robert Reed (*F&SF*, 11-12/15)

"The Empress in her Glory", Robert Reed (*Clarkesworld*, 4/15)

Sunset Mantle, Alter S. Reiss (Tor)

"A Murmuration", Alastair Reynolds (*Interzone*, 3-4/15)

Slow Bullets, Alastair Reynolds (Tachyon)

"Murder Goes Hungry",
> Margaret Ronald (*Beneath Ceaseless Skies*, 9/17/15)

"Auburn", Joanna Ruocco (*Lady Churchill's Rosebud Wristlet*, 6/15)

"The Old Man in the Kitchen", Patricia Russo (*The Dark*, 8/15)

"Trapping the Pleistocene", James Sarafin (*F&SF*, 5-6/15)

"Of Golden Birds and Caged Dreams", Ken Scholes
> (**Blue Yonders, Grateful Pies & Other Fanciful Feasts**)

"Gypsy", Carter Scholz (**Gypsy**)

"The Exile of the Eldest Son of the Family Ysanne",
> Kendra Leigh Spedding (*Beneath Ceaseless Skies*, 8/6/15)

"Trickier With Each Translation",
> Bonnie Jo Stufflebeam (*Lightspeed*, 6/15)

"The Pyramid of Krakow", Michael Swanwick (*Tor.com*, 09/30/15)

"Lock Up Your Chickens and Daughters, H'ard and Andy are Come to Town",
> Michael Swanwick and Gregory Frost (*Asimov's*, 4-5/15)

"Tea Time", Rachel Swirsky (*Lightspeed*, 12/15)

"The Boatman's Cure", Sonya Taaffe (**Ghost Signs**)

"Acrobatic Duality", Tamara Valdomskaya, (*Tor.com*, 2/15)

"The Lily and the Horn", Catherynne M. Valente (*Fantasy*, 12/15)

"On the Road with the American Dead",
> James Van Pelt (*Black Static*, 7-8/15)

"Bannerless", Carrie Vaughn (**The End Has Come**)

"Sinseerly a Friend & Yr. Obed't",
> Thomas M. Waldroon (*Beneath Ceaseless Skies*, 4/16/15)

"Builders of Leaf Houses", Catherine Wells (*Analog*, 12/15)

"The Beast Unknown to Heraldry", Henry Wessells
> (*Lady Churchill's Rosebud Wristlet*, 6/15)

"Walking to Boston", Rick Wilber (Asimov's Oct/Nov)

"Kaiju Maximus®: 'So Various, so Beautiful, so New' ",
> Kai Ashante Wilson, (*Fantasy*, 12/15)

"On the Night of the Robo-Bulls and Zombie Dancers", Nick Wolven
> (*Asimov's*, 2/15)

"No Placeholder for You", My Love", Nick Wolven (*Asimov's*, 8/15)

"Incubator", Gene Wolfe (**Onward, Drake!**)

"Rock, Paper, Scissors, Love, Death",
> Caroline M. Yoachim (*Lightspeed* 11/15)

"Seven Wonders of the Once and Future World",
   Caroline M. Yoachim (*Lightspeed*, 9/15)
"Partible", K. J. Zimring (*Analog*, 4/15)

PUBLICATION HISTORY

ABOUT THE AUTHOR

Rich Horton is an associate technical fellow in software for a major aerospace corporation and the reprint editor for the Hugo Award-winning semiprozine *Lightspeed*. He is also a columnist for *Locus* and for *Black Gate*. He edits a series of best of the year anthologies for Prime Books, and also for Prime Books he has co-edited *Robots: The Recent A.I.* and *War & Space: Recent Combat*.